# Contents

# Consultants and Contributors

GENERAL EDITOR

**Barrie Hughes**, author and editor

ASSOCIATE EDITORS

**Jane Drury**, BA, book editor

**Margaret Barrett**, book editor and writer

SPECIALIST CONSULTANTS

**Phillip Adams**, AO, FRSA, broadcaster, newspaper columnist, film producer and author

**John Curtain**, BA, BEd, associate professor of publishing and director of the Centre for Publishing Studies, Royal Melbourne Institute of Technology

**Gary Dean**, former chief sub-editor at the Melbourne *Age*, and editor of *The Age Style Book*

**Arthur Delbridge**, AO, MA, HonDLitt, emeritus professor of linguistics, Macquarie University, and editor-in-chief of *The Macquarie Dictionary*

**Max Harris**, AO, BA, BComm, writer, publisher, and founder and editor of several literary journals; Max Harris died in 1995

**Michael Kitson**, NDD, MCSD, senior lecturer in computer graphics at the Centre for Industrial Design, Monash University

**Stephen Knight**, MA, PhD, professor and head of English Literature at the University of Wales, Cardiff, former professor of English at the University of Melbourne, and author of works on modern popular culture and English usage

**Leonie Kramer**, AC, DBE, BA, DPhil, chancellor of the University of Sydney, emeritus professor of Australian literature at the University of Sydney, and author of studies in Australian literature

**Elizabeth Manley,** OBE, FAIM, FIDA, FRSA (Lond), former president of the Australian Institute of Management, South Australia, and former commissioner of Telecom Australia

CONTRIBUTORS

Judith Arthy
Margaret Barca
Kerry Cannon
Neil Conning
Vicki Hamilton
Anne McDougall
Sandra Zurbo

RESEARCHERS AND ADVISERS

Australian Copyright Council
John and Susan Barrett
Geoffrey Bills
Ceremonial and Hospitality Unit,
Department of the Prime Minister and Cabinet
Sarah Dawson
Henry, Mandy and Simon Drury
Dan Eaves
Cathy Gowdie
Jeffrey Grey
Alan Gunther
David Jones
Mallesons Stephen Jaques
Terry Monagle
Maureen O'Brien
Ken Ruthven
Paul Savage
David Wells
Lee White

# Acknowledgements

The publisher wishes to thank the following people and organisations for permission to reproduce or adapt copyright material: Melbourne *Age*, for some short entries from Gary Dean (ed.), *The Age Style Book*, David Syme, Melbourne, 1987; Commonwealth of Australia, for the table 'Symbols for Correcting Proofs', in *Style Manual for Authors, Editors and Printers*, 4th edn, Australian Government Publishing Service, Canberra, 1988; Australia Post, for illustrations of correctly addressed envelopes; Geoffrey Dutton, for index extracts from *Snow on the Saltbush*, Viking, 1984; Andrew Green, for an extract from Dorothy Green, 'Henry Handel Richardson', in Marilyn Lake and Farley Kelly (eds), *Double Time: Women in Victoria – 150 Years*, Penguin, 1985; Macquarie Library Pty Ltd, for the table 'Weights and Measures', in *The Macquarie Dictionary*, 2nd edn, Macquarie University, Sydney, 1991; Melbourne Cricket Club, for its logo; Paul Slessor and Collins/Angus & Robertson Publishers, for the first verse from Kenneth Slessor, 'South Country', in *Selected Poems*, Angus & Robertson, Sydney, 1975.

# Introduction

H. W. Fowler has an entry in his famous *Dictionary of Modern English Usage* contrasting what he calls 'working words' with 'stylish words'. Working words are often the simple ones, the ones most appropriate for clear communication; stylish words, by Fowler's definition, are the ostentatious ones inappropriate in everyday contexts.

Clear communication and appropriateness are what *The Penguin Working Words* is all about. The book aims to promote good, plain English and to show that some words function more effectively than others in particular situations. Entries frequently distinguish between the kinds of language suitable for formal prose, informal expression, public speaking and conversations at the supermarket. In casual conversation, gestures and tone of voice help to make meaning clear, slang comes into its own, and tidy sentences are relatively unimportant. Formal writing and speech are far more open to criticism. Careless English suggests careless thinking, and the formal word, whether in speech or on paper, requires precise, unambiguous expression.

The focus of *Working Words* is primarily the printed word because, even in an age of advanced sound and image recording, it remains the most enduring medium. Words work best for both writer and reader if the writer not only understands the most appropriate context for them but knows what they really mean, how to spell them, and where to locate them in a sentence. English is a complex language, and few people have encyclopaedic knowledge of it or an infallible instinct for the right word. *Working Words* therefore deals with word use and spelling, sentence structure, punctuation and the parts of speech. There are detailed articles on clauses, commas and nouns, for instance, and shorter ones on commonly confused words such as *flaunt* and *flout*, *affect* and *effect*. Pronunciation guidance has been given where necessary.

There are hundreds of examples of word use in the book. Sometimes the editors found that a grammatical point could be illustrated by a simple phrase, but often sentences were required. Examples of what *not* to do were considered helpful in many cases. One of the difficulties for compilers of style guides is avoiding examples that assume prior knowledge on the part of the reader. A range of familiar sources is essential. Sporting events, travel experiences, weather reports and the more startling snippets of daily news provided a ready supply of raw material, but the net had to be flung much wider to catch the diversity of Australian society: old and young, female and male, recent immigrant and Australian-born.

The rapidly changing technology of turning words into print has meant that hot-metal typesetting has vanished, and computer typesetting and desktop-publishing systems have taken over. The editors felt that *Working Words* should include substantial entries on desktop publishing and associated subjects such as layout and typography. A number of entries define the technical terms needed by everyone in publishing from writers and editors to designers and printers. These terms too are working words, tools of trade in the business of communication.

Though *Working Words* is not an encyclopaedia, it does bring together useful information that can be hard to gather from scattered sources. The abbreviated names of numerous organisations and companies, for example, have been spelt out because too often they appear in print without amplification. Other entries cover subjects such as copyright, indexing, the writing of formal letters, and the marks to use in proof correction. Australian place-names that are so similar in spelling that they could be confused are placed side by side for easy comparison, and descriptions of broad geographic regions in and near Australia have also been included.

A North American teacher working in South Australia wrote in 1992 to the journal *Australian Style* complaining about immigrants being required to observe 'the local Australian ways of spelling and punctuating even if they're full of inconsistencies and exceptions to rules that have been learned elsewhere'. His solution, not surprisingly, was to advocate the adoption here of the rules he had been taught elsewhere. *Working Words* argues that Australians need feel no obligation whatever to adopt the conventions of the United States or any other country, and that they can find in reference works such as *The Macquarie Dictionary* and the Australian Government Publishing Service's *Style Manual for Authors, Editors and Printers* – and *Working Words* itself – authoritative guidance on Australian usage and style.

Different English-speaking countries have colloquialisms that are readily recognised by the outside world, particularly when they are voiced in the accents of those countries. National distinguishing marks are less conspicuous in the written word, but the distinctions are real nevertheless. Even when American spelling is altered, as it is in British editions of works, American English retains a certain flavour of its own, whatever the subject matter. The same is true of Australian English.

Spoken English in Australia has been bombarded for decades by films and television from the United States, but written English has been affected less noticeably. British English, the language the first white settlers brought with them, remains predominant, though not unchanged. Modern Australian English is the product of two centuries in which Australians of Aboriginal, Anglo-Celtic, European and Asian descent contributed words, idioms and nuances of meaning to the language. Whatever the future impact of English imported from other parts of the English-speaking world, these native influences will continue to be at work, and the distinctive tone of Australian English will continue to be heard.

In his foreword to the 1992 second edition of *The Macquarie Dictionary*, Donald Horne wrote that 'Any dictionary is a snapshot of one moment in an ever-changing process'. The editors of *The Macquarie* – the dictionary most frequently consulted in the preparation of *Working Words* – emphasise the point that entries are based on usage in Australia, not subjective judgement; in general they record contemporary practice rather than recommend for or against a particular use. The function of *Working Words* is rather different. Its role is to guide the reader to acceptable English in modern Australian contexts; to emphasise one approach over another if necessary (or to indicate where two approaches have equal value); and to make recommendations that are based on the research and experience of Australians who constantly work with words. Sometimes it lays down the law, as in the joint entry for *disinterested* (impartial) and *uninterested* (not interested): 'These adjectives are never synonymous'. *The Macquarie*, on the other hand, includes the phrase '*Colloq*. uninterested' in its entry for *disinterested*. People unaware that dictionaries are often descriptive rather than prescriptive mistakenly believe they are being told that *disinterested* should be used to mean *uninterested* when the context is informal. One of the functions of *Working Words* is to help readers to distinguish between valid usage and usage that has arisen through ignorance.

It could be argued that the battle for distinctions of this kind has already been lost, or that the battle is barely worth fighting. But people who care about the way they write and speak want guidelines such as *Working Words* provides, even though, like the book, they accept that a living language will keep changing.

Certainly words and phrases are shaped by the use women and men make of them. *Gender* is a word clearly in transition. Some Australians now use it instead of the traditional word *sex* in phrases such as 'a person of the opposite sex'. In *Working Words* either word is stated to be acceptable in this sense, but the book's own references stick with tradition. On this point, and a host of others, readers will of course make up their own minds.

Any group of people foolhardy enough to put together a usage guide know that some of their judgements will be challenged. The compilers of *Working Words* welcome debate on matters raised in the book and hope that readers will express their views by writing to the publisher. Future editions will take account of comments and continue to reflect the latest developments in Australian English.

[illegible]

[illegible]

[illegible]

[illegible]

[illegible]

# A to Z WORKING WORDS

# Aa

**a/an** The grammatical term for *a* or *an* is the indefinite article. Use *a* before words beginning with a consonant, or a vowel that sounds like a consonant:

a tree    a hovercraft    a eulogy    a union    a one-sided affair

Use *an* before words beginning with a vowel, or a consonant that either sounds like a vowel or is not sounded at all:

an egg    an umbrella    an X-ray    an heir

Traditionally *an* was often used before words beginning with *h* if the first syllable was unstressed and the *h* sound dropped:

an hotel    an historian    an habitual liar

Today it is more common to sound the *h* in such words and therefore to use *a* before them. Similarly, sound is the key to choosing *a* or *an* before figures, acronyms and abbreviations:

a 400 hectare property    a Unicef conference    a VIP lounge
an $80 fine    an Asio file    an NRMA van

Except in cases of special emphasis, the word *a* should be pronounced like the *u* in *under*, not the *ay* in *hay*.

**AA** Alcoholics Anonymous.

**AAL** Aborigines Advancement League Inc.

**AAMI** Australian Associated Motor Insurers Limited.

**AANT** Automobile Association of the Northern Territory.

**AAP** Australian Associated Press.

**AAT** Administrative Appeals Tribunal; Australian Antarctic Territory.

**ABA** Australian Booksellers Association; Australian Broadcasting Authority.

**abattoir** Note the single *b* and *-tt-*, and the fact that the plural form *abattoirs* may be used to mean one slaughterhouse only. The recommended pronunciation is '**abba**-twah' rather than 'abba-tor'.

**abbreviations and contractions** An *abbreviation* is a shortened form of a word (or words) that consists of the initial letter alone, or the initial letter followed by letters other than the final one:

p. a.m. Mon. approx. vol. Vic. etc. op. cit. P. D. James

Abbreviations are usually followed by a full stop. Those made up of a group of initial capitals have traditionally had a full stop after each capital:

M.P. N.S.W. H.M.A.S. A.B.C. P.L.O.

Today, however, the trend is towards lighter punctuation and the stops are usually dropped:

MP NSW HMAS ABC PLO

Note that *acronyms* are abbreviations of this kind that form words:

CHOGM OPEC SALT

Some have come to be written with an initial capital only:

Nato Anzac Unesco

Another exception in the matter of stops comprises internationally recognised units of measurement, whose abbreviations – regarded as symbols – do not take full stops:

cm (centimetre) A (ampere) g (gram) L (litre)

Then there are the abbreviations that have lost their full stop for no logical reason:

per cent *not* per cent. 50c *not* 50c.

A *contraction* is a shortened form of a word (or words) that ends in the same letter as the word itself:

Mr Dr Qld we're Cwlth Pty Ltd

Contractions are not followed by a full stop unless they end a sentence.

Note that *vol.* is an abbreviation but that its plural form, *vols*, is a contraction and therefore is not followed by a full stop. Here are some other plurals to note:

p. (page) pp. (pages)
MP (member of parliament) MPs (members of parliament)
km (kilometre) km (kilometres)
Mr (Mister) Messrs (more than one 'Mister')

There is no apostrophe in plurals such as *MPs*.

Some abbreviations and contractions are more often used than the full words:

a.m. *not* ante meridiem
Mr Barnes *not* Mister Barnes
Quickfix Pty Ltd *not* Quickfix Proprietary Limited

Some people prefer to write *a.m.* (as well as *p.m.*, *i.e.* and *e.g.*) without the stops. If you adopt this style it is necessary to ensure that *am* cannot be mistaken for the first person singular form of the verb *to be*.

In contractions such as *I've*, *she'll*, *we're*, *they'd* and *can't* an apostrophe indicates the dropping of letters. Note that there are irregular contractions, such as *shan't* (from *shall not*) and *won't* (from *will not*). Be sure to place the apostrophe correctly: *wouldn't* not *would'nt*. These forms are common in spoken English and informal writing, but in more formal prose normally appear only in reported conversations.

The purpose of abbreviations and contractions is to save time and space – letters, memos, notes, bibliographies and tables are full of them. In more formal contexts there will be fewer, but measurements in a biological text, for instance, are usually abbreviated, and contractions such as *I've* and *you'll* abound in fictional conversation. Whether or not to abbreviate *New South Wales* to *NSW* will partly depend on the likely distribution of the publication. Remember that *NSW* is as meaningless to most Americans as *Pa* (Pennsylvania) is to most Australians.

Some subject matter calls for many abbreviated or contracted names. It may be necessary to list them at the beginning or end of the text, but it is often sufficient to spell out the less familiar ones (with the shortened form in brackets), then use only the initials. Some people prefer to give the shortened form in the first instance, with the full name in brackets.

The European Free Trade Association (EFTA) . . .
*or* EFTA (European Free Trade Association) . . .
*then* EFTA met during the week . . .

Everyday conversation is full of words and phrases that are abbreviated in a more general sense – *mozzies* for *mosquitoes*, *metho* for *methylated spirits*. These examples would be unusual in formal prose (except for fiction), but many abbreviations of the same kind are accepted without question:

| | | | | | |
|---|---|---|---|---|---|
| plane | *for* | aeroplane | vet | *for* | veterinary surgeon |
| piano | *for* | pianoforte | fax | *for* | facsimile |

See also **acronyms**; **ampersand**; **apostrophe**; **capitalisation**; **compass points**; **degrees and diplomas**; **ranks, titles, honours and awards**; **weights and measures**.

**ABC** Australian Broadcasting Corporation (Commission until 1983).

**Aberfeldie, Vic.** (3040) Compare with *Aberfeldy*, Vic. (3825).

**ability/capability/capacity** These nouns are similar in that each broadly means competence, but there are subtle differences. Strictly speaking, *ability* should only be attributed to living things: *Greg's ability to play the piano*. It has the additional meaning of proficiency or talent:

Greg's musical ability astounded the audience.

*Capability* suggests possession of the necessary qualities, as yet unused, to do something:

The ship has a nuclear capability.

Mandy has the capability for success in any field.

*Capacity* suggests the power, not just the potential, to experience, produce, receive or contain something:

He remarked on his friend's capacity for forgiveness.

The machine's heating capacity is high.

It may also mean function: *in my teaching capacity*; maximum amount: *working to capacity*; or volume: *10 litre capacity*.

**abjure/adjure** These are rather ponderous verbs. *Abjure* means to renounce or repudiate:

I'll abjure drinking if you'll abjure eating.

*Adjure* means to bind solemnly or command:

The doctor adjured him to give up alcohol.

**-able/-ible word endings** These word endings (suffixes) are used to form adjectives, usually from verbs. There are many more *-able* than *-ible* suffixes.

Some sources offer a set of rules to help us predict the likely suffix for a particular word, but the rules are neither watertight nor easy to interpret. Guidelines for adapting the root of a word before adding the suffix are also quite complex. Instead of rules, here is an alphabetical list of the most frequently used words with *-able* or *-ible* endings.

abominable
accessible
actionable
adaptable
adducible
admissible
adorable
advisable
agreeable
amenable
analysable
appreciable
apprehensible
arguable
ascribable
assessable
atonable
audible
available
bearable
believable
blamable
*or* blameable
bribable
bridgeable
calculable
capable
changeable
chargeable
coercible
collapsible
collectable
*or* collectible
combustible
comfortable
compactable
compatible
comprehensible
compressible
conceivable
condensable
conferrable
consolable
contemptible
contractible
controllable
convertible
corrodible
corruptible
credible
curable
debatable
*or* debateable
deducible
deductible
defensible
deferrable
definable
delineable
demonstrable
desirable
despicable
destructible
detectable
*or* detectible
detestable
diffusible
digestible
dilatable
dirigible
discernible
dismissible
dispensable
dispersible
dissolvable
distendible

distinguishable
distractible
divisible
drinkable
drivable
*or* driveable
durable
dutiable
eatable
edible
educable
eligible
endorsable
endurable
enforceable
equable
evadable
evincible
excisable
excitable
excusable
exhaustible
expansible
expendable
expiable
expressible
extendable
*or* extendible
extensible
extractable
*or* extractible
fallible
feasible
flammable
flexible
forcible
foreseeable
forgettable
forgivable
framable
*or* frameable
frangible
fusible
gettable
giveable
governable
gullible
hireable
horrible
illegible
illimitable
immeasurable
immersible
immiscible
immovable
*or* immoveable
immutable
impalpable
impartible
impassable
impeccable
impenetrable
imperceptible
impermeable
impermissible
imperturbable
implacable
implausible
impossible
impracticable
impressible
impressionable
improvable
inaccessible
inadmissible
inalienable
inapprehensible
inaudible
incalculable
incombustible
incompatible
incomprehensible
inconceivable
inconsolable
incontestable
incontrovertible
inconvertible
incorrigible
incorruptible
incurable
incredible
indefatigable
indefeasible
indefensible
indelible
indescribable
indestructible
indetectable
*or* indetectible
indigestible
indiscernible
indispensable
indistinguishable
indivisible
indubitable
inducible
inedible
ineligible
inestimable
inexcusable
inexhaustible
inexorable
inexpressible
infallible
inflammable
inflatable
inflexible
infrangible
infusible
ingestible
inimitable
inoperable
insensible
inseparable
insubmissible
insufferable
insuperable
insupportable
insuppressible
insurmountable
insusceptible
intangible
intelligible
interruptible
intolerable
invertible
invincible
inviolable
invisible
irascible
irreconcilable
irreducible
irreplaceable
irrepressible
irresistible
irresponsible
irretrievable
irreversible
justifiable
knowledgeable
laughable
legible
leviable
likable
*or* likeable
livable
*or* liveable
lovable
*or* loveable
malleable
manageable
manoeuvrable
marriageable
measurable
miscible
movable
*or* moveable
namable
*or* nameable
negligible
nondeductible
notable
noticeable
objectionable
obtainable
operable

palatable
passable
payable
peaceable
penetrable
perceptible
perfectible
perishable
permeable
permissible
personable
persuadable
persuasible
plausible
pleasurable
possible
practicable
preferable
prescribable
preventable
*or* preventible
probable
producible
pronounceable
provable
ratable
*or* rateable
readable
reasonable
receivable
reconcilable
rectifiable
reducible
registrable
regrettable
reliable
remissible
removable
replaceable
reprehensible
repressible
reproducible
reputable
resistible
responsible
retractable
retrievable
reversible
revertible
risible
salable
*or* saleable
seasonable
sensible
serviceable
sizable
*or* sizeable
solvable
storable
submergible
submersible
suggestible
suitable
supportable
suppressible
surmountable
susceptible
tamable
*or* tameable
tangible
teachable
tenable
terrible
tolerable
traceable
tradable
transferable
translatable
transmissible
transmittable
treasonable
tunable
*or* tuneable
unbelievable
uncomfortable
unconscionable
uncontrollable
undeniable
undesirable
undetectable
unendurable
unenforceable
unexceptionable
unforgettable
unforgivable
unforseeable
unframable
*or* unframeable
ungovernable
unintelligible
uninterruptible
unjustifiable
unknowable
unmanageable
unmentionable
unmistakable
*or* unmistakeable
unobjectionable
unobtainable
unpronounceable
unreadable
unreliable
unscalable
unreasonable
unseasonable
unserviceable
unshakable
*or* unshakeable
unsuitable
untamable
*or* untameable
untenable
untraceable
untransferable
untranslatable
unutterable
usable
*or* useable
vendible
visible
washable
winnable

**ABM** antiballistic-missile missile.

**Aborigine/Aboriginal** The recommended term for Australia's original inhabitants is *Aborigine(s)*. *Aboriginal* is the adjective. Both noun and adjective have an initial capital:

He is an Aborigine of the Arunta tribe.

She is a noted Aboriginal poet and activist.

Some Aborigines prefer to be called by names from their own languages. Names now in common use include *Koori* (or *Koorie*), which simply means 'our people' and is widely favoured in the eastern States; *Murri* in Queensland

and northern New South Wales; *Yolngu* in the Northern Territory; *Aranda* in central Australia; *Nyunga* in Western Australia; and *Nungga* in South Australia. There are alternative spellings for many of these.

The words *aborigine* and *aboriginal* (with a lower-case initial) describe the original inhabitants of any country.

See also **black**.

**about/around** *About* and *around* are synonymous in some instances, although *about* is preferred in Australian English when we want to say approximately:

We must leave the cafe at about 3 p.m.

Note that *about* is superfluous where approximation has already been expressed: *about 3 or 4 p.m. About* is used in informal English to mean almost (usually preceded by *just*):

We are just about ready.

Either *around* or *about* may be used to mean in the vicinity:

The waiter is somewhere around [*or* about].

There is no need to use both words, as some people do in speech: *The waiter is somewhere around about.*

See also **around/round**.

**above/over** *Above* means on a higher level or in a higher position (than):

Our plane flew above the clouds.

*Over* means directly above or across:

Our plane flew over Sydney.

We drove over the Sydney Harbour Bridge.

In some instances these prepositions are synonymous:

The students live above [*or* over] the milk bar.

The use of *above* as a noun, adverb or adjective to describe something already mentioned is more acceptable in business letters or down-to-earth handbooks than in elegant texts:

For further details see the above [noun].

*or* For further details see above [adverb].

*or* Quote the above [adjective] reference number.

*but* We have already described this process in some detail, and . . .

See also **below/beneath/under/underneath**.

**ABPA** Australian Book Publishers' Association.

**abridgement/abridgment** The word means a shortened version of something written, or the creation of the shortened version. Either spelling, with or without the *-e* of *abridge*, is acceptable.

**abrogate/arrogate** *Abrogate* means to annul or repeal (usually a law or a treaty):

After the execution we urged the government to abrogate the death penalty.

*Arrogate* means to claim unduly for oneself or to seize without justification:

The chief of the defence forces arrogated the powers of government.

**ABS** Australian Bureau of Statistics.

**abscess** Note the *-sc-*.

**absorption** Note the *-p-* in this noun. *Absorb* is the verb.

**ABT** Australian Broadcasting Tribunal (since October 1992, the Australian Broadcasting Authority: ABA).

**abuse/misuse** The noun *abuse* can mean wrong, improper or illegal use: *abuse of power*; *drug abuse*. It can also mean insulting language, or injurious behaviour:

The politicians shouted abuse at each other.

Child abuse is a criminal offence.

The noun *misuse* also means wrong use, in the sense of something being inappropriate or misapplied, but it is a much less emotive word: *the misuse of one's leisure*; *the misuse of grammar*. As verbs the words keep the same distinction:

The student abused the library's honour system by exceeding the time limit.

He misused the screwdriver in trying to make a chisel of it.

Pronounce the end of the nouns with a soft *s* ('ab-**yoos**', 'mis-yoos') and the verbs with a 'z' sound ('ab-**yooz**', 'mis-**yooz**').

**ac** alternating current (electricity).

**a/c** account.

**academic** The noun *academic* means a teaching member of an institution of higher education: *an academic from an interstate university*. The adjective *academic* means relating to scholarship; or theoretical, irrelevant, impractical; or conforming with tradition:

Academic standards are slipping.

In view of the warm public response, the committee's criticism is academic.

He was an academic painter with a conservative style.

**ACC** Australian Chamber of Commerce.

**accede** Note the *-cc-*. This verb means to agree or to take up high office. It is pronounced 'ak-**seed**'.

**accelerator** Note the *or* ending.

**accents** These marks are used in some languages to indicate pronunciation or stress. Foreign words used in English are sometimes written with their accents and pronounced – by some speakers, at any rate – as in the original language. A number of foreign words are unusual enough to be italicised in print, and some dictionaries indicate their preferred style. The following are the most common accents likely to be needed:

- acute (ʹ), which indicates that the *é* is pronounced 'ay'

  passé  sauté  élan
- grave (`), which indicates a falling pitch when it is applied to *e*

  chère [pronounced 'share']  à la [pronounced 'ah lah']
- cedilla (¸), which softens a hard *c* to make it sound like 's'

  façade [pronounced 'fa-**sard**']  soupçon [pronounced '**soop**-son']
- circumflex (ˆ), which lengthens a vowel sound

  crêpe suzette [pronounced 'krape soo-**zet**']

  bête noire [pronounced 'bate nwar']
- diaeresis (¨), which usually indicates that the second of two adjacent vowels is pronounced separately

  naïve [pronounced 'nie-**eev**' *or* 'nay-**eev**']
- umlaut (¨), which indicates a change in a vowel sound

  *Mann* [pronounced 'mahn'; German for *man*]

*becomes*

*Männer* [pronounced 'menner'; German for *men*]

While there is no overall ruling on whether or not to use accents on foreign words in English, there are two useful rules of thumb.

- If the word or phrase is so unusual as to warrant setting in italics, accents are generally used:

  *idée fixe*  *crème de la crème*
- If the omission of accents from the commoner foreign words set in roman might result in mispronunciation of the word, it is better to use them – especially acute accents:

  attaché  fiancé  cliché

But note that we are quite accustomed to leaving the accents off some words without having problems with pronunciation:

elite  regime  cafe

If a word requires accents, ensure that it receives its full complement:

pâté  résumé  crème brûlée

Only the pedantic would insist on accents for well-assimilated words such as *fete*, *premiere*, *role* and *bric-a-brac*. Note that *naïve* is often written without the diaeresis over the *i* – possibly because the pronunciation is now so well known.

Dictionaries sometimes recommend alternative styles of setting for foreign words (accents or no accents; italic or roman), and authorities differ. Moreover these words may change style as they become more widely used in English.

See also **foreign words and phrases**; **italics, use of**.

**accept/except** These verbs are occasionally confused. *Accept* has a range of meanings that include to take or receive; or to agree (to), admit or believe:

The television hostess will accept the award on behalf of her show.

Her competitors accept the judges' decision.

*Except* means to leave out or exclude:

Vaccinations are compulsory and the school can except no student.

This example illustrates the rather institutional tone of the verb. We are more likely to use a different form of the word:

Vaccinations are compulsory for students, with no exceptions.

See also **except**.

**access** The broadest meaning of the noun *access* is the ability to reach or be admitted to something:

Even the window-cleaner had access to the Minister's private papers.

The lane gave access to the stage door.

The use of *access* as a verb belongs to computer jargon and means to locate information in or obtain it from a computer:

Can you access these files for me?

We need to access the book's sales figures before deciding on a reprint.

In non-computer contexts prefer verbs such as *consult*, *approach* or even *read*.

**accessary/accessory** In law an *accessary* is someone connected with a crime although not present at the time it was perpetrated:

The guard was charged as an accessary.

An *accessory* is a minor fitting or attachment, such as a computer mouse, a car mirror or a woman's handbag. However, it is becoming increasingly common to use this spelling for both meanings. Many authorities recommend it.

**accommodate/accommodation** Note the *-cc-* and *-mm-*, which can trip even the copywriters for the best hotels.

**accompanist** Not 'accompanyist'.

**ACDRE/Air Cdre** Air Commodore.

**ACER** Australian Council for Educational Research.

**acetic/aesthete/aesthetic/ascetic** Only the middle two words are related. *Acetic* is a chemical term usually linked with the word *acid*: *acetic acid*, for instance, is the basis of vinegar. Pronounce it 'a-**see**tik'.

The noun *aesthete* means a person who cultivates an appreciation of beauty:

A true aesthete, she loved both Bach and Byron.

The adjectival form, *aesthetic*, means relating to beauty or good taste. The US spellings *esthete* and *esthetic* are not recommended. Pronounce the words '**ees**-theet', 'ees-**thet**tik'; or '**ess**-theet', 'ess-**thet**tik'.

The noun *ascetic* refers to a person who practises self-denial, originally a monk or hermit. As an adjective it means abstemious. Pronounce the word 'a-**set**tik'.

**ACF** Australian Conservation Foundation.

**acknowledgement/acknowledgment** Either spelling, with or without the final *-e* of *acknowledge*, is acceptable.

See also **acknowledgements**.

**acknowledgements** The authors of some printed works acknowledge the help of others in a section headed *Acknowledgements* (or *Acknowledgments*), or in a preface to the work.

See also **acknowledgement/acknowledgment**; **foreword/preface**; **publications, parts of**.

**ACM** Air Chief Marshal.

**ACN/A.C.N.** Each letter in this abbreviation for *Australian Company Number* was originally followed by a full stop, but the stops are now optional. Public and private companies registered in Australia are issued with a nine-digit ACN by the Australian Securities Commission and are required to print the abbreviation and number on every 'public document' and 'eligible negotiable instrument' – for instance letterhead, cheques, invoices and the company seal. A company's publications have to carry the ACN, but commercially produced books do not.

**ACOSS** Australian Council of Social Service (not 'Services').

**acquaint** Note the *-cqu-*. You should *acquaint* someone *with* (not *of*) the facts, but the simpler verb *tell* (or *inform* in official contexts) is often preferable.

**acquiesce** Note the *-cqu-* and the *-sc-* in this verb meaning to agree. Note also that a person acquiesces *in* something, not *with* or *to*:

> Since Tuan would have to put our proposals into practice, we hoped she could acquiesce in them.

**acreage** The *-e* of *acre* is retained.

**acronyms** An *acronym* is a word made from the initial letters (and occasionally syllables) of other words. It may be a made-up word (*EFTPOS*) or may coincide with a real word (*BASIC*). Most authorities use this term for such a letter group only when it is pronounced as a word (*CAT*, *TEAS*); if it is pronounced as a series of initials (*AMP*, *VIP*), the term used is *abbreviation*. Other authorities use the term *acronym* in both cases. Acronyms usually start as groups of capital letters and, if accepted generally enough, become words in their own right, with only an initial capital:

NATO (**N**orth **A**tlantic **T**reaty **O**rganization)    Nato

Others lose even the initial capital; they are usually formed from lower-case letters anyway:

LASER (**l**ight **a**mplification by **s**timulated **e**mission of **r**adiation)    laser

However, it is advisable to retain the full capitals if there is any possibility of confusion: *SALT, WHO*.

Other examples of completely assimilated words are *radar* (**ra**dio **d**etection **a**nd **r**anging), *sonar* (**so**und **n**avigation **a**nd **r**anging), *quasar* (**quas**i-stell**ar**) and *scuba* (**s**elf-**c**ontained **u**nderwater **b**reathing **a**pparatus). Established Australian acronyms include *Anzac* (**A**ustralian **a**nd **N**ew **Z**ealand **A**rmy **C**orps), *Qantas* (**Q**ueensland **a**nd **N**orthern **T**erritory **A**erial **S**ervices), *Asio* (**A**ustralian **S**ecurity **I**ntelligence **O**rganization), *ACOSS* (**A**ustralian **C**ouncil **o**f **S**ocial **S**ervice) and *NIDA* (**N**ational **I**nstitute of **D**ramatic **A**rt).

Thc current trend is for more and more acronyms, with every new organisation or pressure group feeling it will miss the public eye if it does not concoct a name that can be twisted into an acronym. Some relatively recent examples are *ASH* (**A**ction on **S**moking and **H**ealth), *SIDS* (**S**udden **I**nfant **D**eath **S**yndrome) and *ATOM* (**A**ustralian **T**eachers **o**f **M**edia).

Be sparing in your use of unusual acronyms and provide the reader with the complete form of all but the most familiar of these shortened expressions, at least on first mentioning them.

See also **abbreviations and contractions**.

**acrostic** An acrostic is a message or word spelt out by initials in a series of lines, such as the following Advice to New Employees:

The kinds of people who last only a few weeks in this office
**D**on't usually listen to what they are told
**U**nderstand little when they do
**D**elay action as long as possible and
**S**ulk most of the time

The initials do not necessarily fall at the beginning of the lines, but a pattern needs to be discernible.

**ACs** See **author's corrections**.

**ACT** Australian Capital Territory.

**act/action** These words both refer to something that is being done. *Act* emphasises the thing done but *action* is concerned with the process of doing, which may involve a number of *acts* and possibly a longer time:

Sean's first act on arriving home was to eat a high-calorie meal.

He and his mates were planning a night of action at the skating rink.

**active voice/passive voice** Many verbs may appear in either the *active voice* or the *passive voice*:

The farmer sows [active voice] the wheat.

The wheat is sown [passive voice] by the farmer.

In the first example the subject of the sentence, farmer, performs the action; in the second the action is undergone by the subject, wheat. Here is a slightly more complex example:

The police will identify and prosecute [active voice] drink-drivers.

Drink-drivers will be identified and prosecuted [passive voice] by the police.

A verb in the active voice gives a basic sentence the simplest sequence: subject, object, verb. The passive voice reverses the order and complicates the sentence. Choosing the active voice rather than the passive also helps to give your writing vigour and immediacy. Putting verbs invariably into the passive voice is liable to send the reader to sleep. However, the passive voice is useful when the identity of the doer is unknown or irrelevant, or when an impersonal tone is desired. It is nevertheless often used excessively in technical and bureaucratic writing to distance the writer from what is being said:

Overtime payments will no longer be made by this company.

Compare this with the more direct statement:

This company will no longer pay for overtime.

See also **case (grammar)**; **subject/object**; **verbs.**

**ACTU** Australian Council of Trade Unions.

**actual/actually** The adjective *actual* and the adverb *actually* are valid words when used to indicate what is real and not imagined or fake; or to suggest surprise:

They brought back an actual piece of the Berlin Wall.

She actually passed that difficult exam.

However, they are often misused as meaningless fillers: *Actually I've been to the pictures*; *in actual fact*. The phrase *in actual fact* should be avoided in any case because it is a tautology.

**actualise** A verb from *actual* that is frowned on by many people.

**actually** See **actual/actually**.

**acute/chronic** An *acute* problem is brief and severe, generally requiring prompt attention, and a *chronic* problem is one that has continued for some time or is recurrent:

His dehydration was acute but an intravenous drip quickly eased it.

The financial problems of public transport systems are chronic rather than recent.
The use of *chronic* to mean awful (*a chronic rock group*) is strictly informal.

**AD** Australian Democrats.

**AD/BC** *AD* is an abbreviation of the Latin *anno Domini* (in the year of the Lord) and is placed before the year: *AD 1991*. *BC* stands for *before Christ* and is usually placed after the year: *44 BC*. People of non-Christian religions often prefer to use *CE* (Common Era or Christian Era) and *BCE* (before the Common Era or before the Christian Era) instead of AD and BC. Many archaeologists use the term *BP* (before the present), which is an age indicator that is related to radiocarbon dating, not the calendar.

Some typographers use small capitals rather than full capitals for these abbreviations: AD 1993.

See also **centuries**; **dates**.

**adaptation/adaption** *Adaptation* is the preferred noun for the act or result of adapting: *a modern adaptation of the play. Adaption* is now restricted to a specialised usage in sociology.

**adapter/adaptor** Either spelling is acceptable for the word meaning a person who adapts something, or an electrical or mechanical device.

**adaption** See **adaptation/adaption**.

**adaptor** See **adapter/adaptor**.

***ADB*** *Australian Dictionary of Biography*.

**ADC** aide-de-camp (pronounced 'ay-d'com').

**addendum** This noun means something that is to be added; the plural is *addenda*.

**address** The verb *to address* has one well-known usage that is not recommended: the tendency of people in public life to *address* issues rather than to *tackle*, *face* or *deal with* them.

**addressing envelopes** The principal concern in addressing envelopes is clarity. As many postal articles are electronically sorted, it is wise to follow Australia Post guidelines.

- Restrict the name and address to three or four lines wherever possible (normally, only the last two lines are scanned for location information).

- Write the address in the centre of the envelope, with the left-hand margins aligned.
- Do not use end-of-line punctuation.
- Do not underline.
- Use capital letters for the last line of the address.
- Use the correct postcode.
- Keep the bottom 15 millimetres of the envelope clear for automatic sortation index printing.
- Include a return address, either on the front top left-hand corner of the envelope, or on its reverse.

The following examples illustrate the style recommended by Australia Post. Note that the layout for machine-addressed envelopes differs from that of hand-addressed ones.

See also **letters, formal**.

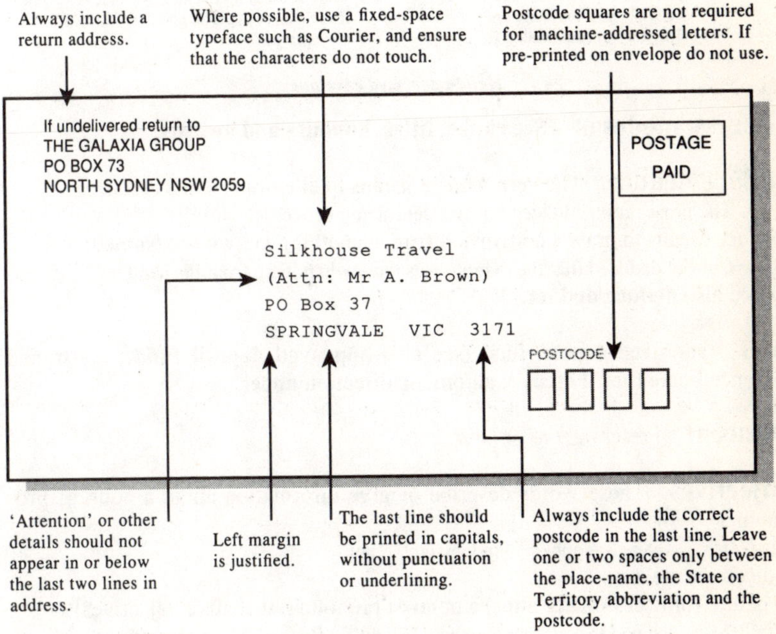


***Machine-addressed envelope***

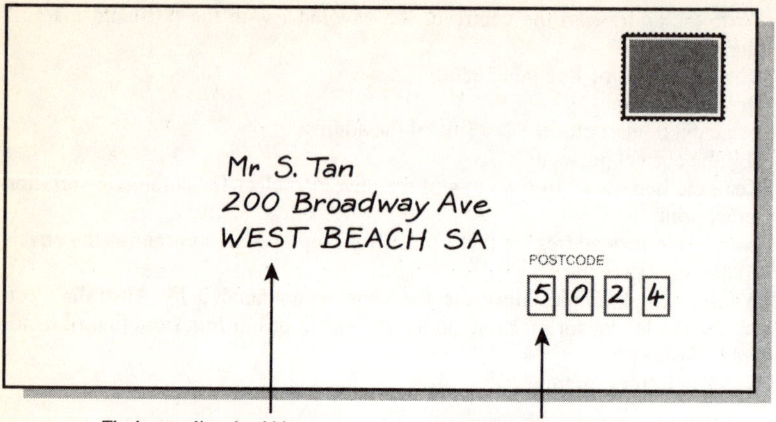


The bottom line should be in capitals and include only the place-name or post office of delivery, and the State or Territory in abbreviated form.

Write the postcode clearly in the four postcode squares. Do not use the squares when addressing letters for overseas – even if the overseas postal code can fit into the squares.

***Hand-addressed envelope***

**address, modes of** See **ranks, titles, honours and awards**.

**adduce/deduce** The verb *adduce* means to cite or present as proof:

The prosecution adduced faulty scientific evidence.

*Deduce* means to draw a conclusion from something known or assumed:

Gabriel deduced that the magpie was tame when it ate from his hand.

See also **deduce/deduct**.

**ADF** approved deposit fund (see also **approved deposit fund**); Australian Defence Force (not 'Forces'); automatic direction finder.

**adjacent** Prefer *next to* or *near*.

**adjectives** These words describe or give information about a noun or pronoun:

fat    clean    wobbly    indecisive    apt

Adjectives are used:

- before (or occasionally after) a noun or pronoun (attributive adjectives)

  the *brown* paddocks    *indispensable* help    *Poor* me!    a ship *afloat*
- after a verb (predicative adjectives)

  The paddocks look *brown*.    Help was *indispensable*.    The ship was *afloat*.

Some adjectives are derived from pronouns (possessive adjectives):

*your* shin    *her* ingenuity    *their* cakes

Some have a special function in specifying things and people (demonstrative adjectives):

Does the government value *these* rainforests?

*That* member has taken a stand.

You can combine many of them with other adjectives, nouns and adverbs (compound adjectives):

| | |
|---|---|
| white-hot steel | heavy-hearted refugees |
| sea-green curtains | well-framed etchings |
| overconfident contestants | an understaffed office |

The hyphenation of such compounds is discussed under **hyphenation**. Note that although many compound adjectives end in *d* or *ed*, there are numerous exceptions.

Some adjectives can be used as nouns:

the rich    the powerful

Adjectives should be selected with care in order to avoid

- tautology: *true facts*; *an unexpected surprise*; *a round circle*
- clichés: *masterly understatement*; *valiant efforts*; *a close call*; *thick as thieves*
- faulty combinations: *cheap prices* [use *low prices*]
- vagueness: *a nice girl*; *a terrific party*
- overuse

The last point is taken up in Sir Ernest Gowers' *The Complete Plain Words*: 'If a *crisis* is always *acute* and an *emergency* always *grave*, what is left for those words to do by themselves?'. Always ask yourself whether an adjective will add anything of value to the word it qualifies.

Absolute adjectives such as *perfect*, *complete*, *total*, *extreme*, *entire* and *unique* cannot be modified by adverbs like *very*, *utterly*, *totally* and *extremely*, but some can be modified by the adverbs *almost* or *nearly*:

| | | |
|---|---|---|
| | almost perfect | nearly complete |
| *not* | totally perfect | very complete |

Here are some other absolute adjectives:

| | | | |
|---|---|---|---|
| absolute | extreme | immaculate | total |
| basic | ideal | impossible | ultimate |
| complete | fatal | inevitable | unanimous |
| empty | final | perfect | unique |
| entire | full | simultaneous | universal |
| equal | fundamental | supreme | whole |

Be careful not to use an adjective when an adverb is required:

The home team played more strongly [adverb] than the visitors.

*not* The home team played stronger [adjective] than the visitors.

Particularly when an adjective and adverb look different, as *strong* and *strongly* do, it is important to understand the role the word is playing. If it is referring to a noun (as in *strong team*) the word must be an adjective (*strong*); if to a verb (*played* in this sentence), it must be an adverb (*strongly*). The suffix *-ly* distinguishes adverb from adjective in many cases, but far from all. Note that words such as *fast*, *late* and *early* look the same whether they are acting as adjectives or adverbs:

The fast [adjective] train went by.

He ran fast [adverb] to catch the train.

Others such as *high* and *clear* can act as adjectives or adverbs, and also have an *-ly* form for an adverb with a different meaning:

It was a high [adjective] wall.

She threw the ball high [adverb].

We value your work highly [adverb].

See also **adverbs**; **clause**; **comparative and superlative**; **hyphenation**; **phrase**.

**adjure** See **abjure/adjure**.

**ad lib** This term means freely or as one pleases (Latin: *ad libitum*). Its most common use in informal contexts is as a verb meaning to improvise, an adjective meaning improvised, or an adverb meaning spontaneously. It may be written as one word without a full point, but as an adjective and an adverb it is usually two words.

The prime minister stumbled when he had to adlib during the debate.

This comedian is capable of a brilliant ad lib performance.

When rain interrupted play the commentators rattled on ad lib for hours.

**ADM/Adm.** Admiral.

**administer/administrate** Prefer *administer* to *administrate* when the meaning is manage:

Helen wanted to administer the company herself.

*Administer* is the right word when you mean provide:

Sanjay was about to administer first aid.

The verb *administrate* is rarely used, unlike the associated noun *administration.*

**admission/admittance** These words both mean permission to enter. Only *admission* may involve a charge, and have the separate meaning acknowledgement or confession: *an admission of guilt.*

**admit** Do not use the preposition *to* with this word in the following construction:

Admit your mistake. *not* Admit to your mistake.

You may, of course, have to *admit your mistake to the supervisor* or ask the doorman to *admit you to a club.*

**admittance** See **admission/admittance**.

**admonitory** This adjective is often misspelt. It means cautionary or reproving: *an admonitory message about noisy parties.*

**adolescence** Note the *-sc-* and the *-nce.*

**adopted/adoptive** A child is *adopted*; those who adopt the child are *adoptive* parents.

**ADP** automatic data processing.

**ADT** automatic data transmission.

**advantageous** The *-e* of *advantage* is retained.

**adverbs** These are words that tell *how, when, why* or *where*, and their role is to modify:

- verbs

  sang *sweetly* arrived *late* stepped *sideways*
- adjectives

  *very* bracing *too* sunny *nearly* impossible
- other adverbs

  *most* diligently *rather* soon *quite* brilliantly

Most adverbs are formed by adding *-ly* to an adjective:

fortunately weirdly mysteriously cheerfully

It is harder to identify those that are not:

here there everywhere also

Many adverbs take the same form as the adjective or preposition:

| | |
|---|---|
| *much* [adverb] happier | *much* [adjective] mess |
| he flew *upward* [adverb] | an *upward* [adjective] glance |
| the firm went *under* [adverb] | *under* [preposition] a gum |

When a few words such as *well* and *ill* are used as adverbs in combination with past participles to make compound adjectives, a hyphen usually links them if they occur before a verb, but not after:

A well-made suit lasts for years.

*but* This suit is well made.

In similar situations the many adverbs that end in *ly* never have a linking hyphen, whether they appear before or after a verb:

This rarely seen portrait will attract attention.

The portrait is rarely seen.

As a general rule, place the adverb where it sounds best in a sentence:

The cat *stealthily* advanced on the bird.

*or* The cat advanced *stealthily* on the bird.

*or* *Stealthily* the cat advanced on the bird.

*or* The cat advanced on the bird *stealthily.*

But do not place an adverb between the parts of an infinitive if there is a satisfactory alternative:

The cat tried to advance *stealthily.*

*rather than*

The cat tried to *stealthily* advance.

Note that the position chosen for an adverb may affect the meaning of a sentence:

Sam decidedly prefers spicy foods.

Putting *decidedly* before *prefers* makes it clear that Sam's preference is strong. If *decidedly* belongs with *spicy* you must put the words side by side:

Sam prefers foods that are decidedly spicy.

Avoid overloading your prose with adverbs. Where possible, choose an appropriate verb and eliminate the adverb:

I *relished* the thought of his vintage port.

*rather than*

I *greatly enjoyed* the thought of his vintage port.

As Graham Greene is reputed to have said, 'If you get the verbs right you don't need adverbs at all'.

See also **adjectives**; **clause**; **comparative and superlative**; **hyphenation**; **phrase**; **split infinitive**.

**adversary** Put most stress on the first syllable: '**ad**-versary'.

**adverse/averse** *Adverse* means unfavourable, hostile or against one's interests. It is only used to describe things:

Adverse weather conditions ruined our camping holiday.

The critics destroyed the play with adverse reviews.

*Averse* means disinclined, reluctant or opposed to. It can only be used of people:

A pacifist is averse to violence.

Note that *averse* must always be followed by *to*. When *not* precedes it, *averse* is often being used ironically:

Most people are not averse to flattery.

**advert/avert** *Advert* is a very formal verb that means mention or refer to:

The barrister said he would advert to your evidence.

*Avert* means to prevent or turn away:

The intervention of the police will avert an accident.

**advice/advise/counsel** The first two words are frequently confused. *Advice* is the noun, *advise* the verb:

The travel agent gave us sound advice regarding our holiday.

She can advise you on obtaining a passport.

Note that *inform* is not a synonym for *advise*, though the words are closely related: you *inform* students of examination dates; you *advise* them to prepare their work in good time.

The verb *counsel* also means to *advise* but has a different shading. It is more formal and tends to mean the offering of judicious advice or of comfort. Practitioners in the religious, medical, legal and social-guidance fields may *counsel* rather than *advise*:

> You must counsel Angelica if she is unsure of her rights.

See also **council/counsel**.

**adviser/advisor** Prefer *adviser*, but the adjective is *advisory*.

**ae/oe/e** Influenced by US English, the digraphs *ae* and *oe* in words such as *encyclopaedia* and *foetus* are tending to be dropped in favour of the simple *e*. The sound represented by these digraphs is usually 'ee', but in *manoeuvre* is pronounced 'oo'.

The possibility of mispronunciation is in fact the main objection to this trend: the fourth syllable of *encyclopedia* can occasionally be heard to rhyme with *head*, the first syllable of *fetus* with *pet*. In Australian English (as in British and US English) there is no clear-cut answer to the question of which form to use. The major Australian, British and US dictionaries give preferences and alternatives, although the US favours the *e* spellings.

See also **digraph/diphthong/ligature**.

**aer-** *Aer-* comes from the Latin and Greek words for air. Note the spelling of *aerate* (not 'airate', 'airiate' or 'aeriate'), which means to expose to the action of air or gas (*aerated waters*); and *aerial*, which means of or in the air (*aerial spraying*).

**aerobic/anaerobic** The adjective *aerobic* means requiring oxygen to live or be active. Its opposite, *anaerobic*, means not requiring oxygen. The activity that is called *aerobics* is intended to improve participants' use of oxygen by strengthening their heart and lungs.

**aesthete/aesthetic** See **acetic/aesthete/aesthetic/ascetic**.

**AFC** Australian Film Commission.

**affect/effect** These words are frequently confused. *Affect* is normally used only as a verb, meaning to influence, move (emotionally), impress; or, less commonly, to assume a pose, make a pretence of:

> The new traffic regulations will affect everyone.
>
> He affected a look of surprise when booked for speeding.

*Effect* as a verb means to bring about, accomplish:

The Minister effected many beneficial changes in road regulations.

*Effect* is also used as a noun, to mean a result:

The effect of the new traffic regulations was to lower the death toll on the roads.

The plural noun *effects* can mean more than one result; or goods (*our personal effects*).

**affectation/affection** *Affectation* is the putting on of airs and graces, an assumed manner:

The commercial traveller's affectation of gentility amused his country customers.

The most common meaning of *affection* is love or a kindly feeling: *parents' affection for their children.*

**affinity** This noun means a liking for, or likeness to, people or things. Note the prepositions preferred in the following:

There was an affinity *between* Peter and Paul, and both had an affinity *with* Mary.

*but not*

Peter has an affinity *for* [or *to*] Paul and Mary.

Using *for* or *to* in examples such as the last would seem to imply that affinity can be a one-sided matter, which is incorrect.

**afflict/inflict** The verb *to afflict* means to distress with mental or bodily pain; it is followed by *with*:

Why did the teacher afflict the class with his dreadful verse?

This verb is often turned around: *afflicted with blindness.*

To *inflict* means to impose something or someone unpleasant on another; *on* is the preposition to use after it:

The teacher intends to inflict his verse on the class.

Note that it is the *verse*, not the *class*, that is inflicted.

**AFI** Australian Film Institute.

**AFIC** Australian Financial Institutions Commission.

**aficionado** Note the *-ion-* (not '-ian-'). The plural is *aficionados*. This word, meaning a devotee, may also be spelt *afficionado*. Pronounce the *-fic-* 'fish'.

**AFL** This is the abbreviation for *Australian Football League* (formerly VFL, Victorian Football League, 1896–1989), the major organisation in Australian Rules football. In 1992 the AFL teams and their nicknames were as follows: Adelaide (Crows); Brisbane (Brisbane Bears); Carlton (Blues); Collingwood (Magpies); Essendon (Dons, Bombers); Fitzroy (Lions); Footscray (Bulldogs); Geelong (Cats); Hawthorn (Hawks); Melbourne (Demons); North Melbourne (Kangaroos); Richmond (Tigers); St Kilda (Saints); Sydney (Sydney Swans); and West Coast (West Coast Eagles).

**Afrikaans/Afrikaner/Afrikander** Note the *-k-* in each. *Afrikaans* is the language of the *Afrikaners*, who are white South Africans, especially of Dutch descent. An *Afrikander* is a South African breed of cattle or sheep.

**afterwards** Prefer this spelling to *afterward*.

**AGC** Australian Guarantee Corporation Limited.

**ageing/aging** Either spelling, with or without the *-e* of *age*, is acceptable, *ageing* being more common in Australian English. The relatively new terms *ageism* and *ageist* are still under probation.
See also **discriminatory language**.

**agenda** This noun (the plural of the Latin *agendum*) means things to be done; it is now treated as singular, with the plural form *agendas*. Avoid overusing it in phrases such as *hidden agenda* (for secret motives) and *on the agenda* (for under discussion).

**aggravate** In formal speech and writing *aggravate* means to make worse or more severe, and should be used to describe things, not people:

The pollution aggravated his asthma.

However, the informal use of the word to mean irritate or annoy has a long history and is firmly entrenched, even if some disapprove of it:

She was aggravated by his snoring.

**aggressive** This adjective may mean hostile or destructive, but also energetic, bold and assertive – in which case it is approving. Be careful that the context conveys your meaning.

**AGM** annual general meeting.

**ago/since** To use *ago* and *since* in combination is tautological:

I was at school ten years ago.

*or* It is ten years ago that I was at school.

*or* It is ten years since I was at school.

*but not*

It is ten years ago since I was at school.

See also **as/since/because/for**.

**AGPS** Australian Government Publishing Service.

**agreeable** Note the *-eea-*.

**agreement** There are no such words as 'agreeance' or 'agreance'.

**AHA** Australian Hotels Association.

**AI** Amnesty International; artificial insemination; artificial intelligence.

**AIATSIS** Australian Institute of Aboriginal and Torres Strait Islander Studies.

**aid/aide** Both spellings are acceptable for the noun describing a person who helps or assists, but *aide* is now preferred, particularly since the arrival of the acronyms *AID* (*artificial insemination by donor*) and *AIDS (acquired immune deficiency syndrome)*.
See also **AIDS**.

**AIDC** Australian Industry Development Corporation.

**aide** See **aid/aide**.

**AIDS** acquired immune deficiency syndrome; also *Aids*.
See also **HIV**; **syndrome**.

**AIF** Australian Imperial Force.

**AIM** Australian Inland Mission; Australian Institute of Management.

**AIS** Australian Institute of Sport.

**AJA** Australian Journalists' Association (since 1992, Media, Entertainment and Arts Alliance).

**AJC** Australian Jockey Club.

**aka** This is an acronym for *also known as*. It is synonymous with *alias*, and is sometimes used to introduce a disparaging nickname:

David Cornwell, aka John le Carré.
Trevor Green, aka the Holy Terror.

**à la** In English the French phrase *à la* is used to mean according to or after the fashion of:

His books were witty à la Thackeray.

It is not necessary to set *à la* in italic, but the grave accent should be retained.

**à la carte/prix fixe/table d'hôte** These French phrases respectively mean according to the card, price fixed and table of the host, and are all common restaurant terms. An *à la carte* menu offers an individually priced choice of dishes; some menus have fixed-price courses or combinations that might be described as *prix fixe*; and a *table d'hôte* is the only menu available to guests at some hotels, though the name might be applied to any fixed-price menu with a very limited choice in each course. The terms are all printed in roman type, but the accents in the first and last are retained.

**albino** Plural *albinos.*

**Alexandra, Vic.** Compare with *Alexandria*, NSW.

**alga** Plural *algae.*

**alias** Plural *aliases.*

**alibi** This word is Latin for *elsewhere*. As a legal term it means that a person accused of a crime was elsewhere when it was committed. However, it is perfectly acceptable to use the word informally to mean an excuse (*an alibi for being late*).

**the Alice** Alice Springs.

**alkali** Plural *alkalis.*

**all/all of** It is unnecessary (although common in US English) to insert the preposition *of* between *all* and words such as *the*, *this*, *that*, *these*, *those* and *our*:

all the wombats *rather than* all of the wombats
all these T-shirts *rather than* all of these T-shirts
all our remarks *rather than* all of our remarks

However, *of* should be used before pronouns such as *them*, *us* and *my*, and *whom*, *whose* and *which*:

all of them are going *not* all them are going
the girls, all of whom we had seen *not* the girls, all whom we had seen

**allay/alleviate/assuage/relieve** All these verbs mean to give relief in some way, but there are subtle differences in their application. *Allay* is most often used in relation to fear, *alleviate* to pain or sorrow (though the relief is often only temporary) and *assuage* to worry, grief, thirst or hunger. If in doubt use *relieve*, which is comfortable in all these contexts; it can also suggest, as the other verbs do not, the removal of a problem's cause. Thus:

Robyn's fear of doctors was *allayed* by the surgeon's kindly manner, and drugs *alleviated* the pain. Her worries were *assuaged* next day, moreover, when she learnt that further treatment would *relieve* the inflammation altogether.

**allegory** In literary contexts an *allegory* is a story ('an extended metaphor', says *The Shorter Oxford English Dictionary*) whose narrative has an underlying, often symbolic, significance: Bunyan's *Pilgrim's Progress* and Orwell's *Animal Farm*, for example. A work of art may be an allegory also. Do not confuse *allegory* with *analogy*.

See also **analogy/analogous**; **metaphor**.

**alleviate** See **allay/alleviate/assuage/relieve**.

**alliteration/assonance/onomatopoeia** These terms all refer to the use of sound in words or word combinations. Skilful writers – and poets in particular – have exploited the first two devices brilliantly, but the less gifted need to treat them with care and restraint. Unintended alliteration and assonance do not usually enhance the sentences they occur in.

*Alliteration* is the repeated use of a sound, particularly that of a consonant, at the commencement of two or more words in the same phrase or sentence:

> Wet winters are wearisome, and sweet spring lifts the spirits.

*Assonance* is the use of identical or similar sounds, mainly in the accented and following vowels:

> 'And the foetid air and gritty of the dusty, dirty city' (A. B. Paterson)

*Onomatopoeia* (note the spelling) is the forming of a word by imitation of a sound that describes or suggests a quality of the subject:

> cuckoo quack sizzle hiss ting-a-ling

The word is pronounced 'onna-matta-**pee**-a'.

**all-ordinaries index** Abbreviated *all-ords*, this is an index of the price of shares listed on the Australian Stock Exchange. The sharemarket's movements are gauged by thirty-one different indexes, which measure the progress of industrial or mining shares, or of specific sectors such as paper and packaging. Among these is a composite index of 235 ordinary shares across all sectors, commonly referred to as the *all-ordinaries index*.

See also **Dow Jones index**; **Nikkei**.

**allot/allotted/allotting** Note the single *t* in the first word and the *-tt-* in the other two. The related noun is spelt *allotment*.

**all ready/already** The phrase *all ready* refers to the readiness of a group of people, animals or things:

> Are the cows all ready to be taken to the saleyard?

*Already* means before this or that time, or as early as this:

> The cows are already there.

**all right** *All right* is correct in all instances. *Alright*, though frequently seen, is not recommended.

**all together/altogether** *All together* means as a group, all at the same time or in the same place:

My three sisters travelled all together in the one car.

*Altogether* means entirely:

The chef served an altogether different menu last week.

**allude/elude/evade** Since *allude* means to speak of something without directly mentioning it, do not use it to mean refer:

When Rumpole mentioned 'She Who Must Be Obeyed' he was alluding to his wife.

*Elude* most commonly means to avoid skilfully, sometimes by trickery:

The company eluded its creditors by declaring itself insolvent.

A second, slightly different meaning is to escape the comprehension of, to baffle:

The significance of the questions in Form E eluded the creditors.

*Evade* means much the same as *elude*, but seems to imply more deliberate artifice and deception, sometimes involving action:

The company's accountant helped it to evade both creditors and tax authorities.

See also **allusion/illusion/delusion**; **allusive/elusive/illusive**.

**allusion/illusion/delusion** An *allusion* is an indirect mention of something:

Georgiana made an allusion to her ancestry.

An *illusion* is a misleading impression or false image:

Georgiana's manner gave the illusion of confidence but she was very insecure.

A *delusion* is a false belief or mistaken opinion, and the word is often used to describe a state of mind that is abnormal:

Georgiana's delusion as to the worth of her ancestry led her to put on airs and graces.

A mirage is an *illusion*, but if you were convinced that it was real you would be suffering from a *delusion*.

See also **allude/elude/evade**; **allusive/elusive/illusive**.

**allusive/elusive/illusive** The adjective *allusive* refers to something mentioned indirectly:

The parent's letter was allusive but failed to focus on the real problem.

Something that is *elusive* is hard to define, or grasp mentally or physically – perhaps a perfume, a butterfly, the name of a song.

The adjective *illusive* (or, more commonly, *illusory*) describes a misleading impression or false image:

The guru's power over his followers was illusive [*or* illusory], and collapsed with his arrest.

See also **allude/elude/evade**; **allusion/illusion/delusion**.

**alongside** Do not follow *alongside* with *of*.

**along with/together with** These are prepositional phrases, which have a kind of parenthetical role and do not affect verb agreement in the way that the conjunction *and* does. The verb remains singular whether or not the words are marked off by commas. Compare the following:

The plumber and his apprentices *are* coming to check the pipes.

*but* The plumber, along with [*or* together with] his apprentices, *is* coming to check the pipes.

*and* A tree root along with [*or* together with] the downpour *is* responsible for the damage.

Reserve *along with* and *together with* for situations where emphasis is required; *and* (followed by a plural verb) often suffices.

Watch out for ambiguity in using either phrase: *We gave birdseed to the canary, along with the pheasant.* For the sake of plain English as well as the canary's digestion, link the names of the birds with *and* instead.

See also **singular or plural.**

**a lot** This informal phrase is always expressed as two words.

See also **lot.**

**ALP** This is the abbreviation for *Australian Labor Party.* The *ALP* has spelt *Labor* with an *-or* since its present title was adopted throughout Australia in 1918.

See also **labor/labour.**

**ALRC** Australian Law Reform Commission.

**already** See **all ready/already.**

**also** Use *also* as an adverb, not a joining word:

Please also deliver the birdcages.

*not* Please deliver the table, also the birdcages.

It is perfectly all right, however, to make *also* part of the joining phrase *and also*, particularly where emphasis is needed:

Please deliver the table, and also the birdcages.

Sentences should not begin with *also*:

We also had chocolates with the coffee.

*not* Also we had chocolates with the coffee.

Inverted sentences sometimes start this way: *Also in attendance were . . .* It is preferable to rework them:

The bishop and his coadjutor were also in attendance.

*Also* should sometimes be eliminated in the interests of elegance:

We will not grant the request, nor can we allow more time.

*rather than*

We will not grant the request, and also we cannot allow more time.

**altar/alter** An *altar* (noun) is a structure on which religious rites are performed. The verb *to alter* means to change or modify.

**alternate/alternative** As adjectives these two are frequently confused. The primary meaning of *alternate* is by turns, or every second one:

I go overseas in alternate years.

A secondary meaning is substituting, in the sense of taking over a role turn-by-turn:

Smith is an alternate director for Jones.

In a similar kind of sentence *alternative* is the better word if you mean providing a choice – substituting in the sense of taking over someone else's role completely:

Smith would make a good alternative director to Jones.

Use *alternative* only when a choice is offered, not simply as a synonym for *other*.

*Alternative* is now also commonly used to mean departing from traditional practice: *alternative lifestyle*; *alternative medicine*.

The noun *alternative* traditionally meant a choice arising from two possibilities, but is now accepted as embracing two or more – even though purists would prefer a word like *option* in the latter case:

I have the alternative of travelling by first, business or economy class.

The phrases *no other alternative* and *different alternatives* are tautological.

Note that when *alternate* is used as a verb (*We will alternate our shifts*) instead of an adjective, the pronunciation changes: '**orl**ta-nate' instead of 'orl-**ter**nit'.

**although/though** Both conjunctions mean in spite of the fact or notwithstanding, and are interchangeable in many instances:

We went to the park although [*or* though] it was raining.

*Though* is somewhat less formal and can be used in more ways than *although* – for example, at the end of a sentence as a substitute for *however*:

We didn't get very wet, though.

It can be combined with *even* to add emphasis:

We didn't get very wet even though it was raining.

*Though*, and sometimes *although*, can mean *yet* or *but*:

We hoped it would stop raining, though [*or* although] that was unlikely.

**altogether** See **all together/altogether**.

**alumina/aluminium** *Alumina* is aluminium oxide; it is not the plural of *aluminium*. The US spelling of *aluminium* is *aluminum*.

**alumna/alumnus** *Alumna*, a female graduate, and *alumnus*, a male graduate, are the singular forms; the plural is *alumni*, which now means female and male graduates. The words are much less commonly used in Australia than in the US but have some official currency:

> The alumni of Flinders University were invited to join staff and present students at the ceremony.

**Alzheimer's disease** This is an organic brain disease that can strike anyone from middle age onwards. It is the cause of most pre-senile dementia.

**AM** Air Marshal; amplitude modulation (radio); Medal of the Order of Australia (see also **ranks, titles, honours and awards**).

**a.m./p.m.** As a general rule, include the full stops in these abbreviations of the Latin *ante meridiem* (before noon) and *post meridiem* (after noon):

> 7 a.m. 10 p.m. 11.45 a.m.

Sometimes, as in extensive listings of opening hours and in many newspapers, the abbreviations are set without full stops and close to their related numerals: *7am, 10pm.*

See also **numbers in figures or words; time of day**.

**AMA** Australian Medical Association.

**amateur/amateurish** An *amateur* pursues an activity for pleasure rather than professionally – that is, for money. The adjective *amateurish* usually means poor or incompetent, however. Pronounce these words '**amma**-ter' and '**amma**-terish'.

**ambidextrous** See **dexterous/dextrous**.

**ambience** Meaning the atmosphere or character of a place, this word has become misused and overused in recent years. Like *atmosphere*, *ambience* needs an adjective or context: *a Parisian ambience*; *an ambience of wealth*. To say that a restaurant has *ambience* is too vague; the most squalid public lavatory also has *ambience*.

Though the word is derived from the French *ambiance* you may sound priggish if you pronounce it the French way. Say '**am**-bee'nce'.

**ambiguous/ambiguity** An *ambiguous* statement has more than one meaning (or an obscure meaning), which may be intended or accidental. *Ambiguous* words help to make up puns, innuendo and double entendre in humorous writing, and in the hands of skilled writers add depth and richness to language. Advertising copy-writers often use *ambiguity* to make a point. A banking advertisement might state, *If we're honest, we have very little interest in your money*, playing on the word *interest* to suggest that the bank's customers get the bulk of the money that it earns on their investments.

Most ambiguity, however, is accidental and arises from careless expression. Unintended ambiguity can slow readers down or lead them astray. Avoid this sort of problem:

Watching television often leads to eyestrain.

This can mean two things:

Frequently watching television leads to eyestrain.

*or* Watching television leads to eyestrain in a number of cases.

See also **ambivalent**; **double entendre**; **pun**.

**ambivalent** This word is not synonymous with *ambiguous*. It describes someone with simultaneous but conflicting emotions, or something with simultaneous but conflicting elements in it:

The daughter's feelings towards her mother were ambivalent, a complex mixture of love and hate.

Some authorities allow *ambivalent* to describe simple mixed feelings or a state of indecision, but it would be better to choose another word or expression:

I'm in two minds [*not* ambivalent] about Bartok's music.

See also **ambiguous/ambiguity**.

**AMEB** Australian Music Examinations Board.

**ameliorate** This verb is slightly pompous; use *improve* instead.

**amend/emend** These verbs are similar in meaning. *Amend* means to alter, change for the better or correct in general (your character, the situation, a shopping list):

The government will amend the Fisheries Act.

Mike has promised to amend his behaviour.

Note the noun: *amendment*.

*Emend* has a narrower meaning: to remove errors from a written or printed text:

Is it too late to emend the index before printing begins?

Note the noun: *emendation*.

**America/United States/Latin America** Although strictly speaking the name *America* refers to the landmass that includes North, Central and South America, it is almost universally understood to mean the *United States of America* (the *US* or the *USA*). The term *the States* is informal.

The expression *the Americas* is sometimes used to denote the various countries of the two American continents. *Latin America* consists of the parts of Central and South America where Spanish or Portuguese is spoken.

*American Indians* has been the traditional term for the original inhabitants of both American continents, but *native Americans* is now regarded as more acceptable. *Amerindian* has some currency in anthropology but is not a word for general use.

See also **discriminatory language**.

**American English** See **US English**.

**American spelling** See **US spelling**.

**Americas Cup/America's Cup** The form of these sporting trophy names is confusing. The *Americas Cup* for golf has no apostrophe, but the *America's Cup* for yachting, first won by the yacht *America*, does have one.

**amiable/amicable** Both these adjectives mean friendly, agreeable or pleasant, but only *amiable* is used to describe people:

> Since Ann is usually amiable, her grumpiness puzzled us.
> Since everyone tried hard to be amiable, the meeting was amicable.

**amid/among** Use *amid* mainly with indivisible things or mass (*amid a sea of students*) and *among* mainly with countable items (*among the students*).

See also **among/amongst; among/between**.

**amniocentesis** *Amniocentesis* is a medical procedure in which a sample of the amniotic fluid surrounding an embryo is removed, usually to test for abnormality in the embryo.

**amok/amuck** Either spelling is acceptable but *amuck* is preferred. The word comes from Malay, and is generally used as an adverb to mean frenzied: *running amuck*. However you spell the word, pronounce it 'amuck'.

**among/amongst** Either form is acceptable, though *amongst* sometimes sounds rather 'literary' for everyday writing. Some authorities suggest using *among* before consonants and *amongst* before vowels: *among these valleys*; *amongst our relatives*.

See also **amid/among; among/between**.

**among/between** The traditional view was that *among* expressed a relationship involving three or more things, while *between* related to only two:

> The fishing dispute was among countries in the South China Sea.
> The trade relationship between Australia and New Zealand was strengthened.

Modern usage allows *between* to act also as a general substitute for *among* when describing an exact position or precise relationships, no matter how many things are involved:

> The Anzus treaty between Australia, New Zealand and the United States was signed during the Korean War.

See also **amid/among; among/amongst; between**.

**amongst** See **among/amongst**.

**amoral/immoral** Note the *-m-* in *amoral* and the *-mm-* in *immoral*. *Amoral* means beyond morals. Amoral people are neither moral nor immoral; they are unconscious of moral codes and have no sense of right and wrong. Infants are *amoral*; so are some psychopaths.

*Immoral* means not moral, and people who are *immoral* are consciously breaking moral codes. *Amoral* people would not realise that they were committing *immoral* acts.

**amount/number** *Amount* is used to describe a quantity or mass (that is, in the singular): *a fair amount of money*; *an excessive amount of caution*. *Number* is used with quantities (that is, in the plural): *a number of 5 cent pieces*; *a number of warnings*.

**AMP** Australian Mutual Provident Society.

**ampersand** An *ampersand* (&) is the typographic device that stands for *and*. It is not normally used in text unless it is part of a registered trade name, or the preferred style of a company: *Black & Decker*; *Weidenfeld & Nicolson*. It is acceptable as a space-saver in headlines, bibliographies and tabulations.

**amuck** See **amok/amuck**.

**an** See **a/an**.

**anaerobic** See **aerobic/anaerobic**.

**anagram** An *anagram* is a word or phrase formed by the rearrangement of letters from another word or phrase. Inventing complex and clever anagrams is a popular feat among literary gymnasts, but for the simplest of examples you could make the anagram *drop* from *prod*, and the anagram *scared* from *sacred*.

**analogy/analogous** An *analogy* points to something that is partly similar to or comparable with something else in specified ways, often using a word picture to do so: you could draw an *analogy* between the human lungs and a pair of bellows, for example. Do not confuse *analogy* with *allegory*.

The adjective *analogous* should not simply be used to mean similar, comparable or like when the likeness is not specified:

> Her writing style was like [*not* analogous with] mine.

The preposition following *analogous* can only be *with* or *to*.

Pronounce *analogy* with a soft *g*, *analogous* with a hard one.

See also **allegory**; **simile**.

**analyse** The Australian spelling is *-se*, not *-ze* (US English). To *analyse* something means to examine it critically or to study it closely by investigating the various parts making up the whole: you can *analyse* the contents of a drug or the usefulness of a new appliance. However, the word is often misused to inflate the importance of the investigation where *discuss* or *examine* would be more appropriate.

See also **analysis/synthesis**.

**analysis/synthesis** *Analysis* is the noun relating to the verb *analyse* and therefore it means critical examination, or close study through investigation of the various parts making up the whole:

> An analysis of the play revealed high drama, low comedy and knockabout farce.

It is a perfectly good word that has been overused by people who want to make a trivial action or investigation appear more important than it is by writing *in the ultimate analysis* or *in the final analysis* when all they mean is *in the end*, *at last* or *finally*. The plural is *analyses* (pronounced 'analla-**seez**').

*Synthesis* is the antonym of *analysis*; it refers to the combining of parts into a whole:

> The play was a synthesis of drama, comedy and farce.

The plural is *syntheses* (pronounced 'sintha-**seez**').

See also **analyse**.

**ANARE** Australian National Antarctic Research Expeditions.

**ANC** African National Congress.

**ancillary** Note the *-ll-* and the *-ary*. This adjective means supplementary, and is often used in institutional contexts: a hospital's *ancillary* services may include social work.

***AND*** *The Australian National Dictionary*.

**and** The belief that the conjunction *and* should never begin a sentence is out of step with modern usage. *And* is a legitimate opener; it can be a way of reinforcing the sentence before, or emphasising the words that follow:

> Sarah was left to finish all the letters. And Sarah can't type.

If you begin too many sentences with *and* you will soon bore the reader, of course. Similarly, do not overuse *and* in the one sentence. It is better to make an additional sentence, or break up ideas with colons or semicolons.

*And* is otherwise used to link words or groups of words: *bread and butter*; *long ago and far away*. It must always join words and phrases that have a similar function in a sentence. A mistake to watch for is the unrelated series.

> He was an archaeologist, soldier and writer, and he died in 1936.
>
> *not* He was an archaeologist, soldier, writer [nouns] and died [verb] in 1936.

It is equally wrong to put this: *He was an archaeologist, soldier and writer and died in 1936*. Note that a comma has been inserted before the second *and* in the correct first example to separate the unrelated final clause from the preceding series.

Watch out also for possible ambiguity or confusion; a comma is usually enough to straighten it out:

The explorers were Stuart, McKinlay, and Burke and Wills.

*not* The explorers were Stuart, McKinlay and Burke and Wills.

Although it is usual to put *and* between the last two elements in a list, it may occasionally be left out, particularly when you want to suggest that the list is incomplete:

He bought wrapping paper, tinsel, decorations, presents galore.

Note that a comma follows rather than precedes *and* when it is one of a pair:

There was little seating and, while some guests found chairs, most people sprawled comfortably on the floor.

Here the comma precedes *and* because it is not one of a pair:

There was little seating, and most people sprawled comfortably on the floor.

This rule applies to other conjunctions also – *but*, *or*, *when* and so on.

In formal writing (and preferably in conversation too) *and* should not be used in place of *to*:

Why don't we try to fix it? *not* Why don't we try and fix it?

The important role of *and* in determining verb agreement is illustrated in **singular or plural**.

See also **and/or**; **and which**; **comma**; **semicolon**.

**and/or** The device *and/or*, in which the words are joined by a solidus (a diagonal or oblique stroke, or slash), is common in very informal writing. Such forms of shorthand are not appropriate in formal work, and are too open to misinterpretation for use in commercial or legal documents such as contracts. In any context you must avoid ambiguity:

They can go on Saturday and/or Sunday.

Does this mean they can go on both days (Saturday *and* Sunday) or only on one day (Saturday *or* Sunday)? Rephrase the sentence to clarify your meaning.

See also **solidus**.

**and which** If you need to link two clauses by means of *and* (or *but*) followed by *which* (or other relative pronouns such as *that*, *who*, *whom* and *whose*), make sure that both clauses are adjectival and that the first clause includes a matching relative pronoun (the same one, or a version of it; you might have *who* in the second clause but *with whom* in the first):

Sue sat in her favourite chair, which had been brought by her mother from Scotland and which she had inherited.

*not* Sue sat in a chair brought out from Scotland by her mother and which she had inherited

Note that although the relative pronoun must be included in the *first* clause, it is neater to omit it from the *second* when the sentence is simple:

> It is Sue's favourite chair, which is comfortable and [which] gives her happy memories.

The *and which* kind of construction can seem rather stiff, and simpler sentences are preferable provided that they observe all the rules.

**anemone** Note the spelling.

**ANL** Australian National Line.

**annex/annexe** *Annex* is the verb, meaning to add, attach or join; or to take without permission:

> I intend to annex this clause to my will.
> There is a plot to annex the nearest islands.

*Annexe* is the noun, meaning a subsidiary building; or anything that is added. Both the verb and the noun are spelt *annex* in US English, and this spelling has traditionally been an option in British and Australian English.

**annual/biennial/perennial** Used as nouns, these words have specific meanings of interest to gardeners. An *annual* is a plant that flowers and dies in one year: petunias and marigolds are *annuals*. A *biennial* is a plant that flowers and dies in its second year: foxgloves and stocks are *biennials*. A *perennial* is a plant other than a tree or shrub that lives for several years: bulbs, and herbaceous plants like Easter daisies and delphiniums, are *perennials*.

See also **bi-**.

**annul/annulled/annulling** Note the single *l* in the first and the *-ll-* in the other two. The related noun is spelt *annulment*.

**annunciation/enunciation** *Annunciation* is an infrequently used synonym for *announcement*. *The Annunciation* (with an initial capital) refers specifically to a religious feast commemorating the appearance of the Archangel Gabriel to the Virgin Mary, when he announced the incarnation of Christ.

*Enunciation* means a particular way of pronouncing words, or a precise statement, or a proclamation:

> The enunciation of both his words and his philosophy was clear.

**anomaly** Note the single *n* and the *-aly* in this noun, which means a deviation from the normal:

> Since the accounts are fastidiously kept, the missing $20 from the company funds is a strange anomaly.

**anorexia** Someone suffering from *anorexia* has lost the desire for food. *Anorexia nervosa* is a mental disorder that causes patients to develop an intense dislike of food, an aversion sometimes leading to their death by starvation. The adjective is most often spelt *anorexic*, but *anorectic* is an accepted alternative.

**ANSTO** Australian Nuclear Science & Technology Organisation (in 1987 replaced AAEC: Australian Atomic Energy Commission).

**Antarctic/Arctic** Note the *arc* in both words. Pronouncing this syllable clearly will help you to spell the names correctly.

**ante-/anti-** The prefixes *ante-* and *anti-* are often confused. *Ante-* means before: *antenatal*, *antebellum*, *anteroom*. *Anti-* means against, opposed to, or the opposite of: *anticlockwise*, *antidepressant*, *anti-abortion*, *anti-inflationary*. A hyphen is used after the prefixes *ante-* or *anti-* if the next letter is a vowel.

Avoid the common error 'antinatal' for *antenatal*: *antenatal nurse*; *antenatal clinic*. The opposite of *ante-* is *post-* (after); the opposite of *anti-* is *pro-* (for). *Anti* and *pro* are sometimes used informally as words in their own right: *She's anti insecticides; he's pro*. Pronounce *anti* 'antee', not 'anteye'.

**antecedents** Your *antecedents* are the events in your history rather than the people in it, who are your *ancestors*:

> There are antecedents for Roger's absence on Mondays.

The word is also police jargon for a person's criminal history:

> The sergeant told the constable to check the prisoner's antecedents.

**antenna** Plural *antennae* (of insects), *antennas* (for radio, television).

**anti-** See **ante-/anti-**.

**anticipate** *Anticipate* traditionally means to look ahead and prepare for something or forestall it:

> The townspeople anticipated the cyclone by boarding up windows.

Some authorities disapprove of using the word as a synonym for *expect*, arguing that to expect something is not necessarily to do anything about it. However, many dictionaries now allow this usage:

> We anticipate that the plane will be late because of the turbulent weather.

**antiseptic/aseptic** An *antiseptic* is an agent that destroys the micro-organisms causing sepsis. *Aseptic* is an adjective describing objects free from such micro-organisms or other contaminating matter:

> Washing the bandages in antiseptic will make them aseptic.

**antithesis** The meaning of this noun is contrast, or the very opposite (usually of ideas or actions):

> Bankruptcy was the antithesis of his money-making dreams.

The plural of *antithesis* is *antitheses*, and it is pronounced '**an-titha-seez**'.

**antonyms and synonyms** An *antonym* is a word with a meaning opposite to that of another word; a *synonym* is a word with the same or similar meaning. For example, antonyms for *happy* include *sorrowful*, *sad*, *melancholy* and *unhappy*; synonyms include *joyful*, *glad*, *delighted* and *cheerful*. The English language is rich in antonyms and synonyms, partly because it has been borrowing words from other languages for centuries. Many words with similar meanings have different origins – for example, *dead* (Old Norse), *defunct* (Latin) and *kaput* (German). Thesauruses contain lists of antonyms and synonyms, as well as words and phrases with related meanings. A well-indexed thesaurus is an invaluable resource for writers seeking to vary overworked phrases or to find the most appropriate words for the meaning or atmosphere they wish to convey.

See also **thesaurus**.

**anybody/anyone** These pronouns may be used interchangeably to mean *any one person*. To be grammatically correct, any verb or pronoun governed by *anybody* or *anyone* should be singular:

> Anybody may come if he or she is insured.
> Has anyone here lost his umbrella?

Some people dodge the question of whether to use the sex-specific *his* or *her* (or both) by substituting a plural pronoun for the singular:

> Anybody may come if they are insured.
> Has anyone here lost their umbrella?

Such usage has always been common in speech, but is frowned on in formal English.

Note that the two-word form *any one* is always used in reference to *things*. The word is also split when it is followed by *of* and refers to *people*.

> You can watch any one of these videos.
> Any one of the players could have kicked that goal.

See also **discriminatory language**; **every/everybody/everyone**; **gender**; **he/she**; **pronouns**; **their/them/they**.

**any more** In Australian and British English the expression *any more* is two words in all senses:

> If he eats any more cake he'll feel ill.
> The trees grew so big that she could not prune them any more.

*Anymore* as one word is sometimes used in US English to mean any longer: *I can't stand it anymore*.

**anyone** See **anybody/anyone**.

**anything/anywhere** Each of these is always expressed as one word.

**any way/anyway** The expression *any way* is always two words when it means in any direction or manner:

They could not control the yacht in any way.

When it means in any case it becomes one word:

I was too late for the first half of the recital, but I went anyway.

**anywhere** See **anything/anywhere**.

**ANZ** Australia & New Zealand Banking Group Limited.

**ANZAAS** Australian and New Zealand Association for the Advancement of Science.

**Anzac** This is an acronym for the *Australian and New Zealand Army Corps* of World War I, which landed at Gallipoli in 1915. The name is also applied to members of this Corps, though it was extended to Australian and New Zealand soldiers in later campaigns and wars. *Anzac Day* is 25 April.

**ANZUS** This is an acronym for *Australia, New Zealand and the United States* (particularly in relation to the security pact of 1951; New Zealand became a non-participant in 1985). It is also expressed as *Anzus*.

**AO** adults only (TV classification); Officer of the Order of Australia (see also **ranks, titles, honours and awards**).

**AOC** Australian Olympic Committee.

**AOTC** Australian and Overseas Telecommunications Corporation.

**apartheid** This Afrikaans word was coined to describe the South African government's policy of separate development for different racial groups. Pronounce it '**apar**-tite' or '**apar**-tate'.

**apartment** Note the single *p*.

**APEC** Asia Pacific Economic Cooperation.

**apex** Plural *apexes* or, less commonly, *apices*.

**apiary/aviary** An *apiary* is where you keep bees, an *aviary* is for birds.

**APM** Australian Paper Manufacturers.

**APN** Australian product number.

**apologia** An *apologia* is a formal explanation of beliefs and conduct, in speech or writing. It is not an apology, though it may contain one. Pronounce the word 'appa-lo-ja'.

**a posteriori/a priori** *A posteriori* (Latin, meaning from the latter) describes an argument reasoned from effect to cause, based on observation:

The people were not starving therefore there must have been food.

*A priori* (Latin, meaning from the previous) is the opposite, describing an argument that looks forward from cause to effect, based on assumption:

Since there is no food, the people will starve.

It is advisable to confine these terms to the specialised contexts in which they will be understood.

See also **deduction/induction**.

**apostrophe** The *apostrophe* has two main uses: to indicate the omission of letters (*she'll*, *he'd*, *can't*); and – a much more complicated matter – to indicate possession in nouns.

The rule governing possession in the case of *most singular nouns* is to place *an apostrophe and s* after the word:

the boy's hat    an octopus's garden
the pilot's dilemma    Dylan Thomas's poetry

Traditional exceptions to this rule include some classical or biblical names ending in *s*, where only an apostrophe is added:

Jesus' disciples    Hercules' strength    Moses' old age

The guidelines on how to treat other names ending in *s* are not watertight, and many of them relate to the way the name sounds. *Dylan Thomas's poetry* has been used in the example above because it is easy to say *Thomas's*. *Euripides's plays* is hard to say; write *Euripides' plays* instead. A much shorter name, *Menzies*, is nevertheless a mouthful if we try to say *Menzies's biographer*; write *Menzies' biographer*.

Sound also dictates the dropping of the possessive *s* in the expressions *for goodness' sake* and *for conscience' sake*.

The rule governing possession in the case of *most plural nouns* is to place *an apostrophe only* after the word. The majority of plurals end in *s*:

all the boys' hats    the ponies' tails
the pilots' strike    the Joneses' camellias

Plural nouns that do not end in *s* are among the exceptions. They take *an apostrophe and s*:

the mice's droppings    children's books    women's studies

So do nouns with the same form in the singular and plural:

two sheep's fleeces    three deer's antlers

Use apostrophes in the plurals of abbreviations only when they have a possessive role:

the MPs' new suites    the POWs' stretchers

*but* all the MPs *not* all the MP's

the POWs ran *not* the POW's ran

Joint possession requires the apostrophe only in the last name:

our mother and father's anniversary Lerner and Loewe's musicals

When the possession is not joint, both names take an apostrophe:

the butcher's and the baker's deliveries Wagner's and Verdi's operas

If there is any doubt whether the possession is joint or individual it is better to use some other way of indicating your meaning:

the musicals of Smith & Brown

the butcher's deliveries and the baker's

Note that you can say *the butcher's deliveries and yours* but not *yours and the butcher's deliveries.*

A modern trend is to omit the apostrophe in plural nouns ending in *s* when they are considered to be adjectival rather than possessive:

Teachers Union jockeys caps drivers licence

Some authorities view this trend (and the rationale for it) with suspicion, believing it can lead to confusion and inconsistency. The apostrophe has been officially dropped by some organisations, for example the *Federated Clerks Union*; others, like the *Australian Workers' Union*, retain it. In cases where you are unsure whether or not to add an apostrophe, follow traditional usage and you cannot go wrong – grammatically at least:

Teachers' Union jockeys' caps driver's licence

However, you must retain the apostrophe in plural nouns that do not end in *s*, even when they are clearly adjectival rather than possessive:

children's books *not* childrens books

women's studies *not* womens studies

The apostrophe has been dropped from most Australian place-names and street names: *Connells Point*; *Wilsons Promontory*; *Browns Lane*.

Many brand-names have also abandoned the apostrophe: *Taubmans*, *Pears*. Others such as *Kellogg's* retain it as an important part of their trademark. Or it might be a typographical device in a product's name – *Peter Jackson 30's* (even though this is used incorrectly).

Misuse of the apostrophe is widespread, particularly in advertising and journalism. One common error is the omission of apostrophes:

last year's fashion *not* last years fashion

The apostrophe is optional when more than one year is involved, however:

ten years service *or* ten years' service

Another common error is the unnecessary inclusion of apostrophes. Pronouns such as *yours*, *hers*, *its*, *ours* and *theirs* have a possessive sense built in and do not need apostrophes. One of the commonest traps is *its* because we often see *it's*, the contraction of *it is* or *it has*. If it makes sense to substitute *it is* or *it has* for *it's*, the apostrophe is correct; otherwise the word is *its*.

The 'roving apostrophe' sometimes slips into a plural noun or a verb and should be eliminated:

Fish and chips sold here *not* Fish and chip's sold here
*Fairstar* sails in June *not* *Fairstar* sail's in June

Although letters have been dropped from words such as *phone*, *flu* and *plane*, we no longer use an apostrophe to indicate the omission – they have become words in their own right.

One oddity that is widely accepted involves expressions such as *do's and don'ts*; *the old so and so's*; *minding your p's and q's*; and *crossing your t's and dotting your i's*. The apostrophes here do help our understanding.

See also **abbreviations and contractions**; **its/it's**; **nouns, plurals of**; **possessives**; **singular or plural**; **they're/there/their**.

**apotheosis** See **epitome/apotheosis**.

**appal/appalled/appalling** Note the single *l* in the first and the *-ll-* in the other two.

**apparatus** The plural is *apparatus* or *apparatuses*. Pronounce the word 'appa-**rah**-t's' or 'appa-**ray**-t's'.

**apparent** Note the *-pp-* and *-ent*.

**appeal** Do not use the US form *appeal the decision*; say *appeal against the decision*.

**appeasement** The second *e* of *appease* is retained.

**appendices/appendixes** Both are accepted as plurals of *appendix*. Used in the sense of supplements to a printed work, *appendixes* is today gaining ground over the more traditional *appendices*.

See also **publications, parts of**.

**application/program/package** In computer terminology the words *application*, *program* and *package* are broadly interchangeable, all referring to software – for example page-makeup, word-processing and graphics programs, spreadsheets and computer games.

See also **hardware/software**.

**APPM** Associated Pulp & Paper Mills.

**apposition** A word or phrase is said to be *in apposition* when it is placed next to another word or phrase to extend or modify meaning; it must be capable of replacing the original. Commas, brackets or dashes are used to mark off the *appositional* word or phrase:

Scott, *the best scoutmaster they'd had*, left the town.

The old dog (*Bluey*) put his nose on my knee.

The Melbourne Cup – *Australia's best-known horse race* – is run on the first Tuesday in November.

See also **brackets**; **clause**; **comma**; **dashes, use of**; **phrase**.

**appraise/apprise** To *appraise* is to assess or evaluate:

Two examiners appraised his thesis.

*Apprise* means to inform or notify:

They apprised him of the fact that his thesis had been given a pass.

The examiners are more likely to have *told* him: *apprise* is not an everyday kind of word, and it needs the bulky extra phrase *of the fact*.

**appreciate** The verb *to appreciate* has one straightforward meaning, to increase in value: *Our superannuation is appreciating*. Its other meanings are more abstract. If you *appreciate* something you are grateful for it, or place a high value on it. *Appreciate* in that sense is rapidly becoming overused. On the other hand, the writers of business letters who say *We would appreciate your prompt attention in this matter* are probably overstating the case: this is often a euphemism for 'pay up or else'.

A more recent development is using *appreciate* instead of *realise* or *understand*:

I appreciate that you should have your say too.

The choice of the word *appreciate* rather than *realise* in this context is often deliberate, implying the opposite of what is said. The speaker really means 'I'm damned if I think you should have your say too'.

**apprehend/comprehend** In one of its senses, *apprehend* means to grasp, or to recognise, something without necessarily understanding it fully:

She attempted to apprehend God's wisdom.

To *comprehend* is to understand fully the nature or meaning of something:

Though unable to share her faith, he comprehended her theological arguments.

**apprise** See **appraise/apprise**.

**approved deposit fund** Special tax treatment is provided for an *approved deposit fund* (abbreviated *ADF*), a type of fund permitted by government to receive eligible termination payments from superannuation funds and other sources.

**APRA** Australasian Performing Right Association (not 'Rights').

**April Fools' Day** Note the position of the apostrophe; the date is 1 April.

**a priori** See **a posteriori/a priori**.

**apropos** This term comes from the French *à propos*, which means to the purpose. It has been fully assimilated into English and is spelt as one word without an accent. Its sense is with reference to:

> What is the law apropos [*or* apropos of] the migration of business investors to Australia?

Notice that *apropos* is never followed by *to*. The pronunciation is '**apra**-po'.

**apt/liable/prone/likely** When these four adjectives are followed by *to* they all express probability or a tendency. The first three mostly imply some degree of unpleasantness and hark back to past experiences, whereas *likely* has a more neutral tone and does not necessarily reflect any experience in the past; it also suggests the most probable outcome. Any of the words could be interchanged with the one chosen (and marginally preferred) in the first three of the following examples. In the last example *likely* is the only possible choice.

> Alan is apt to spend too much on presents at Christmas time.
> Alan is liable to regret his generosity once January arrives.
> Alan is prone to bouts of depression over money.
> Alan is likely to look for a better job soon so that he has more money to spend.

See also **prone/prostrate/supine.**

**aqueduct** Note the *-que-* (not 'aquaduct').

**arabic numerals** The digits 1, 2, 3 and so on are *arabic numerals*.
See also **numbers in figures or words**; **roman numerals.**

**arbiter/arbitrator** In US English, and increasingly in Australian English, *arbiter* and *arbitrator* are synonymous, both indicating a person empowered to decide a dispute. Traditionally an *arbiter* was someone who had an influence in a general sense: an *arbiter* of taste, of fashion, of morals. Careful users of the language still like to preserve the distinction.

**arbitrate/mediate** *Arbitrate* means to decide or determine a specific question, usually between opposing parties:

> The judge was appointed to arbitrate the matter disputed by the two trade unions.

*Mediate* means to act as an intermediary between opposing parties in an attempt to bring about an agreement:

> He tried to mediate between the unions but the case still had to go to the Arbitration Commission.

**arbitrator** See **arbiter/arbitrator**.

**archetype** The most common meaning of this noun is the original model (prototype) on which other things are based. Some dictionaries include 'a typical example' among the meanings, but there is usually a better word.

An improved harpsichord was the archetype of the grand piano.

Her romantic novel was a typical [*not* the archetype of a] bodice-ripper.

Note that you usually have an archetype *of* something but a prototype *for* it. Pronounce the word '**ar**ka-type'.

**archipelago** The plural is *archipelagoes* or *archipelagos*. Pronounce it 'arka-**pella**-go'.

**Arctic** See **Antarctic/Arctic**.

**argot/dialect/jargon/lingua franca** *Argot* now means the spoken language of a particular group, such as fishing enthusiasts or the younger children in a family, but the word was originally applied to the slang of thieves and vagabonds, who kept their plans to themselves by using words unfamiliar to others. Pronounce it 'argo'.

A *dialect* is the version of a language spoken in a specific region, with a distinctive vocabulary, pronunciation, and often grammar. Residents of the British Isles, as well as visitors from other countries, may have difficulty understanding some of the many dialects spoken there.

*Jargon* is the written or spoken language peculiar to a trade, profession or other group. It can be the technical terminology of scientists, essential for clear communication; or the euphemisms of real-estate agents, who unashamedly refer to a ruin as a 'renovator's opportunity'; or the mystifying exchanges of the pop-music world. Many people are irritated by jargon other than their own, simply because it makes them feel left out. Some jargon is certainly no more than a debased form of the language.

The *lingua franca* was originally a blend of languages including Italian, French, Spanish and Greek used by traders in the Mediterranean. It now means a common language adopted by speakers of a range of different languages: French was once the *lingua franca* of diplomacy; English is the *lingua franca* of the airline business. Pronounce the phrase 'ling-gwa franka'.

See also **colloquialisms**; **commercialese**; **gobbledegook**; **idiom**; **journalese**; **officialese**; **pidgin/pigeon**; **slang**.

**arise/rise** Problems, difficulties, questions, doubts and other abstract things generally *arise*:

If the nasty question of the deficit arises, it must be debated.

*Rise* is the more literal verb, and is used in most other cases:

Prices rise as surely as the sun rises every morning.

See also **raise/rise/raze**.

**Armadale, Vic. and WA** Compare with *Armidale*, NSW.

**armful/armfuls** Note the single *l* in both, and the form of the plural (not 'armsful', 'armsfull' or 'arms full').

See also **compound nouns, plurals of**; **-ful**.

**aroma** An *aroma* is a pleasant smell (*the aroma of freshly baked bread*). It is not just any smell and definitely not an unpleasant one, which is more likely to be an *odour*, or even a *stench*.

**around/round** When used as adverbs and prepositions these words are often interchangeable, though there is some feeling that *around* is a shade more formal than *round*:

We saw Malcolm running around [*or* round] the lake.

Sonja wore a scarf around [*or* round] her neck.

But we would say *play around* rather than *play round*, and *all year round* rather than *all year around*.

We tend to use *round* when a revolving or circular motion is implied, and *around* when something is being surrounded.

The ferris wheel went round and round.

The children crowded around the fire.

See also **about/around**.

**arouse/rouse** Both of these verbs can mean to excite, or to awaken from sleep, but *arouse* is the better word for the first and *rouse* for the second.

Her lectures on biology always arouse the students' interest.

You'll have to rouse him early if he is to attend the lecture.

**arrant/errant** *Arrant* means downright, and is used to imply a sense of notoriety:

That fellow is an arrant liar who has deluded even his friends.

*Errant* means moving in an aimless way, or straying from acceptable standards:

Even if he changes his errant ways he is unlikely to win back his friends.

The original meaning of *errant* was journeying or travelling, as in the phrase *a knight errant*.

**arrogate** See **abrogate/arrogate**.

**artefact/artifact** Either spelling is correct but *artefact* is recommended. The word describes an object made by human hand. It is not correct to describe old bones, fossils or rocks as *artefacts*.

**arteriosclerosis** Note the spelling of this noun, which means hardening of the arteries.

**ARTF** Australian Road Transport Federation.

**artifact** See **artefact/artifact**.

**artiste/artist** The spelling *artiste* has been replaced by *artist* in nearly all cases, which some people regard as regrettable since *artiste* once meant simply a professional performer and had no connotations of quaintness or mediocrity.

See also **discriminatory language**.

**artpapers** See **paper sizes and weights.**

**AS** This abbreviation for *Australian standard* is usually followed by a reference number (for example *AS 1234*), which relates to an index of standards published by an organisation called *Standards Australia*. These standards may be specifications for products, testing methods and codes of practice, and they are applicable to many fields.

**as** There are many jobs for this word to do, and plenty of traps. Choosing the right pronoun after *as* is sometimes difficult:

> She is as strong as they [*not* them].

*They* is the correct word in written English, even though most people are more comfortable using *them* in conversation. The sentence really means:

> She is as strong as they *are*.

Identifying the missing word or words will help you to choose the right pronoun:

> You are as slow as I [am].

*but* He respects you as much as [he respects] me.

Make sure you do not omit an essential *as*:

> The chocolates are as dear as [*not* as dear], or dearer than, champagne.

But do not add an unnecessary *as* either:

> Much as [*not* As much as] we love him, we can't buy him chocolates.
>
> Dried fruit is equally [*not* equally as] delicious and much cheaper.
>
> Chandra has not bought her books yet [*not* as yet].
>
> She will be at university from [*not* as from] next week.

However, *as from* is sometimes used in agreements and accounting:

> The salary increase is payable as from today.

Never use the expression *as what*:

> He is as keen to start as [*not* as what] I am.

Note that the construction *as . . . as* is sometimes ambiguous: *Rodney can throw the ball as far as his twin*. Rephrase to make your meaning clear.

Use *as* or *as if*, not *like*, when either means similar to and it is attached to a verb:

> We worked hard, as [*not* like] our parents *did*.
>
> She ran as if [*not* like] her life *were* dependent on it.

Note the subjunctive *were*, not *was*, in the last example, indicating that the situation was hypothetical, not actual. You can use *like* only when it is attached to a noun or pronoun rather than a verb:

We worked hard like our *parents*.

She ran like the *wind*.

Note the difference in meaning in the following, depending on whether *as* or *like* is the preposition:

As Sharon's swimming coach, Fred supervised her diet.

Like Sharon's swimming coach, Fred supervised her diet.

See also **as/since/because/for**; **as follows**; **as for/as to**; **as if/as though**; **as well as**; **equally**; **like**; **regard**; **seeing that**.

**as/since/because/for** Any of these words may be used as conjunctions to introduce an explanatory clause. *As* and *since* are most often placed at the beginning of a sentence when the reason is already known or is less important than the main statement:

As [*or* Since] we are already late, we will go by car.

*Because* emphasises the reason:

Because it is so hot we will not go at all.

*For* comes between the main statement and the reason, and places equal weight on each:

He never knew the truth, for she left Australia without telling anyone.

Note that *as* is a conjunction that can express either cause or time:

As Sally was watching television, her friends left.

Did the friends leave *because* Sally was watching television or *while* she was watching television? Ambiguity can be avoided by replacing *As* with either *Because* or *While* (and deleting the comma).

Because Sally was watching television her friends left.

While Sally was watching television her friends left.

*Since* is also occasionally ambiguous because it may refer to either cause or time: be sure to make your meaning clear.

See also **as**; **because**; **seeing that**.

**asap** This is an informal acronym for *as soon as possible*.

**ASC** Australian Securities Commission (until 1990, NCSC: National Companies and Securities Commission).

**ascender** See **type**.

**ascent/assent/consent** The noun *ascent* means the act of upward movement or rising: *the slow ascent of the balloon*.

*Assent* and *consent* can both be used as nouns meaning agreement; *consent* puts extra emphasis on permission:

We could not release the statement without the director's assent.

Katrina could not go to the nightclub without her mother's consent.

*Assent* and *consent*, used as verbs, mean to agree. You can *assent to something* but not *assent to do something*, while *consent* can be followed by either the noun or the infinitive.

The director assented to our proposal.

Katrina's mother consented to her outing.

*or* Katrina consented to return by 2 a.m.

**ascertain** This verb means to find out in order to know for certain; do not use it if you merely mean find out:

I'll ascertain that the opals are safe.

*but* I'll find out what the opals are worth.

**ascetic** See **acetic/aesthete/aesthetic/ascetic**.

**ASCII** *ASCII* (pronounced 'ass-kee') is an acronym for *American Standard Code for Information Interchange*. In the 1960s ASCII became the means by which computers could 'talk' to each other. Before this time a computer had to convert any other computer's characters into its own set of codes to do this. The development of this internationally recognised computer industry standard means that every letter in the alphabet, every number and every special keyboard character is represented by a number between 0 and 255. For instance, a lower-case *m* is stored in the computer as the number 109.

Note that ASCII codes for formatting characters (such as bold, italic and tabulation) may not be standard on all computers; therefore using ASCII for transferring a word-processing file may result in some loss of formatting detail, although the text will remain intact.

See also **bureau (desktop publishing)**; **disk conversion**.

**ascribe/subscribe** If you *ascribe* something you attribute it to a cause or source:

She ascribed her fine voice to her father's musical family.

However, you would probably prefer the word *attribute*.

*Subscribe* suggests agreement, which may involve payment: you *subscribe* to a magazine or to a particular view.

**ASEAN** Association of South East Asian Nations.

**aseptic** See **antiseptic/aseptic**.

**as follows** This introduction to a list of points or examples is always singular (that is, never 'as follow'): *The new rules are as follows.*

**as for/as to** The expressions *as for* and *as to* are useful at the beginning of a sentence to bring a topic into prominence:

As for the greenhouse effect, it is a matter that concerns us all.

As to its influence on Australian weather, we are unsure.

When such emphasis is not needed, a single-word preposition is preferred:

She has lofty ideas about [*not* as to] behaviour.

They had been critical of [*not* as to] his report.

*As to* is not necessary before *whether*:

He must decide today whether [*not* as to whether] to resign.

**Asian/Asiatic** Prefer *Asian* to *Asiatic* when describing the people of Asia. The word *Asiatic* is often considered to be racially offensive now.

See also **discriminatory language**.

**aside from** Prefer *apart from*.

**as if/as though** These are similar enough in meaning to be interchangeable in most sentences:

She spoke as if [*or* as though] she meant it.

In formal writing both phrases need to be followed by *were* (the subjunctive), not *was*, when expressing something that is a possibility or an imaginary case rather than a fact:

It looked as if [*or* as though] the delivery boy was likely to be promoted.

*but* The delivery boy acted as if [*or* as though] he were general manager.

Use *as if* rather than *as though* in exclamations:

As if I could help it!

See also **subjunctive mood**.

**ASIO** Australian Security Intelligence Organization (note the *-z-*); also *Asio*.

**ASIS** Australian Secret Intelligence Service; also *Asis*.

**ASPAC** Asian and Pacific Council; also *Aspac*.

**asphalt** Note the spelling (not 'ashphelt').

**assemble** See **together**.

**assent** See **ascent/assent/consent**.

**assertive** This adjective has become such a cliché, particularly in recruitment advertising, that its primary meaning – stating as true or defending a matter – is often superseded by its secondary meaning of positive and, by extension, constructively aggressive. Do not be afraid to use it when it seems right, however:

Members should be assertive but not vociferous, the president said.

**assimilate** Note the *-mi-*.

**assonance** See **alliteration/assonance/onomatopoeia**.

**assume/presume** Although these verbs may seem to be virtually identical when used to mean suppose or take for granted, there are cases where one is better than the other. *Assume* is preferred where something is supposed without any evidence to back up the supposition; *presume* is preferred where there is some evidence to go on:

We assume [*or* presume] you will not be leaving the firm.

*but* We assumed [*rather than* presumed] that you could not afford to leave the firm.

*and* We knew how large the redundancy package was and presumed [*rather than* assumed] that you could afford to leave the firm.

**assurance/insurance** Traditionally a life *assurance* policy provided financial support in the event of the policyholder's death (which is a certainty), in contrast to a general *insurance* policy, which provided recompense in the event of occurrences such as theft, fire, accident or sickness (which are only possibilities):

Let's see the agent about life assurance; insurance for the house will have to wait.

The distinction is disappearing in Australian, British and US English, where *insurance* tends to be used in all cases. The noun *assurance* (from the verb *assure*) also has the more general meaning of confidence or a guarantee.

See also **assure/ensure/insure**.

**assure/ensure/insure** These three verbs all mean to make safe or certain, but there are slight differences. To *assure* is to convince, or declare something positively:

The previous owner of the car assured me that the brakes were safe.

To *ensure* is to make certain:

I had the brakes checked to ensure that they were safe.

To *insure* is to guarantee financially against possible loss or damage:

I thought I should insure the car even though the brakes were safe.

In US English *insure* is often used instead of *ensure*. This confusing use of the word may sometimes be heard in Australia but is not recommended.

See also **assurance/insurance**.

**asterisk** The most common use for an *asterisk* (*) in books and articles is as a reference mark. To indicate footnotes it is placed at the end of the phrase or sentence that is being noted, and at the beginning of the footnote. Put it outside the full stop or closing quotation mark when it occurs at the end of a sentence:

Exhibition ends 30 January.*

An asterisk should not break the flow of a simple sentence, but may need to when the sentence is more complex:

Exhibition* ends 30 January, but pictures available through Nature-art Gallery.

The footnote in both cases is *Etchings on Bush Themes.

It is important, if you are an editor or proofreader, to make sure that the footnote implied by a textual asterisk exists, and that it is on the correct page.

Sometimes more than one reference mark is needed on a page; see the entry **reference marks** for additional symbols to use. In cases where there are still more references, it may be desirable to use small numbers (superior figures) instead of reference marks; see the entry **notes**.

Asterisks were once commonly used to indicate the omission of letters in (usually) quoted material that readers might find offensive:

He said, 'That politician is a f***ing no-hoper'.

Long dashes are recommended instead, though many writers and publishers now spell out such words.

Asterisks are sometimes used in narrative text to indicate a change of theme, time, place or thought (though it is now more common to leave a two-line space blank). Three asterisks are placed about 15 millimetres apart with a line space above and below:

*    *    *

This device should not appear at the start of a new page.

See also **inferior characters/superior characters**; **notes**; **reference marks**; **references**.

**asthma** Note the *-sth-*. Pronounce the word 'assma'.

**as though** See **as if/as though**.

**astronaut** Note the *-ron-* (not 'astranaut').

**astronomy/astrology** *Astronomy* is the science of the 'heavenly bodies'; *astrology* is the study that interprets their supposed influence on humans.

**as well as** This prepositional phrase has a kind of parenthetical role and does not affect number agreement in the way that the conjunction *and* does. The verb remains singular whether or not the words are marked off by commas.

Lauren and Carla have cats.
*but* Lauren as well as Carla has a cat.
*and* Lauren, as well as Carla, has a cat.

Add the verb *does* to the end of the following sentence to avoid ambiguity: *Lauren loves her cat as well as Carla.*

See also **singular or plural**.

**ASX** Australian Stock Exchange.

**at/in** As a general rule use *at* before the names of small towns and *in* before cities, States and countries:

Grandma lived at Longreach in Queensland.

Our friend Patrick lived in China for many years.

When referring to your own town or city, use *in*:

I live in Kalgoorlie.

Use *in* for an area, such as a suburb, and *at* for a particular address:

They live in Hakea at 38 Shrub Street.

Note these further examples: *in a flat*; *in a mansion*; *at the Windsor Hotel*; *at Atherton House*.

**-athon** The suffix *-athon* has in recent times been borrowed from *marathon* to describe various fundraising feats of endurance: words such as *sportathon, walkathon* and *swimathon* now test the endurance of the listener.

**ATM** automated teller machine.

**ATSIC** Aboriginal and Torres Strait Islander Commission.

**attain** This verb means to achieve or accomplish by continued effort, and suggests the reaching of a desired goal:

Women attained the vote after decades of struggle.

It should not be used to describe an undesirable state: you would not *attain* bankruptcy, for example.

**at this moment in time/at this point in time** These phrases are undesirably roundabout ways of saying *now*.

**attorneys-general** Note that the first word indicates the plural.

See also **compound nouns, plurals of**.

**attribute** The verb means to give credit for, or ascribe; the noun means a quality or feature:

We attribute Joan's success to her remarkable attributes.

Pronounce the verb 'a-**trib**-yoot' and the noun '**at**-ribyoot'.

**attribute (typesetting)** An *attribute* in typesetting is a special feature, usually of a typeface; bold, italic, decorative initial capitals, small capitals and point size are attributes of this kind.

**auger/augur** An *auger* is a tool with a spiral groove for drilling holes:

They'll need a new auger to get through red gum.

An *augur* is a soothsayer or prophet; the verb *to augur*, which is much more often seen than the noun, means to divine or predict:

A good degree augurs well for her future.

**au naturel** Note the *-el*. The context should tell you whether this French phrase means naked, uncooked or plainly cooked.

**aural/oral** *Aural* refers to the ear or to hearing:

> Dogs have an aural capacity that enables them to hear higher notes than humans.
> In their aural test the piano students must listen to a tune then sing it.

*Oral* refers to the mouth or to speaking:

> Oral hygiene centres on cleaning your teeth regularly.
> Aboriginal tales of the Rainbow Serpent are part of an oral tradition.

As the words are pronounced similarly, be careful not to confuse them in speech.
See also **oral/verbal.**

**AUS** Australian Union of Students.

**auspicious** Reserve this slightly pompous word for times when you mean favourable or propitious, rather than special or important:

> Alistair regarded the conjunction of planets as auspicious for his exam.
> Gran's ninetieth birthday was a special [*not* auspicious] occasion.

**AUSSAT** This is the name (also *Aussat*) of the organisation formed by the federal government and Telecom in 1981 to operate Australia's domestic satellite system.

**Australasia** *Australasia* comprises Australia and New Zealand and their associated islands.

**Australia** *Austral* means south. As parts of the theoretical Great South Land (*terra australis*) were proved to exist, the Dutch called what they found New Holland and the British used the name New South Wales. Matthew Flinders proved that both were part of the same landmass, which he called *Australia*, although the title of his 1814 book was *A Voyage to Terra Australis*. Lachlan Macquarie (governor, 1810–21) first used the name *Australia* officially, and that was its geographical designation until 1901, when by an Act of the British Parliament the colonies became States of the Commonwealth of Australia.

**Australia Council** Originally established in 1968 as the Australian Council for the Arts, the *Australia Council* became a statutory authority in 1975. It is the federal government's chief funding and advisory body for the arts, and provides annual grants and fellowships through its specialist Boards: Aboriginal Arts; Community Arts; Crafts; Design Arts; Literature; Music; Theatre; and Visual Arts.

**Australia Felix** In 1836 Thomas Mitchell gave the name *Australia Felix* (*felix* is Latin for fruitful, blessed or fortunate) to a large part of western Victoria, including what is now called the Western District. Later writers used the name for all of what became the colony of Victoria.

**Australiana** Written material relating to Australia is called *Australiana*. In recent years the term has been extended to include objects of special interest or rarity (such as colonial cedar chairs) that originate in or relate to Australia. It should not be used of just any Australian item.

**Australian ballot** This term is often used erroneously as a synonym for the preferential system of voting. *Australian ballot* means simply, and only, secret ballot.

**Australian English** The grammar of Australian English is virtually identical with that of British English, though usage sometimes differs. When it comes to spelling, Australian English seems to be having a bet each way, using British spelling for some words and US spelling for others. Many people, for instance, tend to use US spellings for *honor* and *program*, but British for *centre* and *theatre*. Sometimes Australians have made clear choices between the British and US words, retaining the British *tap* and *petrol* (in preference to *faucet* and *gas*), for instance, but adopting the US *freeway* and *sedan* (instead of *motorway* and *saloon*).

What sounds like linguistic confusion is merely the result of the strong currents flowing from two major sources. British and US English have also accepted (and rejected) changes to words, spelling and usage in apparently inconsistent ways over a much longer period.

For many years British critics regarded all specifically Australian words as mere slang. In 1945 Sidney J. Baker refuted this opinion in his book *The Australian Language*, in which he described the evolution of a distinctively Australian form of English, with its own vocabulary, idiom and usage. *The Australian National Dictionary*, published in 1988, records the development of the 10 000 words (noted in about 6000 entries) it considers constitute the Australian contribution to English.

Like the colonists of North America, the first European settlers in Australia had to find words for things unknown in Britain. They adopted or adapted many Aboriginal words, and words were formed from compounds to describe the new environment and occupations: *outback*, *bottlebrush*, *ironbark*, *overlander*. Some British words were given Australian applications: *station* for sheep and cattle property; *paddock* for field. Other words were adapted from the argot of the convicts or were variants of nineteenth-century English colloquialisms: *swag*, *fair dinkum*, *cobber*, *larrikin*, *barrack*. Imports from the Californian gold rush of the mid-nineteenth century included *digger*, *prospector*, *pan out* and *cradle*.

Early Australian inventiveness with slang is often attributed to the large proportion of Irish and Cockney convicts, both groups having a love of language and being quick to turn a new phrase. The creative Australian approach to swearing was also noted at an early stage. According to the *Bulletin*, 'The true Australian oath was a thing of beauty, providing a means of relief for depression, exasperation, hard luck... It was descriptive, vigorous and decisive'.

Some language-watchers believe that the spirit of Australian linguistic improvisation is now languishing. For example, since decimal currency was introduced in 1966, not a single denomination has received a widely recognised nickname, whereas the imperial *pound* was familiarly a *quid*; a *shilling* a *bob* or *deener*; *sixpence* a *zack*; and *threepence* a *trey*. Much of the slang entering Australian English today is of American origin. Surprisingly, European immigrants and their languages seem to have had little direct linguistic impact, mainly contributing words describing new foods.

Some authorities divide the patterns of Australian speech into three categories: Cultivated, General and Broad. Cultivated Australian is an approximation of the Received Pronunciation (RP) of southern England and is spoken by about one-tenth of the population. General Australian is spoken by just over half the population and Broad Australian by the rest. In Australia, as in the US, pronunciation is not necessarily linked with social standing or occupation, and all three types may be present in the one family.

An essential difference between Cultivated (or adapted RP) and Broad – and, to a lesser extent, General – Australian is found in the vowel sounds. For example, the sound of 'ay' in *today* becomes relaxed into 'ie' as in *die*; and the 'ie' moves towards 'oi' as in *boy*. Thus *I'll buy a pie today* sounds in Broad Australian like 'oil boy a poy todie'. The rounded sound of 'o' in *home* becomes the slackened, more open and yet nasalised 'howm'. Speakers of Broad and General Australian also run words together and omit syllables, as was illustrated in *Let Stalk Strine* (1965) by Afferbeck Lauder (the pseudonym, standing for Alphabetical Order, of Alistair Morrison): *air conditioner* becomes 'egg nishner' and *glorious home* is 'Gloria Soame'. Consonants such as *t* often become *d* in words such as *matter*, which becomes 'madder'.

When looking at the question of correct or incorrect pronunciation (within the framework of variations in accent), it is worth remembering that language is a living thing and that changes do and will occur. The reasons for change are sometimes evident – for instance, the growing long-term influence of US film and television on all varieties of English. Some words whose stress has been changing because of this are '**con**-troversy' (US 'con-**trov**-ersy'), '**dec**-ade' (US 'dec-**ade**'), '**in**-tegral' (US 'in-**teg**-ral'), '**in**-ventory' (US 'in-**vent**-ory' or 'invent-**ory**'), '**prem**-ature' (US 'prema-**ture**' or '**pre**-mature') and '**temp**-orary' (US 'tempor-**ary**').

But the Americans cannot be blamed for the numerous mispronunciations that are simply a result of ignorance or careless articulation. The following are notable examples:

| | | | | | |
|---|---|---|---|---|---|
| 'haitch' | *for* | the letter *h* | 'pronounciation' | *for* | pronunciation |
| 'Orstrieyia' | *for* | Australia | 'umberella' | *for* | umbrella |

| | |
|---|---|
| 'Orstrielyun' *for* Australian | 'hyderainga' *for* hydrangea |
| 'sekatary' *for* secretary | 'adver**tize**ment' *for* ad**ver**tisement |
| 'Febewary' *for* February | 'stastistics' *for* statistics |
| 'burgular' *for* burglar | 'eksetra' *for* etcetera |
| 'Chooseday' *for* Tuesday | 'fillum' *for* film |
| 'pitcher' *for* picture | 'chimley' *for* chimney |
| 'mischeeveeous' *for* mischievous | 'know-en' *for* known |
| 'Ahtic' *for* Arctic | 'arksed' *for* asked |
| 'vunerable' *for* vulnerable | 'bronikal' *for* bronchial |
| 'fith' *for* fifth | 'artitekt' *for* architect |
| 'strenth' *for* strength | 'asparagrass' *for* asparagus |
| 'anythink' *for* anything | 'krippeling' *for* crippling |
| 'rekkanise' *for* recognise | 'pacific' *for* specific |

A good dictionary will provide the best guide to the most widely accepted pronunciation. *The Macquarie Dictionary* uses phonetic alphabet symbols to provide comprehensive pronunciation guidance, based on usage in the Australian community, for every headword. The *Heinemann Australian Dictionary*, with its simple, non-phonetic pronunciation system, is recommended for those who find phonetics difficult. People involved in public communication or the study of linguistics and phonetics will find *Everyman's English Pronouncing Dictionary* by Daniel Jones invaluable for its record of the pronunciation used in the RP of British English.

See also **British English**; **slang**; **US English**; **US spelling**.

**author** Do not use this noun as a verb: *She has just authored her third novel.*

**authoritarian/authoritative** These adjectives are often confused and misspelt. *Authoritarian* means favouring strict obedience to authority as opposed to individual freedom, and is usually disapproving:

> Many Third World countries are run by authoritarian regimes.

*Authoritative* means having the sanction or weight of authority, and is often a term of approval:

> The report was an authoritative document in which we could all have faith.

**author's corrections** *Author's corrections* (abbreviated *ACs*) are changes made during production to typeset material, other than those necessitated by typesetting errors. Publishers, editors and designers as well as authors may contribute to these changes, but they are billed to the publisher. If the changes requested by authors exceed the proportion allowed for in their contract, the publisher is entitled to pass on some of the cost to them.

See also **proofs**.

**autocracy/autonomy** *Autocracy* is government by, or control exercised by, one person (an *autocrat*) with unlimited powers; *autocracies* are countries governed in this way:

Nearly all the offshore islands are autocracies.

*Autonomy* is self-government by a country or group; or the freedom of individuals to decide things for themselves:

Nearly all the offshore islands have autonomy but their leaders are autocrats.

Surely I can have autonomy in my own kitchen!

**automaton** Plural *automata* or *automatons*.

**autonomy** See **autocracy/autonomy**.

**autopsy** An *autopsy* is *performed* or *done*, not *held*.

**AV** audio-visual; Authorised Version (of the Bible).

**avenge/revenge/vengeance** The verbs *avenge* and *revenge* both relate to retaliation for wrongs done, but with a subtle distinction that is often overlooked. *Avenge* usually implies acting on behalf of someone else:

Hamlet vowed to avenge his father's murder.

*Revenge*, a slightly stronger word, usually means acting on your own behalf:

I will revenge myself at any cost.

*Vengeance* is the noun from *avenge*. *Revenge* has the same form for verb and noun, and many people would substitute *take revenge* for *revenge myself* in the last example.

**average/mean/median** In common parlance all these words can mean in the middle: *average ability*; *a mean acceptable to all*; *the median strip*. As statistical terms they are not interchangeable, however, and can be very confusing to the uninitiated. The 'average' obtained by totalling a group of figures then dividing by the number of items in the group is statistically known as the *arithmetic mean*. But there are also 'averages' such as the *harmonic mean* and the *geometric mean*, which have specific uses. *Median* as a statistical term means the middle item in a series. A textbook of basic statistical method can supply definitions and examples.

**averse** See **adverse/averse**.

**avert** See **advert/avert**.

**aviary** See **apiary/aviary**.

**AVM** Air Vice Marshal.

**avocado** Plural *avocados*.

**AWA** Amalgamated Wireless (Australasia) Ltd (from 1988, AWA Limited).

**await/wait** *Await*, meaning to wait for, is a slightly more formal word than *wait*:

The architect will await your approval of the new designs.

*Wait* must be followed by *for* when used to mean *await*:

The groom has to wait for the bride.

*Wait on* means to serve or be attendant on:

He waited on his uncle hand and foot.

The job of a restaurant waiter is to *wait*, not to 'waiter'.

**awake/awaken/wake/waken** Used as verbs all these words have the primary meaning to rouse, or to emerge, from sleep (or, sometimes, inactivity); a secondary meaning is to come to a realisation of, or to become aware of.

*Awake* and *awaken* are preferred for figurative use, as in poetry:

awake not the dawn    as Spring awakens

*Awake* used as an adjective means vigilant, aware, or not asleep:

I was awake to the danger of the rotten floorboards.

I lay awake all night.

*Wake* and *waken* are the most common everyday forms:

Will this noise wake the baby?

This noise would waken the dead.

Note also the informal expression *a wake-up to*:

We were a wake-up to their ulterior motives.

**award-winning** This compound adjective has reached plague proportions, particularly in the fields of advertising, literature and the visual arts. Some awards are not particularly prestigious, and the implication that something is good because it has been given an unspecified award could be misleading.

**aware** This adjective means conscious (of something):

He was aware of the folly of swimming in shark-infested waters.

*Aware* has become a cliché describing (with approval) a vaguely defined state of mind or being. *He's an aware person* might mean that he is observant, sensitive or knowledgeable, and this comment will therefore mean little unless the context is made clear.

**awful/awfully** Both words have drifted a long way from their source in the word *awe*, meaning reverence for or fear of the grand or sublime, and using them in the original sense would risk being misunderstood. *Awful* now means extremely bad or unpleasant; *awfully* has become a synonym for *very*:

Travelling with small children is awful.

Their parents will be awfully glad when the trip is over.

**AWL/AWOL** The traditional Australian form of abbreviation for this military term meaning absent without leave seems to be *AWL* (in contrast to the US

*AWOL*). Either form of the abbreviation has some general as well as military currency:

Because they couldn't get the day off, they went AWL [*or* AWOL].

**AWU** Australian Workers' Union.

**axe** Do not overuse this colloquial verb; remember alternatives such as *dismiss*, *terminate* and *cut*.

**axis** The plural is *axes*, pronounced '**ak**-seez'.

**ayatollah** An *ayatollah* is a leader of the Shiite sect within the Islamic faith. The word needs an initial capital when used as a title:

The Ayatollah Khomeini died in 1989.

Pronounce it 'eye-a-**tolla**'.

**Ayers Rock** See **Uluru**.

# Bb

**bachelor** This noun is occasionally misspelt 'batchelor' in Australia, probably because of the long-established Australian spelling *batch* for *bach*, a colloquial verb that means to live on one's own.

**bacillus** The plural is *bacilli*. The *c* is soft.

**back formation** This is the process of forming new words by shortening existing ones: for example, the noun *editor* became the verb *edit*. It is the reverse of the normal process of derivation, in which prefixes or suffixes are added to root words to make new ones: the noun *atom* plus *ic* became the adjective *atomic*, for instance.

Most back formations are verbs derived from existing nouns or adjectives: *burgle* from *burglar*; *laze* from *lazy*; *scavenge* from *scavenger*; *resurrect* from *resurrection*; *enthuse* from *enthusiasm*.

Some people welcome new verbs formed in this way, while others dislike and resist them. Back formations are usually accepted when time has shown that there is a genuine need for them.

See also **verbs**.

**back matter** See **publications, parts of**.

**back to back** This is a confusing and unnecessary recent synonym for *successive* or *successively*:

> That's three premierships they've won back to back.

What strange game were they playing?

See also **consecutive/successive**.

**backup** A computer *backup* is an electronic copy of a file, folder, floppy disk or hard disk. Backups can be made onto another floppy disk or hard disk, a digital audio tape, cartridge or compact disk. It is important to make regular backups – at least once a day – to guard against problems such as system crashes and virus damage.

See also **crashed/gone down**; **save**.

**backward/backwards** The adjective is always *backward*: *a backward step*. The adverb can be either, but *backwards* is preferred: *walking backwards*.

**bacteria** The singular is *bacterium*.

**bail/bale** The spelling of these two words, which can both be used as either nouns or verbs, is interchangeable in some cases. British and American dictionaries do not agree with each other, and neither totally agrees with Australian usage, of which the following are examples:

Bail was set at $8000.
Brigands bailed us up in the desert and robbed us.
The wicketkeeper removed the bails.
Heather got the cow into its bail and we soon had milk.
You'll have to bale [*or* bail] out the dinghy occasionally.
The plane is too high up for us to bale [*or* bail] out.
We sold two thousand bales of wool.

**baited/bated** Sorting out the spelling of *baited* and *bated* is easy if you remember that *baited* is much more common; *bated* usually appears in only one phrase: *bated breath*.

Uncle Bill baited his line with garfish.
The interviewer baited the celebrity with provocative questions.
The couple awaited the bank manager's decision with bated breath.

**baksheesh** Strictly speaking this Middle Eastern word means money given as a present, but it is widely used to mean a bribe.

**Balaclava, Vic.** Compare with *Balaklava*, SA.

**balance of trade** The *balance of trade* over a certain period means the difference between the value of a nation's exports and its imports. It is said, perhaps misleadingly, to be 'favourable' or 'unfavourable' – depending on whether the value of exports exceeds, or is lower than, the value of imports.

**bale** See **bail/bale**.

**baleful/baneful** *Baleful* means menacing or malevolent:

Cheated of the last cream cake, Amy shot a baleful look at her little brother.

*Baneful* is an out-of-date word for destructive or pernicious:

Blackberries were a baneful addition to the Australian bush.

This adjective comes from the noun *bane*, which means something that causes misery or ruin:

Hayfever is the bane of his life in spring.

**balk/baulk** This verb, meaning to stop (at an obstacle or before taking a step) or shirk, can be spelt either way, but *baulk* is generally preferred in Australia. It is always followed by *at*.

**ballot/balloted/balloting** Note the *-ll-* and single *t* in all three.

**balmy/barmy** *Balmy*, stemming from *balm*, means soothing, soft, mild or fragrant:

The Whitsundays are balmy in July but hot in December.

*Barmy* is slang for crazy:

My cousin's barmy ideas will get him certified.

**banana republic** Originally the name given to a number of small Central American countries economically dependent on the US, *banana republic* is now used to describe any small nation that is politically unstable and dependent on trade with rich and powerful countries. It has occasionally been used facetiously of Australia – and colloquially to describe Queensland.

**bandaid solution** Note the lower-case initial for *bandaid* (unhyphenated) in this phrase. Derived from the registered trade name *Band-Aid* (plaster strip), the term – now a cliché – describes any temporary or superficial response to a problem.

**baneful** See **baleful/baneful**.

**banister/bannister** Either spelling, with one *n* or two, is acceptable but *banister* is more common in Australian English. The plural *banisters* is often used instead of the singular to mean the same thing – the handrail and supporting posts of a staircase: *sliding down the banisters*.

**bankruptcy/factoring/liquidation/receivership** When people are pronounced insolvent by a court of law, their *bankruptcy* is said to have been declared. When a company or business sells all or part of its 'accounts receivable' to a finance institution in order to inject money into the business, it is *factoring* its debts. The finance company deducts a commission from the debt payments. The term *factoring in* has a special sense in finance circles; it means taking into account (the influence of an expected rise in interest rates, for example). When a company is in *liquidation* it is in the process of paying off debts and accounts by selling all assets, with a view to winding up the company as a result of court action by creditors. *Voluntary liquidation* occurs when a company decides of its own accord to settle all debts and wind up business. When a company is in *receivership* it is being managed by someone from outside the organisation who has been appointed, usually by a court of law, to take charge of the business until its financial position is resolved.

**banquet/banqueted/banqueting** Note the single *t* in all three.

**barbaric/barbarous** These adjectives both mean uncouth or uncivilised, but they are used in slightly different ways. *Barbaric* sometimes implies little more than unsophisticated or primitive; it may be used to condemn, or to express admiration:

> There was a barbaric vigour about Cecil B. De Mille's biblical films.

The word *barbarian*, as noun and adjective, has the same range of connotations as *barbaric*. *Barbarous*, on the other hand, condemns outright, implying cruelty or brutality:

> The torture of the political prisoners was barbarous.

**barbecue/barbecued/barbecuing** The spelling *barbeque* is not recommended. The shortened forms *BBQ* and *bar-b-q* are strictly informal.

**bar code** The series of bars of different thickness now printed on the wrapper, cover or container of many products is called a *bar code*. The bars are coded to identify the product and give information on matters such as price; the bar code is read by an optical scanner, usually at the point of sale.

**barely** See **double negative**; **hardly**.

**barmy** See **balmy/barmy**.

**Barney Point, Qld** Compare with *Barneys Point*, NSW.

**barrel/barrelled/barrelling** Note the single *l* in the first and the *-ll-* in the other two.

**base/basis** These nouns both mean the foundation, the starting point or the groundwork, or something that supports other things. *Base* more often refers to tangibles than intangibles:

> The base of the lamp was broken.

*Basis* refers only to intangibles and is therefore mainly figurative:

> The basis of applied philosophy is logic.

The plural of both words is spelt *bases*, but the plural of *base* is pronounced '**bay**-s'z', and of *basis*, 'bay-**seez**'.

See also **base/bass**.

**base/bass** *Base* (*base motives*) and *bass* (*a bass bassoon*) both rhyme with *face*, but the fish *bass* rhymes with *lass*.
See also **base/basis**.

**baseline** See **leading; type**.

**BASIC** In computer terminology this is an acronym for *Beginner's All-purpose Symbolic Instruction Code*.

**basically** Used to mean fundamentally, *basically* is a valid adverb:
His first proposition was basically wrong.
However, like *actually* and *anyway*, it is too often turned into a meaningless filler, a piece of verbal punctuation: *Basically, I don't like the cold weather*. Try to avoid such words in formal English.

**basis** See **base/basis**.

**bass** See **base/bass**.

**bated** See **baited/bated**.

**bath/bathe** The verbs *to bath* and *to bathe* both mean to wash or immerse the body, but Australians do not normally say *bathe* when they mean have a bath, or give one:
Jan will do the ironing then bath the baby.
*but* The children can bathe in the river.
Note also the usage *to bathe a cut*.

**bathos/pathos** These nouns are often confused. *Bathos* is occasionally replaced – to the annoyance of the author – with *pathos* (the more common word) by a puzzled sub-editor, typesetter or proofreader. The primary meaning of *bathos* is a sudden, ludicrous descent from the lofty to the commonplace: in general, an anticlimax. It is most often used in a literary or artistic context:
In the last episode Martha dies of starvation and her house-plants succumb to overfeeding – such bathos!
*Bathos* can also mean false sentimentality, triteness, or the lowest point of something.
*Pathos* is a quality evoking genuine pity or sadness:
The pathos of the refugee's plight brought tears to his eyes.
See also **pathetic**.

**baud rate** A measure of computer data transmission speed.
See also **bits per second**.

**baulk** See **balk/baulk**.

**bazaar/bizarre** The noun *bazaar* means marketplace. *Bizarre* is an adjective that means strange, odd or singular in appearance or character:

> Jo's luminous green hair looked bizarre, especially at the office.

**BBC** British Broadcasting Corporation.

**BC** See **AD/BC**.

**BDR** Bombardier.

**because** Since the conjunction *because* means for the reason that, it would be superfluous to use it with a similar phrase of explanation:

> She is late because her watch is slow.
>
> *or* The reason she is late is that her watch is slow.
>
> *not* The reason she is late is because her watch is slow.

Be careful when using *because* after a negative clause, as this may result in ambiguity: *She didn't love him because he was wealthy*. Did she dislike his wealth? Or did she love him for reasons other than his wealth? Rewrite the sentence to make the meaning clear.

Avoid using *just because* when you mean the fact that:

> The fact that [*not* Just because] he's unmarried doesn't mean he's lonely.

See also **as/since/because/for**; **because of/owing to/due to**; **reason**.

**because of/owing to/due to** Grammatical arguments concerning the use of these phrases are complex, but here are some simple guidelines. *Because of* and *owing to* are often interchangeable and may be used in various positions in a sentence:

> Because of [*or* Owing to] the traffic jam, we were delayed.
>
> We were delayed because of [*or* owing to] the traffic jam.

*Due to* is not nearly so versatile. It should not start a sentence; must always be used as an adjective linked with a preceding noun; and is most safely used to mean *caused by*:

> Our delay was due to the traffic jam.
>
> The delay due to the traffic jam made us late.

If in doubt, use *because of* or *owing to*.

*Due to* is also used in phrases such as *fees due to the club*, where it means owing to.

Avoid the verbose phrase *owing to the fact that* and use *because* instead.

**beg the question** Someone who *begs the question* is neither raising nor evading it, but attempting to prove an argument or draw a conclusion by assuming the truth of the very thing that has yet to be proved:

The Bible is true because the Bible says so.

She is sure to be elected because most people will vote for her.

See also **leading question; rhetorical question**.

**beige** Note the *-ei-*.

**Beijing** The old name, *Peking*, now has mainly historical use. Pronounce Beijing 'bay-jing'.

**Bel Air, NSW** Compare with *Belair*, SA.

**beleaguered** Note the spelling of this verb meaning besieged or surrounded.

**belligerent** Note the *-ll-* and the *-erent*.

**below/beneath/under/underneath** All these words, which are used here as prepositions, convey the meaning lower than, but there are fine differences. *Below* contrasts with *above* and is often used in relation to levels:

Her office is on the floor below mine.

Thomas was below me at school.

*Beneath* can often be interchanged with the other three, but it is the only real choice when you mean unworthy of:

Polishing his own shoes was beneath his dignity.

*Under* often contrasts with *over* and may literally mean covered by:

The money was found under the couch.

You can substitute *underneath* for *under* in that kind of context. *Under* can also mean subject to:

Local councils are under government control.

Of the four words, *under* is used in the widest range of idioms, some of which relate only loosely to the primary meanings:

Under this schedule there will be plenty of time for a rest.

She travelled to Paris under an assumed name.

With a hectare under strawberries they needed lots of pickers.

The sloop limped home under diesel power.

I was born under Leo but am hardly lionhearted.

See also **above/over**.

**beneficent/beneficial** See **benevolent/beneficent/beneficial/benign**.

**benefit/benefited/benefiting** Note the single *t* in all three.

**Benelux** The name is a compound of the first letters of the names Belgium, the Netherlands and Luxembourg, and refers to these countries collectively or to the non-political unions they have made.

**benevolent/beneficent/beneficial/benign** These adjectives all derive from the Latin *bene* (well) and convey the sense of desiring to do good or actually doing it, but there are nuances of meaning. *Benevolent* means wishing to do good for others: *a benevolent institution*; *a benevolent fund*. *Beneficent*, like *benevolent*, means charitable or generous, but the emphasis is more strongly on action than intent. It is also more often used to describe people than things:

A beneficent industrialist helped the work of the Sisters of Charity.

Something that is *beneficial* may promote well-being, but can also have the meaning advantageous. It is used to describe things, not people, and does not necessarily have the altruistic touch of *benevolent* or *beneficent*:

Vitamin C is believed to be beneficial to health.

The agreement proved beneficial for all concerned.

The meaning of *benign* varies according to its context:

Autumn is benign [mild] in the southern States.

Luckily the tumour was benign [not malignant].

Try to catch the boss when she's feeling benign [genial].

**Bentleigh, Vic.** Compare with *Bentley*, NSW and WA.

**bereaved/bereft** The past participle of the verb *bereave* has two forms, *bereaved* and *bereft*. To be bereaved usually means to be deprived of a person who has died:

The bereaved father visited his son's grave.

*Bereft* usually means deprived of an important non-material thing and it is a more forceful word, implying utter loss and desolation:

The poor man was bereft of all companionship.

*Bereft* should not be used simply as a synonym for *without*:

I am without [*not* bereft of] mathematical ability.

**Berridale, NSW** Compare with *Berriedale*, Tas.

**Berrima, NSW** Compare with *Berrimah*, NT.

**beside/besides** *Beside* is a preposition that usually means at the side of or next to: *beside the lake*. To be *beside oneself* is to be extremely excited or upset. When something is *beside the point* it is irrelevant.

*Besides* is a different word altogether. Used as an adverb it can mean moreover:

Besides, we didn't plan to stay late.

Used as a preposition it can mean in addition to, or except for:

Besides the usual menu there are daily specials.

She has no family besides her mother.

**between** The preposition *between* creates problems for many people. Here are some guidelines.

Pronouns following *between* should be in the objective case:

between you and me *not* between you and I
between him and her *not* between he and she
between them and us *not* between they and we

*Between* traditionally implies a relationship involving two things, though modern usage allows the relationship to include more than two in some cases (see **among/between**). That notion of a relationship suggests that *between* should be followed by a plural: *between the posts*; or by words joined by *and*: *between each post and the next*. Note that *between each post* or *between every post* would be incorrect.

Do not use any linking word other than *and* after *between*:

I must choose between buying a video *and* renting one.
*not* I must choose between buying a video *or* renting one.

Similarly, write:

The house was between 80 and 90 years old.
*or* The house was 80–90 years old.
*not* The house was between 80–90 years old.
*or* The house was between 80 to 90 years old.

See also **among/between**.

**b.f.** bloody fool; bold face (typography; see also **type**); brought forward (also *b/f*).

**BGDR/Brig.** Brigadier.

**BHP** The Broken Hill Proprietary Company Limited.

**bi-** In most cases the prefix *bi-* conveys simply and clearly the idea of *two*: *binoculars*, *bicycle*, *bilateral*, *bisect*. However, when used with units of time it can cause confusion. Note the following examples and use the less ambiguous alternative wherever possible:

*biannual* means twice a year; use *twice yearly*
*biennial* means every two years; use *every two years*
or it can mean lasting for two years; use *for two years*
*bimonthly* can mean every two months; use *every two months*
or it can mean twice a month; use *twice monthly*
*biweekly* can mean every two weeks; use *fortnightly*
or it can mean twice a week; use *twice weekly*

A *bicentenary* is a 200th anniversary, and the adjective *bicentennial* describes either a 200th anniversary or something lasting 200 years. Note the *-ten-* in *bicentenary* (pronounced 'teen' or 'ten') and the *-tenn-* in *bicentennial* (pronounced 'ten').

**biannual** See **bi-**.

**bias/biased/biasing** Note the spelling.
See also **bias/prejudice**.

**bias/prejudice** The nouns *bias* and *prejudice* can both mean irrational inclination, but *bias* is most often used when the inclination is favourable and *prejudice* when it is unfavourable: *a bias in favour of school uniforms*; *a prejudice against school uniforms*.
See also **bias/biased/biasing**.

**Bible/bible/biblical** When *Bible* has an initial capital it refers to the sacred writings of the Christian religion, which consist of the Old and New Testaments. A *bible* (with a lower-case initial) is any authoritative work. The adjective *biblical* always has a lower-case initial.

**bibliographic style** This relates to the manner in which notes, references and bibliographies are presented. The most important things to remember when setting out bibliographic information are to be clear and consistent, and to provide enough information to enable interested readers to trace books and journals and to find the text cited. Some aspects of bibliographic style depend on the nature of the publication and the publisher's preference. The bibliographic style of a library is likely to differ in some ways from that of a book publisher.
See also **asterisk**; **bibliographies**; **notes**; **reference marks**; **references**.

**bibliographies** A *bibliography* may be a list of the works of an author or publisher; a list of works relating to a particular subject; or a detailed listing of the sources used specifically or consulted marginally in the preparation of a work. Authors and editors need some guidelines, such as the following, on recommended ways of presenting the third type of bibliography.

Non-fiction books for the popular market – for example handbooks on antique-collecting, Australian frogs, organic gardening – often need a bibliography because many readers like to pursue aspects of the subject in greater detail. This kind of bibliography is sometimes labelled *Further reading*.

Scholarly books and substantial articles frequently require a bibliography because their authors consult many more works than they refer to in notes: a *List of references* covers only the latter. (See the **notes** and **references** entries in this book for further information.) A bibliography is placed near the end of a book – usually just before the index if there is one.

A writer's sources of information may include a wide range of written materials – for example newspapers, journals, books, unpublished manuscripts, theses, private letters and transcripts of interviews. Many writers list all these diverse works together (alphabetically, by author's surname) in their bibliography, but subsections for the various categories may be more helpful, particularly in a very long bibliography.

The following examples of entries in a bibliography cover most of the peculiarities likely to be encountered. Many entries will be simpler than these, but the same rules for capitalisation, punctuation and sequence apply. Chapter 9 of the AGPS *Style Manual* (4th edition) deals with bibliographies, and the manual's own bibliography is also instructive. Note that for a standard bibliography a full stop follows the author's name, the name of the work, the precise edition and the last word of the entry. The bibliography for an article or book referenced under the author–date (Harvard) system (see **references**) has a slightly different format – the same as for the list of references required by that system.

Abbott, J. H. M. *Tommy Cornstalk*. Longman Green, London, 1902.

*Advertiser* (Adelaide). 1970–80.

*Advertiser* (Bendigo). 1972–78.

*Ararat Advertiser*. 1970–76.

Attwill, Miss Merri. Reminiscences of 1910–1920. Taped at Airlie Beach, Qld, 23 January 1992. (Tape in writer's possession.)

Australia, House of Representatives 1977. *Debates*, vol. HR103.

Bean, C. E. W. *The Australian Imperial Force in France, 1917*. Angus & Robertson, Sydney, 1933. (*The Official History of Australia in the War of 1914–1918*, ed. C. E. W. Bean, 12 vols, 1921–42, vol. 4.)

Biblioteca Nacional, Rio de Janeiro. Codex 2/2-19, f. 368. Quoted in A. R. Disney, *Twilight of the Pepper Empire: Portuguese trade in southwest India in the early seventeenth century*. Harvard University Press, Cambridge, Mass., & London, 1978.

de Garis, B. K. '1890–1900'. In F. K. Crowley (ed.). *A New History of Australia*. Heinemann, Melbourne, 1974.

D'Urso, Janet. 'The social construction of woman: western mythic and religious stereotypes'. *Hecate*, vol. 1, no. 1, January 1975, pp. 23–30.

Eddy, J. & Schreuder, D. (eds). *The Rise of Colonial Nationalism: Australia, New Zealand, Canada and South Africa first assert their nationalities, 1880–1914*. Allen & Unwin, Sydney, 1988.

Foster, Leonie. High hopes: the men and the motives of the Australian Round Table. PhD thesis, La Trobe University, 1985.

Hancock, W. K. *Australia*. 1930, reissued Jacaranda Press, Brisbane, 1961.

La Meslee, E. Marin. *The New Australia (L'Australie Nouvelle*, 1883). Trans. and introd. by R. Ward. Heinemann, London & Melbourne, 1973.

New South Wales, Legislative Council. *Votes and Proceedings*, 1836.

Victoria, Parliament. Royal Commission on State Banking 1895. *Report. Parliamentary Papers 1895–96*, vol. 4.

Webb, Beatrice. Diary, January–February 1895. Microfilm in writer's possession of typescript copy at the British Library of Political and Economic Science, London.

Winner, Major V. C. Personal interview by writer at Queenscliff, Vic., 13 August 1991.

Wotherspoon, Garry. 'Some impacts of homosexual and gay sub-cultures in Australia'. *Journal of Australian Studies*, no. 28, March 1991, pp. 56–62.

See also **bibliographic style; references; titles of publications, and literary, artistic and musical works.**

**bicentenary/bicentennial** See **bi-**.

**bid** As a synonym for nouns like *try*, *attempt*, *move* and *effort* this word has become overused, particularly in newspapers (*runner in 1500 m record bid*; *Everest bid fails*). Choose an appropriate alternative.

**biennial** See **bi-**; **annual/biennial/perennial**.

**billet/billeted/billeting** Note the single *t* in all three.

**billet-doux** French for love-letter; plural *billets-doux*.

**billion** In Australia, as in Britain, a *billion* traditionally meant a million million ($10^{12}$). In the US a *billion* means a thousand million ($10^{9}$), and this is now becoming Australian usage too, although it is not universally accepted. Because confusion could be disastrous, avoid *billion* and deal in millions instead: *$2100 million profit* rather than *$2.1 billion profit*.

See also **currency**; **numbers in figures or words**.

**bimonthly** See **bi-**.

**bio-** This prefix indicates life or living: *biology* (the science of living things); *biodegradable* (able to be broken down by living organisms); *bioethics* (ethical issues involving human life).

**BIOS** basic input/output system (computer term).

**bipartisan** This adjective, broadly meaning agreed on by two parties, is often misunderstood. Prefer *common*, *joint*, *two-sided*, *mutual* (agreement, decision, statement).

**bird's-eye view** Note the hyphen, and the position of the apostrophe in this expression, and in *worm's-eye view*.

**bisect/dissect** *Bisect* (one *s*) means to cut into two, while *dissect* (double *s*) means to cut up – into any number of parts – for analysis. The pronunciation of *bisect* is always 'bie-**sekt**' but *dissect* may be 'dis-**sekt**' (preferred) or 'die-**sekt**'.

**bit** This is an acronym for *binary digit*. Binary digits (0 and 1) are used in a numbering system for computer operations.

See also **bits per second**; **byte**.

**bitmap** The noun *bitmap* is a computer term that describes an image produced by using dots (pixels). When printing text, if the PostScript font is unavailable, the bitmapped font will be printed instead, resulting in a rough-edged ('jaggy') image.

See also **dots per inch; font; jaggies; pixel; PostScript**.

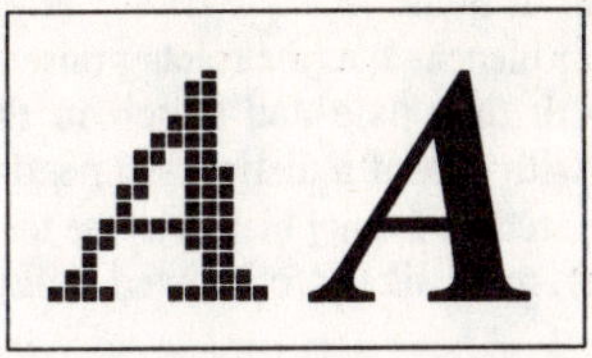

***A bitmapped character contrasted with a PostScript one***

**bits per second** This is a measure of computer data transmission speed (abbreviated *BPS*), just as *baud rate* is.

See also **bit**.

**bivouac/bivouacked/bivouacking** Note the *-c* in the first and the *-ck-* in the other two. Both the noun and the verb *bivouac* relate to a temporary camp, used by soldiers, for example.

**biweekly** See **bi-**.

**bizarre** See **bazaar/bizarre**.

**BL** British Library.

**black** Some people in Australia use the noun *black* (or *Black*) to describe Aboriginal people, but many Aborigines now prefer to be called by names such as *Koori* (or *Koorie*) that derive from their own languages. *Black* is, however, the preference of many Afro-Americans and British people of Afro-Caribbean origin. Some Aborigines choose to identify with these groups by calling themselves blacks too.

See also **Aborigine/Aboriginal; discriminatory language; negro**.

**Blackall, Qld** Compare with *Blackalls*, NSW.

**black economy** The term describes a cash-based underground economy that does not show up in the national accounts of a country. It mainly involves unrecorded cash payments that are made to people but not declared by them for income tax purposes.

**Black Hill, SA and Vic.** Compare with *Black Hills*, Tas.

**blame** Blame a person or thing *for* something; do not blame something *on* a person.

**blanch/blench** Both words can mean to become pale, and *blench* has the additional meaning to flinch or quail:

The student blanched [*or* blenched] as the teacher raised the cane.

As many people would both turn pale and flinch in these circumstances you should choose your words with care if a distinction needs to be made:

Pale though he was, the student did not blench as the teacher raised the cane.

The word *flinch* is, however, more likely to be used today.

**blatant/flagrant** The meaning of these adjectives overlaps, but only *blatant* can be used of people as well as things. Something or someone *blatant* is offensively conspicuous, shameless or brazen: *a blatant error*; *a blatant crook*. *Blatant* should not be used as a synonym for *obvious*:

It was obvious [*not* blatant] that the foundations of the house were weak.

Something that is *flagrant* is scandalous, notorious or reprehensible, and more likely to outrage moral values than something that is merely *blatant*:

The builder had shown a flagrant disregard for the engineer's advice.

**bleed** In the context of printing, *bleed* or *bleed off* means to run off the edge of a page; as a noun *bleed* means running off, or the extent of the running off. If it is intended that an image should run to the edge of a page, 4 millimetres of bleed should be added beyond the trim marks.

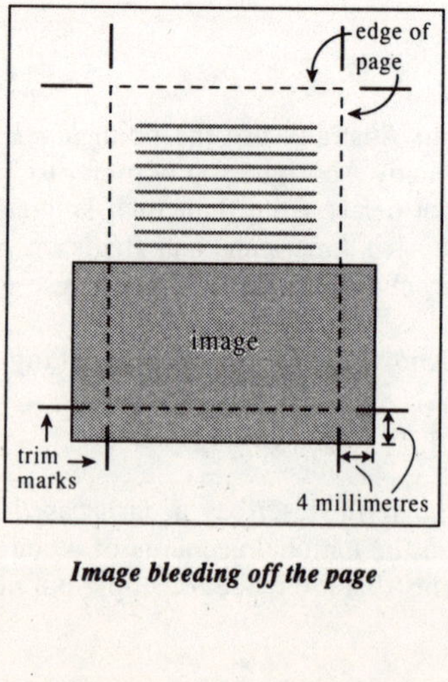


***Image bleeding off the page***

**blench** See **blanch/blench**.

**BLF** Builders' Labourers Federation.

**bloc/block** A *bloc* is a group of countries, States, political parties or people united by some common factor: *the South-East Asian bloc*; *the anti-logging bloc*. *Block* has numerous meanings, and in US English one of them is *bloc*. However, in Australian English the distinction between the two words is maintained.

**blond/blonde** This word means light-coloured or having light-coloured hair (and sometimes skin). Traditionally it was spelt *blond* when the subject was masculine, *blonde* when feminine. For a mixed group it is spelt *blond*: *blond children*. The trend now seems to be towards using *blond* whenever the adjective is required, but the fair-haired girl or woman is likely to remain *a blonde*.

**blue chip/gilt-edged** These terms are not interchangeable. *Blue chip*, in investment circles, means high-quality, low-risk securities (which can nevertheless drop in value). *Gilt-edged* traditionally refers to government (and sometimes bank-backed) securities, which can be regarded as completely safe.

**bluish** Note the spelling of this adjective (not 'blueish').

**blurb** A *blurb* is descriptive information such as is printed on the cover or jacket of a book, written by the publisher to encourage the potential reader to buy the book. A book blurb might be a synopsis of the plot, a listing of highlights, or a compilation of laudatory reviews.

**BM** British Museum.

**BMA** British Medical Association.

***BMJ*** *British Medical Journal*.

**BMX** bicycle motocross.

**boat/ship** A *ship* is a large *boat*, but exactly when one becomes the other is unclear. Inshore vessels of small to medium size are usually boats: *rowing boat*; *tug boat*; *fishing boat*. Large deep-sea vessels are usually ships, but even the biggest racing yachts are boats. Note that submarines are always called boats and that you can be shipwrecked even if the vessel involved is tiny.

**body copy** This typographical term refers to the standard text material of a publication.

**bogey/bogy/bogie** A *bogey* in golf can mean either par (the number of strokes a good player might require on a particular hole or course); or one over par. A very different *bogey* (or *bogie*) is a swim or a swimming hole in Australian English; the swimming hole may sometimes be known as a *bogeyhole*. Then there is the well-known march 'Colonel Bogey', made popular in the film *The Bridge on the River Kwai*.

A *bogy* (or *bogey*) is an evil spirit or goblin; or a bugbear.

A *bogie* may be the wheeled part of the undercarriage of a railway vehicle; or a small railway truck.

**bold type** See **type**.

**Bolwarra, NSW** Compare with *Bolwarrah*, Vic.

**bona fide/bona fides** *Bona fide* is the Latin for in good faith, and is mainly used as an adjective in English to describe something that is genuine or sincere:

> Are you sure it is a bona fide organisation, with real members?

*Bona fides* is a singular noun, not the plural of *bona fide* as is often thought. It means genuineness, good faith or sincerity:

> His bona fides is supported by good references.

Note the singular verb in this example.

Pronounce *bona fide* '**bo**-na **fie**-dee' and *bona fides* '**bo**-na **fie**-deez'.

**bon mot** The plural is *bons mots*. A *bon mot* (French for good word) is a clever, witty or particularly appropriate remark. Pronounce both singular and plural 'bon mo'.

**book type** See **type**.

**boost** As a noun *boost* has been overused to the point where it has come to mean any *rise*, *increase* or *lift*. Use it judiciously.

**boot** In computer parlance the term *boot* is used to describe the sequence of operations that takes place automatically inside a computer between the time it is turned on and when it can be used. The word is derived from *bootstrap*, the computer being seen to 'pull itself up by its bootstraps' after start-up.

**born/borne** Both *born* and *borne* are past participles of the verb *to bear*, but *born* is used only in the passive voice, when referring to someone or something brought forth by birth:

> She was born in 1950.
>
> Methodism was born in song.

*Borne* is mainly used to mean endured, carried, or having given birth to:

He has borne all the inconvenience cheerfully.

Our lemon tree has borne fruit throughout the year.

At twenty-three she had already borne [*not* born] five children.

Note that *borne* in the last example is in the active voice.

**borrow** Sticklers for correct usage will not let you *borrow* something *off* them, but will happily (and correctly) let you *borrow* something *from* them.

**both** This word refers to two people or things; do not use it, therefore, when describing more than two:

She is tall, slim and elegant.

*not* She is both tall, slim and elegant.

Avoid using *both* when you mean each:

There was a jetty on each side of the river.

*not* There was a jetty on both sides of the river.

Watch out for ambiguity:

We were each given a book.

*not* We were both given a book.

You may of course have both been given the same book (to share), in which case the last sentence would be correct.

When you are using *both* as a conjunction with *and*, make sure that you are linking grammatically similar things:

Giulietta is both hard-working [adjective] and studious [adjective].

*not* Giulietta is both hard-working [adjective] and a student [noun].

Note that it is necessary to write *the responsibility of both* not *both their responsibility*.

*Both* is often superfluous. Remove it from the following examples:

The two girls are (both) equally intelligent.

Her parents are (both) flying together to Adelaide.

Ron and Jim (both) live in the same suburb.

All of the following are acceptable:

We will both go to the preview.

Both of us will go to the preview.

Both of the girls will go to the preview.

The word *of* is commonly omitted in the last example before the noun (*girls*) but is essential before the pronoun (*us*) in the second example.

Never use the phrase *the both of us*.

**bottleneck** If it is necessary to use this tired noun, which means a narrowing or constriction, think first of the neck of a bottle. It does not make much sense to write of *an enormous bottleneck* or of *smoothing out the bottleneck*.

**bottom line** This was originally the final row of figures in a set of accounts but now it is jargon for any aim or result: *The bottom line is that we've got to win the premiership*. Do not use this expression in formal English.

**bought/brought** *Bought* comes from the verb *to buy*, and refers to the exchange of money for goods:

I bought some crumpets at the supermarket.

*Brought* comes from the verb *to bring*, and refers to carrying or taking:

The shearers' cook brought his own saucepans.

Think of the *br-* in *brought* and *bring*, and you should never get *bought* and *brought* confused again.

**bouillon** The name of this clear soup is pronounced 'bwee-yon'.

**bouncy** Note the spelling.

**bourgeois** The adjective *bourgeois* means belonging to the middle class (or *bourgeoisie*). People often give *bourgeois* a derogatory slant that implies the meaning materialistic, conventional or boring. Pronounce *bourgeois* '**boor**-jwa' and *bourgeoisie* 'boor-jwar-**zee**'.

**Bourke, NSW** Compare with *Burketown*, Qld.

**boutique** A boutique is a small shop that sells fashionable and luxurious goods, especially for women. The word is now commonly used (though not officially sanctioned) as an adjective to mean small (and probably exclusive) in phrases such as *boutique hotel* and *boutique wine* (the latter is not necessarily expensive, but comes from a small winery). Pronounce the word 'boo-**teek**'.

**bp** boiling point.

**BPS** See **bits per second**.

**bracket/bracketed/bracketing** Note the single *t* in all three.

**brackets** *Round brackets* or *parentheses* are the commonest kind: (  ). They are used to enclose material that provides additional information or comment, and the sentence must be grammatically complete without the bracketed interpolation:

Turn to chapter 9 (page 42) for a discussion of engraving.

Plant willow-leaved hakea (*Hakea salicifolia*) as a windbreak.

He was elected president (and it was by secret ballot) but he did not stay in office long.

In some instances commas or dashes are an alternative to brackets, which tend to indicate a more definite break than commas and have similar weight to dashes. Commas would work as well in the second example, and dashes would be quite as suitable in the second and third.

When you enclose material in brackets, punctuation within the sentence remains the same:

I set up the easel, laid out my paints and selected a brush.

I set up the easel (which I had recently purchased), laid out my paints and selected a brush.

Note the position of the comma: after the closing bracket, never before.

Punctuation within the brackets also follows the normal rules:

She refused to go without her cat (why, we asked ourselves?).

When a whole sentence is in brackets it starts with an initial capital and the full stop (or question mark or exclamation mark) falls within the closing bracket:

She refused to go without her cat. (We didn't know she even liked it.)

Round brackets are also used to enclose numbers and letters in itemised lists.

*Square brackets* are used quite often: [ ]. Their most important function is to enclose material that was not written by the author of the sentence. Explanations within direct quotations and editorial comments or queries come into this category:

'I always swear [wear?] black and blue', said the vicar.

The naturopath believed it [ginger] cured travel sickness.

He wrote, 'It was a forgone [*sic*] conclusion'.

Sometimes an author needs to add an explanation to material that is already in parentheses. Square brackets are often used within round brackets for this purpose, but the AGPS *Style Manual* points out that this may be ambiguous: readers will not know whether the explanation is the author's or an editorial one. The *Style Manual* suggests using round brackets for both:

Most liquidambars will become too big for suburban gardens (perhaps 60 feet (18 metres) or more).

This is not a satisfactory solution, and it would be better either to replace the internal brackets with dashes or to rewrite the sentence:

Most liquidambars will become too big for suburban gardens; they may in fact grow to more than 60 feet (18 metres).

*Braces* look like curly brackets: { }. They should only appear in technical writing.

See also **apposition**; **clause**; **comma**; **dashes, use of**; **phrase**; ***sic***; **singular or plural**.

**brand names** See **business names/trade names/trademarks**.

**Branxholm, Tas.** Compare with *Branxholme*, Vic.

**breach/breech** A *breach* is a break or rupture. It can be visible:

The storm has caused a breach in the sea wall.

or invisible:

The company was accused of a breach of contract.

The verb *breach* means to break:

The action of the waves will breach the sea wall.

The company may breach the contract

A *breech* most often refers to the lower rear part of the body, though it can mean the part of a gun behind its barrel. In a *breech birth* a baby emerges with its buttocks or feet first, instead of its head. *Breeches* (sometimes spelt as it is pronounced, 'britches') are trousers, especially ones extending only to the knee.

**breakthrough** An overused noun, particularly in science and technology.

**breech** See **breach/breech**.

**briquette** This is a lump of compacted coal dust used for fuel. It is roughly shaped like a small brick but has nothing to do with house bricks.

**Britain/Great Britain/United Kingdom/British Isles** *Britain* is a shortened form of *Great Britain*, which consists of England, Scotland and Wales.

The *United Kingdom* (or *UK*) consists of Great Britain *and* Northern Ireland. It is the official title of that political entity (the *United Kingdom of Great Britain and Northern Ireland*). Note that Northern Ireland is often called Ulster, which is the Irish name of a province only six of whose original nine counties comprise Northern Ireland. While the people of the UK are all *British*, the internal distinctions – English, Scottish, Welsh and Northern Irish – should be carefully observed.

The *British Isles* is the geographical name for the United Kingdom, the Republic of Ireland (Eire), the Isle of Man and the Channel Islands.

**British English** As the parent of all varieties of English, British English has traditionally been considered to be the 'correct' or standard form of the language. However, its rapid spread and its adaptation in numerous countries have changed conceptions of what constitutes standard English. In many parts of the world British English is no longer the indisputable norm by which other varieties are judged.

British English is itself a hybrid language, part Germanic (German and Old Norse) and part Romance (Latin and French). English did not originate in the British Isles. It was brought to Britain in the middle of the fifth century by tribes of Angles, Saxons and Jutes, who conquered the Celtic-speaking inhabitants and drove them westwards. The invaders spoke dialects of *Englisc* which, though unintelligible to English-speakers today, formed the basis for the language now spoken by more than 750 million people throughout the world, though barely half of those speak it as their first language.

English developed from Englisc in three stages, termed Old English or Anglo-Saxon (up to about 1100), Middle English (up to about 1450), and Modern English (from then on). During this evolution many Greek, Latin and Scandinavian words entered the language, and thousands of words were taken from French, which was the official state and legal language of England for about three hundred years after the Norman conquest of 1066. The introduction of printing in the fifteenth century helped to form a fairly standard version of written English, but numerous attempts to rationalise the wildly inconsistent spelling were unsuccessful.

In the eighteenth century English grammar and usage became matters of public interest, and Samuel Johnson's two-volume *Dictionary of the English Language*, which contained idiosyncratic definitions of and historical evidence for 40 000 words, was published in 1755. In 1828 another version of English appeared in Noah Webster's *American Dictionary of the English Language*. Some expressions in this dictionary that were labelled 'Americanisms' by defenders of British English were shown, however, to include old English words that had become obsolete in England but had lived on in America – words such as *fall* (for *autumn*); *gotten* (for *got*); and *guess* (for *imagine*). In the nineteenth century many American words such as *telephone* and *typewriter* were absorbed into British English without argument, but others were resisted strongly.

The first edition of the *Oxford English Dictionary* (*OED*), published in instalments between 1884 and 1928, contained ten times the number of words in Johnson's dictionary. It demonstrated the richness, flexibility and cosmopolitan nature of English, and also the chaotic nature of its spelling, which four hundred years of trying has not simplified. To add to the complications, English has the largest vocabulary of any language. The twenty volumes of the second edition of the *OED*, published in 1989, contain more than 600 000 word forms.

One characteristic of British English that distinguishes it from other varieties is the diversity of dialects spoken within the British Isles. The user of one dialect is sometimes virtually incomprehensible to the user of a different one. The same cannot generally be said of English in Australia, the United States, Canada, New Zealand, South Africa or anywhere else.

Probably the best-known British accent is Received Pronunciation – often called BBC English – which the BBC has made familiar to millions of radio listeners around the world. Another well-known British accent is Cockney, the working-class East London speech famous for its rhyming slang: *loaf = loaf of bread = head*; *soldiers = soldiers bold = cold*; *butchers = butcher's hook = look*. It could be said that George Bernard Shaw's observation in the preface to *Pygmalion* that 'it is impossible for an Englishman to open his mouth without making some other Englishman despise him' is as true today as it was when the play was first performed in 1914.

See also **Australian English**; **US English**; **US spelling**.

**British Isles** See **Britain/Great Britain/United Kingdom/British Isles**.

**Bro./Bros** The abbreviation *Bro.* is most often seen in monastic titles: *Bro. O'Brien*. The plural form is *Bros* (no full stop), which is common in company names: *Scalli Bros*.

**broach/brooch** The most common meanings of the verb *broach* are to tap or pierce, and to mention or suggest: *to broach the beer barrel*; *to broach a* *topic of conversation*. A *brooch* is a clasp or an ornament for a dress. Both words rhyme with *poach*.

**broadcast** Use *broadcast* rather than *broadcasted* for the past tense.

**broadsheet** See **paper sizes and weights**.

**broccoli** This is the plural of *broccolo*, the Italian for a sprout. Pronounce it '**brokk**a-lee'.

**bromide** *Bromide* is light-sensitive photographic paper used to produce photographic, illustrative or typographical images. The images themselves on such paper are called *bromides*. Camera-ready art is prepared from bromide prior to the platemaking process that is part of a printer's job.

See also **camera-ready art/camera-ready copy**.

**brooch** See **broach/brooch**.

**brought** See **bought/brought**.

**brussels sprouts** Note the lower-case initial and the *s* at the end of the first part of this name.

**BSI** British Standards Institution.

**Buckley's** This Australianism (sometimes expanded to *Buckley's chance*, *choice*, *hope* or *show*) means either a slim chance or no chance at all. It may commemorate the convict William Buckley, who escaped to the bush in 1803 and lived with the Aborigines for thirty-two years. However, since the first recorded use of the expression was in the 1890s, it seems more likely that it has its origins in the name of the Melbourne firm *Buckley & Nunn*, founded in 1851. The phrase 'two chances, Buckley's and none' is probably a pun on the business name.

**budget/budgeted/budgeting** Note the single *t* in all three.

**budget deficit** A *budget deficit* is the amount by which the government's spending exceeds its income during a specified period of time, usually one year.

**buffer** This computer term means a temporary storage area for data; a *buffer* is used to compensate for the different speeds at which parts of the system operate. For example, data is stored in a buffer prior to printing because a printer works more slowly than a computer.

See also **spooler**.

**bug** An error, malfunction or defect in a computer program or system is called a *bug*. The term *debug* means to rectify a bug.

See also **virus**.

**bulk** This noun refers to mass rather than number:

The bulk of the shipment was saved
Most of [*not* The bulk of] the articles in the container were saved.

For publishers and printers *bulk* has additional meanings: either the thickness of paper (as compared with its weight) or the 'fatness' of a publication once it is printed and bound.

**bulletin board** A *bulletin board* is a central computer that receives and holds information such as software news, computer hints and lists of public domain software, all of which can be accessed by subscribers via a modem. Some bulletin boards accept information from subscribers (for example, new games or other software created by them); others only install information gathered by operators at the central unit.

See also **electronic-mail**; **modem**; **user groups**.

**bullets and boxes** *Bullets* and *boxes* are open (○ □) or closed (● ■) dots and squares that are used for itemising points in text. While handy devices, bullets and boxes should not be overused or their effect will be diminished. Moreover if too many bulleted items follow the introductory phrase or sentence, the reader may forget the point that was made there. A bulleted series of items would sometimes be more effectively presented as ordinary run-on text. Bullets or boxes should not be too large or too small for the text. Bullet and box size, as well as type size, should be included in specifications for the typesetter.

The punctuation at the end of bulleted or boxed items can cause problems. Since there are no firm guidelines, the normal rules of punctuation should be applied where possible; sensible compromises are usually acceptable, provided they are followed consistently. If the items are complete sentences in themselves, it is usual to start each with an initial capital and end with a full stop. If the items are effectively part of a single sentence, each may begin with a lower-case initial and end with a semicolon, or there may be no punctuation at all. If the items constitute a simple listing, punctuation is not required at the end of each.

Please bring the following:

- tent
- waterproof groundsheet
- insect repellent and sunscreen
- walking shoes
- small rucksack

Desktop publishers should avoid using the numerous other indicating devices found in dingbat packages: pointing fingers, stars and so on, which can make text resemble a railway timetable. If your word-processing package or printer cannot generate a bullet or box, a hyphen or dash is preferable to an asterisk or full stop.

See also **pi font**.

**bulrush** Note the single *l* (not 'bullrush').

**bumf** Sometimes genteelly spelt *bumph*, the word is short for bum-fodder. Paperwork, especially of the bureaucratic kind, is often considered deserving of the name.

**Bunya, Qld** Compare with *Bunyah*, NSW.

**buoy/buoyant** Note the *-uo-*. A *buoy* is an anchored float. *Buoyant* means floating or uplifted; it has the secondary meaning cheerful:

> Justin felt buoyant after receiving the good news.

Note also the spelling of *lifebuoy*.

**bureau** The plural is *bureaus* or *bureaux*. Pronounce both of the plural versions 'bew-rose'.

**bureaucracy** Note the *-eau-* and the *-cy*. *Bureaucracy* means a system of government by officials (*bureaucrats*), but it often has pejorative overtones of inefficiency, unnecessary documentation and inflexibility. Pronounce *bureaucracy* 'bew-**rok**ra-see' and *bureaucrats* '**bew**ra-krats'.

**bureau (desktop publishing)** A *bureau* is a business that offers at least some of the following services: disk conversion from one system to another (for instance from IBM to Apple or vice versa); data retrieval; word processing; disk duplication; and scanning of hard copy onto disk. Bureaus can supply laser proofs, bromide, film and colour proofs, and they will extract information from a corrupted disk.

When submitting a job to a bureau for output to laser proofs, bromide or film, list every typeface you have used, make sure that the bureau has all the typefaces you need, and indicate which version of a particular program you are using. Most bureaus carry all the middle-range and high-end programs, and a wide range of font families. Let the bureau know whether or not you want crop marks on each page, and what size your page will be. Send hard copy of the entire job so that the bureau can check its output against yours.

**burglar** Note the spelling, and pronounce it '**berg**-lar' (not '**berg**-yoo-lar').

**burgle/rob/steal** To *burgle* is to break into and enter premises with the intention of stealing:

> He set out to burgle the flats.

A *burglar* commits a *burglary*. The US verb *to burglarise* is not yet universal in Australian English but has been given the nod by *The Macquarie Dictionary*.

To *rob* is to deprive someone of something, and usually involves unlawful force or the threat of violence. *Rob* can also be used figuratively:

Those who rob taxi-drivers are liable to be caught.

The years robbed Maria of her beauty.

To *steal* is to take something wrongfully or dishonestly. It too has figurative uses:

Don't steal their newspaper; borrow mine.

The children were intent on stealing the limelight.

**burned/burnt** These are alternative spellings for both the past tense and past participle of the verb *to burn*. *Burnt* is generally preferred in Australian English:

He burnt his old manuscripts.

The meal was a burnt offering.

*Burned* is recommended if the verb has no object, and for figurative use:

The house burned fiercely.

Her eyes burned with passion.

**business/busyness** *Business* has many meanings associated with commercial and personal affairs, but *busyness* is simply the state of being busy. The first is pronounced '**biz**-n's' and the second '**bizee**-nes'.

**business names/trade names/trademarks** Writers, editors and publishers should be aware that some words are business names, trade names or trademarks. Writing registered trademarks without an initial capital may imply that the name is for general use, and the product's manufacturer may consider that you have infringed its trademark status, which is legally protected. Among the hundreds of such names, the following are some well-known examples:

| | | |
|---|---|---|
| Aspro | Fibro | Plexiglas |
| Bakelite | Gladwrap | Polaroid |
| Band-Aid | Hoover | Primus |
| Besser Block | Kleenex | Pyrex |
| Biro | Laminex | Sanforised |
| Bri-Nylon | Laundromat | Sellotape |
| Cellophane | Levi's | Spam |
| Coca-Cola, Coke | Linotype | Technicolor |
| Dacron | Masonite | Terylene |
| Dictaphone | Orlon | Thermos |
| Driza-Bone | Perspex | Valium |
| Elastoplast | Ping-Pong | Vaseline |
| Esky | Plasticine | Xerox |

Some of these names – *biro*, *cellophane*, *ping-pong*, for example (written without an initial capital) – are so thoroughly entrenched in English as words of generic or general use that prosecution would be most unlikely. There are other names that have become everyday verbs: *to hoover*, *to nugget*, *to tippex*. Unless you are referring to a specific product, however, trade names are best avoided. Alternatives can readily be found for most: *tissues* for Kleenex, *plastic wrap* for Gladwrap, *ovenware* for Pyrex, *photocopy* for Xerox.

Remember that, while the whole world knows that *Levi's* are jeans, many trade names are not recognised outside their country of origin. For example, *Masonite* is meaningless in the UK, where the equivalent product is described as *hardboard*.

There is no need for us to adopt the increasingly prevalent US habit of adding a superscript ™ or ©, or to use the symbol ®, at the end of every reference to a registered trademark in an advertisement. An initial capital is all that is required.

See also **copyright**.

**busyness** See **business/busyness**.

**but** Although *but* is most often used as a conjunction, it may become a preposition in some sentences and an adverb in others.

When *but* is a conjunction it must join contrasting ideas:

Lots of investors collect coins, but few buy books on the subject.

Do not combine *but* with words like *however*, *nevertheless*, *nonetheless* or *yet*. They all indicate contrast, and it is superfluous to use more than one:

The meat should be fried but the rice must be steamed.

*not* The meat should be fried but the rice, however, must be steamed.

Beginning a sentence with the conjunction *but* can be very effective, though it should be used in moderation:

Caviar is expensive, I know. But can you think of anything nicer?

In the following example *but* is a preposition combined with a noun:

Nobody can see it but the astronomers.

Here it is combined with a pronoun, which must be in the objective case:

Nobody can see it but me.

*not* Nobody can see it but I.

Note that *but* is an adverb in the following example:

They all but gave up.

You may hear some Australians use the adverb *but* to mean *though* at the end of a sentence: *I decided not to go, but*. This is definitely not recommended.

See also **cannot/can't; case (grammar); not only . . . but also**.

**buzz words** These are voguish, overused terms that are intended to arouse or impress. Most of them have everyday, unemotional uses too; it is usually the context that turns them into buzz words: *aware*; *bizarre*; *caring*; *environmental impact*; *lifestyle*; *quantum leap*; *trauma*; *smear*; *user-friendly*.

**bv** brick veneer (house); also *BV*.

**BWIU** Building Workers' Industrial Union.

**by** See **with/by/of**.

**by-/bye-/bye** *By-* is combined with many nouns to add the meaning incidental, secondary or near: *by-product*, *by-law*, *by-election*. Sometimes the hyphen is dropped: *bypass*, *bystander*. *Bye-* is an option in a few combinations: *bye-law*, *bye-election*.

The word *bye* may be a shortening of *goodbye*, or a sporting term. The expression *by the by* may be spelt *by the bye*, but note that *by and by* and *by and large* do not have any optional form.

**by-line** A *by-line* is a line giving the name of the writer of a newspaper or magazine article.

**BYO** bring your own (alcohol).

**byte** In computer terminology a *byte* is a unit consisting of a group of *bits* (binary digits), usually eight, which makes up a character (for instance a letter, number or punctuation mark) on a computer. The size of a computer's memory is measured in *kilobytes* (*K*) or *megabytes* (*Mb*). A kilobyte is approximately a thousand bytes (technically $2^{10}$ or 1024 bytes or, in practical terms, about 170 words); a megabyte is approximately a million bytes (technically $2^{20}$ or 1 048 576 bytes).

See also **memory**.

**byword** Note the *by* (never 'bye'). The most common use of *byword* is to designate someone or something that is an excellent or typical example of a characteristic: *Her work is a byword for precision*.

# Cc

**C** Celsius *or* centigrade (see also **Celsius/centigrade/Fahrenheit**); century (also c.; see also **centuries**); 100 (roman numeral; see also **roman numerals**); children 6 to 13 (TV classification); common time (music).

**c** cent or cents.
See also **currency**.

**c.** century (also C; see also **centuries**); copyright (often printed without the full stop and encircled: ©; see also **copyright**).

***c.*** This abbreviation means about (shortened from the Latin *circa*); it is italicised: *c.* 1951.
See also ***circa***.

**CAC** Corporate Affairs Commission.

**cactus** Plural *cacti* or *cactuses*.

**CAD** This is the abbreviation for *computer-aided design*, the use of computer software to produce two-dimensional and three-dimensional drawings for design professionals such as architects and engineers.

**caddie/caddy** A *caddie* (or *caddy*) is someone who carries a player's clubs on a golf course. A *caddy* is a small container, usually holding tea.

**caesarean** Note the spelling and the lower-case initial.

**caffeine** Note the *-ei-*.

**CAI** Confederation of Australian Industry.

**calendar/calender/colander** A *calendar* is a tabular arrangement of the days, weeks and months of the year. A *calender* is a press used for smoothing or glazing materials such as cloth or paper. A *colander* is a perforated bowl-shaped strainer for food; it is less commonly spelt *cullender*. *Colander* may be pronounced '**kol**'nda' or '**kul**'nda'.

**calf** Plural *calves*.

**calibre** This is the preferred Australian spelling (not the US *caliber*). The word literally means the diameter of a cylindrical body: the *calibre* of a gun describes its bore, not its weight. Figuratively *calibre* may indicate ability or character: *impressive calibre*.

**Calista, WA** Compare with *Kallista*, Vic.

**calligraphy** *Calligraphy* is handwriting as an art. The adjective *calligraphic* is applied to some decorative type fonts as well as to the art itself. A number of these calligraphic fonts emulate the variable stroke widths of a broad-nibbed pen, one of the best-known being Zapf Chancery (designed by the German typographer Hermann Zapf):

> *Zapf Chancery is a calligraphic typeface.*

While the beauty of calligraphic type is obvious, such faces should be used sparingly. They are best reserved for invitations, scrolls and so on.

See also **type**.

**callous/callus** The adjective *callous* describes a hardened or insensitive mental state:

> It would be callous to reduce the income of pensioners.

A *callus* is a hardened or thickened area of skin or bark. It is correct to write of *calloused skin* (skin made hard) or *callused skin* (skin marked by calluses), but there is no such thing as a *callus nature*.

**CAM** computer-aided manufacturing.

**Cambodia** Use this name for the country called Kampuchea 1970–1989.

**camera-ready art/camera-ready copy** *Camera-ready art* (or *camera-ready copy*, abbreviated *CRC*) is a publishing term that refers to material (principally text and drawings) that is presented to a printer for the photographic process that precedes platemaking and printing. The names *finished artwork* (or *finished art*) and *artwork* are also commonly used for the same material.

See also **bromide**; **makeup**; **paste-up**.

**camouflage** Note the *-ou-*.

**can/may** Many people ignore the difference between *can* and *may* when they are speaking, but it is sometimes important to observe it even then. It is highly desirable to do so in formal writing. If you choose *can*, you are putting emphasis on the ability to do something:

Can I pass this exam? [Have I the ability to . . .?]

When you use *may*, there is a stronger sense of permission or likelihood:

May I leave the room? [Have I your permission to . . .?]

These are simple examples, but it is sometimes difficult to avoid ambiguity. In the following sentence either ability or permission could be involved:

There can be no correspondence on this matter.

In the next the ambiguity is between likelihood and permission:

Unqualified players may not take part in the finals.

Rewrite the sentences to make your meaning clear.

*Put* We are unable to deal with correspondence.
*or* Correspondence is not permitted.
*Put* Unqualified players are not likely to take part in the finals.
*or* Unqualified players will not be permitted to take part in the finals.

See also **may/might**.

**cancel/cancelled/cancelling** Note the single *l* in the first and the *-ll-* in the other two.

**canister** Note the single *n*.

**cannon/canon** A *cannon* is a large gun; a stroke in croquet; or a shot in billiards.

A *canon* is an ecclesiastical law, or a set of rules that may be non-ecclesiastical; a clergyman attached to a cathedral; a style in musical composition; a list of sacred books; or the authentic list of works by a writer.

**cannot/can't** In a rather old-fashioned idiom, *cannot*, or its contraction *can't*, may be used before *but*:

She cannot [*or* can't] but grant his request.

and before *help*:

She cannot [*or* can't] help granting his request.

However, avoid a combination of the two negatives: *She cannot [*or *can't] help but grant his request*.

Note that *cannot* is written as one word, and that *can* and *not* sometimes fall side by side when they do not belong together. Rephrase to avoid this:

She not only sings but dances as well.
*not* She can not only sing but dance as well.

*Can't*, like most contractions, is best avoided in formal writing.

Watch out for ambiguity when using *cannot* or *can't*. The common admonition *You can't be too careful* is intended to warn that you must be careful; literally it suggests inability to be too careful.

**canon** See **cannon/canon**.

**can't** See **cannot/can't**.

**Cantab.** This is an abbreviation of the latinised *Cantabrigiensis*, which means of Cambridge University: *Florence Richards, MA (Cantab.)*.
See also **Oxon**.

**cantaloupe** This fruit is called rock melon in some parts of Australia. The spelling *cantaloup* is also acceptable. The preferred pronunciation is '**kanta**-loop', not '**kanta**-lope'.

**canvas/canvass** *Canvas* (mainly a noun or adjective) is a heavy fabric: *a canvas tent. Canvass* (mainly a verb) means to solicit votes, donations, subscriptions, orders or opinions, or to investigate thoroughly:

> The Salvation Army canvassed the district for flood relief.
> Our Hall Committee is canvassing local opinion: repaint or rebuild?

**cap** capital letter: S, T, in contrast to s, t (*caps* is the plural).
See also **capital letters, setting of**; **type**.

**capability/capacity** See **ability/capability/capacity**.

**Cape York Peninsula, Qld** Compare with *Yorke Peninsula*, SA.

**cap height** See **type**.

**capital/Capitol** The noun *capital* has numerous meanings, from the city that is a State or country's centre of government to the wealth of an individual, company or country.

The *Capitol* is the temple of Jupiter in ancient Rome; or, today, the collection of buildings occupied by the US Congress in Washington DC, or (with a lowercase initial) by any US State legislative body.

**capitalisation** While there are conventions governing the use of capital letters, the most important point for a writer or editor to remember is to be consistent. Few readers will object to finding *federal parliament* written without initial capitals; many, however, will be irritated to see *Federal Parliament* two lines later. Initial capitals are optional in this example (depending on the kind of publication), but capitalisation is necessary in many other instances in spite of a trend towards lower case.

Initial capitals should be used:

- at the beginning of a sentence, and at the beginning of a whole sentence quoted within a sentence or enclosed within parentheses

  There was a notice on the door: 'Gentlemen must wear ties'.

  We invited Michael after all. (And we hoped he would come.)

  but not when only a phrase is quoted

  He described them as 'ridiculously outmoded'.
- for people's personal names (watch out for unusual surnames like *de Berg* that combine capital and lower-case initial letters) and their official titles (main words only)

  Dame Joan Sutherland    the Lord Mayor of Perth

  Her Majesty the Queen    the Minister for Education, Mr Oaks

  the President of France    Snugglepot

  but not when the title is used in a general sense or in the plural

  He wanted to become lord mayor.

  Two of the richest women in the world are queens.

  Were any presidents of France born in Lyon?

  and selectively when there is a risk of ambiguity

  Mr Oaks, a Uniting Church minister, became Minister for Education.
- for adjectives derived from proper names

  Orwellian characters    Australian athletes

  Thatcherite policies    Iraqi jets

  but note that some words and phrases have lost the initial capital they once had

  furphy    boycott    anglicise

  venetian blinds    french windows
- for family titles used in direct speech

  'Thank you, Uncle.'    'This is my Aunt Sally.'    'Please, Mum.'

  but not when references are indirect

  He is a kind uncle.    My aunts arrived.    She asked her mum.
- for nicknames and epithets

  the Iron Lady    the Little Digger    the Smart Young Things
- for civil and military honours, professional distinctions, academic degrees, awards and prizes

  Kate O'Brien, AM (Member of the Order of Australia)

  Dimitri Skuros, CGM (Conspicuous Gallantry Medal)

  Lyn Tan, FRACS (Fellow of the Royal Australasian College of Surgeons)

  David Reid, MBA (Master of Business Administration)

  the Brownlow Medal

  the Pulitzer Prize
- for the official titles of public buildings and locations

  the Australian War Memorial    the Sydney Opera House

  Townsville Town Common

  but not when a name is used in a general sense or pluralised

  a war memorial erected in 1920    the opera houses of Sydney and Vienna

- for days of the week, months, holidays, religious festivals and regular gatherings of various kinds

  Wednesday June Australia Day Yom Kippur the AFL Grand Final

  but not the seasons, unless they are personified

  It's a very dry summer. 'Come, gentle Spring!'
- for historical, cultural and geological eras

  the Dark Ages the Renaissance the Palaeozoic era

  but not when the name of a period is used in a general sense

  renaissance painting and sculpture
- for the names of languages, religions and ethnic groups

  Yiddish Swahili Greek Orthodox Islam

  Caucasians Negroes Aborigines Celts

  but *Aborigines* becomes *aborigines* when used to mean the original inhabitants of any country
- for trademarks and registered business names

  Coca-Cola Vegemite Move Records
- for the points of the compass, and directions that are part of a proper name

  N S W E NE SSW Wangaratta South East Perth

  but not for the directions spelt out and used generally

  heading east trudging towards the north-west border
- for the names of countries, real or fictitious

  Belgium the People's Republic of China Lilliput
- for political entities and geographical names

  the Federal Government the Ottoman Empire

  South-East Asia Bass Strait

  the Rock of Gibraltar the Campaspe River

  but not when the names are descriptive, unofficial or in the plural

  federal powers

  an empire centred on Constantinople

  the Loddon and Campaspe rivers
- for the names of supreme beings (and personal pronouns associated with them, like *Thou*)

  Allah Buddha God

  but not when they are used in a non-religious, general sense

  The little boy had a round fat face like a buddha's.

  Don't make money your god.
- for the names of ships, aircraft and other vehicles

  HMAS *Melbourne* the yacht *Ragamuffin* a Daisy Moth

  a Concorde a Holden Commodore the *Orient Express*
- for most of the formal scientific names in botany and zoology

  the family Mimosaceae the genus *Acacia*

  *Hardenbergia* 'Happy Wanderer' the class Insecta

  but never for species names (which follow genus names), even when they are derived from the names of people or places; and not for common names, except when they are derived from the names of people or places (names that identify specific Australian birds are, however, given initial capitals, according to the convention established by the Royal Australasian Ornithologists Union and widely followed)

*Acacia mitchellii*, Mitchell's wattle

*Morelia spilotes*, the diamond python

an acacia   an azalea   a dusky coral-pea

a Bogong moth   a White-eared Honeyeater

- for abbreviations and acronyms

  ABC   CSIRO   ACOSS   WASP   TAFE

  but note that some acronyms are usually written in lower-case letters or with an initial capital only

  laser   sitcom   Unesco   Qantas
- for the titles of books, newspapers, magazines, films, plays, poems, songs and other musical compositions (see the entry **titles of publications, and literary, artistic and musical works** for detailed information on capitalisation within such titles)
- for parts of a book, such as chapter, foreword and section, *only* when they begin a sentence or heading, or there is any possibility of ambiguity

  Chapter 1: How it all began   This information is found in appendix II.

  Turn to figure ix.   The page numbers are indicated in the Contents.

Dealing with the capitalisation of the names of companies, organisations and institutions – particularly government bodies and initiatives – is quite complex. Written in full, these names take initial capitals (main words only):

Zappy Zips Pty Ltd   Friends of the National Library

the University of Sydney   Australian Taxation Office

the Department of Civil Aviation   the Royal Commission on Hygiene in Hotels

When such names are reduced to a shortened form it is often safest to retain the initial capital:

There will be a meeting of the Friends tonight.

He is moving from Defence to Civil Aviation.

Under the Commission's terms of reference there will be scope for public discussion.

More capitalisation is used in official publications produced by the Australian Government than in general ones. The words *Government* and *Parliament*, for instance, are always given an initial capital when they are referring to specific bodies:

the Western Australian Government   the Government in Adelaide

the Queensland Parliament   In Parliament the Premier of Tasmania . . .

a joint venture by the Australian and New Zealand Governments

the Commonwealth Government and the State Governments

In non-official and general publications it is acceptable to use lower-case initials for any of these bodies when the title is not complete: for example, *the government in Western Australia*. Lower-case initials are also appropriate when the references are general:

Two governments lost office within a few weeks of each other.

These two members brought some humour into parliament.

She was a popular premier.

He will get to university, you may be sure.

Surely we need a royal commission on transport!

The practice of giving the following names an initial capital, particularly in official publications, ensures clarity in any kind of text:

| | | | |
|---|---|---|---|
| the Treasury | the Budget | the Crown | the Bar |
| the Bench | the Cabinet | the Chair | the Constitution |

Give the words *State* and *Territory* an initial capital when they are referring to the geographical and political entities that make up the Commonwealth of Australia, whether the reference is formal or abbreviated:

| | |
|---|---|
| the State of New South Wales | a matter affecting all States |
| the Northern Territory | the dry season in the Territory |

Give *state* a lower-case initial when it is used to mean nation (*a state in the Asian region*) or government (*a state-controlled education system, not a private one*). Give *territory* a lower-case initial when it simply means land or district.

The words *Act*, *Bill*, *Treaty* and *Conference* belong to a category in which the initial capital is necessary only for the specific or formal, provided that no ambiguity is possible:

| | | |
|---|---|---|
| the Trade Practices Act | *but* | amendments to many acts |
| the Treaty of Versailles | *but* | a treaty with the Aborigines |

See also **abbreviations and contractions**; **acronyms**; **business names/trade names/trademarks**; **capital letters, setting of**; **degrees and diplomas**; **proper nouns**; **ranks, titles, honours and awards**; **titles of publications, and literary, artistic and musical works**.

**capital letters, decorative initial** *Decorative initial capital letters* are sometimes used at the beginning of the chapters or sections of a book or magazine. They are most effective when used sparingly. The *drop capital* and the *raised capital* are the two main types, and the following word or words are often set in small capitals or full capitals. For a special effect an 'alien' initial (one from a contrasting typeface) may be used. The positioning of the initial capital is important. The base of the letter is usually aligned with a line of text, and the space around a drop capital can often be made optically equal at the side and bottom. Some letters require the contouring of adjacent type to give a visually pleasing effect. Avoid opening quotation marks with decorative initial capitals.

See also **capital letters, setting of**; **capital letters, small**; **type**.

ATTRACTIVE chapter openings are sometimes achieved by the use of decorative initial capitals. The drop capital and the raised capital are the two main types. Small capitals or full capitals, instead of lower-case letters, may follow the initial.

ATTRACTIVE chapter openings are sometimes achieved by the use of decorative initial capitals. The drop capital and the raised capital are the two main types. Small capitals or full capitals, instead of lower-case letters, may follow the initial.

Attractive chapter openings are sometimes achieved by the use of decorative initial capitals. The drop capital and the raised capital are the two main types. Small capitals or full capitals, instead of lower-case letters, may follow the initial.

***Decorative capitals: drop capital and full-size capitals, top left; raised capital and small capitals, top right; script capital, bottom***

**capital letters, setting of** Care should be taken in the use of capital letters, particularly in headings. Words set in lower case are easier to read than those in capitals because the eye tends to recognise a variable outline more quickly:

HOW TO PROCEED How to proceed

If words in capitals are used in text, small capitals are often preferred to full capitals, which may look disproportionately large:

The instructions were headed HOW TO PROCEED.

Words set in capitals require fine kerning for satisfactory letter spacing, and sometimes further adjustment once they are set.

See also **capitalisation**; **capital letters, decorative initial**; **capital letters, small**; **kerning**; **type**; **word spacing**.

**capital letters, small** These are often preferred to full-size capital letters when a word or phrase is capitalised within text because they are less intrusive; they may also be used in headings or combined with full capitals there. Small capitals are often obtained by using a special font. See the entries **capital letters, decorative initial** and **capital letters, setting of** for examples.

See also **capitalisation**; **kerning**; **type**.

**capital punishment/corporal punishment** *Capital punishment* means punishment by death (that is, the death penalty). *Corporal punishment* means punishment by the infliction of pain on the body (by beating, for example).

See also **corporal/corporeal**.

**Capitol** See **capital/Capitol**.

**cap line** See **type**.

**cappuccino** Note the spelling. The plural is *cappuccinos*.
See also **espresso**.

**CAPT/Capt.** Captain.

**caption** The explanatory copy usually printed above or below an illustration is called its *caption*. The best captions are economically expressed, and consistent in style with the text. Captions that are incomplete sentences should not be followed by a full stop, and some publishers prefer not to conclude any caption with a full stop – even when it consists of several sentences. Other publishers have a full stop at the end of all captions that include at least one full sentence – in spite of the inconsistency that a mixture of non-sentence and sentence captions will produce.

It is usually an editor's job to ensure that captions are unambiguously keyed to the relevant illustrations and pages before a publication goes to press. The source of an illustration should be acknowledged somewhere other than in its caption; a heavily illustrated publication may need a page-by-page list of picture credits printed at the end.

**carat/caret** A *carat* is a unit for measuring the weight of precious stones or the proportion of gold in an alloy: *9 carat gold*. A *caret* is a proofreader's mark made in printed matter to show where something is to be inserted: ⋌ . The Latin word *caret* means *it is missing*.

**carburettor** Note the *-tt-* and the *-or*.

**carcase/carcass** Both spellings are acceptable. The most common meaning of the word is the body of a dead animal.

**cardinal numbers/ordinal numbers** *Cardinal numbers* indicate quantity but not sequence: *7 mullet*; *113 cakes*; *69 letters*. *Ordinal numbers* denote position in a sequence: *the 7th mullet*; *the 113th cake*; *the 69th letter*. Both kinds of numbers may be written as words (*seven*, *seventh*) as well as figures (7, *7th*). Factors such as the type of text (narrative? scientific?) will help you to decide which is preferable.

See also **first/firstly**; **numbers in figures or words**.

**caret** See **carat/caret**.

**cargo** Plural *cargoes*.

**caring** In the sense of being concerned or compassionate about the welfare of others, the word *caring* has been overworked in recent years, particularly in the field of social welfare.

**carpal tunnel syndrome** See **RSI**.

**carpet/carpeted/carpeting** Note the single *t* in all three.

**case** Much used in circumlocutory speech and writing, this word is often superfluous.

*Put* Will you be at home tomorrow?
*not* Is it the case that you will be at home tomorrow?
*Put* Let me know if you can't come.
*not* In the case of something preventing your attendance, let me know.
*Put* Our cyclists are more optimistic than they were last week.
*not* Our cyclists are more optimistic than was the case last week.

*Case* is correct in the following sentences:

Her case baffled medical science.
Bring your lunch in case we stay all day.

See also **case (grammar)**.

**casebound** See **hardback/paperback**.

**case (grammar)** *Case* is a grammatical term involving the relationship between nouns (or pronouns) and verbs. In English grammar it is a simpler matter than it is in some other languages, and the *subjective* (or nominative) *case* and the *objective* (or accusative) *case* are the ones we need to bother about most. English nouns do not change their form according to case, but some pronouns do. The following examples illustrate the pronouns concerned and their *subjective* and *objective* forms:

I [subjective] love her [objective].
We [subjective] love him [objective].
He [subjective] loves me [objective].
She [subjective] loves us [objective].
They [subjective] love them [objective].

Note that the verb *to be* and all its forms (including *am*, *are*, *is*, *was*, *were*, *will be* and *would be*) take a *complement*, which is always *subjective* when written:

If you are looking for the manager, it is I [subjective].
It was we [subjective] who decided.
It would be she [subjective] who did the work.

In conversation, the colloquial forms *it is me*, *It was us* and *It would be her* are generally regarded as being more natural.

The *objective case* is always used after a preposition:

This secret must be *between* Zoe and *me* [objective].

Sit *behind us* [objective] at the film.

She was a woman *with whom* [objective] most men could work.

They looked *up to her* [objective].

The children ran *towards him* [objective].

There was no one left *but them* [objective].

For guidelines on choosing *who* or *whom* in various sentences, see **who/whom**.

The wrong case is often used in sentences that are more complex than the ones above. If you are not sure whether a pronoun should be subjective or objective, strip the sentence down to basics:

They chose Mary, the quickest, Barbara, the prettiest, and her, the most efficient.

Eliminate everyone else, and you know that *her*, the objective case, is correct:

They chose her.

Similarly:

Would you be so good as to allow my spaniel, Matey, and me to get through?

Eliminate the polite words and your dog, and *me* is obviously the right word:

Would you allow me . . . ?

The following example is more complex, but just remember that *were* (part of the verb *to be*) takes the subjective case:

Talking before the preview were the critics, some of the stars, and I.

See also **gerund**; **-ing forms**; **prepositions**; **pronouns**; **subject/object**; **who/whom**.

**cash management trust** A *cash management trust* pools the funds of small investors and invests them in short-dated securities such as Treasury notes and bank bills, which offer a high return coupled with low risk.

**cast/caste** *Cast* as a verb and noun has numerous meanings. *Caste* is a noun (often used adjectivally) that refers to divisions within a social or religious class: *the untouchables in the Hindu caste system*.

**caster/castor** Use either spelling for the fine sugar and its dispenser, and the small swivelling wheel on furniture, but only *castor* for the purgative oil.

**cast-off** A *cast-off* is an estimate, based on manuscript, of the number of pages a published work will contain after typesetting. Computers can be used for these calculations and they give accurate results.

See also **character count/word count**; **extent**.

**castor** See **caster/castor**.

**CAT** This acronym stands for *computer-assisted typesetting*; and for *computerised axial tomography* (a *CAT scan* is a form of high-speed layered X-ray).

**cataclysm/catastrophe** A *cataclysm* is a violent upheaval, especially of a social, military or political kind:

The military coup was a cataclysm for the government.

A *catastrophe* is a sudden and widespread disaster or a disastrous end:

Cyclone Tracy was a catastrophe for Darwin and surrounding areas.

Neither word should be used to describe mundane incidents, except jocularly: some people might joke that the unexpected birth of triplets was a *cataclysm*, or possibly a *catastrophe*, in their household.

**catalogue/catalogued/cataloguing** The US spelling is *catalog*.

**catalyst** This scientific word, related to chemical reactions, has been adopted to describe a person, thing or event that provokes significant change:

The student riot was a catalyst for the violent suppression of free speech.

Do not use it just as a synonym for *cause*.

**catastrophe** See **cataclysm/catastrophe**.

**catchline** *Catchlines* are used in typesetting to provide information on manuscripts and proofs. A catchline might include a working title, date, the typesetter's name, client's name, job number or computer file name.

See also **running heads/running feet**.

**Catholic/catholic** *Catholic* needs an initial capital when you are referring to the Catholic Church, its teaching or its adherents:

Lutherans, Catholics and Anglicans were present at the Congress.

In this era of ecumenicalism the term *Roman Catholic* is rarely used except in certain theological contexts.

The word *catholic*, with a lower-case *c*, is an adjective meaning universal or wide-ranging:

He had a catholic taste in art and literature but a limited appreciation of music.

**caulk** This spelling is preferred, though you may also see *calk*. The word means to fill or close a seam: *Caulk the gaps with fibreglass*. Pronounce it 'kork'.

**caviar** Australian English favours this spelling rather than *caviare*.

**CB** citizen band (radio).

**CBA** Commonwealth Bank of Australia; cost benefit analysis.

**CBD** central business district.

**c.c.** carbon copy.

**CD** compact disc (or *compact disk* in computer contexts; see also **disk, optical**); diplomatic service (French: *corps diplomatique*).

**Cdr/CMDR/Com./Comdr** Commander.

**CDRE/Cdre/Cmdr.** Commodore.

**CD-ROM** Compact disk read-only memory.
See also **disk, optical**; **read-only memory**.

**Celluloid** Note the spelling of this trademark.

**Celsius/centigrade/Fahrenheit** The names *Celsius* and *centigrade* are interchangeable for the temperature scale on which water freezes at 0° and boils at 100°. On the *Fahrenheit* scale, water freezes at 32° and boils at 212°. In accordance with its adoption of the metric system in the late 1960s, Australia today uses the Celsius scale:

ten degrees Celsius *or* 10°C

The Fahrenheit equivalent is expressed as:

fifty degrees Fahrenheit *or* 50°F

Some Australians continue to use the Fahrenheit scale, which remains the official scale in the US. In the UK there is a gradual move to Celsius, but Fahrenheit is used by most people. It is important, therefore, to indicate the scale you are using. Note that *Celsius* and *Fahrenheit* should be spelt with an initial capital, as these are the names of the scientists who devised the scales.

See also **imperial system**; **metric system**; **numbers in figures or words**; **weights and measures**.

**cemetery** Note the *-etery*. Pronounce it '**semma**-tree'.

**censer/censor/censure** A *censer* is a container in which incense is burnt:

The priest carried the censer down the aisle.

The verb *censor* means to examine material such as literature and films, and to ban it or remove parts considered to be immoral, libellous, seditious, or contrary to government or official policy. The noun *censor* means the person who does this job:

This obscene book has been censored.

The film censors discussed the rating for *Silence of the Lambs*.

*Censure* may also be a verb or a noun, and refers to strong criticism or disapproval:

The umpire censured the players for shoving.

The players incurred the umpire's censure for shoving.

**centenary/centennial** *Centenary* as a noun means a 100th anniversary or its celebration; as an adjective it describes a 100th anniversary or something lasting 100 years: *Adelaide's centenary in 1936*; *Adelaide's centenary celebrations in 1936*. In Australian usage *centennial* is an adjective that means the same as the adjective *centenary*. We do not use *centennial* as a noun, as US English does.

Note the *-ten-* in *centenary* (pronounced 'teen' or 'ten') and the *-tenn-* in *centennial* (pronounced 'ten').

See also **centuries.**

**centigrade** See **Celsius/centigrade/Fahrenheit.**

**central processing unit** The *central processing unit* (abbreviated *CPU*) is the part of a computer that coordinates and controls all the other parts of the system.

**centre/centred/centring** Note the *-tr-* in all three. The US spellings *center*, *centered* and *centering* are not recommended.

See also **centre/middle; centre on.**

**centre/middle** In many instances these nouns are interchangeable:

> Domenica stood in the centre [*or* middle] of the stage.
>
> Ian was at the centre [*or* in the middle] of the controversy.

However, *centre* is preferred when the location is more precise than this:

> The light came from the centre of the sphere.

*Middle* often suggests the meaning midway between, especially when the exact position of the centre may be difficult to ascertain: *in the middle of a discussion*; *down the middle of the road*.

See also **centre/centred/centring; centre on.**

**the Centre/the Red Centre** *The Centre* and *the Red Centre* are popular names for that part of the Northern Territory centred on Alice Springs and noted for the redness of its soil.

**centre on** Discussions, interests, arguments and other matters can *centre on* (or *upon*) things; buildings, organisations and institutions can be *centred in* or *at* a place:

> The committee's talks centred on [*or* upon] the budget.
>
> Support groups for patients are centred in private homes.

Since a centre cannot literally lie around something, avoid the common expression *centre around* and use *centre on* (or *upon*) or *revolve around* instead.

See also **centre/centred/centring; centre/middle.**

**centuries** These are periods of 100 years, calculated from the year AD 1 in all Christian and many non-Christian countries. The first century AD was AD

1–100; the twentieth century is AD 1901–2000. The new millennium (a 1000-year period) will start on 1 January 2001 (but will no doubt be celebrated incorrectly on 1 January 2000).

Centuries BC are counted in reverse from AD 1, Julius Caesar being assassinated in 44 BC (that is, in the first century BC) and Alexander the Great dying in 323 BC (that is, in the fourth century BC).

See also **AD/BC**; **bi-**; **centenary/centennial**; **dates**.

**CEO** chief executive officer.

**cereal/serial** A *cereal* is a plant yielding edible grain, hence a *breakfast cereal*. A *serial* is anything published or broadcast in instalments (that is, a series): *a radio serial about station life*.

**ceremonial/ceremonious** The word *ceremonial*, used as an adjective, describes something marked by or relating to ritual or ceremony and suggests formal observance:

> The dawn services on Anzac Day are ceremonial occasions.

The adjective *ceremonious* is used of people as well as things and means carefully observant of ceremony; it can suggest a tendency towards pomposity or excessive formality in some contexts:

> Members of the club paid ceremonious attention to the rules.
> Angela is a trifle ceremonious at the breakfast table: must I wear a tie?

**CES** Commonwealth Employment Service.

**c/f** carried forward *or* carry forward (accounts).

**cf.** compare (Latin: *confer*).

**CFC** The abbreviation *CFC* is better known (and easier to spell) than the name *chlorofluorocarbon*, a chemical often used as a refrigerant and an aerosol propellant, and now considered to be harmful to the earth's atmosphere.

**CGA** colour graphics adapter.

**ch.** chapter; check (chess).

**chair** Some people dislike the use of *chair* as a noun in place of *chairman*, *chairwoman* or *chairperson*, but as it is both short and sex-neutral such objections are surprising. *Chair* used as a verb (*She will chair the meeting*) is acceptable to all.

See also **discriminatory language**; **gender**; **-person**; **spokesperson**.

**Chamber of Manufactures** Not 'Manufacturers'.

**chamois/chammy/shammy** The name of the antelope is spelt and pronounced in the French way: *chamois* and '**sham**-wah' respectively. The soft leather polishing cloth may be spelt *chamois, chammy* or *shammy*, but is pronounced '**sham**-ee'.

**changeover** No hyphen; *change* will usually do.

**Channel Country** The *Channel Country* is a geographic region of south-west Queensland, so named because of the many channels that cross the plains.

**chaperon/chaperone** Either spelling is recommended but, regardless of which you choose, pronounce the word '**shappa**-rone'.

**character** This noun describes the sum of the qualities that distinguish a particular person or thing from others:

> John was noted for his loyal character.
>
> The renovation ruined the character of the Federation house.

*Character* is used idiomatically in a variety of ways, but also in pretentious or unnecessarily verbose statements: *actions of a questionable character* (for *questionable actions*); *productions of an artistic character* (for *artistic productions*).

**character (typesetting)** Any letter, figure, punctuation mark or symbol in a typeface is referred to as a *character*. For the purpose of character-counting, all space bars, tabs and carriage returns are also called characters.

See also **character count/word count**.

**character count/word count** These terms mean calculation of the number of characters or words in a manuscript to determine matters such as the extent of the publication or the cost of typesetting.

The traditional procedure is as follows. If the type in the manuscript is unjustified, it is first necessary to take a page of the copy and establish the average line length. Draw a vertical line through the copy at this point and count the number of characters (including word spaces) or words up to your line. Count the number of lines on the page and multiply this figure by the number of characters or words per line. Once the number of characters or words per page is established, multiply this figure by the total number of pages in the manuscript. Allowance will have to be made for short pages, headings, artwork and so on, of course. If the manuscript type is justified, the average number of characters or words in five lines supplies the basis for your calculation. An alternative to counting the actual words in a line is to divide the number of characters (and word spaces) in a line by six to obtain the number of 'average' words to be counted.

In desktop publishing most word-processing programs can do all the calculations automatically. All characters are counted, including spaces, punctuation and carriage returns. This is useful for an operator charging for word-processing by the number of keystrokes.

See also **cast-off**; **character (typesetting)**; **extent**.

**charisma** This noun has become debased in recent years, being misused to describe the impact of almost anyone, pop star or politician, who performs well on television. *Charisma* (from the Greek word for grace or gift) in fact means a divinely conferred power or talent. It is correctly used of those rare people who have the ability to inspire devotion and enthusiasm for good, and strictly speaking should not be applied to those who arouse less admirable instincts. Nor should it be used simply as a synonym for words such as *attraction*, *likeability* and *popularity*.

**Charleston, SA** Compare with *Charlestown*, NSW.

**chassis** Singular and plural.

**chateau** The plural is *chateaux* or *chateaus*. The French word *château* means a castle or large country house. The circumflex over the first *a* is usually omitted in Australian English and the word need not be set in italics. Pronounce it '**shat**-o' (plural '**shat**-oze').

**chauffeur** Note the spelling.

**chauvinism/chauvinist** These nouns derive from the name of Nicolas Chauvin, a French soldier who was an ardent admirer of his leader, Napoleon Bonaparte, and a fanatical patriot. *Chauvinism* is thus belligerent patriotism or zealous devotion to some other cause. A *chauvinist* displays these attitudes.

The word was adopted by the feminist movement in the 1970s to use in the expression *male chauvinist pig*, which meant a man considered to hold sexist views. The first and last words of the term were later dropped, and an entire generation now uses *chauvinist* as a synonym for a sexist person, usually male.

**cheap** Goods may be *cheap*; prices may not.

**check/cheque/chequered/chequers** The pattern of small squares is a *check* in Australian, British and US English. Our bank *cheque*, *chequered* history (or flag) and game of draughts (or Chinese *chequers*) are respectively spelt *check*, *checkered* and *checkers* in US English.

**chemical symbols** The following are the *chemical symbols* for some common elements.

| | | | | | |
|---|---|---|---|---|---|
| Ag | silver | H | hydrogen | Pt | platinum |
| Al | aluminium | He | helium | Pu | plutonium |
| As | arsenic | Hg | mercury | Ra | radium |
| Au | gold | I | iodine | S | sulphur |
| B | boron | K | potassium | Sb | antimony |
| Ba | barium | N | nitrogen | Se | selenium |
| C | carbon | Na | sodium | Si | silicon |
| Ca | calcium | Ne | neon | Sn | tin |
| Cd | cadmium | Ni | nickel | Sr | strontium |
| Cl | chlorine | Mg | magnesium | Ti | titanium |
| Co | cobalt | Mn | manganese | U | uranium |
| Cr | chromium | Mo | molybdenum | W | tungsten |
| Cu | copper | O | oxygen | X | xenon |
| F | fluorine | P | phosphorus | Zn | zinc |
| Fe | iron | Pb | lead | Zr | zirconium |

**cheque/chequered/chequers** See **check/cheque/chequered/chequers**.

**chilblain** Note the single *l* in *chil-*. The association between chilly weather and the development of *chilblains* on fingers, toes and ears may lie behind the common misspelling 'chillblain'.

**child** Prefer *child* or *children* to *kid* or *kids*, which many adults – and quite a few children – find offensive.

**childish/childlike** *Childish* means appropriate to a child or behaving like a child. It is often used to criticise someone (young or old) who is acting immaturely or displaying some of the less attractive characteristics of childhood:

> The teller was childish to throw a tantrum over $5.

It may, of course, be used of a child without implying criticism:

> She held out her hands for the present with childish glee.

It would be tautological to call a child *childlike*, but when used of an adult the word suggests the attractive qualities of childhood:

> The artist is childlike in her enthusiasm, and she paints wide-eyed figures that are essentially childlike too.

See also **juvenile/puerile**.

**Chile/chilli** *Chile* is a Spanish-speaking country in South America. In English the name is pronounced '**chil**-ee', not 'chil-**ay**'. *Chilli* is the spelling in Australian English for the hot spice, or the capsicum from which the spice is made (plural *chillies*).

**China/Chinese** Australian newspapers – and Australians generally – call the People's Republic of China by its old name, *China*. The island of Formosa off the coast of China, which styles itself the Republic of China (it is the home of Nationalist Chinese), is called Taiwan by outsiders.

*Chinese* as an adjective refers to anything from China, including its people: *Chinese pottery*; *Chinese students*. As a noun it refers to the various languages of China, and also to its people: *Let's try to learn Chinese*; *a restaurant full of Chinese*.

The term *Chinaman*, seen as something of a colonial leftover, is not acceptable today.

See also **discriminatory language**.

**chisel/chiselled/chiselling** Note the single *l* in the first and the *-ll-* in the other two.

**chlorophyll** Note the spelling.

**CHOGM** Commonwealth Heads of Government Meeting.

**choleric** This adjective means irascible or angry. It does not describe someone with cholera: that adjective is usually *choleraic*.

**cholesterol** Note the spelling.

**chook** The colloquialism *chook* for the domestic fowl is unlikely to be understood outside Australia, except by overseas fans of Barry Humphries (in all his disguises) and of the Australian novelist Tim Winton. Use *fowl, hen* or *chicken* instead if immediate recognition by non-Australians is important.

**chord/cord** *Chords* in music, but vocal *cords*.

**Christian name** See **given name/Christian name**.

**chronic** See **acute/chronic**.

**chrysalis** The plural is *chrysalises*, *chrysalids* or *chrysalides*. A *chrysalis* is a pupa: *the chrysalis from which a butterfly will emerge*. Pronounce it '**krissa**-liss'.

**chutzpah** Note the spelling of this Yiddish word meaning gall or brazen self-confidence. The *ch* sounds like 'h' and the *utz* rhymes with *puts*.

**CIA** Central Intelligence Agency (US).

**CIB** Criminal Investigation Branch (the name most commonly used by Australian police forces).

See also **CID**.

**CID** Criminal Investigation Department (especially in Britain).
See also **CIB**.

**c.i.f./CIF** The initials stand for *cost, insurance, freight*. This is a trading term meaning that insurance and freight as well as the cost of the goods are covered in the price quoted by the seller.
See also **f.i.s./FIS**; **f.o.b./FOB**.

**C-in-C** commander-in-chief.

**CIP** The *CIP* (*cataloguing-in-publication*) data that is printed, for the guidance of libraries, on the reverse of the title page of many Australian books is supplied to publishers (on request) by the National Library in Canberra.
See also **publications, parts of**.

**cipher/cypher** Either spelling is correct, but *cipher* is recommended. The commonest meaning of the noun is a method of secret writing, a secret message, or the key to it. A person who is described as a *cipher* is, however, a nonentity.

***circa*** This italicised Latin word meaning about (and sometimes abbreviated to *c.*) is most often used in connection with dates:

He was a sculptor, born *circa* 1860.

**circumlocution** Also known as *periphrasis*, *circumlocution* is a roundabout way of saying things. It is a common style fault, closely linked with verbosity in that more words are used than are necessary. Writers of official and academic prose are often guilty of *circumlocution*, but anyone may need an occasional reminder to write:

no *rather than* the answer is in the negative
we believe *rather than* we are of the opinion
even if *rather than* notwithstanding the fact that

A little circumlocution may, of course, encourage cooperation:

I wonder whether you would mind moving along.

*rather than*

Move along there!

See also **clichés**; **commercialese**; **euphemisms**; **fillers**; **officialese**; **tautology/pleonasm**.

**circumstances** The expressions *in the circumstances* and *under the circumstances* both mean because of the situation. *In the circumstances* is slightly better when the emphasis is on the *existence* of the situation:

In the circumstances it is best to say nothing.

Prefer *under the circumstances* when you are referring to a *link* between the situation and something that follows it:

Australia needed to sell its coal, and under the circumstances was justified in requiring more information from its rivals.

**CIS** This is the abbreviation for the *Commonwealth of Independent States*, which developed after the dissolution of the Union of Soviet Socialist Republics (USSR). There were ten member states early in 1993.

**cite/site** The verb *cite* can mean refer to as an authority, or quote: *The economist cited Keynes*; or commend: *The corporal will be cited for bravery*; or enumerate: *Cite the virtues of the princess*.

*Site* used as a noun means location: *a site on the hilltop*; as a verb it means locate: *Site the shed near the river*.

**civic/civil** These two adjectives have the same Latin root (*civis*, citizen) but are not synonymous. *Civic* means relating to a city or town and its residents: *Brisbane's civic centre*; *the mayor's civic duties*. *Civil* encompasses the notion of a country or State and its citizens (*civil war*; *civil rights*) and, by extension, denotes the difference between what is religious and what is not (*a civil wedding ceremony*); and indicates something that is non-military (*civil defence*).

If you are being *civil* you are showing politeness without necessarily being particularly warm: *His ex-wife is civil but that is all*.

**CJ** Chief Justice.

See also **ranks, titles, honours and awards**.

**clad/clothed** Either word may be used as the past tense and past participle of the verb *to clothe*, but *clad* sounds archaic if used in reference to people and is best reserved for knights of yore *clad in chain-mail* rescuing damsels *clad in fine raiment*. Its main modern usage relates to inanimate objects: *a steel-clad furnace*; *a glass-clad building*. You may, however, jokingly say that you went out *clad in your best bib and tucker*.

**claim** The verb *to claim* means to demand as a right, or as something you believe is due to you. You can *claim* your luggage, an inheritance, or a Christmas bonus. *Claim* is often used as a synonym for *allege*, *state* or *say*, any one of which would be more appropriate in the following example:

> The sales representative said [*not* claimed] that the personal computer was under warranty for a year.

Newspaper journalists are warned that using the word *claim* about a statement implies a degree of scepticism. It is suggested that they might choose a more neutral word:

> The pastrycook said [*not* claimed] that he turned off the oven.

**classic/classical** Something that is *classic* is of the highest class, and often serves as a model in its field; it is unlikely to be affected by changing fashion:

This tile is a classic piece of art deco pottery.

*All Quiet on the Western Front* is a classic war novel.

Chanel's suits are subdued but classic.

*Classical* relates to the literature, languages, art and architecture of ancient Greece and Rome, all of which may be studied under a *classical education*. *Classical* also describes things of elegance or refined form from, or modelled on, the taste and standards of those times. *Classical music* is serious music composed between the mid-eighteenth and early nineteenth centuries, or serious music of high quality from any period. Note that both *classic* and *classical* may apply to the same thing, for instance a splendid Roman vase.

**clause** A *clause* is a group of words that has a subject and a verb. A complete sentence must contain at least one clause that can stand alone and make sense: the *main clause*.

The following simple sentences each have one main clause:

The window is open.

We put your shoes by the fire.

Bruno does not like rain.

Sentences may have two or more main clauses joined by words such as *and*, *but*, *or*, *nor* and *whereas*. The sentences above have been extended to include two main clauses each:

The window is open *and* the rain is coming in.

We put your shoes by the fire *but* we can lend you ours.

Bruno does not like rain, *nor* does he want the furniture to get wet.

If you make sure that every sentence you write includes a main clause, you will avoid a common error, the *unintended sentence fragment*.

Since a string of main clauses soon becomes monotonous, a *subordinate clause* may be used to link ideas effectively. A subordinate clause, as the name implies, is dependent on the main clause in the sentence. It has a subject and a verb, but it cannot stand alone. Three kinds of subordinate clause are illustrated in the following simple sentences:

- the *adjectival clause*, which is introduced by words such as *when*, *who*, *which* and *that*, and relates to a noun or pronoun in the main clause (or to a whole clause)

  We chose a day *when the weather was fine*.

  I invited Keiko, *who will bring a friend*, to stay to lunch.

  She wore a green scarf, *which matched her jacket perfectly*.

  The hotel will accept anyone *that can pay the bill*.

  but note the special guidelines on the use of *that* and *which* at the end of this entry, and the fact that *who* is an option in the last example
- the *adverbial clause*, which is introduced by words such as *where*, *because*, *until* and *as*, and relates to the verb (or an adjective or adverb) in the main clause; it tells us where, why, when and how

He walked *where his mother used to walk.*

*Because she is fond of animals* she will feed this stray.

Wait on the footpath *until I can join you.*

Grant apologised *as a gentleman should.*

- the *noun clause*, which is introduced by words such as *whether*, *why* and *how*, and can form the subject of the main clause

  *Whether the road could be completed in time* was doubtful.

  *Why the council delayed the work* seemed inexplicable.

  *How we might deal with the matter effectively* gave us food for thought.

  or it can form the object of the main clause

  We asked *whether the road could be completed in time.*

  No one could say *why the council delayed the work.*

  Please tell us *how we may deal with the matter effectively.*

Note that words such as *when* and *where* can introduce an adjectival, adverbial or noun clause, depending on the relationship of that clause with the rest of the sentence.

When sentences are complex, subordinate clauses sometimes relate to words in other subordinate clauses and it becomes difficult to decide what kind they are. The important thing to remember is that even the most complicated sentence needs a sound structure. The inclusion of at least one main clause – the group of words that can stand alone and make sense – is, as indicated earlier, the key to avoiding incomplete sentences.

Adjectival clauses introduced by *that* and *which* need special care. Fowler said in *Modern English Usage* that 'if writers would agree to regard *that* as the defining relative pronoun and *which* as the non-defining, there would be much gain both in lucidity and in ease'. Not everyone supports this view, but maintaining the distinction seems worth while and is therefore recommended.

A *defining* adjectival clause (using *that* as the relative pronoun) 'defines' a previous element in the sentence, usually a noun or pronoun. In the following sentence the clause *that she likes best* defines the noun *cheese*, adding essential information.

Let's buy the kind of cheese that she likes best.

A *non-defining* clause (using *which* as the relative pronoun) does not define, but simply provides additional, non-essential information, as in the following variation on the first sentence:

Let's buy brie, which she likes best.

Note the comma that must precede *which* in this kind of construction.

Sometimes the meaning of two sentences, identical in every other way, is radically changed by the replacement of the defining *that* by the non-defining *which* and a pair of commas:

Rice that is grown in Australia is the staple diet of Asia.

Compare this with:

Rice, which is grown in Australia, is the staple diet of Asia.

The first sentence tells us that Australian rice constitutes the staple diet of Asia, a statement that is patently untrue. The second sentence tells us that rice is the staple diet of Asia, and it provides the additional, non-essential information that rice is grown in Australia. This is the statement the writer surely intended to make.

Adjectival clauses introduced by any other word (*when*, *where*, *who*, *whom*, *whose* and so on) are similarly defining or non-defining, and it is only the comma preceding the relative pronoun that identifies the non-defining ones. Note the difference the comma (and the second one completing the parenthesis) makes to meaning in the following:

Children who behave badly will not be admitted to the circus.

The defining clause (*who behave badly*), which is not marked off by commas, 'defines' the noun *children*.

Children, who behave badly, will not be admitted to the circus.

The non-defining clause, marked off by commas, appears to be providing additional, non-essential information about children in general, but in fact is telling us that all children behave badly. This is surely *not* the statement the writer intended to make.

There is further discussion on the role of these commas in the entry **comma**. Defining and non-defining phrases introduced by *like* are discussed in the entry **phrase**. Note that some people use the name *restrictive* instead of *defining*, and *non-restrictive* instead of *non-defining*.

See also **apposition**; **comma**; **phrase**.

**Clayton's** This uniquely Australian word is derived from the name of a non-alcoholic drink, *Clayton's Tonic*, which was marketed as 'the drink you have when you're not having a drink'. Used as an adjective, *Clayton's* means illusory (or a substitute), describing anything that appears to be something that it is not:

It was a Clayton's auction: the estate agent and the vendor were the only bidders.

**clean/cleanse** As verbs both words mean to free from dirt or filth, but *cleanse* has the added meaning purify, and is often used figuratively:

We must cleanse our minds of disloyal thoughts.

Advertisers have added another layer of refinement to two nouns derived from these verbs. While detergent-makers are still content to sell lavatory *cleaners*, cosmetic companies sell skin *cleansers*.

**clichés** These stereotyped expressions have usually lost most of the power they had when coined. Clichés sound too automatic to be the result of careful thought and often seem like the lazy way out. They can consequently raise doubts in a reader's mind about a writer's ability and, perhaps, credibility.

In formal or official writing clichés obscure the precise communication of information and ideas: writing that is full of *possible scenarios*, *strategic approaches* and *high profiles* is not going to hold a reader's attention for long. In speech, clichés like *by and large*, *to all intents and purposes* and *far be it from me* are common circumlocutions. Most listeners will rapidly lose interest unless such expressions are strictly rationed.

It is difficult, indeed unnecessary, to avoid the use of clichés altogether. Some serve a useful role in communicating ideas economically, summoning up vivid images that may be beyond the power of the writer or speaker to invent: *a needle in a haystack* or *the thin end of the wedge* may say it all.

See also **circumlocution**; **colloquialisms**; **commercialese**; **fillers**; **idiom**; **journalese**; **metaphor**; **officialese**; **simile**.

**client/customer** Lawyers, architects, accountants and some other members of the professions have *clients*; shops, markets and other trading establishments have *customers*. In recent times the former word has become something of a genteelism, with department stores, frock shops and banks preferring the sound of clients rather than customers. A *clientele*, pronounced 'klee-on-**tel**', comprises the people who deal with a particular business.

**climactic/climacteric/climatic** *Climactic* is the adjectival form of *climax*, which means the point of greatest intensity or the culmination; it does not necessarily mean the end:

> Singing at the royal wedding was the climactic moment of her career.

The use of *climax* as a verb in the expression *Did you climax*? (meaning have an orgasm) is strictly informal.

The noun *climacteric* means a critical stage in human life; it is used of a woman's menopause, for example.

*Climatic* is the adjectival form of *climate* and refers to weather:

> Climatic conditions suggest that it will be a wild night.

**clip art** *Clip art* (also known as *click art*) is a collection of computer graphics available on disk. Though the resolution and quality of the artwork are not always first-rate, clip art is useful for operators who do not have graphic skills or the budget to employ a graphic designer or illustrator.

**clique** Pronounce this word meaning a select group to rhyme with *creek*, not *brick*.

**clone** Originally a horticultural term defining a group of plants produced from the one stock, *clone* was adopted by genetic science to mean an asexually reproduced individual, genetically identical with the donor of the original body cell. *Clone* is now often used, and probably overused, to describe people or objects that are identical or close copies:

> She was a Marilyn Monroe clone.
> My wristwatch is a clone of a much more expensive one.

**clone (computer)** A computer that is functionally identical with an IBM personal computer is called a *clone* (or a *compatible*).

**clothed** See **clad/clothed**.

**CMDR/Cmdr** See **Cdr/CMDR/Com./Comdr**.

**CMF** Citizen Military Forces.

**CML** Colonial Mutual Life.

**CND** Campaign for Nuclear Disarmament.

**CNS** central nervous system.

**CO** commanding officer.

**Co./Coy** *Co.* may be the abbreviation for *Company*: *Blenkins & Co.*; or *County*: *Co. Cork*. *Coy* is the military contraction for *Company*: *B Coy, 10th Battalion*.

**co-** Preferred modern usage is to drop the hyphen in most words beginning with the prefix *co-*: *cohabit*, *coincide*, *coefficient*. In US English the dropping of the hyphen extends to such unusual conjunctions of letters and syllables as *coworker*, *costarring*, *copilot*, all of which have a hyphen in Australian and British English. Many people prefer to retain the hyphen when *co-* is followed by *o*, as in *co-operate* and *co-ordinate*, and there is logic in this: even the Americans often hyphenate *co-opt* and *co-op*. But *cooperate* and *coordinate* are very commonly used, and this form is recommended.

**c/o** care of (in addresses); also *c/-*.

**coalesce** Note the spelling of this word, which means (literally or figuratively) to blend:

> The factions coalesced and a single body emerged.

**coarse/course** *Coarse* is an adjective that means common or inferior in quality and, by extension, rough or crude: *coarse cloth*; *coarse language*.

The noun *course* has numerous meanings, including an onward movement or direction; part of a meal; a series of lectures or classes; and a race track. The verb *to course* refers to the so-called sport in which hares are hunted by hounds; and to the movement of a liquid:

> They swam for exercise and coursed for thrills.
> The spilt water coursed across the floor.

**coat of arms** No hyphens.

**COBOL** Common Business-Oriented Language (computer term).

**coca/cocoa/coconut** The dried leaves of the *coca* shrub yield cocaine and other alkaloids. *Cocoa* consists of the roasted and ground seeds of the cacao tree; it is used to make the drink of the same name, and chocolate. A *coconut* is the fruit of a coconut palm.

**COD** cash on delivery; *Concise Oxford Dictionary* (when italicised).

**codeine** Note the *-ei-*.

**co-ed** Note the hyphen. This word is an abbreviation of the adjective *co-educational*. A *co-educational school* is one that takes pupils of both sexes. In US English a *co-ed* is a female pupil of such a school.
See also **co-**.

**coerce** Note the spelling of this verb meaning to force.

**C. of E.** Church of England.

**cognisant** Note the *-s-* in this rather formal adjective that means aware (of something): *The director is cognisant of Elaine's qualifications.*

**COL/Col.** Colonel.

**Colac, Vic.** Compare with *Coolac*, NSW.

**colander** See **calendar/calender/colander**.

**coliseum** This is the accepted modern spelling for the word meaning a large stadium or theatre (from the Latin *colosseus*, gigantic, hence the ancient Colosseum in Rome).

**collaborate/cooperate** *Collaborate* is the stronger of these two verbs, and it is usually applied to actions entailing cooperation in a creative enterprise:

> They collaborated on an Oscar-winning script.

But it is also possible for citizens of an invaded country to *collaborate with the enemy*.

*Cooperate* is more often used as a general term relating to mutual help:

> Landowners and tenants will cooperate to get a reduction in rates from the council.

Note that it would be superfluous to add the word *together* to either of these.
See also **co-**; **corroborate**.

**collective nouns** These nouns refer to groups of people, animals or things, and include words like *crowd*, *audience*, *parliament*, *crew*, *navy*, *army*, *herd*, *swarm*, *minority* and *collection*.

Some collective nouns that are really classes of things – *crockery*, *cutlery*, *underwear* and *luggage* – always take a singular verb:

The crockery is on the shelves; the cutlery is in the drawer.

Other collective nouns, those of multitude, present a problem when it comes to choosing a singular or plural verb. The deciding factor is the way in which the writer views the noun in the particular context.

- When the group is seen as a unit, use a singular verb:

  The government has been defeated and will stand down tonight.

- When the group is seen as a set of individuals capable of individual action, use a plural verb:

  The government were unable to agree on the issue and some of the members crossed the floor.

Beware of treating a collective noun as both singular and plural in the same sentence or passage:

The team *is* being sent to Greece, where *it* will represent Australia.

*not* The team *is* being sent to Greece, where *they* will represent Australia.

A related matter of consistency sometimes arises. Hotel staff, for instance, may be a thing (impersonal and singular) or people (personal and plural). Choose one or the other:

We have a reliable staff, *which has* given the hotel a good name.

*or* We have reliable staff, *who have* given the hotel a good name.

See also **nouns**; **nouns, plurals of**; **singular or plural**.

**collision/collide** Careful users of English argue that in a *collision* all the objects must be in motion: for example, a motor cycle cannot *collide* with a fence, only with another moving object, such as a car. You will nevertheless hear many people say *The motor cycle collided with the fence*; even the most casual is unlikely, however, to say *The fence collided with the motor cycle*.

**colloquialisms** Words, phrases or expressions that are widely used and acceptable in informal circumstances, but not generally used in formal contexts, are called *colloquialisms*. Because they are friendlier, more amusing or more colourful than formal words, colloquialisms are an essential ingredient of everyday speech. What may be *extremely irritating* formally might *drive us up the wall* colloquially; we may *bend over backwards to help* a friend who is *as sick as a dog*, but promise *as much assistance as possible* to a business colleague who is *seriously ill*.

In formal writing colloquialisms should be used sparingly, if at all. Formal speech, however, may need colloquialisms as much as informal chatter does. Winston Churchill's dramatic public appeal to Franklin Roosevelt in 1941, 'Give us the tools, and we will finish the job', might not be remembered today if he had said, 'Give Great Britain the guns and ships and it will defeat the Germans'.

See also **clichés**; **idiom**; **journalese**; **slang**.

**colon** The *colon* (:) is the punctuation mark that is most often used to introduce something. Note that modern convention has done away with the combined colon and dash (:–), though a dash is sometimes a suitable alternative to a colon (as it would be in the first three examples below). You will normally put a colon before the following:

- a list

  We need vegetables: some potatoes, a capsicum and a couple of carrots.

- an explanation

  Two things are certain in life: death and taxes.

- an example (or examples)

  Simon likes Australian rock bands: INXS, Midnight Oil and Cold Chisel.

- a substantial quotation or piece of direct speech (though a comma is often sufficient for shorter quotations, and some need no punctuation at all)

  The treasurer was quoted as saying: 'We may turn into a banana republic if industry does not become more competitive'.

- dialogue in a play

  *Lady Bracknell:* A handbag?

- a summary or a recapitulation

  This is the gist of her speech: she agreed to . . .

- a subtitle

  *Centennial Park: A History*

A colon is also used to indicate a ratio: *the scale of 2:1000*; and the distinction between chapter and verse in the Bible: *Psalms 9:1*.

An unusual but legitimate use of the colon is to link two grammatically complete clauses when the second marks a step forward from the first:

Writing style is not just words: style is using words well.

You may put anticipatory phrases like *such as*, *including* and *namely* instead of colons in the middle of a sentence; it is optional to put a colon after such phrases when the examples are set out on a new line. Thus you may write the following in several ways:

Keep notes on birds of prey such as eagles, falcons, harriers, kites and goshawks.

*or* Keep notes on birds of prey: eagles, falcons, harriers, kites and goshawks.

*or* Keep notes on birds of prey such as:

eagles
falcons
harriers
kites
goshawks

Do not disrupt a sentence by placing a colon between a verb and its object or complement: *The decorator changed: the wall colours, the curtains and the rugs*.

Note that words other than proper nouns following a colon have a lower-case initial except when they introduce a quotation that begins with a capital letter, dialogue in a play, direct speech or a subtitle (as already illustrated).

See also **comma**; **dashes, use of**; **full stop**; **semicolon**.

**colonnade** Note the single *l* and the *-nn-*.

**colophon/logo** A *colophon* was originally a paragraph at the end of a book describing its typography and other aspects of its production. Such information is now usually found on the reverse of the title page. In modern times a *colophon* has become a publisher's symbol or trademark (often called a *logo*): for example, the bird from which Penguin Books draws its name, the ship of Viking, and the coats of arms of various university presses.

The word *logo* is short for *logotype*, originally a term used in hot-metal typesetting to describe a set of letters or a word cast as one body. Today a *logo* is a set of specially designed letters (sometimes linked with a symbol) that represents a company's name or a product, though, as noted above, it is commonly used as a synonym for *colophon*. The logo of the Melbourne Cricket Club is illustrated here.

See also **publications, parts of**.

**colours in printing** Four-colour printing uses combinations of *process colours*: black and the three primary colours, cyan (blue), magenta (red) and yellow. If a special colour is required it is chosen from an international standard of inks known as the Pantone Matching System (PMS); these colours are often called *PMS colours*.

**columns** See **layout**; **measure**.

**comic/comical** Note the difference in meaning between these two adjectives. There is a planned funniness about something that is *comic*: *a comic act that brought down the house*. Something that is unintentionally funny should be described as *comical* rather than *comic*: *a comical mixture of terrier and poodle*.

**comma** The *comma* (,) is the punctuation mark that provides the shortest pause. In many ways it is the most important mark. By separating words and word-groups within a sentence, the comma helps to indicate a writer's exact meaning. Misuse or neglect of the comma often leads to confusion and ambiguity. Although commas are now used much less liberally than they once were, some commas, including the following, are regarded as essential by traditional grammarians and careful writers.

• Those that separate nouns, adjectives, adverbs or word-groups:

Fish, chicken, beef and game are on the menu.

It was a warm, cosy, welcoming, safe nest.

Dinner will be quickly, efficiently and graciously served.

Those present included boys and girls, teachers and advisers, and parents.

- Those that separate long main clauses:

  They hoped to stay out of sight, but their giggling could be heard easily.

- Those that follow adverbial clauses of reason and condition:

  Since you cannot decide, let me make up your mind for you.

  If you refuse, I have only one option.

- Those that isolate clauses, phrases and words supplying additional but inessential information; note that *two* commas, one before and one after, are needed when the clause or phrase is in the middle of a sentence:

  Be sure, when you reach the market, to buy the bread first.

  Fulvia, the fruiterer's daughter, married the butcher.

  Pay attention, children, to what I am saying.

  Is that you, Margaret?

  You'll never win a cent, that's for sure.

  Blow me down, we won the lottery!

- Those that prevent ambiguity:

*Put* Our meal consisted of braised oxtail topped with peppercorns, and strawberry ice-cream.

*not* Our meal consisted of braised oxtail topped with peppercorns and strawberry ice-cream.

*Put* While we watched, strangely dressed tribesmen filed past.

*not* While we watched strangely dressed tribesmen filed past.

*Put* He doesn't hate me, because I'm your friend.

*not* He doesn't hate me because I'm your friend.

*Put* We compared the music of Sondheim, Webber, and Gilbert and Sullivan.

*not* We compared the music of Sondheim, Webber and Gilbert and Sullivan.

- Those that follow, or surround, *however* when it is acting as a sentence connecter (when you use *however* as an adverb it never has a comma after it):

  However, he stuck to the road even though it was hard.

  Try this road, however, and you should reach Wangaratta by lunchtime.

  However [adverb] hard the road is, he must stick to it.

  But note the comments on words like *moreover*, *nevertheless* and *thus* near the end of this entry.

In the following examples commas are recommended but not essential.

- To separate medium-length main clauses:

  Judith felt elated, but there was nobody to tell.

- As an alternative to dashes or brackets:

  Mr Kostas, the new postmaster, settled in quickly.

*or* Mr Kostas – the new postmaster – settled in quickly.

*or* Mr Kostas (the new postmaster) settled in quickly.

Some commas are appropriate in one sentence but not in another that may seem similar.

• Between short main clauses:

He packed, and went home in a huff.

*but* He packed and went home.

• After long introductory phrases:

In a desperately hard winter with no rain between May and August, animals get really short of feed.

*but* In winter there may be a shortage of feed.

• Before the final *and* in a series that mixes nouns, adjectives or phrases in the following ways:

*Put* Let's order chaff, layers pellets and lucerne hay.

*but* Let's order chaff, layers pellets, and as much lucerne hay as we can afford.

*Put* Geraldine is capable, articulate and keen.

*but* Geraldine is capable, articulate, and keen to do well.

• Before the final *or* in a similar series:

For $20 the hairdresser can do a stylish cut, highlights, or an economy perm.

There are certain places where a comma should *not* go; outstanding instances follow.

• Not where a pair of main clauses needs linking; use a semicolon instead, or rewrite the clauses as two sentences:

Bob cast his line at once; the fish were biting.

*or* Bob cast his line at once. The fish were biting.

*not* Bob cast his line at once, the fish were biting.

The last example illustrates a common error known as a *run-on sentence*.

• Not where the comma would break the flow of a sentence; for instance, a single comma should not separate the subject of a clause from its verb, nor the verb from its object:

*Put* Anyone who called was invited in.

*not* Anyone who called, was invited in.

*Put* The shop having closed, Garth could not buy his socks.

*not* The shop, having closed, Garth could not buy his socks.

*Put* The ironbarks, wattles and native grasses made a lovely picture.

*not* The ironbarks, wattles, and native grasses, made a lovely picture.

• Not where a couple of main clauses are joined by *therefore*; you need either a semicolon or no punctuation at all, depending on whether the two clauses are strongly separated or not:

The economic outlook is exceedingly bleak in this country; therefore we must make some constructive plans.

*or* The outlook is bleak therefore we must plan carefully.

• Not, as a general rule, after words like *moreover*, *nevertheless*, *thus* and *meanwhile* (as noted, commas are required after *however* when it is a sentence connecter):

The train was delayed. Moreover it stopped at every station. We nevertheless had allowed plenty of time and thus arrived before lunch. Meanwhile those who drove were caught up in a traffic jam.

- Not between adjectives that are very closely related to each other or to the noun they qualify:

*Put* The shed has a strong, unyielding frame.
*but* The shed has a solid steel frame.
*Put* They were asked to use a sharp, non-smudgy pencil.
*but* They were asked to use a sharp blue pencil.

A helpful test of the relationship between such words is to ask yourself whether *and* could separate them. If the answer is yes, a comma is probably necessary.

Note the position of the comma in relation to conjunctions such as *but* in the following construction:

You will certainly need your coat but, if it rains, you will want your umbrella too.
*or* You will certainly need your coat, but if it rains you will want your umbrella too.
*not* You will certainly need your coat, but if it rains, you will want your umbrella too.
*or* You will certainly need your coat, but, if it rains, you will want your umbrella too.

Commas can make important distinctions in meaning between defining and non-defining clauses (and phrases). A comma preceding an adjectival clause (or phrase) – or a pair marking it off – means that the clause (or phrase) is non-defining. Note the difference the commas make to the meaning of the adjectival clause in each of the two following examples;

My sister who lives in Adelaide is an architect.

The absence of commas marking off the clause *who lives in Adelaide* implies that she is not my only sister, merely the one who lives in Adelaide. The clause 'defines' my sister.

My sister, who lives in Adelaide, is an architect.

The presence of commas marking off the clause implies that she is my only sister. The clause *who lives in Adelaide* simply adds information about her.

The same is true of adjectival phrases: *my sister Ruth* implies that she is not my only sister; *my sister, Ruth* implies that she is.

The terms *defining* and *non-defining*, and the preference for *that* over *which* as a defining relative pronoun, are explained in the entry **clause**; another problem with commas in defining and non-defining constructions is also explained there.

See also **and**; **apposition**; **brackets**; **colon**; **dashes, use of**; **phrase**; **sentence**; **singular or plural**.

**command** A statement or word such as 'print' or 'copy' that sets in motion a series of instructions to a computer is called a *command*.

**commando** Plural *commandos.*

**commence** Unless the context is decidedly formal, do not *commence* things; *begin* or *start* them. Some institutions, however, have *Commencement Week* rites.

**commercialese** This is the name given to the dry, mechanical kind of language used in some business writing, particularly correspondence. It is typified by circumlocution and unnecessary (usually Latin) abbreviations, and looks distinctly old-fashioned today. Happily most businesses have discovered this and now use plain English in their communications, writing *Thank you for your letter of 16 October* rather than *Acknowledgement is made for yours of the 16th ult. to hand*; and *As I said in my last letter* rather than *As per our most recent communication.* While commercialese should be avoided because it is often difficult to understand, and sounds impersonal and insincere, care must be taken that the informal approach does not seem rude or abrupt.

See also **circumlocution**; **gobbledegook**; **Latin words and phrases**; **letters, formal**; **officialese**; **re**; **reports and submissions**.

**commitment** This must be one of the most frequently misspelt words in the English language. Note the single *t* in the second syllable. There is no alternative spelling, even in US English; but note *committing*, *committed* and *committal.* Because *commitment* is an overworked word, try alternatives such as *concern, belief, devotion* and *dedication.*

**common/mutual/reciprocal** The adjective *common* has a number of different meanings (including ordinary, widespread and vulgar) besides the one sometimes confused with that of *mutual.* In the following example it means belonging to, or shared by, two or more:

> My neighbour and I have a common desire for a new fence.

*Mutual* implies *interaction* between two or more:

> My neighbour and I have a mutual desire for a closer relationship.

*Common*, used instead of *mutual* in the second example, would not only be incorrect but, because of its other possible meanings, might imply that the shared desire was somewhat vulgar. Note that expressions such as *mutual agreement* and *mutual cooperation* are tautological.

The word *reciprocal* has the same meaning as *mutual*, and sometimes also the sense *responsive* (to something initiated by another):

> The croquet club lent its urn to the bridge group, which made the reciprocal offer of its card tables.

**common sense/commonsense** The compound noun is two words:

> Jane's mother had great common sense.

The adjective is one word:

> This is a commonsense proposition.

**Commonwealth** The *Commonwealth of Australia* is a federation of States and Territories with powers and responsibilities constitutionally divided between a central government and the governments of its constituent parts. The central government is today often called the *Federal* or *Australian Government* rather than the *Commonwealth Government*. For a comprehensive essay on the origin and use of the term *Commonwealth* in the Australian context, see Stephen Murray-Smith's *Right Words*.

The (British) Commonwealth of Nations is the residue of the British Empire, and it consists of a free association of independent nations acknowledging the British monarch as head of the Commonwealth but mostly not as head of state.

**comparable** Pronounce this adjective '**komp**ra-b'l', not 'kom-**pair**a-b'l'.

**comparative and superlative** When two or more things are compared, we use special forms of adjectives to convey the degree of comparison. The form that compares only two things (or two sets of things) is called the *comparative*:

> She was the stronger of the two girls.
> Cheetahs are faster than lions.

The form that compares more than two is called the *superlative*:

> She was the strongest of the five girls.
> Cheetahs are the fastest of the four-legged animals.

The *comparative* and *superlative* forms of adjectives and adverbs are illustrated by the following examples. The sequence is *normal* form, then *comparative*, then *superlative*:

- adjectives

| | | | |
|---|---|---|---|
| *one syllable* | strong | stronger | strongest |
| *same form as adverb* | fast | faster | fastest |
| *irregular* | good | better | best |
| *another irregular* | bad | worse | worst |
| *two syllables, -y ending* | pretty | prettier | prettiest |
| *two syllables, -le ending* | humble | humbler | humblest |
| *two syllables, -ow ending* | shallow | shallower | shallowest |
| *two syllables, -er ending* | clever | cleverer | cleverest |
| *all others with two syllables* | pompous | more pompous | most pompous |
| *all others with three or more syllables* | discerning | more discerning | most discerning |

• adverbs

| | | | |
|---|---|---|---|
| *different form from adjective* | strongly | more strongly | most strongly |
| *same form as adjective* | fast | faster | fastest |
| *irregular* | well | better | best |
| *another irregular* | badly | worse | worst |

Watch out for *absolute adjectives*, and the adverbs formed from them, neither of which can be comparative or superlative. They include words like *empty*, *fatal*, *impossible* and *unique*. While it is possible to modify absolutes by using words such as *almost* or *nearly* (*almost fatal* or *nearly impossible*), it is nonsense to refer to something as *more fatal* or *more impossible*.

Take care not to use *more* (comparative) when you mean *most* (superlative), and vice versa:

> She is the most [*not* more] lively of the triplets.
>
> She is the more [*not* most] lively of the twins.

Be sure to avoid doubling up comparatives or superlatives: *more brighter*; *most quickest*.

Note also the 'advertiser's comparative', which never completes the comparison: *Yum Yum bars taste better!*. Better than what, one might well ask. It is not difficult for writers outside the commercial world to make the same error by saying baldly that a certain tomato is *much more juicy*, for instance.

See also **adjectives**; **adverbs**; **more**; **most**.

**comparatively/relatively** These two adverbs are used interchangeably, meaning in comparison with a standard:

> He is a comparatively [*or* relatively] placid dog for his breed.

Neither should, strictly speaking, be used as a synonym for *fairly* or *rather*:

> It was a fairly [*not* comparatively *or* relatively] short storm.

It is worth noting also that we should write about there being *comparatively few gales*, not *a comparatively few gales*.

**compare to/compare with** Use *compare to* when emphasising the way in which people or things are similar to others:

> By comparing himself to Jesus Christ he upset the Christians in the audience.

Use *compare with* when both similarities and differences are being considered, assessed or discussed, particularly when debate is likely:

> When we compare ourselves with Christ we see how unforgiving we are.
>
> Experts on the New Testament will compare the new translation with the work of earlier scholars.

When using *compare with*, make sure that like is compared with like. In the following example music cannot be compared with people, only with other music.

Let us compare Bach's music with that of his contemporaries.

*not* Let us compare Bach's music with his contemporaries.

See also **contrast**.

**compass points** The *points of the compass* are abbreviated *N*, *S*, *W*, *E*, *NE*, *SSW* and so on. In combination with a proper name the abbreviation is followed by a full stop: *S. Melbourne*. The initial capital is used when the direction, expressed in full, is part of a proper name: *the South China Sea*; and when a whole area is customarily designated as a region: *the West Coast of South Australia*. Otherwise use a lower-case initial: *south of the island*; *on the west coast of Tasmania*; *a fence to the north-east*; *flying south-south-west*.

**compatible** See **clone (computer)**.

**complacent/complaisant** The primary meaning of *complacent* is self-satisfied, but it can also simply mean pleasantly satisfied, agreeable – though this is a fairly uncommon use of the word:

His complacent smirk irritated people.

She remained complacent in spite of her children's noisy demands.

*Complaisant* means agreeable, disposed to please:

We have found James complaisant in negotiation – an easy man to deal with.

Use these words carefully because the secondary meaning of *complacent* is quite close to the meaning of *complaisant*, and they sound the same. You would not want to confuse either with the primary meaning of *complacent*, which is usually uncomplimentary.

**complement/compliment/supplement** All three may be used as nouns or verbs. The first two words are frequently confused. A *complement* is what is needed to complete something or make it perfect; *to complement* means to make complete:

The softball club lacked its full complement of players.

Red wine will complement a beef dish.

A *compliment* is a word of praise; *to compliment* is to praise:

Helga's dress got more than one compliment.

The children were complimented on their good behaviour.

Remembering the *comple-* of *complete* helps to prevent confusion between *complement* and *compliment*.

A *supplement* is an addition to something already considered complete; *to supplement* means to add to something:

They produced a magazine supplement for the Sunday newspaper.

It is necessary to supplement your pension to live comfortably.

See also **complement (grammar)**.

**complement (grammar)** The grammatical term *complement* has the same meaning (that which is needed to complete something) as the word normally has, but its application is quite narrow. A grammatical complement may be a word, phrase or clause. For instance, a preposition such as *with*, *about* or *under* needs a complement: *with him*; *about the house*; *under water.*

Linking verbs such as *be*, *seem* and *taste* need a complement: *He is a biologist*; *It seems close to home*; *That toffee tastes delicious.*

See also **case (grammar)**; **clause**; **complement/compliment/supplement**; **phrase**.

**complex** A *complex* is something composed of interconnected parts, such as an *airport complex* or a *housing complex*. Some authorities suggest that the term should be used to describe physical structures or areas designed for a variety of purposes (*a complex of shops and offices*) rather than closely related functions, as in the kind of conglomerate they would prefer to call an *arts centre*, *office block* or *block of flats*. The distinction would not always be easy to make.

The psychoanalytical meaning of *complex* is a group of repressed ideas or impulses causing an abnormal mental condition. This sense of the word is commonly extended to describe any obsessive state:

> She has a complex about being overweight.

See also **complex/complicated**.

**complex/complicated** As adjectives both words mean intricate. *Complex* is the more neutral word; it suggests something that is *naturally* intricate:

> The brain is the most complex part of the body.

Something that is *complicated* is often difficult to understand, and the word implies that it is *unnecessarily* intricate and could be made simpler:

> Our complicated legal system is beyond most people's understanding.

Note that something may be *complicated to do*, but cannot be *complex to do*.

See also **complex**.

**compliment** See **complement/compliment/supplement**.

**compose/comprise/constitute** These verbs are similar in that they refer to parts making up a whole, but each has its own idiomatic use. When we talk about a whole (for example the alphabet) being made up of a number of parts (the letters), we may say:

> The alphabet is composed of 26 letters.

*or* The alphabet comprises 26 letters.

*not* The alphabet is comprised of 26 letters.

Conversely, when we talk about a number of parts making up a whole, we may say:

> Twenty-six letters compose the alphabet.

*or more usually*

Twenty-six letters constitute the alphabet.

*not* Twenty-six letters comprise the alphabet.

To avoid misusing *comprise*, remember that it can only mean to consist of.

**compound nouns, plurals of** Two or more words can form a unit of meaning and become a compound noun. In most cases at least one is already a noun:

poet laureate passer-by blackberry

Here are a few compound nouns that do not include a noun in their composition:

close-up stand-in summing-up standoff

Compounds often start life as distinct words, go through a period of being hyphenated, then end up as one word. An example of this transition is *best seller* becoming *best-seller* then *bestseller*.

The plurals of compounds are generally formed by adding *s* (or the normal plural ending) to the noun part, if there is one noun only:

poets laureate passers-by blackberries

If there is more than one noun, *s* is usually added to the last part of the compound:

film buffs donkey-rides gin-and-tonics screenwriters

But here are two exceptions:

tugs-of-war sisters-in-law

The compounds that do not include a noun in their make-up usually have *s* added to the last part:

close-ups stand-ins standoffs

But one exception is *summings-up*.

A number of the one-word compounds end in *ful*: *handful*, *spoonful*. Their plural is formed by adding *s*: *handfuls*, *cupfuls*, *spoonfuls* (not 'handsful', 'cupsful' or 'spoonsful').

It is often necessary to pluralise both parts of a compound when *woman* or *man* is one of the parts:

women doctors men friends menservants

But there are also *woman-haters* and *manhunts*, for instance.

For the use of the hyphen in compound words, see **hyphenation**.

See also **nouns**; **nouns, plurals of**.

**comprehend** See **apprehend/comprehend**.

**comprise** See **compose/comprise/constitute**.

**compulsive/compulsory** The adjective *compulsive* describes behaviour that is caused by a strong impulse, often uncontrolled:

He was a compulsive roulette player.

*Compulsory* describes something that is forced on a person or people by others:

Voting is compulsory in Australia but optional in New Zealand.

**computers – and words** The impact of computer technology on writing is predominantly through the use of word-processing and desktop-publishing programs. Such programs enable the entry, manipulation, editing, display, merging, storage, retrieval and printing of text. The ease with which changes can be made enables the production of several drafts of a document in considerably less time than would be needed for rekeying on a typewriter. Desktop-publishing programs enable text and graphics to be combined and converted into typeset pages ready for printing.

See also **desktop publishing**.

**computer typesetting** The modern typesetting procedure that makes use of computers and photographic processes rather than hot metal is called *computer typesetting*. Other common terms for it are *filmsetting*, *phototypesetting* and *photocomposition*.

See also **hot-metal setting**.

**conceit** Note the *-ei-*.

**conceive** Since, biologically, something can be conceived only once, avoid adding words such as *first*, *initially* or *originally* to this verb.

**concept** This noun has journeyed a long way from its original meaning of an idea, thought or notion formed by generalising from particular instances:

> Our concept of the solar system is based on the observation of natural phenomena.

It is now widely used, particularly by advertisers, as a synonym for any kind of *idea*, *design* or *plan*:

> Try the latest concept in sound systems.
> This is the newest concept in inner-city living.

Although some people object to such usage, it is firmly entrenched. Nevertheless you should choose the less pretentious word *idea* if that is all you mean. Similarly, prefer the verbs *imagine*, *understand* or *visualise* to the lofty *conceptualise*:

> The town-planner cannot understand [*not* conceptualise] your design for the city.

**concerning** See **re**.

**concerto** The plural is *concertos* or, more rarely, *concerti*. Pronounce the word 'kon-**cher**to'.

**concomitant** This word is frequently misspelt or misunderstood. It means existing or occurring together, but can often be replaced by the more familiar *accompanying*.

**condensed type** See **type**.

**condition/precondition** When it means something demanded as an essential part of an agreement, a *condition* can be fulfilled before or after the agreement is made:

We will send the goods on condition that you pay within seven days.

A *precondition* is a provision that must be met *before* the agreement is made:

A precondition for delivery of the goods is payment in advance.

**condone** This verb means to forgive or overlook (an offence), not to approve or agree (with something).

The company condoned Steve's lateness because his children were sick.

**confidant/confident** A *confidant* (male or female) is a person to whom secrets are confided or with whom intimacies are discussed; the form *confidante* (for a woman) has little usage now:

Everyone needs a confidant, but a sympathetic ear is hard to find.

*Confident* means certain or assured:

Miguel was confident of success after all his training.

**confrontation** This emotive word has been worked to exhaustion by journalists and sub-editors attempting to instil drama into mundane meetings that lack the hostility and defiance of a genuine *confrontation*. The word needs a rest: replace it with *conflict*, *argument*, *disagreement* or *dispute*, for example.

**congenial/genial** *Congenial* means agreeable or compatible:

They were a congenial group of like-minded friends.

*Genial* means cheerful or cordial:

He's always genial after lunch and will agree to anything.

**congenital/genetic** A medical problem that is *congenital* originated at birth; one that is *genetic* was inherited.

**conjunctions** The work of *conjunctions* is to join words; there are two main types:

- coordinating conjunctions such as *and*, *but*, *or*, *nor* and *whereas*, which join grammatically equal words, phrases or clauses

  bread *and* circuses [words] over the hills *and* far away [phrases]

  Mother laughed *but* I cried [main clauses].

- subordinating conjunctions such as *when*, *where*, *if*, *because* and *although*, which join subordinate clauses to main clauses

  I gave him the job [main clause] *because* he needed it [subordinate clause].

It is quite legitimate to begin some sentences with *or*, *and* or *but* provided that you do not make a welter of it.

See also **clause**; **phrase**.

**connecter/connector** Either spelling is correct for this noun when it means something that connects: *The wire connecter [*or *connector] was broken.* However, the noun meaning a person who does the connecting is generally spelt *connecter.*

**connection/connexion** Either spelling is correct, but *connection* is recommended.

**connector** See **connecter/connector**.

**connexion** See **connection/connexion**.

**connive** The verb *connive* means to conspire (followed by the preposition *with*), or to disregard or tolerate (followed by the preposition *at*):

> Our aunt connived with our cousin to allow cake for breakfast.
>
> Our easy-going aunt connived at our eating cake for breakfast.

Spell the noun *connivance* rather than *connivence*.

**connoisseur** Note the *-nn-* and *-ss-*. This noun is used today to describe a sound judge of anything from football tackles to beer, but in formal English it should be restricted to refined taste and the arts. Pronounce it 'konna-**ser**'.

**connote** See **denote/connote**.

**conscience** Take care in spelling this word.

**conscientious** Note the *-t-*, and do not confuse the spelling with that of *conscience*.

**consecutive/successive** *Consecutive* is the better word when things occur one after another without interruption. *Successive* things occur one after another, even though there may be intervals between them.

> The band went on a hectic tour of Queensland, performing in Brisbane, Surfers Paradise, Townsville and Cairns on four consecutive nights.
>
> Labor won four successive elections – in 1983, 1984, 1987 and 1990.

See also **back to back**.

**consensus** This has nothing to do with a census. Belief that it does has resulted in one of the most frequent misspellings in English: the non-word 'concensus'. *Consensus* – from the same root as *consent* – means concord or a general agreement:

> The prime minister won the consensus of unions and business.

The terms *general consensus* and *consensus of opinion* are tautologies.

**consent** See **ascent/assent/consent**.

**consequent/consequential/subsequent** These adjectives all loosely mean following, but they are not interchangeable. *Consequent* means following as a direct result (hence *consequences*):

Walter enjoyed the lasagne but not the consequent indigestion.

*Consequential* means following as an indirect result. If your car is stolen and your insurance policy indemnifies you against *consequential loss*, the cost of hiring a replacement vehicle, for example, should be covered.

It also means important or self-important (*the consequential Mr Micawber*), though its opposite, *inconsequential*, is probably more common (it means insignificant):

The journal *Nature* rejected his article as inconsequential.

*Subsequent* simply means following in time:

On a subsequent visit to the Italian restaurant Walter chose a dish without garlic.

However, it is often better to use the simpler word *later* instead of *subsequent*, and *then* instead of its adverb, *subsequently*.

**consider** This verb can simply mean to think, and in this sense it is never followed by *as:*

We considered it essential [*not* as essential] to attend.

I consider her an ideal tutor [*not* as an ideal tutor].

*Consider* can also mean to envisage in a certain role; in this sense it may be followed by *as:*

We considered Zandra as lawyer and diplomat, and she was clearly the best person for the job.

See also **regard**.

**considerable** When you say that you had *considerable difficulty*, or that someone has *considerable talent*, the nouns involved are abstract. If you link *considerable* with concrete nouns it is necessary to use the word a little differently: *a considerable quantity of oil* (not *considerable oil*); *a considerable number of houses* (not *considerable houses*).

*Considerable* sometimes means important or worthy of respect, and in this sense can be attached to personal nouns: *a considerable orator*; *a considerable mathematician*.

**consideration** This word is often part of unnecessarily wordy or formal phrases: *give consideration to* could become *consider*; *is under consideration* could become *is being considered*.

**consignor** This is the preferred Australian spelling for the word meaning a person who sends or transmits something; the recipient is a *consignee*.

**consist in/consist of** *Consist in* roughly means to exist in; it is usually followed by abstract concepts:

The strength of this novel consists in its skilful characterisation.

*Consist of* means to be made up of; it is often followed by concrete nouns:

A synopsis may consist of an introduction and some chapter headings.

**consonant** See **consonants, doubling of**; **vowel/consonant**.

**consonants, doubling of** A suffix is a letter or syllable that can be added to the end of an existing word to extend its meaning. *Park* becomes *parking* if we add the suffix *-ing*; *blur* becomes *blurred* if we insert an additional *r*, then the suffix *-ed*. Some other relevant suffixes are *-en*, *-er*, *-est*, *-y*, *-dom*, *-ful*, *-ment* and *-less*.

The problem is whether or not to double the final consonant when a suffix is attached: in the case of *park* it is not doubled; in the case of *blur* it is. Here is an outline of the rules for the most troublesome suffixes.

*Double the final consonant* where the suffix is *-y* or begins with a vowel, and the following conditions apply:

- when a single-syllable word ends in a single consonant preceded by a single vowel

  run, runny    stop, stopped    bit, bitten    big, bigger    hot, hottest
- when a multi-syllable word ends in a single consonant preceded by a single vowel, provided that the stress is on the last syllable

  occur, occurred    commit, committing    forget, forgetting
- when a compound word ends in a single consonant preceded by a single vowel, and does not have the stress on the last syllable but retains a full vowel sound in it

  kidnap, kidnapped    zigzag, zigzagging
- when the final consonant *l* is preceded by a single vowel

  fulfil, fulfilled    jewel, jeweller    travel, travelling

*Do not double the final consonant* in the following cases:

- when the suffix begins with a consonant

  delight, delightful    top, topless    commit, commitment

  but note exceptions such as *open*, *openness*; *drunken*, *drunkenness*
- when a word ends in two consonants

  part, parted    curl, curler    accept, accepting
- when there are two vowels before the final consonant

  retreat, retreated    hoot, hooter    tread, treading    hoar, hoary

  but note the exception *wool*, *woollen*, *woolly*
- when the stress in a multi-syllable word is on a syllable other than the last

  limit, limited    delimit, delimited    cellar, cellarer    letter, lettering

  but note the exception *worship*, *worshipped*, *worshipping*

See also **prefixes and suffixes**; **stress**; **US spelling**; **vowel/consonant**.

**constitute** See **compose/comprise/constitute**.

**contact** There are two meanings of *contact* that are relatively modern. One is to get in touch with:

> I'll contact you next week.

The other is to describe a person who might be useful:

> Leonora is a good business contact.

Both uses are acceptable in formal as well as informal contexts.

**contagious/infectious** *Contagious* diseases are transmitted by physical contact between people or things: mumps is *contagious*. *Infectious* diseases are transmitted by organisms in air or water, or by insects – in fact by any means, including contagion: influenza is *infectious*. Used figuratively the words are synonymous:

> The crowd's enthusiasm was contagious [*or* infectious].

**containerise** To *containerise* is to transport cargo in large standard-size box-shaped containers.

**contemporary** The primary meaning of the adjective *contemporary* is living or occurring at the same time; as a noun it means a person living at the same time as another:

> Tom Roberts and Arthur Streeton were contemporary artists; Albert Tucker and Arthur Boyd were contemporaries of a later generation.

A secondary meaning, living or occurring at the *present* time, has resulted in the widely accepted connotation of up-to-the-minute modernity:

> The unit has delightful contemporary furnishings.

Since the twofold meaning may produce ambiguity, use the adjective carefully. A contemporary opinion of Rembrandt's works could mean the opinion of one of his seventeenth-century contemporaries, or of a twentieth-century critic.

**contempt** *Contempt* consists of words or conduct that are considered likely to obstruct or interfere with the fair administration of justice; or that show disrespect for, or disobedience to, the ruling of a court, whether the proceedings are criminal or civil.

Journalists in particular are urged to keep abreast of the latest implications of this law, as infringements may lead to very costly and time-consuming prosecution.

Misreporting court proceedings can constitute contempt if it is likely to prejudice a fair trial. Under the sub judice rule, publication of articles that prejudge issues in a pending trial, or that reveal any investigation of a crime before or during a trial, is a contempt of court. Comments on the character or behaviour of an accused person that are likely to influence jurors or potential jurors and therefore prejudice a fair trial may also be in contempt of court.

It does not have to be proved that a published article actually prejudiced a trial for it to amount to contempt; it is enough to show that its publication was likely to do so. Where a published article is held to be in contempt, not only the writer but anyone associated with its publication – the newspaper owner, publisher, editor, printer or distributor – may be held liable.

In Australia journalists cannot claim *privilege,* or the right to withhold details about the source of their information, although a court can be requested to make an order preserving such confidentiality. A journalist who does not comply with a court order to disclose the name of a source may be held in contempt of court and face the possibility of a gaol sentence, a fine, or both.

The law of contempt also applies to both houses of the Federal Parliament and some State Parliaments, which have the power to punish offenders who obstruct or interfere with their duties or their members. A contempt can include an attempt to 'exert improper influence' on a member or a parliamentary witness; unauthorised publication of evidence taken by a parliamentary committee in camera, or of a confidential document; and a wilful misrepresentation of parliamentary proceedings.

See also **defamation**.

**contemptible/contemptuous** *Contemptible* means deserving contempt:

> The murder of prisoners of war is contemptible.

*Contemptuous* means showing contempt, scorn or disdain:

> Contemptuous glares followed the person who jumped the TAB queue.

Use the construction contemptuous *of*, not *about*.

**contents** See **publications, parts of**.

**continent/Continent** There are seven landmasses known as *continents*. Europe is one of them, but it is the only one referred to as *the Continent*. The adjectives *continental* and *Continental* maintain the distinction.

**continual/continuous** These two are not quite interchangeable. *Continual* means recurrent, usually at short intervals:

> Continual noisy disturbances made concentration impossible.

*Continuous* describes an uninterrupted sequence:

> During our walk we heard continuous birdsong.

Note that *continuous* (not *continual*) should be used in an example such as the following:

> He unwound a continuous length of wire from the coil.

**continue** See **still**.

**contractions** See **abbreviations and contractions**.

**contracts** These are formal agreements, oral or written, between two or more parties. In publishing, *contracts* set out matters such as financial arrangements and the terms and conditions under which copyright material may be used. Oral contracts may be upheld in a court of law, but it is advisable for writers and publishers (or film and stage producers) to put their agreements in writing because oral agreements are very difficult to prove. Furthermore copyright law does not recognise an unwritten assignment of rights.

If a contract is set out clearly, and all parties understand the same thing by its terms, there are usually no difficulties. Writers should read contracts very carefully to make sure they understand exactly what rights they are licensing or assigning (selling), and what warranties and indemnities they are committing themselves to. *Licensing* and *assignment* are further explained below.

It is recommended, therefore, that a writer should seek expert advice before signing a contract. Writers who have literary agents acting for them have such expertise on tap, but there are other sources of help. The Australian Society of Authors and the Australian Writers' Guild have prepared standard contracts, which at least suggest a basis for negotiation, and both provide a contract advisory service. The Australian Copyright Council offers a free contract review service as well as useful literature. Most publishers and producers have standard house contracts that can be used as they stand or adapted to suit all parties; or a negotiated agreement may be drawn up.

Publishing contracts may include clauses dealing with such things as the date for the delivery of manuscript; time and methods of payment; specification of the rights granted; grounds for terminating the contract; and processes for settling disputes. To avoid any possible ambiguity about the licensing or assignment of rights, contracts should include a clause specifying that any legal rights not expressly given up or otherwise affected by the contract are reserved (that is, retained) by the author. It is also important for writers to know whether or not they retain ownership of copyright in their works.

Book contracts sometimes give a date for intended publication. Those that are signed prior to receipt of a manuscript usually allow the publisher an opportunity for final approval of the manuscript on its arrival, to ensure that the work is up to standard. The contract should specify whether or not the writer is required to repay any advance royalties received, and whether or not he or she is free to offer the work to another publisher if the manuscript is rejected at this point. Script contracts should also cover the conditions under which a script 'buy back' would operate if a play or film were not produced within a specified time.

***Licensing and assignment*** An important part of any contract is the clause covering the *licensing* or the *assignment* of rights in a work. The writer is generally the first owner of copyright and can dispose of this right in various ways, either by licensing others to use the work for a certain purpose or time or in a specified place, or by assigning the right (that is, selling it as a whole or in part). A licence of copyright permits the licensee to use the copyright material under certain terms and conditions, whereas assignment transfers the ownership of the specified rights to the other party. A licence can be exclusive (that is, licensed to one party only) or non-exclusive (that is, licensed to several parties independently). Licensing is often preferable to assignment and in the writer's best interests because the writer thereby retains rights in and control over the use of his or her work. However, some publishers or producers may only be interested in a contract that assigns them the specific right they require, which under the terms of the contract may be the right to publish or produce for the legal term of the copyright or other specified time. Film producers usually insist on ownership of the specific portion of the copyright they require and therefore request an assignment of the rights, because they do not want to put the large sums of money involved in film-making at risk over copyright disputes. If a writer assigns copyright to a publisher or producer, the publisher or producer becomes the owner of that portion of the copyright that has been assigned.

***Subsidiary rights*** The clauses covering subsidiary rights (that is, the rights to translate, serialise, make a film of a book and so on) should be considered carefully. Many writers throw these rights away, not realising that they can be far more valuable than their publication rights. They may be included in a publishing agreement if the writer feels that the publisher is in the best position to exploit them. A contract should state clearly how income derived from the sale of these rights will be divided, as the publisher may be entitled to retain a percentage of the receipts. The contract should also specify the degree of consultation and approval required by the writer prior to the sale of any subsidiary right.

***Royalties and advances*** Book publishers usually pay their writers by way of a royalty, which is a percentage that may be based on the recommended retail price of the book, or the publisher's net receipts, or a combination of the two. If the same percentage is involved, calculations based on the recommended retail price will give the writer the best return. As it can be years after a contract is signed before royalties start to flow from sales, most publishers give the writer advances against royalties. Writers of scripts, articles and short stories are usually paid by fee. Film writers may also be able to negotiate for a share in a film's net profit, but this should be in addition to a fee.

***Other clauses*** Most publishers and producers require writers to warrant in a contract that their work is original, that they own the copyright (that is, their work is not subject to any other agreement), and that the work is not obscene or defamatory. Writers are required to indemnify the publisher or producer against loss or damage resulting from a breach of these warranties, so they must be examined closely and taken seriously by the writer.

A contract may be terminated by either party in circumstances described in the contract itself. The usual reasons for termination are that the writer does not deliver the work as contracted; that the publisher or producer fails to make payments as agreed; or that a book goes out of print and the publisher fails to reprint within a specified time. The methods for settling disputes arising from a breach of contract or other disagreements are usually included in the terms of the contract.

See also **copyright**; **defamation**; **obscenity**.

**contractual** This adjective from *contract* does not have a second *r* (not 'contractural').

**contra deal** An agreement to provide goods or services in exchange for other goods or services rather than money (traditionally called bartering) is sometimes described as a *contra deal*.

**contrast** The verb means to distinguish by comparing different or opposite qualities; the noun means the distinction or emphasis of difference:

> The reporter contrasted the winter temperatures of Darwin and Hobart, and noted the contrast between clothes being worn in the two cities.

A contrast is a kind of comparison, but comparison includes likeness as well as difference.

See also **compare to/compare with**.

**control keys** These are special computer keys used to modify the functions of other keys, usually when they are pressed at the same time.

See also **function keys**.

**controversy** Put the stress on *con-*.

**convalescence** Note the *-esc-* and *-ce*.

**convener/convenor** Either spelling is acceptable, but *convener* is preferred.

**converse/inverse/obverse/reverse** The following examples illustrate the different uses for these four words, which as nouns and adjectives reflect aspects of the word *opposite*. *Converse* expresses the reversal of an action or idea:

> You tell me that you are happy with Peter, but is the converse true: is Peter happy with you?

*Inverse* may have a technical or a general meaning:

> The inverse order of 123 is 321.
>
> Inverse snobbery made her refuse the invitation to the vice-regal garden party when it finally came.

*Obverse* is the most often misunderstood:

> Make sure you photocopy the obverse [that is, the face] of the form; the other side [the reverse] is blank.

The word can also be used to mean counterpart.

*Reverse* can be used more generally than the other three; it may be a verb as well as a noun and adjective:

> They reversed the trend towards high-rise flats by building many small houses to be rented cheaply.
>
> Yesterday was hot; today it is the reverse – bitterly cold!
>
> Put the car into reverse gear and back into that space.

See also **reversal/reversion**.

**conversion tables** See **weights and measures**.

**converted graphics files** In desktop publishing, graphics files may have to be converted before being placed in other software programs because different programs require different types of file. Some of the typical formats include EPS file (which means Encapsulated PostScript file); TIFF (Tagged Image File Format); RIFF (Raster Image File Format); and PICT (an abbreviation of *picture*).

See also **encapsulated PostScript; graphics**.

**conveyer/conveyor** Either spelling is acceptable, but *conveyor* is recommended.

**convince/persuade** To *convince* people of something is to make them believe in it:

> Emma's arrival at the party convinced Olaf that she had completely recovered from the fever.

To *persuade* people to do something is to induce them to, even if they do not believe in it:

> I persuaded the ballerina to come to the football, although she was not convinced that she would enjoy it.

*Persuade* may be followed by *of*, *that* or *to*. *Convince* may be followed by *of* or *that*, but must not be followed by *to*, although some journalists have an unhappy tendency to assume that it can be.

**Coolac, NSW** Compare with *Colac*, Vic.

**Coonawarra, SA and NT** (Naval Base) Compare with *Koonwarra*, Vic.

**cooperate** See **collaborate/cooperate**.

**copy editing** This procedure entails the assembling, checking, and where necessary correcting of text for publication. Its chief purpose is to ensure that the writer's message is expressed clearly, and to minimise errors that would be expensive to rectify later in the production process. In book publishing an editor often oversees the production of a book from its conception to the receipt of printed copies. A second editor is sometimes entrusted with the copy editing since it may be more time-consuming than any other part of the work. Any editor is likely to be described as a copy editor while engaged in editing copy, even if some other title (such as senior editor) normally applies.

The principles of copy editing are the same whether you are marking a typescript with a pen or, as is increasingly common today, keying in corrections on a word processor. The main tasks of a copy editor are as follows:

- to assess the structure of the work with regard to its organisation and completeness
- to ensure that the work is accurate (though this is primarily the author's responsibility) and expressed clearly
- to check that it does not contain any material that is libellous or in breach of copyright
- to identify and correct inconsistencies, grammatical errors, and infelicities of style such as repetition, ambiguity and jargon
- to ensure that the material sent to a typesetter is complete, and that any instructions are clearly marked
- to make sure that production deadlines are met
- to brief the designer on the most appropriate look for the publication; in desktop publishing there may be no designer and the editor is likely to be responsible for the design, often in conjunction with the keyboard operator (this procedure is not recommended, however)

The main qualifications for a copy editor include the following.

***Language skills*** A sound knowledge of the English language and its more subtle points of style is a fundamental qualification for a copy editor.

***Sensitivity*** As most authors expend a good deal of thought and effort on their work, an editor should be tactful when suggesting and making changes to the text. The editor is an intermediary only, and he or she should not interfere gratuitously with the author's style or the content of the material. The urge to rewrite an author's work completely must be resisted.

***Common sense*** The editor need not be an expert in the subject of the text but should approach it as an intelligent lay reader and query anything that is confusing or unintelligible. However, provided that the text is accurate and consistent, there is no merit in making numerous unnecessary changes.

***Flexibility*** Every publication has its own requirements and point of view, and an editor must remain open-minded about the most appropriate style, structure and form of presentation in each case. While there are firm rules about consistency in spelling and grammar, each work should in other respects be judged on its own terms.

***Attention to detail*** Much of the process of copy editing involves fairly time-consuming checking and tidying up of small points such as consistency in spelling, hyphenation and capitalisation. While this can be tedious it is very important, for inconsistency in apparently minor points will jar on the reader.

There are a few basic editing procedures that apply to all texts.

- Check, as soon as the manuscript arrives, that every page is numbered. An unnumbered manuscript dropped on the floor can take a long time to reassemble.
- First look quickly through the text to get a sense of its flow and the organisation of its main points. Any comments or suggestions on structural changes should be pencilled on the manuscript for discussion with the author, who often then carries out the decisions made, although some people are happy to delegate the task to a trusted editor.
- Detailed copy editing requires a scrupulous reading of the text for sense as well as for grammar, spelling and consistency. An invaluable aid is an editorial style guide, divided into alphabetical sections, in which you note the preferred style of spelling, capitalisation etc. for each variable word. The publisher's preferences on various points (the 'house style') will dictate some of these, but factors such as the tone of the work (educational, conversational, official?) will suggest others.
- If the preliminary pages are part of the copy editor's duties, imprint page details such as production acknowledgements and library cataloguing data (CIP) must be prepared.
- Check the selection and positioning of any illustrations or tables, and ensure that all headings, captions, notes, cross-references and bibliographic references are useful, accurate, consistent, and in the correct order. Grade headings A, B, C etc. to help the designer to understand their roles.
- If the text is to be typeset from hard copy, editorial changes should be marked clearly in ballpoint or felt-tip pen once firmly decided. Write them as close as possible to the original words, using the margins for spillover only. Queries for the author or designer should be written in pencil so that they can be erased before typesetting. Any instructions should be circled so that they are not mistaken for part of the text to be typeset.
- If the text is to be given to the typesetter in the form of a computer disk accompanied by hard copy, it is advisable to write final corrections for the disk, and special instructions for the typesetter, in a conspicuous colour. Try not to obscure the existing type with your corrections.

For complex texts with many elements, it is often advisable to draw up a checklist of the editorial tasks to be done, incorporating all the points made here and any others peculiar to the particular publication (there may be copyright permissions to be sought, for example).

See also **bibliographic style**; **bibliographies**; **caption**; **copy, presentation of**; **copyright**; **defamation**; **desktop publishing**; **indexing**; **layout**; **marking up**; **notes**; **obscenity**; **permissions**; **proofs**; **publications, parts of**; **quotations**; **reference marks**; **references**.

**copy, presentation of** Good presentation of copy simplifies the early stages in the publishing process, and can save time and money. Manuscripts that are typeset in the traditional way from hard copy are prepared and presented quite differently from those that are supplied in electronic form – on computer disk, or directly via a modem into the typesetter's computer.

***Traditional presentation of copy*** All manuscript (including footnotes, captions and any other special material) should be typed, double-spaced, on one side of the paper only, with generous margins around the copy. Paper should be sufficiently heavy to withstand substantial wear and tear, and be of a uniform size, preferably A4. Do not staple, pin or tape the pages, but keep them together in a folder, perhaps secured with an alligator clip.

Textual amendments should be clearly written or typed within the copy. Try not to write in the margins. If alterations are lengthy it is often necessary to retype a section and paste the new copy over the original. If the alteration is longer than the original, an additional page may be slotted in: if it follows page 95, for example, label it 95a. Every page, of course, needs a number. Handwritten copy should be avoided, except for textual amendments. Do not leave unmarked blank sections at the tops or bottoms of pages as these may be mistaken for the endings of sections or chapters, or thought to indicate missing copy: always join blank sections to preceding or following copy with a run-on line.

If any part of the copy is unusual – for example, eccentric word usage or intentional misspelling – indicate it by placing a tick over the word or words concerned. A tick placed above a hyphen occurring at the end of a line tells the typesetter to retain it. End-of-line words that are to be closed up in the typeset version should be indicated with linking marks. All instructions to the typesetter should be circled to prevent their being mistaken for part of the text. Chapter titles and text subheadings should be clearly indicated, and even at this stage may be graded A, B, C (and so on) and marked accordingly.

The top copy should be submitted for editing and setting; a second copy may be required by the publisher. Always keep a photocopy (a backup disk needs to be kept if the hard copy was generated by computer).

***Presentation of copy on computer disk*** If copy is being presented on a computer disk for typesetting or desktopping, there are certain procedures that will generally save time and expense. One of the most important is that authors should supply, with their disk, a printout that exactly matches the disk in every way – content, wording and sequence. This manuscript can then be edited on the hard copy and corrected on screen, or edited and corrected on screen. Authors need to discuss details of presentation with their publishers, because requirements differ. The following guidelines will not suit all cases but are a basis for discussion.

- On a disk to be presented to a typesetter, use hard carriage returns only at the ends of headlines, subheadings or paragraphs. Soft or hard returns can be used as required if the disk is to be presented to a desktop publishing (DTP) operator. It is preferable not to add a line of space between paragraphs, as this only inserts an unnecessary hard return. If the writer has inserted double returns, perhaps for ease of reading either on the screen or from hard copy, it is a simple matter to use the 'search and replace' facility to remove them and substitute singles.

- If presenting a word-processed disk to a traditional typesetter, do not use hard page breaks because they insert a code that will have to be deleted. It is acceptable to use them if the disk is being presented to a DTP operator.
- Do not use tabs to indent the beginning of a paragraph. Use no more than one tab to separate columns of text or figures, even if the columns do not line up on screen, otherwise all extraneous tabs will have to be removed – an unnecessary expense. The columns can be lined up by using the tabbing facility of the word-processing package. A DTP operator can insert the correct tabs at the time of page makeup.
- If presenting work to a traditional typesetter, do not justify type. A DTP operator can accept justified or unjustified type. Some word-processing programs, particularly for DOS-based platforms, are sold with justification as the default setting. If most of your work is going to be handled by a traditional typesetter, it may be worth changing the default to unjustified – either permanently when you install the program or before you start your word processing.
- If presenting a word-processed disk to a traditional typesetter, you should use hyphens only for compound nouns and compound adjectives. Do not break words at the end of a line. In desktop publishing, hyphenation at the end of a line is acceptable, but only if you use soft hyphens. Otherwise hyphenate as for traditional typesetters.
- If presenting a disk to a traditional typesetter, any codes for automatic running heads or feet, or for page numbering, should be removed after printing out the final hard copy. This is not necessary if presenting a disk to a DTP operator.
- If presenting copy to a traditional typesetter, do not use attributes such as italic, bold and underlining; mark your requirements on the hard copy. However, it is acceptable, even preferable, to use the attributes if presenting a disk to a DTP operator.
- If you are presenting copy to a traditional typesetter, dashes are best represented by a hyphen or double hyphen with a space on either side. These can then be marked up on the hard copy as en or em dashes as appropriate. For DTP, the appropriate dash can be generated by a keyboard command and requires no further conversion. If the writer or word-processing operator has keyed in the dash as 'space hyphen space', which is a common practice, it is a simple matter to search this out and replace it with the appropriate dash, with or without spaces on either side, depending on the design specifications.
- If the disk is to be presented to a traditional typesetter and your keyboard only has word-processing double inverted commas (sometimes called 'rabbit's ears') and an apostrophe, use the double quotation marks in preference to two apostrophes. This is not necessary when word processing for DTP. There are keyboard commands for a true inverted comma – single or double, opening

and closing – and for a true apostrophe, the latter being the same as a single closing inverted comma.

- For a traditional typesetter, accents are best written on the hard copy and brought to the attention of the typesetter. However, in DTP this is not usually necessary. If the work is word processed on a Macintosh, for example, and the DTP will be performed on a Macintosh, the accents can be keyed in by the writer or word-processing operator. Accents can be inserted using keyboard commands.
- Use a single space after a full stop, not the two spaces often used by typists in writing letters, for example. Never use spaces where tabs should be used, or to line up columns of text or figures.
- Divide your disk copy into manageable and recognisable files of no more than about thirty printed pages. A new file for each chapter or major section is usually the best sort of division. Provide the typesetter or the DTP bureau or operator with a printout of the directory (that is, list) of files on the disk you are sending.
- Make backup copies of your disks and keep them in a safe place. It is a good idea to keep a copy in a place other than your working premises if possible. Never rely on your hard disk as your only backup.

See also **ASCII**; **bureau (desktop publishing)**; **copy editing**; **desktop publishing**; **disk conversion**; **marking up**.

**copy protection** Companies producing computer software discourage infringement of software copyright by a system of *copy protection* that makes illegal copying of the disk, usually referred to as *pirating*, difficult – sometimes impossible. Different programs have different methods of maintaining copy protection.

See also **copyright**; **pirating**; **software copyright**.

**copyright** *Copyright* is the protection afforded to the creator of an original work under the *Commonwealth Copyright Act 1968*. This provides protection for a wide range of literary, musical, dramatic and artistic works, which includes sound recordings, films, television and radio programs, and published editions. For copyright purposes literary works include catalogues, instruction manuals and computer software as well as novels, poetry and song lyrics. Copyright protects the original form of expression in a work, but does not protect the ideas or information the work contains.

To qualify for copyright in Australia, a work must be original and created by an Australian citizen or resident, or first published in Australia. Works by authors of other nationalities are protected if their countries have reciprocal copyright arrangements with Australia under the Berne Convention for the Protection of Literary and Artistic Works, or the Universal Copyright Convention.

*Original* means that the work must be the author's own, not copied; it does not have to display 'original' ideas, be particularly inventive or of any great quality. For example, a letter between friends or the wording of an advertisement is granted the protection of copyright. Copyright in Australia applies automatically the moment a work is recorded in some way: the work does not have to be published, and there are no formalities or registration procedures.

Copyright law in other countries is not identical with Australia's, and it is essential to seek advice from the publisher prior to publication there. This is especially important if an Australian author is considering publishing first overseas, given recent amendments to the Australian Copyright Act with regard to importing books into Australia.

It is not obligatory in Australia to place a notice of copyright claim on all publicly distributed copies of a work, but it is strongly recommended that this be done – to ensure copyright protection, and to make it easy to trace the copyright owner when applying for permission to use the work (though it is preferable to contact the publisher in the first instance). The internationally recognised form of the notice consists of the © symbol, followed by the name of the copyright owner and the year of first publication, as in:

© Penguin Books Australia Ltd 1993

This claim should be included on the reverse of the title page of a published work.

*Copyright ownership* The first owner of copyright in a work is its author or creator, except when the work is created in an individual's capacity as an employee, in which case the employer owns the copyright. However, when the author is a journalist employed by a newspaper, the employer owns copyright only for publication in a newspaper or magazine, or for broadcasting; the journalist retains the rights for other purposes, such as publication in a book (the rules regarding split ownership were, however, under review in late 1992). If an author creates a work as an independent contractor for a newspaper, the copyright remains with the author. Note that where a work is created or first published under the direction or control of the Government, the Government owns copyright. In cases other than these, the ownership of copyright in a particular publication can be a matter of agreement between the parties involved.

*Copyright assignment* Copyright is personal property and a divisible asset. The owner can dispose of copyright by assigning (selling) it or just a part-interest of it; can license someone – such as a publisher – to use it for a limited period or purpose; and can bequeath it in a will, like any other asset. Copyright is assigned by contract, which should specify the rights assigned. For instance, the author of a novel may assign exclusive television rights to one producer and theatrical rights to another.

*Copyright duration* Copyright in a literary, dramatic or musical work published during the creator's lifetime exists from the date of publication until fifty years after the creator's death (at the end of the calendar year). If a work is published after the creator's death, copyright exists for fifty years after publication. Where there are two or more creators, copyright continues until fifty years after the death of the creator who dies last. These rules apply regardless of whether or not the copyright has been assigned to another party. Copyright duration for material other than literary, dramatic or musical works is different, however.

***Fair dealing*** The permission of the owner or owners is required by law if a copyright work is to be used by another party, unless an exception applies, such as the *fair dealing* provisions of the Copyright Act. The Act provides for a portion of a work to be reproduced without permission for the non-commercial purposes of criticism or review, news reporting, or research and private study. Unfortunately there is no provision in the Act for deciding what is a fair portion, and the only safe course is for the intending user to seek permission for any substantial reproduction. Even if a relatively small part of a work is used, it is wise as well as polite to acknowledge the source. Anyone needing advice on the use of copyright material can contact the Australian Copyright Council, Suite 3, 245 Chalmers Street, Redfern, NSW, 2016.

***Photocopying*** Photocopying can be an infringement of copyright, although the Copyright Act makes exceptions in certain cases. Educational institutions may make multiple copies of copyright works for teaching purposes by virtue of a compulsory licensing procedure under which they pay a fee to the Copyright Agency Limited, which disburses money to authors and publishers based on a sample of copying. Photocopying for the purpose of research or private study is also permitted if it comes under the Act's fair dealing provisions. The Copyright Agency Limited is at Level 19, 157 Liverpool Street, Sydney, NSW, 2000.

See also **business names/trade names/trademarks**; **contracts**; **copy protection**; **permissions**; **quotations**; **software copyright**.

**cord** See **chord/cord**.

**cordial** In Australia this is a soft drink but in the US it is an alcoholic liqueur.
See also **liqueur/liquor**.

**co-respondent/correspondent** A *co-respondent* is a person alleged to have committed adultery with the respondent in a divorce case. Since the passage of the *Commonwealth Family Law Act 1975*, co-respondents have ceased to be legally relevant. The prefix *co-* is pronounced separately as 'ko'.

A *correspondent* is a person who communicates by letter, or who is the official supplier of news reports from a distant area, or of copy on a specific subject such as gardening.

**corollary** Note the spelling. Technically speaking, a *corollary* is a proposition that follows from another that has been proved; it is more commonly used simply to mean a result:

> Drought in Australia may be a corollary of the El Nino phenomenon in the Pacific.

**corporal/corporeal** These adjectives both refer to the human body but are not interchangeable. Sensations affecting the body are often called *corporal*:

*corporal pleasures*; *corporal punishment*. The tangible nature of the body – physical in contrast to spiritual – may be described as *corporeal*:

They believed that after the soul had left, what remained was purely corporeal.

See also **capital punishment/corporal punishment**.

**corporate raider** A *corporate raider* is someone who makes a practice of buying large parcels of shares in listed companies in order to imply that a take-over is imminent; then, having forced up the price, the raider sells at a profit. Corporate raiding was rampant in the 1980s.

**corps/corpse/corpus** All these nouns mean body, but they are not interchangeable. Note the following examples: *army corps* (rhyming with *core*); *a rotting corpse*; *a corpus of writing* (meaning a collection).

**correlate** Note the spelling. *Correlate* most commonly means to place or be placed in a mutual or reciprocal relationship:

Australian scientists will correlate international findings on the drug.

Pronounce it '**korr**a-late', not '**ko**-relate'.

**correspondence** See **letters, formal**.

**corrigenda** See **errata/corrigenda**.

**corroborate** This verb meaning to make certain or confirm should not be confused with *collaborate:*

The hockey umpire asked the goalie to corroborate her view that a goal had been scored.

See also **collaborate/cooperate**.

**corrupt** In computer parlance the terms *corrupt* and *corruption* refer to a fault in a program or file that may render it useless. Corruption is an important reason for making backup copies.

See also **backup; data retrieval**.

**cosmetic** Strictly speaking, the adjective *cosmetic* means beautifying the body (especially the face). It has become a cliché for a superficial or small change in anything from a recipe to legislation. Alternatives worth considering are *small*, *minor*, *token*, *inconsequential* and, of course, *superficial*.

**cosset/cosseted/cosseting** Note the single *t* in all three. *Cosset* is a kindly synonym for *pamper*: *cosseting my dear old mother.*

**cost/price** These nouns are frequently interchangeable, although *price* is more literal than *cost*, which is more commonly used for abstract things and overall amounts:

the price of books *but* the cost of education
the price of groceries *but* the cost of living

Either word may be used to describe a sacrifice or effort needed to achieve something:

No price is too high for freedom.
We shall defend our homeland, whatever the cost may be.

**council/counsel** A *council* (a noun, never a verb) is a group of people meeting for discussion: *a council of war*; or a body appointed to serve in an advisory or administrative capacity: *a municipal council.* Members of the second kind of *council* are called *councillors.*

The noun *counsel* means judicious advice: *wise counsel.* Someone who provides it is a *counsellor*: *marriage guidance counsellor. Counsel* (singular only) is also the name given to a barrister or group of barristers advising on legal points and representing someone in court: *counsel for the defendant.* To *keep your own counsel* means to keep your opinion to yourself. Note also the verb *to counsel*:

The doctor counselled him on his drug problem.

See also **advice/advise/counsel.**

**counterfeit** Note the *-ei-* in the final syllable.

**course** See **coarse/course.**

**court martial** This term for a military court follows one of the normal rules for compound nouns when they are in the plural: *courts martial.* When the term is used as an adjective or verb a hyphen is added: *a court-martial matter*; *to be court-martialled.*

See also **compound nouns, plurals of.**

**Coy** See **Co./Coy.**

**CPA** Communist Party of Australia (disbanded 1991).

**CPI** This is the abbreviation for *consumer price index*, a series of numbers that shows, in relative terms, the extent to which the prices of certain goods and services, in successive periods, have increased since a given earlier period (the base period). The prices are those of a fixed collection (*basket*) of retail goods and services purchased by 'typical' metropolitan households.

**CPL/Cpl** Corporal.

**CPO** Chief Petty Officer.

**CPU** See **central processing unit.**

**CRA** CRA Limited (before 1980, Conzinc Riotinto).

**Cranbrook, Qld, Tas. and WA** Compare with *Cranebrook*, NSW.

**crashed/gone down** When a computer is said to have *crashed* or *gone down*, it has stopped working or is not working properly. Crashing is usually caused by a fault in the system or the program software.
See also **hung (computer)**.

**CRC** See **camera-ready art/camera-ready copy**.

**credibility gap** This near-cliché means the difference between what is said or promised (often by a politician) and what is meant or done:

> There was a credibility gap between the government's statements on conservation and its attitude to logging.

**credible/creditable/credulous** *Credible* means believable or trustworthy; its opposite is *incredible*:

> Marietta's autobiography was astonishing but credible.
> Ahmed will be a credible witness.
> It was incredible that the deckhand could have swum 25 kilometres.

*Creditable* means bringing credit, praiseworthy; its opposite is *discreditable*:

> Putting out the bushfire so quickly was a creditable feat.
> Starting a bushfire – even unintentionally – is a discreditable act for a firefighter.

*Credulous* means gullible, too ready to believe; *incredulous* (*at* or *of*) means unable to believe:

> The credulous students expected selling encyclopaedias to be easy.
> The students were incredulous at the poor demand for encyclopaedias.

See also **incredible/incredulous**.

**crescendo** A *crescendo* is a gradual increase in loudness (particularly in music) or intensity; it describes the movement towards a climax, but not the climax itself:

> The crescendo of the percussion reached a thunderous climax.
> Publicity for the project brought about a crescendo in donations, from $500 a week to $5000.

Note that the phrase *a rising crescendo* is tautological, and that you cannot *reach a crescendo*. Pronounce the *sc* in *crescendo* as 'sh'.

**crevasse/crevice** A *crevasse* is a deep cleft, especially in the ice of a glacier: *The sled plunged into a crevasse.* A *crevice* is a narrow cleft in, for example, the earth, a rock or ice: *Tiny wildflowers filled the crevice.*

**crippling** Pronounced '**krip**-ling', not 'krip-el-ing'.

**crisis** A *crisis* is a decisive stage in the course of anything, or a turning point:

> The people's support of Solidarity caused a political crisis in Poland.
>
> The crisis in her pneumonia came at dawn.

*Crisis* is often misused to describe a situation that is merely difficult or worrying. Especially try to resist using the cliché *crisis of confidence*. The plural of *crisis* is *crises* (pronounced '**kry**-seez').

**criterion** The plural is *criteria*. Note that a *criterion* is a standard or principle by which something is judged; it is not a mere requirement:

> Gina grew carrots that matched the criterion of the seed packet photograph.
>
> Klaus will be aiming high to meet the criteria of honesty and diligence set by his uncle.

There is no such thing as 'a criteria' (use the singular *a criterion*), or 'criterias'.

**critic/critique** A *critic* is a person who judges something, especially literary or artistic works:

> The critics praised the Australian Ballet's production of *Le Carnaval*.

In other contexts a *critic* is understood to be someone whose judgements are always unfavourable:

> Improved trade figures will quieten the government's critics.

A *critique* is an article or essay judging something; the word is often used where *review* would be more appropriate:

> Her review [*not* critique] of opportunities in the building trade was timely.

Do not use *critique* as a verb.

**critical/crucial** In the sense of involving a decisive stage or a turning point, these adjectives are virtually synonymous:

> Some people believe that the Eureka Stockade was a critical [*or* crucial] event in Australia's history.

*Crucial* is the stronger word. It should not be used merely to mean important.

**critique** See **critic/critique**.

**Cromalin proofs** A *Cromalin proof* (referred to as a *Cromalin*) is a colour proof made from separated film for a client to approve (and as a guide to the printer) before the film goes for platemaking. This is an expensive form of proofing and is not recommended for the early proofing stages. A Cromalin is essential for final proofing of book covers, magazines, high-quality brochures, colour material in books – in fact any work that is using full colour – before the commencement of the print run.

**crop marks** *Crop marks* (sometimes called *trim marks* or *cut marks*) are used in printing to indicate the boundaries of each page – that is, where pages are to be trimmed. Fine lines 5–10 millimetres long will do.

If you are a desktop publisher outputting to bromide or film, advise your bureau that you want A4 output with crop marks. If you do not specify crops your A4 page will be sitting in the middle of large amounts of white space, and either you or the printer will have to make up a grid and mark every page for crops, a time-consuming and costly exercise.

If your page is smaller than A4 most page-makeup programs will ask you whether or not the document is to be printed with crop marks. Setting up a template for your document will automatically provide you with crop marks on these smaller pages.

See also **bureau (desktop publishing); template**.

**cropping** This word has a specific publishing sense: the elimination of parts of an illustration not required for reproduction. A designer might decide, for instance, to *crop* the photograph of a man at his waist or just below his tie.

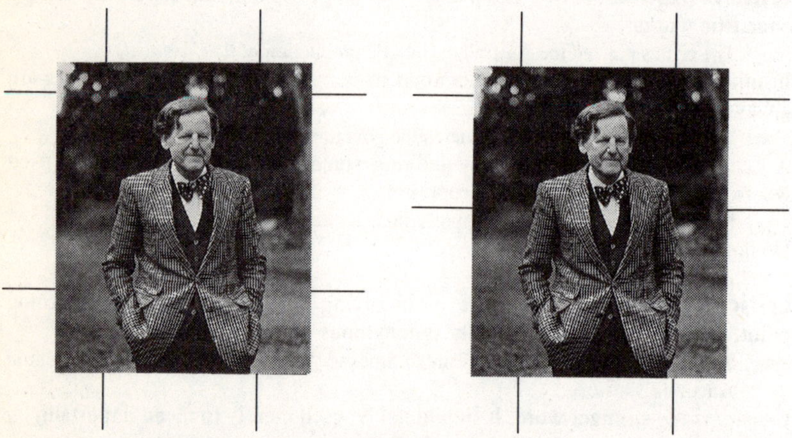

***Alternative croppings of a photograph (at waist or chest level)***

**cross-section** A non-technical meaning of the word *cross-section* is a typical or representative sample showing all characteristic parts:

The sample was a cross-section of viewers' opinions.

*Cross-section* should always be hyphenated.

**Crown/crown** Give the institution an initial capital, but the royal headware lower case.

**crucial** See **critical/crucial**.

**crux** The plural of *crux* (Latin for cross) is *cruxes* or *cruces*. The *crux* of something is a basic or decisive point in it: *the crux of the problem*. Remember that *crux* rhymes with *ducks*, not *chooks*.

**cryo-** This prefix is derived from a Greek word that means frozen – hence *cryogenics*, the study of materials and phenomena at very low temperatures. The term *cryopreservation* has been popularised because of its application in the freezing of sperm, ova and embryos.

**CSIRO** Commonwealth Scientific and Industrial Research Organisation.

**CSM** company sergeant-major.

**CSR** CSR Limited (until 1973, the Colonial Sugar Refining Co. Limited).

**CST** Central Standard Time.
See also **time zones**.

**cuisine** The French word *cuisine* is too often used where the perfectly good English words *cookery* or *cooking* would be more appropriate. It is correct, however, to describe the style of cooking of a particular country, region or restaurant as its *cuisine*: *Thai cuisine*. Some specialised forms of cooking – *cuisine minceur* and *nouvelle cuisine*, for example – have retained their French names long after spreading from their country of origin. The word is pronounced 'kwee-**zeen**'.

**culminate** This verb means to reach the highest point of development:

> Her studies in engineering culminated in the award of a doctorate.

*Culminate* does not mean to conclude: industrial strife cannot *culminate in a compromise*, but it may *conclude* or *end* in one.

**cultivated/cultured** Both *cultivated* and *cultured* may refer to refinement, the first implying a degree of deliberation and the second particularly relating to appreciation of the arts:

> Her cultivated manners were the result of hard work, not upbringing.
> The truly cultured have no need to show off their knowledge.

Another meaning of both words is grown or produced: note that we speak of *cultivated plants* but *cultured pearls*.

**cumquat/kumquat** Either spelling is acceptable for this citrus fruit, but the first is recommended.

**curb/kerb** The verb *to curb* means to restrain or control: *Curb your appetite and remain willowy*. A *kerb* is the edge of a pavement, hence *kerbing* and *kerbstones*. Do not use the US spelling *curb* for this word.

**curio** Plural *curios*.

**Currajong, Qld** Compare with *Kurrajong*, NSW.

**currency** Australian currency is expressed in dollars and cents. The recommended style for figures is as follows:

$5 *or* $5.00 (for full dollars)

$5.05 $100.75 (for dollars and cents)

5c 75c (for cents)

Note the lower-case *c*; no full point; no space between the number and the *c*. The US cent sign (¢) is not used in Australia.

Millions of dollars may be written as:

$1 000 000 *or* $1m *or* $1 million

$1 250 000 *or* $1.25m *or* $1.25 million

Many people still use a comma to mark off groups of three digits, but a single space between each group is recommended instead, except where the total number of figures is only four, in which case no space is required:

$1 000 000 $125 234 $6007 $8315

It is necessary, however, to include a space between the first two digits of a four-digit figure when sums of money are set out in columns, so that the columns line up properly:

| $ |
|---:|
| 13 923 |
| 4 210 |
| 29 875 |
| 8 946 |

To distinguish between Australian currency and other dollar-denominated currencies, insert the capital letter A between the $ symbol and the amount: *$A50.*

Before February 1966 Australia's currency was expressed in pounds, shillings and pence, using the symbols £ s d (from the Latin *librae*, *solidi*, *denarii*). There were twelve pence (12d) in a shilling; twenty-four pence (24d) in a florin; two shillings and sixpence (2s 6d) in a half-crown; 240 pence or twenty shillings (20s) in a pound; and twenty-one shillings (21s or £1 1s 0d) in a guinea. The recommended style for Australia's former currency is £10 7s 6d, not £10/7/6.

Particular care should be taken when calculating decimal equivalents for pre-1966 currency in historical texts. Absurdities can easily arise. To write that *a farmhand earned £1 [$2] a week in 1870* takes no account of the real value of £1 in 1870 vis-à-vis today's currency.

The following is a select list of international currencies and their symbols.

| *Country* | *Currency* | *Symbol* |
|---|---|---|
| Argentina | Austral | ₳ |
| Australia | Dollar | $A |
| Austria | Schilling | Sch |
| Belgium | Franc | BF |

| *Country* | *Currency* | *Symbol* |
|---|---|---|
| Brazil | Cruzado | Cz |
| Cambodia | New Riel | C Rl |
| Canada | Dollar | C$ |
| China | Yuan | ¥ |
| Denmark | Krone | D Kr |
| Egypt | Pound | £E |
| Fiji | Dollar | $F |
| France | Franc | Fr |
| Germany | Deutschmark | DM |
| Greece | Drachma | Dr |
| Hong Kong | Dollar | HK$ |
| India | Rupee | IR |
| Indonesia | Rupiah | Rp |
| Iran | Rial | lR |
| Iraq | Dinar | ID |
| Ireland | Punt *or* Irish Pound | I£ *or* IR£ |
| Israel | New Sheqel | NIS |
| Italy | Lira | L |
| Japan | Yen | ¥ |
| Korea, North | Won | NK W |
| Korea, South | Won | SK W |
| Laos | Kip | Kp |
| Malaysia | Ringgit | M$ |
| Mexico | Peso | Mex$ |
| Netherlands | Guilder *or* Florin | Gld *or* Fl |
| New Caledonia | Franc | CFP Fr |
| New Zealand | Dollar | $NZ |
| Norway | Krone | N Kr |
| Pakistan | Rupee | PR |
| Papua New Guinea | Kina | K |
| Philippines | Peso | PP |
| Portugal | Escudo | Esc |
| Russia | Rouble | Rub |
| Saudi Arabia | Riyal | SR |
| Singapore | Dollar | S$ |
| South Africa | Rand | R |
| Spain | Peseta | Pa |
| Sweden | Krona | S Kr |
| Switzerland | Franc *or* Franken | S Fr |
| Taiwan | New Dollar | NT$ |
| Thailand | Baht | B |
| Tonga | Pa'anga | $T |
| Turkey | Lira | TL |

| *Country* | *Currency* | *Symbol* |
|---|---|---|
| UK | Pound *or* Pound stg | £ |
| USA | Dollar | $US |
| Vietnam | New Dong | D |

See also **billion; numbers in figures or words**.

**current/currently** Both the adjective *current* and the adverb *currently* are useful words that refer to the present time:

Current jet-engine technology is making new planes quieter.

The rock band is currently on tour but will take a break next year.

Often, however, these words unnecessarily duplicate the meaning of a verb: *I am currently employed by BHP*. If stress is really needed, *at present* or *now* may be more effective than *currently*.

See also **presently**.

**curriculum** Plural *curricula* or *curriculums*.

See also **cv**.

**cursor** A *cursor* is an electronic marker on a computer screen – usually a short blinking line or small rectangle – that shows where the next character to be typed will appear. The cursor moves along the line automatically as more characters are typed, or it can be moved to a new position by the operator, who uses arrow keys or a pointing device such as a mouse.

See also **mouse; trackball**.

**customer** See **client/customer**.

**cut in** Write a *cut in* pay rates, not a *cut to* pay rates.

**cv** This is an abbreviation of the Latin *curriculum vitae* (literally, the course of one's life). It is a brief description of a person's career, often required by potential employers. Another name for a cv is a résumé; neither is italicised. *Curriculum vitae* is pronounced 'ka-**rik**-yoolum **vee**-tie'.

See also **curriculum; résumé**.

**cv.** cultivar (botany).

**CWA** Country Women's Association.

**Cwlth** Commonwealth.

See also **Commonwealth**.

**cyan** The process colour blue, used in four-colour printing.

**cynic/sceptic** It is easy to confuse these two nouns (and their respective adjectives *cynical* and *sceptical*), partly because many *cynics* are also *sceptics* and vice versa. A *cynic* denies or doubts human goodness, and may demonstrate this by sarcasm or sneering:

> The philosophy lecturer was a cynic who declared that all churchgoers were hypocrites.

A *sceptic* doubts the validity of accepted beliefs, perhaps even his or her own:

> The social worker was a sceptic, unconvinced that medical science had changed life for the better.

The US spelling *skeptic* is not acceptable in Australian English, even though the word is pronounced '**skep**-tik'. Do not confuse *sceptic* with *septic*, an adjective that means infected by or dependent on bacteria (*septic sores*; *septic tank*).

**cypher** See **cipher/cypher**.

**cypress/Cyprus** The coniferous tree is the *cypress*; the island in the eastern Mediterranean is *Cyprus*.

**Czechoslovak** This is the adjective (not 'Czechoslovakian') as well as the noun.

# Dd

**D** 500 (roman numeral).
See also **roman numerals**.

**d** penny or pence (abbreviated from the Latin *denarius* or *denarii*).
See also **currency**.

**d.** date or dated (see also **dates**); dead or died.

**dais** Pronounce this name for a small platform '**day**-iss'.

**dangling participles/dangling phrases** There are two kinds of participle, present and past. The regular verb *to cook*, for example, has the present participle *cooking* and the past participle *cooked*; the irregular verb *to throw* has the participles *throwing* and *thrown*. Participles are often used as adjectives attached to the subject of the following verb. But sometimes they dangle, seemingly attached to the wrong word or totally unattached:

> Thrown out by the tenants, I knew the chair must be broken.

In this case the dangling participle *Thrown* appears to belong to the subject *I*, but really refers to *chair*. There are two correct versions of this sentence:

> Thrown out by the tenants, the chair, I knew, must be broken.

*or* I knew that the chair, thrown out by the tenants, must be broken.

Descriptive *phrases* are also left sadly dangling at times:

> A tall, strong young man, his mother knew he would be good at basketball.

The dangling phrase *A tall, strong young man* appears to belong to the subject, *his mother*. Rewrite as:

> He was a tall, strong young man and his mother knew he would be good at basketball.

Long use has allowed some phrases to be regarded as prepositions or conjunctions and therefore to bypass this rule. Here are some of the acceptable expressions:

*Speaking of* Belinda, she will be staying with her brother.

*Provided that* the chef is well, there will be a smorgasbord on Sunday.

*Given the circumstances*, you should be allowed to leave early.

*To tell the truth*, the wind is too strong for hang-gliding today.

See also **-ing forms**; **participles**.

**dashes, types of** There are two kinds of *dashes*: the *em rule* and the *en rule*. It is important for an editor to indicate the type of dash required. The *em rule* (—) is the longer dash, being the width of the square of the type body. The *en rule* (–) is approximately half the width of an *em* rule.

The punctuation type of dash, shown in all the examples in the following entry, **dashes, use of**, may be typeset in one of three ways, depending on the preference of the publisher. The 'house style' of the Australian Government Publishing Service is an *unspaced em rule*:

Smith was a man—a truly remarkable man—who knew no fear.

Others might choose a *spaced em rule*:

Smith was a man — a truly remarkable man — who knew no fear.

The house style of Penguin Books (and therefore of *Working Words*) is the *spaced en rule*:

Smith was a man – a truly remarkable man – who knew no fear.

The em rule is sometimes doubled in length to form a *2 em rule*. This is useful in a bibliography to indicate that the author's name is to be repeated:

Horne, Donald. *Money Made Us*. Penguin, Ringwood, 1976.

——*Winner Take All?*. Penguin, Ringwood, 1981.

A 2 em or 1½ em rule replaces letters or figures omitted for reasons of secrecy, or to avoid offending readers:

The agent met D—— at the restaurant in December 19——.

The bouncer was alleged to have told the men to f—— off.

The *en rule* is the more versatile dash. As well as being used by some publishers in a punctuating role, as we have seen, it has specific applications in:

- spans (to replace the word *to*)

  the years 1989–1992 pages 98–103 60–70 kilograms
- compound expressions where a hyphen would not do because the words retain a separate identity

  a Sydney–Melbourne flight Japan–Australia talks a boy–girl relationship
- compound expressions in which at least one of the items has two parts (the *en rule* must be *spaced* when this happens)

  a Sydney – Blue Mountains cycling tour

  an Australia – New Zealand agreement

  but such constructions should be rewritten where possible

  cycling from Sydney to the Blue Mountains

  an agreement between Australia and New Zealand
- capitalised headings, where it may be preferred to a hyphen, which often looks too small when surrounded by capitals

In desktop publishing all forms of dashes and rules can be generated from the computer keyboard, using keyboard commands. Do not use a hyphen as a dash.

See also **dashes, use of**; **ellipsis**; **em/en**; **hyphenation**; **numbers in figures or words**.

**dashes, use of** The *dash* is used as a punctuation mark in a variety of situations. Material set apart by dashes will emerge more prominently or become more emphatic. Dashes make most impact when used sparingly, however. A pair of dashes can be used to mark off parenthetical material when something slightly more forceful or abrupt than commas or brackets is required (though the three kinds of punctuation have very similar weight in some sentences). One way of testing whether you have placed a pair of dashes correctly is to visualise the sentence without them or the words they enclose; if it remains grammatically complete, all is well. The following are some of the ways in which dashes are used:

- for clear, decisive parenthesis that elaborates on something

  The tropical fish – a vivid shoal of them – darted among the coral.
- to gather together a group of words and lead into a summation of them

  The iron roof, the shady verandah, the criss-crossed railings, the luxuriant purple bougainvillea – his childhood home stood before him.
- for a dramatic or melodramatic ending

  The countess slipped gracefully from her horse – into a deep puddle.
- to introduce an afterthought

  She was singing a song – a rather jolly song, I remember.
- for an abrupt change or interruption in speech

  'I can't wait to start my strict new diet – but what's for dinner?'

  'The ticket office will close soon – let's go now!'

In the following sentence the complex parenthetical phrase, dotted with commas, needs to be marked off by dashes rather than further commas:

> She found that her humanities lectures – fine arts, Japanese, and the history and philosophy of science – were all before lunch.

The only punctuation that can appear just before a dash is a closing bracket, exclamation mark or question mark:

> Give the shrub a good watering (preferably by hand) – unless it rains.
>
> Keep up the watering – what a chore! – unless it rains.
>
> Ask Josh – would you mind? – to do the watering.

See also **apposition**; **brackets**; **colon**; **comma**; **dashes, types of**; **semicolon**; **singular or plural**.

**data** Authorities disagree on whether to treat *data*, which means a collection of facts or items for analysis, as singular or plural:

> The data on divorce rates is [*or* are] ready.

Although *data* is indeed the plural of *datum*, a word rarely used except in specialist fields such as surveying and cartography, it is most often used as a collective noun these days, taking a singular verb (particularly if the *data* is stored in a database).

Do not overuse the word; sometimes *facts* or *information* may suffice. *Data* is pronounced '**day**-ta' or '**dar**-ta' (the latter especially in the US).

**database** A computer *database* is a collection of related information organised in such a way that items can be selected and updated as required. For example, a retail business might keep a database of customer information, a manufacturer might list stock, and a botanic garden its plants. Data can then be sorted in any way – for instance customers by postcode for the retailer, stock by type or trade name for the manufacturer, and plants by genus for the garden.

See also **spreadsheet**.

**data retrieval** This is a computer term. To retrieve data (any information on a disk) means to rescue it on either a floppy or hard disk when the computer has crashed or gone down. It is not always possible to retrieve the data. However, if you use a program on your own system or send it to an appropriate bureau immediately a crash occurs without attempting to add material to your disk, you have a good chance of retrieving most and sometimes all of the apparently lost data. The best way to prevent complete loss or to minimise it is to save regularly and make a backup copy at least once a day on a different disk, hard or floppy.

The term *data retrieval* is also used in reference to recovering archival information from files or databases.

See also **backup**; **bureau (desktop publishing)**; **crashed/gone down**; **save**; **undo command**.

**dates** Figures are acceptable for the expression of dates in most descriptive and narrative contexts, although legal documents usually require the written form. Preferred style is day, month, year, which is logical in sequence and requires no punctuation:

> 24 September 1988

When a sentence starts with the day of a month, spell out the words:

> The twenty-fourth of September [*or* Twenty-four September] is my son's birthday.

When a sentence ends in a date, use the ordinal form with either words or figures:

> Alexander's birthday is on the twenty-fourth [*or* 24th].

Avoid beginning a sentence with a year expressed in figures; it is acceptable at the end of the sentence, however:

> The year 1983 brought the end of the drought.
>
> The drought ended in 1983.

If the day of the week precedes the date, insert a comma:

> Saturday, 24 September 1988

Use a full stop rather than a solidus (slash) between figures when writing dates in numerals:

> 7.1.91 *not* 7/1/91

But note that while 7.1.91 means 7 January 1991 in Australia and the UK, it means 1 July 1991 in the US, Canada and some other countries. This is the default date style of most US word-processing and spreadsheet computer programs, but it can usually be changed and should be.

Centuries may be written in figures or words:

the 20th century *or* the twentieth century

The abbreviation *BC* (before Christ), if required, should follow the year; the abbreviation *AD* (anno Domini) goes before the year:

44 BC AD 1991

Decades should be written thus:

the 1990s

*rather than*

the nineteen-nineties *or* the nineties

Avoid the forms *the 1990's*; *the '90s*; and *the 'nineties*. Note that *the 1990s* has no apostrophe because it is a plural, not a possessive.

Spans of years should be written as follows:

1988–89 *or* 1988–1989

Do not use the forms *1988–9*; *1988/89*; *1988/9*; or *1988/1989*. Note also:

1991–2001 1700–04 *or* 1700–1704

Spans of days follow similar rules:

9–24 September 24–25 September

Do not use the forms *24–5 September* or *24/25 September*.

Use an en rule, not a hyphen, to separate figures. Insert a space on either side of the en rule if either part of a span of dates contains words as well as figures:

24 September 1988 – 13 October 1993

The International Organization for Standardization (ISO) has designed a system of date-writing to expedite international communication. This system follows a descending order of year, month and day. The date 15 August 1992 would be written thus:

19920815 *or* 1992–08–15 *or* 1992 08 15

See also **AD/BC**; **centuries**; ***circa***; **decades**; **em/en**; **numbers in figures or words**.

**daylight saving** This system of putting clocks forward in summer extends the usable period of daylight at the end of each day. The months of daylight saving vary between States.

See also **time of day**; **time zones**.

**daytime/night-time** Make one word of *daytime*, but hyphenate *night-time*.

**dc** direct current (electricity).

**DDT** dichlorodiphenyltrichloroethane (insecticide).

**de-** The prefix *de-* can indicate removal or separation, as in *dethrone*; negation, as in *demerit* and *destabilise*; reducing or lowering, as in *devalue*; and reversal, as in *de-activate*. This handy prefix is constantly being used to form new words, such as *decontrol* and *demonetise*, but some oddities result. Many people would prefer to be asked to leave an aircraft rather than to *deplane*, for example, but some of these expressions take more getting used to than others.

**debar/disbar** To *debar* is to exclude or prevent:

> The pledge taken by the young man debarred him from having a beer with us.

*Disbar* has a very specific meaning: to deprive a lawyer (especially a barrister) of the right to practise.

**debauch/debouch** To *debauch* is to corrupt, pervert or seduce:

> Violent films may debauch the young.

To *debouch* is to emerge from a narrow opening:

> The lava debouched from a fissure in the volcano.

Pronounce *debauch* 'd'**borch**'. *Debouch* is generally pronounced 'd'**boosh**' in Australia.

**debonair** Note the spelling. This adjective means stylish, carefree or affable, and tends to be used especially of men.

**debouch** See **debauch/debouch**.

**debug** See **bug**.

**deca-/deci-** *Deca-* is a prefix meaning ten times, hence *decathlon* (an athletic contest involving ten events); *decasyllabic* (having ten syllables); and the *Decalogue* (the Ten Commandments).

*Deci-* means one-tenth, hence *decimate* (reduce by a tenth); *decibel* (one tenth of a bel, a unit used in measuring sound or power levels); and *decimal* (pertaining to tenths or the number ten, or the number system that has ten as its base).

**decades** A *decade* is any period of ten years. A *new decade* begins, strictly speaking, with the numeral one (1901–10, 1981–90), though many people use it to describe periods beginning with nought (1900–09, 1980–89). The pronunciation '**dek**-ade' is recommended.

See also **centuries**; **dates**.

**deceitful/deceptive** These two adjectives both mean misleading, but *deceitful* practices are designed to cheat or trick, whereas something that is *deceptive* is often unintentionally so:

The substitution of kangaroo meat for beef was deceitful, though the resemblance between the two is deceptive.

The adverb *deceptively* is sometimes misused. It is correct to say that someone is *deceptively calm* when he or she appears to be calm but is not, but it is incorrect to call the weather *deceptively fine* if you merely mean that it is *surprisingly* fine for the time of year.

**deci-** See **deca-/deci-**.

**decidedly/decisively** The primary meaning of *decidedly* is unquestionably, although the word can overlap with *decisively*, which means resolutely or with great determination:

Churchill decidedly enjoyed cigars.

Churchill acted decisively, inspiring the British people.

Churchill decidedly [*or* decisively] influenced the outcome of World War II.

**decimate** This verb literally means to reduce by one-tenth. It originally referred to the Roman practice of killing one in ten mutinous or cowardly soldiers to discipline the others. Today it is generally accepted that *decimate* can mean to destroy a large number or sizeable proportion:

The earthquake decimated the city's population.

*Decimate* should not be used to describe total annihilation or destruction, nor should it be used of an individual:

Not a tree remained standing after a cyclone destroyed [*not* decimated] the forest.

Achilles slew [*not* decimated] Hector.

Careful writers also avoid the word when specifying the degree of damage:

Fifty per cent of the apple crop was ruined [*not* decimated].

**decisively** See **decidedly/decisively**.

**deconstruction** In literary and cultural studies, *deconstruction* means the unmasking of concealed assumptions and unnoticed contradictions in the language of a text. Introduced in 1968 by the French philosopher Jacques Derrida, deconstruction began as a process of linguistic analysis. In radical and feminist usages, however, the term has broadened to describe the uncovering of hidden political assumptions, especially with respect to class, gender and race. Journalists sometimes use the word in a vague and alarmist way to denigrate any form of contemporary cultural critique.

**decry/descry** To *decry* is to disparage or condemn:

It is easier to decry typographical errors than to eliminate them.

*Descry* is a rather archaic word meaning to see something, usually with difficulty:

Captain Cook was able to descry the coastline through the mist.

**deduce/deduct** To *deduce* is to draw a conclusion from something known or assumed:

I could deduce from her accent that she was Scottish.

To *deduct* is to subtract, as from a total or amount. The noun from both *deduce* and *deduct* is *deduction*.

See also **adduce/deduce**; **deductive/inductive**.

**deductive/inductive** These adjectives describe two types of reasoning. *Deductive* reasoning proceeds from general principles to specific conclusions:

Vegetables must have water for good growth; these lettuces are growing poorly because they have received no water.

*Inductive* reasoning moves in the opposite direction; it draws a general principle from specific instances:

The lettuces that received no water are growing poorly; water must therefore be essential for vegetable-growing.

See also **a posteriori/a priori**; **deduce/deduct**.

**deem** This verb has specific formal uses but informally, meaning simply to think or consider, it is best avoided unless you are being facetious.

**defamation** *Defamation* occurs when one party makes a damaging statement about another to a third party (who may be one person or thousands of newspaper readers) – a statement that tends to lower the person it concerns in the estimation of ordinary 'right-thinking' people, or to hold that person up to 'hatred, ridicule or contempt'. A defamatory statement can be spoken (slander) or written (libel). Slander is actionable only in certain circumstances, and defamation laws vary between the Australian States.

Despite the differences in legislation, there are basic principles common to all. Defamation is actionable only if there is a defamatory statement – usually in words, although a film, cartoon or photograph can be considered a statement. The defamatory statement must be published – that is, communicated to a third party. Moreover the person defamed must be identifiable, though not necessarily named.

If a court should find that the reputation or integrity of a plaintiff has been damaged, or that the plaintiff has been held up to hatred, ridicule or contempt, penalties against the defamer may be substantial. In the case of printed articles, liability for defamation falls on the writer, publisher and printer.

There are four main defences that allow the publication of defamatory material. The defences do not make the material less defamatory but they do provide a defence to any claim for liability in defamation.

***Absolute privilege*** This applies to statements made in parliamentary proceedings, to official reports of these proceedings (in Hansard), and to papers and reports printed by order of Parliament; to statements made in judicial proceedings;

and to statements made in communications between officers of state (such as ministers and heads of departments). In these instances there can be no action for defamation, even if the statements made are untrue or malicious.

***Qualified privilege*** This extends to fair and accurate reports and summaries of parliamentary and judicial proceedings, and certain other public proceedings (such as royal commissions). However, journalists relying on this defence need to ensure that there is genuine public interest in their reports, not just vulgar curiosity. This defence is also unavailable if what the law calls 'malice' in this context can be attributed by the defendant. Malice in the law of defamation has a somewhat different meaning from that which the word has in everyday language. In the eyes of law, malice means a lack of good faith on the part of the person publishing the defamatory words. This may mean that, for example, a publisher was motivated by a desire to injure the party defamed, but may equally involve recklessness as to whether the material published was true or false, failure to inquire as to its truth, actual knowledge that the material was false, or 'the deliberate introduction of irrelevant material to the occasion of qualified privilege'.

Qualified privilege also extends to professional and business communications in which information is passed to those with a genuine interest in receiving it: for example, in a job reference or a report between medical practitioners. However, such information must not be malicious.

***The truth as a defence*** This defence (also known as justification) may be successfully raised if the defendant can establish the truth of every relevant material fact in a statement: a court has to be satisfied that the words are 'true in substance and in fact'. This defence fails if any material fact is shown to be untrue. In some States the truth of a statement is not by itself an adequate defence; the statement must also be shown to be in the public interest or benefit.

***Fair comment*** In a matter of public interest, fair comment can be a defence, but it must be shown that the words used are comments, not facts, and that the comments are fairly supported by facts that are true and were known to be true at the time the statement was made. Malicious comments, even if based on facts, are not protected by this defence.

It is no defence to claim reasonable error or lack of intention to defame. Thus the disclaimer often seen in film credits or on the imprint page of novels that 'no reference is intended to any actual person' may give some protection, but does not of itself absolve the author from potential liability. If a character a writer believes to be imaginary is defamed, and a real person could reasonably be thought by others to be that character, the writer can be held liable. It is also possible to defame someone unintentionally when referring to another person of the same name. Any 'Dr Brown' whom people might reasonably believe to be the 'Dr Brown' defamed in, for example, a newspaper article, may take action, even though reference was to another doctor of the same name. It is, therefore, essential to give full names and addresses and as much identification as possible in reports containing material that is possibly defamatory.

Everyone concerned with the writing and distribution, or republishing, of defamatory matter may be liable – the writer, editor, publisher, printer and, to some extent, distributor, although it is a defence if secondary distributors such as librarians and newsagents prove they did not know that the publication contained defamatory matter.

See also **contempt**; **contracts**.

**default** In computer language the term *default* (or *default setting*) describes certain preset elements that are used each time a new program or document is opened. For example, a word-processing program would have default settings for the number of characters in a line, the number of lines on a page, the margins, the tab sizes and so on. Such settings are easily changed, however, and most programs can be adapted permanently to suit the user's requirements.

The same term is used when your printer attempts to access an unavailable typeface. In this situation a message on the screen tells you that the computer is defaulting to another typeface.

**defective/deficient** The adjectives *defective* and *deficient* both mean inadequate in some way, but as a general rule *defective* applies to quality and *deficient* to quantity. A *defective iron*, for instance, is inadequate because it has a mechanical or structural fault. A *deficient power supply*, on the other hand, is inadequate because there is not enough power to meet a certain level of demand.

**defence/defense** In Australian and British English the noun *defence* is spelt with a *c*, in US English with an *s*. But note the adjectives *defensive* and *defensible*, which are spelt with an *s* in all varieties of English.

**deficient** See **defective/deficient**.

**defining clause** See **clause**.

**defining phrase** See **phrase**.

**definite/definitive** Something *definite* is clearly defined, precise or exact:

> When our holiday plans are definite we can make bookings.

Something *definitive* is conclusive or final; more than that, it is authoritative and comprehensive. The word should not be used lightly.

> This is the definitive biography of Patrick White.

**defoliation/deforestation** *Defoliation* is the removal of the leaves from trees and plants; *deforestation* is the removal of the trees themselves (a more cheerful word is *reafforestation*, the replanting that restores forests).

**defuse/diffuse** The verb *defuse* means to remove the fuse from something or (used figuratively) to calm a situation or action:

> Our host defused a tense moment by opening the champagne.

The adjective *diffuse* means dispersed or spread widely, and (figuratively) discursive:

The foyer's diffuse lighting created a soft glow.

Your diffuse style of writing obscures your meaning.

Pronounce it 'dif-**yoos**'.

**degrees and diplomas** There are three main levels for most *degrees*: Bachelor (ordinary or honours), Master and Doctor. Doctorates are subdivided further: the Doctor of Philosophy degree (PhD, called DPhil by Oxford University) is the lower of the two, and it may relate to any branch of scholarship (philosophy in this context simply means learning); the higher grade includes Doctor of Letters (DLitt, which relates to the Humanities), Doctor of Science (DSc), Doctor of Medicine (MD), Doctor of Laws (LLD) and Doctor of Divinity (DD).

A prerequisite of many *diplomas* is a degree at Bachelor level. Diplomas taken by students who have not completed a Bachelor's degree are sometimes called *certificates*.

For the sake of typographical neatness it is recommended that the initial letters and abbreviations for degrees and diplomas be set solid and without full stops:

Mark Cohen, BA, DipEd Amy Cheng, MB, BS, DPH

Such post-nominal initials are usually placed after the holder's name in the order of conferment. The name of the institution that granted the qualification is sometimes added. An honours degree is usually indicated:

Patricia O'Connell, BSc (Adel.), DipAgSc (La Trobe)

Tony Miotto, BEc (Hons), MBA (Melb.)

Here is a list of abbreviations for some of the common degrees and diplomas available in Australia in the 1990s. Preference in the list has been given to abbreviated forms consisting entirely, or almost entirely, of initial letters, as their meaning may not be immediately obvious. Note too that some of these have alternative versions.

BA Bachelor of Arts
BAO Bachelor of Obstetrics
BArch Bachelor of Architecture
BBus Bachelor of Business
BCE Bachelor of Civil Engineering
BChE Bachelor of Chemical Engineering
BCL Bachelor of Civil Law
BCom Bachelor of Commerce
BCS Bachelor of Computer Science
BD Bachelor of Divinity
BDS Bachelor of Dental Surgery
BE Bachelor of Engineering
BEc Bachelor of Economics
BEd Bachelor of Education
BEE Bachelor of Electrical Engineering
BFA Bachelor of Fine Arts
BJ Bachelor of Journalism
BME Bachelor of Mechanical Engineering
BMet Bachelor of Metallurgy
BMetE Bachelor of Metallurgical Engineering

BMus Bachelor of Music
BPharm Bachelor of Pharmacy
BPhil Bachelor of Philosophy
BS Bachelor of Surgery
BSc Bachelor of Science
BScAgr Bachelor of Science in Agriculture
BSc(Med) Bachelor of Science in Medicine
BTh Bachelor of Theology
BVSc Bachelor of Veterinary Science
ChB Bachelor of Surgery
ChM Master of Surgery
DA Diploma in Anaesthesia
DCH Diploma in Child Health
DCh Doctor of Surgery
DCL Doctor of Civil Law
DCPS Diploma in Computer Science
DD Doctor of Divinity
DDS Doctor of Dental Surgery
DDSc Doctor of Dental Science
DIH Diploma of Industrial Health
DipABS Diploma in Accounting and Business Studies
DipCrim Diploma in Criminology
DipEd Diploma of Education
DipEEng Diploma of Electrical Engineering
DipEnv Diploma of Environmental Studies
DipFor Diploma of Forestry
DipJ Diploma of Journalism
DipPE Diploma of Primary Education
DipPhysEd Diploma in Physical Education
DipPubAd Diploma of Public Administration
DipSoc Diploma of Sociology
DipTCP Diploma in Town and Country Planning
DipVA Diploma of Visual Arts
DLD Diploma of Landscape Design
DLitt Doctor of Letters
DM Doctor of Medicine
DMD Doctor of Dental Medicine
DMR Diploma in Medical Radiology
DMus Doctor of Music
DO Diploma in Ophthalmology
DPH Diploma in Public Health
DSc Doctor of Science
DTh Doctor of Theology
DTRP Diploma in Town and Regional Planning
DVMS Doctor of Veterinary Medicine and Surgery
DVSc Doctor of Veterinary Science
EdD Doctor of Education
LittD Doctor of Letters
LLB Bachelor of Law(s)
LLD Doctor of Law(s)
LLM Master of Law(s)
MA Master of Arts
MAgrSc Master of Agricultural Science
MArch Master of Architecture
MASc Master of Applied Science(s)
MB Bachelor of Medicine
MBA Master of Business Administration
MCh Master of Surgery
MChE Master of Chemical Engineering
MCom Master of Commerce
MD Doctor of Medicine
MDS Master of Dental Surgery
MEc Master of Economics
MEd Master of Education
MEng Master of Engineering
MME Master of Mechanical Engineering
MJ Master of Journalism
MPH Master of Public Health
MPhil Master of Philosophy
MPs Master of Psychology
MS Master of Surgery
MSc Master of Science
MSW Master of Social Work
MTCP Master of Town and Country Planning

| | | | |
|---|---|---|---|
| MusB | Bachelor of Music | PhD | Doctor of Philosophy |
| MusD | Doctor of Music | PTC | Primary Teacher's Certificate |
| MusM | Master of Music | STB | Bachelor of Sacred Theology |
| OD | Doctor of Optometry | ThD | Doctor of Theology |

See also **Doctor, the title**; **ranks, titles, honours and awards.**

**deign** Those who *deign* to do something are usually condescending about it:

> The managing director may deign to photocopy his own letter.

Pronounce the word to rhyme with *plane*.

**deja vu** These two French words (*déjà vu*, meaning already seen) have been absorbed into English and are therefore usually printed in roman type without the accents. The expression may be used as a noun to mean something new that feels as if it has been experienced already:

> As Bernard walked into the Irish village he had a sense of deja vu.

As an adjective it usually means unoriginal:

> As her inspiration declined, Olivia's paintings became distinctly deja vu.

Pronounce the phrase 'day-**jar** voo'.

**delimit/limit** The first of these verbs is a little more precise than the second. To *delimit* is to establish or fix the boundaries of something that is restricted (it is often used in a geographical or territorial context). To *limit* is merely to restrict:

> The Minister must delimit the expenditure at $500 000.
>
> The Minister must limit the scope of the project.

See also **limited.**

**delusion** See **allusion/illusion/delusion.**

**demi-bold type** See **type.**

**demise** The most common meaning of *demise* is death, though it is a euphemism that may sound facetious. Another valid meaning is termination:

> Polluted water was blamed for the demise of fishing in the cove.

Avoid using *demise* to mean downfall:

> The Watergate scandal caused the downfall [*not* demise] of Richard Nixon.

Pronounce the word 'd'**mize**' (not 'd'**mice**' or 'd'**meeze**').

**demonstrable** If you spell this word correctly you will pronounce it correctly (not 'demonstratable').

**demur/demurred/demurring** Note the single *r* in the first and the *-rr-* in the other two. The verb means to object, or to demonstrate reluctance; the noun means objection:

The old lady demurred at the idea of an hour's walk.

The old lady accepted a lift without demur.

Do not confuse *demur* with the unrelated adjective *demure*, which means decorous or unnaturally modest.

Pronounce *demur* 'd'**mer**' (and *demure* 'd'**mew**er').

**denote/connote** These verbs are not interchangeable, although they both refer to meaning in words. To *denote* is to provide the basic, primary meaning. To *connote* is to expand a basic meaning, through associated meanings. For example, the word *mother* simply denotes a female who has had a child, but it *connotes* maternal love, tenderness, nurture and protection for many people.

**denouement** Note the spelling. In relation to the plot of a literary work, the *denouement* is the final unravelling of the story. Because this French word has been assimilated into the English language, it is not italicised and the acute accent on the first *e* has been dropped. Pronounce it 'day-**noo**-mon'.

**deny/refute/rebut** *Deny* and *refute* are frequently confused. One meaning of *deny* is to declare something to be false:

The Minister denied accepting the bribe.

To *refute* a charge is to prove it to be false:

The testimony of an independent witness enabled him to refute the charge.

Therefore, while it is possible to *deny* an allegation vehemently, it cannot be *refuted* unless there is proof positive.

*Rebut* takes things a step further, where a point or allegation is not only disproved, but is answered with an opposing argument or *rebuttal*:

Having cleared himself to the satisfaction of the House, the Minister rebutted the charge with evidence of the Opposition's deceit.

**dependant/dependent** The noun *dependant* (sometimes spelt *dependent*) means a person who is supported (usually in a financial way) by another:

Karen is a single mother with three dependants.

The adjective *dependent* means relying on someone or something for assistance or support:

Many elderly people are dependent on social services.

In US English either the *-ant* or *-ent* spelling may be used for the noun.

See also **independent**.

**deplore** This verb means to express regret or to disapprove of. It should always refer to a thing rather than a person:

I deplore his bad manners.

*not* I deplore him because of his bad manners.

**deprecate/depreciate** Although these verbs are sometimes used interchangeably, the distinction between them is worth preserving. *Deprecate* means to express earnest disapproval of or to protest against:

> On democratic grounds he deprecated the Church's refusal to ordain women.

*Depreciate* means to disparage or belittle:

> Kate was secretly impressed by her husband's attempts to learn Japanese, but depreciated them among her friends.

When *depreciate* is an intransitive verb it can also mean to decline in value or worth:

> My computer depreciates by a hundred dollars a year.

If you are *self-deprecating*, you are critical of and modest about yourself; if *self-depreciating*, you belittle your own worth. In these constructions the two words come closest to being synonymous.

**deprived** As a synonym for *poor* or *underprivileged*, *deprived* is overused:

> Many deprived children lack adequate schools.

Since *deprived* means divested of, this usage incorrectly implies that the children have lost rights of some kind that they once had. More explicit adjectives are preferable in any case.

**deregulation** This is the process of removing the restrictions placed on certain activities. *Deregulation* usually refers to the lifting of government regulations in the hope of improving market competition or increasing efficiency.

**de rigueur** Note the spelling (not 'rigeur') of this French phrase meaning essential or compulsory. Pronounce it 'de ree-**ger**'.

**derisive/derisory** Both adjectives mean ridiculing, mocking, or characterised by derision. Some authorities draw a subtle distinction between them, defining *derisive* as conveying derision, and *derisory* as inviting, or worthy of, derision:

> The goalkeeper's error was greeted with derisive yells.
>
> The film's attempt at recreating the landing at Gallipoli with a handful of people was derisory.

*Derisory* is also used to mean absurdly small or not worth serious consideration:

> A pension increase of 20 cents a fortnight is derisory.

Pronounce *derisive* 'd'**rie**-ziv' and *derisory* 'd'**rie**-zaree'.

**derv** This is an acronym for *diesel-engined road vehicle*; in the UK it is the common name for the fuel itself.

**descendant/descendent** In Australian and British English the noun is *descendant*, the adjective *descendent*; in US English both forms are usually spelt *descendent*. A common error is to confuse *descendant* with *ancestor*: you are the *descendant* of your *ancestors*, although in time you will become the *ancestor* of your *descendants*.

**descender** See **type**.

**descry** See **decry/descry**.

**desert/dessert** A *desert* is a dry, barren region such as the *Simpson Desert*. The verb *desert* means to abandon: *She would not desert her child.* To *receive one's just deserts* is to get what one deserves. The sweet course at the end of a meal is called *dessert*.

Stress the second syllable of all these words except the sandy type of *desert*.

**desiccate** This is one of the most frequently misspelt words in the English language: note the single *s* and *-cc-*. It means to dry up. The adjective is *desiccated*, as in *desiccated coconut*.

**designer** Used as an adjective describing expensive and fashionable (but usually mass-produced) goods such as watches, jeans and sunglasses, this word has become a joke. Any manufacturer, retailer or advertising agency that still uses it deserves a designer deficit on the balance sheet.

**desktop publishing** *Desktop publishing* (abbreviated *DTP*) is a relatively inexpensive system of typesetting and page composition using small but powerful computers, and word-processing, page-makeup and graphics software. Many books are now produced on desktop by publishers, as is much of the printed material issued by government and commercial enterprises throughout Australia: magazines and journals, reports, training manuals, catalogues, letters and business cards. You do not have to be a designer to operate this equipment, but some knowledge and understanding of design principles are obviously an advantage.

There are many DTP page-makeup programs on the market, the best known of the high-end programs being QuarkXPress, PageMaker, Ventura, FrameWorks and ReadySetGo!. Popular graphics packages are Adobe Illustrator, Aldus FreeHand, Corel Draw and Photoshop. Some of the most commonly used word-processing packages are Microsoft Word, WordPerfect, Claris Works, WordStar Professional and MultiMate Advantage. There are also spreadsheet programs, for instance Lotus 1-2-3 and Microsoft Excel, and databases such as FileMaker. Programs are constantly being upgraded and new programs regularly appear on the market.

Before purchasing a DTP package you should list your requirements, which may, of course, change with time. Your software needs should always be considered first; once they are established, you can choose the hardware. There may be only a couple of hardware options appropriate to the software you require (for example, Apple or DOS). If the choice is wider, selection might be based on such factors as price, ease of operation, compactness of the equipment and the after-sales service offered.

All DTP packages are graphics-based, giving you complete WYSIWYG (what you see is what you get) facilities in page formatting, graphics and text manipulation. From the very beginning of a project you can see what your document will look like. All elements of the work can be moved around until you are satisfied and ready to print out.

Although most DTP programs can be used with dot-matrix printers, they are generally intended for PostScript black and white or colour laser printers.

The development of desktop publishing has given many people – publishers, self-publishers, keyboard operators, designers, traditional typesetters – the potential to produce, or to have produced, commercial-quality typesetting at relatively low cost. An added advantage, in some situations, is that all parts of the work – design, word processing, page makeup and proofreading – can be done at the one location.

However, the results obtained by inexperienced operators are often poor. This is not the fault of the programs, which in the main are well designed and reasonably simple to use. There are highly specialised skills to be learnt if clear and attractive, professional results are to be obtained. It is necessary to understand at least the basics of typography, design and proofreading to make the leap from typing and word-processing skills to those needed in desktop publishing. Here are some guidelines.

- *Set up a layout grid or template for the entire publication.* This is your first task. Use the tools of your DTP program to lay out margins, columns, rules, running heads, typeface and size, leading, indents and so on. DTP and graphics programs have a library of templates and styles from which the inexperienced operator can choose.
- *Be generous with white space.* Pages that are crammed with text from margin to margin are uninviting and difficult to read; they need white space to frame the type.
- *Provide good contrast between headings and body copy and ensure that there is adequate space around headings.* Avoid enclosing headings in heavy boxes, and do not allow them to be so large as to dwarf the text below. Headings set in capitals, particularly in serif faces, have a 'boxing' effect that may make them difficult to read. A combination of capitals and small capitals is often more effective. Long headings set in two lines are visually more attractive if the space between the lines is smaller than normal (the words should not, of course, be hyphenated at the end of a line, or the lines justified).
- *Use graphics with care.* The fact that graphics can easily be incorporated into a DTP document does not mean that they always should be. If a graphic does not help to tell the story, leave it out. Avoid overuse of the decorative fillers, boxes, rules, dingbats and so on that are supplied with programs or can be purchased separately as clip art.

- *Avoid mixing typefaces unnecessarily.* If variety is needed, use different weights or sizes from the same font family.
- *Ensure that line leading is adequate.* It should allow sufficient space between ascenders and descenders. Leading one to two points larger than the type size usually makes the copy most readable.
- *Avoid setting long runs of copy in bold or italic type.* Roman type is much easier to read and looks more pleasant. Save bold and italic for special purposes (for example, bold for headings, italic for subheadings, titles and emphasis).
- *Avoid underlining words in headings or copy.* Italic or bold type is preferable to underlining when emphasis is needed in text.
- *Use reverse type sparingly.* White type set against a black background is often difficult to read and not necessarily attractive. Above all, never reverse serif fonts that are small in point size.
- *Use devices such as rules and screens sparingly.* Lines, vertical rules, blocks or screens can be effective in breaking up a page covering different topics, but they should be used in moderation. In general the finer the line or rule, and the lighter the density of a screen, the better.
- *Select line length carefully.* Choose a suitable line length for the dimensions of the page. In book work, text that is about seventy-two characters wide is the most readable. Excessively long lines slow down reading, and increase the likelihood of readers getting lost moving from the end of one line to the beginning of the next. It may be appropriate to divide an A4 page of text into two columns for such work as training manuals or reports, whereas three columns may be suitable for newsletters. Justified and unjustified type are both suitable as long as the type size is carefully chosen.
- *Use the kerning and tracking facilities of your DTP program.* These facilities vary in scope from program to program, but most DTP and graphics programs now permit fine kerning and tracking adjustment, which can make all the difference to the appearance of a document.
- *If your program's hyphenation dictionary is a sound one, use it for word division when setting justified text.* Keep an eye open for rivers of white space running through justified copy, and do not break words at the end of more than two consecutive lines.
- *Avoid setting large slabs of text in sanserif type.* Sanserif faces such as Helvetica and Avant Garde may appear to be neater or cleaner than serif faces such as Times and Garamond, but they are more difficult to read. Reserve sanserif typefaces for headings and captions, and display work such as leaflets or brochures.
- *Learn from others.* When you are starting out, examine other publications, and copy or modify their best design points. Remember, however, that if you take a bit from here and a bit from there, you could end up with a mess: keep your design simple.

DESKTOP NEWS July 1993

Effective Page Design

Desktop publishing programs can produce effective layouts in the hands of a knowledgeable operator, but it is preferable to draw on the skills of a professional at least for the initial concept. A common defect of layouts produced without the aid of a designer is that they indiscriminately take up too many of the available options, such as a wide range of typefaces,and are so cluttered that the author's message is obscured.

Layout

Layout should take account of at least the following basic elements:

format – which is the size and shape of a publication

type area – which may be in one block or divided into columns for easier reading

margins – which should be as generous as the type of publication allows

illustrations – which may lie within the page area or 'bleed' (that is, run off the page)

In publications with a variety of headings, illustrations, tables and captions or other non-text matter, it is necessary to devise a modular plan or grid that incorporates all these elements. This ensures visual harmony throughout the work and also serves as a reference for the various people involved in the production process. Grids should show all the features common to every page, such as page size, margins, column widths, text and illustration areas, and the position of headings and folios (page numbers). Once the grid has been established the designer can manoeuvre the text and illustrations within it until the desired result, in both aesthetic and practical terms, is achieved. While the grid provides a prototype for each spread, a skilful designer can introduce variations within the basic framework to avoid monotony. For large projects such as books, the grid is usually printed on sheets to ensure that all dimensions are accurate and consistent. As grids become the designer's layout sheets, on which type is pasted and illustrations are positioned, they should be printed in pale-blue ink, which does not reproduce during the printing process.

In desktop publishing the grid is called a template.

However you choose to produce your material, remember to keep your layout simple, since your aim is to impart information. You may not excite your readers but you will not confuse or offend them.

Designer of the month, Beth McKinlay

DTP STYLE GUIDELINES FOR A PROFESSIONAL RESULT

To produce clear and attractive, professional copy the desktop publisher needs to understand at least the basics of typography and design. Here are some guidelines.

**Be generous with white space.** Pages that are crammed with text from margin to margin are uninviting and difficult to read; they need white space to frame the type. Avoid mixing typefaces unnecessarily. If variety is needed, use different weights or sizes from the same font family.

**Ensure that line leading is adequate.** It should allow sufficient space between ascenders and descenders. Leading one to two points larger than the type size usually produces the most readable copy.

**Avoid setting long runs of copy in bold or italic type.** Roman type is much easier to read and looks more pleasant. Save bold and italic for special purposes (for example, bold for headings, italic for subheadings, titles and emphasis).

**Use reverse type sparingly.** White type set against a black background is often difficult to read and not necessarily attractive. Above all, never reverse serif fonts that are small in point size.

**Use devices such as rules and screens sparingly.** Lines, vertical rules, blocks or screens can be effective in breaking up a page covering different topics, but they should be used in moderation. In general the finer the line or rule, and the lighter the density of screen, the better.

**Use the kerning and tracking facilities of your DTP program.** These facilities vary in scope from program to program, but most DTP and graphics programs now permit fine kerning and tracking adjustment, which can make all the difference to the appearance of a document.

**Avoid setting large slabs of text in sanserif type.** Sanserif faces such as Helvetica and Avant Garde may appear to be neater or cleaner than serif faces such as Times and Garamond, but they are more difficult to read. Reserve sanserif typefaces for headings and captions, and display work such as leaflets or brochures.

continued over page



*A poorly designed page with a confusing layout*

The criterion for all type is readability. To use every gimmick and font available might be fun for the operator, but in most cases it will only irritate or confuse the reader. Given even, well-leaded setting in an appropriate font, plenty of paragraphs and enough white space, your document will convey its message as clearly as the words allow.

See also **capital letters, setting of**; **clip art**; **copy editing**; **copy, presentation of**; **font**; **hyphenation dictionary**; **indention**; **justified type/unjustified type**; **kerning**; **layout**; **leading**; **marking up**; **measure**; **pi font**; **printer**; **proofs**; **running heads/running feet**; **template**; **tracking**; **type**; **typesetting**; **underlines/ underscores**; **word division**.

**despatch/dispatch** Either spelling is acceptable, but *dispatch* is recommended.

**despite/in spite of** Used to mean notwithstanding, the two may be interchanged:

> We were on time despite [*or* in spite of] the road conditions.

Note that *despite* is not followed by a preposition: *despite of* is incorrect.

**despoil/despoliation** Note the spelling change from *-oil* to *-ol-* when the verb (meaning to plunder) becomes a noun.

**dessert** See **desert/dessert**.

**destined** The adjective *destined* (which traditionally meant predetermined, or having a specific destination) and the noun *destiny* (a predetermined course of events) have drifted apart in modern usage. *Destined* is sometimes used as a synonym for *intended* or *designed* when one or other of these words would be better:

> These bricks are intended [*rather than* destined] for my new house.
>
> This is a film designed [*rather than* destined] for the under-25s.

**deteriorate** If you spell this word correctly you will pronounce it correctly (not 'deteriate').

**deterrent** Note the spelling (not 'deterrant'). Pronounce it 'de-tair'nt'.

**detract/distract** To *detract* from is to diminish (usually something of quality, value or reputation):

> The tenor's poor performance this week will detract from his reputation.

To *distract* means to draw the attention away from or divert:

> Do not distract me from my clarinet practice.

**devaluation** Official *devaluation* of a nation's currency occurs when the set exchange rate is altered by a government, with the result that a unit of the currency can buy fewer units of foreign currency.

**device/devise** *Device* is a noun meaning a contrivance; an object such as a tool; a plan; or an ornamental pattern or emblem. *Devise* is a verb meaning to contrive or invent; it does not have the option of an *ize* ending.

> The multi-bladed knife is a handy device.
>
> Ali devised a clever system for processing the orders as they came in.

Pronounce *device* 'd'**vice**' and *devise* 'd'**vize**'.

**device (computer)** *Device* is another name for a piece of hardware (printer, screen, mouse, scanner) attached to the central processing unit.

**devil's advocate** A *devil's advocate* is someone who defends the more unattractive side of a particular argument. This is not the same as making a good thing out of something bad, or whitewashing it. Nor does it mean acting as an agent of the devil, enticing people into evil.

**devise** See **device/devise**.

**Dewey Decimal System** Named after the American Melvil Dewey, who died in 1931, this is a method of classifying and numbering books in libraries. There are ten main subject categories: 000–099 General Works; 100–199 Philosophy; 200–299 Religion; 300–399 Social Science; 400–499 Language; 500–599 Pure Science; 600–699 Applied Science; 700–799 Fine Arts; 800–899 Literature; 900–999 History, Biography, Geography. The *Dewey Decimal System* is used by many libraries in the English-speaking world.

**dexterous/dextrous** Either spelling, with or without the second *-e-*, is acceptable, but *dexterous* is preferred. The word means skilful or nimble. Note that *ambidextrous* (equally skilful with either hand) has no alternative spelling.

**df** This is the abbreviation (also *DF*) for *double-fronted*, a real-estate term usually applied to a detached Victorian or Edwardian house with two major rooms facing the road.

**diaeresis/dieresis** Either spelling is acceptable; in the plural the last syllable becomes *-ses* (pronounced 'seez'). This accent, which consists of two dots above a vowel, usually indicates that the second of two adjacent vowels is pronounced separately. The diaeresis is rarely seen in English today, but is sometimes used in the word *naïve*.

See also **accents; ae/oe/e**.

**diagnosis/prognosis** In a medical context a doctor studies a patient's symptoms and makes a *diagnosis* of the problem – that is, he or she identifies it. Note that the problem is diagnosed, not the patient:

Asthma is diagnosed in many children.

*not* Many children are diagnosed as having asthma.

The *prognosis* is a doctor's forecast of the course of a medical problem and the likely outcome for the patient:

The specialist's prognosis is that the symptoms will soon disappear.

Both words may be used of problems other than medical ones:

The plumber diagnosed a leak in the cistern.

The economist's prognosis indicated a gradual recession.

The last syllable in both *diagnosis* and *prognosis* becomes *-ses* in the plural (pronounced 'seez').

**diagonal** See **solidus**.

**dialect** See **argot/dialect/jargon/lingua franca**.

**dialogue** This word (a noun, not a verb) is rapidly replacing *discussion*, *talk* or *conversation* on occasions where the exchange is *meaningful* or *constructive*. Such Pentagonspeak is best avoided, except possibly where opposing parties are attempting to work out an agreement or treaty and need the shield of obscurantism.

**dialogue box** A *dialogue box* is a boxed area that appears on a computer screen and contains a message to which the operator is required to respond by answering questions or making decisions.

**diarrhea/diarrhoea** Either spelling is acceptable.

**dice/die** *Dice* is the plural of the little-known noun *die*, the small cube used in gambling games. Today *dice* is the form used for one or more cubes. The singular appears in the phrase *the die is cast*, meaning that an irrevocable decision has been made. A *die* is also, for example, a device for cutting or forming material: *a die stamper*; *a die press*.

**dichotomy** A *dichotomy* is a division into two parts and the word is correctly used to describe two things that are mutually exclusive or sharply contrasted: *the dichotomy between clear-felling and forest preservation*. It should not be used to describe a simple difference (particularly of opinion) between two things.

**dictionary** A *dictionary* contains the words of a language set out in alphabetical order, giving parts of speech, meanings, pronunciation, origins, forms of spelling and so on. It can also list the words of one language translated into another (a French–English, English–French dictionary), or explain the vocabulary of special subjects (for example a dictionary of nautical terms). The word is also used to describe books containing a collection of entries on a common topic (as in the *Australian Dictionary of Biography* and *A Dictionary of Politics*). Samuel Johnson's *Dictionary of the English Language* (1755), Noah Webster's *American Dictionary of the English Language* (1828), and the monumental *Oxford English Dictionary* (published in instalments from 1884; 2nd edition 1989) laid the groundwork for the proliferation of English-language dictionaries published today. In Australia *The Macquarie Dictionary* (1st edition 1981; 2nd edition 1992) has gained acceptance in many quarters as the national dictionary. The AGPS *Style Manual*, for instance, recommends that Commonwealth Government publications should in general follow the spelling given in *The Macquarie Dictionary*.

Other excellent Australian dictionaries are published by Oxford University Press, Collins and Heinemann.

See also **thesaurus**.

**die** See **dice/die**.

**dieresis** See **diaeresis/dieresis**.

**diesel** Note the *-ie-*.

**dietician/dietitian** Either of these spellings is acceptable. The science of diet is called *dietetics*.

**differ/diverge** To *differ* is to be unlike (someone or something), or to disagree. Note the prepositions in the following examples:

> The care of Australian plants differs *from* that of exotics.
> Landscape designers differ *on* the role of Australian plants in gardens.
> Janet differs *from* Steve *on* whether to prune grevilleas.
> Horticulturists differ *with* gardeners *on* many details.

*Diverge* means to move in different directions from a common point:

> Experts generally agree that some Australian plants need fertilisers, but their views diverge as to the best type.

**different** This word is often superfluous, as in the following examples: *many different kinds of experience*; *various different supermarkets*; *five different species of frogs*.

See also **different from/different to**.

**different from/different to** The recommended usage is *different from*, especially in formal writing, although *different to* has sometimes been used by established writers and is often heard in speech. *Different than* is common in US English but is not acceptable in Australian or British English.

My viewpoint is different from yours.

*or informally*

My viewpoint is different to yours.

See also **different**.

**differential** There are a number of scientific and technical uses for the word *differential* but as an everyday noun it means a factor that makes a distinction between comparable things; it is not just an imposing alternative to *difference*:

The differential between allowances for single and married students was slight.

As an adjective it is most commonly applied to the difference in wages paid to people in the same industry but with different skills and working under different conditions:

Differential rates of pay for black station hands and white rouseabouts caused unrest in the pastoral industry.

**different to** See **different from/different to**.

**diffuse** See **defuse/diffuse**.

**digraph/diphthong/ligature** A *digraph* is a pair of letters (vowels or consonants) representing a single speech sound, as in the *ea* of *seat*, *ae* of *encyclopaedia* or *th* of *bath*. A *diphthong* is a speech sound consisting of a glide between two vowels within one syllable, as in the *ou* of *cloud*. A *ligature* is a pair of letters printed as a single character, such as *æ*. This typographic device is now rarely used in English-language printing.

See also **ae/oe/e**.

**dilemma** A *dilemma* is a situation where a person is faced with a choice between two unattractive options:

Athalie's dilemma was whether to stay in an unsatisfying job or resign and risk unemployment.

It is acceptable today to use *dilemma* where more than two choices are involved, in spite of the *di-* (Greek for two) in the word, provided they are all unsatisfactory. However, the word is unsuitable for describing a simple problem or predicament:

Athalie's problem [*not* dilemma] was whether she could afford a new car.

Pronounce the word 'dil-**emma**'.

**dilettante** *Dilettante* is the singular noun; the plural is *dilettantes* or *dilettanti*. The word is also used as an adjective. A dabbler in the arts or sciences risks being called a *dilettante* if the involvement is essentially casual rather than professional:

His steady flow of novels proved he was no dilettante.

**Dimboola, Vic.** Compare with *Dimbulah*, Qld.

**dimension** This noun refers to magnitude, size and measurement, and is overused figuratively to mean aspect, particularly in advertising copy that urges you to *add a new dimension to your life* by means of a holiday or a new car.

**diminutive/diminution** Take care over the spelling of *diminutive* (meaning small) and *diminution* (meaning reduction in size or intensity).

As a noun *diminutive* is a grammatical term for a word that conveys the idea of small size (or little importance) through the use of a suffix such as *-ette* (*kitchenette*) or *-let* (*farmlet*).

**dingbats** See **pi font**.

**dinghy/dingy** A *dinghy* is a small boat, whereas the adjective *dingy* means dark, drab or dirty, and is commonly used to mean shabby. Pronounce the boat '**ding**-gee' and *dingy* '**din**-jee'.

**dingo** Plural *dingoes* or *dingos*.

**dingy** See **dinghy/dingy**.

**diphtheria** Watch the spelling. Traditionally the *ph* at the end of the first syllable was pronounced 'f', but it is acceptable now to say 'dip-**theer**ia'.

**diphthong** See **digraph/diphthong/ligature**.

**diplomas** See **degrees and diplomas**.

**directory** A computer's *directory* is a list of the files on a hard or floppy disk. The structure of a directory is usually hierarchical – that is, the directory contains a list of subdirectories, each of which contains further subdirectories or files. A directory or subdirectory in any window-based program can be viewed as an icon or a written list. A well-planned and logically arranged directory structure is essential to a computer user.

See also **file**; **icon**.

**disable (computer)** See **enable/disable**.

**disassemble/dissemble** *Disassemble* means to take something apart:

> Please disassemble the toaster and repair it.

*Dissemble* means to behave hypocritically or to conceal the real nature of something:

> Although he disliked the play, he dissembled by praising the scenery.

**disastrous** Spell this word correctly (not 'disasterous') and you will pronounce it correctly.

**disbar** See **debar/disbar**.

**disbursement** The *-e* of *disburse* is retained.

**disc/disk** Because of the prevalence of US computer technology, *disc* has largely given way to the US spelling *disk* in the computer context: *floppy disk*. Australian English favours *disc* in all other cases: *compact disc* (the sound-recording kind); *disc brakes*; *slipped disc*.

**disciplinary** Note the *-ary*.

**discomfit/discomfort** There is some overlap in the meaning of these two words but they should not be confused. The slightly archaic verb *discomfit* means to thwart, disconcert or make uneasy:

> The confidence of the batsman discomfited the bowler.

The verb *discomfort* (much less common than the noun) means to make uncomfortable or uneasy; the latter meaning gives rise to the possible overlap. You could say that *the children's new shoes discomforted them*, but it would be more natural to say that *the children suffered discomfort from their new shoes*.

**discreet/discrete** Although these adjectives are very different in meaning, their spelling is frequently confused. *Discreet* (the more common word) means prudent or circumspect: *a discreet friend who keeps a secret*. *Discrete* means separate: *discrete particles of dust in a sunbeam*. A memory-jogger is the fact that the letter *t* separates the first and second *e* in the word that means separate. Care must be taken in speech because the words sound the same. If there is any possibility of confusion, avoid the less familiar of the two.

> I have been making discreet [cautious] inquiries.

*but* They have been making separate [*rather than* discrete] inquiries.

**discrepancy/disparity** A *discrepancy* is a difference or inconsistency, usually small:

> There is a slight discrepancy in the bank accounts.

A *disparity* is a difference, usually considerable, that focuses on inequality:

> There is a marked disparity between their salaries.

**discrete** See **discreet/discrete**.

**discretionary hyphen** See **hard hyphen/soft hyphen**.

**discriminating/discriminatory** Although the noun *discrimination* can mean either discernment or prejudice, the two adjectives related to it diverge sharply from each other. Someone who is *discriminating* is discerning, capable of making fine distinctions:

Margot is a discriminating judge of colonial art.

*Discriminatory* primarily means prejudiced, capable of making distinctions unfavourable to one party:

Discriminatory attitudes against locally grown wines will ruin the industry.

See also **discriminatory language**.

**discriminatory language** Writers and editors should be aware of the role language can play in reinforcing prejudice and inequality, particularly when they are producing texts for teaching or reference, or preparing advertising copy or media reports. For instance, some words and usage are considered inappropriate today because of the wide variety of racial and national groups in Australia and the changing status of women in society. It is desirable to eliminate expressions that are likely to offend the sensibilities of any group, and stereotypes that perpetuate prejudiced attitudes.

Avoiding the use of discriminatory language is largely a matter of good sense coupled with an awareness of the terms preferred by the groups involved: *Kooris* or another Aboriginal name rather than *blacks* for *Aborigines*; *disabilities* not *handicaps*; *non-drinkers* not *wowsers*. Many people would, however, consider it inappropriate to substitute *the unwaged* for *the unemployed*, for example.

Elderly people do not necessarily appreciate the euphemism *senior citizen*, even though they resent the kind of discrimination that is termed *ageism* – discrimination against old people solely because they are old. Ageism seems to be largely an attitudinal rather than a linguistic problem, however.

When editions of non-fiction works that do not have the status of literature are being revised for reprinting, outmoded and discriminatory descriptions or examples should, within reason, be removed and more acceptable words substituted. School texts, for instance, should reflect the mixed origins of the Australian people, not only the country's Anglo-Saxon and Celtic traditions and characters. Depictions of stereotyped female and male roles and behaviour should be replaced with more balanced and up-to-date images. Such 'editing' requires great skill and common sense: care must be taken that a historian's interpretation is not distorted or facts discarded simply to reflect current preoccupations or taste. The main danger is the replacement of longstanding prejudices by a new set. Literature should never be given this treatment: if a novel, for instance, is worth printing (or reprinting) it should stand as written, prejudices intact.

***Racist language*** Racist terms such as *wog*, *dago*, *abo* or *yid* are obviously offensive, but so are racial or national stereotypes that depict people as violent, ignorant, habitually drunk, avaricious, stupid or slovenly because of their background alone. To describe someone as *foreign-looking* immediately creates a perception of 'us versus them', and the implications of the term are questionable in a country where approximately two out of five people were either born overseas or had a parent born overseas. Statements like *Her behaviour was typical of her race* or *His racial characteristics come to the fore in these situations* show prejudice because they attribute differences between human beings solely to their racial or national origins.

***Sexist language*** It is this area that poses the greatest problems for the writer and editor. So-called sexist expressions have been part of our language – indeed our cultural heritage – for so long that we often use them without thinking. Such expressions can discriminate against women or men by fixing them in typecast roles or behavioural patterns. However, most instances of sexist language disparage women rather than men, either by excluding them or by portraying them as subordinate or inferior to men.

Because the word *man* is used in two senses in English – to describe an adult male human, and humanity in general – and because *he*, *him* and *his* have traditionally been used generically for male and female, women appear to miss out in phrases like *the family of man*, *man's dreams and aspirations*, *man's discoveries in science* and, in the oft-quoted oddity, *Man is a mammal who suckles his young*. To many people nowadays the word *man* is so closely associated with the adult male human that its use as a generic term is no longer acceptable, either by itself or in a compound. It is preferable, therefore, to use sex-inclusive words or phrases (that is, those that can include both males and females) rather than sex-exclusive ones. Here are some examples.

| ***Exclusive*** | ***Inclusive*** |
|---|---|
| mankind | humanity, humankind, human beings |
| manpower | workers, the workforce, personnel |
| the man in the street | the average citizen, ordinary people |
| sportsmanlike | fair, sporting |
| policeman | police officer |
| salesgirl | shop assistant |

Some critics have ridiculed such changes to established usage, saying that we will be forced to use words like *one-up-personship* and *personhandle*, and that we will no longer be free to fall down a *manhole* but only an *access hole* or *utility hole* (to cite an example from the controversial chapter on non-sexist language in the fourth edition of the AGPS *Style Manual*). Again common sense must prevail: obviously some words and phrases cannot be adapted gracefully to include both sexes, and writers and editors must retain good judgement and an awareness of what reads well.

Qualifiers such as *woman* dentist and *lady* doctor make women sound like oddities in a profession, as *male* nurse does for men. Another common example of sex discrimination in language is the portraying of women as appendages of men: *Mark Merrivale and his wife, Ann*. It is preferable to call them simply *Mark and Ann Merrivale*, or *Ann and Mark Merrivale*, unless it is necessary to indicate that they are not brother and sister but *the couple Ann and Mark*

*Merrivale*. And then there is *Mrs Harris, widow of Herbert Harris*. She should be *Henrietta Harris* or perhaps *the widow Henrietta Harris*.

Describing women by their physical appearance when describing men according to their intellectual attributes or occupation is yet another anomaly: *the brilliant scientist Edward Burton and his striking blonde wife, Rita*. Rita's talent or career may be as noteworthy as her husband's; her looks are usually irrelevant. Thus:

> The Burtons are an impressive couple: Rita is a splendid pianist, Edward an outstanding scientist.

It is obviously desirable and sensible to put men and women on an equal footing in the language: to write about *human achievement* instead of *man's achievement*; and *our pioneer ancestors* or *forebears* rather than *our forefathers*.

When referring to a person who could be of either sex you will have to take special care to avoid this kind of exclusive language:

> The examinee should give his paper to the supervisor.

Change to the plural:

> Examinees should give their papers to the supervisor.

Or recast the sentence completely, avoiding the use of a pronoun:

> Give examination papers to the supervisor.

There are other devices for getting around the problem of sex-specific language, but few are completely satisfactory. The combination of *she or he*, *his or her* and *her or him* is cumbersome when used repeatedly, though it is sometimes needed to prevent any possible confusion, as in legal documents. The use of *they*, *them*, *their* and *theirs* as what might be termed honorary singular pronouns linked with indefinite singular words such as *anyone*, *someone*, *each* and *whoever* is gaining ground today, even in formal writing:

> If *anyone* complains, it will be *their* own fault.
>
> *Someone* is knocking. Tell *them* I'm not here.
>
> *Each* person is telling me *they* are right.
>
> *Whoever* reaches camp first will receive *their* rations first.

The practice is nevertheless unacceptable to many careful writers.

The gimmick of changing the sex of the personal pronoun in alternate chapters (or paragraphs) of a non-fiction book so that both sexes receive what might be seen as fair treatment is irritating to the reader and should be resisted. It is equally undesirable to refer to a human as *it*. The device *he/she* should be restricted to official documents and forms.

Suffixes may give rise to difficulties. Many people consider that the suffixes *-ess* (*authoress*), *-ette* (*usherette*) and *-trix* (*executrix*) are unnecessary, denoting not simply the sex of a person but a sub-group of their category. There certainly are not many *poetesses* around these days, but there are still many *actresses*, *waitresses* and a few *heiresses*, some of whom object to being called *actors*, *waiters* and *heirs*. There is no simple solution to the suffix problem. Use the preference of the person you are writing about if you know it. In other cases use the form that sounds correct: *authoress* and *aviatrix* have an archaic ring today but *actress* does not. In some instances a new term has solved the problem: *flight attendant* is an intelligent way around the sex-exclusive *stewardess* (and *steward*, for that matter).

Arbitrarily assigning primary or secondary roles to men or women should be avoided. The typecasting of men as the sole supporters of the family and women as housewives is an inaccurate reflection of today's society. Stereotyping is unfair to both sexes.

See also **Aborigine/Aboriginal**; **America/United States/Latin America**; **anybody/anyone**; **Asian/Asiatic**; **black**; **chair**; **China/Chinese**; **discriminating/ discriminatory**; **each**; **either**; **ethnic**; **every/everybody/everyone**; **female/ feminine/feminist**; **gender**; **he/she**; **Jew/Israeli/Israelite**; **male/masculine**; **man/mankind**; **Ms**; **negro**; **New Australian**; **-person**; **pronouns**; **racism/ racialism/ racist/racialist**; **spokesperson**; **their/them/they**; **woman**.

**disfranchise** The spelling *disenfranchise* allowed by some authorities is not recommended for this verb, which most commonly means to deprive of the right to vote.

**disinformation/misinformation** *Disinformation* is inaccurate or misleading information, deliberately given. *Misinformation* may or may not be deliberate, but can be equally inaccurate or misleading.

**disingenuous** See **ingenious/ingenuous**.

**disinterested/uninterested** These adjectives are never synonymous. *Disinterested* means impartial:

> Because the judge must remain disinterested, her son is not competing today.

*Uninterested* simply means not interested:

> Some of the onlookers are uninterested in the sheepdog trials and will watch the wood-chopping instead.

See also **indifferent**.

**disk** See **disc/disk**; **disk, magnetic**; **disk, optical**.

**disk conversion** In desktop publishing *disk conversion* means the converting of a computer program from one system to another – for example from a Microsoft Word file on a DOS platform (IBM or compatible machine) to Microsoft Word on Apple. Software and, where necessary, cabling are available for a wide range of platforms and programs to allow disk conversion inhouse, or disks can be sent to a bureau for conversion.

See also **ASCII**; **bureau (desktop publishing)**; **file conversion**.

**disk copy** See **copy, presentation of**.

**disk drive** The *disk drive* in a computer is the device in which a disk is held for reading from and writing data to. The disk is spun at high speed and a read/write head is moved over its surface, in and out from the centre to the edge, so that any section of the disk can be located in a very short time for reading or writing data. The disk drive may be a unit separate from the main computer but plugged into it (*external disk drive*), or it may be part of the computer's central processing unit (*internal disk drive*). The greater the capacity of the disk drive, the larger the amount of information that can be stored.

See also **disk, magnetic**.

**diskette** See **disk, magnetic**.

**disk, magnetic** *Magnetic disks* or *diskettes* are used in computer systems for the storage, transfer, writing, reading and copying of data. So-called *floppy disks* – some of which are flexible (5¼ inches in diameter) and others firm (3½ inches in diameter) – are completely portable. They are placed in a disk drive to enable an operator to perform any of the functions mentioned, and are removed from the drive when work with them is completed. Floppy disks of both diameters come in a range of storage capacities, from 360 kilobytes to 1.4 megabytes.

*Hard disks* are usually fixed units within the computer, but they may be separate, attached by cable to the back of the computer. Hard disks have far greater storage capacity than 'floppies'; they are also faster and more reliable. Hard disks can store a large number of programs and data files, which avoids frequent changing of floppy disks.

Despite their power and capacity, hard disks are delicate and can crash without warning. It is wise to have backup files (on floppy disks or another hard disk, for instance) of all the material on them.

See also **backup**; **disk drive**; **disk, optical**.

**disk operating systems** See **MS-DOS**; **operating system**.

**disk, optical** An *optical disk* is a computer disk that uses optical techniques instead of magnetic ones for data storage. On an optical disk the data is stored in such a way that it can be read by a laser beam. Also called *compact disks*, optical disks can hold much larger quantities of data than magnetic disks of the same physical size. CD-ROM (compact disk read-only memory) allows data to be accessed and read, but not altered.

See also **disk, magnetic**.

**disorient/disorientate** Either form is acceptable for this verb, which means to confuse, especially with regard to direction, but *disorientate* is preferred.

See also **orient/orientate**.

**disparity** See **discrepancy/disparity**.

**dispatch** See **despatch/dispatch**.

**dispel/disperse** Both verbs can mean to scatter or drive off. *Dispel* tends to be used of abstract things – fears, suspicions, illusions, doubts:

> Life in a cramped cottage dispels romantic illusions of cosiness.

*Disperse* is used of people, and of things that tend to be concrete:

> Decentralising this department will disperse the experts and their equipment throughout the State.

*Disperse* can also mean vanish:

> The thick fog dispersed by midday.

**display type** See **type**.

**disputation/dispute** Do not use the word *disputation* – which means a very formal kind of argument – when you are referring to a simple disagreement, which is better described as a *dispute*.

**dissatisfied/unsatisfied** Both adjectives mean not satisfied. A *dissatisfied* person is discontented:

> Daniel is dissatisfied by his lack of promotion.

An *unsatisfied* person has unfulfilled needs but is not necessarily grumpy about the situation:

> Ingrid remains unsatisfied by the answers to her question.

**dissect** See **bisect/dissect**.

**dissemble** See **disassemble/dissemble**.

**dissociate** *Dissociate* means to disregard, or break an association with, something:

> I wish to dissociate myself from these local rivalries.

Some authorities allow *disassociate* as an optional spelling for this word.

**distil/distilled/distilling** Note the single *l* in the first and the *-ll-* in the other two.

**distinct/distinctive** These adjectives are not synonymous. *Distinct* means definite or clearly distinguishable:

> There are two distinct paths across the paddock.

*Distinctive* means characteristic:

> This large hole is the distinctive work of a wombat.

**distract** See **detract/distract**.

**distrust/mistrust** These words, used as both verbs and nouns, may nearly always be interchanged. *Distrust* is the more commonly seen of the two, and puts more emphasis on suspicion. Choose *mistrust* when the suspicion is less marked, or directed towards one's own feelings or abilities:

We distrusted the chef's proficiency after tasting his soup.

Kim mistrusted her ability to choose a ripe mango and consulted the fruiterer.

**disturb/perturb** To *disturb* is to interrupt, disarrange or trouble (mentally or physically):

It was forbidden to disturb the nuns at prayer.

Your toddler disturbed my neat bookshelves.

Cosmo says that Eva's ambitions disturb him.

Because *perturb* means to trouble mentally (but not physically), it could replace *disturb* in the third example.

**dived** In Australian English the past tense of *dive* is *dived*. *Dove* (pronounced to rhyme with *cove*) is not acceptable.

**diverge** See **differ/diverge**.

**diverse/divers** *Diverse* means varied or unlike:

Their diverse opinions meant that compromise was necessary.

*Divers* is a rather old-fashioned word meaning several or sundry:

The migrants spoke in divers languages.

It is pronounced '**die**-v'z'.

**divorcee** A *divorcee* is a divorced person of either sex. The French forms *divorcé* (male) and *divorcée* (female) are rarely used in Australian English today. Pronounce the word 'd'vor-**see**'.

**DIY** do it yourself.

**DJ** disc jockey.

**DLP** Democratic Labor Party.

**DMZ** demilitarised zone.

**DNA** This term, an abbreviation of *deoxyribonucleic acid*, refers to the long threadlike molecules, found in chromosomes and viruses, that are responsible for storing the genetic code of most organisms. Because DNA structure is unique to each organism, scientific analysis of DNA is becoming an accepted means of identifying people through a test known as a *DNA fingerprint*.

**do** The informal use of the verb *do* to replace a more precise word is widely accepted, but it is less appropriate in formal English:

Did you do [wash] the floor?

Do they do [serve] lunch?

They will do [study or perform] Brecht.

The other parts of the busy *do* family are also used informally in various ways:

They did [robbed or cheated] me.

He's doing time [serving a prison term].

It was a great do [party or other social event].

In conversation some people feel obliged to complete a verb with *do* rather than abbreviate or repeat it: *Mother told us not to replace the jug we broke, but we will do.* The word is unnecessary here, but is legitimately combined with *so* for emphasis:

She doesn't want us to buy a new jug, but we intend to do so.

**Doctor, the title** The title *Doctor* attached to someone's name is normally abbreviated to *Dr*. Physicians have long been given the courtesy title *Dr* even when they hold only bachelor's degrees, not doctorates. Surgeons, on the other hand, have generally preferred to style themselves *Mr*, *Mrs*, *Miss* or *Ms* – even when they hold a doctoral degree. In recent years Australian dentists and veterinarians (with one bachelor's degree apiece) have attempted to improve their status by calling themselves *Dr*. Universities sometimes award honorary doctorates to distinguished citizens who lack academic qualifications altogether; the use of titles in such cases is for the recipient to decide, but many regard it as inappropriate. (Many highly qualified academics are also awarded honorary doctorates, of course.)

Note that professors who happen to have doctorates are addressed and referred to as *Professor*, not *Dr*.

See also **degrees and diplomas**; **ranks, titles, honours and awards**.

**document** In computer terminology a *document* is a collection of data on disk.

**dodo** Plural *dodoes* or *dodos*.

**doggerel** Note the *-el*. *Doggerel* is trivial (usually comic) verse in irregular style; or drivel, nonsense: *He talked doggerel*.

**doily** The preferred Australian spelling for the little (often lacy) ornamental mat is *doily*. The plural is *doilies*.

**dominate/domineer** People or things may *dominate*, and the verb does not imply criticism of the dominator:

The Romans dominated the ancient world for four centuries.

Japanese cars dominate the market.

People only, not things, may *domineer*, and this verb always has a pejorative tone; the adjective *domineering* has similar restrictions on its use:

He is a tyrant who will domineer over staff and family alike.

**domino** The plural is *dominoes* for the game; *dominoes* or *dominos* for the masks or hooded cloaks worn by those (also called *dominoes* or *dominos*) who wear such outfits at a masquerade.

**DOS** disk operating system.

See also **MS-DOS**; **operating system**.

**do's and don'ts** Note the position of the apostrophes, which are regarded as essential in this expression.

**dot-matrix printer** See **printer**.

**dots per inch** Most computer printers use a rectangular pattern or matrix of dots to form the characters they print. The number of *dots per inch* (abbreviated *dpi*) of printed line indicates thc resolution (that is, the clarity) with which characters are formed by a printer. The more dots per inch (that is, the higher the resolution), the better the printed image. Most laser printers reproduce text and graphics at 300 dots per inch, though 600 dpi and 1000 dpi are also available. The output from image setters is most commonly 1200 dpi. Even at 300 dpi there is considerable variation in quality; however, there are many satisfactory applications for 300 dpi, including the production of memos, manuals, reports and books.

See also **bitmap**; **image setter**; **jaggies**; **pixel**; **printer**.

*Image at 300 dpi*

*Image at 1200 dpi*

**double entendre** This French expression (meaning to hear double) is used in English of words and phrases that have a double meaning, one of which is often in dubious taste.

See also **ambiguous**.

**double negative** Most people recognise that constructions like *I didn't say nothing* and *She hasn't got no money* are incorrect because the two negatives make a positive by cancelling each other out: if you didn't say *nothing* then you must have said *something*. The real objection to such constructions is that they are slipshod rather than that they are misleading or ambiguous.

The part-negative adverbs *scarcely, hardly* and *barely* may give rise to similar errors that are not necessarily confusing: *He travelled without hardly any money* clearly means that the traveller took little money with him. However, the following kind of construction is unacceptable: *He had barely not enough money for his fare*.

It is important to avoid doubling up negatives in a way that conveys a meaning opposite to the one intended, or makes the sentence puzzling:

> The board was unprepared to accept denials that the players had not taken drugs.

Remove the *not* and the sentence, though too complex, has the right meaning; simplify it and the meaning becomes easy to understand:

> The board continued to believe that the players had taken drugs.

It is legitimate to use double negatives in phrases or sentences such as these:

> Camilla is not unattractive.     Clive is not unintelligent.

In this kind of construction they modify ideas or impart a subtlety of meaning.

A colloquialism such as *I'm not going today*, *I don't think* is rarely ambiguous and is generally acceptable in informal spoken English.

See also **hardly**; **negative words**.

**double possessive** See **possessives**.

**doubling of consonants** See **consonants, doubling of**.

**doubtful/dubious** These two adjectives are often interchangeable, but *doubtful* is the more everyday word and it has a more neutral tone:

> The success of the talks remains doubtful.

Using the word *dubious* suggests that there is some suspicion (of unreliability or immorality) attached to the person or thing in question:

> Roger is a dubious ally because he weakens under pressure.

It is idiomatic to follow *doubtful* by *whether*, not *if*, in constructions of this kind:

> It is doubtful whether the record will be broken.

**doubtless/undoubtedly/indubitably** All these adverbs mean without a doubt, but *doubtless* conveys only grudging acceptance, even a hint that there may after all be some doubt. *Undoubtedly* (note the spelling – not 'undoubtably') is considerably more forceful than *doubtless*, indicating that there is no doubt at all. The strongest word (though a rather stagy one) is *indubitably*:

> Doubtless she will do well in the race, though she is out of form.
> She will undoubtedly win the race for she is in good form.
> Her performances as a hurdler have indubitably improved.

Most authorities object strongly to the form *doubtlessly*.

**douse/dowse** *Douse* means to plunge or be plunged into water, or to drench; and, colloquially, to extinguish: *Please douse the lights*. An accepted variant spelling is *dowse*, which is the only recommended spelling for the word that means to search for underground water or minerals with a divining rod.

**Dow Jones index** At the New York Stock Exchange the main index of share price movements is known as the *Dow Jones index*. Also called the *Dow Jones Industrial Average*, it is based on the daily average price of thirty leading stocks.

See also **all-ordinaries index**; **Nikkei**.

**download** To *download* means to transfer data from one computer to another or from a computer to a printer. You can download any computer file – for example, applications, databases, typefaces, utilities and games.

**downloadable font** *Downloadable fonts* in desktop publishing are those purchased and loaded into your system; they are accessed by your printer as required.

See also **font**; **printer font/screen font**; **resident font**.

**downplay** Prefer *play down*.

**downside** This overworked piece of US business jargon is now applied to the negative aspects of almost anything: *The downside of the job is that you have to work hard*. The opposite of *downside* is, naturally, *upside*. Avoid both words.

**Down syndrome** This is the recommended form (not *Down's*) for the name of the chromosomal abnormality once known as Mongolism.

See also **syndrome**.

**downward/downwards** The adjective is always *downward*: *a downward trend*. The adverb may be either *downward* or *downwards*: *walking downward [*or *downwards]*; *everyone from the president downward [*or *downwards]*.

**dowse** See **douse/dowse**.

**doyen/doyenne** The *doyen* is the most senior member of a particular group, not nécessarily the best: *the doyen of British paediatricians*. The feminine form *doyenne* is still used to describe women in this category.

See also **discriminatory language**.

**DP** data processing (computer).

**dpi** See **dots per inch**.

**Dr** debtor (on accounts); Doctor as a title before a name, normally abbreviated (see also **Doctor, the title**).

**draconian** Use a lower-case initial for this adjective (meaning harsh).

**draft/draught** In Australian and British English *draft* and *draught* cause many problems. We have the *draft* of a manuscript; *draft* legislation, and a *draftsman* (or *draftsperson*) who *drafts* it; a *draft* of soldiers; and a *draft* involving money. On the other hand there are *draughtsmen* or *draughtswomen*, who draw up technical plans; the *draught* of a ship; *draught* beer; a *draught* horse; a *draught* of air under a door; and the game of *draughts*.

In US English all these words, with the exception of the game of draughts (which is called checkers), are spelt *draft*.

**dramatic** Do not overuse this adjective to mean amazing, extraordinary or extreme, but if you feel you must use it, be sure that it is appropriate. You might refer to a *dramatic* downturn in the economy, for instance, but a *noticeable* price rise.

**drank/drunk** Note the forms of this verb:

> They drank [*not* drunk] lime and bitters.
> They have drunk [*not* have drank] lime and bitters.

See also **drunk/drunken/drunkenness**.

**dreamed/dreamt** Either form is acceptable as the past tense and past participle of the verb *to dream*, but *dreamt* is recommended.

**drier/driest** See **dry/drier/driest/dryer**.

**drop capital** See **capital letters, decorative initial**.

**drunk/drunken/drunkenness** The adjective *drunk* has two forms, *drunk* and *drunken*. *Drunk* is generally the one to use after a verb:

> We all became drunk on six or seven martinis.

*Drunken* is generally used before a noun:

He was only a two-pot screamer, not a drunken lout.

There is also a difference in meaning: *drunk*, the weaker word, implies a state of temporary insobriety, while *drunken* implies a habitual state. Note the spelling of *drunkenness*, with its *-nn-*.

See also **drank/drunk**.

**dry/drier/driest/dryer** *Drier* and *driest* are the comparative and superlative, respectively, of *dry*. Mechanical drying devices (*hair drier*; *clothes drier*) are normally spelt like the comparative, but *dryer* is also acceptable.

**DTP** desktop publishing.

See also **computers – and words; desktop publishing**.

**DT's/d.t.'s** Both are common forms of abbreviation for *delirium tremens*, a psychosis suffered by some alcoholics.

**dual/duel** *Dual* means pertaining to two: *dual controls*; *a dual nature*. A *duel* is combat with deadly weapons, arranged between two people to settle a dispute. An intellectual skirmish is sometimes described as *a duel of wits*.

**dubious** See **doubtful/dubious**.

**duel** See **dual/duel**.

**due to** See **because of/owing to/due to**.

**dumb** The word *dumb* (and the expression *deaf and dumb*) needs to be used very carefully in reference to anyone who is unable to speak, because of its past connotation of stupidity.

See also **discriminatory language**.

**dummy** To publishers and printers a *dummy* is an unprinted book made from the paper, and to the size, specified in a printer's quotation. Dummies may have a few printed pages and illustrations added to them for the information of potential buyers (book clubs, for example), who often need to see the material long before a printed book is available.

**Dutch/the Netherlands/Holland** The *Dutch* are the people of the political entity called *the Netherlands*, which is popularly known as *Holland* (originally a small coastal province of the Low Countries).

**dwarf** The plural is *dwarfs* except for those associated with Snow White, traditionally called the *Seven Dwarves*.

**dwelled/dwelt** Either form is acceptable as the past tense and past participle of the verb *to dwell*, but *dwelt* is preferred.

**dyeing/dying** *Dyeing*, from the verb *to dye*, is the process of colouring cloth. *Dying*, from the verb *to die*, means approaching death.

**dyelines** This term refers to the photographically produced proofs (on special paper) that printers provide for their clients just before a publication goes to press.
See also **proofs**.

**dynamic** This adjective and its noun *dynamics* have lost all their dynamism in recent years. Give them a rest.

**dynamo** Plural *dynamos*.

**dynasty** Pronounce this word '**din**-astee', not '**dine**-astee'.

**dysentery** Note the spelling.

**dyslectic/dyslexic** *Dyslectic* is the preferred Australian spelling for the adjectival form of the noun *dyslexia*, which is the name of a reading disability. A *dyslectic* is a person suffering from that disability.

# Ee

**e/ae/oe** See **ae/oe/e**.

**each** When *each* precedes the noun or pronoun to which it refers, treat it as singular and follow it with a singular verb and pronoun. When *each* follows the noun or pronoun, treat it as plural:

Each girl brings her own lunch. Each of them brings her own lunch.

*but* The girls each bring their own lunch. They each bring their own lunch.

The position of *each* in the second pair of examples makes the sentences slightly awkward, and some people would choose to rephrase without that word:

All the girls bring their own lunches.

When the sex of the person to whom *each* refers is unknown, or the word is attached to a mixed group, there may be problems with pronouns. The *he or she* construction may be considered necessary to avoid the sexist *he* but it is clumsy; using *their* after a singular subject means that you must flout the traditional rules of grammar. Careful writers will opt for the plural throughout the sentence:

The skiers will each follow their own map.

*or* All the skiers will follow their own maps.

*not* Each skier will follow his or her [*or* their] own map.

See also **discriminatory language**; **each other/one another**; **gender**; **he/she**; **pronouns**; **singular or plural**.

**each other/one another** Few authorities now hold that *each other* ought only to be used in reference to two things, and *one another* for more than two. In general the phrases are interchangeable:

Our manager and your director will talk to each other [*or* one another].

Everybody in the press gallery knew each other [*or* one another].

When *each other* is used as a unit it is treated as singular:

They disliked each other's [*not* each others'] philosophy.

Note also the following:

The twins each know what the other is feeling.
*not* The twins know what each other is feeling.
See also **each**.

**E & OE** The abbreviation for the old-fashioned phrase *errors and omissions excepted* is still occasionally found at the bottom of accounts and advertisements. The letters and ampersand are often closed up: *E&OE*.

**Earnest** The double entendre title of Oscar Wilde's famous comedy involving Ernest Worthing is *The Importance of Being Earnest*, not '*Ernest*'.
See also **double entendre**.

**Earth/earth** Use an initial capital when referring to the planet *Earth* as opposed to Mars, Uranus and the rest, but otherwise make it lower case: *on this earth*; *flat-earth theories*.

**East/east** See **compass points**.

**Eastlake, Qld** Compare with *Eastlakes*, NSW.

**eatable/edible** It is possible to eat (with or without pleasure) something that is either *eatable* or *edible*. In some contexts *edible* has an additional meaning, fit to eat (that is, not poisonous):

The meal was certainly eatable but I wondered whether the mushrooms were of an edible variety.

***EB*** *Encyclopaedia Britannica*.

**ebullient** Someone who is *ebullient* is overflowing with enthusiasm or excitement – at boiling point, figuratively speaking. Pronounce it '**ee-bul**-y'nt', with the 'bul' rhyming with either *full* or *hull*.

**EC/EEC** *EC* and *EEC* are abbreviations for the *European Community* and the *European Economic Community* respectively. The *European Community* is the present name of what before 1957 was called the *European Economic Community* or, informally, the *Common Market*. Member countries early in 1993 were Belgium, France, Germany, Italy, Luxembourg, the Netherlands, Denmark, the United Kingdom, Republic of Ireland, Greece, Spain and Portugal. The EC is often just called the *Community*.

**ECG** electrocardiogram; electrocardiograph.

**echo** Plural *echoes*.

**eco-** This prefix, taken from the word *ecology* – the study of living things in relation to their environment – is useful in compounds such as *ecosystem* and *ecosphere*, but is now tacked onto many words that have only a tenuous or indirect link with that study: *eco-freak*, *eco-babble*, *eco-lifestyle*, *eco-food*, *eco-jargon, eco-hoon*. Such words are suffering from overexposure.

**ecology/environment** Do not use the word *ecology*, which means the study of living things in relation to their environment, when you really mean *environment*, the natural surroundings (in this context).

See also **environment**.

**economic/economical** The adjective *economic* means relating to finance or the economy:

> Economic mismanagement has ruined the company.

*Economical* means thrifty:

> Economical habits make food and drink go further.

The two words are mistakenly interchanged by some people, particularly in speech, but the distinction is worth maintaining. Confusingly, *economically* is the adverb relating to both *economic* and *economical*. Moreover their opposites *uneconomic* and *uneconomical* can mean the same thing: unprofitable. Pronounce the *e* in all these words 'ee' or 'e' (as in *egg*).

See also **uneconomic/uneconomical**.

**economic rationalism** This is a rather imprecise term, but it is generally taken to mean the belief that whole economies and their constituent parts (markets, and the production and distribution processes) work best when the role of government is kept to a minimum.

**ecstasy** There are no variant spellings: 'extasy' is for X-rated video covers only, where it is usually 'eXtasy'.

**ECT** electroconvulsive therapy.

**ECU** European Currency Unit.

**-ed/-t word endings** Where verbs such as the following can form the past tense or past participle with either *-ed* or *-t*, give preference to the *-t* in Australian English: *dream/dreamt*; *spell/spelt*; *kneel/knelt*; *learn/learnt*.

**edible** See **eatable/edible**.

**editing** See **copy editing**.

**edition/impression/reprint** A book may be printed once and never reprinted. In this event the *first edition* remains the only edition. Reprinting the book would provide a *second impression* or a *reprint*. Reprints become *new editions* when there are substantial changes to the original. For example, a large number of corrections might be necessary; a hardback edition might become a paperback or a lavish limited edition; or the original might be revised, abridged or enlarged. Some books may run to many impressions and several editions.

See also **publications, parts of**.

**EDP** electronic data processing.

**-ee/-er word endings** When an *-ee* ending is attached to a verb, the noun it makes usually refers to a person to whom the action of the verb happens: a *trustee* is trusted; an *amputee* has had a limb amputated; something is referred to a *referee*.

When *-er* is attached to a verb, the noun it makes usually refers to a person who carries out the action: an *employer* employs someone; a *jogger* jogs; a *player* plays. An exception dating back three centuries and formed from a verb now obsolete is *refugee*. *Escapee* is widely accepted today, but many authorities have argued for the more logical *escaper*. *Retiree* (*retirer*?) has some currency and may be accepted in time.

See also **-er/-or word endings**.

**EEC** See **EC/EEC**.

**EEG** electroencephalogram; electroencephalograph.

**EEO** equal employment opportunity, as in *EEO officer*, *EEO program*.

**eerie/eyrie** The adjective *eerie* means inspiring fear:

> A bustling airport becomes slightly eerie when empty.

An *eyrie* is the high, inaccessible nest of a bird of prey such as an eagle. It has the extended meaning remote hideaway:

> The tower at Sissinghurst Castle made an eyrie for Vita's writing.

Variant spellings of *eyrie* are *aerie*, *aery* and *eyry*. It is pronounced '**ee**-ree', '**air**-ee' or '**eye**-ree'.

**effect** See **affect/effect.**

**effective/effectual/efficacious** These adjectives are similar in meaning but have distinctions worth noting. *Effective* means producing an intended or desired result or making a striking impression:

> We think the advertisement will be effective in selling the product, and it looks effective too.

*Effective* is also used of people who get results: *an effective president*; of people who perform roles nominally filled by others: *the effective manager*; and in phrases such as *a regulation effective from 1 January*.

*Effectual* also means producing an intended or desired result (with more definite success, perhaps); it is a relatively formal word:

> A petition presented by residents was effectual in drawing attention to zoning breaches.

*Efficacious* is similarly formal, and tends to be used of remedial treatment or action, especially medical:

> The prolonged course of treatment proved efficacious.

**effete** Modern usage has added the meanings decadent and effeminate, but this adjective basically means lacking in vigour, worn out. Use it carefully to avoid confusion: a fiscally bankrupt nation might truly be said to be *effete*, but it is not necessarily decadent. The word originally meant exhausted by bearing children, but it is not applied to women now.

**efficacious** See **effective/effectual/efficacious.**

**EFT** electronic funds transfer.

**EFTA** European Free Trade Association.

**EFTPOS** electronic funds transfer at point of sale.

**e.g./i.e.** The abbreviation *e.g.* (Latin: *exempli gratia*) means for example, and should not be confused with *i.e.* (Latin: *id est*), which means that is: *popular tourist destinations, e.g. Bali and Singapore*; *popular tourist destinations, i.e. ones that become overcrowded in season.* Note that there is a comma just before both *e.g.* and *i.e.* but not after them.

These shortened forms are best restricted to notes, footnotes and tabulations, or where space-saving is important. They should not be used in formal narratives. The full stops are sometimes omitted in modern usage, but retaining them is recommended.

Note that it is tautological to use *e.g.* with words or phrases like *including*, *etc.*, *such as* or *as in*.

**ego** Plural *egos.*

**egoism/egotism** These words have distinct though overlapping meanings. *Egoism* can simply mean self-interest; or it can mean the ethical theory that self-interest is the foundation of behaviour; hence an *egoist*, an adherent of this philosophy. *Egotism* (the more pejorative word) is self-centred or boastful behaviour, hence an *egotist*.

**EIS** environmental impact statement (or study).

**either** Most functions of this word involve the meaning one of two possibilities:

Either milk or water may be added.

If there are more than two possibilities use *any* or *any one*:

Any [one] of three spices may be added.

When used as an adjective or pronoun *either* takes a singular verb:

Tell me if either [adjective] man rings the bell.

*or* Tell me if either [pronoun] of the men rings the bell.

*not* Tell me if either of the men ring the bell.

In the *either...or* construction, when both subjects are singular use a singular verb:

Either Tony or George takes messages.

When both subjects are plural, use a plural verb:

Either the receptionists or the porters take messages.

When there is a combination of singular and plural subjects, the verb agrees with the subject nearest to it:

Either Tony or the porters take messages.

The same principle applies when pronouns seem to require different forms of a verb:

Either you or he is [*not* are] to take the messages.

The *either...or* construction is difficult to use satisfactorily when the subjects are not of the same sex, because it is often impossible to observe number agreement while avoiding both sexist language and over-complexity. Rewriting is recommended – you can sometimes, for example, reverse the sentence as follows:

A soft chair will be needed if either Sam or Naomi comes.

*not* If either Sam or Naomi comes *they* will need a soft chair.

Neither of the following examples is entirely satisfactory but such constructions may be unavoidable:

If either Sam or Naomi comes *he or she* will need a soft chair.

If either Sam or Naomi comes *she* will need a soft chair.

The careful writer will always place *either* in a position that balances the alternatives:

Dilute the scotch either with water or with soda.

*or* Dilute the scotch with either water or soda.

*not* Dilute the scotch either with water or soda.

Note that *either* may be used as an adverb, following a negative:

My sister does not like sweet coffee; I don't either.

The first syllable of *either* may be pronounced to rhyme with *fly* or *flee*.

See also **discriminatory language**; **gender**; **he/she**; **neither**; **or**.

**the Ekka** A popular name for the annual Brisbane Exhibition.

**elder/eldest/older/oldest** The adjectives *elder* and *eldest* are used only of people, and generally only in the context of family relationships: *my elder brother*; *her eldest sister.* Note, however, that *elder* cannot be used with *than*: *a sister older [*not *elder] than me*. *Elder* is also used, sometimes as a noun, to describe people of achievement, experience or age: *an elder statesman*; *an Aboriginal elder*; *church elders*. *Older* and *oldest* are used of things as well as people in any context: *my older brother*; *the older dog*; *the oldest building*.

See also **comparative and superlative**.

**electric/electrical/electronic** Literally speaking, anything that uses electricity as a source of power is *electric*: *an electric blanket*; *an electric clock*. *Electrical* is a more general word: *an electrical engineer*; *an electrical shop*. *Electronic* is used of systems in which an electric current is directed through a device such as a thermionic valve or semiconductor: *an electronic game*; *electronic data processing*.

**electronic mail** This is a method of sending messages in electronic form from one computer to another, via a cable network, telephone lines or satellite. The message is typed at the sender's computer, then transmitted electronically to a storage area. At any time the person for whom the message was destined can log into the storage computer and retrieve the message. Coded addresses and passwords are used to enhance security and accurate directing of messages. The term *electronic mail* is often abbreviated to *e-mail*.

See also **bulletin board**; **local area network**.

**elegy/eulogy** An *elegy* is a plaintive or melancholy poem or song, often a lament for the dead. The adjective is *elegiac* (not 'elegaic'). A *eulogy* is a formal tribute, spoken or written, often to someone who has died.

**elemental/elementary** Both these adjectives primarily mean pertaining to basic principles, but they are not interchangeable. *Elemental* refers mainly to the forces of nature:

> The elemental power of the hurricane was awesome.

*Elementary* means simple or rudimentary:

> Elementary grammar is most easily learnt at school.

**elicit/illicit** The spelling of these two words is sometimes confused. The verb *elicit* means to draw out or bring forth:

> The clown tried to elicit a reaction from the shy little boy.

The adjective *illicit* means illegal or not approved:

> The illicit cassettes were cheap but shoddily produced.

See also **illegal/illegitimate/illicit**.

**ellipsis** *Ellipsis* (plural *ellipses*) is the omission of words that would have completed a sentence or clarified its construction. It makes for brevity in casual exchanges:

Shame you can't come. Call you Monday.

And it avoids repetitiveness:

The receptionist is expected to answer the phone and [is expected to] type letters.

Headlines and cryptic notices make use of ellipsis:

Smoking rate down!  NO CARS ON BEACH

Problems can arise from ill-considered ellipses:

- in ambiguous constructions, where the reader cannot be sure that ellipsis has taken place

For lunch Granny gave us bread and sardines, both fresh.

*not* Granny gave us fresh bread and sardines [straight from the sea, or tinned?] for lunch.

- where the omitted part of a compound verb plays a different role from the part expressed

That dog never has *been* and never will be friendly.

*not* That dog never has and never will be friendly.

- in constructions from which a relative pronoun has been omitted

The heart-rate of athletes is lower than *that of* inactive people.

*not* The heart-rate of athletes is lower than inactive people.

- in constructions from which a preposition has been omitted

She skates as well as or better than the instructor.

*not* She skates as well or better than the instructor.

An *ellipsis* is also a printing device (. . .) used to indicate that words have been omitted from a quoted passage:

'Alas! poor Yorick. I knew him, Horatio . . . he hath borne me on his back a thousand times . . .'

It may indicate an unfinished sentence or hesitant speech:

'Could you perhaps . . . er . . . I was wondering . . .'

Use three dots only, even at the end of a sentence; no full stop is added but a question mark or exclamation mark may follow ellipsis. The space before, between and after the dots should be equal.

See also **quotations**.

**elude** See **allude/elude/evade**.

**elusive** See **allusive/elusive/illusive**.

**em/en** These are typesetting terms. An *em* is a *variable* measurement that is based on the square of the type body. For example, in 14 point type the width of an *em* is 14 points. In mark-up a *pica* (which is a *fixed* measurement of 12 points) is sometimes called a *pica em* or simply an *em*, but this practice is very misleading. An *en* is half an *em*. In typesetting jargon an *em* is called a *mutton* and an *en* a *nut*. See the entry **points** for an illustration of em and en measures compared with picas, points and inches.

See also **dashes, types of**; **pica**.

**e-mail** See **electronic mail**.

**embargo** The plural is *embargoes*. An *embargo* is a prohibition imposed in areas such as commerce, publicity and shipping.

**embarrass/embarrassment** Note the *-rr-* and *-ss-*.

**emend** See **amend/emend**.

**emigrant/immigrant/migrant** *Emigrants* leave their native land to live somewhere else; *immigrants* come into another country to settle there. Thus *emigrants* become *immigrants* on arrival in their adopted land:

> Many of the Italians were emigrants [*not* immigrants] from Sicily.
>
> Australia receives many immigrants [*not* emigrants].

Referring to *immigrants* as *migrants* is a singularly Australian usage that has enabled people to skirt around the difference between *emigrant* and *immigrant*. Strictly speaking, a *migrant* is a person or animal that travels from one place to another: *a migrant from the inner city to the suburbs*; *birds that are seasonal migrants*.

Note that an *émigré* is usually someone who has become an emigrant for political reasons.

**eminent/imminent/immanent** *Eminent* means high in station, distinguished, or conspicuous: *an eminent surgeon*; *eminent fairness*. *Imminent* describes something that is threatening or about to happen: *an imminent attack*; *their imminent return*. Take care not to confuse *imminent* with the lesser-known word *immanent*, meaning indwelling or inherent. In Christian theology God is said to be *immanent*: that is, pervading the universe and dwelling within people.

**emissary** Note the single *m* and the *-ss-*. An *emissary* is a messenger or representative.

**emotional/emotive** Use *emotional* to suggest the displaying or experiencing of emotion:

> It is difficult to remain calm when others are openly emotional.

Use *emotive* to suggest the arousing of emotion:

> Anti-vivisection is an emotive cause.

Some people use the word *emotive* when *emotional* would be the better choice:

> Rosemary is an emotional [*not* emotive] sort of person, joyful one moment and depressed the next.

**empathy/sympathy** *Empathy* is a perception of another's feelings that involves a close mental connection with them or a sharing of them. *Empathy* should not be used in mundane contexts as a synonym for *understanding* or *sympathy*:

He had a great understanding of [*not* empathy with] koalas.

*Sympathy* involves a compassionate feeling towards the problems of another. Many Australians have *sympathy* for the underfed peoples of the world but few would have *empathy* with them.

**en** See **em/en**.

**enable/disable** These words have special meanings in the context of computers. To *enable* a function of a computer program is to turn it on. For example, if you want to highlight all the keyboard characters, including the carriage returns, space bars and tabs, you can enable the function by turning it on in the appropriate dialogue box.

To *disable* a function is to turn it off. For example, if you do not want to use automatic hyphenation in your document, you can disable it by turning it off in the appropriate dialogue box.

**encapsulated PostScript** Converting a graphics file into an *encapsulated PostScript* file (abbreviated to *EPS*) enables a computer operator to import the graphics file into a program with a different format, for example a page-makeup program.

See also **converted graphics files**; **graphics**.

**encumbrance** Note the spelling (not 'encumberance'). A variant spelling is *incumbrance* (with *incumber* a variant of *encumber*); this is far less commonly used, however.

**encyclopaedia/encyclopedia** Either spelling is acceptable.

**ended/ending** Use *ended* when a period is in the past, *ending* when referring to future events:

Records were kept for the year ended June 1992.

They will be away for the fortnight ending at Christmas.

**endmatter** See **publications, parts of**.

**endnotes** See **notes**; **reference marks**; **references**.

**endorsement** The final *e* of *endorse* is retained.

**endpapers** Some books, especially hardcover editions, have *endpapers* joining the body of the book to the covers. The inner half of the first endpaper is called the *flyleaf*.

**end product/end result** The word *end* is usually superfluous in both of these phrases.

**energising/enervating** Some people treat these words as synonyms but they are actually antonyms. *Energising* means supplying energy or rousing into activity. *Enervating* means weakening, depriving of vitality.

> Extroverts find parties energising; introverts find them enervating.

**enforceable/enforcement** Both words retain the final *e* of *enforce*.

**enormity/enormousness** Dictionaries give *enormity* the meanings outrageousness, monstrous wickedness, abnormality and enormousness, but stylists tend to disapprove strongly of the last. To avoid controversy (or to align yourself with the stylists) you may prefer to use words like *enormousness*, *vastness* and *immensity* when you mean great size:

> Neglect of the mentally ill is an enormity.
>
> The enormousness of health costs is a budgetary burden.

**enquiry/inquiry** *Inquiry* is the preferred spelling.

**enrol/enrolled/enrolling** Note the single *l* in the first and the *-ll-* in the other two. The related noun is *enrolment*.

**ensconce** If you spell this word correctly you are unlikely to mispronounce it 'esconce'.

**ensure** See **assure/ensure/insure**.

**enthral/enthralled/enthralling** Note the single *l* in the first and the *-ll-* in the other two.

**enthuse** The verb *enthuse* (a back formation from the noun *enthusiasm*) has been around for a long time in US English but has yet to find formal acceptance in Australian or British English. Use it in informal writing only, and otherwise choose *be enthusiastic* or *excite enthusiasm* (in others).

**entomology/etymology** *Entomology* is the study of insects, *etymology* the study of word derivations.

**entrepreneur** Watch the spelling, and pronounce it '**on**tra-pr'n-**er**'.

**enunciation** See **annunciation/enunciation**.

**environment** Note the *-onm-*. *Environment* is one of the great buzz words of the late twentieth century and is in danger of becoming debased, popping up in contexts where it has no serious application. The phrase *environmentally friendly* is also overused; indeed it has been exploited by advertising agencies to describe products from unbleached lavatory paper to biodegradable plastic bags.

See also **ecology/environment**.

**envisage/envision** Forget *envision* and use the much commoner word *envisage*, but use it properly. It means to visualise, not simply to expect:

The planners envisage nature trails criss-crossing the national park.

The planners expect [*not* envisage] little opposition to the zoning.

**envy/jealousy** The noun *envy* means the desire to possess someone else's advantage or success, and the discontent arising from frustration of that desire. It may range from admiration to dangerous resentment:

Christine's self-control was the envy of her friends.

Envy aroused by his wealth led to plotting among the prince's friends.

*Jealousy* involves the resentment, suspicions and fears aroused by rivalry; and it may mean assiduous care in the protection of one's own possessions:

Jealousy of his brother soured Martin's outlook.

The villagers knew of the squire's jealousy in guarding his fishing rights.

Note that you might feel *envy* because your neighbour has a new car, but not *jealousy*. The neighbour, on the other hand, might demonstrate *jealousy* of the precious vehicle by locking it up at night.

**EPA** Environment Protection Authority.

**EPAC** Economic Planning and Advisory Council.

**epic** This word has descended with a thump from its original meaning, a lengthy narrative poem describing heroic deeds (such as Homer's *Iliad*). Today it is an adjective popular with journalists describing anything unusually large or impressive – from a football match to a meal in an expensive restaurant – but careful writers will still use it selectively, for serious or jocular purposes:

The breaking of the sound barrier was an epic moment in the history of aviation.

Walking across the room was an epic journey for our toddler.

**epigram/epithet/epitaph** An *epigram* is a comment or poem that is short and witty. Alexander Pope produced many epigrams – for instance the line from *The Dunciad*, 'A brain of feathers, and a heart of lead'.

An *epithet* may be a descriptive word or phrase attached to a name, as in *Edward the Confessor*; or it may be a term of abuse: *dole-bludgers*.

Most dictionaries define an *epitaph* as a 'commemorative inscription' on a graveyard monument or elsewhere: *A loved mother, wife and friend.* Pithy descriptions summing up a person or thing are also sometimes termed epitaphs: *'Always late' will be his epitaph.*

**epitome/apotheosis** *Epitome* most commonly means a typical example or embodiment of something (but not necessarily something good):

> The social worker was the epitome of bureaucratic bungling.

Note that a typical example is not the same as the best possible example. A common error is to use *epitome* as a synonym for *culmination*: *the epitome of his acting career.* The word is pronounced '**e**pi**tt**a-mee'.

*Apotheosis*, unlike *epitome*, means the best possible example of a person or thing:

> Mother Teresa seemed the apotheosis of selflessness.

**EPNS** electroplated nickel silver.

**eponyms** Words derived from the names of real or imaginary people are called *eponyms* (from a Greek word meaning named after). Well-known examples include *bloomers* (Amelia Bloomer, 1814–94), *braille* (Louis Braille, 1809–52), *boycott* (Captain Charles Boycott, 1832–97), *cardigan* (7th Earl of Cardigan, 1797–1868), *morse* (Samuel Morse, 1791–1872), *quisling* (Vidkun Quisling, 1887–1945), *sandwich* (4th Earl of Sandwich, 1718–92), *watt* (James Watt, 1736–1819), *herculean* (Hercules) and *quixotic* (Don Quixote). An Australian example is *furphy* (rumour), derived from the brand-name Furphy, which appeared on water-carts whose drivers spread gossip among Australian soldiers in World War I.

In general, eponyms are written with a lower-case initial letter; exceptions include *Celsius* (Anders Celsius, 1701–44) and *Fahrenheit* (Gabriel Fahrenheit, 1686–1736). The adjective is *eponymous*:

> The coffee-house of Edward Lloyd was the meeting-place for the eponymous underwriters [Lloyd's].

**EPS** See **encapsulated PostScript**.

**equable/equitable** *Equable* means placid or uniform:

> An equable disposition makes for harmony in human relationships.
>
> The climate on the island is equable because of the narrow temperature range.

*Equitable* means just:

> An equitable division of assets will give them one-third each.

**equal/equalled/equalling** Note the single *l* in the first and the *-ll-* in the other two.

**equally** Do not combine *equally* and *as*. Write:

The vet and her assistant were equally kind.

*or* The vet was just as kind as her assistant.

*not* The vet was equally as kind as her assistant.

**equal to/equal with** To be *equal to* something is to be capable of it: *equal to the task*. To be *equal with* something or someone is to reach the same level: *equal with our opponents*.

**equitable** See **equable/equitable**.

**equivocal** See **unequivocal**.

**-er/-ee word endings** See **-ee/-er word endings**.

**-er/-or word endings** When the suffix *-er* is added to verbs or altered versions of them, it turns them into nouns describing people or things that perform the action of the verbs: *do*, *doer*; *blend*, *blender*; *run*, *runner*.

In some instances the suffix *-or* has the same effect. Although *-er* is the more common ending, verbs that end in *t* and *ct* usually take *-or*: *audit*, *auditor*; *act*, *actor*; *dissect*, *dissector*. So do verbs ending in *ate* and *ute*, but they drop their *e* first: *calculate*, *calculator*; *emulate*, *emulator*; *contribute*, *contributor*.

Some words can have either an *-er* or an *-or* suffix and retain the same meaning: *adviser/advisor*; *convener/convenor*. Others have different meanings according to the ending: *sailer* (a vessel with sails) or *sailor* (someone whose occupation or pastime is sailing).

As there are so few clear rules on whether to use *-er* or *-or*, it is best to check the spelling in a dictionary when in doubt (bearing in mind the fact that US and Australian usage are often different).

See also **-ee/-er word endings; -or/-our endings**.

**-er/-re word endings** See **US spelling**.

**ergonomics** The study of the efficiency of people in their working environment is called *ergonomics*. *Ergonomist* is the latest name for the person who used to be called a *time-and-motion technician*.

**errant** See **arrant/errant**.

**errata/corrigenda** Either of the Latin plurals *errata* (singular *erratum*, meaning error) or *corrigenda* (singular *corrigendum*, meaning a thing to be corrected) may be used to head a list of mistakes discovered in a book just before (or just after) printing.

**erupt/irrupt** To *erupt* is to break out:

The chicken pox erupted overnight.

To *irrupt* is to break or burst (into):

The alarm irrupted into my dream of Venice.

**escalate** This verb means to increase or develop by stages. It has become overused as a synonym for *rise*, *expand* or *intensify*. Choose instead the most suitable of those words.

**Eskimo** Plural *Eskimos* or *Eskimo*.

**ESL** English as a second language.

**ESP** extra-sensory perception.

**especially/particularly** These adverbs should usually be placed as close as possible to the word they modify as their position may dictate the meaning of a sentence:

Dave especially [*or* particularly] doesn't like pumpkin.

Dave doesn't like pumpkin especially [*or* particularly].

Intonation in speech can often make your meaning clear, but when writing it is essential to place the words correctly to avoid ambiguity. A similar problem may occur with words like *even*, *only*, *simply* and *merely*.

See also **especially/specially**.

**especially/specially** Although often used interchangeably, these adverbs have a distinct difference in meaning. *Especially* means particularly or exceptionally:

She is especially fond of her grandmother.

The dinosaur exhibition was especially interesting.

*Specially* means specifically, or for one purpose:

Zoology students went to town specially to see the exhibition.

The bridal gown was made specially for her.

It could, of course, also be *an especially beautiful gown*.

See also **especially/particularly**.

**espresso** Not 'expresso' (coffee-machine or coffee).

See also **cappuccino.**

**Esq.** This polite title, used in place of *Mr* in addresses (*Clem McCluskey Esq.*), is rare today. It is an abbreviation of *Esquire*.

**EST** Eastern Standard Time.

See also **time zones.**

**the Establishment** *The Establishment* is the name often given to a long-established segment of society; its usually conservative views and values are widely influential.

**estimate** It is tautological to combine this noun or verb with words like *about* or *approximately* because *estimate* includes this sense: *an audience estimated at [*not *estimated at about] 500.*

**ETA** estimated time of arrival.

**et al.** This is an abbreviation of the Latin phrase *et alii*, which means and others (that is, other people). It is printed in roman type:

Parker, Kalamakis, Bloch et al. always arrive in time for drinks.

Lee et al. are authors of a study called *Hong Kong Traders*.

If you see *et al.* printed in italic it is probably the abbreviation of another Latin phrase, *et alibi*, which means and elsewhere.

See also **bibliographies**; **notes**; **references**.

**etc./et cetera** The Latin phrase *et cetera*, which is usually abbreviated to *etc.* (or, more rarely, *&c.*), means *and the rest* or *and other similar things*; it is always printed in roman type:

Vittorio bought bread, olive oil, milk, salt etc. at the corner store.

The word is used to refer to things rather than events or people. It is not appropriate in formal writing, where *and so on* or *and so forth* may replace it. Do not write *and etc.*, or use it at the end of a list preceded by *such as* or *for example*. *Etc.* should always end with a full stop, but is preceded or followed by a comma only when the sentence structure demands it:

The bread etc., to say nothing of the fruit and beer, cost too much.

*Etceteras* (one word) are various extra things or people.

Do not pronounce *etc.* 'eksetra'.

**ETD** estimated time of departure.

**ethnic** This adjective is used to describe the attributes of any group or race, and matters such as its culture, language and food. In Australia it has become a debased word, used as a label (originally well meant) for people from non-white or non-English-speaking countries. Because *ethnic* usually categorises people according to colour or race, it is more offensive in its own way than the comparatively innocuous term *New Australian*, also originally well meant, that it has largely replaced (and which applied to immigrants from anywhere). To use the word as a noun – *He [*or *She] is an ethnic* – may not be as bad as saying *He [*or *She] is a dago*, *chink* or *nigger*, but the implication is much the same: he or she is certainly not of white Anglo-Saxon, Celtic or Nordic stock. Because of its current state in the language the word is best avoided where possible, even in such seemingly innocent but meaningless phrases as *ethnic radio*, *ethnic food* and *ethnic clothes*. If you have Greek neighbours, eat Indian food, or have just listened to a program in Swahili, then say so plainly and simply.

See also **discriminatory language**; **New Australian**.

**et seq.** This abbreviation means and the following (Latin: *et sequens* or *et sequentes*). Its most common use is in references: *pp. 185 et seq.*, which means page 185 and the pages following. It is not italicised.

See also **references**.

**etymology** See **entomology/etymology**.

***Eucalyptus*** If you want to refer to a tree that belongs to this genus, call it a *eucalypt* (plural *eucalypts*). Note that not all eucalypts are, strictly speaking, gum trees (some are peppermints, for example, others ironbarks).

**eulogy** See **elegy/eulogy**.

**euphemisms** These roundabout, toned-down or vague words or phrases are used to avoid what Fowler in *Modern English Usage* calls 'blunt precision or disagreeable truth'. Families might be said to be *in a low-income group* rather than *poor*; to live in *sub-standard housing* rather than *slums*; to have some members spend time in *correctional facilities* rather than *prisons*; and to suffer from the *outplacement* rather than *sacking* of other members.

Euphemisms are often used as genteel substitutes for words that are considered indelicate: *lavatory* is the classic instance, turning up as, for example, *powder room*; *smallest room*; *little boys'* or *little girls' room*; and *toilet*. To *die* is to *pass on* or, if one is an American, *experience a terminal episode*. The US is in fact the home of the imaginative euphemism, with the Pentagon the forcing ground of many examples: *tactical air support* for *blanket bombing*; *destabilisation* for *subversion*; *tactical redeployment* for *retreat* or *defeat*; *inoperative combat personnel* for *dead* or *wounded soldiers*; and *collateral damage* for *dead civilians*.

See also **circumlocution**; **lavatory/toilet**.

**European Community/European Economic Community** See **EC/EEC**.

**euthanasia** The Greek root of this word means good death (that is, a gentle death), and *euthanasia* and *mercy killing* have become synonyms meaning the painless putting to death of the brain-dead or those with an intolerably distressing incurable disease.

**evade** See **allude/elude/evade**.

**even** The adverb *even* should usually be placed as close as possible to the word it modifies as its position can dictate the meaning of a sentence:

Even I prefer beer to champagne.

I prefer even beer to champagne.

I prefer beer even to champagne.

Intonation in speech can often make your meaning clear, but when writing it is essential to place the word correctly to avoid ambiguity. Note that a similar problem may affect other words such as *merely*, *only*, *simply*, *especially* and *particularly*.

**eventuate** Much used by politicians and public servants, *eventuate* is a slightly pretentious way of saying *happen*, *occur*, *result* or *come about*.

**ever** Some people disapprove of using *ever* in phrases such as *the most surprising election ever*. They argue that *ever* includes the future, which is unpredictable. This is pedantic: such usage is idiomatic and generally acceptable. It would be tautological, however, to write *the first election ever held by the bingo club*: *first* says it all.

See also **how ever/however**.

**every/everybody/everyone** To be grammatically correct, any verb and pronoun governed by *every* should be singular:

Every girl carries her own camera.

Every birdwatcher has his or her own binoculars.

Note that to avoid sex-exclusive language *his or her* may be used when the sex of the subject is unknown, but this construction is too clumsy for frequent use. Replacing *his or her* with *their*, as some prefer to do, flouts the traditional rules of grammar. The sentence should be recast in the plural if possible:

All the birdwatchers have their binoculars.

*Everybody* and *everyone* are interchangeable and, like *every*, should be used with a singular verb and singular pronoun; otherwise the sentence is better recast in the plural:

Everybody [*or* everyone] has his or her own binoculars.

*or* All have their own binoculars.

But note that the two-word form *every one* is always used in reference to things. The word is also split when it is followed by *of* and refers to people:

The guide carried every one of the raincoats.

Every one of the hikers has a raincoat.

Take care when using *every* in the following construction:

Put a full stop at the end of every line.

*not* Put full stops at the end of every line.

See also **anybody/anyone**; **discriminatory language**; **gender**; **he/she**; **pronouns**; **their/them/they**.

**evince/evoke** *Evince* means to demonstrate clearly or reveal (especially qualities):

The company's generosity to the accountant evinced its loyalty to staff.

*Evoke* means to call up or produce (memories or feelings):

Adelaide always evoked happy memories for her.

**exaggerate** Note the *-gg-* and single *r*.

**exceedingly/excessively** *Exceedingly* means very much but *excessively* means too much.

**excel/excelled/excelling** Note the single *l* in the first and the *-ll-* in the other two.

**except** The preposition *except* means apart from, and any pronoun attached to it must be in the objective case:

Everybody has had coffee except me [*not* I].

Some careful writers dislike the use of *except for* to mean *without* or *but for*; either of those is to be preferred:

I would have got nowhere without [*or* but for] your help.

*rather than*

I would have got nowhere except for your help.

See also **accept/except**; **case (grammar)**.

**exceptionable/exceptional** *Exceptionable* is a fairly uncommon adjective that means objectionable:

Those remarks are exceptionable; please apologise.

*Exceptional* means very unusual, well above the average or extraordinary:

She is an exceptional chess player for one so young.

It was exceptional for so much rain to fall in summer.

The negative of both words – *unexceptionable* (inoffensive) and *unexceptional* (ordinary) – causes considerable confusion, and it is necessary to be particularly careful where the context would allow either. An exhibition of paintings could be *unexceptionable* or *unexceptional*. The first of these two words is again much less common than the second.

**excess** Avoid the cliché *in excess of*; use *more than*.

**exclamation mark** An *exclamation mark* (!) is the punctuation mark that conveys any strong feeling. *Exclamation marks* are commonly used in the following ways:

- to express surprise, disbelief or annoyance, for instance

It's amazing! He couldn't have! How dare he!

Why didn't you tell me you'd be so late!

- to praise or condemn

  How lovely!     What an appalling waste!
- after interjections, oaths, toasts, and words expressing noises

  Oh!     Damn you!     Long live the Queen!     Bang!
- after commands and to express alarm

  Stop!     Lie down!     Help!

Some writers scatter exclamation marks throughout their work instead of choosing vivid phrases that need no such emphasis. Overuse of what in the typesetting business are known variously as *startlers*, *shrieks* or *screamers* will annoy most readers. As one is usually more than enough, they should never be doubled (!!) or trebled (!!!).

**exclusive language** See **discriminatory language**.

**exhausting/exhaustive** *Exhausting* means extremely tiring:

> Cycling from Perth to Adelaide was an exhausting experience.

*Exhaustive* means comprehensive and thorough:

> An exhaustive study of roads, roadside facilities and weather patterns would be helpful to cyclists.

**exhilarate** Note the *h* after *ex-*.

**existent** See **extant/existent**.

**exorbitant** Note that there is no *h* after *ex-*.

**exotic** The primary meaning of the adjective *exotic* is foreign in origin or character, hence *exotic* plants (those brought in from another country) as opposed to the *native* species. Today the word is also legitimately used to describe anything unusual, exciting or colourful.

**expanded type** See **type**.

**expatiate/expostulate** To *expatiate* (on) means to enlarge on or explain in detail (a theme or topic):

> The geologist expatiated at length on his new theory.

*Expostulate* means to remonstrate or reason with someone:

> The geologist's assistant expostulated with him about his failure to mention her contribution.

**expatriate** The Latin phrase *ex patria* (out of one's native land), from which *expatriate* is derived, may be a useful reminder that the word is not spelt 'expatriot'. An *expatriate* is someone who has chosen to live in a country other than his or her own (the word may also be used adjectivally or, less commonly, as a verb):

The Australian writer Christina Stead was an expatriate for more than forty years, but late in life she returned to her homeland.

**expedient/expeditious** *Expedient* means advantageous, appropriate or convenient in the circumstances, often implying self-interest; *expeditious* means characterised by speed or promptness:

The maintenance manager found it expedient to overlook the cheekiness of the cleaner because her expeditious working habits saved so much time.

**experiment** Since an *experiment* is something that is by definition *tried*, it should always be *made* or *undertaken* rather than *tried*.

**expertise** Do not forget synonyms such as *skill*, *ability* and *knowledge*.

**explicable/explicate** *Explicable* is an adjective meaning able to be explained:

The high price of the small Christmas turkey was explicable only in terms of the demand.

The verb *explicate* means to make clear, analyse or interpret (matters such as a theory or viewpoint):

The teacher attempted to explicate the theory of atoms.

The word is regarded as pretentious when used as a synonym for *explain* in a general or mundane context.

**explicit/implicit** *Explicit* means clearly and unequivocally expressed:

The leaflet provided explicit instructions for assembling the new shelves.

The phrase *explicit scenes* is widely understood as shorthand for *explicitly sexual or violent scenes* in films.

*Implicit* primarily means not explicit – that is, implied rather than directly stated:

Her friendliness was implicit in her warm tone of voice.

A secondary meaning is unquestioning or absolute:

We had implicit trust in her good sense.

**exploitative** This (not 'exploitive') is the adjectival form of the verb *to exploit*.

**export/import** In desktop publishing to *export* a file from a graphics program means to save it in a particular format so that it can be placed in a word-processing or page-makeup document.

To *import* text means to bring material produced in one program (for instance a word-processing, graphics or spreadsheet program) into another program (such as a page-makeup program).

**expostulate** See **expatiate/expostulate.**

**extant/existent** Both adjectives mean existing, but *extant* has the added connotation of survival:

So many whales had been killed that only one species was extant in the area.

Regulations to protect the whale were existent but needed enforcing.

**extempore/impromptu** Both these adjectives mean without preparation. *Extempore* (pronounced 'ex-**tem**pa-ree') usually refers to an unprepared speech or performance: *an extempore lecture*. *Impromptu* is the better word for unexpected action in general: *an impromptu meal*; *an impromptu change of plan*. Note that music played spontaneously (that is, composed as it is being played) is said to be *improvised* rather than *extempore* or *impromptu*.

**extended type** See **type**.

**extent** The finished length of a publication.
See also **cast-off**; **character count/word count.**

**extenuating** This adjective, commonly used in the expression *extenuating circumstances*, means lessening the culpability of someone for something bad, not eliminating blame or excusing the person.

**exterior/external/extraneous** The adjectives *exterior* and *external* both mean pertaining to the outside; they are often synonymous:

They decided to do the exterior [*or* external] renovations before the interior.

*but* She suffered external [the better word] bruising when the ladder slipped.

*Extraneous* (note the spelling) refers to something that is beyond the relevant or essential (that is, it is coming from outside the matter):

The report is too long because it contains extraneous material.

**extraneous** See **exterior/external/extraneous.**

**extraterrestrial** Note the *-r-* in the second-last syllable, and be sure you include it in both spelling and pronouncing the word. As an adjective it means happening beyond the earth's atmosphere; the noun means a being from somewhere other than Earth.

**extrinsic/intrinsic** These adjectives are opposite in meaning. *Extrinsic* (the less common word) means originating or operating from outside something (not part of its essential being). *Intrinsic* means belonging to something as a permanent part of it. For example, an art dealer might appreciate only the *extrinsic* value of a fine painting – that is, its market value; an art lover might be more strongly attracted by the painting's *intrinsic* value – that is, its visual or emotional appeal.

**extrovert/introvert** Note the *-tro-* in both nouns, which are derived from Jungian psychology and are popularly used to describe contrasting types of personality or behaviour. *Extroverts* are people whose interests and thoughts are directed outside themselves; sociable and outgoing, they appear confident and unreserved:

> A natural extrovert, Omar mixes readily with all sorts of people.

*Introverts* are more concerned with their own thoughts and emotions than with society at large; they can appear withdrawn, preferring quiet reflection to social activity:

> Chloe is such an introvert that she hates meeting people.

The adjectives are also *extrovert* and *introvert* (or *introverted*).

**eyrie** See **eerie/eyrie.**

# Ff

**F** Fahrenheit.
See also **Celsius/centigrade/Fahrenheit**.

***f*** loud (music), abbreviated from the Italian *forte*.

**f.** female *or* feminine (see also **female/feminine/feminist**); focal length; folio (see also **fol./ff.**); franc (see also **currency**).

**fabulous** This adjective (and its abbreviation *fab*) has become so overworked as a synonym for *marvellous* that it is now dormant, awaiting a revival of its earlier meanings – celebrated in fable, or incredible.

**facade** The cedilla accent on the *c* is often dropped from this French word and it is not italicised. *Facade* means front (*an imposing Victorian facade*) or superficial appearance (*a calm facade hiding a tempestuous nature*). It is pronounced 'fa-**sard**'.

**face/face up to** *To face* something is to confront it, or to have it ahead of you:

> The climbers of Mt Blanc faced a great challenge.
> We face grave economic times in the next decade.

Some people dislike the expression *face up to*, but it does indicate a little more than confrontation – there is a greater determination to deal with or accept something unpleasant:

> The government has faced up to the problem of salination in the Murray–Darling basin.

**facetious** *Facetious* people and *facetious* comments may be lightly amusing, but they are often more annoying than entertaining because of their flippancy or poor taste:

Peter Bull insists on making facetious remarks about his virility.

The word itself is a curiosity, being one of the few in the English language containing all the vowels, only once and in alphabetical order.

**facile** Because this adjective, which means easily done, is now so often used derogatively to imply superficiality, it is safest to use words such as *skilful* or *effortless* when you want the ease to sound like a virtue:

Jim's facile writing carries no conviction.

*but* Carmel's skilful [*not* facile] turn of phrase brings life to her descriptions.

Pronounce the word '**fass**-ile'.

**facilitate** To *facilitate* something means to make it easier; you can *facilitate* events or actions but not people:

The instructions on the box will facilitate our building of the glider.

*but* The local scouts helped [*not* facilitated] the searchers.

**facility/faculty** The noun *facility* means being able to do something easily because of acquired skill:

Campbell has developed notable facility as a composer of film scores.

*Faculty* is a natural ability to do something easily:

Our Cambodian neighbour has a faculty for languages and has become an interpreter.

The use of *faculty* to describe a section of a university or college, such as *the faculty of architecture*, is long established, but *facility* does not have the same acceptance as a synonym for *premises*, *factory*, *base*, *station* or *office*.

**factious/fractious** *Factious* means acting in the interests of a faction, and therefore divisive:

Factious quarrelling threatened to split the union.

*Fractious* means peevish or unruly:

The crowd was fractious because rain interrupted the Test match.

**factitious/fictional/fictitious** There is a degree of artifice about things that are *factitious*, *fictional* or *fictitious*, but these adjectives are not synonymous. *Factitious* means contrived or sham. *Fictional* primarily means relating to or belonging in fiction, while something that is *fictitious* is intended to mislead.

Welfare payments were reduced on the factitious grounds that unemployed people would thenceforward try harder to find work.

Hughie Darcy is a fictional character in some of Ruth Park's novels.

Meg felt guilty about giving the supervisor a fictitious reason for her absence.

It is possible, however, for the three adjectives to apply to the one noun: a letter of gratitude may be at the same time *factitious* (sham in sentiment), *fictional* (occurring in fiction) and *fictitious* (deceitful).

**factoring** See **bankruptcy/factoring/liquidation/receivership**.

**facts** The terms *actual facts*, *true facts* and *real facts* are all tautological: the adjectives simply duplicate the meaning of the noun.

**faculty** See **facility/faculty**.

**Fahrenheit** See **Celsius/centigrade/Fahrenheit**.

**faint/feint** The adjective *faint* means lacking in strength, clarity or loudness, while the noun and verb relate to loss of consciousness. The less common *feint* means a movement made in order to distract or deceive (it can be a verb as well as a noun):

The boxer's feint tricked his opponent into an error.

**fair dealing** See **copyright**.

**fait accompli** Pronounce this French phrase (meaning accomplished fact) in the French way: '**fate** akkom-**plee**'.

**fantastic** This word is now liable to be misunderstood if used correctly to mean extravagantly fanciful, eccentric or capricious. It has become instead a somewhat overworked term of approval meaning wonderful or 'great': *It was a fantastic party and we had a fantastic time*.

**FAO** Food and Agriculture Organization (UN).

**faq** fair average quality (especially of wheat).

**Far East/Middle East/Near East** Broad geographical areas are covered by these Eurocentric terms. The *Far East* comprises Asian countries such as China, Japan and Thailand; the *Middle East* the area stretching from the eastern shores of the Mediterranean and Aegean to India; and the *Near East* the former Balkan states, Egypt and south-western Asia. Notwithstanding Australia's geographical position they are also Australian terms, although the name *Far East* is giving way to *Near North* or, simply but inaccurately, *South-East Asia*.

See also **South-East Asia**.

**farther/farthest/further/furthest** When referring to distance, both actual and figurative, *farther* is usually interchangeable with *further* and *farthest* with *furthest*.

Melbourne is farther [*or* further] from Cairns than from Adelaide.
It is the farthest [*or* furthest] thing from my mind.

When it means additional or, used as a verb, to advance, *further* is correct:

Further to our letter of 12 June, here is a summary of our discussions.

The group vowed to further the cause of homeless children.

There is no such word as 'furtherest'.

**fast** See **quick**.

**fatal/fateful** Although both adjectives have their origin in the noun *fate*, their meanings are distinct. *Fatal* means causing death or destruction. *Fateful* means involving momentous consequences, which may be good or bad:

The bushwalker suffered a fatal snakebite.

It was a fateful day when Germany invaded Poland.

Note that something that is *fateful* may also be *fatal*:

That one fateful [*or* fatal] error brought death to the toreador.

**Father's Day/Mother's Day** Note the position of the apostrophe in these names. *Father's Day* is celebrated on the first Sunday in September, *Mother's Day* on the second Sunday in May.

**FAW** Fellowship of Australian Writers.

**fax** A *fax* is a document transmitted by a *facsimile* (or *fax*) machine through a method called *fax*: *I received a fax*. The word is also used as a verb: *Please fax it to me*. In a remarkably short time this word as both noun and verb has gained complete acceptance.

**faze/phase** *Faze* is a colloquial verb of US origin meaning to upset or disconcert; its adjectival form, *fazed*, is more common than *faze*:

The guest contralto seemed fazed by her unresponsive audience.

The word is not yet fully acceptable in formal English but may be seen, often incorrectly spelt *phase*, in the popular press.

The noun *phase* means a stage, aspect or development:

The first phase in the building of the Town Hall has been completed.

The verb *phase in* means to plan or introduce something in stages:

The company will phase in the new computers over three months.

**FBI** Federal Bureau of Investigation (US).

**FBT** This is the abbreviation for *fringe benefits tax*, which must be paid by an employer on rewards additional to wages and salaries, such as a company car and travel.

**feasible** Note the *-ible*. This adjective means capable of being achieved or done:

The Very Fast Train seemed feasible to its promoters.

*Feasible* is often used as a synonym for *credible* or *likely*: *Does she have a feasible excuse?*. Careful writers avoid this usage.

**February** Spell this word correctly (note the first *r*) and you will pronounce it correctly.

**feet/foot** The plural of this imperial unit of measurement is *feet*: *six feet tall*. But note the compound adjectival form: *a six-foot man*.

**feint** See **faint/feint**.

**feisty** This US colloquialism means full of spirit, aggressive or quarrelsome. It is a popular newspaper word: *The feisty star slated her critics*. Pronounce it '**fice**-tee'.

**female/feminine/feminist** The adjective *female* simply describes the sex of humans, animals or plants: *a female cat with four kittens*. Its opposite is *male*. *Feminine* normally describes the characteristics of women. A man can be said to show feminine traits (*a feminine eye for detail*), but if his behaviour and appearance follow traditional female patterns he is likely to be described as *effeminate*. *Feminine* (and its opposite, *masculine*) also describes the gender of words: *the third-person feminine pronouns she and her*. The adjective *feminist* describes the movement aimed at putting women on an equal footing with men: *feminist recommendations for sex-inclusive language*. A *feminist* (noun) is a woman or man who subscribes to the views of the feminist movement.

See also **gender**; **male/masculine**; **man/mankind**; **woman**.

**ferment/foment** Although these words (used as both nouns and verbs) have different meanings in a scientific context, most authorities regard them as interchangeable when they are verbs meaning to agitate or incite:

His intention was to ferment [*or* foment] racial discord among the unemployed.

**fetid/foetid** Either spelling is acceptable for this adjective meaning ill-smelling. Pronounce it '**fee**-t'd' or '**fet**'d', whichever spelling you choose.

**fetus/foetus** Either spelling is acceptable, and the same applies to the adjective: *fetal* or *foetal*. The words are pronounced '**fee**-t's' and '**fee**-t'l'.

**fewer/less** Since *fewer* applies to number and *less* to quantity, a good rule of thumb is to use *fewer* with plural nouns (*fewer people*; *fewer worries*) and *less* with singular nouns (*less land*; *less boredom*). Apply the same rule to the phrases *fewer than* and *less than*:

The trio ate fewer than six sausages and drank less than a bottle of wine.

Some measurements, although expressed in the plural, are thought of as single units and require *less than*: *to pay less than $100*; *to swim less than 50 metres*; *to weigh less than 30 grams.*

Note that it is necessary to write *a smaller number* or *fewer in number* rather than *a fewer number.*

***ff*** very loud (music), abbreviated from the Italian *fortissimo.*

**fiancé/fiancée** *Fiancé* is the masculine form and *fiancée* the feminine of a noun that means someone engaged to be married. The acute accent should be retained. Both words are pronounced 'fee-**on**-say'.

**fiasco** The plural of this noun meaning humiliating failure is *fiascos.*

**fictional/fictitious** See **factitious/fictional/fictitious.**

**FID** This is the abbreviation for *financial institutions duty*, a State tax that is imposed on the receipts of all financial institutions. The rate varies from State to State.

**file** In computer terminology a *file* is a collection of information in a storage device (for example a hard or floppy disk). Files should always be clearly named.

**file compression utility** A *file compression utility* is a computer program that will compress files and release them as needed. By compressing all the files not currently in use on a hard disk drive you gain more room to operate large, complicated programs, and the hard drive will operate faster.

See also **disk drive.**

**file conversion** In computer terminology *file conversion* means taking a file from one program and converting it into another program – for example, a database file into a word-processing file, or a word-processing file into a page-makeup file.

See also **disk conversion.**

**filigree** This is the recommended spelling, though variant spellings are *filagree* and *fillagree.* Fine wire is twisted to make the delicate jewellery and other ornamental work known as *filigree.*

**Filipino/the Philippines** A native of the Philippine Islands is a *Filipino* (plural *Filipinos*). The preferred adjective is *Philippine* and the country is known as *the Philippines.* Thinking of that name as a compound of *Philip* and *pines* may help you to spell it correctly, but you must pronounce it 'filli-**peens**'.

**fillers** In the context of spoken English, *fillers* are words or parenthetical phrases that contribute to a relaxed and friendly tone if kept to a minimum, but are capable of annoying or distracting the listener if overdone. Fillers usually add little to the substance of what is said:

> *Actually* it's my birthday on Sunday, *you know*. I'm *kind of* having a few friends over and was wondering, *you know*, if you'd like to come. *Basically* it won't be a big party, *sort of* a few drinks, but perhaps, *hopefully*, a bit of fun, *if you see what I mean*.

It is noticeable that the filler count decreases when people are speaking into a telephone or on the radio. They seem to realise that, without the benefit of eye contact and gestures, they must impart information through the voice alone, and that careless speech bursting with fillers will not hold the interest of a listener for long.

The sentence that we have time to form mentally before writing is usually not complete before we begin speaking. Instead, our unformed thoughts have to be stuck together with a paste of fillers. It is possible, however, to keep fillers in check by thinking before we speak, and by using shorter sentences.

See also **circumlocution**; **clichés**.

**fill in/fill out** In formal Australian English we generally *fill in* a form; informally we – like the Americans – often *fill out* a form. Either is acceptable.

**fillip** One meaning of the noun *fillip* is a flick of the finger, but a much more common meaning is a stimulus or boost:

> The award for best cinematography gave Jenny's career a fillip.

**fill out** See **fill in/fill out**.

**filmsetting** See **computer typesetting**.

**finalise** Some good writers avoid this word altogether; others are willing to use *finalise* when the thing to be completed is a plan of some kind. *Complete*, *conclude* or *finish* are favoured in other contexts:

> The travel agent helped us to finalise our itinerary today.
>
> The construction company has at last completed [*not* finalised] the new freeway.

**first/firstly** Although any of the following forms are acceptable when making a list, the initial one is recommended:

> First, the meat; second, the fish; third, the poultry; and last, the wine.

*rather than*

> First, the meat; secondly, the fish; thirdly, the poultry; and lastly, the wine.

*or* Firstly, the meat; secondly, the fish; thirdly, the poultry; and lastly, the wine.

See also **cardinal numbers/ordinal numbers**.

**First World** See **Third World/First World/Second World**.

**First World War** See **World War I**.

**f.i.s./FIS** These initials stand for *free into store*, a trading term similar in meaning to *f.o.b.*: the price a buyer agrees to pay does not include the cost of insurance or freight, which the seller must cover.
See also **c.i.f./CIF**; **f.o.b./FOB**.

**fish/fishes** Both words are acceptable as plurals, but *fish* is used in general contexts and in references to the food. The form *fishes* is usually restricted to technical publications and those in which species or groups of fish are discussed.

**fix/repair** *Fix*, meaning to mend, is a common synonym for the slightly more formal *repair*. Other uses of *fix*, as in expressions like *I'll fix you a drink* and *I'm in a bit of a fix*, are strictly informal.
See also **repairable/reparable**.

**flagrant** See **blatant/flagrant**.

**flair/flare** *Flair* is unusual talent or aptitude; an additional meaning is elegance or stylishness:

Toby had a flair for picking winners at the races.
The flowing silk costumes epitomised the flair of the show.

The noun *flare* has numerous meanings, all based on the notion of spreading outwards: *a flare of light*; *the flare in her skirt*; *a flare of temper*.

**flak** Do not spell this noun 'flack'. It means anti-aircraft fire or, informally, heavy criticism or abuse. It is an acronym derived from the German ***Fliegerabwehrkanone***, an anti-aircraft gun.

**flamingo** Plural *flamingos* or *flamingoes*.

**flammable/inflammable/nonflammable** Although *flammable* and *inflammable* appear to be opposites like *efficient* and *inefficient*, they are in fact synonymous, both meaning easily set on fire. To avoid any possibility of misunderstanding, *flammable* is preferred as a warning on garments, materials, bottles and so on. Similarly, something that will not burn easily should be marked *nonflammable* rather than *non-inflammable*.

**flannelette** Note the single *l* in the middle of this fabric name.

**flare** See **flair/flare**.

**flaunt/flout** *Flaunt* means to parade or display ostentatiously:

The squatter flaunted his wealth at every opportunity.

To *flout* means to treat with disdain or contempt:

The jolly swagman flouted the law against sheep-stealing.

**flautist** A flute-player is known as a *flautist* in Australian and British English but a *flutist* in US English.

**fledgeling/fledgling** The spelling *fledgling* is preferred.

**FLGOFF** Flying Officer.

**floodwaters** They are *deep*, not high.

**floor/storey** A building that rises above ground level has a series of *floors* or *storeys*: *an office on the sixth floor*; *a building nine storeys high*. Once inside the building we think in terms of *floors* rather than *storeys*. The first storey is called the ground floor while the second storey is called the first floor, so that a building always has one more storey than it has floors. An unambiguous alternative system, which is common overseas though less so in Australia, entails calling the ground floor Level 1, the first floor Level 2 and so on.

See also **storey/story**.

**floppy disk** See **disk, magnetic**.

**flounder/founder** To *flounder* is to struggle clumsily or helplessly:

The calf floundered in the mud until the farmer pulled it free.

To *founder* is to sink, or to fail utterly:

When the ship foundered in heavy seas the crew escaped unhurt.

Both words are often used figuratively in the same context, and awareness of their distinct meanings is important. A company in financial difficulties, for instance, may *flounder* but recover. To fail completely and *founder* is a more serious matter altogether.

**flout** See **flaunt/flout**.

**FLTLT/Flt Lt** Flight Lieutenant.

See also **lieutenant**.

**flu** No apostrophe; short for *influenza*.

**flummoxed** Note the spelling of this colloquial adjective (not '-ixed' or '-uxed'), which means bewildered or confused.

**fluorescent** Note the *-uor-* and the *-sc-*.

**flyleaf** See **endpapers**.

**FM** frequency modulation (radio).

**FO** Foreign Office (UK).

**f.o.b./FOB** These initials stand for *free on board*, a trading term. It means that the price a buyer is prepared to pay does not include the cost of insurance or freight, which the seller must cover.

See also **c.i.f./CIF**; **f.i.s./FIS**.

**focus** The plural is *focuses* or *foci*. The verb-forms *focused* and *focusing* are recommended, but *focussed* and *focussing* are acceptable.

**foetid** See **fetid/foetid**.

**foetus** See **fetus/foetus**.

**FOI** This is the abbreviation for *Freedom of Information*, as in the *Freedom of Information Act 1982*. The phrase does not require initial capitals when used generally: *freedom of information inquiries*.

**fol./ff.** *Fol.* (or *f.*) is an abbreviation for *folio* or *folios*. A folio can be either a page number or the page itself. The abbreviation *ff.* can stand for *folios* or the phrase *and the following*: *page 121 ff.* (that is, page 121 and the following pages).

See also **page numbering**.

**folder** In computer terminology a *folder* has a data-collecting function similar to that of the stationery item.

**follow** *Follow after* is a tautology.

**following** As an adjective or a noun *following* does not usually cause trouble: *the following day*; *a large following*. As a preposition, however, the word is sometimes ambiguous because it may be confused with the present participle:

> Following this tennis match they will be hungry.

In this kind of sentence it is best to choose another word to suit the meaning intended:

> Watching this tennis match they will be hungry.

*or* After this tennis match they will be hungry.

**foment** See **ferment/foment**.

**font** A *font* (or *fount*) is a complete set of letters, figures, punctuation marks and other symbols available in a particular typeface. Font names, designs and sizes vary, depending on the equipment and software being used. A *font family* is a group of fonts with the same name – for example Times. The font Times italic is a member of the Times family.

Commercial typesetters and bureaus have to carry a large number of fonts. There are thousands of digitised fonts available in PostScript format for desktop-publishing equipment. Moderate and casual users will find that about twenty fonts, including both serif and sanserif faces, are adequate for most purposes. If the work consists mainly of books or reports, more serif than sanserif faces should be carried. Basic fonts might include the following, which in spite of their variations are shown in the same point size:

*Serif fonts (having short strokes at tips of some letters)*

Baskerville This is a serif face.

Caslon This is a serif face.

Century This is a serif face.

Garamond This is a serif face.

Plantin This is a serif face.

Times This is a serif face.

*Zapf Chancery* *This is a serif face.*

*Sanserif (without strokes)*

Futura This is a sanserif face.

Gill Sans This is a sanserif face.

Helvetica This is a sanserif face.

Desktop publishers sending a document to a bureau must supply a list of the fonts used, including screen fonts and printer fonts.

See also **bureau (desktop publishing)**; **pi font**; **PostScript**; **printer font/screen font**; **type**.

**foot** See **feet/foot**.

**footnotes** See **notes**; **reference marks**; **references**.

**for** See **as/since/because/for**.

**forbad/forbade** Prefer *forbade* as the past tense of the verb *to forbid*; pronounce it 'for-**bad**'.

**forbear/forebear** To *forbear* means to refrain or be patient:

> Since he is my neighbour I shall forbear from criticising him in public.

Pronounce it with the stress on the second syllable.

A *forebear* is an ancestor. The variant spelling *forbear* is acknowledged by most authorities but is not recommended:

> I have inherited my baldness from my forebears.

Put the stress on the first syllable.

**forceful/forcible** *Forceful* means powerful or vigorous, and is often applied to people and their qualities:

> The teacher's forceful personality kept the boys in check.

*Forcible* means carried out by force, and is mainly applied to actions:

> Forcible extractions for the crocodile seemed the only way to keep tourists safe.

**forceps** Singular and plural.

**forcible** See **forceful/forcible**.

**fore-** The prefix *fore-* means before or in front: *forewarned*, *forecast*, *forethought*, *foreleg*, *forelock*.

**forebear** See **forbear/forebear**.

**foreboding** Note the *-e-*.

**forecast** Use this form rather than *forecasted* for the past tense.

**forego/forgo** To *forego* means to go before or precede, and its forms *foregone* and *foregoing* are the most commonly used:

> The suit was so well made that its high price was a foregone conclusion.

To *forgo* means to do without or give up:

> I will forgo the pleasure of chocolate eclairs today.

**foreign words and phrases** The English language makes use of many foreign words and phrases, some of which add a flavour or meaning that no English word can provide – for example *joie de vivre*; *faux pas*; *alma mater*; *alter ego*; *chutzpah*; *glasnost* and *perestroika*. Since a variety of languages has contributed to the English we know today, it is likely that a number of the words we now call foreign will ultimately be absorbed into it.

In the meantime they should be used in moderation. There is no particular point in writing *idée fixe* when you mean *obsession*, or *con amore* when you mean *with love*. Texts laced with foreign words and phrases give the impression that the writer is showing off. This applies as much to fiction as to non-fiction. No writer should expect readers to be fluent in a foreign language. Moreover if readers do not understand what is being said, they will only be annoyed by the writer's efforts.

Writers should always ask themselves the following questions.

- If the word or phrase is so obscure as to warrant setting in italics, should it be used at all?
- Is there an English equivalent or near-equivalent that does the job as well? Some cookery and food columns in newspapers and magazines contain so many French words that they are virtually unintelligible, even to the initiated.
- Who is going to read the work? A group of lawyers would have little trouble with specialist Latin terms mystifying even to educated readers of a high-quality newspaper.

When foreign words and phrases are used in printed works, they are treated in different ways depending on the degree of their assimilation into English.

- Words that are regarded as still foreign, even if frequently used, are printed in italics and any accents are retained:

  *au courant*    *haut monde*    *à deux*
- Words that have been largely assimilated are not italicised, but accents are sometimes retained as a guide to pronunciation:

  soiree    papier mâché    blasé    in toto
- Words that have been fully absorbed into English are neither italicised nor given their original accents:

  curriculum vitae    smorgasbord    graffiti    entree

English plurals are used for fully assimilated words such as *infernos* and *arias*, though *algae* and *bacteria* are among many others that retain the plural form of the original language (Latin in this case). Others again have optional plurals (*concertos* or *concerti*; *bureaus* or *bureaux*).

It is often difficult to judge the status of a foreign word, as not all dictionaries use italics to specify those regarded as needing them: common sense and the writer's own experience of the particular word must sometimes decide the matter.

English forms are generally used for foreign place-names: *Venice* (not *Venezia*), *Munich* (not *München*). The writer who thinks it clever to write *Firenze* instead of *Florence* may not be knowledgeable or consistent enough to write *Al-Qāhirah* instead of *Cairo*.

See also **accents**; **italics, use of**; **Latin words and phrases**; **loan words**.

**Forestdale, Qld** Compare with *Forrestdale*, WA.

**forever/for ever** In Australian English *forever* is generally written as one word, but some writers prefer the two-word form when they mean eternally: *I won't live for ever.*

**foreword/preface** A *foreword* is sometimes included among the first few pages of a printed work (usually between the imprint page and contents list) and is generally an endorsement of it written by someone other than the author. Avoid the common misspelling 'forward'.

If the work has a *preface*, it too occurs early – following the contents list but before the beginning of the text. The preface is written by the author, who sometimes wants to explain the purpose of the book or provide important background information, and may also use part of the preface to acknowledge help from others.

See also **acknowledgements**; **introduction**; **publications, parts of**.

**for example** See **e.g./i.e.**

**formatting** There are a number of different uses for the word *formatting* in the computer context. For example it may mean taking a used or clean disk, inserting it into the disk drive and telling the system to organise the structure of the disk according to operating requirements. (Note that formatting a disk will erase any material already there.) These days many disks come preformatted and ready to use.

In desktop publishing *formatting* has additional meanings – for example the enhancement of text with the designer's style specifications (such as typeface, leading, line length and page size). The word *format* is also used in desktop publishing in relation to the platform the material was produced on or the program that produced it.

For publishers *format* most often means the size, shape and general appearance of a publication.

See also **copy, presentation of**; **desktop publishing**; **layout**.

**former/latter** It is only possible to use the terms *former* and *latter* if two things have previously been mentioned:

> I can't eat cream or pineapple: the former is fattening and the latter gives me indigestion.

The formality of this kind of reference is not always appropriate, however:

> If I could holiday in Samoa or Hawaii, I would choose the former.

Rewrite in the following way:

> I would rather holiday in Samoa than Hawaii.

For three or more things, use *first*, *first-mentioned*, *first-named*; or *last*, *last-mentioned*, *last-named*.

Overuse of any of these terms is irritating to a reader.

**formula** The plurals are *formulas* in general contexts and *formulae* in scientific work.

**forte** This noun meaning strong point is pronounced '**for**-tay'.

**forthcoming** Use this adjective rather than the comparatively new but already overworked *upcoming*.

**FORTRAN** In computer terminology this is an acronym for *Formula Translation*.

**fortuitous/fortunate** Things that happen by chance – lucky accidents or unhappy ones – may be called *fortuitous*; the adjective is applied to things, not people:

The fortuitous meeting of Smith and Brown led to a profitable venture.

Fortuitous events brought disaster to Jack and Jill.

Good fortune – but not misfortune – is involved in the idea *fortunate*, which can be applied to things or people:

Albert was satisfied with what he called his fortunate life.

Ambiguity is inevitable when chance events are described as *fortuitous* unless the context indicates whether they are a matter of good fortune or not.

**forward/forwards** The adjective is always *forward*: *forward planning*; *a forward child*. The singular noun, verb and adverb are also *forward*, except when the adverb is describing movement towards a place, as in the last of the following examples: *our best hockey forward*; *please forward the information*; *from this day forward*; *run forwards into the water*.

**founder** See **flounder/founder**.

**fount** See **font**.

**four-letter words** See **vulgarisms/four-letter words**.

**fp** freezing point.

**Fr** Father (the honorific for a priest).

See also **ranks, titles, honours and awards**.

**fracas** Pronounce this noun meaning a noisy quarrel or disturbance '**fra**-kah', not '**fra**-k's'.

**fraction** This word means any part of a whole number, or a small amount:

Three-fifths was too high a fraction of his salary to spend on rent.

We spent only a fraction of our money at the market.

Additional phrases such as *only a* are recommended if *a small amount* is meant. Discounted goods are sometimes advertised as being available at a fraction of their normal price: the fraction in such circumstances is not necessarily small.

See also **per cent/percentage**.

**fractious** See **factious/fractious.**

**Frankenstein** The creator of the monster in Mary Shelley's novel, not the monster itself.

**free** Try to avoid the expression *for free*: something is either *free* or has been acquired *for nothing*. The phrase *free gift* is a tautology.

**-free** This adjective is tacked onto many words – by means of a hyphen – to indicate the absence or elimination of something undesirable: *lead-free*, *chemical-free*, *pollution-free*, *duty-free*. Such formations are acceptable in formal contexts.

**freeze/frieze** To *freeze* is to turn into ice. A *frieze* (note the *-ie-*) is a decorative strip on a wall.

**Fremantle, WA** Not 'Freemantle'.

**fresco** Plural *frescoes* or *frescos*.

**frieze** See **freeze/frieze.**

**frolic/frolicked/frolicking** Note the *-c* in the first and the *-ck-* in the others.

**frontispiece** This is the name given to an illustration that may appear opposite the title page of a book.
See also **publications, parts of.**

**front matter** See **publications, parts of.**

**FRS** Fellow of the Royal Society.

**fruition/fructification** *Fruition* means the attainment of something desired or the bearing of fruit (metaphorically speaking):

All our dreams came to fruition when we bought our bush block.

*Fructification* is literally the fruiting of a plant:

Fructification of tomato plants will be speeded by hot weather.

**FSGT** Flight Sergeant.

**fuchsia** Note the spelling of this plant-name. The pronunciation is '**few**-sha'.

**-ful** For nouns ending in *-ful* – such as *roomful*, *handful* and *spoonful* – use the plural form *-fuls*: *roomfuls*, *handfuls*, *spoonfuls*. Note the single *l* in both the singular and the plural forms.
See also **compound nouns, plurals of.**

**fulfil/fulfilled/fulfilling** Note the single *l* in the first and the *-ll-* in the other two. The related noun is *fulfilment*.

**Fullarton, SA** Compare with *Fullerton*, NSW.

**fullness** This is the Australian spelling (not 'fulness').

**full out** This typesetting instruction (abbreviated *f.o.*) means that copy should be set to the full measure of a line – that is, not indented.

**full stop** The *full stop* (.) is the punctuation mark used to indicate the end of sentences that are neither questions nor exclamations. It is alternatively called a *stop*, *period*, *point* or *full point*. Full stops are also normally used at the end of abbreviations (but not contractions): *approx.*, *vol.*; as decimal points: *0.25 kilograms*; in the expression of times: *6.35 a.m.*; and in one form of date: *12.11.90*. The trend towards light punctuation has allowed some abbreviations to lose their traditional full stops, for example *SA*, *AMA*, *faq* and *PTO*.

Full stops are not generally placed at the end of book, play, film or chapter titles; after headings, headlines, or lines displayed in special type; at the end of short captions; at the end of index entries; or after people's signatures.

See also **abbreviations and contractions**; **caption**; **colon**; **comma**; **dates**; **ellipsis**; **exclamation mark**; **question mark**; **semicolon**; **sentence**; **weights and measures**.

**fulsome** An early meaning of *fulsome* was abundant, and some people still use it in that sense:

> The fulsome detailing in the wood-carvings was impressive.

But the word is now generally used pejoratively to mean excessive or insincere:

> His fulsome praise did not ring true.

If there is any possibility of misinterpretation or ambiguity, use another adjective.

**fun** Used as an adjective before nouns – *fun person*, *fun time*, *fun food* – this word is strictly informal.

**function** This seems such a *functional* word that we are tempted to overuse it. Instead of the verb sometimes try words such as *work*, *operate*, *act* or *perform*; instead of the noun try *role* or *duty*.

**function keys** In computer terminology the *function keys* of a keyboard are those that enable the user to carry out an action rather than type a character – for instance there is a function key (or combination of keys) for copying data and another for printing. A function key can often be reprogrammed by the operator to perform a different role from its original one: it might be used for inserting a graphic element, for example.

Function keys can also be used with what are known as smart-key programs. If, for example, a lengthy group of words needs to be typed throughout a document, a function key, together with the appropriate smart-key software, can do it for you. For instance, if the name 'Canberra International Mining and Exploration Co. Pty Ltd' is allocated to a single function key, you strike that key every time the name is required. This saves the time needed for typing each character and avoids the possibility of error in that group of words.

See also **control keys**; **keyboard commands**.

**fundamental** This adjective means basic or underlying, and should not be used as a synonym for *major* or *important*:

The fundamental meaning of democracy is government by the people.

*but* The battle of El Alamein was a major [*not* fundamental] turning point in World War II.

**fungous/fungus** *Fungous* is the adjectival form of *fungus*, the plural of which is *fungi* (or, more rarely, *funguses*). Mildew and mushrooms are both *fungi*. The *g* is hard, and the *i* of *fungi* may be pronounced to rhyme with *me* or *my*.

**furore/furor** Prefer the British spelling, *furore*, for this noun meaning uproar, or an outburst of enthusiasm or anger. However, it is usually pronounced the American way, '**few**-ror', rather than the British way, 'few-**ror**-ree'.

**furphy** *Furphy* is a uniquely Australian word meaning rumour, gossip, or (by extension) a false story. It is derived from the name of John Furphy, a manufacturer of water-carts in Victoria. During World War I troops gathered around Furphy's carts for a drink and a gossip.

**further/furthest** See **farther/farthest/further/furthest**.

**fwd** forward.

# Gg

**G** a grand (US colloquialism for $1000, now used in informal Australian English); for general exhibition (film and TV classification).

**the Gabba** The Woolloongabba district and cricket ground in Brisbane are colloquially *the Gabba*.

**gaiety** Note the *-aie-*.

**Gairdner, WA** Compare with *Gardiner*, Vic; *Gardiners Bay*, Tas.

**galley proof** See **proofs**.

**gambit** The original meaning of this noun was an opening move in chess by which a player sacrificed a pawn or other piece to gain an advantage. Many authorities consider that the ideas of both earliness and sacrifice have receded, however, and a *gambit* may now be taken to mean any strategem by which it is hoped to obtain some advantage:

> The lads tried to raise money by the gambit of hailing cars at traffic lights.

**gamble/gambol** To *gamble* is to bet on an outcome, usually with money. To *gambol* is to skip about or frolic.

**gaol/jail** The preferred Australian spelling is *gaol*, even though it has been known on many occasions to give rise to the typographical error 'goal'. Contrary to popular opinion, *jail* is not an Americanism but was used by Samuel Johnson and John Milton among others as a variant of *gaol*.

**garish** Pronounce the first syllable of this adjective to rhyme with *bear* or *bar* (the word means excessively showy and bright).

**garlic** Note the *-ck-* in *garlicky.*

**GATT** General Agreement on Tariffs and Trade.

**gauge** Note the *-au-* in this noun meaning a measurement or estimate. The verb means to measure.

**gay** Many male homosexuals now use *gay* as an adjective and noun to describe themselves: *a gay club*; *a well-known gay.* This usage has gained universal currency and it would be a stubborn or naive person who still used the word in its old sense, merry or cheerful.

See also **homosexual; lesbian**.

**gazump** This informal verb may mean either to sell real estate at a higher price to someone other than the agreed purchaser, or to sell anything at a higher price than was agreed to.

**GB** Great Britain.

See also **Britain/Great Britain/United Kingdom/British Isles.**

**GDP** gross domestic product.

**gelatin/gelatine** Either of these spellings is acceptable. Pronounce the word '**jell**a-tin' or 'jella-**teen**' depending on which spelling you choose.

**GEN/Gen.** General.

**gender** This is the grammatical term used to classify nouns according to whether they are masculine, feminine or neuter. Gender plays only a small part in English but is fundamental to the structure of many other languages. In languages where gender is important, words attached to or referring to nouns – such as articles, adjectives and pronouns – change in accordance with the gender of the noun; thus in French a white wine is *un vin blanc* (*vin*, the word for wine, is masculine), and a white skin is *une peau blanche* (*peau*, the word for skin, is feminine).

It may be said that English has *natural* as opposed to *grammatical* gender. For example, the pronouns *he*, *she*, *it* are used according to whether the nouns they refer to are male, female or inanimate: *father*, *mother*, *table*.

The use of *gender* as a synonym for *sex* is a controversial matter. Many feminists prefer the word *gender*, particularly when alluding to the differences between females and males. In respected academic circles, too, *gender* is being used in describing the formation of sex-associated identities, which may or may not relate to physical characteristics; gender studies discuss the formation (and implications) of notions of gender, masculine as well as feminine. Nevertheless the traditional word, *sex*, has been used throughout this book because it seems to be more widespread in the general community at the present time; *gender* may well replace it increasingly in the future. Either is acceptable in the following examples:

> Some professions retain a strong sex-bias [*or* gender-bias].
>
> Women should not be discriminated against because of their sex [*or* gender].
>
> The new laws should not be sex-specific [*or* gender-specific].

See also **discriminatory language; female/feminine/feminist; male/masculine**.

**genealogy** Note the spelling (not '-eol-'). It means the pedigree of a family or the detailing of it in written form.

**genetic** See **congenital/genetic**.

**genial** See **congenial/genial.**

**genius** The plural is *geniuses*. The word *genii* is the plural of *genie* (a spirit).

**genocide** Note the spelling of this noun, which means the deliberate extermination of a racial or national group.

**genus** Plural *genera*.

**Georgetown, NSW, Qld and SA** Compare with *George Town*, Tas.

**geriatric** The adjective relates to *geriatrics*, the branch of science dealing with the medical and social care of old people. As a noun the word means an elderly person, especially one who has become incapacitated by age. *Geriatric* has also become a jocular synonym for anything old, decrepit, dilapidated or broken-down: *a geriatric washing-machine*. Used this way the word is derogatory, adding regrettable overtones to both adjective and noun in their customary applications.

**germane/material/relevant** All three of these adjectives can mean pertinent or related to the matter in hand. *Material*, but not the other two, may be used to mean of great importance or essential:

> The colour of the carpet is germane [*or* material *or* relevant] to our decision on wall colour.
>
> Availability of the carpet we want is the material problem.

Note the spelling and pronunciation of *relevant*: not 'relavent' or 'revalent'. Avoid the same traps in its opposite, *irrelevant*.

**gerrymander** This word of US origin and the practice it describes are well known in Australia. The verb means to manipulate the boundaries of constituencies in order to gain an electoral advantage, and the noun refers to such manipulation.

**gerund** A *gerund* (or verbal noun) has the same form as the present participle of a verb (*eating*, *seeing*, *hoping*) but acts as a noun rather than an adjective.

See also **-ing forms**; **participles**; **verbs**.

**get/got** Both present and past tenses of the neat, multi-purpose verb *to get* have a bad reputation for overuse and imprecision, and more specific words are often available:

> After we receive [*rather than* get] the contract tomorrow we shall obtain [*rather than* get] legal advice on when to have [*rather than* get] the property insured.

Whether the tense is present or past, the word is nevertheless difficult to replace in many idiomatic expressions including the following: *get out of the way*; *get into bed*; *get down to discussion*; *get over the disappointment*.

*Got* is usually superfluous when combined with *has* or *have* to indicate possession or necessity: *She has got a pen*; *They have got to buy pens*. It is usually retained, however, when *has* or *have* is abbreviated: *She's a pen* does not mean the same as *She's got a pen*. In Australian English the word *gotten* is acceptable only in phrases such as *ill-gotten gains*.

**GG** Governor-General.

See also **governors-general**; **ranks, titles, honours and awards**.

**ghetto** Plural *ghettos* or *ghettoes*.

**GHQ** General Headquarters.

**GI** US private soldier (from *government issue*).

**gibber** A *gibber* (derived from an Aboriginal word) may be a large or small stone; *gibber plains* in inland Australia are sometimes covered with actual boulders. The *g* is hard.

To *gibber* is to speak fast and incomprehensibly. The *g* is soft.

**gibe/jibe** To *gibe* is to jeer or scoff; the noun, meaning a taunt, is also *gibe*. An alternative spelling is *jibe*.

The spelling *jibe* is, however, the most common one for the sailing term, which is used as a noun or verb (*gybe* and, more rarely, *gibe* are also seen).

Whatever the spelling or meaning, the initial letter sounds like the *j* in *jam* and the word rhymes with *tribe*.

**giddy/giddily/giddiness** Note the spellings.

**gild/guild** To *gild* means to coat with gold, gold leaf, or something gold in colour. The cliché *to gild the lily* (derived from Shakespeare, though not a direct quote) means to spoil something beautiful by adding to it unnecessarily. It does not mean to improve something drab or dull.

A *guild* is an organisation of people with common interests, often professional or commercial.

See also **misquotations**.

**gilt-edged** See **blue chip/gilt-edged**.

**GIO** GIO Australia Holdings Limited (the initials stand for *Government Insurance Office*).

**gipsy/gypsy** Either spelling is acceptable.

**girl** See **woman**.

**Girraween, NSW** Compare with *Girrawheen*, WA.

**given name/Christian name** In a secular country such as Australia, with its many racial, national and religious groups, it is obviously desirable to use a neutral term such as *given name* to refer to the name or names given at birth (as opposed to the surname or family name), particularly on official forms and documents. The traditional *Christian name* is often unacceptable to non-Christians, and *first name* and *forename* do not take account of the many people now living in Australia who place the names given at birth *after* the family name. *Christian name* is still appropriate on specifically Christian documents such as baptismal certificates.

**gladiolus** Plural *gladioli*.

**glasnost** This Russian word, now adopted into English, describes the new Russian openness in relationships dating from the rise to power of Mikhail Gorbachev in the USSR in the late 1980s. The word is associated with the adjective *glasnyi*, which originally meant known or obvious to everyone, unhidden.

See also **perestroika.**

**glossary** See **publications, parts of**.

**glower** As a verb it means to stare angrily, as a noun the stare itself. Pronounce *glower* to rhyme with *flower*, not *mower*.

**glue/gluey/glueing** The *-e* of *glue* is retained.

**glycerin/glycerine** Either spelling of this word is acceptable. Pronounce it '**glis**sa-rin' or 'glissa-**reen**' depending on which spelling you choose.

**GM** general manager; Grand Master (at chess; of Masonic Lodge).

**GMT** This is the abbreviation for *Greenwich Mean Time*, which is the mean solar time of the meridian of zero longitude that passes through the London suburb of Greenwich. It is widely used as the basis for international time-reckoning.

See also **latitude/longitude**; **time zones**; **UT**.

**GNP** This is the abbreviation for *gross national product*. A country's gross national product is the total value of its products and services in any one year.

**go** Try to avoid the combination *going to go*, and use instead constructions like *[He] will go* or *[She] intends to go*.

**gobbledegook/gobbledygook** Either of these spellings is acceptable. This noun means impenetrable officialese, particularly of a circumlocutory type. It is also a name for the nonsense text sometimes used by typesetters in sample setting.

See also **commercialese**; **officialese**.

**GOC** General Officer Commanding.

**God/god** When used in reference to the deity or supreme being worshipped in monotheistic religions, *God* is customarily written with an initial capital. Traditionally pronouns referring to God – *He, Thou, Thee, Thy* – have been treated likewise, though some people prefer to give them lower-case initials now. In compounds such as *godchild*, *godfather*, *godforsaken* and *god-fearing* the initial is lower case, as it is for beings worshipped in polytheistic religions: *the Hindu temple gods*; *like a Greek god*.

**Gold Coast** The *Gold Coast* in Queensland is one of Australia's most thoroughly developed and popular resort centres. It extends for roughly thirty-two kilometres, from Southport in the north to Coolangatta in the south, and has a population of some 84 000. Its best-known urban centre is Surfers Paradise.

See also **Sunshine Coast**.

**Gondwana** Also known as *Gondwanaland*, this ancient continent of the Palaeozoic and Mesozoic eras included Australia, Antarctica, India, South America and parts of Africa.

**gorilla/guerilla/guerrilla** A *gorilla* is a very large ape.

Either spelling, *guerilla* or *guerrilla*, is acceptable for the name of the fighter in an independent force that wages irregular warfare:

The guerillas [*or* guerrillas] attacked, then disappeared into the jungle.

The word is pronounced 'ger-**rill**a'.

**got** See **get/got.**

**gourmand/gourmet** The distinction between these two words has been blurred, particularly by food writers in Australian newspapers and magazines. A *gourmand* is a glutton. A *gourmet*, however, is a good judge of fine food.

**Gov.** Governor.
See also **ranks, titles, honours and awards.**

**governors-general** Note that the first word indicates the plural.
See also **compound nouns, plurals of.**

**GP** general practitioner (see also **Doctor, the title**; **ranks, titles, honours and awards**); gross profit.

**GPCAPT/Gp Capt** Group Captain.

**GPO** General Post Office.

**graceful/gracious** The adjective *graceful* means characterised by grace of form, manner, movement or speech:

Torvill and Dean's performance on the ice was amazingly graceful.

*Gracious* implies kindness, benevolence or courtesy:

A gracious contribution is much appreciated by the opportunity shop.

It can also suggest condescension; therefore ensure that the context makes your meaning clear. The word is part of a cliché much used by advertisers to describe elegant lifestyles: *gracious living*.

**graffiti** Note the *-ff-* and single *t*. Although *graffiti* is the plural of an Italian word, *graffito* (meaning a little scratch), it is acceptable in English for both singular and plural and takes a singular verb. The messages and drawings (mainly on walls) that we call *graffiti* are not necessarily disgusting or insulting:

This boy's graffiti is a work of art.

**Grantville, Vic.** Compare with *Granville*, NSW and Qld.

**graphical user interface** The term *graphical user interface* (abbreviated *GUI*) describes a system of computer program management that uses icons or graphic images on the screen. These usually represent familiar office objects such as a sheet of paper, to symbolise a text file; a paintbrush, to symbolise a graphics file; and a rubbish bin, to suggest the dumping of files. If you want to open any of the graphically represented files or programs showing on the screen, select it by using a mouse, trackball or other pointing device and double-clicking.

See also **file**; **icon**.

**graphics** In general computing and desktop-publishing terminology, the word *graphics* means any image created by way of a graphics program. The enormous range of possibilities includes simple line graphs or bar graphs in black and white, the most complex full-colour three-dimensional illustrations in magazines or on book covers, and equally complex engineering diagrams. Output of such work can be by means of black and white or colour laser printer, colour photocopy, bromide or film. In addition, slides and overhead projector transparencies of very high quality can be produced for use in presentations.

Graphics can be generated as new artwork or scanned onto disk from original art; manipulated to change their shape; or have colour or text added. Photographs can be scanned at high resolution in either black and white or full colour and imported into a document.

The quality of the graphics images will depend on the resolution of the output device. At the 300 dots per inch (dpi) rate of the average laser printer, the quality of a simple line drawing or halftone is generally adequate for most desktop publications, but higher resolutions are essential for better-quality work.

Graphics files take up large amounts of disk space – enormous amounts if you have complex artwork and are using colour.

See also **converted graphics files**; **scanning**.

**graphics files** See **graphics**.

**graphs** *Graphs* provide an effective way of presenting complex information in a simple diagrammatic form. Types of graphs include the *line graph*, *bar chart* or *histogram*, and the *pie chart*. The line graph and bar chart have vertical and horizontal axes between which the information to be collated is set out. The information on a line graph is used to show changes or trends, not separate events, with the plotted points joined by a line usually starting in the bottom left-hand corner. A bar chart uses vertical or horizontal bars of various lengths to provide information about quantities at set intervals. A pie chart uses segments of a circle to show relative quantities.

All kinds of graphs can be created by means of desktop-publishing graphics programs. Some programs allow you to key in the data and then select the most suitable type of graph for depicting the information.

A line graph, a bar chart and a pie chart are illustrated on the following page.

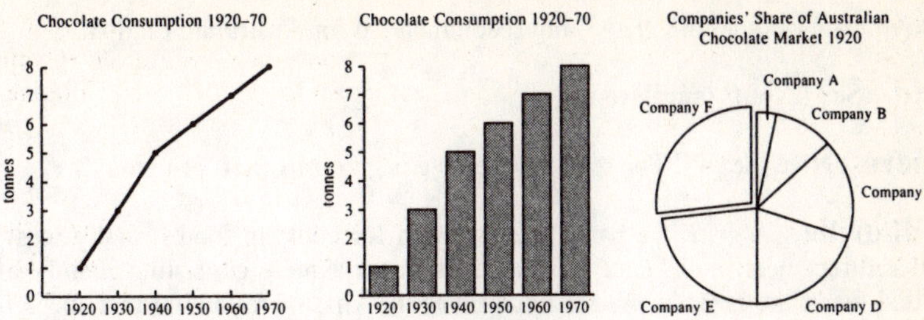


***Line graph*** ***Bar chart*** ***Pie chart***

**gratuitous** The meanings of *gratuitous* are quite distinct: given freely or, more commonly, unjustified. They do not include grateful.

Diana's gratuitous trip to France was a reward for long service.

Duncan's unkind remarks and gratuitous criticisms are hard to take.

**Great Britain** See **Britain/Great Britain/United Kingdom/British Isles.**

**the Great War** See **World War I**.

**green** When applied to politicians, political parties, protesters and so on this word indicates a concern for the environment. Hence *greenies* is a colloquial term for *environmentalists*. Colloquialisms not associated with the conservation movement include the expressions *a bit green* (inexperienced), *turning green* (when seasick) and *green with envy*.

**Greenacre, NSW** Compare with *Greenacres*, SA.

**greenhouse effect** The air in a greenhouse is warmed when heat from the sun is trapped under the glass. The term *greenhouse effect* is used to describe the alleged rise in the temperature of the earth that is believed to be associated with the increased amount of carbon dioxide and various pollutants in the atmosphere that, like the glass, trap the sun's heat.

**green paper/white paper** Both terms refer to documents presented to parliament by a government as a basis for discussion. A *green paper* is a preliminary statement on a particular subject and is not necessarily a declaration of government policy. A *white paper* is a statement of government policy, and it is usually presented to parliament just before, or accompanying, the introduction of a related Bill. The names are derived from the colour of the paper used.

**Greenwich Mean Time** See **GMT**.

**grey** The US spelling *gray* is not recommended for Australian English.

**grid** See **layout**; **template**.

**grieve** Note the *-ie-*. The related adjective is *grievous* (not 'grievious').

**grill/grille** A *grill* is a barred device used for cooking food (usually meat) under direct heat, and hence the name given to a meal consisting mainly of grilled meat, the meat itself, and sometimes the kind of restaurant that specialises in grilled meat.

A *grille* is an openwork screen (usually made of metal and often ornamental), a grating, or a car radiator cover.

**grisly/gristly/grizzly** *Grisly* (note the *-s-*) means horrible or gruesome, while *gristly* (note the *-st-*) means containing gristle (cartilage). Something that is greyish in colour may be called *grizzly*, but the word is most often used of the North American *grizzly bear.* Hair that has turned grey is more appropriately described as *grizzled. Grizzly* (from *grizzle*) is also used colloquially to mean whimpering or whining: *a grizzly child.*

**gross** Pronounce this word 'groce'; it does not rhyme with *cross*.

**grotto** Plural *grottoes* or *grottos*.

**ground** When *ground* means reason, cause or basis, distinguish between singular and plural: *divorced on the ground of separation*; *several grounds for his action.*

**groupings** The following are commonly accepted names for groups of people, animals, and various items.

| | | | |
|---|---|---|---|
| *People* | | *Animals* | |
| actors | company, troupe | bees | swarm |
| angels | host | birds | flock |
| bishops | bench | cattle | herd, mob |
| dancers | troupe | chickens | clutch, brood |
| magistrates | bench | cubs | litter |
| singers | choir | deer | drive, herd |
| thieves | gang | dogs | kennel, pack, team |
| worshippers | congregation | fish | aquarium, school, shoal |
| | | foxes | skulk |
| *Miscellaneous* | | geese | flock, gaggle, (in flight) skein |
| aeroplanes | flight, squadron | hounds | kennel, pack |
| bells | peal | kittens | brood, litter |

| *Miscellaneous* | | *Animals* | |
|---|---|---|---|
| cakes | batch | leopards | leap |
| concerts | series | lions | pride |
| eggs | (for hatching) clutch | locusts | cloud, swarm, plague |
| flowers | bouquet, bunch, posy | monkeys | troop |
| grapes | bunch, cluster | oxen | herd, span, team, yoke |
| keys | bunch | pups | litter |
| limousines | fleet | rabbits | warren |
| playing cards | deck, pack | sheep | flock, herd, mob |
| ships | fleet, flotilla, squadron | whales | gam, herd, pod, school |
| stars | constellation | wolves | pack |
| steps | flight | | |

**growth** This word is disliked by some when it is used as an adjective in expressions such as a *growth industry*. Whatever its merits, it is certainly overworked. Replace it with others such as *increasing*, *expanding* and *developing*.

**gsm** See **paper sizes and weights**.

**GSO** General Staff Officer.

**GST** goods and services tax.

**GT** a touring car (adapted from the Italian *gran turismo*, which means grand touring).

**guerilla/guerrilla** See **gorilla/guerilla/guerrilla**.

**GUI** See **graphical user interface**.

**guidelines** Do not overuse this word. Remember alternative nouns such as *instructions*, *advice* and *policy*.

**guild** See **gild/guild**.

**gut** Used as an adjective to mean instinctive or intuitive, *gut* should be restricted to informal contexts: *a gut feeling*; *a gut reaction*.

**gutter** In the context of printing, a *gutter* is the blank space (comprising the inner margins) between two opposite pages, or the space between a pair of columns of text. The outer edge of a book's pages (opposite the binding) is called the *fore-edge*.

See also **desktop publishing**; **layout**.

**guttural** Note the *-ur-* (not 'gutteral').

**gymnasium** Plural *gymnasiums* or *gymnasia*.

**gynaecology/obstetrics** *Gynaecology* is concerned with the functions of, and diseases in, women (*gynecology* is a variant spelling). *Obstetrics* is concerned with the treatment of women before, during and after childbirth.

**gypsy** See **gipsy/gypsy**.

# Hh

**H** hard (pencils).

**h** This letter is pronounced 'aitch', not 'haitch'.

**habit** Since the noun *habit* includes the sense *usual* or *customary*, these words should not be attached to it.

**hacker** In its popular usage this term describes someone who breaks into computer systems for fun, using dial-in telephone lines and a modem. The traditional definition within the computing fraternity is quite different. There a *hacker* is a highly skilled programmer, and a *hack* is a piece of programming that is both clever and elegant. Hackers of the traditional sort argue that the word *cracker* should be used for the newer variety, because breaking into computer systems requires little beyond great patience.

**had** See **have/had**.

**haemo-** The word element *haemo-*, derived from the Greek *haima*, meaning blood, retains the *a* of the digraph *ae* in Australian English (the form *hemo-* is principally US usage). Note the following difficult spellings: *haemodialysis*, *haemoglobin*, *haemophilia*, *haemorrhage* and *haemorrhoid*.

See also **ae/oe/e**.

**hail/hale** *Hail* has a number of meanings including greet (verb) and balls of frozen rain (noun). *Hale* means healthy or vigorous, but it is rarely used except in the expression *hale and hearty*.

**halcyon** Note the spelling of this adjective, which means tranquil, carefree or joyous. It is pronounced '**hal**-see'n'.

**hale** See **hail/hale**.

**half** When referring to a singular noun or pronoun, *half* is followed by a singular verb; when it refers to a plural noun or pronoun, a plural verb follows:

Half the watermelon was eaten.

Half the peaches were eaten.

Note that it is equally acceptable to say half *of* the peaches were eaten.

Compounds beginning with *half* are usually hyphenated: *half-life*, *half-pay*, *half-yearly*, *half-back*. Exceptions include *halfpenny*, *halftone*, *halfwit* and *halfway*. Note also *half an hour* but *a half-hour*; *the bottle is half empty* but *a half-empty bottle*.

Although the expression *cut in halves* is strictly more correct, *cut in half* is more idiomatic.

**halftone** In the context of printing, photographs are described as *halftones*. They must be rephotographed through a screen so that their tonal variations can be interpreted as dots and therefore printed. Non-photographic illustrations that have continuous tone (that is, are not composed of dots or lines) are also called halftones and screened for printing.

**hallo/hello/hullo** All three spellings of this greeting are acceptable, but *hallo* and *hello* are preferred.

See also **Hi**.

**hallucinatory/hallucinogenic** Both adjectives relate to *hallucinations* – sensory perceptions that have no basis in reality – but they are not synonyms. *Hallucinatory* describes matters pertaining to hallucinations: *hallucinatory fears*. *Hallucinogenic* describes substances that cause hallucinations: *hallucinogenic drugs*.

**halo** Plural *haloes* or *halos*.

**H & J** hyphenation and justification.

See also **hyphenation dictionary**; **justified type/unjustified type**.

**hands-on** This compound adjective means practical, as opposed to theoretical:

Have you had any hands-on computer experience?

The only real objection to the term is that it is overused and often superfluous, particularly in recruitment advertising: most jobs are by their nature *hands-on*.

**hangar/hanger** A *hangar* is a large shed, especially one used for housing aircraft. A *hanger* is someone (such as a *paperhanger*) who hangs something; or an object (such as a *coat-hanger*) that has things hung from it.

**hanged/hung** The form of the past tense and past participle of the verb *to hang* is *hung*, except when the word refers to death by hanging or is used in a certain slang expression where it means damned:

They hanged Ned Kelly.
I'm hanged if I'm going to eat stale bread.

**hanger** See **hangar/hanger**.

**hanging indent** See **indentation**.

**Hansard** This is the unofficial name given to the daily printed reports of Australian, British, Canadian and New Zealand parliamentary debates. The name comes from that of Luke Hansard (1752–1828) and his sons, early printers of the House of Commons journals. Although Hansard purports to be a verbatim transcription of proceedings, members of parliament may improve the grammar or clarity of their recorded utterances. They are generally not permitted to change the content.

**harakiri** Note the recomended spelling of this Japanese word meaning ritual suicide.

**harangue/tirade** A *harangue* is a long, vehement speech; a *tirade* is a harangue that is abusive or denunciatory. Hitler was a master of both. Note that the phrases *a long harangue* and *a tirade of abuse* are tautological. The words are pronounced 'h'**rang**' and 'tie'**rade**' respectively.

**harass** Note the spelling. The word is pronounced '**harr**'ss' or 'h'**rass**'.

**hardback/paperback** A *hardback* (or *casebound*) book is bound between heavy pieces of stiff cardboard, usually covered in cloth. The sections are usually sewn together. A *paperback* book has flexible, light cardboard covers and, although sections may be sewn, the book is most often bound adhesively – commonly using a technique called *perfect binding*.

**hard copy** *Hard copy* is the term given to typewritten manuscript or any output (that is, printed material) from a computer.

See also **copy, presentation of**; **desktop publishing**.

**hard disk** See **disk, magnetic**.

**hard hyphen/soft hyphen** These are the two kinds of hyphen that can be inserted into a desktop-publishing document. *Hard hyphens* should only be used in permanently hyphenated words such as *non-appearance*. *Soft hyphens*, sometimes referred to as *discretionary hyphens*, should be used for word breaks at the end of lines because, if the line-ending changes, they will automatically disappear rather than turn up in the middle of a line where they are not wanted.

See also **hard return/soft return**; **hyphenation dictionary**; **hyphenation**; **word division**.

**hardly** The most common meanings of this adverb are barely (*hardly arrived*) and not quite (*hardly adequate*). Because *hard* can function as either adjective (*hard beds*) or adverb (*to be hit hard*), the form *hardly* is rarely needed in that sense (but note that the alternative form of the expression *hard done by* is *hardly done by*). In any case the word must be used with care: *hardly affected* might in some contexts suggest *badly affected* even when *scarcely affected* is intended.

As *hardly* has a strong negative sense, it does not require a second negative:

The oil-covered penguin could hardly swim.

*not* The oil-covered penguin could not hardly swim.

The same applies to *scarcely* and *barely*.

*Hardly* is often used ironically:

I can hardly wait for that lukewarm cup of tea.

Note that *when*, not *than*, follows *hardly*:

They had hardly finished packing when [*not* than] the taxi arrived.

See also **double negative**; **negative words**.

**hard page break/soft page break** A *hard page break* in desktop publishing is a page break that is inserted by the operator before the natural end of the page appears. A *soft page break* is the natural end of a page. When this point is reached in a page-makeup program, the text will flow into the next page.

See also **hard return/soft return**.

**hard return/soft return** A *hard return* in computer terminology is a normal carriage return inserted by the operator. A *soft return* is inserted to force a line-ending when, near the end of a line of justified type, the next word will not fit and hyphenation is inappropriate or impossible. A soft return will make the problem word roll over to the next line, and the line from which it has been moved will justify.

See also **justified type/unjustified type**.

**hardware/software** The computer term *hardware* describes the physical components of a computer system – for instance the central processing unit (the computer box), the keyboard and the screen. *Software* means the programs or instructions that control the working of a computer. System software controls access to disk drives, printers and so on, and also controls the running of other programs. Application software is designed to carry out particular tasks such as word processing, page makeup, disk conversion and virus detection.

**harebrained** Note the spelling.

**Harvard system of referencing** See **notes; references.**

**has** See **get/got.**

**have/had** Separately these words cause much less difficulty than they do in combination. The verb *to have* (*They will have a quick meal*) should not be confused with the auxiliaries *have* and *had*, which help other verbs to form tenses including the perfect and past perfect (*They have eaten*; *They had eaten*). The two varieties sometimes come together, of course, in sentences such as *They have had a quick meal.*

It is when you find yourself saying or writing *had have* that you are in trouble. Note the following, with its *if* construction:

If they had stopped for lunch they would have felt less tired.

*not* If they *had have* stopped for lunch they would have felt less tired.

The legitimate *they would have*, however, looks the same as the incorrect *they had have* when abbreviated to make *they'd have*. There is nothing wrong with the following sentence, in which *they'd have* stands for *they would have*:

If they had stopped for lunch they'd have felt less tired.

The *would have* construction must nevertheless not lead on to a superfluous *have*:

They would have liked to stay for dinner.

*not* They would have liked to *have* stayed for dinner.

Note the alternative correct form:

They would like to have stayed for dinner.

See also **get/got; of.**

**Hawthorn, SA and Vic.** Compare with *Hawthorne*, Qld.

**HAZCHEM** A sign reading *HAZCHEM* should be placed on the outside of any building where *hazardous chemicals* are stored or used in quantity, as a warning to the fire brigade and other authorities.

**HB** hard and black (pencils).

**Hb** haemoglobin.

**HD** hard disk (computer).
See also **disk, magnetic.**

**HE** His Eminence; Her (or His) Excellency.
See also **ranks, titles, honours and awards.**

**he/him** The correct pronoun to use before and after various verbs is explained in the entry **case (grammar)**.

See also **he/she**.

**he/she** In English there is no third-person singular pronoun that can serve both sexes equally. Traditionally *he*, *him* or *his* has been used as the generic pronoun in constructions such as the following, where *man*, *he* and *his* refer to people generally, male and female:

When man damages his environment he usually suffers for it.

Every man has his price.

Since this convention is sometimes misleading or absurd, and is now widely considered discriminatory, it is preferable to avoid it. Here are some ways around the problem:

- using *he or she*, *him or her*, *his or her* (a solution too clumsy for repeated use)

  The child should complete the task in his or her own time.
- using *he/she*, *his/her* (even clumsier, but acceptable in notes or forms)

  The child should complete the task in his/her own time.
- making the subject plural (more stylish, but unsuitable for legal documents)

  Children should complete the task in their own time.
- recasting the sentence to avoid the pronoun altogether (the most satisfactory answer in most situations)

  The task should be completed in the child's own time.

Choose the construction that is best suited to the context: there is no simple, all-purpose solution.

See also **anybody/anyone**; **case (grammar)**; **discriminatory language**; **each**; **every/everybody/everyone**; **gender**; **man/mankind**; **pronouns**; **their/them/they**.

**head up** People who are said to *head up* a department could just as easily *head* or *lead* it.

**Hebrew/Yiddish** *Hebrew* is the language of the Jewish religion and its scriptures, the official language of modern Israel, and one of the two languages specifically spoken by Jews. The other is *Yiddish* (a mixture of German, Hebrew and various Slavic languages). There is no *Jewish* language as such.

See also **Jew/Israeli/Israelite**.

**HECS** Higher Education Contribution Scheme.

**HECT** Hydro-Electricity Commission of Tasmania.

**heifer** Note the *-ei-*.

**heinous** Note the spelling (the word means hateful or vile). It is pronounced '**hay**-n's' or '**hee**-n's'.

**heir** Note the *-ei-*. An *heir apparent* is a person whose right to succession or inheritance cannot be negated by any possible birth; an *heir presumptive* can be displaced by the birth of an heir with a stronger claim.

**Helensvale, Qld** (4210) Compare with *Helenvale*, Qld (4871).

**hello** See **hallo/hello/hullo**.

**help** See **cannot/can't**.

**hence** The adverb *hence* is most often used today to mean therefore:

> Chiu wants high marks, hence his huge effort this term.

Another reasonably common meaning is from this time: *six months hence*. Meanings now regarded as archaic are go away (*hence!*); and from this place (*hurry hence*). Note that *from* is part of the meaning of *hence* and does not therefore precede it.

See also **thence; whence**.

**hereditary/heredity** People sometimes use the adjective *hereditary* when they mean the noun *heredity*. Note the following correct usage:

> Is intelligence hereditary or due to upbringing?
> Intelligence could be influenced by heredity, upbringing or environment.

**hero** Plural *heroes*.

**hew/hue** To *hew* is to chop or strike (as with an axe or sword). A *hue* is a shade or tint. Note that it is also used in the expression *hue and cry*, which has nothing to do with colour.

**hf** high frequency (electromagnetic waves, as in radio and TV); also *HF*, *h.f.*

**HH** Her (or His) Highness; His Holiness (the Pope).

See also **ranks, titles, honours and awards**.

**Hi** The informal greeting *Hi* is frowned on by many people but is commonly heard in Australia.

See also **hallo/hello/hullo**.

**HIA** Housing Industry of Australia.

**hiatus** The plural of this noun meaning gap is *hiatuses* or simply *hiatus*.

**hiccup/hiccough** Although either spelling is acceptable, *hiccup* is the preferred spelling and pronunciation in Australian English. Other forms of the verb are *hiccupped* and *hiccupping*.

**hierarchy** Note the *-ie-* and the *-ch-*. A *hierarchy* is a graduated system of organisation, especially in scientific terminology, religious or secular government, and the ranking of angels. The *ch* sounds like 'k'.

**high-end program** In the context of computers *high-end programs* are the most sophisticated – that is, they have the greatest number of features and give the most professional results.

**highlight** When you *highlight* words, numbers or graphic elements displayed on a computer screen, you are selecting them in order to change them. For example you can cut the highlighted material and paste it in another position, or delete it. Highlighting is sometimes called *blocking*. On a computer screen the highlighted section of text looks something like the following:

> When you *highlight* words, numbers or graphic elements displayed on
> a computer screen, you are selecting them in order to change them
> in some manner

**high profile/low profile** Both these terms are now acceptable in formal contexts. They may be used as compound nouns or (hyphenated) as compound adjectives, and describe a conspicuous and inconspicuous presence respectively:

> Becoming mayor gave Sue a high profile in the town.
>
> Low-profile products tend to bring low returns.

Do not consider using either compound as a verb.

See also **low-key**.

**Hilldale, NSW** (2420) Compare with *Hillsdale*, NSW (2036).

**him/his** See **-ing forms**.

**historic/historical** Although people often confuse these closely related adjectives, their meanings are distinct. *Historic* means well known or important in history:

> Elizabeth Farm at Parramatta is a historic building.

*Historical* means relating to, belonging to, or concerned with history:

> She needed a grant for historical research on the sheep industry.

Both words may sometimes be applied to the same noun:

> The historical landing at Botany Bay was historic.

**histrionic/hysterical** There is a high level of emotion in behaviour that is either *histrionic* or *hysterical*. *Histrionic* behaviour is excessively dramatic, sometimes in order to mislead:

> He was prone to histrionic declarations of affection, which never fooled his friends for long.

*Hysterical* is the adjectival form of *hysteria*, an uncontrollable state expressed in outbursts of various kinds: *hysterical laughter*.

**hitherto/previously** *Hitherto* is an old-fashioned adjective that means until or before now:

> Hitherto there has been no proper planning, but this will change.

*Previously* means until or before then:

> They lived in a hut but previously had had only a tent.

**HIV** This acronym stands for *Human Immunodeficiency Virus*, the virus responsible for AIDS. It should not be referred to as the HIV *virus*.

See also **AIDS**.

**HM** Her (or His) Majesty.

See also **ranks, titles, honours and awards**.

**HMAS** Her (or His) Majesty's Australian Ship.

**HMS** Her (or His) Majesty's Service; Her (or His) Majesty's Ship.

**HMSO** Her (or His) Majesty's Stationery Office, the British equivalent of the Australian Government Publishing Service.

**hoard/horde** A *hoard* is a collection of something saved for future use: *a hoard of gold*. A *horde* is a very large crowd or group: *a horde of grasshoppers*.

**Hobson's choice** This expression means no choice at all – you take what is offered or go without. Customers of the sixteenth-century stable-keeper Thomas Hobson were in exactly that position: they had to accept or reject the horse they were offered for hire – there were no options.

**hoi polloi** This Greek phrase (literally the many) is used as a derogatory term for the uneducated masses; it does not mean the educated elite. Although *hoi* means *the*, it is now considered acceptable to refer to *the* hoi polloi. The phrase is printed in roman, not italic, type.

**holistic** This adjective (from the noun *holism*) is a buzz word much used and misused by proponents of such things as organic food, herbal medicines and unbleached lavatory paper. *Holism* is the philosophy that sees a whole as greater than the sum of its parts, and the concept of wholeness is behind the vogue for *holistic* as a word to describe wide-ranging matters affecting the whole body. *Wholistic* and *wholism* are alternative spellings accepted by some authorities.

**Holland** See **Dutch/the Netherlands/Holland**.

**holocaust** Note the spelling. The word primarily means enormous loss of life, especially from fire. It should not be used to describe just any disaster. In recent times the word has been applied to the mass murder of Jews by Germans during World War II. In that context it is normally spelt with an initial capital. Pronounce it '**holl**a-kost' or '**holl**a-korst'.

**homely** Take care to use this adjective in a way that makes your intention clear. It can mean homelike or unpretentious:

> The cottage has a warm, homely atmosphere.

Or it can mean plain or unattractive:

> The new gardener has a fine physique but a homely face.

**homogeneous/homogenous** These words can both mean having components of the same kind; *homogenous* has an additional meaning – having components of the same kind because of their common origin.

> We were a homogeneous [*or* homogenous] group of the same background and age; we had in fact all gone to school together.

Each word also has a technical meaning, in mathematics and biology respectively. The opposite of *homogeneous* is *heterogeneous*. In *homogeneous* and *heterogeneous* the stress is on the *-ge-* (pronounced 'jee'), and the *-e-* in *-neous-* is pronounced 'ee'. In *homogenous* the *-mog-* (pronounced 'modge') gets the emphasis.

**homosexual** This word is derived from the Greek prefix *homo-*, meaning the same, not from the Latin word *homo*, meaning man. The noun or adjective refers to a person, male or female, who is physically attracted to members of the same sex. *Homosexual* is, however, used particularly of men; women homosexuals are called *lesbians*. The first two syllables of *homosexual* are pronounced '**home**-o' or '**homm**-o'.

See also **gay**; **lesbian**.

**honorifics** See **ranks, titles, honours and awards**.

**honourable/honorable/honorary/honorific** *Honourable* is spelt with or without the *u* in Australian English, *honorary* and *honorific* always without it. *Hon.* is the abbreviation of *Honourable* in the honorific (title) *the Honourable*, and of *Honorary* in *Hon. Sec.*:

> The Honourable [*or* Honorable *or* Hon.] Doug McDougal, Minister for the Arts.
> The club's honorary secretary, Jill Brown, signed the letter Jill Brown, Hon. Sec.

Note that *honorary* in the last example simply means unpaid, and spelt out in this way always takes a lower-case initial.

See also **ranks, titles, honours and awards**.

**hoof** Plural *hoofs* or *hooves*.

**hopefully** The traditional meaning of the adverb *hopefully* is optimistically:

Farmers are watching hopefully for signs of rain.

Today's farmers are, however, quite likely to say:

Hopefully it will rain before long.

By this they mean that they hope (or perhaps hope and expect) that it will rain before long. Many people object strongly to this relatively new usage and the speed with which it has spread. Nevertheless it is likely some day to attain the respectability of the adverb *naturally*, for which either *in a natural manner* or *it is natural that* could be substituted.

Those who find the modern use conveniently concise and impersonal, particularly in conversation, are unlikely to abandon it because there is a slight possibility of ambiguity on some occasions. The common practice of making it the first word in a sentence largely eliminates ambiguity, but here is an example of the problem:

We will hopefully arrive before dark.

Does this mean that our mood will be optimistic when we arrive or that, with luck, we will arrive while it is still light?

**horde** See **hoard/horde**.

**horrendous/horrific/horrible/horrid** These adjectives all mean much the same thing: arousing horror. *Horrendous* and *horrific* are regarded as being stronger than the other two; they are certainly overused. Overblown journalistic clichés to be avoided in formal English include the *horrendous price rise* and *horrific tax increase*. Both words should be reserved for things that are genuinely shocking: *a horrendous earthquake*; *a horrific road accident*.

The weaker *horrible* and *horrid* are appropriately used to describe something unpleasant or disagreeable.

**hors d'oeuvre** Note the spelling; the plural is *hors d'oeuvres*. This French phrase (meaning apart from the work) is commonly used in English to mean appetiser. Pronounce it 'or **derv**'.

**hospitalised** There are alternatives: *taken to hospital*; *admitted to hospital*; or perhaps simply *in hospital*.

**hot-metal setting** A method of typesetting, now largely superseded, that uses and re-uses molten metal.

See also **computer typesetting**; **printer**.

**how** The word *about* is superfluous in the following construction:

She told us (about) how she made the documentary.

**however** When *however* means nevertheless it is traditionally separated from the rest of a sentence by commas:

We were, however, determined to continue.
However, we were determined to continue.

*However* needs the commas here because, unlike other connecters such as *moreover*, *furthermore* and *yet*, which do not require commas, it has alternative meanings: in whatever way and no matter how. When the meaning is not nevertheless, *however* is not followed by a comma because there is no chance of ambiguity:

We wanted to help however we could.
However tired we became, we were determined to continue.

Avoid putting *however* and *but* into the same construction: *But when we arrived, however, it was too late*. Remove one or the other.

See also **how ever/however**.

**how ever/however** The rule that tells you the difference between *how ever* and *however* applies to a group of words that are often associated with *ever*. When *ever* is used colloquially, expressing feelings such as surprise and disgust, to emphasise interrogative words such as *how*, *what*, *when*, *where* and *who*, it must not be joined onto them but written separately:

How ever will you get home?
What ever have you bought now?
When ever did they arrive on time?
Where ever did she find that hat?
Who ever would have guessed it?

In all other cases the two parts are joined to make one word:

However busy you are, and whatever else is on, come whenever possible.

See also **ever; however.**

**HP** high pressure; hire-purchase; horsepower.

**HQ** headquarters.

***HRA*** *Historical Records of Australia*.

**HRH** Her (or His) Royal Highness.

See also **ranks, titles, honours and awards.**

**HRT** hormone replacement therapy.

**hue** See **hew/hue.**

**hullo** See **hallo/hello/hullo**.

**humor/humour** Either spelling is acceptable, but *humour* is recommended. Note the spelling of *humorous* and *humorist*.

**hung** See **hanged/hung**.

**hung (computer)** When your computer is *hung* the software has 'jammed' and will not work. The current window and the cursor will remain on the screen but you will not be able to move anything or execute any keyboard commands. The only solution is to turn your computer off then on again. Any work not saved at the time your computer hangs will be lost.

See also **save**.

**Huntley, NSW** Compare with *Huntly*, Vic.

**hygiene** Note the spelling.

**hype** Exaggerated publicity that is used to stimulate demand for a product is sometimes called *hype*. The word may be derived from *hypodermic needle* (which suggests stimulus); or from the noun *hyperbole* (implying exaggeration); or from the prefix *hyper-* (implying excess). *Hype* may be used colloquially as a noun but is less acceptable as a verb:

> The film was all hype and no content.

**hyper-/hypo-** The prefix *hyper-* means over, and implies excess: *hyperbole* (obvious exaggeration); *hypersensitivity* (extreme sensitivity); *hyperthermia* (a high body temperature). *Hypo-* means under, and implies deficiency: *hypo-activity* (diminished activity); *hypo-allergenic* (having low allergenic properties); *hypothermia* (a low body temperature).

**hyperbole** This is the use of exaggerated terms for the sake of emphasis: *'I've asked you to do this a thousand times'*. It is pronounced 'hie-**per**ba-lee'.

**hypercritical/hypocritical** *Hypercritical* means excessively critical:

> We are hypercritical of our leaders but fawn on our film stars.

The first two syllables are pronounced 'hie-per'.

*Hypocritical* means pretending to have standards or beliefs one does not possess:

> It is hypocritical to denounce the building of freeways that we intend to use.

The first two syllables are pronounced 'hippa'.

See also **hypocrisy/hypocrite**.

**hypertension/hypotension** The first of these medical terms means abnormally high blood pressure, the second abnormally low blood pressure.

**hyphenation** This is a contentious subject. Some people use very few hyphens; others use too many. Even the authorities differ in their recommendations. A good starting point in any discussion of hyphenation is Fowler's observation that 'the hyphen is not an ornament but an aid to being understood, and should be employed only when it is needed for that purpose'. The implication is that many hyphenation decisions depend on the context. Few modern writers would disagree with Fowler on that point, and modern practice is to omit the hyphen where it is reasonable to do so. The possibility of misleading the reader because of ambiguities sometimes dictates its inclusion in places where it would not ordinarily be necessary. Common sense and a good, up-to-date dictionary are helpful when you are unsure whether to hyphenate a specific word.

There are three stages in the development of many compound words: separate (*horse power*); hyphenated (*horse-power*); and closed up or solid (*horsepower*). In US English, compounds usually reach the closed-up stage sooner than elsewhere. Sometimes hyphenation is a matter of what people get used to, sometimes a matter of aesthetics. Consider some compounds that have so far remained separate words: *post office*; *charity worker*; *general store*. Then there are those that are hyphenated in some dictionaries but not others: *flame-thrower*, *mast-head*, *wrong-doer*. There are also words that are generally closed up: *crossword*, *housekeeper*, *bookmaker*. Compounds like *ice-cream* frequently appear as *ice cream* or *icecream*, and a writer must choose one form and use it consistently in a given work.

The AGPS *Style Manual* provides a comprehensive analysis of the rules underlying the formation of compounds. The following guidelines are widely accepted.

Use a hyphen, rather than treat words as separate or closed up:

- in compounds where the words are to be read together because they have a single meaning

| | | |
|---|---|---|
| a down-and-out | happy-go-lucky | the brush-off |
| a get-together | marking-ink | to house-hunt |

  but note that there are many exceptions, for example the separate forms *bubble bath* and *loading bay*, and the closed-up forms *pushover*, *inbred* and *downwind*
- in the majority of compounds used as adjectives, whether they come before or after the word they are attached to

| | |
|---|---|
| blue-black [adjective + adjective] | The berries were blue-black. |
| travel-weary [noun + adjective] | The refugees were travel-weary. |
| high-sounding [adjective + present participle] | The phrases are high-sounding. |
| able-bodied [adjective + past participle] | The men are able-bodied. |

| | |
|---|---|
| mind-boggling [noun + present participle] | The proposals are mind-boggling. |
| price-controlled [noun + past participle] | The milk was price-controlled. |

but note exceptions that are closed-up forms, for example *footsore* and *housebound*

- in many other compounds used as adjectives, when they come before but not after the word they are attached to, and provided that there is no ambiguity involved

| | | |
|---|---|---|
| a barbed-wire fence | *but* | The fence was made of barbed wire. |
| a down-at-heel fellow | *but* | He was decidedly down at heel. |
| hard-to-get items | *but* | Some items are hard to get. |

- in compounds used as adjectives and involving adverbs such as *ill*, *well*, *little* and *long*, when they come before but not after the word they are attached to

| | | |
|---|---|---|
| an ill-disguised tramp | *but* | The tramp was ill disguised. |
| a well-planned excursion | *but* | The excursion was well planned. |
| a little-known novelist | *but* | This novelist is little known. |
| his long-dead brother | *but* | His brother was long dead. |

Some authorities recommend omission of the hyphen when the compound occurs either before or after the attached word in the case of this last group when an adverb such as *very* or *rather* modifies the compound, or where the compound is in the comparative or superlative. But these constructions are so often ambiguous (because a word like *ill* may be an adverb or adjective) that it is much safer to retain the hyphen consistently. It is certainly essential in the following:

a very ill-disguised tramp
a rather little-known novelist
a better-planned excursion
his longest-dead brother

Note that adverbs ending in *ly* that are involved in compounds used as adjectives are not likely to be mistaken for adjectives themselves and therefore will not produce ambiguity if unhyphenated. This is one case, in fact, where hyphens should definitely not be used in either of the possible positions:

| | |
|---|---|
| the slowly turning wheel | The wheel is slowly turning. |
| freely given advice | The advice is freely given. |

Many compounds (especially those involving a pair of nouns) that are normally separated before the word they are attached to need a hyphen to avoid ambiguity when modified:

food store suppliers
*but* Efficient food-store suppliers call daily.
wood collection areas
*but* There were widely dispersed wood-collection areas throughout the forest.

Hanging hyphens should be avoided by rewriting where possible, but an occasional instance is acceptable:

Turn on the cold-water taps and the hot ones too [*rather than* the cold- and hot-water taps].

The car is available with right- and left-hand drive.

The hyphen must be included in both parts of the sentence in examples such as the second; omitting the one after *right* is no solution to the problem.

Hyphens are also required:

- in number compounds

    sixty-five (and all written numbers of this kind)
    four-fifths (fractions)
    thirty-odd
    80-fold (figures only: note tenfold; a hundredfold)
    a nine-point plan
    a ten-year-old child
    pre-1788

- after certain prefixes, for instance *ex-* (when it means former), *half-*, *self-* and *semi-*

    ex-husband half-digested self-pity semi-educated

    but note exceptions such as *halfway*, *selfsame* and *semicircular*

- between many prefixes and the root word where there are adjoining vowels, particularly the same vowel, or where pronunciation assistance is necessary

    anti-immigration pre-election re-entry co-author

    but note that for some very common words with the prefix *co-*, many authorities drop the hyphen and close up the word

    cooperation coordination coexistence

- after single initial capitals forming compounds

    A-frame M-rated P-plate

- with a prefix followed by an initial capital, a word set in italics or one within quotation marks

    un-Australian post-Renaissance
    pre-*déjeuner* non-'pukka'

    but note that phrases like the following do not require a hyphen or hyphens:

    *in flagrante delicto* situations 'quick fix' solutions

- after *great* and before *in-law*

    great-grandson father-in-law

- to differentiate between meanings

    re-lay (to put down again) *and* relay (to transmit)
    re-form (to form again) *and* reform (to bring reform)
    re-creation (reconstruction) *and* recreation (relaxing activity)

- in most compound titles denoting rank or office

    attorney-general vice-chancellor governor-general

Consult your dictionary because there are many exceptions to these rules and usage is changing constantly.

Note that in the following examples an *en dash* rather than a *hyphen* joins the words or figures:

a Hobart–Launceston flight 1923–52 pages 99–104

A very important function of hyphens is to break words at the end of lines. This is discussed in the entry **word division**.

See also **compound nouns, plurals of; dashes, types of; hard hyphen/soft hyphen; hyphenation dictionary; numbers in figures or words; prefixes and suffixes; re-; word division**.

**hyphenation dictionary** Computer software that determines word breaks is called a *hyphenation dictionary*. It is usually supplied as a standard part of the word-processing or page-makeup package. However, hyphenation dictionaries are not always acceptable as many of their word divisions differ from those favoured in Australia. Hyphenation may be turned off during the production of a document and soft (discretionary) hyphens added.

See also **hard hyphen/soft hyphen; hyphenation; word division**.

**hypo-** See **hyper-/hypo-**.

**hypocrisy/hypocrite** Both words are often misspelt. Note the *-isy* in *hypocrisy* (not 'hypocracy'), and the *e* at the end of *hypocrite*.

See also **hypercritical/hypocritical**.

**hypocritical** See **hypercritical/hypocritical**.

**hypotension** See **hypertension/hypotension**.

**hypothesis** Plural *hypotheses*.

**hysterical** See **histrionic/hysterical**.

# Ii

**I** one (roman numeral; see also **roman numerals**).

**I/me** Choosing the correct pronoun before and after various verbs is explained in the entry **case (grammar)**.

Note, however, that the strictly incorrect *It's me* common in conversation is more acceptable than the correct but stilted *It is I*. In another phrase often heard, *between you and me*, *me* is the only option.

**IAC** Industries Assistance Commission.

**IATA** International Air Transport Association.

**ibid.** This abbreviation (Latin: *ibidem*) means in the same place. It is always printed in roman type, given a lower-case initial, and followed by a full stop. A useful convention for traditional-style notes and references, it is not used in modern schemes such as the Harvard system of referencing. It means that the work being quoted is the same as in the previous note; the page numbers may differ:

> [1]A.W. Reed, *Place Names of Australia* (Sydney, 1973), p. 25.
> [2]ibid., p. 44. [same book, another page]
> [3]ibid. [same book, p. 44]

See also **notes; references**.

**-ible word endings** See **-able/-ible word endings**.

**IBM** International Business Machines Corporation.

**i/c** in charge; in command (*second in command* is expressed as *2IC*).

**-ic/-ical word endings** The suffixes *-ic* and *-ical* are added to some nouns or stems to form adjectives: *poetic*, *botanic*, *classical*, *farcical*. Sometimes the *-ic* and *-ical* words are synonymous – *botanic* and *botanical*, for instance – although one form usually gains wider favour. Sometimes such words have different meanings: *economic* and *economical*, *historic* and *historical*, for example.

**ICBM** intercontinental ballistic missile.

**ICFTU** International Confederation of Free Trade Unions.

**ICI** Imperial Chemical Industries Australia Limited.

**ICJ** International Court of Justice.

**icon** In computer terminology an *icon* is a graphic symbol displayed on a screen to represent a folder, file, program or game. Most computers provide the option of displaying the material stored on their disks as either textual lists or icons.

**ID** identification.

**identical to/identical with** Either preposition is acceptable:

> My car is identical to [*or* with] the one I saw outside.

**identify** There are well-established meanings for the verb *to identify*, but also a couple of modern ways of using the word that are convenient – if slightly overdone. One is to associate closely:

> They identified the company with advances in laser technology.

The other is to recognise and appraise:

> Our study identified major parking problems.

**idiom** Naturalness of expression in a language is the primary meaning of this word (*idiomatic* is the adjective). The accepted *idiom* is *I enjoy singing*, not *I enjoy to sing*; *a cup of strong black coffee*, not *a cup of the black strong coffee*. Idiom is formed by time and tradition, and often logic and the rules of grammar have little to do with it. Because much of it is vivid, idiom has been called the life and spirit of language.

Popular expressions that may occur in formal or informal writing or in speech are also called *idioms* (*colloquialisms* are idioms that are suitable only for informal contexts). This kind of idiom includes colourful phrases such as *spick and span*; *as thick as thieves*; *clutching at straws*; *sticking to your guns*; *playing with fire*; *champing at the bit*; and *holding the fort*. (Of course, most of these are regarded as clichés, not to be overused.)

Some idioms of Australian origin are *chucking a mickey*; *up the country*; *wild and woolly*; *hard yakka*; *on the outer*; *as game as Ned Kelly*; *going walkabout*; and *mad as a cut snake*.

Another meaning of *idiom* is the language form peculiar to a specific area: *the idiom of Lancashire*; *the idiom of Alsace–Lorraine*.

One meaning, distinctive character, is not necessarily related to language at all: *the idiom of Walter Burley Griffin*; *the idiom of flamenco music*.

See also **argot/dialect/jargon/lingua franca**; **clichés**; **colloquialisms**; **metaphor**; **simile**; **slang**.

**idiosyncrasy** Note the idiosyncratic spelling of this word.

**IDL** International Date Line.

**idle/idol/idyll** You may choose to be *idle* rather than busy; worship an *idol*; or create an appealing scene (especially a rustic one) that might be described as an *idyll* in words, music or paint (pronounced '**idd**'l' or '**eye**-d'l').

**i.e** See **e.g/i.e.**

**IEL** Industrial Equity Limited.

**if** Although the conjunction *if* is often used interchangeably with *whether*, the following sentences have slightly different meanings:

> Let your aunt know whether you have passed the exam.

This means *whether or not* (that is, there are two possibilities).

> Let your aunt know if you have passed the exam.

This means *only if* (that is, there is only one possibility).

When *if* occurs in the following kind of sentence it often produces ambiguity:

> The girl would make a good cook, if not an executive chef.

It is impossible to tell whether this means *although not an executive chef* or *perhaps even an executive chef* (or even *provided she is not an executive chef*). Use an unambiguous substitute that conveys your intention.

See also **as if/as though**; **doubtful/dubious**; **if and when**; **if it was/if it were**; **whether**.

**if and when** This is a contradictory stock phrase. Use one conjunction or the other:

> I'll let you know if [*or* when] I get the facts.

**if it was/if it were** When something is a fact or probability, use *if it was*:

> If it was time for dinner I always stopped work.

When something is merely possible or hypothetical, and not a fact, use *if it were* (subjunctive):

> If it were possible to turn back the clock, I would do so.

In general, if *would* is in the sentence, use *were*.

See also **subjunctive mood**.

**ignoramus** The plural is *ignoramuses*. Pronounce the word 'igna-**ray**-mus'.

**ilk** This noun once exclusively meant a place of the same name, denoting the estates of the landed gentry in Scotland: *McNolty of that ilk* meant *McNolty of McNolty*. Today *ilk* is a synonym for *type*:

William dines with financiers and others of that ilk.

**illegal/illegitimate/illicit** These three adjectives all mean unlawful and they overlap to some extent, but there are differences in their application. *Illegal* may mean contrary to the law or to regulations: *illegal demolition*; *illegal immigration*; *illegal parking*.

*Illegitimate* was once primarily used to describe the status of children born outside wedlock, but the word *exnuptial* has replaced it in societies where *illegitimate* no longer has legal significance in this sense. *Illegitimate* can still mean forbidden by law, and has the additional meaning irregular or defying logic: *illegitimate use of taxi vouchers*; *an illegitimate excuse*.

*Illicit* covers activities that might be legal if conditions laid down by the law were complied with, such as *illicit gambling* in a State where legal gambling also exists. *Illicit* may describe activities that contravene social mores and yet are not illegal: *illicit sex*.

See also **elicit/illicit**.

**illegible/unreadable** What is *illegible* is hard or impossible to read because it is poorly handwritten, typed or printed; or because the letters have been partly obliterated:

He failed the exam because of his illegible handwriting.

Something *unreadable*, on the other hand, may be impeccably presented but is so incompetently phrased or constructed that the reader does not want to persist with it:

The manuscript was rejected because the author's style made it unreadable.

If you use *unreadable* as a synonym for *illegible* it will be necessary to make your meaning clear:

The appalling photocopy made the document unreadable.

**illegitimate** See **illegal/illegitimate/illicit**.

**illicit** See **elicit/illicit**; **illegal/illegitimate/illicit**.

**illiterate/innumerate** Both these adjectives relate to educational deficiencies (*illiteracy* and *innumeracy* are the deficiencies). *Illiterate* primarily means unable to read or write, though another meaning is badly educated: either in general

(*Half the students leave school illiterate*) or in a specific field (*He is culturally illiterate*). *Illiterate* can also be a noun. *Innumerate* means ignorant of the procedures of mathematics or science.

**illusion** See **allusion/illusion/delusion**.

**illusive** See **allusive/elusive/illusive**.

**ILO** International Labour Organisation.

**IM/IV** These are the abbreviations for the medical terms *intramuscular* and *intravenous* respectively. If you spell *intravenous* correctly you will pronounce it correctly (not 'intravenious').

**image setter** In desktop-publishing terminology an *image setter* is the high-end output device. A laser printer outputs at 300 to 1000 dots per inch (dpi) onto ordinary paper, whereas an image setter outputs at 1200 to 3600 dpi onto bromide paper or film. Some equipment and software will output pages imposed in eight-page sections.

See also **dots per inch**; **output device**; **printer**.

**imaginary/imaginative** The adjective *imaginary* means existing only in the imagination, not real:

> Before he went to sleep Alexander always talked to the imaginary dragon that lived under his cot.

*Imaginative* means able to imagine creatively, or describes something produced by a creative imagination:

> Shakespeare's imaginative use of metaphor is conspicuous in all his plays.

Both words may apply to the same noun. An *imaginary* clown (that is, one who exists in someone's imagination) may also be an *imaginative* clown (that is, one who performs innovative tricks).

**imbroglio** The plural is *imbroglios*. An *imbroglio* (Italian for confusion) is a difficult or perplexing state of affairs. The word is pronounced 'im-**brole**-ee-o'.

**imbue/infuse/instil** As the verb *to imbue* means to inspire or saturate, its object (usually human) is always followed by *with*, not *into*:

> The self-help group imbued its members with confidence.

*not* The self-help group imbued confidence into its members.

*Infuse* and *instil* have a similar meaning, but their object (usually inanimate) is always followed by *into*:

> The self-help group infused [*or* instilled] confidence into its members.

See also **inculcate**; **instil/instilment**.

**IMF** International Monetary Fund.

**immanent** See **eminent/imminent/immanent.**

**immigrant** See **emigrant/immigrant/migrant.**

**imminent** See **eminent/imminent/immanent.**

**immoral** See **amoral/immoral.**

**immovable/immoveable/irremovable** The first two spellings are normally interchangeable (the legal term spelt *immoveable* is an exception). *Immovable* means incapable of being moved: *an immovable object. Irremovable* means impossible to remove: *an irremovable stain.*

See also **movable/moveable.**

**immunity/impunity** These words are sometimes confused because both mean exemption. *Immunity* is exemption from an unwelcome duty: *immunity from jury service*; from laws that apply to others: *diplomatic immunity*; or from susceptibility to a disease: *immunity to cholera. Impunity* has a narrower meaning, exemption from harmful consequences: *charging excessive prices with impunity.*

**impact** This noun has lost much of its impact since it became a newspaper catch-all for *impression*, *influence* or *effect*: *TAX IMPACT BITES*. *Impact* is not widely accepted as a verb: *High taxes impact on disposable income.*

**imperative mood** Verbs used in commands or requests are said to be in the *imperative mood*:

> *Get* back in the boat and please *sit* still.

See also **mood.**

**imperial/imperious** *Imperial* means relating to an empire, emperor or empress; it can also mean domineering, but *imperious* is the better word for this. *Imperious* is unambiguous and conveys the sense of tyranny more strongly, whether it is applied to a supreme ruler or an overbearing waiter.

**imperial system** Australia began to phase out this British system of measurements in the late 1960s, and replaced it with a metric system. Imperial measures included feet and inches (length), pounds and ounces (weight), gallons and pints (capacity), and Fahrenheit (temperature).

See also **metric system; weights and measures.**

**imperious** See **imperial/imperious**.

**impinge/infringe** *Impinge* (on) and *infringe* can mean much the same thing: encroach on. But note that while *impinge* is always followed by *on* or *upon*, *infringe* is not:

This work is impinging on my free time.

*but* Parking there infringes the local regulations.

The noun *infringement* retains the *-e* of *infringe*.

**implement** Remember the synonyms for this verb: *do*, *accomplish*, *carry out*, *fulfil* and *execute*.

**implicit** See **explicit/implicit**.

**imply/infer** These verbs have completely different meanings and are in no way interchangeable. To *imply* is to hint at or suggest something that is not explicitly stated:

The arrival of a load of bricks implied that building would soon start.

To *infer* is to deduce or draw a conclusion (from something):

We inferred from the arrival of a load of bricks that building would soon start.

The words are used of various circumstances, of course, but – in the context of communication – a speaker or writer *implies*; a listener or reader *infers*.

See also **indicate**.

**importantly** This adverb may be used to mean in an important manner, or significantly:

The butler announced us importantly.

Importantly for the trio, this violinist works well with other musicians.

Be careful in using this word because either of the meanings may be possible in some contexts:

Importantly, he wore his full regalia.

See also **hopefully**.

**import (computer)** See **export/import**.

**imposition** To publishers and printers *imposition* means the arrangement of pages that will ensure their correct sequence once they have been printed and folded.

**impostor** Do not spell this noun 'imposter'.

**impracticable/impractical** See **practicable/practical**.

**impresario** Note the single *s* in this noun meaning an organiser or manager of various public entertainments. The plural is *impresarios*.

**impression** See **edition/impression/reprint**.

**imprint page** See **publications, parts of**.

**impromptu** See **extempore/impromptu**.

**impugn/impute** To *impugn* means to call into question, or to doubt, the veracity of something:

If you impugn my honesty in public I shall sue you.

To *impute* is to attribute something (usually discreditable) to a person:

The bus company imputed the theft to its ticket clerk.

**impunity** See **immunity/impunity**.

**impute** See **impugn/impute**.

**in** See **at/in**; **in to/into**.

**in-** See **non-**.

**in addition to** This prepositional phrase has a kind of parenthetical role and does not affect verb agreement in the way that the conjunction *and* does:

A sharp pencil and a red pen *are* required.

*but* A sharp pencil, in addition to a red pen, *is* required.

The verb remains singular whether or not the words are marked off by commas. Phrases like *in addition to* are useful for emphasis, but *and* often suffices.

See also **singular or plural**.

**inapt/inept** *Inapt* means inappropriate or unskilful: *inapt clothing*; *inapt manoeuvres*. *Inept* has the same meanings, with the addition of clumsy, incompetent or foolish; only *inept* can be used of a person: *inept questioning*; *an inept negotiator*.

**inasmuch as/in so far as/in so much that** These are the recommended forms of three closely related and rather stilted phrases (note the prepositions), whose most common uses are best illustrated in context:

Inasmuch as Con had prepared a meal, we felt obliged to stay.

In so far as they apply to us, the rules seem fair.

We felt obliged to stay, in so much that Con had prepared a meal.

The last phrase is the least often seen and the most liable to be misunderstood.

**in attendance** Use *present* or *there*.

**inaugurate** *Inaugurate* strictly means to install formally in office, but also to begin. It is, however, too ponderous a word to use in everyday contexts as a synonym for *begin* or *start*:

We started [*not* inaugurated] the new baby-sitting roster last week.

The adjective *inaugural* is often mispronounced 'in-or-gral' and therefore misspelt 'inaugral'. Note the second *u*.

**Inc.** Incorporated (as a company).

**inchoate/incoherent** Both adjectives mean lacking in organisation, but in different senses. *Inchoate* means just beginning or undeveloped:

All he could suggest was an inchoate scheme requiring weeks of refinement.

Pronounce it 'in-**ko**-ate'.

*Incoherent* means disjointed or rambling, and is generally used of thoughts or speech:

After a third martini her comments on other guests became incoherent.

**in close proximity** As proximity means nearness in place, time or relation, the phrase *in close proximity* is a tautology; prefer *close to* or *near to*.

**inclusive language** See **discriminatory language**.

**incoherent** See **inchoate/incoherent**.

**incredible/incredulous** *Incredible* means unbelievable, and it mostly applies to things:

Superman's adventures were incredible.

Note also the colloquialisms *incredible [amazing] luck* and *an incredible [very good] party.*

*Incredulous* means unable to believe, and is mostly applied to people:

Jodie was incredulous when she saw the falling star.

But note also phrases such as *an incredulous stare*, where the word refers only indirectly to a person.

See also **credible/creditable/credulous**.

**inculcate** Ideas, beliefs, habits, concepts and rules are *inculcated in*, *into* or (less commonly) *upon* a person; a person is not *inculcated with* anything:

The notion of fair play was inculcated into the child.

*not* The child was inculcated with the notion of fair play.

See also **imbue/infuse/instil**.

**incumbent** The phrase *present incumbent* is tautological because an *incumbent* is the *present occupant* (of a position).

**indefinitely** Note the *-ite-*. When we remember that *indefinitely* means possibly forever, it becomes obvious that the phrase *almost indefinitely* is nonsensical.

**indention** In typesetting there are two main types of *indention*, the *paragraph indent* and the *hanging indent*.

In a *paragraph indent* the first line, like this one, is set in from the left margin to indicate the beginning of a new paragraph. The paragraph indent is an important aid to legibility, particularly in book text. It should be used in preference to a line space between paragraphs. There is usually no paragraph indent at the beginning of a chapter, under a heading, or after a gap in narrative designed to indicate a distinct break in its flow.

A *hanging indent* has the first line, like this one, set full out to the left margin and subsequent lines indented – as in this paragraph. It is sometimes useful in reference works where a headword is to be emphasised, or to introduce a series of bulleted or highlighted points.

See also **paragraphs**.

**independent** This adjective cannot be spelt 'independant'. Many people make this error, however, probably because of the confusion between its opposite, the adjective *dependent*, and the noun, which is usually spelt *dependant*.

See also **dependant/dependent**.

**in-depth** It is surprising that anyone can still use the overworked expression *in-depth* (ostensibly meaning thorough or profound) without a titter. Veto it.

**indexes/indices** Either is acceptable as the plural of *index*, but *indexes* is more common in general contexts and *indices* in scientific or mathematical work.

See also **indexing**.

**indexing** An *index* is an alphabetical listing of all references to particular items – from people and places to events and concepts – that are scattered throughout a book. Indexes follow the text, usually at the very end of the volume (the list of contents, which some people confuse with the index, sets out the main topics to be covered and is located early in the work). The importance of a good index, particularly in a reference book or manual, cannot be overemphasised. Responsible publishers and editors spend a great deal of time ensuring that the indexes of the books they produce are both logically arranged and comprehensive.

Indexes are usually compiled from page proofs, when the text has been finalised and page numbers allocated. However, a preliminary index – without final page numbers – can be prepared at an earlier stage, even from manuscript.

Many word-processing programs have the capacity to generate indexes at typescript stage, when they can be a valuable aid in the organisation of material. However, such indexes do not advance the publication process if substantial rewriting and reordering occur at the editing stage. In that event every reference will need to be checked again, with little time being saved.

The indexing of large and complex works has traditionally been the responsibility of professional indexers, but simpler indexes can usually be compiled by editors or authors. The main thing to remember is that an index exists for the convenience of the reader. There are a number of basic principles that apply to the process of compiling any index.

***Coverage and systems*** An indexer should always bear in mind the audience intended for the book. It is necessary to consider not only the items readers are likely to look for, but also the most accessible form for them. It is important to decide early whether the book needs more than one index. Indexes dealing separately with, for instance, the scientific and common names of plants can pointlessly double a reader's search. But handbooks that provide separate listings of, for example, the wheelchair access and cuisine offered by restaurants named in a general index are genuinely helpful.

The system of alphabetical order to be followed must also be decided at the outset. The sequence of entries may be word-by-word or letter-by-letter.

| ***Word-by-word*** | ***Letter-by-letter*** |
| --- | --- |
| public buildings | publications |
| public hygiene | public buildings |
| public meetings | public hygiene |
| public service | publicity |
| publications | public meetings |
| publicity | public service |

Here are some general guidelines on indexing by traditional methods, which can easily be adapted by people whose computers have suitable programs.

***Procedure*** First, read the text through quickly, if you are not familiar with it, to get a broad understanding of level and content, and to identify the main themes and topics. The scope and length of the index are matters for early consultation with the publisher.

Then mark (by underlining, circling or highlighting) the items you think should be included in the index. These decisions will often need revision: many indexers find that they begin by treating the material in far too much detail.

When a satisfactory selection has been made, write each item at the top of a separate index card. Each heading (entry) in the index should be a noun or phrase, the most important word coming first. The standard form for main headings is as follows:

*Family Herald*, 201
Farwell, George, 176
fascism, 28
Faust, Beatrice, 128

Fellowship of Australian Writers,
172, 211

The heading is usually separated from the page reference or references by a comma, but a space may be substituted for that comma. Topics closely related to a heading are usually linked to it as subheadings (sub-entries), which are placed on a separate line below it and indented or, to save some space, run on between semicolons. Unlike the main heading, subheadings may begin with the definite or indefinite article (*the*, *a* or *an*), adjectives, prepositions or conjunctions, which are sometimes essential for showing how they are related to the main entry:

Ferguson, George, xi, 230, 233
  on George Robertson, 222
  publishing in London, 255–6
film industry, xi, 36–7
  patronage, 208
Finniss, M. M., 125–6
FitzGerald, R. D., 244, 272
  early Australian literary
    influences, 48, 53

Here is the same series of headings and subheadings in run-on style:

Ferguson, George, xi, 230, 233; on
  George Robertson, 222;
  publishing in London, 255–6
film industry, xi, 36–7; patronage,
  208
Finniss, M. M., 125–6
FitzGerald, R. D., 244, 272; early
  Australian literary influences,
  48, 53

If the first entry had had no general page references to George Ferguson, it would have read like this:

Ferguson, George
  on George Robertson, 222
  publishing in London, 255–6

*or* Ferguson, George: on George
  Robertson, 222; publishing in
  London, 255–6

The material may be broken down further, to include sub-subheadings:

Ferguson, George, xi, 230, 233
  on George Robertson, 222
    his grandfather, 142
    as publisher, 231, 252,
      287–8, 290

*or* Ferguson, George, xi, 230, 233; on
  George Robertson, 222, (his

grandfather) 142, (as publisher)
231, 252, 287–8, 290

Note that, under the second style, the bracketed words precede the page numbers to which they refer.

If the reader is likely to look up more than one word when searching for a particular topic, or if there are any related entries, a cross-reference should be provided:

publishers at Angus & Robertson,
*see* Ferguson, George;
Robertson, George
FitzGerald, R. D., 244, 272
*see also* Australian poets

*or* FitzGerald, R. D., 244, 272; *see*
*also* Australian poets

***Alphabetical order*** The word that a reader is most likely to look up should come first in an index heading (as opposed to a subheading or sub-subheading). Any articles, prepositions or conjunctions are ignored in the alphabetical arrangement of subheadings. Remember that whether you choose the word-by-word or letter-by-letter system, it must be followed consistently. Family names starting with *Mac* or *Mc* are usually arranged as if spelt *Mac*.

***Style*** Every aspect of an index must in fact be consistent. The headings and subheadings should be identical with the text in spelling, hyphenation, capitalisation and punctuation, though space-saving devices such as initials instead of given names are acceptable.

Each page reference is listed, in numerical order. If the topic being indexed is discussed continuously over two or more pages an inclusive reference may be given (125–6). The devices *ff.* and *passim* are occasionally necessary: the reference *113 ff.* means that a lengthy discussion of a topic begins on page 113 and continues for some pages; the entry *Australian literature*, *passim* means that Australian literature is discussed here and there throughout the book. *Passim* is always printed in italic.

References to illustrations and notes should be distinguished from references to the main text. Illustrations might be indicated in bold type, notes by the abbreviation *n* in italic:

Finniss, M. M., 125–6, **144**
FitzGerald, R. D., 244, 272, 300*n*

If these devices are used there should be an explanatory note at the beginning of the index.

***Typography*** In order to save space, indexes are usually set two or three points smaller than the text and arranged in columns. Subheadings are indented 1 em (or a smaller space decided by the designer) and turnovers and sub-subheadings a further 1 em each according to the indented style most commonly used. If entries are in run-on style, every line below the heading is indented 1 em only. Runs of page numbers (125–6) are joined by an en rule, not a hyphen. There is no full stop at the end of an entry, or any part of it. The alphabetical sections are generally separated by a line space, though a half-line space is sufficient if there is not enough room for more.

See also **indexes/indices; publications, parts of**.

**indicate** This verb can only be used instead of *said* when its subject implies rather than states something:

The prime minister seemed to indicate that the election would be held in May.

*but* He said [*not* indicated] that he wanted to hold it before the president's visit.

See also **imply/infer**.

**indicative mood** See **mood**.

**indices** See **indexes/indices**.

**indifferent** This is a tricky adjective that is sometimes ambiguous. *Indifferent* (to) can mean uninterested: *indifferent to your fate*; or unimportant: *an indifferent posting*; average or poor: *an indifferent performance*; or impartial: *an indifferent judgement*. Use the word carefully, and make sure that the context indicates your intended meaning.

See also **disinterested/uninterested**.

**indiscriminate/undiscriminating** Both adjectives mean not discriminating (that is, not making fine distinctions), and in some contexts they are interchangeable:

Wayne buys CDs with indiscriminate [*or* undiscriminating] enthusiasm.

When you mean random and the connotation is unpleasant, prefer *indiscriminate*:

Indiscriminate spraying killed bees as well as wasps.

In this sentence *undiscriminating* is better:

Jacqui is undiscriminating about flatmates and gets on with all of them.

**indoor/indoors** *Indoor* is the adjective: *indoor swimming pool*. *Indoors* is the adverb: *swimming indoors*.

**indubitably** See **doubtless/undoubtedly/indubitably**.

**inductive** See **deductive/inductive**.

**indulgences** Not 'indulgencies'.

**inept** See **inapt/inept**.

**inequity/iniquity** These two nouns not only look similar but share the meaning injustice. *Iniquity*, however, primarily means a wicked act.

The partners were equal in status but there was inequity in their sharing of costs.

The community regards the kidnapping of children as an iniquity.

*Iniquitous*, the adjectival form of *iniquity*, is often used to mean unjust and wicked in equal portions:

It is iniquitous to charge excessively high rents for dingy houses.

**in fact** Use this phrase when you need emphasis, not just absent-mindedly. The same applies to words like *actually* and *really*.

**infamous/notorious** Both adjectives are used of people or deeds that incur condemnation. *Infamous* means of evil repute or detestable:

Stalin's infamous purges of opponents were hidden for years.

*Notorious* emphasises the amount of publicity a person's bad behaviour has attracted (it is legitimate but inadvisable to use the word simply to mean well known – you are likely to be misunderstood):

Notorious for his drinking and brawling, he was no longer welcome at the club.

Journalists should be aware that neither word should be applied to a living person, even in jest: defamation actions are costly.

**infectious** See **contagious/infectious**.

**infer** See **imply/infer**.

**inferior characters/superior characters** *Inferior* and *superior characters* (also called *subscripts* and *superscripts*) are typeset in a smaller point size than the main text. *Inferior characters* are positioned below the baseline of type, and *superior characters* are positioned above it. Inferior and superior characters (in this case figures) are often used in mathematics and chemistry:

$4^2 \times 10^3 = 16\,000$

$H_2SO_4$ (sulphuric acid)

Superior characters are used to indicate footnotes or references:

A new approach to the study of international agreements was suggested by the same author.[36]

[36]ibid.

The results of a new study on asthmatics and air pollution* were surprising.

*Reported in the *Age*.

In display advertising, superior characters are frequently used for the dollar sign and for cents in product prices:

WINDCHEATERS $^{\$}14^{99}$ CELERY $85^{c}$

See also **asterisk; notes; reference marks; references**.

**infinitive** An *infinitive* is the basic form of a verb, which usually begins with *to*: *to go*; *to help*; *to be*; *to meet*. Sometimes the *to* is hidden: *I can go [am able to go]*; *you may help [are permitted to help]*; *they must be [are obliged to be]*;

*we should meet [ought to meet]*. Unlike other verb-forms the infinitive does not have a subject, though it may itself be the subject or object of another verb – that is, it can act as a noun: *To delay is impossible*; *She chose to resign.*

See also **case (grammar)**; **split infinitive**; **verbs**.

**inflammable** See **flammable/inflammable/nonflammable**.

**inflation** The term *inflation* means an increase in the general level of prices, usually expressed as an annual percentage change or rate of change: *Inflation in 1991 was 3 per cent.* Note, however, that this may mean that prices in 1991 were 3 per cent higher than in 1990, or that prices rose by 3 per cent during 1991. The phrase *during the course of the year* is often used to convey the latter meaning more precisely: *During the course of 1991 the rate of inflation was 3 per cent.*

Similarly the statement *In the June quarter of 1991 the annual rate of inflation was 4 per cent* may mean that prices in the June quarter of 1991 were 4 per cent higher than a year before, or that prices in the June quarter were 1 per cent higher than in the previous March quarter and were therefore rising at an annual compound rate of around 4 per cent. It is important to use enough words to make the meaning clear. Note too that, except for small numbers, multiplying the quarterly percentage change by four does not result in an accurate statement of the annual compound rate of change. A 4 per cent change in prices from one quarter to the next means an annual inflation rate of 17 per cent, not 16 per cent.

A fall in the rate of inflation does not denote a fall in prices; it simply indicates a fall in the rate of increase in prices. Note that if the rate of inflation increases from 10 per cent to 15 per cent, it is not correct to say that inflation has increased by 5 per cent, as the increase in the *rate* of inflation is 50 per cent. The increase in the rate of inflation is correctly described as an increase of 5 *percentage points*.

**inflection/inflexion** Either spelling is acceptable. A change in the pitch of a voice is one meaning of *inflection*:

> A rising inflection indicated his anger.

In grammar, *inflection* is the term for variant forms of a word denoting such functions as gender, tense, voice, number, person and case; the process of change involved is also called *inflection*. Here are some words with possible inflections:

| | |
|---|---|
| a *goose*; a *gander* [gender] | you *see*; you *saw* [tense] |
| she *pushes*; she *is pushed* [voice] | a *table*; *tables* [number] |
| *I* play; *she* plays [person] | *We* like Gavin; Gavin likes *us* [case] |

**inflict** See **afflict/inflict**.

**inform** Use *tell* instead of *inform* unless the context is appropriately formal:

> I'll tell [*not* inform] you when he comes.
>
> You must inform the embassy of your address.

**informant/informer** An *informant* supplies information to anyone about anything; an *informer* supplies information to the police (or to some other organisation with regulatory powers).

**infra dig** This expression means undignified (Latin: *infra dignitatem*, below one's dignity). The term is not generally used in formal writing.

**infra-red** Note the hyphen; *ultraviolet* is one word.

**infrastructure** This word is much used by politicians, public servants, sociologists and petty officials to make something basic or banal sound important. It is often possible to replace it with *framework*, *parts*, *foundation* or *structure*, or to omit it altogether. The first example shows an acceptable use of the word.

Roads and other parts of the transport infrastructure need funds.

*but* The living-and-learning centre needs reorganising.

*rather than*

The infrastructure of the living-and-learning centre needs reorganising.

**infringe** See **impinge/infringe**.

**infuse** See **imbue/infuse/instil**.

**-ing forms** All verbs have *-ing forms*: *have/having*; *be/being*; *see/seeing*. The *-ing form* of a verb on its own never has a subject but can have an object:

I saw her smoking a cigarette [object].

There are two kinds of *-ing form*, the *gerund* (verbal noun) and the *present participle*.

The *gerund* acts like a noun and can be the subject or object of a verb:

Smoking [subject] is not allowed.

I do not allow smoking [object].

Even when it is simply part of a verb – *He is smoking* – the *present participle* acts like an adjective and describes a noun or pronoun:

The old man sat outside, smoking [describes *old man*].

Please move to the smoking area [describes *area*].

We don't like to see him smoking [describes *him*].

When a word ending in *ing* is preceded by a pronoun, it is not always easy to know which form of the pronoun is correct. There are two options:

I enjoy him playing the trumpet.

*or* I enjoy his playing the trumpet.

The deciding factor is the job the *-ing* word is doing. In this example it is a gerund, acting as a noun: I enjoy the *playing*, not *him*. Whose playing? *His*. Thus:

I enjoy his playing the trumpet.

In this kind of construction the pronoun preceding the word *playing* could be *his*, *its*, *their*, *my*, *your* or *our*.

In the following example *playing* has a different job to do:

I found him playing the trumpet.

Here it is a present participle, acting as an adjective: I found *him*, not the *playing*, which merely describes *him*. In this kind of construction the pronoun preceding the word *playing* could be *him*, *it*, *them*, *me*, *you* or *us*. The pronoun *her* would be used whether the -ing word was a gerund or a past participle.

See also **case (grammar)**; **gerund**; **participles**; **pronouns**; **verbs**.

**ingenious/ingenuous** The adjective *ingenious* (noun *ingenuity*) means inventive or clever:

They produced an ingenious cipher machine.

*Ingenious* is pronounced 'in-**jeen**-ee-us'.

*Ingenuous* (noun *ingenuousness*) means innocent, artless or without guile:

The fellow seemed ingenuous but had already served two years for fraud.

*Ingenuous* is pronounced 'in-**jen**-yoo-us'. Note that *disingenuous* is not exactly the opposite of *ingenuous*; it means *pretending* to be ingenuous.

**in-group** Note the hyphen in this colloquial term for an exclusive group.

**inhuman/inhumane** Though these adjectives are similar in meaning, *inhuman* is the stronger word. To be *inhuman* is to lack all human qualities, literally or figuratively:

An inhuman shriek woke the explorers.

It was an inhuman act to deprive the prisoner of water.

*Inhumane* means lacking in compassion or kindness towards our fellow creatures (human or otherwise):

It was inhumane to deprive the prisoner of visitors.

Some people regard the caging of birds as inhumane.

**iniquity** See **inequity/iniquity**.

**initial/initialled/initialling** Note the single *l* in the first and the *-ll-* in the other two.

**initial capitals** See **capital letters, decorative initial**.

**in lieu of** Prefer *instead of*, except where one thing is being replaced with another of equivalent value (*lieu* is French for place):

I'll give you shares in lieu of cash.

*but* He had a sandwich instead of [*not* in lieu of] a full meal.

**innocuous** Note the *-nn-* and single *c*. The word means harmless.

**innovation** It is tautological to write of a *new innovation*.

**innuendo** The plural is *innuendoes*. An *innuendo* is a hint of an unfavourable kind – an insinuation.

**innumerate** See **illiterate/innumerate**.

**inoculate** This verb (and the noun *inoculation*) is one of the most frequently misspelt words in the English language. Note the single *n* and *c*.

**in order to/in order that** Both these phrases are formal, and quite often verbose.

*Put* She climbed over the fence *to* avoid the long walk round.

*rather than*

She climbed over the fence in order to avoid the long walk round.

*Put* A section was reserved *so that* some passengers could smoke.

*rather than*

A section was reserved in order that some passengers might smoke.

*In order that* (but not *so that*) has to be followed by *may*, *might*, *shall* or *should* instead of *can*, *could*, *will* or *would*, and this is an additional reason to avoid it.

While *so that* can generally replace *in order that*, it is sometimes necessary to use *in order to* rather than *to* for the sake of clarity:

In order to be heard by everyone you must speak loudly.

**input/output** In general usage the word *input* is voguish but can easily be replaced if you are allergic to such words. *Output*, on the other hand, is entrenched in the language and acceptable to all.

**input/output (computer)** In general computing and desktop publishing *input* is any data entered into a computer for processing by a program. *Output*, also called printout or hard copy, is the printed material produced.

**inquiry** See **enquiry/inquiry**.

**insertion point** In computer terminology the *insertion point* is the current position of the cursor – usually a short blinking line or small rectangle – in the text. This is where the next character entered will appear.

See also **cursor**.

**in short supply** The word *scarce* is usually adequate.

**inside/outside** When they are used as prepositions, *inside* and *outside* are never followed by *of*: *inside the factory*; *outside these limits*. It is a different matter when they are nouns:

The inside of the factory was painted yellow; the outside of it was white.

Note that the *of it* near the end of the example is optional.

See also **of**.

**insider trading** This occurs when shares are traded because of privileged information about forthcoming or hidden events that could influence the share price.

**insidious/invidious** *Insidious* means deceitful or stealthily spreading:

We noticed too late the insidious patch of oil under the car.

*Invidious* means causing ill will, resentment or offence:

The caretaker resigned because of invidious remarks about dusty corners.

**insignia** The preferred plural form (as well as the singular).

**in so far as/in so much that** See **inasmuch as/in so far as/in so much that**.

**insouciance** This noun means nonchalance or unconcern and is pronounced with both *c*s soft. The adjective is *insouciant*.

**in spite of** See **despite/in spite of**.

**install/instalment** With the exception of *instalment*, all forms of *install* have the *l* doubled (including *installation*).

See also **instil/instilment**.

**instantly/instantaneously** Although these adverbs are interchangeable in meaning, the shorter is preferable.

**instil/instilment** All other forms have the *l* doubled (including *instillation*).

See also **imbue/infuse/instil; install/instalment**.

**instrumentality** Do not overuse this term. Government *instrumentalities* usually have more specific names.

**insurance** See **assurance/insurance**.

**insure** See **assure/ensure/insure**.

**integral** The adjective *integral* is superfluous in the cliché *integral part* because *integral* means being part of a whole thing. Therefore you can say:

The index is an important part of this book.

*but not*

The index is an integral part of this book.

Note that integral is often followed by *to*: *The hub is integral to a wheel.* Put the stress on *in-*, not *-teg-*, when pronouncing the word.

**integrate** Note the spelling (not 'intergrate').

**intelligentsia** Note the *-t-* in the fourth syllable of this noun, which means the intellectual elite in a group or country.

**Intelsat** International Telecommunications Satellite Organization (Consortium until 1973).

**intense/intensive** *Intense* means extreme in degree, force or feelings:

> The intense heat of the midday sun was unbearable.
>
> Terry is so intense that we regard him as emotionally unstable.

*Intensive* means thorough or concentrated:

> An intensive examination of the mural revealed minute flaws.

**inter-/intra-** The Latin words *inter* and *intra* have supplied these prefixes to the English language. *Inter-* means between: *inter-company*, *inter-dominion*, *intermolecular. Intra-* means within: *intramural*, *intra-uterine*, *intramolecular*.

**interactively** The word *interactively*, used of computer programs, means simultaneously. You can, for instance, use a word-processing program and page-makeup program interactively.

***inter alia*** This Latin phrase (usually italicised) means *among other things*:

> The box contained cutlery *inter alia.*

The expression may sound pretentious in unsophisticated circles and writing, and the English version is often preferable.

**intercede** Note the *-cede*. This verb means to come between opposing parties as a mediator.

**interface** An *interface* is a connection or link, especially between parts of a machine. In a computer system it describes the circuitry that enables the central processing unit to communicate with a peripheral device such as a disk drive, printer or screen. Its figurative use as a synonym for the nouns *interaction*, *communication* or *cooperation* and the verbs *interact*, *communicate* or *co-operate* has been tediously overdone. Try to avoid it:

> The communication [*not* interface] between the teacher and his pupils was good.
>
> The two teams cooperated [*not* interfaced] in the fundraising.

The word will no doubt continue to be found in that repository of junk English, the recruitment advertisement.

**interjection** An *interjection* is the part of speech that expresses strong emotion, in one word or more: *Hey! Stop thief!*. The words themselves are also called interjections. Written interjections are usually followed by exclamation marks, but not everything that is followed by an exclamation mark is an interjection.

**interment/internment** *Interment* is a formal word for burial: *The interment will take place at 3 p.m. Internment* means the imprisonment or confinement of enemy aliens in wartime; it can also be used of prisoners of war, or of hostile troops in a neutral country: *internment during the hostilities*.

See also **intern/internee**.

**in terms of** Radio interviews are often punctuated with this phrase, which means regarding or expressed by:

> They interpreted job vacancy figures in terms of misery for the young.

A single word can often replace the phrase, however:

> What solutions do you recommend for [*not* in terms of] youth unemployment?
> The government is troubled by [*not* in terms of] youth unemployment.

**intern/internee** *Intern* is the traditional name in the US for a recent medical graduate living and working in a hospital to complete his or her training, and the term is becoming common in Australia. An *internee* is someone imprisoned or confined in wartime.

See also **interment/internment**.

**internecine** Since this adjective means destructive to both parties, it should not be applied to petty disagreements:

> Internecine strife within the freedom movement threatened the cause itself.

Pronounce the word 'inter-**nee**-sine'.

**internment** See **interment/internment**.

**interpersonal** This adjectival compound means between people. It is overused in the stock phrases *interpersonal relationships* and *interpersonal skills*, and has become something of a joke. When it is clear that the relationships referred to are between people, the word is superfluous.

**Interpol** International Criminal Police Organization.

**interpretative/interpretive** Either spelling is acceptable. This adjective means involving or providing interpretation.

**interstate/intrastate** *Interstate* means between States (of a country), but *intrastate* means within a State. It may be a costly error to send a parcel at *interstate* rates when it is for *intrastate* delivery.

**interval** An *interval* is a gap between two boundaries or events; it is not simply any period:

There was an interval of three years between her first and her second child.
*not* You will need an interval of two months for this job.

**in the circumstances** See **circumstances.**

**in the near future** This is a verbose way of saying *soon*.

**in this day and age** Prefer less cliché-like equivalents, such as *now*, *today* and *nowadays*.

**in to/into** Use the two-word form when the *to* belongs essentially to the verb preceding it:

I was called in to dinner.
I moved closer in to see what was happening.

Use the one-word form when the *to* belongs essentially to the noun or pronoun following it:

She walked into the shop.
The seat dug into me.

If you cannot decide which word *to* belongs to, either form will probably do. Some people use the test of pausing after *in*; if the pause seems natural, the word can probably be split.

Using *into* to mean enthusiastic about something (*We are into health food*) is colloquial and therefore inappropriate in formal contexts.

**in toto** This Latin phrase meant *on the whole* to the Romans but has long meant *completely* in the English language. It no longer needs to be italicised.

We declined their enthusiastic invitations in toto.

It seems most natural to use it with verbs that have a negative sense: *decline*, *veto*, *censor*, *reject*, *disagree*.

**intra-** See **inter-/intra-**.

**intrastate** See **interstate/intrastate**.

**intravenous** See **IM/IV**.

**intrinsic** See **extrinsic/intrinsic**.

**introduction** An *introduction* is sometimes included among the first few pages of a printed work – usually just before the beginning of the text. It is written by the author, who may explain there the scope of the work and set out its main arguments, for example (the information in a *preface* is normally less detailed and more general).

See also **acknowledgements; foreword/preface; publications parts of.**

**introvert** See **extrovert/introvert.**

**intrude/obtrude/protrude** *Intrude* means to bring in or go in without sufficient reason:

She advised us not to intrude personal views into official statements.

They will not intrude on our discussions.

To *obtrude* is to thrust oneself or an object forward without warrant; the verb is not often seen but the adjective – *obtrusive*, meaning unpleasantly noticeable – is quite common:

Flashing lights in a shop may be obtrusive rather than helpful.

*Protrude* simply means to stick out:

The ladder protruded from the back of the van.

**invaluable** This adjective is not the opposite of *valuable*; in fact it means extremely valuable.

**inveigh/inveigle** *Inveigh* means to speak violently (against):

Rhonda inveighed against the radical new English syllabus.

Pronounce it 'in-**vay**'.

*Inveigle*, pronounced 'in-**vay**-g'l' or, more rarely, 'in-**vee**-g'l', means to entice or tempt, often in a deceitful manner:

He inveigled me into joining an offshore investment scheme that failed.

**inventer/inventor** Either spelling is acceptable, but *inventor* is recommended.

**inverse** See **converse/inverse/obverse/reverse.**

**inverted commas** See **quotation marks/inverted commas.**

**investor** Note the *-or*.

**invidious** See **insidious/invidious.**

**invite** Do not use this word in place of the noun *invitation* in formal contexts:

They sent the premier an invitation [*not* invite].

**invulnerable** See **vulnerable**.

**inward/inwards** *Inward* is the adjective: *an inward movement*. *Inwards* is the adverb: *Push the gate inwards*.

**IOC** International Olympic Committee.

**IOU** I owe you; an *IOU* is a note recording a debt.

**IPA** International Phonetic Alphabet.

**ipso facto** This Latin phrase (meaning by the same fact or act) has some currency in formal contexts:

> When he climbed through the window he was ipso facto liable for a breaking and entering charge.

The phrase is usually not italicised.

**IRA** Irish Republican Army.

**Irian Jaya** This Indonesian province occupies the western part of the island of New Guinea, bordering Papua New Guinea.

**iridescent** Note the single *r* and the *-esc-*.

**iris** Plural *irises*.

**irony/ironic/ironical/ironically** *Irony* is the use of words whose literal meaning is the opposite of what is meant. The tone of irony is mocking, and it is often intended to amuse and sometimes to instruct; it does not have the wounding intensity of *sarcasm*. Subtle irony tends to go undetected by the naive; heavy irony may border on the sarcastic. There is irony in the title *The Fortunes of Richard Mahony*, since the book focuses on the *misfortunes* of Richard Mahony.

The term *dramatic irony* describes a theatrical convention in which the implications of what is happening on stage are understood by the audience but not by some or any of the characters in a play.

Some authorities regard the adjectives *ironic* and *ironical* as synonymous. Prefer *ironic*, however, when gently mocking either oneself or others; and *ironical* when you are describing an incongruity between what was expected and what actually happened:

> His ironic telegram, 'Sorry about your broken hands', reminded her of her promise to write.
>
> It was ironical that the worst typist instead of the most proficient was given the new word processor.

Avoid using *ironical* to mean unexpected or coincidental: *It's ironical that we both go to the same dentist.*

The adverb *ironically* is used in the same way as the adjectives:

> She looked at the plump infant and remarked ironically, 'Looks as if he could do with a square meal'.
>
> Ironically, the worst typist instead of the most proficient was given the new word processor.

Do not use *ironically* when you merely mean oddly enough: *Ironically, they never saw him again.*

**irregardless/regardless** The word *irregardless* is accepted as a colloquialism by some authorities, but people who care about the English language will shun it in any context. *Regardless* should be used in all instances, as adjective and adverb:

> Regardless of the risks involved, they went on diving in the caves.
>
> They went on diving regardless.

**irrelevant** See **germane/material/relevant**.

**irremediable** See **remediable/remedial**.

**irremovable** See **immovable/immoveable/irremovable**.

**irreparable/unrepairable** Note the spelling of *irreparable* (not '-repair-'). Use this adjective for abstract nouns (*irreparable harm*) and *unrepairable* in describing objects such as your refrigerator. Put the stress on the second syllable (*-rep-*) of *irreparable*.

**irrespective** This adjective is most commonly used in the phrase *irrespective of*, which means without regard or reference to:

> The policy was to accept all immigrants, irrespective of colour, class or creed.

Note that the adverb *irrespectively* should not be followed by *of*:

> He'll come irrespectively, whether we're here or not.

*not* He'll come irrespectively of whether we're here or not.

**irrevocable** Put the stress on the second syllable (*-rev-*) of this adjective meaning unable to be recalled or altered.

**irrupt** See **erupt/irrupt**.

**ISBN** This stands for *International Standard Book Number*, a ten-digit number given to each edition of a book or pamphlet published anywhere in the world to enable identification by publishers, booksellers and libraries. The ISBN for the paperback edition of this book is 0 140 51351 5. The first digit (0 in this case) indicates the language in which the book is written; the 140 is the prefix for the publisher, Penguin Books; the 51351 is the title number; and the 5 is a check digit that guards against computer error. An ISBN should be printed on the reverse of the title page (that is, on the imprint page) and as part of the bar code on the back cover or jacket. To obtain ISBN numbers, publishers should apply to the ISBN Agency, National Library of Australia, Canberra, ACT, 2600.

See also **ISSN**; **publications, parts of**.

**ISD** International Subscriber Dialling.

**-ise/-ize word endings** Either *-ise* or *-ize* is acceptable for the suffix added to the roots of many words, but *-ise* is now widely preferred in Australia and is recommended here (the same applies to other forms such as *-ising* and *-izing*, *-isation* and *-ization*):

organise recognising civilisation

The *-ize* suffix has the disadvantage that it is not an option in a number of cases, so that those who choose it must identify the exceptions – for instance *advertise*, *arise*, *comprise*, *compromise*, *despise*, *exercise* and *surprise*. A few words such as *capsize*, *size*, *prize* and *seize* have *ize* at the end, but it is not a suffix there.

Many people dislike the numerous verbs created from nouns and adjectives by the addition of *-ise* (or *-ize*): *containerise, pedestrianise*. Some of these verbs are here to stay, but it is wise to avoid using them in formal contexts until they have gained general acceptance.

See also **verbs**.

**Islam/Muhammad/Muslim** The prophet of the religion known as *Islam* was *Muhammad* (rather than *Mohammed* or *Mahomet*). Followers of Islam are called *Muslims* (rather than *Moslems*). They are not referred to as *Muhammadans* because *Islam* means submission to the One God, not to the prophet *Muhammad*, and *Muslim* means one who submits.

**-ism** Originally a suffix denoting a practice, a state, a kind of behaviour and so on, as in *baptism*, *realism* and *criticism*, *-ism* is tacked onto many words today (too many perhaps) to indicate some form of discrimination: *sexism*, *heterosexism*, *ageism*, *classism*.

**ISO** Companion of the Imperial Service Order (see also **ranks, titles, honours and awards**); International Organization for Standardization.

**Israeli/Israelite** See **Jew/Israeli/Israelite**.

**ISSN** This is the abbreviation for *International Standard Serial Number*, a ten-digit identifying number given to serial publications such as newspapers, periodicals and annual reports.

See also **ISBN**.

**issue** Somewhere in the world there is an institution teaching its students that there are no such things as *subjects*, *topics*, *concerns*, *questions*, *matters* or *points* – there are only *issues*. This overworked word needs a rest. Choose one of the alternatives.

**isthmus** Note the spelling; the plural is *isthmuses*. An *isthmus* is a narrow strip of land connecting two comparatively large areas.

**it** The impersonal pronoun *it* is so common in everyday speech that we are often unconscious of its imprecision:

> She placed the chair on the table then sat on it.

Did she sit on the chair or the table?

> Fred can have this ticket if he feels like it.

Fred may have difficulty feeling like a ticket. Recast the sentence if there is any likelihood of ambiguity or confusion.

See also **its/it's**.

**it/its** See **-ing forms**; **its/it's**.

**italics, use of** The house style of a particular publisher may determine otherwise, but the following rules for italicisation have been widely adopted. Italics are indicated in a manuscript by underlining. Use italic rather than roman type in printed text for

- the titles of books, plays and long poems; newspapers and magazines; musical works; films; and works of art:
  *The Man Who Loved Children*  *The Removalists*
  *Prometheus Unbound*  *Courier-Mail* [not *The Courier-Mail*]
  *Wildlife Research News*  *Phantom of the Opera*
  *The Sting*  *Spring in the You Beaut Country*
- foreign words and phrases not yet assimilated into the English language:
  *coup de grâce* [*but* cafe]  *Deo volente* [*but* ad hoc]
- the scientific names of plants and animals, but not common names or family names (or other parts of names left in roman type in the following examples):
  the ghost gum, *Eucalyptus papuana*, family Myrtaceae
  *Allocasuarina* sp. [species]
  a very attractive helipterum, *Helipterum albicans* ssp. [subspecies] *albicans* var. [variety] *incanum*
  the red kangaroo, *Macropus rufus*, family Macropodidae
- the names of specific trains, ships and aircraft, but not terms like HMAS, or makes and models:
  the *Orient Express*  the *Princess of Tasmania* [*but* HMAS *Melbourne*]
  *Southern Cross* [*but* a Boeing 747]
- legislation, when using the exact title (note the format details):
  the *Copyright Act 1968* (Cwth)

- court cases (note the format details):
  *Commonwealth v. Trip and Trap* or *Commonwealth* v. *Trip and Trap*
- cited letters or words:
  the second *m* in *accommodate*
- emphasised letters or words:
  Now we must *un*do the damage.
  I said we'd go *today*, not next week.
- the cross-references *see* and *see also* in an index:
  polyester, *see* synthetic fabrics
  synthetic fabrics, 45, 78–9; *see*
  *also* clothing imports
- stage directions, usually placed in square brackets:
  [*Gondoliers exit left*]

Italics are an option, dictated by design considerations, for such elements in printed texts as headings, quoted verses and dedications.

See also **foreign words and phrases; titles of publications, and literary, artistic and musical works; type.**

**italic type** See **type.**

**its/it's** These two words are often confused. *Its* is the possessive pronoun:

The cat hasn't drunk its milk [the milk belonging to it].

*It's* is the contraction of *it is* or *it has*:

We can see when it's [it is] wrong.
We can see where it's [it has] gone wrong.

See also **it.**

**IUD** intra-uterine device.

**IV** See **IM/IV.**

**IVF** in-vitro fertilisation.

**IWW** Industrial Workers of the World.

**-ize word endings** See **-ise/-ize word endings.**

# Jj

**J.** judge; Justice (placed after a judge's name: *Smith J.*).
See also **ranks, titles, honours and awards**.

**jackaroo/jackeroo** Either spelling is acceptable for this indigenous Australian word. A *jackaroo* is a young man, usually with managerial ambitions, who works as a labourer on a sheep or cattle station to obtain practical experience.
See also **jillaroo**.

**jaggies** In computer slang *jaggies* are the rough edges around type or artwork seen either on screen or on dot-matrix and some laser-printed pages. The higher the number of dots per inch of the output device, the less *jaggy* the output will be.
See also **bitmap**; **dots per inch**; **printer**.

**jail** See **gaol/jail**.

**jargon** See **argot/dialect/jargon/lingua franca**.

**J-curve** In economics a *J-curve* describes the situation that occurs when a country's currency falls in value or is devalued. Initially the trade balance deteriorates but, as imports decrease and exports increase, the balance improves. In graphs the shape represented by these movements resembles the letter *J*.

**jealousy** See **envy/jealousy**.

**jeopardy** Note the *jeo-*. Pronounce it '**jepp**a-dee'.

**jerrybuilt** Something that is *jerrybuilt* has been constructed cheaply or with shoddy materials by a *jerrybuilder*.

**Jervis Bay** This is an area of Commonwealth territory situated south of Nowra on the New South Wales coast. The commonly accepted pronunciation of the first part of the name is 'jarvis', although the Australian Broadcasting Corporation recommends 'jervis'.

**Jew/Israeli/Israelite** A *Jew* is one whose religion is *Judaism*. Use *Jew* in reference to both sexes as the word *Jewess* is not regarded with favour today. An *Israeli* is a citizen of the Jewish state of Israel, created in 1948 from parts of what was Palestine. The *Israelites* are the descendants of Jacob (also called Israel). Do not describe a *Jew* as an *Israelite* or *Hebrew*.
See also **discriminatory language**; **Hebrew/Yiddish**.

**jewellery** Not 'jewelry', as in the US.

**jibe** See **gibe/jibe**.

**jihad** Traditionally this word applied to holy wars conducted by Muslims against unbelievers. It has been broadened to include any strong campaign undertaken to promote or defend a principle. An alternative spelling is *jehad*. It is pronounced 'j'**had**'.

**jillaroo** A *jillaroo* is a young woman, usually with managerial ambitions, who works as a labourer on a sheep or cattle station to obtain practical experience.
See also **jackaroo/jackeroo**.

**JJ.** Justices.
See also **ranks, titles, honours and awards**.

**jodhpurs** Note the *-dhp-*.

**join** See **together**.

**journalese** This is a derogatory term applied to the shallow and cliché-ridden kind of writing that many people associate with newspapers. The most offensive kind of journalese is the racy sensationalism of the tabloid press, where politicians *tiff* or *tough it out*; investigators *probe* or *access*; jobs are *axed*; speculators *bid*; and metaphors are mixed: *Heads roll as PM shuffles Cabinet pack*. The aim of journalese is to catch attention and impart information without taxing a reader's concentration, imagination or intelligence: atmosphere is conjured up in a few well-worn phrases, a lifetime in an adjective-rich sentence, World War III in a headline. Today, as the circulation of the tabloids shrinks and various newspapers close, journalists in radio and television become increasingly conspicuous users of journalese in Australia.
See also **clichés**; **colloquialisms**; **idiom**; **metaphor**.

**JP** Justice of the Peace.
See also **ranks, titles, honours and awards**.

**judgement/judgment** Either spelling, with or without the *-e* of *judge*, is acceptable except in law, where *judgment* is traditional.

**judicial/judicious** *Judicial* means relating to judgment in the courts, or to the administration of justice:

The judicial process was lengthy and costly.

*Judicious* means discreet, prudent, or showing good judgement:

Gita's friendliness made her a judicious choice for the position of student adviser.

*Judicial* decisions should, of course, be *judicious* also.

**juncture** The phrase *at this juncture* is a verbose way of saying *now*.

**junk bond** In investment parlance a *junk bond* is a high-risk, high-yield security of the type often used to finance company takeovers.

**jurist/juror** A *jurist* is an expert in the law; a *juror* is a member of a jury.

**just** The adverb *just* can mean in the time immediately preceding; at this moment; exactly; narrowly; only; or absolutely (in colloquial English):

We have just eaten dinner.
They rang to say they were just leaving.
That is just what I intended saying.
She just missed the boat by minutes.
The children have been just twice to the zoo.
The news is just marvellous.

Its position in a sentence can alter the meaning entirely:

Brad and Matt have just gone to Perth.
Just Brad and Matt have gone to Perth.
Brad and Matt have gone just to Perth.

Place the word as close as possible to the part of the sentence it modifies. The same usually applies to words like *even*, *merely*, *only*, *particularly* and *simply*.

Note that the expression *just exactly* is tautological. Use one or the other:

We were just [*or* exactly] on time.

In the following sentence the *have* is essential in Australian English:

We have just walked back from the beach.
*not* We just walked back from the beach.

**just deserts** Not 'desserts', though pronounced that way.
See also **desert/dessert**.

**justified type/unjustified type** *Justified type* is type set flush against both right-hand and left-hand margins (as in this paragraph, and this book generally). When type is justified, care must be taken to ensure that the spaces between words do not vary too greatly between one line and the next. Breaking words at the end of lines and hyphenating them are often necessary to achieve this: see the entry **word division** for guidelines on appropriate word breaks. Note that the hyphenation programs available in word-processing and page-makeup packages are not always acceptable as many of their word divisions differ from those recommended in Australia. It is important to watch for rivers of white space running through any slab of justified text.

*Unjustified* or *ragged type* may be set flush against only the left-hand margin, only the right, or neither.

This paragraph is set in the first of these three styles – flush against the left-hand margin (and therefore called *ragged right*). The advantages of unjustified type are even word spacing, elimination of (or much reduced) hyphenation at line ends, and simplicity of setting. Its main disadvantage is its inconsistency of line length, which results from long words being taken over if hyphenation is not used. There is no definite ruling on how ragged unjustified setting should be but dramatic variations in line length are best avoided. This can be achieved by fixing a minimum as well as a maximum measure. If this is done, any word reaching the minimum measure but going beyond the maximum will be hyphenated, as in justified setting. Unjustified setting is also made more attractive if the indefinite article *a* sitting on or near the maximum measure at the end of a line is taken over to the next line. It is best to hyphenate manually rather than use a hyphenation program in unjustified setting. Combine this with tracking to ensure an acceptable-looking series of lines.

See also **hard hyphen/soft hyphen**; **hyphenation dictionary**; **measure**; **tracking**; **word division**; **word spacing**.

**juvenile/puerile** The adjective *juvenile* means young or related to the young. It implies criticism only if applied to adults and their behaviour:

> The children preferred chess to juvenile games.
>
> The juvenile naivety of the Senate report undermined our faith in its authors.

*Puerile* strictly means like a boy (from Latin: *puer*, boy) or a child, but the pejorative meaning childishly silly or trivial is now much more common. *Puerile* should therefore not be used unless criticism is intended:

> The play's puerile humour offended the audience.

See also **childish/childlike**.

# Kk

**K** kilobyte.
See also **byte**.

**Kampuchea** See **Cambodia**.

**karri/kauri** *Karri* is a Western Australian tree, *kauri* a Queensland and New Zealand tree.

**KC** This abbreviation for the legal distinction *King's Counsel* (when the monarch is a man) has the plural form *KCs*; *King's Counsel* has no plural form: *three KCs*; *three King's Counsel*.
See also **QC**; **ranks, titles, honours and awards**.

**Kenmare, Vic.** Compare with *Kenmore*, NSW and Qld.

**kerb** See **curb/kerb**.

**kerning** *Kerning* is adjustment of space between pairs of letters, to achieve tightness or evenness of appearance, particularly with capitals in headings. Type may be *kerned* or *unkerned*. High-end page-makeup programs have default kerning between specific pairs of letters, and a facility to enable kerning between any additional pair (or group) of letters.
See also **capital letters, setting of**; **tracking**; **type**.

| | |
|---|---|
| ***Kerned*** | YOUTH AWARDS ANNOUNCED TODAY |
| ***Unkerned*** | YOUTH AWARDS ANNOUNCED TODAY |

**kerosene/paraffin** *Kerosene* is the Australian and US word for the fuel oil called *paraffin* by the British. The spelling *kerosine* is also acceptable.

**key/quay** The *key* used in a lock and the *quay* that is a wharf are pronounced in the same way.

**keyboard commands** *Keyboard commands* are combinations of two to four keys used to give an instruction to a computer. The combination usually includes a command key – the apple key on an Apple, the control key (abbreviated CTRL) on an IBM or clone – in addition to other keys. Command keys are used, for example, for changing highlighted text from roman to italic. On systems using window-based software, most keyboard commands can be performed by using a pointing tool such as a mouse, but it is quicker to use the keyboard commands. Many keyboards have function keys to which commands are already allocated. Utility software, which allows users to define their own keyboard commands, is also available.

See also **function keys**.

**KGB** This is the abbreviation for *Komitet Gosudarstvennoi Bezopasnosti*, the Soviet Committee of State Security (or secret police).

**kibbutz** Plural *kibbutzim* (Israeli agricultural communes).

**kid** See **child**.

**kilobyte** See **byte**.

**kilometre** Much hot air has been expended on the pronunciation of the word *kilometre*, with opposing camps arguing for '**kill**a-meeta' and 'kil-**om**-itta'. The Australian Broadcasting Corporation recommends '**kill**a-meeta'.

**the Kimberleys** A vast and rugged area of about 356 500 square kilometres in Western Australia, *the Kimberleys* (also called the *Kimberley Region)* are bounded by the sea to the north and west, the Fitzroy River valley to the south, and the Ord River valley to the east. This diamond-bearing region should not be confused with *Kimberley* in South Africa, where diamonds are mined in great quantities.

**kindergarten** Note the *-t-*. This word is of German origin and literally means children's garden.

**kind of/sort of/type of** The same rules apply to all three phrases, and authorities are unanimous on the following points:

this kind of wren *not* these kind of wren
wrens of this kind *not* wrens of these kind

This rule is commonly broken in speech but should be strictly observed in print.

Most authorities agree on the following, and using either form is recommended here:

these kinds of wren *or* these kinds of wrens

See also **fillers.**

**kneeled/knelt** Either word may be used as the past tense and past participle of the verb *to kneel*, but *knelt* is recommended.

**knots/nautical miles** A *knot* is a unit of *speed*, equal to 1 *nautical mile* per hour, used in marine and aerial navigation. It is not a measurement of distance: a ship's speed, therefore, is written as *12 knots*, not *12 knots per hour*. The *distance* covered by a ship or plane is measured in *nautical miles* (a nautical mile measures approximately 1.9 kilometres). *Knots* and *nautical miles* are international standards and should not be converted to metric measurements.

The expression *at a rate of knots* means very fast and is not confined to nautical contexts.

**knowledgeable** Retain the final *e* of *knowledge*.

**KO** knock-out (boxing); also *k.o.*

**koala** A *koala* is not a bear – but try telling that to children (and many adults). It is certainly an honorary bear.

**Koori/Koorie** See **Aborigine/Aboriginal.**

**Kosciusko** Pronounce the name of Australia's highest mountain 'kozzee-oss-ko'.

**Kt** knight.

See also **ranks, titles, honours and awards.**

**kudos** This singular noun (from the Greek word for glory) means fame or recognition. Pronounce it '**kew**-doss'.

**Ku Klux Klan** Not 'Klu'.

**kumquat** See **cumquat/kumquat.**

# Ll

**L** fifty (roman numeral; see also **roman numerals**); learner-driver.

**label/labelled/labelling** Note the final *l* in the first and the *-ll-* in the other two.

**labor/labour** Either spelling is acceptable, but *labour* is preferred. Note, however, the spelling of the *Australian Labor Party* and *Labor's policies* (but the *British Labour Party* and *Labour's policies*).

See also **ALP**.

**LAC** Leading Aircraftsman.

**lackadaisical** Note the spelling (not 'lacksadaisical'). This adjective means uninterested, or lacking in vitality.

**lacquer** Note the spelling.

**lacuna** The plural is *lacunae* or *lacunas*. There are several specific biological uses for this noun, but it is also a rather formal word for a gap or a missing portion, usually in a manuscript or book.

**LACW** Leading Aircraftswoman.

**laden/loaded** *Laden* is the past participle of the rarely used verb *to lade*, which means to load (with cargo) – hence a *bill of lading*. *Loaded* is the past tense and past participle of the verb *to load*. *Laden* implies that something is weighed down or full to overflowing; *loaded* merely indicates that something has been stocked or filled and is ready for conveyance:

> The laden ship sat dangerously low in the water.

The truck was still half empty after we had loaded it with our apples.

Both of these words may also be used figuratively: *laden [burdened] with sorrow*; *a loaded [unfairly weighted] question*.

**lady** See **madam/madame**; **ranks, titles, honours and awards**; **woman**.

**laissez-faire** This phrase borrowed from the French (literally meaning allow to do) originally described government abstention from interference in the conduct of economic affairs. The term has come to refer to any non-interference in the affairs of others, and may be used as an adjective or (without the hyphen) a noun:

The zoo-keeper's laissez-faire attitude towards children endangered them.

The zoo-keeper adopted a policy of laissez faire towards the children.

The term is not italicised in English. The infinitive form (*laisser*) is also acceptable but *laissez* is preferred.

**lama/llama** A *lama* is a Buddhist monk of the order of Lamaism; a *llama* is a long-haired South American mammal that is used as a beast of burden.

**lamination** In the book trade this term refers to the plasticised coating (and the process of applying it) now generally used on paperback book covers and the dust jackets of hardback books.

**LAN** See **local area network**.

**landscape/portrait** A page that is wider (that is, horizontally) than it is deep (that is, vertically) is said to be in *landscape* format. The term is also used to describe illustrative material (a map, for instance) that is turned sideways and printed parallel to the spine instead of at right angles to it.

By contrast, a page that is deeper than it is wide is said to be in *portrait* format.

**languid/limpid** *Languid* may mean listless, unenthusiastic, or lacking in vigour or spirit:

His languid manner did not inspire confidence.

It may also mean slow and graceful in movement:

The ballerina's languid arm movements echoed those of the dying swan.

*Limpid* means clear or lucid:

High in the mountains the Snowy River is limpid.

The limpid writing helps us to understand the complexities of her text.

**laptop** A *laptop* is a computer that is light, compact and portable.

**larva** The plural is *larvae* (pronounced 'lar-vee'). A *larva* is a creature such as a caterpillar that represents an immature stage in the life cycle of an insect.

**laser** This is an acronym for *light amplification by stimulated emission of radiation*. Do not spell it 'lazer'.

**laser printer** See **printer**.

**last/latest** Take care not to use *last* when you mean *latest*. *The last film he directed* should be *the latest film he directed* unless he is dead or will never again direct a film.

Similarly, avoid using *last* when you are referring to a period ending in the present – that is, now: *the past [*not *last] six months*.

**lat.** latitude.

See also **latitude/longitude**.

**lateral thinking** This expression means dealing with a problem by approaching it from unexpected angles rather than by a more conventional progression of thought. Do not overuse this phrase.

**latest** See **last/latest**.

**lath/lathe** A *lath* is one of the light, narrow strips of wood (or a substitute such as thin metal) used in the framework of, for example, *lath and plaster walls*. It is pronounced 'larth', rhyming with the *rath-* of *rather*. A *lathe* is a machine that facilitates the working of materials such as wood and metal. It is pronounced 'layth', rhyming with *bathe*.

**Latin America** See **America/United States/Latin America**.

**Latin words and phrases** Latin is not studied widely today and many readers have little or no knowledge of the language, in spite of its significant role in the development of English. Certain Latin expressions are, of course, so well established in English that they can barely be regarded as 'foreign'. All kinds of people prefer the term *ad hoc* to the phrase *established for a specific purpose*; *ad infinitum* to *endlessly*; and *per annum* to *by the year*. The abbreviations *e.g.* (*exempli gratia*, meaning for example) and *i.e.* (*id est*, meaning that is) are sometimes confused but are extremely useful as shorthand in informal contexts.

Nevertheless, writing that is peppered with less familiar terms like *ipso facto* (meaning by the same fact or act) and *a priori* (from the previous) is daunting and looks affected. In most cases English equivalents of the less common Latin phrases can be found and should be used: prefer *among other things* to *inter alia*; *at first sight* to *prima facie*; *the state* to *res publica*.

Certain Latin phrases (and their abbreviations) retain a useful place in notes and references – for example *et al.* (from *et alii*, and others) and *ibid.* (from *ibidem*, in the same place); *passim* (throughout) is still used in indexes. The expressions *op cit.* (from *opere citato*, in the work cited) and *loc. cit.* (from *loco citato*, in the place cited) are rarely seen today. The word *sic* (so) in square brackets indicates an error in quoted material. The abbreviation *NB* (from *nota bene*, note well) has wide currency. Even in bibliographies and references there is a move towards using English words rather than the traditional Latin abbreviations. But Latin retains its longstanding role in areas such as scientific terminology, the law and medicine.

See also **foreign words and phrases**; **loan words**.

**latish** Note the spelling of this adjective or adverb meaning rather late (not 'lateish').

**latitude/longitude** *Latitude* is the angular distance on a meridian north or south of the equator. *Longitude* is the angular distance on a meridian east or west of the Greenwich meridian. *Latitude* and *longitude* are measured in degrees (°) and minutes ('). Australia lies between latitudes 10°41'S (Cape York) and 43°39'S (South Cape, Tasmania); and longitudes 113°09'E (Steep Point) and 153°39'E (Cape Byron). In Australian English *longitude* is pronounced with a hard *g*.

See also **compass points**; **GMT**; **numbers in figures or words**.

**La Trobe** Charles Joseph *La Trobe*, Victoria's lieutenant-governor from 1851 to 1854, has had various institutions and places named after him, but the wrong form of the surname has been traditional in some cases: *Latrobe*, Tasmania; and the *Latrobe* Valley and *Latrobe* River, Victoria. It would be more logical for all to become *La Trobe*, as are Victoria's *La Trobe* University, *La Trobe* electorate, *La Trobe* Library (the State Library of Victoria) and *La Trobe* Street (in Melbourne).

**latter** See **former/latter**.

**laudable/laudatory** *Laudable* means deserving praise:

> Saving the children from the fire was not only laudable, it won Li-Teng a medal.

*Laudatory* means containing or expressing praise:

> A laudatory citation accompanied the bravery medal.

**Laurence, Brotherhood of St** Note the spelling of *Laurence* in the name of this charitable organisation founded in Melbourne.

**lavatory/toilet** The room containing facilities for human defecation and urination has attracted a variety of names, many of them euphemistic. In the

UK, *lavatory* is the term used by the upper and middle classes, *toilet* by the lower class; *loo* is widely used in all strata of society. In the US, euphemisms such as *rest room*, *powder room*, *washroom* and *comfort station* are common. In Australia we seem to have opted for *toilet* in formal usage. Max Harris and Stephen Murray-Smith have both offered a spirited defence of *dunny* (from the old British dialect word *dunnaken*) as an Australian colloquialism worth preserving. Whatever you prefer to call it, do not ask for the *Ladies* or *Gents* in the US if you are in a hurry, because the chances are that you will not be understood.

See also **euphemisms**.

**lawful/legal/legitimate** Although both *legal* and *legitimate* may mean the same as *lawful* (that is, allowed by law), the three words are not always interchangeable. *Lawful* is found in formal contexts and, in such terms as *lawful spouse* or *lawful heir*, means rightful. It can imply a higher moral authority than the word *legal*, which pertains more generally to the law of the land. *Legitimate* once applied to children born in wedlock (in contrast to *illegitimate*, born out of wedlock). It has the added meaning valid or logical: *a legitimate absence*; *a legitimate conclusion*; and it is used in the term *legitimate theatre* (meaning plays as opposed to such performances as musical drama and revues).

See also **illegal/illegitimate/illicit**.

**lay/laying/lie/lying** These words frequently cause confusion, which is compounded by the irregular conjugation of *lie* (except when it means to tell lies) and the multitude of colloquial expressions relating to the words *lay* and *lie*.

To *lay* means to put down, to put to rest or to arrange (something or someone). It is nearly always a transitive verb (that is, it has an object):

I *lay* [or I *am laying*] the book on the desk [present tense].

I *laid* the book on the desk [past tense].

I *have laid* the book on the desk [present perfect tense].

The principal exception to the use of *lay* as a transitive verb involves egg-laying, when the object is implied rather than stated:

The hens will not lay [eggs] in winter.

To *lie* can mean to rest or recline. It is an intransitive verb (that is, it does not have an object) and, as noted, it is irregular:

I *lie* [or I *am lying*] down on my bed [present tense].

I *lay* on my bed yesterday [past tense].

I *have lain* here all day long [present perfect tense].

To *lie* also means to tell lies, in which case the present tense is *lie* or *am lying*; the past tense is *lied*; and the present perfect tense is *have lied*.

You may take your choice in the expression *the lay [*or *lie] of the land*, meaning its direction or position. Do not confuse *lay low* (subdue) and *lie low* (hide) in expressions such as *to lay low the enemy* and *to lie low in the bushes*.

See also **tenses; verbs**.

**lay-by** In Australian English the verb *lay-by* means to reserve a particular article in a shop by payment of a deposit followed by a series of part-payments. The noun has the same form: *collecting my lay-by this week*. In British English a *lay-by* is a parking area off a road or motorway.

**layout** In publishing, *layout* is the arrangement of type and illustrations on a page. Layout should be determined by the content, size and shape of a publication, as well as the intended readership. Good design, which encompasses typography as well as layout, can greatly improve the appearance and readability of a publication.

Graphic designers are traditionally responsible for devising the layout of a publication. Although desktop-publishing programs can produce effective layouts in the hands of a knowledgeable operator, it is preferable to draw on the skills of a professional. A trained designer combines aesthetic awareness with a knowledge of technical processes, which together provide the key to successful design. A common defect of layouts produced without the aid of a designer is that they take up too many of the available options – such as a wide range of typefaces – and are so cluttered that the author's message is obscured.

When layouts are devised, whether for a leaflet or a large illustrated book, each set of facing pages (known as a *spread*) is treated as a unit because this is how the material will be viewed by the reader. This approach means that the relationship between the key elements of the layout remains consistent, and helps to ensure that type areas and illustrations are properly aligned. The designer usually prepares a rough layout or 'visual' to indicate the position and scale of the various elements – type, illustrations, columns, captions, headings and so on. In the case of complicated works the designer may assemble the type and illustrations on layout sheets as artwork (a *paste-up*) for the printer. In desktop publishing this traditional method of paste-up has been replaced by page-makeup programs by means of which a designer lays out the pages electronically.

Layout should take account of at least the following basic points:

- format – the size, shape and extent of a publication
- type area – the space allocated for type, which may be in one block or divided into columns
- margins – as generous as the type of publication allows (the central margins, comprising the gutter, should not be so narrow as to be swallowed up by the binding)
- illustrations – which may lie within the page area or 'bleed' (that is, run off one or more sides of the page)

In publications with a variety of headings, illustrations, tables and captions or other non-text matter, it is necessary to devise a modular plan or *grid* that incorporates all these elements. This ensures visual harmony throughout the work and also serves as a reference for the various people involved in the production process. Grids should show all the features common to every page, such as page size, margin and column widths, text and illustration areas, chapter drop, and the position of headings and folios (page numbers). Once the grid has been established the designer can manoeuvre the text and illustrations within it until the desired result, in both aesthetic and practical terms, is achieved. While the grid provides a prototype for each spread, a skilful designer can introduce variations within the basic framework to avoid monotony.

For projects such as complex, traditionally produced books, the grid is usually printed on sheets to ensure that all dimensions are accurate and consistent. As grids then become the designer's layout sheets, on which the type is pasted and illustrations are positioned, they should be printed in pale-blue ink, which does not reproduce during the printing process. In desktop publishing the grid is called a *template* (see separate entry).

By whatever means you produce your material, remember that if your aim is to impart information you must keep your layout simple. You may not excite your readers, but you will not confuse or offend them.

See also **bleed**; **copy editing**; **desktop publishing**; **landscape/portrait**; **paste-up**; **template**; **type**; **typesetting**.

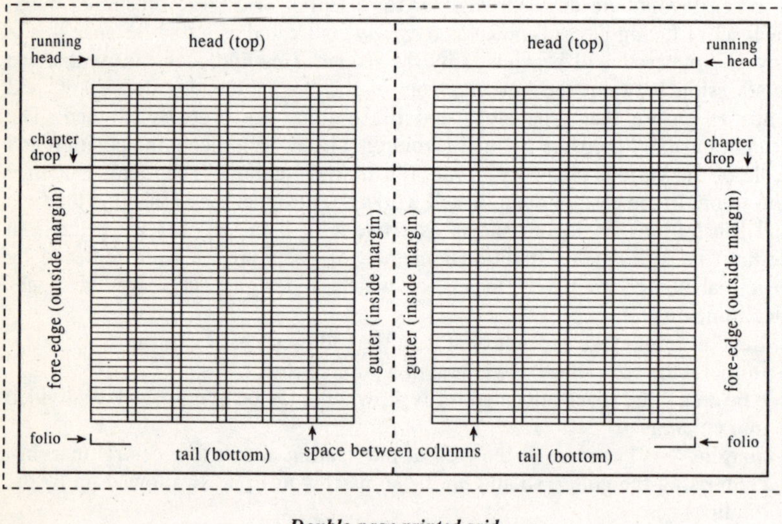


***Double-page printed grid***

**LBDR/L. Bdr** Lance Bombardier.

**l.c.** lower-case type: s, t, in contrast to S, T (upper case).
See also **type**.

**LCD** liquid crystal display.

**LCDR/Lieut.-Comm.** Lieutenant Commander.
See also **lieutenant**.

**LCPL/L. Cpl** Lance Corporal.

**lead/led** These words are frequently confused. The present tense of the verb *to lead* is *lead*:

I lead the team whenever I can.

Pronounce it 'leed', which is also the pronunciation of the noun *lead* in any of its meanings except that of the heavy metal.

The form of the past tense and past participle of the verb *to lead* is *led*:

I led the team last year
The team has been badly led.

Pronounce *led* as it is spelt. The heavy metal called *lead* is also pronounced 'led'.

**leading** In typography the distance between lines of type, measured from baseline to baseline, is called *leading* (pronounced 'ledding'). The word derives from hot-metal typesetting, in which lead slugs between lines of type increased the space. Type size and leading are expressed, for example, as 9 on 10 point or 9/10, the 9 indicating the point size of the type and 10 indicating the leading.

See also **desktop publishing**; **points**; **type**.

**leading question** The intention of a *leading question* is to lead the person questioned into giving the response desired by the questioner. The term does not mean merely a challenging or hostile question. *Leading questions* are seen as manipulative in the courtroom:

You didn't see the defendant pick up the knife, did you?

A barrister asking this leading question would probably be required by opposing counsel to rephrase it:

Did you see the defendant pick up anything?

See also **beg the question**; **rhetorical question**.

**leaned/leant** Either word is acceptable as the past tense and past participle of the verb *to lean*, but *leant* is recommended.

**leaped/leapt** Either word is acceptable as the past tense and past participle of the verb *to leap*, but *leapt* is recommended.

**learned/learnt** Either word is acceptable as the past tense and past participle of the verb *to learn*, but *learnt* is recommended. Note that the adjective *learned* (meaning scholarly), as in *a learned woman*, is pronounced '**ler**-n'd', with both syllables sounded.

**leave/let** There are many uses for the verb *to leave*, but *let* is preferable in the following:

Let [*not* Leave] go of my arm.
Don't let [*not* leave] go of the dog.
We could not paint a room, let [*not* leave] alone the whole house.

**led** See **lead/led**.

**legal** See **lawful/legal/legitimate**.

**legend/myth** A *legend* is a story focused on a famous person, place or event, real or fictional; the story of Lasseter's Reef is something of an Australian legend. The adjective *legendary* is closely linked with the noun.

A *myth* usually involves superhuman or fictitious people or events that have been used to explain natural or social phenomena. The myth, for example, of Ceres and her daughter, Proserpina, was interpreted as accounting for the contrast between winter and summer.

See also **mythical/mythological**.

**legible/readable** See **illegible/unreadable**.

**legitimate** See **lawful/legal/legitimate**.

**Leichhardt** Note the *-hh-* in the name of the river, the places in New South Wales and Queensland, and most other things named after the explorer Ludwig *Leichhardt* (*Leichardt* in Victoria has only one *h*).

**lend/loan** *Lend* is a verb, not a noun:

Please lend me your pen.
*not* Please can I have a lend of your pen.

It is recommended that *loan* be used only as a noun, not a verb:

Thank you for the loan of your pen.
*not* I will loan you my pen.

**lengthways/lengthwise** Either adverb is acceptable:

He sawed the log lengthways [*or* lengthwise].

**lengthy** This adjective means excessively or tediously long and should not be used simply as a synonym for *long*:

The play was so lengthy that the audience became restless.
She had very long [*not* lengthy] fingernails.

**lens** Plural *lenses.*

**lesbian** This term for a homosexual female has a lower-case *l*, even though *lesbian* is derived from the name of the island of Lesbos, where the woman poet Sappho (thought to have had homosexual tendencies) once lived.

See also **gay**; **homosexual**.

**lese-majesty** This compound (derived from the French *lèse-majesté*) means treason or any other subversive behaviour; it is now more often used, jocularly, of any presumptuous behaviour. Pronounce *lese* 'leez'.

**less** See **fewer/less**.

**let** See **leave/let**.

**letters, formal** The writing of formal letters is a daunting exercise for many people who unhesitatingly toss off informal missives to friends. The same people may cheerfully say exactly what they mean when speaking to others, but feel obliged to submerge themselves in officialese when writing formally.

The belief that job applications, letters to and from local authorities, government departments, solicitors and so on must be written in a special language is probably a legacy of the mandarin prose used by officials in past generations to distance themselves from ordinary citizens. Such prose persists in spite of changes in attitude, and government and business urgings to staff to use plain English in correspondence.

People today are more likely to be irritated than impressed by stilted or pompous writing, and will appreciate messages that are brief, easy to understand and pleasantly expressed. The following are some suggestions for overcoming the lure of the impersonal passive voice and achieving an easy, effective style of writing for everyday purposes.

***Be clear*** When replying to a question, make sure you understand it, know what you want to say, and put your answer as directly as possible. Draft the letter first and check it against all the guidelines suggested here. Use English terms rather than Latin: write *at first sight* rather than *prima facie*, and *former* rather than *quondam*, for instance. Choose simple, precise words rather than long, obscure ones.

Prefer, for example:

| | | | | | |
|---|---|---|---|---|---|
| about | *to* | in regard to; in the vicinity of | before | *to* | prior to |
| after | *to* | subsequent to | happen | *to* | eventuate |
| send | *to* | transmit | now | *to* | at this point in time |
| tell | *to* | acquaint; apprise | live | *to* | reside |
| buy | *to* | purchase | start | *to* | initiate; inaugurate |

Plain words and simple structure will help to ensure that your meaning is clear and unambiguous.

***Be concise*** Say as much as you need to in as few words as possible. A concise letter will always have more impact than a longwinded one. Go through your draft and delete superfluous words and phrases such as *very*, *actually*, *particular*, *incidentally*, *it would also be appreciated that*, and *it is of importance to bear in mind*. *We have no powers to investigate* is preferable to *It is not within the parameters of this committee's terms of reference to undertake investigations*.
***Be correct*** Make sure your information is accurate and complete, so that clarifying letters are not needed.

Also check spelling, grammar and punctuation: a job application full of errors, for example, will not produce a good impression. Ensure that names and addresses are right in every detail.
***Be courteous*** Answer letters as soon as possible; apologise for any delays and give reasons. It is important not to make extra work for your reader: if you suggest another point of contact, give the full name and address, not just a recommendation to write to 'the appropriate authority'.
***Be human*** Think of the reader's reaction to the letter. Read it aloud. Is it easy to follow? Does it sound friendly and helpful? Avoid the passive voice and impersonal expressions: *Your correspondence of 4 July is hereby acknowledged. It is regretted . . .* Be positive and matter-of-fact: *Thank you for your letter of 4 July. I am sorry . . .*

Setting a friendly tone does not mean using slang or chatty terms. You can be dignified without being pompous, cordial without being familiar.
***Formats for letters*** Various layouts are suitable for formal letters, and the following is only a guide. Letters should be typed, if possible, not handwritten. Leave at least a 4 centimetre margin on all sides of the page and use single spacing unless the letter is very short. If using a word processor, do not justify the lines but use a ragged right-hand margin. Indicate new paragraphs with a line space rather than an indent.

On business stationery, the location of the company's letterhead often suggests the best position for the date that is to follow it – that is, whether it should be on the right-hand or left-hand side of the page. If there is no printed letterhead, the writer's address, followed by the date, may be ranged right or left.

The name, position and address of the person to whom you are writing comes next, ranged left. The salutation occupies a new line, and is normally the only part of all this preliminary material to end with a comma. Leave a two-line space between each part of the preliminary material.

Always try to obtain the name of the person to whom you are writing, rather than using an official or impersonal designation. If your letter is a reply, copy the address details from the letter you have received as in the following example of a formal salutation.

Ms D. R. Phillips
Managing Editor
Wattle & Daub Publications
3 Eureka Street
Wiribu
Victoria 3999

Dear Ms Phillips,

The title in a salutation should be both courteous and accurate. Not all women wish to be addressed as *Ms*, and a woman's preference needs to be ascertained if possible. Watch out also for titles such as *Sir*, *Dame*, *Professor* and *Dr*. Some people prefer to be addressed by their given name and surname, without any title at all.

If you do not know the name of the person you are writing to you can put *Dear Madam or Sir*, and it is now common to write *Dear Personnel Manager*, or even *Dear Wattle & Daub Publications* if you are unsure which person or department you require. If you cannot find out whether the person is a man or woman it is safest to write *Dear D. R. Phillips*.

If you are replying to a letter, refer in your first paragraph to its date and quote the reference number if one was given.

Concluding material is ranged left. Close the letter with *Yours sincerely* if the person is addressed by name, *Yours faithfully* if not. Phrases such as *With kindest regards* or *With best wishes* are optional, but are normally used only with people you know well or have already had dealings with. The name of the letter-writer is typed under the signature. It is helpful to add your title and position (if appropriate) in parenthesis. The traditional salutation in a letter to the editor of a newspaper or journal is *Sir:* or *Madam:* and the conclusion is not *Yours sincerely* or *Yours faithfully* but *Yours, etc*.

See also **active voice/passive voice**; **addressing envelopes**; **circumlocution**; **commercialese**; **Ms**; **officialese**; **ranks, titles, honours and awards**.

**letter spacing** See **tracking**.

**LEUT/Lieut.** These are the abbreviations for *Lieutenant* in the Royal Australian Navy; note the spelling of the first abbreviation.

See also **Lieut/LT**; **lieutenant**.

**levee/levy** A *levee* may be a raised riverbank or irrigation bank: *a levee built up from silt*; or a reception, usually formal and conducted by people of high rank: *a levee at Government House*. A *levy* is a tax or impost: *the Medicare levy*.

**level/levelled/levelling** Note the final *l* in the first and the *-ll-* in the others. See also **level/mark**; **level playing field**.

**level/mark** These two nouns are used unnecessarily in sentences such as the following:

Children at primary school (level) could easily learn to type.

They hoped to get enrolments up to (the) 500 (mark).

See also **level/levelled/levelling**.

**level playing field** A *level playing field* clearly has advantages in bowls and cricket. To use it whenever you mean equal opportunity (in trade or anything else) is to spoil an otherwise acceptable metaphor. It has become so popular that it is apt to turn up as a mixed metaphor in combinations such as the following, from an ABC commentator: 'Let's not throw the level playing field out of the window'.

**leverage** In general parlance *leverage* is literally and metaphorically the action of a lever. As a business term it is the amount of fixed-interest loan capital compared with share capital that is used in financing an enterprise. Pronounce the general word '**lee**-va-rij' and the finance term '**lev**va-rij'.

**levy** See **levee/levy**.

**lf** low frequency (electromagnetic waves, as in radio and TV); also *LF*, *l.f.*

**liable** See **apt/liable/prone/likely**.

**liaise/liaison** Note the *-iai-*. *Liaise* is overused as a synonym for words such as *cooperate*, *liaison* for words such as *communication*. The verbal form is comparatively new and some authorities disapprove of it: *The two groups will liaise over the union merger*. Choose one of the alternatives wherever possible. Pronounce the words 'lee-**ayz**' and 'lee-**ay**-zon'.

**libel** See **defamation**.

**library** Pronounce the three syllables (not 'lie-bree').

**libretto** The plural is *librettos* or *libretti*. A *libretto* consists of the text, as opposed to the music, of long compositions such as opera.

**licence/license** In Australian and British English *licence* is the noun: *a driving licence*; *poetic licence*. *License* is the verb only: *to license a club*. Note that words derived from the verb also have the *s*. They include the noun *licensee* (someone holding a liquor licence) and the adjective *licensed*. In US English both noun and verb are spelt *license*.

**licorice/liquorice** Either spelling is acceptable. Pronounce it '**likk**a-rish', '**lik**-rish' or '**likk**a-riss'.

**lie** See **lay/laying/lie/lying**.

**Lieut/LT** These are the abbreviations for *Lieutenant* in the Australian Army. See also **LEUT/Lieut.; lieutenant**.

**Lieut. Col./LTCOL/Lt Col/Lt-Col** Lieutenant Colonel. See also **lieutenant**.

**Lieut.-Comm.** See **LCDR/Lieut.-Comm.**

**lieutenant** In Australian English the army and air force ranks are pronounced 'lef-**ten**'nt', the naval rank 'l'**ten**'nt'. The American pronunciation of the word, 'loo-ten'nt', is not recommended.

**Lieut. Gen./LTGEN** Lieutenant General. See also **lieutenant**.

**lifestyle** Although this is a word that many people dislike – probably because of its association with conspicuous consumption and the advertising industry – it has survived the test of time and apparently meets a need in the language. The word may be hyphenated.

**ligature** See **digraph/diphthong/ligature**.

**lighted/lit** Either form may be used as the past tense and past participle of the verb *to light* but *lit* is preferred – except in the old-fashioned usage where it means landed:

> The shipwrecked survivors lighted on a lonely shore.
>
> A blow has lighted on his head.

The form of the past participle used as an adjective is generally *lighted*: *a lighted candle*. When it is modified by an adverb, however, we use *lit*: *a well-lit street*.

**lightening/lightning** The noun *lightening* means a reduction in darkness, weight or seriousness: *a lightening in the paint colour*; *the lightening of his load*; *a lightening of our spirits*. Its spelling should not be confused with that of *lightning*, the flash of light in the sky caused by a discharge of atmospheric electricity.

**light type** See **type**.

**light-year** A *light-year* is the distance light travels in one year, approximately $9.46 \times 10^{12}$ kilometres (or nearly 300 000 kilometres a second). Since it is a measurement of distance, not time, it is not correct to write *That letter was written light-years ago*.

**likable/likeable** Either spelling, with or without the *-e* of *like*, is acceptable, but *likeable* is preferred by many people.

**like** As a preposition, *like* means similar to or resembling. It may be linked to a following noun or pronoun but not a verb:

She runs like a top athlete He laughs like me.

She runs as [*not* like] true athletes can. He laughs as [*not* like] I do.

Note that in the following example *diving*, though a verb-form, is acting as a noun:

She felt like diving into the water.

The pronoun following *like* must be in the objective case, not the subjective:

He laughs like me [*not* I].

The carpenter says that, like him [*not* he], the painter will want a cash deposit.

A common mistake with *like* is to compare things that are not comparable: *Like her brother, her favourite sport was tennis*. Here *her favourite sport* is being compared with *her brother*. Write instead:

Her favourite sport, like her brother's, was tennis.

The same rule applies to *unlike*.

See also **as**; **case (grammar)**; **phrase**; **such/such as/like**.

**likeable** See **likable/likeable**.

**likelihood** Note the spelling.

**likely** *Likely* is most often used as an adjective. When it is used as an adverb it must be qualified by other adverbs such as *very*, *most* and *quite*.

A huge crowd is likely to attend the World Cup final.

*or* A huge crowd will very likely attend the World Cup final.

*not* A huge crowd will likely attend the World Cup final.

See also **apt/liable/prone/likely**.

**limit** See **delimit/limit**.

**limited** Use this adjective when you mean restricted, not just as a synonym for *small*, *brief*, *few* or *rare*:

In thirty minutes you can write only a limited number of words.

*not* He had all day but wrote only a limited number of words.

See also **delimit/limit**.

**limpid** See **languid/limpid**.

**linage** See **lineage/linage**.

**linchpin/lynchpin** Either spelling is acceptable, but *linchpin* is recommended. A *linchpin* keeps a wheel attached to its axle; figuratively, it means the essential element or person:

> The linchpin of the design is its geometrical classicism.
> Pauline had been the linchpin of the committee, which disbanded when she left.

**lineage/linage** The noun *lineage* means the line of descent from one's ancestors: *pride in their lineage*. It is pronounced '**linn**ee-ij'. *Linage* means alignment, and also the number of printed lines: *doing a linage count to see if the manuscript will fit*. It is pronounced '**line**-ij', even when the less common spelling *lineage* is used.

**line length** See **measure**.

**line spacing** See **leading**.

**lingua franca** See **argot/dialect/jargon/lingua franca**.

**liqueur/liquor** A *liqueur* is a strong, sweet alcoholic drink that may follow a meal or be included in cocktails. It is pronounced 'li-**kew**er'. *Liquor* may be any alcoholic drink, but especially one that is distilled (gin, whisky) rather than fermented (wine). It is pronounced '**li**-ker'.

See also **cordial**.

**liquidambar** Note the spelling of the name of this tree.

**liquidation** See **bankruptcy/factoring/liquidation/receivership**.

**liquor** See **liqueur/liquor**.

**liquorice** See **licorice/liquorice**.

**lit** See **lighted/lit**; **literal/literally/littoral**; **typo**.

**literal/literally/littoral** The noun *literal* (abbreviated *lit*) means a printer's error, especially of a single letter or figure. As an adjective *literal* means true to the letter, according to the actual words. In this sense it is the opposite of *approximate* or *figurative*. A person who is *literal* is so tied to the strict meaning of words as to be unimaginative.

The adverb *literally* should be used with care, particularly in formal English. It is generally superfluous, for one thing. For another, it is often misused for emphasis as in the colloquial expression *literally tearing strips off them* (were strips *actually* torn off them?).

A *littoral* is the shore of a lake or the sea. The word is also used as an adjective.

**literati** Note the spelling, and that of *glitterati* and *littérateur*.

**literature** This is probably too grand a word for advertising material. Try *leaflets, brochures, pamphlets, handouts* – and *advertisements*, of course.

**littoral** See **literal/literally/littoral**.

**livid/lurid** Both these words describe colours or combinations of colours, and they have developed distinct figurative meanings. Something or someone *livid* is discoloured or bluish grey, and the word has come to mean very angry:

> She was livid about bottles being tossed from the train.

*Lurid* describes something lit up by an unnatural yellowish glare, and also means sensational or shocking:

> He complained about the lurid films shown on children's TV programs.

**llama** See **lama/llama**.

**load/lode/lodestar/lodestone** These nouns are related in derivation but have quite different meanings. A *load* is a quantity of something or a burden. A *lode* is a deposit of ore within rock, often in the form of a vein. The spellings *lodestar* and *lodestone* are preferred to *loadstar* and *loadstone*. A *lodestar* is, literally and figuratively, something that guides; *lodestone* too has literal and figurative meanings – something that attracts.

**loaded** See **laden/loaded**.

**loan** See **lend/loan**.

**loan words** Words borrowed from another language are called *loan words*. The term is not particularly appropriate as such words, once borrowed, are rarely given back. English is a notably absorbent language that has taken in thousands of words throughout its history, especially from Latin, Greek, French and Scandinavian. But most of the world's languages have made their contribution, and sometimes several are involved in the development of one word: *marmalade*, for instance, comes from a French word adopted from a Portuguese word loosely related to a Latin word adopted from Greek; *tycoon* derives from a Japanese word adopted from Chinese; and *kiosk* comes from a Persian word via Turkish then French.

English has also contributed to other languages, much to the distress of non-English purists – particularly among the French, who regard *Franglais* as a corrupting influence.

See also **Australian English**; **British English**; **foreign words and phrases**; **Latin words and phrases**; **US English**.

**loath/loth/loathe** Both *loath* and *loth* are acceptable spellings for the adjective meaning reluctant or unwilling, but *loath* is recommended:

> Bridget was loath to lay the tiles herself but could not afford a tiler.

*Loathe* is a verb that means to hate, or to feel disgust:

> The children love roast potatoes but loathe boiled cabbage.

Pronounce the *th* in *loath* as in *both*, and in *loathe* as in *scythe*.

**local** Avoid such tautologies as *local residents in this area* and *local neighbourhood.*

**local area network** This term (abbreviated *LAN*) means a group of computers connected by specific network software and cables, and all located at the one site. A network of such machines can share expensive peripherals such as printers and disk drives, and files can be shared and transferred between the computers.

**loc. cit.** This abbreviation (Latin: *loco citato*) means that the particular page (or pages) of a work already cited in notes and references is being quoted again. Even in traditional styles of referencing, however, *loc. cit* is now seldom used.

See also **notes**; **references**.

**lode/lodestar/lodestone** See **load/lode/lodestar/lodestone**.

**lodgement/lodgment** Either spelling, with or without the *-e* of *lodge*, is acceptable, but *lodgment* is recommended.

**logo** See **colophon/logo**.

**long.** longitude.

See also **latitude/longitude**.

**longitude** See **latitude/longitude**.

**Longlea, Vic.** Compare with *Longley*, Tas.

**long-sighted/short-sighted** A *long-sighted* person has poor close-up vision; a *short-sighted* person has poor long-distance vision. Both compounds have figurative uses too. *Long-sighted* can mean having foresight; *short-sighted* can mean lacking it.

**loose/lose** The spelling of these two words is sometimes confused. The adjective *loose* means free of bonds or restraint; lax, not firm: *loose reins*; *loose morals*. The rarely used verb *to loose* means to release or free:

They will loose the stabled horses for grazing in the paddock.

The verb *to lose* means to undergo loss:

They will lose the horses if they don't mend the fence.

**Lord's** Note the apostrophe in the name of this famous cricket ground in London.

**Lorn, NSW** (2320) Compare with *Lorne*, NSW (2439) and Vic.

**lose** See **loose/lose**.

**lot** The phrases *a lot of* (never 'alot of') and *lots of* come so readily to mind that they tend to be overused. Keep them under control, and at the more informal end of the usage scale:

A lot of time has been wasted in all this messing around.

*but* *Much* time has been lost, and the renovations are still incomplete.

We hope lots of people come to the garage sale.

*but* *Many* people who require low-priced goods will attend.

Both *a lot of* and *lots of* may be treated as singular or plural, depending on whether what is referred to is seen as a single entity or as separate items:

A lot of haggling spoils a sale.
A lot of vegetables spoil if not sold.
There is lots of carpet on offer.
There are lots of saucepans in these boxes.

**loth** See **loath/loth/loathe**.

**louvre** Note the spelling.

**low-key** This relatively new adjectival compound meaning restrained or unobtrusive has found general acceptance in Australian English:

Christmas was a low-key affair without the children.

See also **high profile/low profile**.

**low profile** See **high profile/low profile**.

**LP** long playing (record).

**LPG** liquefied petroleum gas; also abbreviated *LP gas*.

**LS** Leading Seaman.

**LSD** lysergic acid diethylamide, a hallucinogenic drug.

**lsd** pounds, shillings, pence (Latin: *librae*, *solidi*, *denarii*); also abbreviated *£ s d*.
See also **currency**.

**LSE** London School of Economics and Political Science.

**LT** See **Lieut/LT**.

**LTAA** Lawn Tennis Association of Australia.

**LTCOL/Lt Col/Lt-Col** See **Lieut. Col./LTCOL/Lt Col/Lt-Col**.

**Ltd** Limited (company).

**LTGEN** See **Lieut. Gen./LTGEN**.

**lurid** See **livid/lurid**.

**luxuriant/luxurious** *Luxuriant* means abundant; or growing vigorously; or ornate:

Elizabeth's garden was full of luxuriant tropical creepers.

There was luxuriant carving on the sideboard.

*Luxurious*, the adjective from *luxury*, suggests sumptuous living; or extravagance; or great comfort:

Oliver's luxurious lifestyle was the result of great wealth.

**lying** See **lay/laying/lie/lying**.

**lynchpin** See **linchpin/lynchpin**.

# Mm

**M** mature audiences (film classification); 1000 (roman numeral; see also **roman numerals**).

**M.** Monsieur.

**m.** male *or* masculine (see also **male/masculine**); married; million *or* millions (see also **numbers in figures or words**); minute *or* minutes (see also **time of day**).

**machismo/macho** *Machismo* is masculinity overtly expressed. Someone who is *macho* (an overused word) is displaying *machismo*: he is aggressively proud of his masculinity. Pronounce the *ch* in both words as in *Charles* or *Chris*.

**macro** In computer terminology a *macro* is a single computer command that incorporates two or more commands. A *function key* can be programmed to execute a macro, which might include a combination of the commands to save, to print, and then to quit.

See also **function keys**.

**macro-/micro-** *Macro-* and *micro-* are prefixes meaning large and small respectively. They were originally restricted mainly to scientific words, such as *macrobiotics* and *microscope*, but now have wider technical uses in terms such as *macro-economics* (study of the economy as a whole) and *micro-economics* (study of the economy with regard to its various sectors).

*Macro-* and *micro-* are often used instead of more readily understandable words such as *large*, *excessive*, *long*, *small* and *tiny* to invent new compounds. A *macro-recession* is a serious recession, possibly a depression; a *macro-length* film is simply long; a *micro-skirt* is a very short version of the *mini-skirt* (a well-established term). This practice does not deserve encouragement.

**madam/madame** A *madam* (plural *madams*) is a woman who manages a brothel. *Madam* is also the polite form of address for a woman, equivalent to *sir* for a man: *May I take your coat, madam?*. It is the title used in a formal letter to a woman whose name is not known: *Dear Madam*. An abbreviation in speech, *ma'am*, has an air of old-fashioned courtesy; it is also the mode of address required by female members of the royal family. Women whose names are unknown are usually addressed collectively as *Ladies*.

*Madame* (plural *Mesdames*) is the French equivalent of the English *Mrs*. *Madame* is usually abbreviated to *Mme* (with no full point) but must be associated with a name (*Mme Gide*). *Madame* is pronounced 'm'**dahm**'; *Mesdames* is pronounced '**may**-dahm'.

See also **Ms**; **ranks, titles, honours and awards**; **woman**.

**maestro** The plural is *maestri* or *maestros*. Italian for *master*, the word has traditionally been used as a title of respect for eminent musicians, particularly composers and conductors. Some people dislike its overuse in other contexts: *a maestro of the boxing ring*.

**Mafia** Give this word an initial capital when referring to the Italian criminal organisation. In figurative use (meaning a clique) – *Irish mafia, literary mafia* – it has a lower-case initial.

**magenta** The process colour red, used in four-colour printing.

**Magna Carta/Magna Charta** Either spelling is acceptable for the name (Latin for *great charter*) of the charter of English liberties granted in 1215, but *Magna Carta* is recommended.

**magnetic disk** See **disk, magnetic**.

**magneto** Plural *magnetos*.

**magnitude** This noun can mean importance or size, but it needs a rest: *the extent* [rather than *magnitude*] *of the country's economic problems*; *the vastness* [rather than *magnitude*] *of the stockpile*.

**Mahomet** See **Islam/Muhammad/Muslim**.

**maize/maze** *Maize* is the US term for Indian corn, a variety of which is commonly called *sweet corn* in Australia. A *maze* is a labyrinth, most popularly an interconnecting arrangement of hedged paths designed as a puzzle; figuratively, a maze is a state of puzzlement (*in a maze over his tax*).

**MAJ/Maj.** Major.

**MAJGEN/Maj.-Gen.** Major General.

**major** *Major* is overused as an adjective, often describing nothing of special importance. Synonyms include *greater*, *larger*, *strong*, *principal* and *serious*. There may be no need for any adjective: the phrase *a major part* often simply means *most*.

**majority/minority** *Majority* and *minority* are used only of people or of things that can be counted; do not use them of a single item.

*Majority* refers to more than half the number; *minority* refers to fewer than half:

The majority of the dates were mouldy.

*but* The greater part [*not* majority] of the batch was mouldy.

*Majority* and *minority* may be treated as singular or plural according to whether the people or items are being considered as a group or as individuals:

A minority of late visitors spoils the fun of the others.

The majority of the visitors are on time.

Avoid the cliché *the vast majority*; use *most* instead.

**makeup** In publishing parlance *makeup* means arranging typeset text and any illustrations into pages.

See also **camera-ready art/camera-ready copy**; **layout**; **paste-up**.

**malapropism** This word is derived from the name of a character in Sheridan's eighteenth-century play *The Rivals*. Mrs Malaprop habitually misapplies words by confusing them with others that sound similar: 'the geometry of contagious countries', for example. Thus a *malapropism* is an unintentional but amusing error of this kind.

See also **spoonerism.**

**Malays/Malaysia** *Malays* make up the main racial group in the political entity of *Malaysia*, which consists of Malaya and parts of Borneo (Sarawak and Sabah). Citizens of Malaysia are called *Malaysians*. The *Malay* language is widely spoken throughout southern Asia.

**male/masculine** The adjective *male* simply describes the sex of humans, animals or plants; its opposite is *female*. *Masculine* normally describes the characteristics of men, though a woman can be said to show masculine traits: *a masculine voice*; *a masculine physique*. *Masculine* (and its opposite, *feminine*) also describes the gender of words: *the third-person masculine pronouns he and him*.

See also **female/feminine/feminist**; **gender**; **man/mankind**.

**malevolent/malicious/malign/malignant** These adjectives all refer to harmful intentions and they are interchangeable in some senses. *Malevolent* specifically means wishing evil on others, and suggests a brooding hostility: *a malevolent attitude towards his cruel father. Malicious* means motivated by vicious or mischievous purposes and suggests spite and ill will: *malicious rumours*; it also has a legal sense: *malicious damage*.

*Malign* means evil in intent or effect: *a malign influence*. *Malignant* is the strongest of the four words, connoting something extremely harmful in influence or effect. It is often used in a medical context, to mean deadly: *a malignant tumour.*

**mall** *Mall* is a fashionable term in Australia for a shopping precinct or car-free pedestrian walk. It is pronounced 'morl' or 'mal'. London's *Pall Mall* is pronounced 'pal mal'.

**the Mallee** This is the name given to certain areas of low rainfall in New South Wales, South Australia, Victoria and Western Australia, where the stunted kind of eucalypt known as *mallee* (with a lower-case initial) is a major component of the vegetation.

**man/mankind** Be aware of the sex bias perceived by many people today when these words are used generically to denote all human beings, both male and female: *Man is not a solitary animal*; *the problems of mankind*; *one man, one vote*. To avoid ambiguity or offensiveness, try to substitute sex-inclusive words: *A human being is not a solitary animal*; *the problems of the human race*; *one person, one vote*. Common sense should always temper such modifications to idiom, however.

See also **discriminatory language**; **gender**; **female/feminine/feminist**; **male/masculine**; **woman**.

**manageable** The *-e* of *manage* is always retained.

**mandarin** Used as an adjective, the word *mandarin* has a sense of bureaucratic aloofness about it: *the mandarin attitudes of some government officials*.

**mandatory** This adjective, which is mainly associated with official worlds, means compulsory, or conveying a command:

> Wearing bicycle helmets is now mandatory, not just optional.

In everyday contexts where officialdom is not involved, *obligatory* or *essential* may be more appropriate:

> Washing your hands before meals is obligatory [*not* mandatory] here.
>
> The study of harmony is essential [*not* mandatory] for an understanding of musical composition.

Pronounce the word '**manda**-tree'.

**mango** Plural *mangoes* or *mangos*.

**manifesto** The plural is *manifestos* or *manifestoes*; the word means a public declaration of policy.

**manikin/mannequin** The primary meaning of *manikin* (sometimes spelt *mannikin* or, rarely, *manakin*) is a small man, a dwarf or a pygmy; an anatomical model may also be called a *manikin*. A *mannequin* is a model – human, or made of materials such as plastic or wood – displaying clothes. Both words are pronounced '**manna**-kin'.

**mankind** See **man/mankind**.

**mannequin** See **manikin/mannequin**.

**manner** This word is sometimes used in verbose phrases: *in a manner similar to* (use *like*); *in a careless manner* (use *carelessly*).

**manoeuvre** Note the *-oeu-* and the forms *manoeuvred*, *manoeuvring* and *manoeuvrable*. A *manoeuvre* is a controlled movement of such elements as personnel and vehicles in warfare or any other situation. Pronounce it 'm'**noo**va'.

***manqué*** This adjective (French for missed) means potential or unfulfilled:

> Such creativity in a family cook indicates a chef *manqué*.

*Manqué* always follows the noun it describes and retains its accent; it is usually italicised. Pronounce it '**mong**-kay' or 'mong-**kay**'.

**mantel/mantle** A *mantel*, as in a *mantelpiece* above a fireplace, has the acceptable variant spelling *mantle* (and therefore *mantlepiece*). The cloak is always spelt *mantle*.

**manuscripts, presentation of** See **copy, presentation of**.

**many** The noun or adjective *many* means a large number. It is generally treated as plural:

> Many are staying overnight.
>
> Many birds have come here to nest.

However, note the singular verb in expressions beginning *many a*:

> Many a tear has fallen since he went away.

Note that *many* is preferred to *a lot of* in formal usage:

> Australia allows many [*rather than* a lot of] overseas students to study here.

See also **lot**.

**margarine** Originally pronounced with a hard *g*, the name of the butter substitute *margarine* is now generally given a soft *g*. The emphasis may be placed on either the first or last syllable.

**marginal** This adjective denotes the edge or border of something; a limit, particularly a lower one; or something that is barely adequate. *Marginal* notes are written in the margin; the vegetation adjacent to a shoreline is called *marginal*; a seat in politics is *marginal* if it is held by a small majority; one extra purchase might add a *marginal* cost; *marginal* land is of little use for primary production.

All these are legitimate uses of the word, but it tends to be overused in some contexts where *small* or *slight* would be more appropriate:

> The teacher says my work shows a slight [*rather than* marginal] improvement.

The verb *marginalise* is a voguish word meaning to relegate to the sidelines and treat or regard as insignificant: *marginalising the achievements of their competitors*. Do not encourage its use.

**margins** See **layout**.

**Marian, Qld** Compare with *Marion*, SA; *Marion Bay*, Tas.

**mark** See **level/mark**.

**marking up** The term used in publishing to describe the annotating of a typescript or printout for the typesetter or desktop-publishing operator is *marking up* or *mark-up*. It includes specifying typefaces and type sizes; attributes such as italic and bold; capital letters; and the spaces required between letters, words, lines and paragraphs. Such global specifications are usually supplied by the designer on a separate *specification sheet*. The identification of elements such as headings, quotations, footnotes or captions is also part of the mark-up.

In book publishing a designer usually devises these typographic specifications and marks up the edited text accordingly. The editor should have drawn the designer's attention to any unusual features of the text, such as a large number of quotations, captions or headings, or the need to fit an excessive number of words into a limited span of printed pages. In desktop publishing the marked-up copy may go straight from the editor to the keyboard operator, which means that all typographic requirements will have to be specified by the editor.

A cardinal rule of mark-up is that all annotations should be comprehensive, legible and unambiguous. Use a ballpoint or felt-tip pen for all text changes and instructions. Queries should be written in pencil so that they can be erased before typesetting. Instructions are circled so that they cannot be mistaken for part of the text to be typeset. As a number of different people may share the setting of the typescript, it is safest to put all instructions (other than items like global specifications and the key to complex heading codes) on the typescript rather than on a separate sheet that may get lost (or be ignored). Most typesetters find it time-wasting to have to refer to a sheet of general instructions.

If there is a substantial amount of material (such as multiple headings or quotations of various kinds) that is to be distinguished from the main text, a coding system will probably be necessary. Use an alphabetical code rather than a colour code where possible, as typescripts are often copied and standard photocopiers do not reproduce colour. Even a simple headings scheme needs to be coded (A for chapter headings, B for the next-level headings, and so on downwards); this is often done at the editorial stage.

Some of the symbols used in correcting proofs are useful in editing and mark-up too. However, editorial amendments to the text should be made primarily between the lines (as close as possible to the original words) rather than in the margin, because some of the margin space will be needed for typesetting instructions, queries, and mark-up devices such as coding.

See also **copy editing**; **copy, presentation of**; **desktop publishing**; **layout**; **marks in proof correction**; **proofs**; **type**.

**marks in proof correction** The importance of using recognised marginal and textual marks for proof correction cannot be emphasised too much. Most typesetters look first for any marginal marks on a galley proof or page proof and then do the corrections indicated in the text; if there is no marginal mark for it a correction is likely to be missed. All proof corrections must be marked in ink, not pencil: ballpoint and felt-tip pens are satisfactory. Use one colour for typesetter's errors (usually red) and another for the author's or editor's additions or corrections (usually blue); always provide a key identifying the colours.

If there are several corrections in a line, divide the marks between left-hand and right-hand margins in the appropriate order; conclude each mark with a diagonal stroke. A mark standing alone may also be followed by a diagonal stroke.

As most typesetters do not read for sense it is important to circle all instructions or queries or you may find such instructions set in the text. This is particularly likely if typesetting is done in countries where English is not the native or first language.

The marks recommended for correcting proofs, an example of typeset copy marked up for correction and the final corrected proof are given on the following pages. For further information see the entries **marking up** and **proofs**.

## Symbols for correcting proofs

| *Instruction* | *Textual mark* | *Marginal mark** |
|---|---|---|
| Correction is concluded | None | / |
| Insert in text the matter indicated in margin | ⅄ | *New matter followed by* / |
| Delete | Strike through ~~out~~ characters to be deleted | ꝺ |
| Delete and close up | Above and below letters to be taken out | ꝺ (with close-up marks) |
| Leave as printed | ~~Under characters to remain~~ (dotted underline) | stet |
| Change to italic | Under characters to be altered (single underline) | ital |
| Change to even small capitals | Under characters to be altered (double underline) | s.c. |
| Change to capital letters | Under characters to be altered (triple underline) | CAPS |
| Use capital letters for initial letters and small capitals for rest of words | Under initial letters and under the rest of words | C. & S.C. |
| Change to bold type | Under characters to be altered (wavy underline) | bold |
| Underline word or words | Under words affected | underline |
| Change to lower case | Encircle (CHA)racters to be altered | l.c. |
| Change to roman type | Encircle (*cha*)racters to be altered | rom |
| Wrong font – replace with letters of correct font | Encircle characters (to) be altered | w.f. |
| Change damaged characters | Encircle (cha)racters to be altered | × |

* Words printed in italics in column below are instructions and not part of the marks.

## Symbols for correcting proofs

| *Instruction* | *Textual mark* | *Marginal mark** |
|---|---|---|
| Substitute or insert† character(s) under which the mark is placed, in 'superior' position | / through character or ⋏ where required | ⋎ *under character* (e.g. x⋎ ) |
| Substitute or insert† character(s) over which this mark is placed, in 'inferior' position | / through character or ⋏ where required | ⋏ *over character* (e.g. x⋏ ) |
| Use ligature (e.g. fi) or diphthong (e.g. œ) | Enclosing letters to be altered | ⁀ *enclosing ligature or diphthong required* |
| Substitute separate letters for ligature or diphthong | Through ligatured letters or diphthong to be altered | *write out separate letters followed by* / |
| Close up – delete space between characters | lin king characters | ⁀ |
| Insert space‡ | ⋏ | # |
| Insert space between lines or paragraphs‡ | > Between lines to be spaced | # |
| Reduce space between lines‡ | ( Connecting lines to be closed up ) | less# close up |
| Make space appear equal between words | Equal\|between \| words | eq.# |
| Reduce space between words‡ | Between \| words | less # |

* Words printed in italics in column below are instructions and not part of the marks.
† The caret mark ⋏ may be used for both – drawn through a character to indicate *substitute* and between characters to indicate *insert*.
‡ Amount of space may be indicated.

## Symbols for correcting proofs

| *Instruction* | *Textual mark* | *Marginal mark* |
| --- | --- | --- |
| Add space between letters* | Between tops of letters requiring space | letter # |
| Transpose | Between characters words or | trs |
| Place in centre of line | Indicate position with | centre |
| Indent one em | | or 1 |
| Indent two ems | | or 2 |
| Move matter to right | At left or right side of group to be moved | |
| Move matter to left | At right or left side of group to be moved | |
| Move matter to position indicated | At limits of required position | move |
| Move to next line or page | | take over |
| Move to previous line or page | | take back |
| Raise lines* | Over lines to be moved ↑ Under lines to be moved | raise |
| Lower lines* | Over lines to be moved Under lines to be moved ↓ | lower |
| Correct the vertical alignment | At left or right of lines to be adjusted | |

* Amount of space may be indicated.

## Symbols for correcting proofs

| *Instruction* | *Textual mark* | *Marginal mark* |
|---|---|---|
| Straighten lines | ~~Through lines to be~~ straightened | ═ |
| Begin a new paragraph | [Before the first word of new paragraph | n.p. |
| No fresh paragraph here | Between paragraphs | run on |
| Spell out abbreviation or figure in full | Encircle word or (figs) to be altered | spell out |
| Insert omitted portion of copy* | Between the⋏adjoining words | out-see copy |
| Substitute or insert† character(s) | / through cha~~tdyrt~~(s) or ⋏ where required | racter / |
| Substitute or insert† comma | / through character or ⋏ where required | ,/ |
| Substitute or insert† semicolon | through character or ⋏ where required | ;/ |
| Substitute or insert† full stop | / through character or ⋏ where required | ⊙/ |
| Substitute or insert† colon | / through character or ⋏ where required | (:)/ |
| Substitute or insert† question mark | / through character or ⋏ where required | ?/ |
| Substitute or insert† exclamation mark | / through character or ⋏ where required | !/ |

* Large amounts of missing copy should be identified on the manuscript page and attached.

† The caret mark ⋏ may be used for both – drawn through a character to indicate *substitute* and between characters to indicate *insert*.

## Symbols for correcting proofs

| *Instruction* | *Textual mark* | *Marginal mark* |
|---|---|---|
| Insert brackets | ⅄ or ⅄⅄ | (/)/ |
| Insert square brackets | ⅄ or ⅄⅄ | [/]/ |
| Insert hyphen | ⅄ | \|-\| |
| Insert en (half-em) rule | ⅄ | \|en\| |
| Insert one-em rule | ⅄ | \|em\| |
| Insert two-em rule | ⅄ | \|2em\| |
| Insert apostrophe | ⅄ | ’/ |
| Insert single quotation marks | ⅄ | ‘/ ’/ |
| Insert double quotation marks | ⅄ | “/ ”/ |
| Insert ellipsis | ⅄ | .../ |
| Insert leader | ⅄ | (..)/ |
| Insert diagonal stroke | ⅄ | (/) |
| Refer to appropriate authority anything of doubtful accuracy* | Encircle words (etc.,) affected | (?) |

* Always set out your query plainly and address it to author, editor or typesetter.

Adapted from ‘Symbols for correcting proofs’, *Style Manual for Authors, Editors and Printers*, 4th edn, Australian Government Publishing Service, Canberra, 1988, pp. 284–87.

## Reader's marked proof

Among serious readers Richardson's status in literature has never been in doubt. She liked to think of herself as a neglected writer, but Arnold Gyde, of Heinemann's, recorded that *Maurice Guest* had always had steady sales. She herself wrote that the last of the trilogy sold 80,000 copies in America and the trilogy itself 30,000 in England. It was highly praised in America by Sinclair lewis. T. E. Lawrence was a great admirer and anticipated the best answer to later critics who pointed out stylistic flaws when he wrote: Only the finest stuff shows specks.

With hindsight one may ask what part the anonymity imposed by her pen-name may have played in denying her first novel early recqnition in her own country She took pleasure in showing that Critics could not as they claimed, detect the work of a woman. Perhaps the joke should have ended with Maurice Guest. Her pen name has certainly hindered proper recognition of her work in feminist literary histories: the brief bibliographical reference in Elaine Showalter's *A Literature of their Own* does not even get her first name right. London reviewers of the ~~recent~~ Virago editions of her work have sometimes been unaware of her sex, while Dorøs Lesslig accused Australians of neglecting her. The facts are otherwise. Nettie Palmer and Leeson Ida wfote about hef from the mid-1920s; HM. Gfddb gave her proper recognition in the first comprehensive account of Australian literature in 1930, and expanded this in his two-volume *History* in 1961. The National Library Centenary Bibliography lists over 600 articles or studies, many of which are by Australians. Australian women have produced two biographical/critical studies one ~~one~~ of them based on completely new material), and a monograph on Richardson's schooldays. She has certainly not been neglected by scholars, either male or female. Richardson was not indifferent to fame and put out feelers to Nettie Palmer about the Nobel Prize, which to date has been won by seventy-one men and 5 women. At the height of Richardson's fame in the early 1930's, the prize went to Sinclair Lewis and John Galsworthy.

Dorothy Green, 'Henry Handel Richardson' in *Double Time/Women in Victoria – 150 Years,* edited by Marilyn Lake and Farley Kelly (Penguin, 1985)

## Revised proof

Among serious readers Richardson's status in literature has never been in doubt. She liked to think of herself as a neglected writer, but Arnold Gyde, of Heinemann's, recorded that *Maurice Guest* had always had steady sales. She herself wrote that the last volume of the trilogy sold 80,000 copies in America and the trilogy itself 30,000 in England. It was highly praised in England, and in America by Sinclair Lewis. T. E. Lawrence was a great admirer and anticipated the best answer to later critics who pointed out stylistic flaws when he wrote: 'Only the finest stuff shows specks.'

With hindsight one may ask what part the anonymity imposed by her pen-name may have played in denying her first novel early recognition in her own country.[13] She took pleasure in showing that critics could not, as they claimed, detect the work of a woman. Perhaps the joke should have ended with *Maurice Guest.* Her pen-name has certainly hindered proper recognition of her work in feminist literary histories: the brief bibliographical reference in Elaine Showalter's *A Literature of their Own* does not even get her first name right. London reviewers of the recent Virago editions of her work have sometimes been unaware of her sex, while Doris Lessing accused Australians of neglecting her. The facts are otherwise. Nettie Palmer and Ida Leeson wrote about her from the mid-1920s; H. M. Green gave her proper recognition in the first comprehensive account of Australian literature in 1930, and expanded this in his two-volume *History* in 1961. The National Library Centenary Bibliography lists over 700 articles or studies, many of which are by Australians. Australian women have produced two biographical–critical studies (one of them based on completely new material), and a monograph on Richardson's schooldays. She has certainly not been neglected by scholars, either male or female. Richardson was not indifferent to fame and put out feelers to Nettie Palmer about the Nobel Prize, which to date has been won by seventy-one men and five women. At the height of Richardson's fame in the early 1930s, the prize went to Sinclair Lewis and John Galsworthy.

Dorothy Green, 'Henry Handel Richardson'
in *Double Time: Women in Victoria – 150 Years,*
edited by Marilyn Lake and Farley Kelly
(Penguin, 1985)

**mark-up** See **marking up**.

**marvel/marvelled/marvelling** Note the single *l* in the first and the *-ll-* in the other two – and in the related adjective *marvellous*.

***Mary Celeste*** The abandoned ship is often incorrectly referred to as the '*Marie Celeste*'.

**masculine** See **male/masculine**.

**masterful/masterly** The primary meaning of *masterful* is authoritarian or imperious:

> His superiors were masterful, his inferiors obsequious.

*Masterly* means extremely skilful:

> We were thrilled by Maria's masterly performance of the cello concerto.

The fact that the two words have drifted together in common usage helps to explain but does not justify a leading cricket commentator's reference during a Test match to 'a masterful day's play'.

**mat/matt** Either spelling is acceptable for this word meaning not glossy, but *matt* is preferred.

**material** See **germane/material/relevant**.

**materialise** This verb means to give physical shape to or, more commonly, to assume physical shape:

> A camel materialised out of the mirage.

It is often used when words such as *happen*, *occur*, *appear*, *develop*, *evolve* or *unfold* would do:

> My birthday cake didn't appear [*rather than* materialise] after dinner.
> Our scheme didn't unfold [*rather than* materialise] as predicted.

**matrix** The plural is *matrices* (pronounced '**may**-triseez') or *matrixes* (pronounced '**may**-triks'z'). There are a number of technical meanings for this word, the most common, perhaps, being the rocky material in which streaks of opal may be found.

**maxi** See **mini-/maxi-**.

**maximal/maximum/maximise** The adjectives *maximal* and *maximum* mean the same thing – the greatest amount possible:

> Today's maximal [*or* maximum] temperature was the highest on record.

They do not simply mean great:

> The team's great [*not* maximal *or* maximum] effort secured victory.

*Maximum* is also a noun (plural *maxima* or *maximums).* Avoid the term *absolute maximum* because *maximum* does not need such emphasis.

The verb *maximise* means to increase to the greatest amount possible:

Constant practice will maximise our goal-kicking potential.

It does not simply mean improve or increase:

Constant practice will improve [*not* maximise] our goal-kicking somewhat.

The factory must increase [*not* maximise] its profits rather than allow them to drop.

See also **minimal/minimum/minimise**.

**may/might** Be careful how you use *may* and *might*. In general, when the present and future are referred to, use *may*:

If they study harder they may succeed.

In general, if the past is referred to, use *might*:

We thought they might succeed if they studied harder.

However, *might* rather than *may* can be used for the present and future to express greater uncertainty: *He might listen to us* is more doubtful than *He may listen to us*. Similarly, *Might we stay?* is more tentative than *May we stay?*. Note, too, that *may have* is used to express a possibility in the past that continues to exist:

They may have built a new house [but I don't know whether they have].

Use *might have* to express a possibility that no longer exists:

They might have been able to build a new house [if a loan had been possible].

Note that the words *possible* and *perhaps* are usually unnecessary in sentences where a possibility is already indicated by *may* or *might*.

See also **can/may; may be/maybe; of.**

**may be/maybe** When a verb is required, the two-word form is used: *They may be injured. Maybe* is one word when it means perhaps: *maybe next week*.

See also **may/might**.

**May Day/mayday** *May Day* is the festival on 1 May; *mayday* is the international radio-telephone distress call (possibly derived from the French *m'aider*, meaning help me!).

See also **SOS**.

**maze** See **maize/maze**.

**Mb** megabyte.

See also **byte**.

**MC** Master of Ceremonies; Military Cross (see also **ranks, titles, honours and awards**).

**MCC** Marylebone Cricket Club; Melbourne Cricket Club.

**MCG** Melbourne Cricket Ground.

**MD** managing director.

**ME** This is the abbreviation for *Middle English*, the English language of the approximate period 1100–1450.
See also **British English**; **OE**.

**me** See **I/me**; **-ing forms**.

**me/my** See **-ing forms**.

**Meadowbank, NSW** Compare with *Meadowbanks*, Tas.

**meagre/mere** *Meagre* means poor or deficient in quality or quantity:

> The survivors' meagre diet lacked essential vitamins.

The adjective *mere* means no more or no better than:

> For all his talk, he is a mere temporary assistant in the laboratory.

**mean** See **average/mean/median**.

**meaningful** This adjective is overused and needs a long rest, if not burial. Hackneyed terms such as *meaningful relationships* or *meaningful experiences* might then become *fruitful*, *significant*, *valuable*, *worthwhile* or *important*.

**means** The noun *means* is always plural when it refers to monetary resources:

> Adrian couldn't live within his means, which were generous.

It can be either singular or plural when it refers to a method:

> Our only means of travel was horseback.
> Our most likely means of travel were horseback and camel train.

**meantime/meanwhile** These adverbs both mean during the intervening time, but *meanwhile* is preferred:

> Meanwhile [*or* meantime] the men did the washing-up.

*Meantime*, but not *meanwhile*, can also be used as a noun:

> In the meantime the men did the washing-up.

Note that it is usually unnecessary to have a comma after words like *meantime* and *meanwhile*, unless it is one of a pair.

**measure** *Measure* is the typographic term for the length of a line of type. The measure is traditionally specified in picas, but any other form of measurement such as millimetres may be used. In *justified* setting a line of type must fill all the space between the left and right limits of the measure. In *ragged right unjustified* setting a line of type must reach as near to the right-hand limit of the measure as possible. Any word that goes beyond must be taken over to the next line. In order to avoid gappy unjustified setting, some designers specify a minimum and maximum measure, preferring a long word to be broken near or on the right-hand limit rather than to go onto the next line.

The relationship between the type size and the width of a measure is important. Small type should be set on a narrow measure, which is why newspapers and magazines use multiple columns. As the type size increases, the measure should too.

See also **indention**; **justified type/unjustified type**; **layout**; **paragraphs**; **pica**; **points**; **type**.

**measures** See **weights and measures**.

**Mecca/mecca** The name of the holy city of the Islamic religion has an initial capital. Given a lower-case initial, the word is a catch-all cliché much used by newspapers to describe a centre of activity or interest. *Tourist mecca* is probably the main offender, but there are many others – all to be avoided.

**mechanical papers** See **paper sizes and weights**.

**media** *Media* is one of the plural forms of the noun *medium*. Radio, television and newspapers are collectively and popularly known as *the media*, but each is a *medium* (that is, a *means*) of communication. Careful speakers and writers use a plural verb with *media*:

> How responsible are [*not* is] the media?

The plural form *mediums* is always used of those who purport to act as intermediaries between the living and the dead. It is an alternative to *media* for some other senses of *medium*, for example *the mediums watercolour, oil and charcoal*.

**mediaeval/medieval** Either spelling is acceptable.

**median** See **average/mean/median**.

**mediate** See **arbitrate/mediate**.

**medieval** See **mediaeval/medieval**.

**mediocre** Note the spelling. This adjective means ordinary: neither good nor bad. Since something is either *mediocre* or not, qualifying the word by using adverbs such as *very* or *quite* is not recommended.

**Mediterranean** The only doubling of letters occurs in the *-rr-*, so think of *terra*, the Latin for *land*, which almost surrounds the *Mediterranean Sea*.

**medium** See **media**.

**medium type** See **type**.

**meet with** Use *meet with* only when you mean experience or receive:

We hope you meet with good fortune.

Otherwise *meet* needs no preposition:

We hope you meet [*not* meet with *or* meet up with] our children.

**mega-** The prefix *mega-* can mean very large, as in *megalith* (a large stone monument); or the factor of $10^6$ or one million, as in *megawatt* (one million watts). The increasing habit of putting *mega-* in front of anything purportedly large or impressive has gone from the silly – *megastore*, *megabucks* – to the ridiculous: *megayummy*, *megatrendy*.

**megabyte** See **byte**.

**megahertz** This is a measurement of frequency equal to one million hertz or cycles per second. In the context of computers, measurement in *megahertz* (abbreviated *MHz*) is an indication of speed: in simple terms, the more megahertz, the faster the computer.

See also **weights and measures**.

**Melanesia/Micronesia/Polynesia** These are terms used to delineate the racial, national and geographical divisions of the peoples and islands of the southern and central Pacific, an area known collectively as *Oceania*. *Melanesia* includes Fiji, New Caledonia and Vanuatu; *Micronesia* includes Nauru, Kiribati, and the Mariana, Caroline, and Marshall island groups; and *Polynesia* includes the Hawaiian Islands, the Cook Islands, Samoa, Tonga, and islands as far south as New Zealand.

**Melburnian** A resident of Melbourne is a *Melburnian*, not a 'Melbournian'.

**melted/molten** *Melted* is the adjectival form, past tense and past participle of the verb *to melt*:

Brush the fish with melted butter.
Our ice-cream melted in the sun.

*Molten* is also a past participle of the verb *to melt*, but as an adjective it is generally used to describe the liquefaction of metals at very high temperatures:

The sculpture was cast in molten bronze.

**memento** Note the spelling (not 'momento'). The plural is *mementos* or *mementoes*.

**memo** The plural of this abbreviation for *memorandums* or *memoranda* is *memos*. Pronounce *memo* '**mem**-mo' or '**mee**-mo'.

**memory** The part of a computer used for storing data and programs is called its *memory*. The size of a computer's memory is measured in kilobytes or megabytes and determines how much information can be dealt with at any one time.

See also **byte**; **random-access memory**; **read-only memory**.

**mendacity/mendicity** *Mendacity* is lying or deception:

> Mendacity is essential in a spy.

The less common word *mendicity* means begging as a way of life:

> Mendicity is the only source of income for many people in India.

A *mendicant* is a beggar.

**menu** In computer terminology a *menu* is a list of options displayed on a computer screen for the user to select from. This may be done by striking an appropriate key (perhaps the first letter of the option selected), or by moving the cursor to the chosen option. The first menu selection may lead to the display of another menu, or sub-menu. Some programs have many levels of menus.

**mere** See **meagre/mere**.

**meretricious/meritorious** Note the spelling of the adjective *meretricious* (not 'merit-'), meaning gaudily attractive or insincere: *meretricious clothing*; *meretricious comments*. *Meritorious* means having merit or deserving praise: *meritorious conduct*.

**merino** Plural *merinos*.

**meritorious** See **meretricious/meritorious**.

**Messiah/messiah** The noun *Messiah* and its adjective *Messianic* (pronounced 'messee-**ann**ik') have an initial capital when used in reference to the expected deliverer of the Jews or to Jesus Christ, but not otherwise: thus *the messiah of the common people* and *messianic reforms*. To arm yourself against know-alls, note that Handel's oratorio is called *Messiah*, not 'The Messiah'.

**Messrs** Plural of *Mr* (actually an abbreviation of the French *Messieurs*).

**metal/mettle** A *metal* is a substance such as gold, silver or copper. *Mettle* means spirit or courage:

> Grandma showed her mettle in the floods when she rowed to safety.

Be sure to use the right word in the expression *on your mettle* (not 'metal').

**metamorphosis** The plural is *metamorphoses*. *Metamorphosis* is a total change of form: caterpillar to moth; pumpkin to glass coach. The emphasis falls on the syllable *-mor-*.

**metaphor** A *metaphor* is a word or phrase that enlivens meaning through imagery: *a close shave*; *the naked truth*; *smelling a rat*. The literal phrase *trying very hard* could be replaced by the metaphor *aiming high*, with its image of projectiles and targets. This kind of metaphor is so well established in the language as to have become an *idiom* – a natural way of expressing something. A metaphor that conveys a somewhat similar meaning in an exaggerated way is *hitching your wagon to a star*, an expression so vigorous that it has become a cliché through overuse.

A *metaphor* differs from a *simile* in that it merely implies meaning through imagery, while a simile uses *like* or *as* to direct attention to meaning through imagery: *hope rising like an arrow*.

Shakespeare was a master of these figures of speech: 'Sleep that knits up the ravelled sleave of care'; 'The slings and arrows of outrageous fortune'; 'It seems she hangs upon the cheek of night/Like a rich jewel in an Ethiop's ear'.

Pitfalls to watch for are the *inappropriate metaphor*: *The town planners called for a complete breakdown of all traffic using the street*; and the *mixed metaphor*, which arises from the uncritical use of ready-made comparisons in such a way that they clash, often ludicrously: *The treasurer is leading the economy up the garden path with his head in the sand*. Mixed metaphors may, of course, be intentionally humorous.

See also **allegory**; **analogy/analogous**; **clichés**; **colloquialisms**; **idiom**; **simile**; **slang**.

**meteorology/metrology** *Meteorology* is the study of weather; *metrology* is the science of weights and measures.

**meter/metre** A *meter* is a measuring device: *water meter*; *barometer*. The basic metric unit of length is a *metre*: *100 centimetres equal 1 metre*; *1000 metres equal 1 kilometre*. *Metre* is also the term for the arrangement of rhythm in verse; confusingly, this becomes *-meter* in words that describe the number of stresses in a line: there are five in a *pentameter*. Note that in US English the spelling *meter* is used for all senses of the word.

See also **weights and measures**.

**methodology** *Methodology* is the science of method – that is, the rules and procedures for analysis and evaluation used in various disciplines. Do not use this word when you simply mean method.

**metre** See **meter/metre**.

**metric system** In Australia this international system of measurements began to be phased in from the late 1960s to replace the *imperial system* inherited from Britain. Metric measures include metres (length), grams (weight), litres (capacity) and Celsius (temperature).
See also **imperial system; SI; weights and measures.**

**metrology** See **meteorology/metrology**.

**mettle** See **metal/mettle**.

**mfg** manufacturing.

**MFP** This is an abbreviation of *multifunction polis*. The technologically avant-garde kind of metropolis that has been dubbed a *multifunction polis* is regarded by some as an Orwellian fantasy, by others as a valid concept and potentially invaluable asset for countries like Australia.

**mfr** manufacture; manufacturer.

**Mgr** Monsignor.
See also **ranks, titles, honours and awards**.

**mgr** manager.

**MHA** Member of the House of Assembly (the lower house in the parliaments of South Australia and Tasmania).
See also **MHR; MLA; MLC; MP; ranks, titles, honours and awards**.

**MHR** Member of the House of Representatives (the lower house in the federal parliament).
See also **MHA; MLA; MLC; MP; ranks, titles, honours and awards**.

**MHz** See **megahertz**.

**MI5** This abbreviation for *Military Intelligence, section five*, is no longer an official designation but remains the popular one for the British Government's counter-intelligence agency.

**MI6** This abbreviation for *Military Intelligence, section six*, is no longer an official designation but remains the popular one for the British Government's intelligence and espionage agency.

**MIA** Murrumbidgee Irrigation Area.

**micro-** See **macro-/micro-**.

**microcomputer** Computers using a single-chip microprocessor as their central processing unit are called *microcomputers*. The first of the microcomputers were released in the late 1970s. At the end of 1981 IBM released its Personal Computer, a name the firm applied to a range of microcomputers. That name, usually abbreviated to PC, has come to mean any IBM or compatible computer, but is used less commonly for Apple Macintosh computers.

See also **central processing unit**.

**Micronesia** See **Melanesia/Micronesia/Polynesia**.

**midday** Also *midnight*, *midweek*, *midyear*, *midsummer* and *midwinter*; but *mid-autumn* and *mid-spring* (and also *mid-January* and so on).

See also **noon**; **time of day**.

**middle** See **centre/middle**.

**Middle East** See **Far East/Middle East/Near East**.

**MIDN** Midshipman (male or female).

**mien** This noun means demeanour or bearing, usually of a person: *a cheerful mien in spite of his problems*. It is pronounced 'meen'.

**might** See **may/might**.

**migraine** Pronounce this word '**my**-grane' or '**mee**-grane'.

**migrant** See **emigrant/immigrant/migrant**.

**milage/mileage** Either spelling, with or without the *-e* of *mile*, is acceptable, but *mileage* is preferred.

**milieu** The plural is *milieus* or *milieux*. This noun means an environment or setting: *a literary milieu congenial to writing*. Though a French word, it is printed in roman, not italic, type. Pronounce it 'meel-**yer**'.

**military units, numbering of** Numerals have mostly been used for the ordinal numbers of military units, except for the very largest of them – like the last two items in this list of army examples:

1st Battalion (Australian Imperial Force, World War I)
2/1st Battalion (Australian Imperial Force, World War II)
First Battalion = 1RAR = Royal Australian Regiment (Vietnam War)

1st Field Ambulance
2/2nd Field Regiment
106th Royal Horse Artillery
4th Brigade
6th Division
I Australian Corps
Second Australian Imperial Force
Eighth Army

Here are some examples of air force numbering:

No. 86 Squadron No. 72 Wing

Here are some examples of naval numbering:

7th Destroyer Flotilla 3rd Cruiser Squadron 1st Battle Squadron

**militate/mitigate** These two verbs have completely different meanings. To *militate* is to have a strong influence – usually adverse:

Political associations may militate against judicial appointments.

*Mitigate* means to reduce or moderate the severity of something:

Daily visits by neighbours mitigated the loneliness while she was ill.

Remember that *militate* is usually followed by *against*, but *mitigate* never is.

**millenary/millinery** *Millenary* is an adjective and noun pertaining to a thousand, particularly a thousand years. *Millinery* is made by a *milliner*; it is the collective noun for women's hats.

See also **millennium**.

**millennium** Note the *-ll-* and *-nn-*; the plural is *millenniums* or *millennia*. A *millennium* is a period of a thousand years. Note the spelling of other members of its word family: *millennial* with *-nn-*, and *millenarian* and *millenary* with *-n-*.

See also **centuries; millenary/millinery**.

**millinery** See **millenary/millinery**.

**MIM** Mount Isa Mines Holdings Limited.

**mimic/mimicked/mimicking** Note the *-c* in the first and the *-ck-* in the other two. A related noun is *mimicry*.

**mini-/maxi-** Popularised by the Morris Mini Minor car in 1959, the prefix *mini-* has become overused as a device for indicating that something is small, interim or unimportant: *mini-skirt*, *mini-budget*, *mini-war*. Its opposite, predictably, is *maxi-*.

**minimal/minimum/minimise** The adjectives *minimal* and *minimum* mean the same thing – the smallest amount possible:

The waiter gave us minimal [*or* minimum] service.

They do not simply mean very little:

Carlos spent very little [*not* a minimal amount of] money.

*Minimum* is also a noun (plural *minimums* or *minima*). Note that the term *absolute minimum* is a tautology.

The verb *minimise* means to reduce to the smallest amount possible:

If we minimise the ticket price we shall have to increase the parking fee.

It does not simply mean reduce :

Even if we reduce [*not* minimise] the ticket price we shall still make a clear profit.

See also **maximal/maximum/maximise**.

**minority** See **majority/minority**.

**minus** Except in mathematical contexts, *minus* is better suited to colloquial than formal uses:

The dog rushed in minus its leash.

*but* Any dog without a registration tag may be impounded.

The noun *minus* means disadvantage:

Long hours are often among the minuses of self-employment.

See also **plus**.

**minuscule** This adjective, meaning tiny, is often misspelt. To avoid the most common error, 'miniscule', remember that something *minuscule* is *minute* in size. The word is pronounced '**minn**a-skewl'.

**miraculous** Genuinely *miraculous* events are exceedingly rare, except in newspapers. There are dozens of more appropriate words to choose from: *unaccountable*, *astonishing*, *extraordinary*, *lucky*, *spectacular* or *uncanny*, for instance.

**mis-** The prefix *mis-*, which indicates that something is mistaken or lacking, is usually attached without a hyphen to the word involved: *misunderstand*, *miscalculate*, *mislead*, *misprint*. Note the resulting *-ss-* when the main word begins with *s*: *misspell*, *misspend*.

**miscellaneous** Note the spelling.

**mischievous** Note the spelling. It is pronounced '**miss**-chiff's', not 'miss-**chee**-vee-us'.

**misinformation** See **disinformation/misinformation**.

**misquotation** In everyday speech and writing there is little wrong with expressions such as 'gilding the lily', 'power corrupts' and 'the best-laid plans', except that they are clichés. The fact that they are misquotations is relatively unimportant because they have a certain liveliness in spite of being overused, and their meaning is clear.

Sometimes exact quotation is distinctly undesirable in such informal contexts. 'To paint the lily' is what Shakespeare wrote, but this is not common knowledge and the exact words may actually hinder communication. Moreover some degree of inexactness is acceptable even in formal writing: *As Lord Acton said, power corrupts*; *As Robbie Burns reminds us, the best-laid plans of mice and men oft go astray*. The misquotation in the first sentence may be regarded as a summary, in the second as a paraphrase.

Inexactness becomes unacceptable when the misquotation is presented as a quotation: *As Lord Acton said, 'Power corrupts'*. Exact writing demands exact quotation; scholarly writing usually demands also the source of the quotation: *As Lord Acton said, 'Power tends to corrupt and absolute power corrupts absolutely' (letter to Bishop Mandell Creighton, 3 April 1887)*; *As Robbie Burns reminds us, 'The best laid schemes o' mice an' men/Gang aft a-gley' ('To a Mouse', 1785)*.

See also **quotation marks/inverted commas**; **quotations**; ***sic***.

**Miss** Plural *Misses*: *the Misses Anderson*.

See also **Ms**.

**missal/missile** A *missal* is the book of prayers and ritual words according to which mass is celebrated in the Catholic Church. Pronounce the word '**miss**'l'. A *missile* is an object or weapon that can be hurled or impelled. The second syllable is pronounced to rhyme with *I'll*.

**misspelled/misspelt** Either spelling is acceptable, but *misspelt* is recommended. Note the *-ss-*.

**mistakable/mistakeable** Either spelling, with or without the *-e* of *mistake*, is acceptable.

**mistrust** See **distrust/mistrust**.

**misuse** See **abuse/misuse**.

**MIT** Massachusetts Institute of Technology.

**mitigate** See **militate/mitigate**.

**MLA** Member of the Legislative Assembly (the lower house in the parliaments of New South Wales, Victoria, Queensland, Western Australia, the Australian Capital Territory and the Northern Territory).

See also **MHA**; **MHR**; **MLC**; **MP**; **ranks, titles, honours and awards**.

**MLC** This is the abbreviation for *Member of the Legislative Council* – the upper house in the parliaments of the Australian Capital Territory, the Northern Territory, and of all States except Queensland, which has no upper house.

*MLC* is also the abbreviation for *Methodist Ladies' College* and *MLC Life Limited* (formerly The Mutual Life and Citizen's Assurance Co. Ltd).

See also **MHA**; **MHR**; **MLA**; **MP**; **ranks, titles, honours and awards**.

**Mlle** Mademoiselle.

**Mme** Madame.

See also **madam/madame**.

**Moama, NSW** Compare with *Moana*, SA.

**moat/mote** A *moat* is a water-filled trench surrounding a structure, usually a fortification, town or castle. A *mote* is a speck, particularly of dust.

**moccasin** Note the *-cc-* and single *s*.

**model/modelled/modelling** Note the single *l* in the first and the *-ll-* in the others.

**modem** A *modem* is a device that enables information from computers to be transmitted along telephone lines. The word is an acronym from **mo**dulator (a device that converts digital information into a form that can be transmitted) and **dem**odulator (a device that converts back to digital form). Two modems are needed for communication between computers, one at each end, to perform the appropriate conversion. Modem transmit and receive software is also needed.

***modus operandi/modus vivendi*** These two Latin phrases (usually italicised) are sometimes confused. *Modus operandi* means a way of operating or working:

> The company's *modus operandi* is explained in this handbook.

*Modus vivendi* literally means a way of living, but is used in English to mean a temporary agreement between conflicting parties:

> The hasty *modus vivendi* satisfied neither the bank nor its customers.

*Modus vivendi* is often misused as a synonym for *reason*:

> My reason [not *modus vivendi*] for this action is personal.

These phrases are best reserved for formal contexts and ones in which they will be readily understood.

**Mohammed** See **Islam/Muhammad/Muslim**.

**molten** See **melted/molten**.

**momentary/momentous** *Momentary* means very brief:

> He had a momentary vision of wealth before realising he'd misread the lottery numbers.

*Momentous* means of great importance:

> Momentous events in Russia have changed the course of history.

**monetarism** According to the theory of *monetarism*, changes in a nation's money supply affect that nation's economy. For example, monetarists believe that rapid growth in the money supply can cause inflation and they therefore advocate a steady reduction in money growth to beat inflation.

**money** The plural is *moneys* or *monies*: *various moneys [*or *monies] allocated.*

**Mongolism** See **Down syndrome**.

**mongoose** Plural *mongooses* (not 'mongeese').

**monitor** In computer parlance a *monitor*, also called a *visual display unit* (or *VDU*), is a television-like screen for displaying computer data. Monitors vary in size and resolution, and are available in monochrome (a single colour against a background) or colour. Some monitors can be tilted or rotated to enable them to be used either landscape (wide) or portrait (tall).

See also **dots per inch**; **landscape/portrait**.

**monogram/monograph** A *monogram* is a decorative device consisting of two or more interlaced letters printed on stationery or embroidered on cloth. A *monograph* is a learned work on a single subject.

**monologue/soliloquy** A *monologue* is a long speech, by means of which one person may sometimes monopolise the conversation. It may be a whole dramatic performance, in which only the one actor speaks. A *soliloquy* is a monologue undertaken regardless of listeners. When a soliloquy occurs in a play, the character's thoughts and feelings are conveyed directly to the audience without regard for other events on stage. This was a dramatic device important to the Elizabethan and Jacobean playwrights. A well-known example is the soliloquy by Jacques in Act II of *As You Like It*, commencing 'All the world's a stage'. The word should not be used to describe just any formal speech or monologue.

**mood** The *mood* of a verb in English may be *indicative*, *subjunctive* or *imperative*. When a verb is in the *indicative* mood it has a straightforward, positive tone, even when it is a question (the *interrogative* is not regarded as a mood):

> He *is putting* the kettle on. *Has* he *put* the kettle on?

A verb in the *subjunctive* mood has a more tentative sound, and it expresses possibility, conditional circumstances or desirability rather than fact. Note the abnormal form of the verbs in the following examples:

They will suggest that she stay [*not* stays] in town.

If I were [*not* was] you I would try to forget the incident.

We wished he were [*not* was] already home.

The *imperative* mood indicates commands:

*Put* the kettle on! *Don't beat* around the bush!

See also **subjunctive mood.**

**Moorland, NSW** Compare with *Moorlands*, SA; *Moreland*, Vic.

**moot** The adjective *moot* means subject to argument or discussion, and is used mainly in the phrase *a moot point*, meaning a point to be debated. The verb *to moot* means to put forward for debate or discussion:

It was mooted that the school should hold a fete to raise money.

**morale/moral/morals** The noun *morale* means a person's level of enthusiasm and confidence:

Friendly letters raised the old man's morale after his telephone was disconnected.

The noun *moral* means a lesson or truth. The adjective *moral* and the noun *morals* both relate to the principles of right and wrong:

The moral of the play was the sanctity of life.

Laws have less bearing on behaviour than one's moral values.

Her morals were worrying even though her genius was beyond question.

**more** Ambiguity is possible when *more* is used before an adjective:

We have more exciting ideas for you to consider.

Rephrase according to which meaning is intended: other exciting ideas *or* ideas that are more exciting.

Avoid adding *more* to adjectives that are already in the comparative: *better* not *more better*; *faster* not *more faster*; *happier* not *more happier*.

When comparing only two items, use *more* not *most*:

I'm not sure whether Tim or Michael is the more easily led.

The phrase *more or less* can mean *approximately* or *either more or less*. Do not allow it to be ambiguous:

Ask her whether the canteen food is reasonably satisfactory.

*or* Ask her whether the canteen food is more satisfactory or less this week.

*rather than*

Ask her whether the canteen food is more or less satisfactory this week.

Note that the phrase *more than one* is always followed by a singular verb:

More than one bus has left.

See also **comparative and superlative**; **most**; **prefer**.

**moreover** See **nevertheless/nonetheless**.

**mores** This is the plural form of a Latin noun whose singular is not used in English. It means the customs that encapsulate the philosophy of a society, group or period: *the mores of the 1960s*. Use the word only in company or contexts where it will be readily understood. Pronounce it '**mor**-aze'.

**moribund** On the point of death is the meaning of this adjective. It is not merely a synonym for *dormant*. A *moribund* company is on its way out, not just inactive.

**mortgage** Because *mortgage* is pronounced '**mor**-gij' it is in danger of being spelt without the *t*. When a *mortgage* is arranged, the *mortgagee* is the lender of the money; a *mortgagor* (or *mortgager*) is the borrower.

**Moslem** See **Islam/Muhammad/Muslim**.

**Mosman, NSW** Compare with *Mossman*, Qld.

**mosquito** Plural *mosquitoes* or *mosquitos*.

**most** Ambiguity is possible when *most* is used before an adjective:

> This garden has the most beautiful flowers in the street.

Rephrase according to which meaning is intended: the greatest number of lovely flowers *or* the loveliest flowers.

Avoid adding *most* to adjectives that are already in the superlative: *speediest* not *most speediest*; *unkindest* not (in spite of Shakespeare's 'most unkindest cut') *most unkindest*; *cleverest* not *most cleverest*.

When comparing more than two items, use *most* not *more*:

> I'm not sure whether Tim, Michael or Martin is the most easily led.

In expressions such as *most obliged I'm sure*, *most* can only mean very. Be careful to avoid ambiguity, however, in other constructions:

> He feels most uncomfortable in low chairs.

Rephrase according to which meaning is intended: very uncomfortable *or* more uncomfortable in low chairs than in any other kind.

The informal US use of *most* to mean almost (*most anyone is welcome*) is not acceptable in Australian English.

See also **comparative and superlative**; **more**; **mostly**; **prefer**.

**mostly** Do not confuse *mostly* and *most*:

> This designer mostly [usually] works from home.
>
> This designer enjoys working from home most of all [rather than in an office].

See also **most**.

**mote** See **moat/mote**.

**Mother's Day** See **Father's Day/Mother's Day**.

**mothers-in-law** Note that the first word indicates the plural.
See also **compound nouns, plurals of**.

**motif/motive** A *motif* (occasionally spelt *motive*) is a recurring theme, subject or design in music, literature or art:

Loneliness is a motif in Henry Lawson's stories.

The most common meaning of *motive* is a reason for doing something, or a goal:

Anna's motive in leaving home was to gain independence.

**motivation** *Motivation* means an incentive or motive; the word is overworked as a substitute for others such as *reason*, *motive*, *ideal* or *belief* – and misused too:

The promised bonus gave the builders the motivation to finish the flats before Anzac Day.

*but* His reason [*not* motivation] for going abroad was to seek foreign investment.

Plain English often supplies substitutes for *motivation* and its forms:

What made her say that? *rather than* What motivated her response?

**motive** See **motif/motive**.

**motto** Plural *mottoes* or *mottos*.

**mould** Do not use the US spelling *mold*.

**Mount Kosciusko** See **Kosciusko**.

**mouse** When it is not a small rodent, a *mouse* is a device moved around with the hand on a flat surface beside a computer keyboard: its control buttons direct cursor movements and the selection of computer functions. Other pointing devices include trackballs, touch screens and light pens.
See also **cursor; trackball**.

**moustache** This spelling is recommended.

**movable/moveable** Either spelling, with or without the *-e* of *move*, is acceptable for general use; *moveable* is preferred in legal contexts.

**mowed/mown** Either word is acceptable as the past participle of the verb *to mow*: *We have mowed [*or *mown] the paddock*. The form of the past participle preferred for adjectival use is *mown*: *a paddock mown but not raked*. The past tense is always *mowed*: *We mowed the paddock*.

**MP** This is the abbreviation for *Member of Parliament*. It is permissible to put *MP* (instead of *MHA*, *MHR* or *MLA*) after the name of a member of any Australian lower house of parliament. Members of State upper houses have *MLC* after their names, while members of the upper house in the federal parliament, the Senate, are simply designated *Senator* ____ .

*MP* is also the abbreviation for *Military Police*.

See also **MHA**; **MHR**; **MLA**; **MLC**; **ranks, titles, honours and awards**.

**mp** melting point.

**MRA** Moral Re-Armament.

**Mrs** This is the abbreviation of *Mistress*, used as a title; the plural is *Mesdames* (*Mesdames Roberts and Kelly*).

See also **madam/madame**; **Ms**.

**MS** multiple sclerosis.

**Ms** This is a title that makes no distinction between the married and unmarried state of women: *Ms* is a contraction of both *Mrs* and *Miss*. Many women nevertheless prefer the traditional titles. In letter-writing there can be no firm rule about which form to use. If a woman's preference is known, that is the deciding factor; if her wishes cannot be ascertained it may be safer to use no title at all and address the woman by her full name.

Pronounce the word 'miz'.

See also **discriminatory language**; **letters, formal**; **madam/madame**.

**MS./MSS.** *MS*. is an abbreviation of the Latin *manu scriptum* (manuscript); *MSS*. is the plural form.

**MS-DOS** This is an abbreviation for *Microsoft Disk Operating System*, an industry-standard operating system for IBM and compatible computers since the early 1980s.

**MSG** monosodium glutamate; also *msg*.

**MTV** modified television version; music television.

**much less/much more** The idiomatic phrase *much less* is shorthand for *and certainly not*. Use it when the first part of the sentence is expressed negatively:

> It is not easy to hold this pony, much less to shoe it.

*Much more* is equivalent to *and certainly*, and it is the correct phrase when the first part of the sentence is expressed positively:

> It is difficult to hold this pony, much more to shoe it.

The same guidelines apply to *still less* (treat like *much less*) and *still more* (treat like *much more*).

**mucous/mucus** A *mucous* membrane (a lubricating membrane in the body) secretes *mucus*.

**Muhammad** See **Islam/Muhammad/Muslim**.

**multi-** This prefix means many. While it has provided good service in such words as *multinational*, *multilingual* and *multicoloured*, it is now overworked in the construction of numerous unnecessary, ugly new words: a *multi-talented performer*, a *multi-role fighter plane* and a *multi-task* or *multi-tasking computer program*. *Multi-* is sometimes joined to its root word by a hyphen, but most of the compounds are unhyphenated and closed up.

**multifunction polis** See **MFP**.

**Murri** See **Aborigine/Aboriginal**.

**Muslim** See **Islam/Muhammad/Muslim**.

**must** The use of *must* as a noun meaning something necessary or vital (*Evening wear is a must on this cruise*) is colloquial and therefore inappropriate for formal writing.

**mutual** See **common/mutual/reciprocal**.

**Myrtle Bank, SA and Tas.** Compare with *Myrtlebank*, Vic.

**myself** Use *I* or *me* rather than *myself* wherever possible:

I patted myself on the back.

*but* Jill and I [*not* myself] wrote the book.

*or* The book was written by Jill and me [*not* myself].

See also **I/me; pronouns; self**.

**mythical/mythological** The primary meaning of *mythical* is pertaining to myth, but it can also mean fictitious: *a mythical dragon*; *mythical excuses for absence*. *Mythological* strictly means pertaining to myth or to mythology: *the mythological Orpheus and Euridice*. Thus, while you might refer to a dragon as either *mythical* or *mythological*, excuses can only be *mythical*.

See also **legend/myth**.

**myxomatosis** Note the spelling.

# Nn

**n.** note.

**n/a** not applicable; not available.

**nadir/zenith** These astronomical terms are also used figuratively. *Nadir* means the lowest point, *zenith* the highest:

> Once your luck has reached its nadir, things can only get better.
> The zenith of the physicist's career was his winning of the Nobel Prize.

Pronounce *nadir* '**nay**-deer'.

**naïf/naïve/naive** The French forms *naïf* (masculine) and *naïve* (feminine) are acceptable for this adjective, which means unsophisticated and artless, but *naive* (without the accent) is recommended. Pronounce it 'nie-**eev**' or 'nay-**eev**'.

The recommended form of the associated noun is *naivety*, but *naiveté* and *naïveté* are also acceptable. All forms of these words are printed in roman, not italic, type.

**naked/nude** The adjective *naked* has a wide range of idiomatic applications: unadorned truth may be called the *naked truth*, an unprotected flame a *naked flame*, and an unclothed body a *naked body*. *Nude* (noun and adjective) applies only to an unclothed person, and is the usual choice where art or indecency is involved: *bathing in the nude*; *nude modelling*; *running nude onto the football ground*.

**named after** Not *named for* (an Americanism).

**naphthalene** Note the *-phth-*. The name of this aromatic hydrocarbon, used in mothballs, is pronounced '**naf**tha-leen'.

**narcissus** Plural *narcissuses* or *narcissi* (members of the genus *Narcissus*, such as daffodils).

**Narembeen, WA** Compare with *Naremburn*, NSW.

**NASA** National Aeronautics and Space Administration (US).

**NATO** North Atlantic Treaty Organization; also *Nato*.

**naturalist/naturist** A *naturalist* is someone who studies natural history, particularly botany or zoology, or is an adherent of the literary, aesthetic or philosophical movement called *naturalism*. A *naturist* is a nudist, or someone who worships nature.

**nature** The word *nature* is often part of several unnecessarily wordy phrases, and should be dispensed with there:

> Their actions were generous [*rather than* of a generous nature].
> Gifts like that [*rather than* of that nature] deserve special mention.
> The gift was a kind of [*rather than* in the nature of a] bribe.

**naturist** See **naturalist/naturist**.

**naught/nought** *Naught* means nothing: *His aspirations came to naught*. *Nought* is the numerical digit 0: *the game of noughts and crosses*. In US English the spelling *nought* is used for both meanings.

See also **zero**.

**nauseated/nauseous/nauseating** *Nauseated* means experiencing disgust or feeling sick (that is, experiencing nausea). *Nauseous* and *nauseating* mean the same thing, causing disgust or nausea; *nauseous* has also come to mean experiencing nausea, but this usage is not universally accepted.

**nautical miles** See **knots/nautical miles**.

**naval/navel** Note the spelling of these words. The adjective *naval* means pertaining to the navy. The *navel* is an abdominal depression containing the scar of the umbilical cord; a *navel orange* has a navel-like pit at its base.

**Nazi** A *Nazi* is a member of the National Socialist German Workers' Party, which came to power under Adolf Hitler. When the word describes people or views sympathetic with but not formally linked with the Party, it sometimes has a lower-case initial. Since this word could be regarded as defamatory, be careful how you use it.

**NB** note well (Latin: *nota bene*).

**NBC** National Broadcasting Company (US).

**NBFI** non-bank financial institution.

**nbg** no bloody good.

**NCA** National Crime Authority.

**NCB** no-claim bonus.

**NCDC** This is the abbreviation for *National Capital Development Commission*, the planning body for Canberra; it has been superseded by the National Capital Planning Authority (NCPA).

**NCO** non-commissioned officer.

**NCPA** National Capital Planning Authority.
See also **NCDC**.

**NCWA** National Council of Women of Australia.

**nearby/near by** *Nearby* is the invariable form of the adjective: *a nearby township*. It is also the preferred form of the adverb: *a woman living nearby*.

**Near East/Near North** See **Far East/Middle East/Near East**; **South-East Asia**.

**NEB** New English Bible.

**nee** The French word for born (*née*), most often seen without its accent and unitalicised, is used to indicate the maiden name of a woman: *Penelope Jones nee Brown*. It is pronounced 'nay'.

**need** To *need* is to require or be obliged:

He needs a rest. He needs to go to bed.

In a question, or a sentence that is in the negative (or has negative implications), the form of the verb may be shortened to *need* in all combinations, with the *to* of the following infinitive dropped:

Does he need to go to bed? *or* Need he go to bed?
He does not need to go to bed. *or* He need not go to bed.
He needs to go to bed only if he is tired. *or* He need only go to bed if tired.

**needless to say** This is a popular filler. It is probably fair to say that it is usually needless to say *needless to say*.

**negative/positive** The word *negative* is overworked as a colloquial adjective meaning hostile or pessimistic. Try some alternatives:

The tennis player's angry [*rather than* negative] reactions to the umpire's decision upset his opponent.

Don't be pessimistic [*rather than* negative] about the future.

The adjective *positive* is acceptable in formal as well as colloquial usage; its meanings include confident and definite:

A more positive attitude will bring promotion.

There was positive improvement in her spelling; her aunt did not just imagine it.

**negative gearing** This is the term given to a situation in which the cost of a loan is not covered by the returns from its use – for example, when someone borrows to buy a house for investment purposes and the rent received does not cover the loan repayments and interest.

The ratio of shareholders' funds to a company's outside borrowings is called *gearing*.

**negative words** Words such as *no*, *never*, *not*, *nobody* and *nothing* express the opposite of, or contradict, something. *Never* and *not*, in particular, must be positioned carefully in a sentence. Different meanings are conveyed by the following:

| | |
|---|---|
| Joe never said he was a builder. | Joe said he was never a builder. |
| Joe did not say he was a builder. | Joe did say he was not a builder. |

The negative is usually placed next to the verb or within the phrase being contradicted, but it is idiomatic to attach it to verbs such as *think*, *suppose*, *believe*, *imagine* and *expect*, even when the negation really belongs somewhere else. Thus it is more natural to write:

I don't suppose they have left yet.

*than* I suppose they haven't left yet.

Negative words can complicate sentences unnecessarily; be more direct if possible:

Notify the ranger before you begin cross-country skiing.

*rather than*

Do not begin cross-country skiing without first notifying the ranger.

Even the great Fowler can be guilty of tangled negatives: 'It is not equally immaterial whether the parenthesis is relevant or not to its sentence . . .'

See also **double negative**; **hardly**; **neither**; **nor**; **not**.

**neglectful/negligent** Both *neglectful* and *negligent* mean failing to provide proper care and attention:

His scuffed shoes suggested that he was neglectful of appearances.

Patrice is fussy about punctuality but negligent with her correspondence.

*Negligent* can mean merely nonchalant, but often has more serious implications than *neglectful*, especially where the failure to provide care becomes a matter for the law:

His driving is not just careless – it's positively negligent.

**negro** The plural is *negroes*. Use the term very carefully. Its association with slavery has caused it to be widely discarded in the US. Many Afro-Americans and British people of Afro-Caribbean origin prefer the name *black* (or *Black*). Avoid *negress* completely; *black woman* may be the best substitute.

See also **black**; **discriminatory language**.

**neither** *Neither* means *not either* and is generally used in reference to one of two possibilities:

Neither my grandmother nor my grandfather could attend the wedding.

Use *none* when dealing with more than two possibilities:

None of the more elderly relatives could attend the wedding.

Used as an adjective or a pronoun, *neither* takes a singular verb:

Neither [adjective] bridesmaid is carrying a posy.

Neither [pronoun] of the bridesmaids is carrying a posy.

In the *neither . . . nor* construction, when both subjects are singular use a singular verb:

Neither the bride nor the groom is here.

When both subjects are plural, use a plural verb:

Neither the bridesmaids nor the pageboys are ready.

When there is a combination of singular and plural subjects, the verb agrees with the subject nearest to it:

Neither the guests nor I am surprised.

The same principle applies when single subjects have different verb-forms:

Neither you nor he is ready.

Pronounce the first syllable of *neither* to rhyme with *fly* or *flee*.

See also **either**; **negative words**; **none**; **nor**.

**nemesis** The word is derived from the name of the goddess of vengeance, *Nemesis*. Your *nemesis* is someone or something whose function is to inflict punishment on you; if a person, he or she is not simply an enemy, a rival, or someone you dislike.

**neo-** New, modern or revived is the meaning of this prefix: *neo-realism*, *neoclassical*, *neocolonialism*.

**neologisms/nonce words** *Neologisms* are new words such as *interface* and *input*, or old words put to new uses, in the way that the nouns *trial* and *source* have become verbs. Such words may be created in numerous ways: by blending existing words (*smoke* and *fog* became *smog*; Lewis Carroll invented *chortle* by combining *snort* and *chuckle*); forming compounds (*own-your-own* flat); using parts of foreign words (the *vit-* in *vitamin* comes from the Latin *vita*, life); and by adding prefixes or suffixes to existing words (*preschool*, *sexism*). Acronyms (*Anzac, radar*) and trade names (often turned into verbs: *to hoover*; *to xerox*) are a rich source of neologisms. If such words meet a need and survive the test of time, they become part of the language. Most of the examples just cited are in fact no longer neologisms.

Many neologisms today are of US origin, deriving from the jargon of technology, business or defence. The Pentagon, US business schools, various US administrations and the computer industry have provided hundreds of neologisms.

*Nonce words* are invented for a single occasion (that is, *for the nonce*), and do not normally win wider currency. Poets and comedians often make use of them, and they are common in household slang and vulgarisms:

> Chocolate is full of *obesogens*.
>
> He needs a good kick in the *barse* to get him going.

See also **colloquialisms; idiom; slang.**

**-ness** Beware of what the cartoonist Arthur Horner calls the Ness Monster: the tendency to turn adjectives into nouns indiscriminately by adding the suffix *-ness*. This is often done in ignorance of perfectly good existing nouns: 'rigidness' for *rigidity*, 'ineptness' for *ineptitude*, 'contriteness' for *contrition*. Of course there are numerous legitimate nouns that end in *ness*: *gentleness*, *greatness* and *friendliness*, for example.

**net/nett** Either spelling is acceptable for this adjective, which means remaining after deductions, but *net* is preferred.

**the Netherlands** See **Dutch/the Netherlands/Holland.**

**nett** See **net/nett.**

**never** See **negative words; nor.**

**nevertheless/nonetheless** *Nevertheless* is always written as one word. Its synonym *nonetheless* has traditionally appeared as three words, but the single word is now generally regarded as the norm.

Do not put a comma after *nevertheless* (or *nonetheless*) unless it is one of a pair – that is, parenthetical:

> Rain delayed the concreting; nevertheless it was finished by Easter.
>
> *but* Rain delayed the concreting; it was finished, nevertheless, by Easter.

The same applies to words like *meanwhile*, *moreover* and *thus*, but see also the entry **however**.

Do not combine *but* and *nevertheless* (or *nonetheless*) because this duplicates the sense of contrast.

**New Australian** Immigrants to Australia after World War II came to be called *New Australians* in the early 1950s. The term was felt to be a friendly substitute for *refugees*, *displaced persons* and *Balts* (refugees from the Baltic states). *New Australian* gradually lost its widespread acceptance, beginning to seem somewhat patronising by the 1980s, and the term *ethnic* became predominant. It too has its problems, described under **ethnic**.

See also **discriminatory language**.

**New England** The *New England* region is an area of northern New South Wales extending roughly from the Queensland border to the Hastings and Liverpool ranges. The area covers about 27 000 square kilometres. Its chief urban centres are Armidale, Glen Innes, Inverell and Walcha.

**news agency/newsagency** A *news agency* such as Reuters or AAP gathers and transmits news. A *newsagency* is a franchise for selling newspapers, usually from a shop called a *newsagency* (run by a *newsagent*) that also retails magazines, stationery, small items of office equipment, and a limited range of books.

**New South Welshman** This is the traditional generic term for someone whose home is New South Wales.

**New Town, Tas.** Compare with *Newtown*, NSW, Qld and Vic.

**NG** New Guinea.

See also **Irian Jaya**; **Papua New Guinea**.

**NHF** National Heart Foundation.

**NHMRC** National Health and Medical Research Council.

**NHS** National Health Service (Britain).

**nice** As an adjective suggesting the meanings pleasant, agreeable or kind, *nice* is about as lifeless a word as can be found. Replace it with more accurate and interesting adjectives wherever possible. The word carries much more weight when used in its earlier sense – precise, delicate, subtle (*a nice distinction*) or proper (often negatived: *not a nice joke*). The noun *nicety* means a fine or subtle point: *a nicety of English grammar*.

**niche** This noun, meaning a shallow recess in a wall or an appropriate place for someone, may be pronounced 'nitch' or 'neesh'.

**NIDA** National Institute of Dramatic Art.

**night-time** Note the hyphen; *daytime* is one word.

**Nikkei** This is an index of 225 industrial stocks listed on the Tokyo Stock Exchange, and the most closely watched Japanese sharemarket indicator. It is equivalent to Australia's all-ordinaries index or the Dow Jones index in the United States.

See also **all-ordinaries index**; **Dow Jones index.**

**no** The plural is *noes* (votes in the negative): *ayes 31, noes 24.*

See also **negative words.**

**no.** number (Italian: *numero*); plural *nos.*

**nobody** See **no one/no-one.**

**noisome** This adjective is derived from *annoy* and therefore has nothing to do with noise. It means offensive or noxious, usually referring to a smell:

> The room was filthy and so noisome they could hardly breathe.

**non-** A prefix meaning not, *non-* provides a neutral antonym of the word to which it is attached: *non-believer*, *non-alignment*. Antonyms formed by *in-* and *un-* often express something stronger: compare a *non-professional golfer* (meaning an amateur) with an *unprofessional golfer* (meaning one who flouts the rules of behaviour or procedure). New words are continually being formed by the addition of *non-*, but a suitable existing word should be used where possible. Prefer *optional* to *non-obligatory*; *secular* to *non-religious*; *tolerant* to *non-critical.* Long-established compounds tend to dispense with the hyphen: *nonconformist*, *nonpareil*, *noncommital*; the newer ones need it, at least for the time being.

**non-breaking space** In desktop publishing a *non-breaking space* is a space inserted to prevent end-of-line breaks between words, numbers and other characters that should be kept intact. A non-breaking space would, for instance, avoid the splitting of a telephone number, a figure such as *1 000 000*, or a person's initials and surname (*A. J. Cronin*).

**nonce words** See **neologisms/nonce words.**

**nonchalant** The *ch* in this adjective meaning casual or relaxed is pronounced 'sh'.

**non-defining clause** See **clause.**

**non-defining phrase** See **phrase.**

**non-discriminatory language** See **discriminatory language**.

**none** It is a mistaken belief that the pronoun *none* must always be singular. It may be singular or plural according to the context. Consider the answers in the following examples:

> Is there any honey? No, there is none [of it].
>
> Are there any eggs? No, there are none [of them].

*None* means *not any* in both answers, yet the first must be singular and the second must be plural to make sense.

When *not one* is implied, the verb is singular:

> None of the students is a better mathematician than your sister.

When *not any* is implied, and it is a matter of number, not quantity, the verb is plural:

> None of the nurses from interstate are better qualified than local ones.

In informal contexts, and particularly in conversation, either the singular or the plural is correct for some constructions:

> None [not one] of our friends has come to see us.

*or* None [not any] of our friends have come to see us.

The second is more idiomatic, even when *not one* is implied.

See also **negative words; neither; singular or plural**.

**nonetheless** See **nevertheless/nonetheless**.

**nonflammable** See **flammable/inflammable/nonflammable**.

**non-racist language** See **discriminatory language**.

**non-restrictive clause** See **clause**.

**non-restrictive phrase** See **phrase**.

**nonsense** Do not say that something is *a nonsense*; simply say that it is *nonsense*.

**non sequitur** *Non sequitur* is Latin for *it does not follow*, but it is a noun in English. A *non sequitur* describes a conclusion that does not follow logically from a previous statement. Assumptions made on unproven grounds give rise to non sequiturs in casual conversation and argument as well as in formal debates. For instance:

> There will be major storms this year on the east coast of Australia because of the earthquakes in Japan.

A connection between storms and earthquakes has not been proved and therefore this conclusion is a non sequitur.

**non-sexist language** See **discriminatory language**.

**noon** There is usually no need to write *12 noon*; *noon* is sufficient. The same applies to *midday* and *midnight*.
See also **time of day**.

**no one/no-one** Both mean nobody. Either form is acceptable, but *no one* is recommended. *No one* is treated as singular, and it can cause problems for those trying to avoid discriminatory language.
See also **anybody/anyone**; **discriminatory language; every/everybody/ everyone; he/she; negative words**; **pronouns.**

**nor** In the *neither . . . nor* construction, *or* cannot be substituted for *nor*:

Neither you nor I like milk.

After other negatives, such as *not*, *never* and *no*, we nearly always use *or* rather than *nor* because the original negative applies to the whole sentence and therefore *nor* is unnecessary:

She did not either laugh or cry. *not* She did not either laugh nor cry.

No dogs or cats allowed. *not* No dogs nor cats allowed.

However, in longer sentences the negative often needs reinforcing, as in the following:

He did not come home for three years, nor did his brother.

The boys did not come home; nor did they go to school.

It is acceptable, and often effective, to begin an occasional sentence with *nor*.
See also **double negative**; **either**; **negative words**; **neither**; **or**.

**normal type** See **type**.

**North/north** See **compass points**.

**not** This word may cause ambiguity if it is not carefully positioned. *All the welders do not work overtime* can mean that only some of them do; or it can mean that no welder works overtime. To avoid ambiguity rewrite:

Not all the welders work overtime.
*or* Some of the welders work overtime.
*or* No welder works overtime.

See also **double negative**; **negative words**; **nor; not only . . . but also.**

**notable/noticeable** Something that is *notable* is worthy of note; it means important or distinguished when applied to people:

Robin Boyd was a notable architect.

*Noticeable* means attracting attention or obvious:

The improvement in paper quality was noticeable.

**notes** *Notes* providing information supplementary to a text are placed at the bottom of the relevant page and keyed to the text by six symbols, which are described under **reference marks**: the first note is given an asterisk, the second a dagger and so on. If more than half a dozen notes are needed on one page the symbols may be doubled for the following six, as in *******Born 1863*. It is preferable, however, to use superior figures for all the notes in this case, so that the seventh one is expressed as [7]*Born 1863*.

When the purpose of the notes is to supply references to the author's sources rather than to add snippets of information, superior figures are almost always used. These referencing notes rarely appear at the bottom of the relevant page in modern printing, but are relegated to the end of the chapter, book or article.

See also **asterisk**; **inferior characters/superior characters**; **reference marks**; **references**; **titles of publications, and literary, artistic and musical works**.

**nothing but** This expression really means *no thing except*, and the verb that follows must be singular:

Nothing but beer and sausages was provided at the barbecue.

**noticeable** See **notable/noticeable**.

**not only . . . but also** Make sure that you link grammatically similar items when you use this expression:

She is not only rich [adjective] but also generous [adjective].

*not* She is not only rich [adjective] but also shares [verb] her money.

Although the four words are generally used, *also* may sometimes be understood rather than stated:

She not only bought her nephew a new house but helped to furnish it.

**notorious** See **infamous/notorious**.

**nought** See **naught/nought**.

**nouns** A *noun* is the part of speech that names people and things:

artist Perth bathroom attitude vegetation

There are innumerable nouns of various kinds. Many fall into more than one category. Some may also function as adjectives (*fruit*; *fruit salad*), others also as verbs (*a push*; *to push*). Yet others may be noun, adjective or verb (*a house*; *a house inspection*; *to house*). Other parts of speech can function as nouns, for instance the present participles of verbs (*Eating* in *Eating gives us pleasure*); pronouns (*he*, *she*, *it*, *you* and so on); and even some adverbs (*Upwards* in *Upwards is the only way to go*).

The following are the main types of noun:

- *common nouns* (the vast majority), which begin with a lower-case letter

  box cockatoo laugh humidity toenail

- *proper nouns*, which name specific people, places and things, and begin with a capital letter

    Judith Wright    Sydney Harbour    the Taj Mahal
- *concrete nouns*, which describe tangible things such as people, objects and substances

    doctor    plate    jacket    alcohol    cheese
- *abstract nouns*, which refer to intangibles such as events, activities, states of mind, processes, times and occasions

    death    walking    pleasure    ageing    bedtime    party
- *collective nouns*, which apply to groups of people, animals or things

    family    committee    flock    cluster    convoy
- *unit nouns*, which refer to things that can be counted (you can put *a* or *an* before one of them, and they have a plural form)

    shoe(s)    emu(s)    idea(s)    birth(s)    pebble(s)
- *mass nouns*, which refer to things that are not thought of as countable (you cannot put *a* or *an* before them, and they usually have no plural form); some of them are collective nouns

    gold    sunshine    bitumen    furniture    intelligentsia

Note that some nouns can be *unit* or *mass* depending on the context:

There was a blond hair [unit noun] on his coat.

His hair [mass noun] is blond.

Nouns are often turned into verbs that many people find unacceptable. This problem is discussed under **verbs**.

See also **collective nouns**; **compound nouns, plurals of**; **nouns, plurals of**; **pronouns**; **proper nouns**.

**nouns, plurals of** The majority of nouns in English form their plurals by adding *s* to the singular:

girls    tables    suspicions    thoughts    hills    employees

There are, however, numerous exceptions to and variations on this general rule.

- For nouns ending in *y*, with a consonant preceding it, change *y* to *ies*:

    majority, majorities    ruby, rubies    family, families

    but not if it is a proper noun:

    Jim Murphy, the Murphys    Kit Carmody, the Carmodys
- For nouns ending in *y*, with a vowel preceding it, simply add *s*:

    donkey, donkeys    day, days    buoy, buoys
- For nouns ending in *s*, *ss*, *sh*, *ch*, *x* or *z*, make the ending *es* not *s*:

    callus, calluses    kiss, kisses    bush, bushes

    crutch, crutches    box, boxes    quiz, quizzes [*z* is doubled]

    but note that some nouns ending in *s* have no plural form:

    news    athletics    politics    mathematics    measles
- Nouns ending in *o* can be tricky. Some change to *oes*:

    potatoes    tomatoes    cargoes    heroes    negroes    echoes and some to *os*:

radios videos folios merinos studios ratios

and others may take either ending, although the *oes* form is traditionally preferred:

dingoes *or* dingos mosquitoes *or* mosquitos
mangoes *or* mangos volcanoes *or* volcanos

- Nouns ending in *f* or *fe* also vary in their plural endings. Some simply add *s*:

  beliefs handkerchiefs roofs proofs safes carafes

  and some change *f* or *fe* to *ves*:

  leaves thieves halves wolves knives wives

  and a few *f* words take either ending:

  hoofs *or* hooves wharfs *or* wharves

- Some nouns have the same form in the plural as in the singular:

  bison deer trout sheep fish [but *fishes* for separate species]

- Some nouns have no special plural ending because they are always used as plurals:

  police clergy poultry cattle vermin

- Some nouns have no plural ending because they never occur in the plural:

  jazz clarity haberdashery motherhood paintwork

- A few nouns retain traditional irregular plural forms:

  child, children woman, women mouse, mice foot, feet

- Many nouns of foreign origin form their plurals in the conventional way by adding *s* or *es* except in technical or scientific writing, where they retain their foreign plural:

  formula, formulas, formulae index, indexes, indices
  focus, focuses, foci antenna, antennas, antennae

- Some nouns of foreign origin retain their foreign plural form in all contexts:

  crisis, crises stratum, strata kibbutz, kibbutzim

- Some nouns of foreign origin have endings that are optional in any context:

  bureau, bureaus, bureaux plateau, plateaus, plateaux

Many troublesome plurals are listed as individual entries. Look up the required word under its singular form.

See also **apostrophe**; **collective nouns**; **compound nouns, plurals of**; **-ful**; **nouns**; **proper nouns**; **singular or plural**.

**nous** Note the spelling. From the Greek word for mind, *nous* means common sense. It rhymes with *mouse*.

***nouveau riche*** The plural of this French expression (usually italicised) is *nouveaux riches*. It literally means new rich, and carries suggestions of brashness, ostentation and lack of culture. Informally it is sometimes shortened to *nouveau*.

**NP** National Party.

**np** new paragraph.

**NRMA** National Roads and Motorists' Association (NSW).

**NSW** New South Wales.

**NT** National Trust; New Testament; Northern Territory.

**NUAUS** National Union of Australian University Students.

**nubile** There are two meanings for this adjective, both applying to girls or women: of marriageable age; and (more recently) sexually alluring. Ensure that the context clearly conveys your intention.

**nuclear** Pronounce this word '**new**-kleer' (not '**new**-kewler').

**nucleus** The plural is *nuclei* or *nucleuses*. A *nucleus* is the centre of something, and the word has specific applications in several branches of science.

**nude** See **naked/nude**.

**Nullarbor Plain** Note the spelling (not 'Nullabor'). *Nullarbor* is not an Aboriginal name: it was formed from the Latin phrase *nullus arbor*, meaning no tree.

**number** See **amount/number**.

**number agreement** See **singular or plural**.

**numbers in figures or words** Numbers may occur in any kind of text, and it is sometimes difficult to know whether to express them in figures or words. In descriptive and narrative text, numbers from one to ninety-nine tend to be written in full, with figures used for 100 and above. In order to save space, many newspapers and magazines use figures from the number 10 upwards. Whichever style you choose, apply it consistently.

As a general rule words rather than figures are used in the following situations:

- at the beginning of a sentence; if necessary, rewrite to avoid the figure
- at the end of a sentence (with the exception of sums of money, and those noted under **dates**)
- in approximations under 100

    six kilometres or so *but* 6 kilometres [exactly]

Numbers are generally expressed in words throughout legal documents.

As a general rule, and in any kind of text other than legal documents, figures rather than words should be used for precise sums of money, times, mass, measures, degrees of inclination and temperature, latitude and longitude, percentages, dates and years:

$10.50    11.15 a.m.    1630 hours    2.75 kg    8 cm    360°    22°C

latitude 36°14' south    45 per cent    6 August    44 BC    1953

As a general rule figures are preferred in technical, scientific, mathematical and statistical writing, and in any other text where there are many numbers. They are also often used in footnotes, bibliographies, references and lists in order to save space.

Where related numbers are used in a sentence, make sure the style is consistent:

Children aged from ten to twelve [*or* from 10 to 12] were chosen.

*not* Children aged from 10 to twelve were chosen.

As these last examples show, age can be expressed in either figures or words. For example, in a text comparing the ages of many people, figures would be more appropriate; if there were few references to age, expressing the numbers in words would be preferable.

Where two sets of numbers are used together, distinguish them by expressing one set in words and the other in figures:

They found that one pie in 20 and two pizzas in 50 contained contaminants.

A comma is often necessary to separate two numbers that have to be expressed as figures:

In 1992, 307 students graduated from this college.

When spans of numbers are required, use as few figures as are necessary to make the meaning clear; note especially the treatment of numbers between 10 and 19 in each hundred:

44–5    pp. 129–32    1000–03

12–13 *not* 12–3

pp. 116–17 *not* pp. 116–7

Exceptions include spans of years (at least two numbers are repeated) and street numbers (not abbreviated at all):

1922–24 *not* 1922–4

35–37 Thomas Street *not* 35–7 Thomas Street

An en rule rather than a hyphen is used to link such spans.

In numbers running into thousands, the traditional comma dividing groups of three digits has largely been replaced by a space, but where the total number of digits is only four, no space is required:

1000    10 000    100 000    1 000 000

In tabular work, however, where the figures are set out in columns, a space is included even in four-digit numbers so that the columns line up evenly:

| |
|---:|
| 1 000 |
| 10 000 |
| 100 000 |
| 1 000 000 |

The same guidelines apply to sums of money, as described under **currency**.

Millions may be expressed in figures, words or both:

14 000 000 *or* fourteen million *or* 14 million

Millions of dollars may be expressed:

$18 000 000 *or* $18 million *or* $18m

When a decimal point is used in a number lower than one, place a nought before the point:

0.75 *not* .75

Fractions and ordinals (numbers indicating sequence) follow the same rules as full numbers. Those below 100 (or 10, if that is the style chosen) should be written out in full:

three-and-a-half days  the eighth century  the forty-seventh customer

Note that in the following kind of expression the figure 47 is used rather than the hyphenated forty-seven to avoid a plethora of hyphens:

a 47-year-old carpenter

See also **between; billion; cardinal numbers/ordinal numbers; currency; dates; dashes, types of; hyphenation; roman numerals; time of day; weights and measures.**

**Nungga** See **Aborigine/Aboriginal.**

**NY/NYC** The first is the abbreviation for New York State, the second for New York City.

**Nyunga** See **Aborigine/Aboriginal.**

**NZ** New Zealand.

# Oo

**O/oh** *O* (always a capital letter) is usually confined to poetry and to invocations addressed to God, or a prophet, saint or muse:

O Lord, have mercy upon us. Hail, O Zeus!

*Oh* is the spelling of the exclamation indicating surprise, pain and so on; it is usually followed by a comma:

Oh, I don't believe you! I need you – oh, please stay!

**oasis** Plural *oases*.

**OAU** Organization of African Unity.

**obeisance** This word, meaning a gesture (often a bow) of respect, deference or reverence, is pronounced 'o-**bay**-s'nse'.

**objective/subjective** The adjective *objective* can mean uncoloured by personal opinion or feelings:

This critic hates modern drama but her job requires her to be objective about it.

Its opposite, *subjective*, means influenced by personal opinion or feelings:

His choice of violets was subjective, because he loves purple.

Do not forget that words such as *disinterested*, *unbiased*, *impartial* and *unprejudiced* are alternatives to *objective* in some contexts.

See also **case (grammar)**.

**objet d'art** The plural of this French term (unitalicised) meaning a small item of artistic interest is *objets d'art* (not 'objects').

**obligated/obliged** Both words mean constrained by conscience, necessity, law or command; they can generally be interchanged:

Diplomatic protocol obligated [*or* obliged] guests to dress formally.

When expressing gratitude, however, use *obliged* not *obligated*:

> I am much obliged to you for your help.

**oblique** See **solidus**.

**oblivious** This adjective means forgetful or unaware, though some people do not accept the second meaning:

> The change of plan was explained to Bob before he left, but he was oblivious of it.
>
> Bob was oblivious of [*or* to] the change of plan because it was made after he had left.

**obscenity** A complete analysis of the multitude of State and Federal laws relating to obscenity is outside the scope of this book. Anyone working with words needs to know, however, that the publication or distribution in Australia of obscene works is an offence that carries penalties of a fine, imprisonment, or both.

The Commonwealth and most States have boards that are empowered to classify publications and ban those they consider obscene. Anyone can refer a publication to these boards. Although the State laws differ in detail, they generally agree in requiring that, while adults may read and view what they wish, they should not be exposed to unsolicited material they might find offensive; and that unsuitable material should not be sold to minors or drawn to their attention.

The laws generally classify publications as follows: suitable for unrestricted distribution; suitable for restricted distribution; and prohibited (among which are works that portray children engaged in sexual acts). The Commonwealth has the power to prohibit the importation of blasphemous, indecent or obscene works.

Matter is regarded as obscene if it is likely to 'deprave or corrupt public morals', or puts undue emphasis on sex, violence, cruelty, horror or crime. The application of this test to publications is influenced by prevailing community standards of taste and levels of tolerance. It would be rare for a writer to be charged with obscenity today, given the general acceptance of visual obscenity. Few writers could match the graphic displays of sex and violence in readily available X-rated videos.

Nevertheless most publishers still require writers to warrant in their contracts that their works are not obscene. If writers also indemnify publishers for losses arising from a breach of this warranty, they will have to compensate the publishers for penalties or losses incurred by confiscation of works, as well as incurring penalties of their own. It is wise, therefore, for writers to take expert advice in the matter if there is the slightest chance that their work might be prosecuted for obscenity. Even an acquittal in court can be a very expensive business.

See also **contracts**; **vulgarisms/four-letter words**.

**obsequious** Note the *-qui-* in this adjective meaning servile: *apparently obsequious but secretly defiant.*

**observance/observation** The meaning of the noun *observance* centres on obedience to a rule or ritual; it can also be the rule or ritual itself:

Religious observance was not compulsory, even though it was a church school.

*Observation* essentially means the process of noticing, or something that is noticed; an *observation* can also be a comment:

Careful observation is vital, and observations must be recorded at once.

He kept making indiscreet observations in a loud voice.

**obsolescent/obsolete** Something *obsolescent* – that is, going out of use – is in the process of becoming *obsolete* – that is, outdated:

Lyn's computer was obsolescent when she bought it and is now obsolete.

**obstetrics** See **gynaecology/obstetrics**.

**obtrude** See **intrude/obtrude/protrude**.

**obverse** See **converse/inverse/obverse/reverse**.

**obviate** This verb means to eliminate (need or necessity); it usually has the sense of forestalling, and does not merely mean to reduce:

The restoration of power supplies obviated the need for candles.

*but* The brightness of the moonlight reduced [*not* obviated] the need for candles.

**OC** officer commanding.

**occur/occurred/occurring** Note the single *r* in the first and the *-rr-* in the other two. The related noun is *occurrence*. Events *occur* or *happen* by chance or accidentally; events that are planned *take place*:

The wedding will take place [*not* occur] on 5 June.

**OCDT** This is the abbreviation for *Officer Cadet* in the Australian Army; the title is abbreviated to *OFFCDT* in the Royal Australian Air Force.

**OCR** See **optical character recognition**.

**octavo** The plural is *octavos*. *Octavo* is the page size that results from folding a broadsheet to make eight leaves.

See also **paper sizes and weights**.

**octopus** Plural *octopuses*.

**oculist/ophthalmologist** Your eye specialist may be called either. Note the spelling of *ophthalmologist* (*oph-*), and pronounce the first syllable 'off', not 'op'.

See also **optician/optometrist**.

**O/D** overdrawn (account); overdraft.

**-odd** Do not omit the hyphen in combinations such as *fifty-odd people* or *twenty-odd glasses*, unless you really mean that the people and the glasses are peculiar and assorted respectively.

**odious/odorous** *Odious* means detestable or offensive:

The children's odious behaviour offended the visitor.

*Odorous* means having a smell:

The decaying compost heap was becoming odorous.

**OE** This is the abbreviation for *Old English* (also called *Anglo-Saxon*), the English language of the period ending about 1100. It was followed by Middle English.

See also **British English**; **ME**.

**oe/e** See **ae/oe/e**.

**OECD** Organization for Economic Cooperation and Development (before 1961, OEEC: Organization for European Economic Cooperation).

***OED*** *Oxford English Dictionary.*

**of** This preposition is often misused, in both conversation and writing. Some people seem to think that the 've' sound in abbreviations such as *could've* and *would've* is really the word *of*, and they therefore write and say 'could of' and 'would of' instead of *could have* and *would have*.

*Put* I should have gone. *or* I should've gone.
*not* I should of gone.
*Put* She would have liked it. *or* She would've liked it.
*not* She would of liked it.

A similar mistake arises from the erroneous 'had've' (the abbreviation of the incorrect *had have*) being taken to mean 'had of', which doubles the problem.

If I had woken earlier I could have had a bath.
*not* If I had of [*or* had've] woken earlier I could of had a bath.

See also **all/all of**; **both**; **have/had**; **inside/outside**; **off**; **possessives**; **with/by/of**.

**off** Note that 'off of' is an unacceptable combination:

He leapt off the train. *not* He leapt off of the train.

Do not use *off* instead of *from* with words like *borrow*, *buy* and *take*:

I borrowed $10 from [*not* off] my uncle.

**OFFCDT** This is the abbreviation for *Officer Cadet* in the Royal Australian Air Force; the title is abbreviated to *OCDT* in the Australian Army.

**offence** The US spelling *offense* is not acceptable in Australian English.

**official/officious** Be careful to use the adjective you really want. *Official* means pertaining to an office or position of authority:

The premier spoke in her official capacity, not as a mere citizen.

People who are *officious* provide or offer their services in an intrusive and self-important way:

An officious porter snatched up my baggage, though I wanted to carry it myself.

**officialese** The obscure, pedantic, verbose or pompous language often found in official letters and forms has come to be known as *officialese*, and is possibly a carryover from the 'us versus them' attitudes of officialdom in earlier times. Today many government departments have simplified their forms, official notifications and standard letters, but some bureaucrats evidently still believe that simplified means undignified. Such people would never *move to another office* but always *transfer to alternative accommodation*. Their letters and memos are full of terms such as *you will appreciate that*; *as at present advised*; *in respect of*; and *in so far as*. Sometimes, of course, officialese is used to blunt unpalatable truths:

The functional responsibilities of this position are not accorded sufficiently high priority to have the role filled within this section's staff allocation.

This just means:

The job is unnecessary.

Official forms, public notices and explanations of new regulations should be written as clearly and simply as possible. This is particularly important in a country such as Australia, where there are many people for whom English is not their native language. The classic work on officialese and its evils is *The Complete Plain Words* by Sir Ernest Gowers (revised by Sir Bruce Fraser).

See also **circumlocution**; **commercialese**; **gobbledegook**; **Latin words and phrases**; **letters, formal**; **reports and submissions**.

**officious** See **official/officious**.

**offprint** An *offprint* is a journal article or book chapter that has been reprinted separately for a special purpose – distribution at a conference, for instance.

**offset printing** This modern printing procedure enables material on a printing plate to be transferred to paper via a rubber-covered cylinder.

**often** *More often* and *most often* are the preferred comparative and superlative forms of *often*, although the ungainly *oftener* and *oftenest* are also correct. Pronounce the word '**off**'n' or '**off**-t'n'.

**oh** See **O/oh**.

**OHMS** On Her (or His) Majesty's Service.

**OK/okay** Either form is acceptable for this informal word, with *okay* preferable in narrative text.

**older/oldest** See **elder/eldest/older/oldest**.

**omelette** Prefer this to the US spelling *omelet*.

**on/upon** Used as prepositions, these words usually mean exactly the same thing, although *on* is less formal and less emphatic than *upon*:

The visitor sat on [*or* upon] a stool.

But both words are part of idiomatic phrases, such as the following, in which *on* and *upon* cannot be interchanged:

On your mark! On the whole I agree.

Upon my word! Once upon a time there was a king.

Note that *upon* becomes two words when elevation is indicated:

Ken climbed up on [*not* upon] the fence.

See also **on to/onto**.

**one** Although members of the royal family may find it convenient, the use of *one* to mean *I* is viewed as pretentious by many people. It can also sound unidiomatic and clumsy:

One doesn't want to impose oneself on one's friends.

This would be better rephrased as follows:

I don't want to impose myself on my friends.

*or* I don't want to impose on my friends.

Even when *one* means people in general rather than *I*, there are more natural-sounding alternatives:

You can only do your best. *or* People can only do their best.

*rather than*

One can only do one's best.

When *one* is the subject of a sentence, use a singular verb:

One in three people *has* influenza.

One in three of the people who have caught influenza this year *was* immunised.

But in the following sentence *who* refers to the plural *people*, not to the singular *one*:

She is one of those people who *are* always on time.

The same rule applies to words such as *which*, *that* and *whoever*.

When *one* is used to specify an actual number of people, or to represent a specific person, the pronoun that follows must be *he* or *she*, or *his* or *her*, not *one* or *one's*:

One of the men eats everything he is offered.

One of the girls is eating her lunch.

The plural of *one* is *ones* (without an apostrophe): *the lucky ones*. However, in the possessive, *one* and its compounds such as *everyone* take an apostrophe and *s*: *one's coat*; *everyone's hats*.

Sometimes *one* is superfluous:

The last day of a holiday is often (a) sad (one).

See also **oneself**; **possessives**; **pronouns**.

**one another** See **each other/one another**.

**oneself** Prefer *oneself* to *one's self*.

See also **myself**; **one**; **self**.

**ongoing** This overused adjective is disliked by many people. Prefer *under way*, *continued*, *continuing* or *in progress*. Above all, avoid the cliché *ongoing situation*.

**on-line/on-stream** These two technical terms – *on-line* from communications and computers, *on-stream* from the oil industry – are disliked by many people when used figuratively to mean in communication (or agreement) with, and in production respectively:

The prime minister was on-line with the treasurer.

The company came on-stream this financial year.

**only** In an idiomatic but ambiguous sentence such as *The band only plays jazz on Fridays*, the speaker's intonation will generally make the meaning clear in conversation; in written work, however, it will usually be necessary to place *only* as close as possible to the word it refers to. This sentence could mean either of the following:

The band plays jazz on Fridays only.

*or* The band plays only jazz on Fridays.

Using *only* as a conjunction in place of *but* is strictly informal: *I intended writing a letter, only I rang instead.*

**o.n.o.** or nearest offer; also *ONO*.

**onomatopoeia** See **alliteration/assonance/onomatopoeia**.

**on-stream** See **on-line/on-stream**.

**on to/onto** When *on* is used as an adverb meaning forward, and is followed by *to*, the words must be kept separate:

The troupe moved on to the next town.

The prepositional form may be *on to* or *onto*:

The actor leapt on to [*or* onto] the stage.

**onward/onwards** *Onward* is the adjective:

Torrential rain checked the onward movement of the locusts.

The adverb, meaning towards a point ahead, is always *onwards*:

Travelling was easier from that time onwards.

**op.** This is an abbreviation of the Latin word *opus*, meaning a work.
See also **opus**.

**o.p.** out of print; also *OP* or *o/p*.

**op. cit.** This abbreviation (Latin: *opere citato*) means in the work cited. The abbreviated words are always printed in roman type, given lower-case initials, and followed by full stops. Op. cit. was once commonly used in notes and references, but the abbreviation of an author's name to surname only has come to be regarded as sufficient to indicate that a work being quoted has already been cited:

[4]Matheson, op. cit., p. 231. *or* [4]Matheson, p. 231.

Compare with the entry **ibid**., and see also **notes and references**.

**OPEC** This is an acronym for *Organization of Petroleum Exporting Countries*. The common phrase *OPEC countries* is tautological.

**openness** Note the *-nn-*.

**operating system** The *operating system* of a computer is the collection of programs that controls the running of the software programs and the peripheral devices. Functions such as the inputting of data via a keyboard, the reading and formatting of disks, and the erasing or copying of files are made possible by the operating system.

**ophthalmologist** See **oculist/ophthalmologist**.

**OPSM** Optical Prescriptions Spectacle Makers Pty. Ltd.

**optical character recognition** This computer term (abbreviated *OCR*) means the process of scanning text and converting it into a form that can be used by a computer. The text can be typed, word processed or handwritten. A document is placed in a scanner, or has a scanning device run over it. The OCR software then interprets the patterns of light and dark as letters and numbers, which it reads into the computer. The error rate in text scanned in this way can be high, and careful proofreading is always necessary.

See also **scanner**.

**optical disk** See **disk, optical**.

**optician/optometrist** An *optician* can make and sell spectacles, but an *optometrist* can test your eyes and prescribe the spectacles, although he or she is not a doctor.

See also **oculist/ophthalmologist**.

**optimal/optimum/optimise** The adjectives *optimal* and *optimum* mean the same thing – the most favourable, or the best compromise (between opposing tendencies):

> Warmth and humidity provide the optimal [*or* optimum] conditions for mould.
>
> The optimal [*or* optimum] amount of logging will supply timber needs yet protect the forests.

If you simply mean *best*, it is preferable to use that word. The noun *optimum* (meaning the most favourable situation) and the verb *to optimise* (meaning to make the most of) have the same restrictions as the adjectives:

> These conditions represent the optimum for mould growth.
>
> We will try to optimise timber production without destroying the forests.

**optometrist** See **optician/optometrist**.

**opus** The Latin word *opus* (plural *opera*) means work, and is used in English (unitalicised) to refer to musical and literary works – sometimes jocularly, in combination with the Latin *magnum*, great: *How's the magnum opus coming along?*. It may be abbreviated to *op.* for musical works classified by number: *Op. 109*.

**OR** This abbreviation stands for *other ranks*, a term referring to members of the armed forces who are not officers; non-commissioned officers are not always considered to be *OR*.

**or** When *or* joins nouns or pronouns that are in the singular, use a singular verb:

> A pineapple or a rock melon is best in this recipe.
>
> He or she always collects the children.

When *or* joins nouns or pronouns that are in the plural, use a plural verb:

Plums or apricots are best in this recipe.

We or they always collect the children.

Where singular and plural are combined, the verb agrees with the noun or pronoun closest to it:

Either the cats or the dog is going to the kennel.

Either the dog or the cats are going to the kennel.

He or they always collect the children.

The same principle applies to different forms of a verb:

Are [*not* Is] you or your sister going to the party?

He or his parents need [*not* needs] to attend to the problem.

In the following construction the noun *colour* and the verb *is* must both be singular because *or* is the link word; they would be plural if the link word were *and*:

The colour red, green or yellow is equally suitable.

*but* The colours red, green and yellow are equally suitable.

The problem of avoiding both sexist language and over-complexity in *or* constructions is dealt with in the entry **either**.

Note that *or* may sometimes begin a sentence for dramatic effect:

They had lost the race. Or had they?

See also **either**; **nor**; **singular or plural**.

**-or/-our word endings** Either *-or* or *-our* is acceptable for the ending of words such as *odour*, *splendour*, *candour* and *labour*, but the *-our* form is recommended. Note, however, the exception in the name of the Australian *Labor* Party. There are also many words whose ending is always *-or*, for instance *conveyor*, *actor*, *mentor* and *author*. Your dictionary will indicate whether a particular word has an optional ending. The compounds of such words also need checking: *glamour* but *glamorise*; *colour* but *coloration*; *humour* but *humorous*.

See also **-er/-or word endings**; **US spelling**.

**oral/verbal** The adjective *oral* refers to the mouth: *oral hygiene*; it can also mean spoken: *an oral agreement made over a drink*. *Verbal* refers to words, which may be spoken or written: *verbal skills*. Misunderstandings may be avoided if, when contrasting something spoken with something written, you use the word *oral* rather than *verbal*. The colloquial noun *verbal* means an oral confession recorded in some way by police. Used as a verb the word implies misuse in court of such an alleged confession: *The cops verballed our Frank*.

Note also the noun *verbiage* and the adjective *verbose*, which both relate to an excess of words.

See also **aural/oral**.

**oratorio** Plural *oratorios*.

**ordinal numbers** See **cardinal numbers/ordinal numbers**; **first/firstly**.

**ordinance/ordnance** An *ordinance* is a decree, rule or regulation: *an ordinance forbidding dogs in parks*. *Ordnance* is the collective term for military weapons and associated equipment: *ordnance stores*.

**organdie** Note the spelling of the name of this fine cotton fabric (not 'organdy').

**orient/orientate** Either form of this word is acceptable, but *orientate* is preferred. The original and literal meaning of the verb is to place something (such as a building) so that it faces east – in modern usage, facing any direction. The word has the additional meaning (sometimes figurative) to align (with) or, by extension, to get one's bearings:

> It is difficult to orientate yourself in an unfamiliar city.

The adjectival form *orientated* (preferably *oriented* in compounds) has become overused, and is often superfluous, in phrases such as *a youth-oriented program* and *a science-oriented project*.

See also **disorient/disorientate**.

**ornaments** See **pi font**.

**orphans and widows** The interpretation of these typesetting terms varies, but the following are among the traditional definitions. An *orphan* is the first or last line of a paragraph standing alone at the top or bottom of a page or column, while a *widow* is a short word (one of fewer than six letters) or the tail of a broken word standing alone on the last line of a paragraph. Some people use *widow* as a blanket term for undesirably short lines in any of these positions.

Orphans and widows are unattractive and should be eliminated by resetting where possible. It is often necessary to add or delete words, but altering end-of-line word breaks may solve the problem. Advanced word-processing and desktop-publishing programs that offer so-called *orphan/widow protection* usually define an orphan as the first line of a paragraph standing alone at the bottom of a page or column, and a widow as the last line of a paragraph standing alone at the top of a page or column. When such protection is used, it will do no more than ensure that at least two lines of a paragraph will end or begin a page or column.

**orthopaedic/orthopedic** Either spelling is acceptable.

**o/s** out of stock; outstanding (accounts).

**ostensible/ostentatious** *Ostensible* means apparent or pretended:

> His ostensible reason for calling was to borrow some milk, but he really just wanted a chat.

*Ostentatious* means showy or pretentious:

Her diamond-studded earings and bracelet looked particularly ostentatious at the local football match.

**OT** Old Testament.

**OTC** Australian & Overseas Telecommunications Corporation (trading as OTC Limited).

**other than** In a construction using *other* and *than* there is no substitute for *than*, whatever the sequence, unless *other* really means opposite:

You can rent any house other than ours.

You can rent any other house than [*not* but *or* except] ours.

The house was on the other side of the road from [*not* than] ours.

However, *but* or *except* may be used if *other* is omitted:

You can rent any house but ours.

They can buy any painting except his.

*Apart from*, *aside from* or *in other respects than* are preferable to *other than* in some sentences; *otherwise* is required in certain constructions:

Apart from [*not* Other than] our cases there is little to carry.

Because there are no taxis we cannot reach the hotel otherwise [*not* other] than by walking.

See also **otherwise**.

**otherwise** When *otherwise* is acting as an adverb it can be attached to a verb, an adjective, or another adverb:

We were offered raw eggs but chose [verb] otherwise.

I was otherwise occupied [adjective].

They might act generously [adverb] or otherwise.

If the sentence can do without the word, replace it with something less formal or leave it out:

They might or might not act generously. *or* They might act generously.

When *otherwise* is acting as an adjective it is attached to a noun:

We were told that there was lots of space but the situation [noun] was otherwise.

When *otherwise* is acting as a conjunction its meaning dictates the punctuation. Use a comma before it if it means or else:

Wash wool carefully, otherwise [*but not* or otherwise] it will matt.

If it means in other ways, use a semicolon:

I need those woollen socks for my feet; otherwise I am warm.

All these complexities make *otherwise* a tricky word to use correctly, and you may prefer to avoid it.

See also **other than**.

**ought** The auxiliary verb *ought* is a strong word (stronger than *should*) expressing obligation and duty. It is nearly always followed by an infinitive such as *to see*:

He ought to see me today.

He not only ought to but can see me today.

The interrogative form is *Ought he*?

Ought he to see me?

The negative form is *ought not*; the *to* of the infinitive may be dropped in this construction:

I ought not to see him. *or* I ought not see him.

When the construction is interrogative or negative *should* is often preferred because it sounds less awkward.

The forms *I didn't ought to* and *Hadn't I ought to?* are always incorrect.

See also **should/would**.

**Ouija** The name of this spiritualist device for conveying 'messages' (often called a *Ouija board*) is a trademark combining the French word *oui* and the German word *ja*, which both mean yes. Pronounce it '**wee**-ja'.

**-our word endings** See **-or/-our word endings**.

**outlay/outlaid/outlaying** Note the spelling.

See also **lay/laying/lie/lying**.

**output** See **input/output (computer)**.

**output device** In computer terminology *output device* is another name for any kind of printer.

See also **printer**.

**outside** See **inside/outside**.

**outward/outwards** *Outward* is the adjective:

An outward composure hid her nervousness.

The adverb meaning towards the outside is usually *outwards*, but *outward* is correct when you mean away from a port:

We walked outwards into the light.

*but* The liner took on its passengers and headed outward.

**over** See **above/over**.

**overall** This adjective means from one end to another, or covering everything:

The overall length of the bridge was 100 metres.

There will be patches of fog but the overall forecast is for fine weather.

The word is often superfluous, as in the following sentence: *The overall result was a win for the visitors.*

**overflow** The past tense and past participle of *overflow* are both *overflowed* (not *overflown*, which is the past participle of *overfly*, an aviation term).

**overkill** If possible, avoid this exhausted word when you mean unnecessary or excessive effort. Substitutes include *excess*, *lack of control* and *intemperance*.

**overlay/overlaid/overlying** Note the spelling.
See also **lay/laying/lie/lying**.

**overly** The combination of *overly* with an adjective (*overly enthusiastic*, *overly indulgent*) often makes rather a mouthful. It is sometimes possible to simplify slightly: *overenthusiastic*, *overindulgent*.

**override** No hyphen.

**overs** *Overs*, a printing term, means the copies of a publication over and above the number ordered by a customer.

**overtones/undertones** Both nouns can be used to describe meanings additional to the obvious ones:

> The tourist brochure had overtones [*or* undertones] of racism.

**overview** This word is much used today where *summary*, *analysis* or *survey* would do. The cliché heading *An Overview of the Situation* at the top of numerous reports by public servants and management consultants is enough to make many readers wince, particularly when it is followed by a list of *Issues to be Addressed*.

**owing to** See **because of/owing to/due to**.

**Oxbridge** This is a combination of the names *Oxford* and *Cambridge*, used when these universities are being considered collectively.

**Oxfam** Oxford Committee for Famine Relief.

**Oxon.** This is an abbreviation of the latinised *Oxoniensis*, which means of Oxford University: *Horace Partridge, DPhil* (*Oxon.*).
See also **Cantab**.

**OYO** own your own (flat, for example); also *o.y.o.*

**ozalids** See **proofs**.

# Pp

**P** pre-school children (TV classification); provisional (driver's licence).

**p** penny, pence (British currency).
See also **currency**.

***p*** soft (music), abbreviated from the Italian *piano*.

**p.** page (see also **page numbering**); per (see also **per**).

**PA** public address (system).

**p.a.** per year (Latin: *per annum*).
See also **per annum**.

**PABX** private automatic branch exchange.

**package** This noun is often used as an adjective to describe an agreement in which acceptance of any of the parts is contingent upon acceptance of the whole: *package deal*; *package holiday*. It is not appropriate, however, to apply the word to just any *plan*, *scheme*, *proposal* or *offer*.

**paean/peon** A *paean* (pronounced '**pee**-an') is a song of praise or triumph: the common expression *a paean of praise* is therefore tautological. The word *peon* (pronounced '**pee**-on') is derived from various words meaning foot. Indian foot soldiers and certain labourers, especially in South America, are described as *peons*.

**page numbering** The technical term for *page numbering* in publishing is *folioing*, and a *folio* is both a single page of a book and its number. All books should be numbered consecutively from beginning to end, with every page, whether printed or blank, accounted for in the total. Blank pages, the half-title page (and its reverse), the title page (and its reverse), the contents pages, and pages introducing sections do not have numbers printed on them and are known as *blind folios*. The number on the right-hand page (called the *recto*) is always odd, on the left-hand page (called the *verso*) always even. In a book that has illustration pages wrapped around or inserted within sections, the extra pages are not usually counted in the total, or given folios. The content would be expressed in a catalogue as, for instance, *160 pp. plus 16 pp. colour*.

The preliminary pages of books (that is, the pages preceding the text) have traditionally been numbered with lower-case roman numerals so that their extent may be altered without the need to renumber the entire book. It is nevertheless acceptable to use arabic numbers right from the start if there is no possibility of such changes. Page numbering for the preliminary pages begins at the half-title page, if there is one; if not, the title page will be the first.

The text of a book, together with all endmatter, is numbered in arabic numerals. If the preliminary pages are given roman numerals, arabic numbering starts at the first page, or the introductory page, of the first section or chapter and continues to the end of the book. Sometimes a substantial introduction is part of the text rather than of the preliminary pages, and therefore receives the first arabic folio.

The traditional position for folios is the top outer corner of a page, either as part of a running heading or alone. In reference books it is particularly important for page numbers to be easy to find and to read. Although a reader will tend to look to the top of a page first, numbers are now frequently placed at the bottom, and that position is essential when illustrations or other important matter needs to be at the top.

Technical books, reports and manuals, particularly those produced in the US, are sometimes numbered by chapter: page 1 of chapter one is labelled 1-1 or 1.1; page 2 is 1-2 or 1.2 and so on. Although this system allows easy insertion of new matter in revised editions (the whole work does not have to be renumbered), in general it is not recommended because in a book with long chapters it can lead to complicated numbers that are difficult for a reader consulting the index to remember. Sometimes paragraphs are designated in a similar way, but the normal page numbering system is retained. There is no doubt that the simpler the page numbering system, the more helpful it is to the reader.

See also **publications, parts of**; **roman numerals**.

**page proofs** See **proofs**.

**PAL** This is the abbreviation for *Phase Alternate Line*, a colour television transmission system.

**palate/pallet/palette** Your *palate* is the roof of your mouth, and the word also refers to taste, both actual and figurative:

My palate is accustomed to hot curries.

I have little palate for grand opera.

A *pallet* is a straw mattress; a portable platform used for storing or transporting goods; or a potter's flat-bladed instrument (there are some less common, technical applications too).

A *palette* (sometimes spelt *pallette* or *pallet*) is the paint-mixing board used by artists, and the range of colours typical of a particular artist:

Gauguin's palette was inspired by the vivid colours he saw in Polynesia.

All three words are pronounced identically, with stress on the first syllable.

**palindrome** A *palindrome* is a word or sentence that says the same thing whether read backwards or forwards: *tenet*; *Hannah*; *sex at noon taxes*.

**pallet** See **palate/pallet/palette**.

**palpable** The original meaning of the adjective *palpable* was tangible, able to be touched:

The palpable coldness of her hand surprised him as he patted it.

A medical extension of the word means evident through touching: *palpable cysts*. *Palpable* also has the more abstract meaning readily perceived or obvious:

Mitya tried to hide her excitement but it was palpable.

**panacea** This noun means a comprehensive remedy (not just a partial one), and the word is generally used figuratively:

Financial handouts are no panacea for Third World poverty.

The word *remedy* would be more appropriate if the problem were a minor or very specific one. For example, something that relieves toothache should not be called a *panacea*.

**Pandora's box** In Greek mythology this was a casket given to Pandora by Zeus containing all the ills of the world – released when she opened the casket. The term is used to describe any source of extensive troubles. It should not be used to designate the origin of good things.

**panel/panelled/panelling** Note the single *l* in the first and the *-ll-* in the other two.

**panic/panicked/panicking** Note the *-c* in the first and the *-ck-* in the others.

**pantihose/pantyhose** Either spelling is acceptable; dictionaries seem to favour *pantihose* and manufacturers are divided between the two.

**paperback** See **hardback/paperback**.

**paper sizes and weights** There are two systems used in Australia for the measurement of paper size, a metric adaptation of the *imperial system* and the *ISO metric system*, devised under the International Organization for Standardization. While the ISO system is in the ascendant and is used exclusively in government publications, the adapted imperial system survives in jobbing printing (invitations, tickets, brochures and so on), partly because of the immense cost of a complete changeover to the ISO system.

The *imperial* or traditional paper size is based on a quad sheet, the complete dimension of which is called a double. Further divisions, formed by folding the sheet, are broadsheet, folio, quarto, octavo, 16mo and 32mo.

Under the *ISO* system, the A-size is the most commonly used. It is based on an AO sheet, which is one square metre in area. Each succeeding size in an AO sheet is exactly half the preceding size, hence A1 is half of AO, A2 half of A1, A3 half of A2 and so on. There are also B-size and C-size sheets, which were originally intended for special items such as posters and envelopes, but are frequently used for general publications.

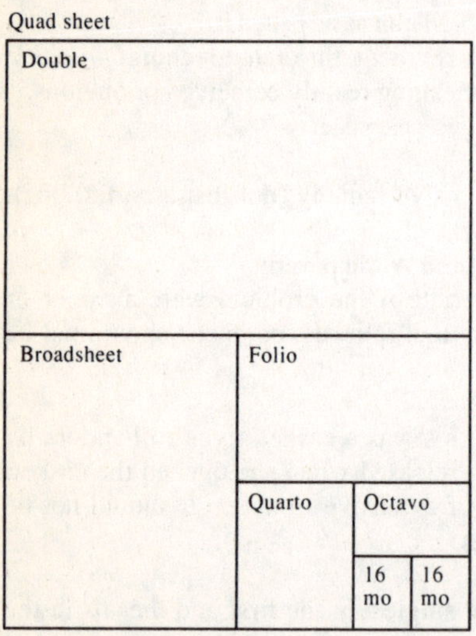


*Imperial paper sizes*

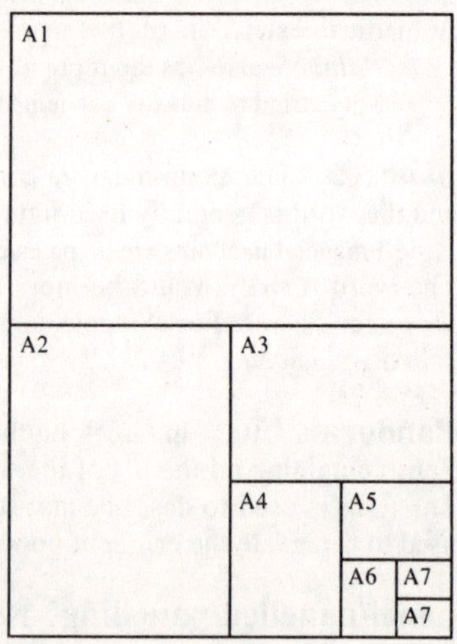


*ISO paper sizes*

In Australia the weight of paper (or grammage) is expressed in grams per square metre, which is abbreviated *gsm* or $g/m^2$. This figure remains constant for any particular grade of paper regardless of sheet size. The weight of paper used in general publications usually ranges between 65 gsm and 140 gsm. Note, however, that papers with the same grammage can vary considerably in bulk. It is a good idea to ask your printer to quote the micron readings (that is, the thickness of the paper in micrometres: 120 micron, for instance) of various papers so that you can compare their bulk as well as price. The three main types of paper used in publishing are as follows:

- mechanical papers (approximately 55–90 gsm; finish is rough and colour often slightly grey) – used for the cheaper paperback titles that have no halftones
- woodfree papers (approximately 70–140 gsm; smoother finish and good white shades) – used for a wide range of publications, including those with halftones
- artpapers (approximately 82–157 gsm; may be glossy or matt) – used for high-quality publications that include colour

The two types of paper most commonly used in offices are *bank* and *bond*. The difference between the two is in the grammage, which is usually below 61 gsm in bank and above 61 gsm in bond. While either bank or bond paper is acceptable for laser and dot-matrix printers, a bond paper of about 80 gsm will give the best results. Lighter papers are more likely to jam in the printing mechanism.

Paper is often the most expensive item in printing, and the advice of a good printer should always be sought in the early stages of planning a publication. Important points to discuss are the shade of 'white' required, and the paper's opacity, finish, strength, stretch, durability and smoothness.

**papier-mâché** This compound word (from the French, chewed paper) may be written without its accents today, and does not need to be set in italics. The material called *papier-mâché* is moulded by a variety of methods from compressed paper, and used in the production of objects such as decorative little bowls.

**Papua New Guinea** This name is written without hyphens and abbreviated *PNG*.

**paradigm/paragon** A *paradigm* is literally a pattern. As a grammatical term it refers to the kind of pattern seen across the tenses of a verb, for instance *show*, *shall show*, *showed*. In an intellectual context a *paradigm* is a major theory that dominates a field for a considerable period: Darwin's theory of evolution provided a *paradigm* for the biological sciences, for instance. Using *paradigm* to mean a typical example is acceptable but can sound pretentious in some contexts. Words such as *model*, *pattern* and *example* are often preferable:

> Government use of recycled paper was a model [*not* paradigm] for the commercial sector.

A *paragon* is a model of excellence, usually a person:

> The secretary of our old scholars' association is a paragon of efficiency.

**paradox** Contradiction, real or apparent, is part of every *paradox*, whether it is centred on people, situations or words. Verbal paradox is what gives bite to the saying 'We won the battle but lost the war'.

**paraffin** See **kerosene/paraffin**.

**paragon** See **paradigm/paragon**.

**paragraph indent** See **indention**.

**paragraphs** The purpose of dividing a body of writing into *paragraphs* is to help the reader absorb the points made, or the events described, by indicating natural breaks. There is no standard length for a paragraph, although it usually consists of more than one sentence. A spate of very short paragraphs can be as irritating as a sequence of very long ones. Effective writing usually involves a judicious mix of long and short. Here are some guidelines on paragraphing.

- A new thought or new step in development usually needs a new paragraph, and the sequence should be logical. The words that link the thought in one paragraph with that in the next need to be varied to avoid a plodding effect.
- Each paragraph should present a unit of thought, whether it takes one sentence or twenty to express. However, the modern trend is against the marathon paragraphs used by some nineteenth-century authors.
- The first line of a new paragraph should be indented from the left margin, unless it begins a new chapter, or immediately follows a heading or a gap in narrative. The practice of leaving a line space between paragraphs instead of indenting the first line is normal in typed correspondence but not recommended for material that is to be published.
- In work being prepared for publication, the type size and width of the final printed column are important considerations. A short paragraph set in 9 point type across a measure of 24 picas (102 millimetres) will look like a very long paragraph if set in 10 point type across a newspaper-size column of a measure of 10 picas (42 millimetres).

See also **indention**; **measure**; **picas**; **points**.

**Paraguay** The *gu* sounds like 'gw'; the last syllable rhymes with *my* or *may*.

**parallel** Note the spelling of this word, and of *paralleled* (and *unparalleled*) and *paralleling*.

**paralyse** Not 'paralyze'.

**parameter/perimeter** *Parameter*, as the following entry indicates, is a technical word. It has several meanings, but essentially describes a constant within a varying set of circumstances:

> Obedience was among the parameters of the sheepdog judging.

*Parameters* has come to be used as a synonym for *limits*, *characteristics*, *constraints* or *framework*, and in that capacity is decidedly overworked. Try to avoid it:

> Building twenty more schools is within the limits [*not* parameters] of the government's resources.
>
> What are the characteristics [*not* parameters] of his argument?

The word *perimeter* also has technical applications, but its most general meaning is boundary: *the perimeter of the oval*.

**parameter (computer)** In computer terminology a *parameter* is a value that can be specified, for example point size and leading, column width and page size, tab indents, and the number of lines required on the page.

See also **default**.

**paranoid** *Paranoia* is a mental disorder characterised by an abnormal tendency to suspect and distrust others, and to have delusions of persecution or grandeur. One who suffers from the disorder is *paranoid*, or a *paranoiac*. Although *paranoid* is often used popularly to describe someone who overreacts or is overanxious about something, specifically psychiatric contexts are more appropriate. Use *anxious*, *obsessed*, *frightened*, *suspicious* – or whatever word accurately describes the person's state of mind.

**paraplegic/quadriplegic** A *paraplegic* is a person paralysed from the waist down; a *quadriplegic* is paralysed in all four limbs. Note the spelling of *quadriplegic* (not 'quadra-').

**parenthesis** Plural *parentheses*.

See also **apposition**; **brackets**.

**parlay/parley** A *parlay* is a bet consisting of an amount successfully wagered plus the winnings from it. As a verb it means making use of someone or something in the pursuit of profit or success:

> By his promotion of its star, the distributor tried to parlay a good run for the film.

A *parley* is a discussion or conference, originally – but no longer exclusively – between enemies. To *parley* is to discuss matters at such a meeting.

**parody/pastiche** *Parody* is humorous or satirical imitation, usually of a creative work: *a Miltonian parody called 'Paradise Tossed'*. The word has an extended meaning – a poor imitation or a travesty:

> Thomson's latest novel was so weak it seemed like a parody of his earlier books.

A *pastiche* is a creative work drawing heavily on the work of at least one other in the same field. The word is normally used pejoratively, implying that such a work is at best plagiaristic, at worst a mess:

> The symphony was only a pastiche but its sources were in the best of taste.

**parsing** See **parts of speech**.

**partially/partly** There is a slight but real distinction between these two adverbs. *Partially* means to a limited degree: *partially deaf. Partly* means in part: *partly glass, partly steel*; *partly in Albury, partly in Wodonga.*

Note that *partially deaf* may suggest impairment of the hearing faculty as a whole, whereas *partly deaf* suggests deafness in only one ear.

**participles** Every verb has a *present participle* and a *past participle*: *eating* and *eaten* respectively in the case of the verb *to eat.*

Both may help to form various tenses – the present continuous, for instance, in the case of the present participle (She *is eating*), and the present perfect, for instance, in the case of the past participle (She *has eaten*).

Both may also act as adjectives, to qualify nouns and pronouns: *squeaking shoe*: *fallen tree*; *myself included.*

*Present participles* are always formed by adding *ing* to the root of the verb:

I am *hoping* so. You are an *amusing* person.

But note that some *-ing* words formed from verbs act as nouns rather than adjectives, in which case they are called *gerunds* or *verbal nouns* rather than present participles:

They did not give up *hoping*. *Amusing* children is his job.

*Past participles* are often formed by adding *ed* to the verb:

| | | |
|---|---|---|
| claim, claimed | film, filmed | hatch, hatched |

The ending in others is simply *d* or *t*:

| | |
|---|---|
| save, saved | smile, smiled |
| mean, meant | burn, burnt |

The many other possible formations include the following:

| | | |
|---|---|---|
| begin, begun | fall, fallen | sing, sung |
| tread, trodden | slide, slid | sit, sat |
| grind, ground | win, won | be, been |

When participles are acting as adjectives it is important not to let them dangle but to link them with the right word:

We could see the ducks flying overhead on their journey south.

*not* Flying overhead, we could see the ducks on their journey south.

See also **dangling participles/dangling phrases**; **-ing forms**.

**particular** The adjective *particular* is often used unnecessarily: *This particular shrub is too prickly* merely means *This shrub is too prickly.*

**particularly** See **especially/particularly.**

**partly** See **partially/partly**.

**parts of speech** The eight main *parts of speech* in English sentences are *adjectives*, *adverbs*, *conjunctions*, *interjections*, *nouns*, *prepositions*, *pronouns* and *verbs*.

They all have distinct roles to play in the structure of a sentence, and the form of a word often varies according to the part of speech required. The verb *to grow*, for instance, has a different form from the noun *growth*. But one word, or something that looks like the one word but has various meanings, may take several roles even in a single sentence:

> The cross [adjective] children cross [verb] the street and mark the fence with a cross [noun].

Identifying words according to their part of speech is called *parsing* them.

For an explanation of the function of each of these parts of speech, see individual entries.

**passed/past** *Passed* is the past tense and past participle of the verb *to pass*:

> We passed the town we once lived in.
>
> We have passed the point of no return.

*Past* is the adjective, adverb, noun and preposition:

> My past [adjective] life flashed past [adverb] as images of a distant past [noun] when I drove past [preposition] my old school.

Note that phrases like *past history*, *past experience* and *past achievements* are usually tautological.

***passim*** This Latin word, meaning throughout, is used in indexes – and occasionally in references – to indicate that a word or concept occurs so often in a text that specific page numbers are not appropriate: in a book on apiary, for example, you might find an index entry that reads bee-keeping, *passim* (always italicised).

See also **indexing.**

**passive voice** See **active voice/passive voice**.

**past** See **passed/past**.

**paste-up** In publishing parlance a *paste-up* is a layout guide traditionally assembled by a graphic designer from galley proofs, which are cut up and stuck onto sheets representing double-page spreads. Complicated books often need an initial ('rough') paste-up and a final one that uses bromide paper and constitutes the camera-ready art that is presented to the printer.

See also **camera-ready art/camera-ready copy**; **layout**; **makeup**.

**pastiche** See **parody/pastiche**.

**patch** See **strip-in**.

**Paterson, A. B.** Note the single *t* in the surname of the writer known as 'the Banjo of the Bush'.

**Paterson, NSW** Compare with *Patterson* and *Patterson Lakes*, Vic.

**pathetic** The colloquial use of *pathetic* to mean worthless or inadequate has overshadowed its formal meaning, pertaining to pity or sorrow, or arousing these emotions:

What a pathetic excuse!
Pathetic stories of the Beijing massacre flowed from China.

See also **bathos/pathos**.

**pathos** See **bathos/pathos**.

**pavilion** Note the single *l*.

**PAX** private automatic exchange.

**PAYE** pay-as-you-earn (income tax).

**PBX** private branch exchange.

**PC** personal computer (see also **microcomputer**); police constable (British); postcard; Privy Council, Privy Counsellor (see also **ranks, titles, honours and awards**).

**p.c.** per cent.
See also **per cent/percentage**.

**p.d.** per day (Latin: *per diem*).
See also **per diem**.

**PE** physical education.

**peaceable/peaceful** *Peaceable* means inclined towards peace. It usually applies only to people or things associated with people:

Their aggressive posture belies their peaceable words.

*Peaceful* means characterised by peace or tranquillity:

The river meandered along its peaceful course.

**peal/peel** Bells *peal*, and you may also hear a *peal* of laughter or thunder. You *peel* an orange and compost the *peel*; skin may *peel* after sunburn. People *keep their eyes peeled* when they need to watch out for something.

**peccadillo** The plural is *peccadilloes* or *peccadillos*. A *peccadillo* is a minor sin or fault. Compared with robbing a bank, speaking with your mouth full is a *peccadillo*.

**pecuniary** Note the spelling of this adjective, which means pertaining to money.

**pedagogue/pedant** The noun *pedagogue* can simply mean teacher, but over the years has taken on the pejorative overtones of *pedant* – someone who is over-fussy about 'correctness' or makes an excessive and tedious show of learning. If you call anyone a *pedagogue*, therefore, be sure that the context conveys your meaning. Note that the second hard *g* of *pedagogue* becomes soft in the adjective *pedagogic* and the noun *pedagogy* – 'pedda-**god**jik' and 'pedda-**god**jee'.

**pedal/peddle/pedlar** We *pedal* a bicycle by using its *pedals* (and a cyclist could be called a *pedaller*). An itinerant salesperson who *peddles* goods is a *pedlar* – unless the goods distributed are illegal drugs, in which case the US spelling *peddler* is now normal.

**pedant** See **pedagogue/pedant**.

**peddle/pedlar** See **pedal/peddle/pedlar**.

**peel** See **peal/peel**.

**peer group** Some people regard this term as sociological jargon that should not be allowed to replace simple words such as *friends*, *equals*, *acquaintances* or *colleagues*. If you do use it, be aware that it means a group of equals (in a category such as age, occupation or income).

**pendant/pendent** Dictionaries allow options, but the following spellings are recommended. Use *pendant* for the necklace or earrings with dangling attachments: *an amethyst pendant around her neck*. Use *pendent* for the adjective that means hanging or impending: *dislodging a pendent rock*; *waiting for a pendent decision*.

**peninsula/peninsular** *Peninsula* is the form of the noun: *the Gove Peninsula*. *Peninsular* is the adjective: *the Peninsular and Oriental Steam Navigation Company*.

**PEN International** An international association of Poets, Playwrights, Editors, Essayists and Novelists.

**penultimate** This adjective means the second last, not the last; it is too pompous, however, for other than jocular and strictly technical use.

**peon** See **paean/peon**.

**people** *People* (plural *peoples*) can be a collective noun referring to a tribe, race or nation, in which case it is usually followed by a plural verb. A singular verb is sometimes more appropriate, however.

They are a primitive people who have much to teach us.

*but* A primitive people needs time in which to comprehend modern society.

When *people* is used of a body of human beings it is almost invariably followed by a plural verb:

The people have the right to be informed.

*People* can also be the plural of the noun *person*:

This person has eaten, but the rest of the people are hungry.

In the expression *no respecter of persons*, and in legal contexts, *persons* is correctly used as the plural of *person*:

The crime was committed by a person or persons unknown.

But users of officialese often say *persons* when *people* would be both accurate and far more natural: this technical term should be used selectively.

**per** The Latin preposition *per* (unitalicised), used in technical terms or – informally – in general contexts, has several meanings. They include by means of: *luggage arriving per plane*; for each: *$250 per week*; and through: *per the kindness of my friend Pete*. Many people prefer the English equivalents, for example *a day* instead of *per day*.

**per annum** This Latin phrase (abbreviated *p.a.*) means for each year, and should be confined to financial or business usage: *insurance costing thousands of dollars per annum*.

**per cent/percentage** *Per cent* is an abbreviation of the Latin *per centum*, meaning by the hundred. It is written as two words, with no hyphen or full point: *58 per cent*; or, in technical contexts, as the symbol %: *58%*.

The noun *percentage* is written as one word and means the rate per hundred, or any proportion. In the second, looser sense the word needs a phrase such as *only a*, *small* or *large* to indicate its approximate size:

Only a percentage of the class turned up.

A large percentage of the class stayed away.

*Per cent* and *percentage* may be followed by a singular or a plural verb, depending on the noun referred to:

Twenty-five per cent of apples are exported.

A small percentage of their time is wasted.

Care should be taken when calculating percentages: a rise in price from $1 to $2 is a rise of 100 per cent, not 200 per cent. See the entry **inflation** for the difference between *per cent* and a *percentage point*.

See also **fraction**; **numbers in figures or words**.

**perceptible/perceptive/percipient** Something that can be perceived or noticed is *perceptible*:

> There was a perceptible flush on his cheek after the kiss.

Someone who has a keen ability to perceive is *perceptive*, and the adjective implies discernment and sensitivity:

> This counsellor is more perceptive about her clients' needs than they realise.

*Percipient* is a somewhat formal synonym for *perceptive*; it may also be used to describe someone whose awareness is outside the normal range of the senses: *a percipient sage*; *a percipient guru*.

Take care not to confuse the adverbs *perceptibly* and *perceptively*:

> Isabel's voice rose perceptibly [noticeably] when she was nervous.
>
> Hsui-Huang wrote perceptively [discerningly] about the countries he had visited.

**per diem** This Latin phrase (literally, by the day) is used as an adverb (meaning daily) or a noun (meaning a daily allowance), but the English equivalents are preferred.

**peremptory/perfunctory** *Peremptory* normally means urgent, dogmatic or imperious: *a peremptory rap on the window*; *a peremptory refusal of the loan*; *a peremptory nod*. As a legal term it means obligatory: *a peremptory order from the judge*.

*Perfunctory* means indifferent, cursory or superficial, and usually refers to an action performed as a routine: *his perfunctory ablutions before bedtime*.

**perennial** See **annual/biennial/perennial**.

**perestroika** This Russian word, now part of the English language, means reconstruction. It describes the restructuring and liberalisation of Russian society dating from the rise to power of Mikhail Gorbachev in the late 1980s. The word was first used in the economic sense, later in social and political contexts.

See also **glasnost**.

**perfect** Try to avoid qualifying the absolute adjective *perfect* with adverbs such as *less*, *more* and *very*, even in conversation.

**perfect binding** See **hardback/paperback**.

**perfunctory** See **peremptory/perfunctory**.

**perhaps** See **may/might**.

**perimeter** See **parameter/perimeter**.

**period** See **full stop**.

**peripheral device** In computer terminology the mouse, screen, keyboard, printer, scanner and other items of hardware connected to the central processing unit (CPU) are called *peripheral devices*. The printer, screen and keyboard are usually plugged in at the back of the CPU, the mouse into the keyboard.

See also **mouse**; **printer**; **scanner**.

**periphrasis** See **circumlocution**.

**permissible/permissive** *Permissible* means allowable, while *permissive* means tolerant (or over-tolerant) – particularly with reference to morals or behaviour:

> Camping in designated areas is permissible.
>
> Parents try to strike a balance between being too restrictive and too permissive.

**permissions** Before reproducing any material from a copyright source it is essential to obtain the permission of the copyright owner. This applies to illustrative materials as much as to text. It is usually the author's duty to obtain such permission and to pay any reproduction fees.

The process of requesting permission should begin at the earliest opportunity as the copyright holder may be difficult to find, and any acknowledgement required will have to be part of the finished manuscript. Initially a letter should be sent to the person most likely to be able to grant the request, for instance the permissions editor at a publisher's office; the director of an art gallery; or the cartoonist whose work you wish to reproduce, care of the newspaper or journal that publishes the cartoons. Describe your work, its publisher, planned date of publication and intended market, and supply full and accurate details of the material you wish to reproduce. It is important to specify fully the extent of the reproduction rights being requested, as this will usually make a difference to any fee payable. The author should discuss with the publisher whether permission should be requested for a single edition or for all editions, local and foreign. It is obviously more sensible, if sometimes more expensive, to request a blanket right of reproduction.

In general it is best to ask permission even if only a small part of a copyright work is required, as the provisions of the Copyright Act are vague about what constitutes fair dealing. Never assume that a work is in the public domain just because it is old and has no obvious copyright notice. Note also that government publications are Crown Copyright and that, unless the half-title page specifies otherwise, permission has to be obtained from the appropriate government agency to reproduce any part of such works.

See also **copyright**.

**Peron, WA** Compare with *Peronne*, Vic.

**perquisite/prerequisite/requisite** A *perquisite* is a gain or a privilege over and above an agreed income or wage; this excessively formal noun is popularly abbreviated to the very informal *perk*:

> The Rolls-Royce was a perquisite of office for the lord mayor.
>
> Hot buns for morning tea are among the perks at the bakery.

A *prerequisite* is a condition that is required beforehand:

> A prerequisite in the finance department is a degree in economics.

A *requisite* is something that is necessary:

> The climbers carried the requisites for any emergency.

**per se** This Latin phrase means in itself:

> I'm not keen on flying per se, but it does get you there quickly.

For some reason Australians love this term; in fact it has become a cliché, sent up by Barry Humphries in particular. It is best avoided.

**persecute/prosecute** *Persecute* means to harass, or to pursue in order to punish:

> The class bully persecuted smaller boys.

*Prosecute* means to institute legal action (against):

> The Environment Protection Authority prosecuted the factory owner for dumping waste in the river.

**persist** See **still**.

**-person** Unimaginative attempts to satisfy anti-discriminatory principles and legislation have led to some absurdities, particularly in the indiscriminate substitution of *-person* for *-man* wherever it may occur. Some people regard offences against idiomatic English as seriously as others view sexist language, and a balanced approach is recommended. *Salesperson* seems a reasonable substitute for *salesman* and is shorter than *sales assistant*. The Swedish word *ombudsman*, on the other hand, should not be meddled with: *ombudsperson* is illogical as well as awkward, and *parliamentary commissioner* is too long-winded an alternative.

*Chair* or *convener* is on a par with *chairperson* (though *chairman* is still the choice of many women). The term *bartender* may be an acceptable substitute for *barperson*; *advocate* for *spokesperson*; *nursery hand* (or *nursery manager*, as appropriate) for *nurseryperson*; and *athlete* for *sportsperson*. When the plural is required, a collective noun such as *staff* is often a more satisfactory general term for employees than compounds using *-persons* or *-people*: *sales staff*.

See also **chair**; **discriminatory language**; **gender**; **spokesperson**.

**personal/personnel** The adjective *personal* is very often superfluous in phrases such as *my personal friend* and *his personal opinion*. It sometimes puts desirable emphasis on a contrast, however:

> I see him on the bus but he is not a personal friend.
>
> Publicly I stand by the choice of site but my personal opinion is against it.

The adverb *personally* is also frequently superfluous.

Note the spelling of *personnel*, a collective noun that is used to describe a body of workers employed by a particular organisation: *airport personnel*; *army personnel*. Avoid using it when you simply mean *staff*, *the workforce* or *employees*. The term *personnel department* is, however, generally acceptable in all contexts, and decidedly better than *human-resources department*, which makes people sound like boxes in a warehouse. Note that *people*, not *personnel*, is the word to use with a definite number:

> The firm employs a thousand people [*not* personnel].

Pronounce *personnel* with the stress on the last syllable.

**personal computer** See **microcomputer**.

**personnel** See **personal/personnel**.

**perspective/prospective** *Perspective* is an adjective or noun referring to spatial relationships, as in *perspective drawing*; and it can mean a mental position or a particular view you have on something: *a new perspective on maths teaching*. Putting something *in perspective* means seeing it in a balanced way:

> The educational requirements of deaf children were put into perspective with their need to mix with children who could hear normally.

The adjective *prospective* means potential or expected:

> The flourmill's prospective profit is larger than last year's achievement.

**perspicacity/perspicuity** The first means discernment or shrewdness, the second lucidity (that is, the ability to be clearly understood).

**persuade** See **convince/persuade**.

**perturb** See **disturb/perturb**.

**peruse** This slightly old-fashioned verb means to study carefully, not to read quickly or glance at. You certainly cannot *rapidly peruse the newspaper* and you must avoid the tautology *peruse carefully*.

**perverse/perverted** Take care not to confuse these adjectives. *Perverse* means wayward: *perverse people* deliberately and persistently go against what is required of them; a *perverse decision* defies logic.

*Perverted* means corrupt, abnormal or unnatural. It is a far more offensive word than *perverse*, and usually has sexual connotations: *perverted desires*; *a perverted pleasure in torture*. Note that *perversity* is the noun from *perverse* and *perversion* the noun from *perverted*.

**PGA** Professional Golfers Association.

**PGR** parental guidance recommended (film and TV classification).

**phase** See **faze/phase**.

**phenomena** See **phenomenon/phenomena**.

**phenomenal** The primary modern meaning of this adjective is remarkable or extraordinary, but it has been debased in becoming a synonym for words such as *excellent*, *enjoyable* and *good*. When someone describes a holiday as *phenomenal* it is possible that the holiday really was outstanding; it is more likely that the speaker is just too lazy to think of a more suitable adjective.

**phenomenon/phenomena** One meaning of the noun *phenomenon* is something observable: *an everyday phenomenon*; it can also be used of someone or something extraordinary:

> The nine-year-old champion was a chess-playing phenomenon.

*Phenomena* is the plural form; there are no such creatures as 'phenomenas', 'phenomenons' or 'a phenomena'.

**the Philippines** See **Filipino/the Philippines**.

**phlegm** Note the spelling of this noun, and pronounce it 'flem'. The *g* is sounded, however, in the adjective *phlegmatic*, meaning unusually calm, sluggish or apathetic.

**phobia** A *phobia* is an excessive and compelling fear or dread of something. The word is a powerful one, describing an extreme psychological state, and it should not be used lightly:

> I dislike [*not* have a phobia about] washing dishes.

**phoney/phony** The recommended spelling for this colloquial adjective meaning false is *phoney*, although *phony* is also acceptable. The plural form of the noun is *phoneys* (*phonies* if you spell the singular *phony*). Note the spelling of the comparative and superlative *phonier* and *phoniest*, and that of the noun meaning insincerity, *phoneyness*.

**photocomposition/phototypesetting** See **computer typesetting.**

**phrase** A *phrase* is a group of words acting as a unit in a sentence but not expressing a complete thought. A *clause* requires a subject and a verb, but a *phrase* does not need either. For example, the first two words in the following sentence make up a clause, and the last three a phrase:

We arrive *in the morning.*

There are several kinds of phrases:

- the *adjectival phrase*, which relates to a noun or pronoun

  It was a day *with sunny breaks.*

  They saw him *in his shady hat.*

- the *adverbial phrase*, which relates to a verb, adverb or adjective

  We'll meet *at the bus stop.*

  We must get there quickly *if possible.*

  Ray is strong *in build* as well as tall.

- the *noun phrase*, which can form the subject or object of a verb

  *Climbing this hill* will tire you.

  Give me *your heavy coat.*

Adjectival phrases introduced by *like* need special care. If they are *defining* phrases (that is, ones that 'define' the previous noun or pronoun), there must be no comma separating the subject from the phrase:

Birds *like the emu and ostrich* are flightless.

Note that the sentence does not make complete sense without the phrase. If phrases introduced by *like* are *non-defining* (that is, ones that simply provide extra, non-essential information), they must be set apart by commas:

Emus, *like ostriches*, are flightless.

Note that the sentence would make complete sense without the phrase.

Some people use the names *restrictive* and *non-restrictive* phrase rather than *defining* and *non-defining*.

See also **clause; comma; sentence; such/such as/like**.

**pica** A *pica* (pronounced '**pie**-ka') is a unit of horizontal measurement used in typesetting. It is divided into 12 points. The term *pica em* is very misleading. See the entry **points** for an illustration of a pica measure compared with ems, ens, points and inches.

See also **em/en; measure**.

**picaresque/picturesque** The adjective *picaresque* (from the Spanish *picaro*, a vagabond) describes a type of episodic fiction dealing with the life of a rogue. Famous examples are Defoe's *Moll Flanders* and Le Sage's *Gil Blas*. *Picturesque* means having visible charm, and sometimes a touch of quaintness too: *a picturesque old mill*. When used of language it means graphic or vivid.

**picnic/picnicked/picnicking** Note the *-c* in the first and the *-ck-* in the others.

**picture element** See **pixel**.

**picturesque** See **picaresque/picturesque**.

**pidgin/pigeon** *Pidgin* is the term applied to a language concocted from other languages. It is used for communication between people who have different first languages. Over time many pidgin languages develop a grammar and syntax of their own, and some become the lingua franca of their countries of origin, as Melanesian Pidgin (or Tok Pisin) has become in Papua New Guinea. (Note the capital initial when *pidgin* is part of a name.) The variant spelling *pigeon* for *pidgin* is accepted by most dictionaries, though rarely seen and not recommended.

A *pigeon* is a plump, short-legged bird, except in phrases such as *that's your pigeon*, where it means responsibility.

See also **argot/dialect/jargon/lingua franca**.

***pièce de résistance*** This French phrase, set in italics and retaining its accents, means the most outstanding event or item in a series, or the main dish of a meal:

> She wrote several novels but the last was her *pièce de résistance*.
>
> Pork fillet braised in soy and ginger was the chef's *pièce de résistance*.

The plural form is *pièces de résistance*.

**pi font** In typesetting a *pi font* is a set of special characters, such as decorative or scientific symbols, that are not provided in a standard font. A pi font might hold a complete range of bullets, boxes, arrows and stars, or a selection of ornaments from which borders can be made. Pi font characters are also known as *dingbats*, *ornaments* or *sorts*. In desktop publishing the pi font most commonly used is Zapf Dingbats.

See also **bullets and boxes; font; type**.

***Samples from Zapf Dingbats***

**pigeon** See **pidgin/pigeon**.

**pigmy/pygmy** Either spelling is acceptable, but *pygmy* (plural *pygmies*) is recommended. A *pygmy* is small in stature or importance; given an initial capital (*Pygmy*), the word refers to someone belonging to a specific race characterised by small size.

**the Pilbara** *The Pilbara* is a mineral-rich area of Western Australia that lies about 1200 kilometres north-east of Perth and covers some 440 000 square kilometres. The area is best known for its immense iron-ore deposits, most notably in the Hamersley Range, and for the offshore oil and gas yielded by the North-West Shelf.

**PIN** This acronym for *personal identification number* (relating to bank accounts) has become, in popular usage, a *PIN number*, even though this duplicates the word *number*.

**pirating** *Pirating* means being the Long John Silver of computer software: obtaining software by copying it from someone else's disks rather than buying it, and thus infringing copyright. There is strict legislation protecting software, and random checks are made on bureaus, government departments, businesses and studios to ensure that their software has been legitimately acquired.

See also **copy protection**; **software copyright**.

**piteous/pitiable/pitiful** These adjectives are usually interchangeable when they mean deserving pity:

> After 100 kilometres all but the fittest of the runners were in a piteous [*or* pitiable *or* pitiful] condition.

However, use *piteous* when you mean pleading for pity:

> She heard the kitten's piteous cry.

Use *pitiable* when you mean wretched or lamentable:

> The neglected children led pitiable lives.

Prefer *pitiful* to *pitiable* when the meaning is distressingly inadequate or contemptible:

> The beggars lived on the pitiful scraps thrown to them.
> The millionaire's donation of $50 was pitiful.

**pixel** This word, short for *picture element*, describes the smallest part of a computer screen that can be individually affected by a program. Combinations of pixel dots form letters or shapes. The resolution of a screen is determined by the number of pixels that can be displayed: the higher the resolution, the easier it is to read the display.

See also **dots per inch**.

**PJT** Prices Justification Tribunal.

**P/L** profit and loss; Proprietary Limited (company).

**placebo** A *placebo* (plural *placebos* or *placeboes*) is a medically neutral substance that may improve a patient's health by psychological means, especially when it is thought to be a real medicine (this result is called *the placebo effect*).

**plaintiff/plaintive** A *plaintiff* is someone who brings an action in a case involving civil law. The adjective *plaintive* means mournful or melancholy: *a plaintive tale of disappointment and rejection.*

**plan** Avoid the phrases *plan ahead* and *future plan*. Both are tautologies.

**plateau** Plural *plateaus* or *plateaux*.

**platform** In the context of computers the word *platform* refers to a computer's hardware and its operating system, for example IBM, IBM compatible or clone (DOS), Apple Macintosh, Atari or Amiga.

**platypus** Plural *platypuses* or *platypus* (not 'platypi').

**plebeian** Note the *-eian*. Derived from the Latin *plebs*, meaning the common people of ancient Rome, this noun (colloquially abbreviated to *pleb*) now refers to a member of the uneducated masses. As an adjective it is used to mean something or someone considered coarse or vulgar.

**plenitude** If you must use this pretentious word, avoid the common spelling error 'plentitude'. The noun *plenty*, *abundance* or *fullness* is preferable.

**pleonasm** See **tautology/pleonasm**.

**plethora** This noun means a superabundance of something, too much or too many, not just a large quantity or number: *too little meat and a plethora of desserts*. Put the stress on the first syllable, *pleth-*.

**pleurisy** Note the *-eu-*.

**PLO** Palestine Liberation Organization.

**plotter** In computer terminology a *plotter* is a graphical output device that draws in colour or black and white using banks of pens. Plotters are mainly used for technical, engineering and architectural drawing.

**plough** Do not spell this word 'plow'.

**PLR** This is the abbreviation for *Public Lending Right*, a government-sponsored scheme under which writers, illustrators, editors and publishers receive an annual payment based on the number of their books estimated to be in Australia's public libraries. The aim of *PLR* is to compensate for royalties lost when books are borrowed from libraries rather than bought. For further information write to The Public Lending Right Scheme, 3rd Floor, Tobruk House, 15 Moore Street, Canberra City, 2601.

**PLTOFF** Pilot Officer.

**plural or singular** See **singular or plural**.

**plus** Except in mathematical contexts, *plus* is better suited to colloquial than formal uses. In the following example it means with the addition of:

Rob's assets consisted of his house plus two cars.

Note that *plus* does not affect verb agreement in the way that the conjunction *and* does:

Rob's house *and* his car *are* to be sold

*but* Rob's house *plus* his car *is* to be sold.

The verb remains singular whether or not the words *plus his car* are marked off by commas.

The noun *plus* means advantage:

Another plus at this factory is the free child care.

Avoid the cliché *plus factor*, the tautology *an added plus*, and the use of *plus* to introduce a clause: *He sold his car, plus he put his house on the market*.

See also **minus**; **singular or plural**.

**PM** post-mortem; prime minister (see also **ranks, titles, honours and awards**).

**p.m.** See **a.m./p.m.**

**PMG** postmaster-general.

**PMS/PMT** The first is the abbreviation for *pre-menstrual syndrome*, the second for *pre-menstrual tension*. *PMS* is also the abbreviation for *Panetone Matching System*, an international standard of inks used in printing (see **colours in printing**).

**pneumonia** Note the spelling.

**PNG** Papua New Guinea (no hyphens).

See also **Papua New Guinea**.

**PO** Petty Officer; post office.

**POA** price on application.

**POD** pay on delivery.

**poinsettia** There is no 'point' in the name of this colourful plant.

**points** An Anglo-American *point* is the basic unit of measurement in Australian typesetting, and it refers to both horizontal and vertical distances. There are 12 points to a pica. The height of type is expressed in points, generally in half-point increments. The most common sizes for text setting range from 9 point to 11 point. Points are also used to measure *leading*, which is the distance between lines of type measured baseline to baseline. A designer's instruction 'Set 9/11' means to use 9 point type with 11 points of leading.

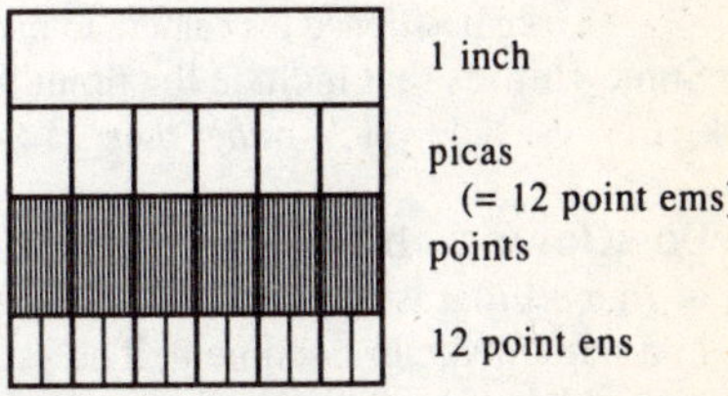


***Points compared with other measurements***

See also **em/en**; **font**; **kerning**; **leading**; **pica**; **tracking**; **type**.

**politic/political** Except in the phrase *body politic*, the adjective *politic* is used today to mean prudent, shrewd or expedient: *a politic move in the circumstances*. A *body politic* is the people as a political entity under a government.

*Political*, the adjective derived from *politics*, ranges in meaning from involved in politics to power-related: *political campaigning*; *a political appointment*.

Note that *polity* is a rather old-fashioned word meaning a form or system of government: *a polity involving both a monarchy and a democracy*.

**Polynesia** See **Melanesia/Micronesia/Polynesia**.

**pore/pour** The verb and noun *pore* is sometimes confused with the verb *to pour*. When you examine a street directory closely you *pore* over it; you have *pores* in your skin. But you *pour* a glass of water.

**portentous/pretentious** *Portentous* means momentous, ominous or (of someone's manner) pompous; the last meaning brings it close to *pretentious*:

> Tanya felt that her twenty-first birthday was a portentous occasion.
>
> The crack in the dam wall was portentous for those who lived in the valley.
>
> His portentous way of introducing himself embarrassed his friends.

*Pretentious* means affecting dignity or importance:

> He is a nonentity, but his manner is pretentious.

See also **pretence/pretension/pretentious**.

**portico** Plural *porticoes* or *porticos*.

**portrait** See **landscape/portrait**.

**POS** point of sale; also *p.o.s*.

**position** Used as a verb, *position* means to place with care and deliberation (not just to put or place):

Bruce positioned his camera to include the house but avoid the clothesline.

Some phrases that include the noun *position* can be replaced by simple verbs:

I can help you. *rather than* I am in a position to help you.

**positionals** In desktop publishing *positional* is the term used for photographs or line art that is scanned onto disk, at low resolution, for temporary positioning in a page-makeup document. The purpose of a positional is to give the operator some idea of how an illustration looks on the page. It is easy to move the image to a different position or replace it with another.

High-resolution scans are, however, used in the production of the final version.

**positive** See **negative/positive**.

**possessives** One of the ways of indicating possession or ownership in English is to use the *possessive* form of a noun, signified by an apostrophe. The broad rule is that when the noun is singular an apostrophe and *s* are added; when it is plural only the apostrophe is added:

one dog's nose two dogs' noses

These are simple examples. The use of the apostrophe is, however, quite complex, and the entry **apostrophe** deals with this in detail.

The preposition *of* can also indicate possession, by joining what is 'owned' to the 'owner':

the nose of the dog the noses of the dogs

Either form of possessive is satisfactory with the names of living things, but the second is preferred for inanimate things:

the man's eye *but* the eye of a needle

Note the odd but legitimate construction known as the *double possessive*, which may occur when an *of* phrase is used with another possessive:

It was a strange habit *of my mother's* [*or* of my mother].

She is a cousin *of Tom's* [*or* of Tom].

A double possessive is not permissible, however, when the 'owner' is an inanimate object, or when *that* comes before *of*:

We were burnt by the heat of the sun [*not* sun's].

A pen similar to that of the teacher [*not* teacher's] was lost.

Pronouns have possessive forms of their own, most of which do not include apostrophes; exceptions are *one's* and its compounds *anyone's* and so on:

| | |
|---|---|
| *my* coat | The coat is *mine*. |
| *your* coat | The coat is *yours*. |
| *his* coat | The coat is *his*. |
| *her* coat | The coat is *hers*. |
| *its* value | *but* *one's* home. |
| *our* coats | The coats are *ours*. |
| *their* coats | The coats are *theirs*. |

Be careful not to confuse *its* with *it's*, the abbreviation of *it is* or *it has*; *your* with *you're*, the abbreviation of *you are*; *their* with *they're*, the abbreviation of *they are*; or *whose* with *who's*, the abbreviation of *who is* or *who has*.

Note that the double possessive is correct in sentences such as the following:

This ring *of mine* [*not* of me] is worth a lot.

The possessive is necessary in some constructions where an *-ing* word is a gerund (verbal noun), as is explained in the entry **-ing forms**. The gerund follows a noun that is a person's name in the first example, and a personal pronoun in the second:

We agreed to Franco's [*not* Franco] buying a computer.

We agreed to his [*not* him] buying a computer.

The non-possessive form may, however, be regarded as more idiomatic when the gerund follows plural nouns, and nouns that are not people's names:

We agreed to our children [*rather than* our children's] buying a computer.

We agreed to our son [*rather than* our son's] buying a computer.

The non-possessive form is used when a gerund follows a demonstrative pronoun (*this*, *that*, *these* or *those*), as it does in the following sentence:

She changed her party to the following week when she found there was no chance of that [*not* that's] clashing with her best friend's holiday plans.

Note that the possessive *s* may have the effect of changing a person's designation into a place:

We shall buy tissues at the chemist's.

*Chemist's* is, of course, an abbreviation of *chemist's shop*.

See also **apostrophe**; **-ing forms**; **pronouns**.

**possible** It is tautological to combine *possible* with *may* (or *might*) in constructions such as the following: *They believe it is possible that the strike may end today*. Delete *it is possible* or replace *may* with *will*.

See also **may/might**.

**post-** The prefix *post-*, from the Latin word meaning after, is often used in English to form new adjectives: *post-Edwardian*, *postnatal*, *post-operative*. It also helps to form verbs such as *postdate* and nouns such as *postscript*. *Postgraduate* may be an adjective or a noun. The prefix never stands alone, but is joined directly onto the relevant word or linked to it with a hyphen.

**posthumous** Note the spelling of this adjective, which is used of events taking place after death: *posthumous awards*. Pronounce it '**poss**-tewm's'.

**PostScript** *PostScript* is a page-description language developed by Adobe Systems in the US. Its main function is to describe to the output device (printer) the shape and position of all the elements on a page. It is not necessary for an operator to have any knowledge of PostScript in order to receive high-quality output.
See also **bitmap**.

**potato** Plural *potatoes*.

**pour** See **pore/pour**.

**POW** prisoner of war; also *PoW*.

**power surge/power drop** These terms have special significance in the context of computers. A *power surge* is a sudden increase in the power supply to a computer; a *power drop* is a sudden drop. Either can cause the computer to crash. Protection against power surges can be obtained by plugging a device called a *power surge protector* into the power point to which the computer is attached.
See also **crashed/gone down**; **uninterruptible power supply**.

***pp*** very soft (music), abbreviated from the Italian *pianissimo*.

**pp.** pages.
See also **page numbering**.

**p.p.** by proxy, through the agency of (from Latin: *per procurationem*).

**ppm** parts per million; also *PPM*.

**PPS** a second postscript (Latin: *post postscriptum*); prescribed payments system (see also **prescribed payments system**).

**PR** proportional representation; public relations.

**practicable/practical** *Practicable* means capable of being done or used:

> A third bricklayer made construction practicable in the time available.
> This route is practicable in dry weather only.

*Practical* has a wide range of meanings, all related to practice or action as opposed to theory. A practical idea, for example, is one that is useful, realistic, and likely to be successful. Note that something *practicable* may not be *practical*:

Finishing the film may be practicable, but it is not practical to invest so much more money in it.

Similar distinctions apply to the antonyms of these words, *impracticable* and *impractical*.

**practically** Take care when using *practically*. Although the word can mean almost, its primary meaning is in a practical manner. Either may be implied in the following example, and the one you intend must be made clear:

The carpenter is practically qualified.

Is the carpenter almost qualified? Or does he or she have practical qualifications?

**practice/practise** The noun is *practice*:

She is joining a medical practice here.

They need more practice at serving.

The verb is *practise*:

He will practise in the country after completing his medical training.

I'm going to practise the guitar.

**pray/prey** To *pray* is to offer prayer to any god, or to entreat a person (in a melodramatic way):

Please pray for his recovery. I pray you, take care.

To *prey* (on) is to hunt with the intention of killing for food:

The lions prey on the young wart-hogs.

People, too, can *prey* on other people, victimising them for advantage. Something that *preys on your mind* worries you deeply. The noun *prey* means victim.

**pre-** The prefix *pre-*, from the Latin word meaning before, is often used in English to form new words. Some are adjectives: *pre-Whitlam*, *prenatal*, *prehistoric*. Some are verbs: *precook*, *preselect*. And some are nouns: *preselection*, *pre-emption*. Note that words like *pre-emption* have no separate existence without the *pre-*. A few authorities object to words such as *prearrange*, *precondition*, *pre-plan* and *prerequisite* because the words *arrange*, *condition*, *plan* and *requisite* all have the *before* idea in them already. The prefix never stands alone, but is joined onto the relevant word or linked to it with a hyphen.

**precede/proceed** To *precede* is to go or come before:

The queen preceded her husband into the ballroom.

The introduction to a book precedes the text.

To *proceed* is to move onwards or to institute legal action:

The royal party proceeded to Sydney after visiting Canberra.

The fraud squad will proceed against the directors.

Do not reverse the endings of these words: common errors are 'preceed' and 'procede'.

**precedence/precedent** *Precedence* usually means priority in importance, or in the rank and order to be observed in a ceremony:

Counter sales take precedence over mail orders.

Members of the clergy were introduced to the bishop in order of precedence.

A *precedent* is an earlier case, in law or in general contexts, that may serve as an example or justification for subsequent cases:

Ordaining women in one State set a precedent for other States.

The preferred pronunciation for the first syllable in *precedence* is 'press'; in *precedent* it can be either 'preece' or 'press'. Stress the first syllable in both words.

**precipitate/precipitous** The adjective *precipitate* means headlong, hasty or rash: *a precipitate entrance*; *a precipitate decision to leave home*. *Precipitous* means extremely steep, like a precipice: *precipitous mountains*. When these two words are confused, the reason is probably that *precipitous* (steep) slopes can cause dangerously *precipitate* (hurried) descents. As an adjective and noun *precipitate* is pronounced 'press-**ippit**'t', as a verb 'pre-**sippa**-tate'.

**precondition** See **condition/precondition**.

**predict/predicate** *Predict* is a common verb meaning to foretell:

It is impossible to predict the winners in horseraces.

*Predicate* is an uncommon and rather formal verb meaning to assert or imply:

Outlandish theories are often easier to predicate than to prove.

In US English *predicate* also means to base (something on):

It will be necessary to predicate the new public health program on government funding.

The passive form is more often seen in Australian English:

The recommendations are predicated on a year's research.

As a verb, *predicate* is pronounced '**predd**i-kate'.

In grammar the noun *predicate* refers to all the words in a clause except its subject:

The noisy children [subject] *disturbed our peace* [predicate].

It is pronounced '**predd**i-k't', with an unstressed last syllable.

**predilection** Note the *-lec-* when both spelling and pronouncing this word, which means preference.

**pre-empt** The hyphen is necessary in this verb, which means to take action in advance of others, thereby establishing a prior right, or to forestall. It does not merely mean prevent:

She pre-empted a vote by pointing out that the meeting did not have a quorum.

**preface** See **foreword/preface**.

**prefer** The verb *prefer* means to like better or to choose rather. *To*, not *than*, should precede whatever is second best:

I prefer watching to [*not* than] playing.

She prefers Mozart to [*not* than] Bach.

The use of gerunds (*watching* and *playing*) in the first example is one way of avoiding the clash that the infinitives *to watch* and *to play* would cause. You simply cannot say: *I prefer to watch to to play.* Other ways of dealing with the problem are to use *rather than*, and to reword the sentence more radically:

I prefer to watch rather than to play.

I choose to watch rather than to play.

I would rather watch than play.

Similarly, *preferable* must be followed by *to*:

Watching is preferable to [*not* than] playing.

Do not use *more* or *most* with *prefer* and *preferable*, which already include a comparative sense:

Which restaurant do you prefer [*not* most prefer *or* prefer most]?

See also **gerund**; **infinitive**.

**prefixes and suffixes** *Prefixes* and *suffixes* (collectively known as *affixes*) are attached to whole words or root words in order to change their meaning.

*Prefixes* are placed before the word or its root: *after-* preceding *noon* makes *afternoon*; *anti-* preceding *climax* makes *anticlimax*; *extra-* preceding *-ordinary* makes *extraordinary*. Other common prefixes include *a-*, *ante-*, *co-*, *de-*, *dis-*, *en-*, *ex-*, *hyper-*, *in-*, *inter-*, *intra-*, *mid-*, *mis-*, *neo-*, *non-*, *post-*, *pre-*, *pro-*, *re-*, *sub-*, *super-* and *un-*.

*Suffixes* are placed after the word or root word: *-ly* added to *woman* makes *womanly*; *-ship* added to *friend* makes *friendship*; *-able* added to *like-* makes *likeable*; *-fold* added to *mani-* makes *manifold*. Other common suffixes include *-dom*, *-ed*, *-en*, *-er*, *-est*, *-ful*, *-hood*, *-ice*, *-ish*, *-ment*, *-ness*, *-ology* and *-y*.

A number of suffixes may change the part of speech of a word. Adding *-er* to *eat* and *preach* changes the verbs into nouns (*eater*, *preacher*), for instance; adding *-ise* to adjectives such as *equal* and nouns such as *vandal* changes them into verbs (*equalise*, *vandalise*).

Many words are formed by adding both a prefix and a suffix to a root word: *mis*concept*ion*, *un*accept*able*.

Many prefixes are closed up with the words they precede; some are closed up with certain words and linked by hyphens with others. Prefixes cannot simply float, unattached in any way. If *post* or *super*, for example, stands alone in a sentence, it is a word in its own right, not a prefix.

See also **back formation**; **consonants, doubling of**; **hyphenation**.

**preliminary pages** See **publications, parts of**.

**premier/premiere** As an adjective, *premier* means foremost or leading:

According to its car licence plates, New South Wales is Australia's premier State.

As a noun, *premier* means the head of a State government.

A *premiere* is the first public performance of a stage show or a film. The word is also commonly used as a verb, although some people dislike this extension:

The film will premiere in ten cities next week.

The words are pronounced '**premm**ia' (not '**pree**-mia') and 'premmee-**air**' respectively.

**premise/premiss** The spelling *premise* rather than *premiss* is recommended for the noun describing a proposition on which an argument is based:

The premise of Claudia's claim was well supported by her reasoning.

In the plural the word means a building and the land belonging to it: *premises ready for inspection by new owners*. The verb is always spelt *premise*.

**prepositions** A *preposition* is one of the parts of speech. Words like *in*, *over*, *before*, *after*, *to* and *of* are *prepositions*. Their role is to relate one word or phrase to others in a sentence, and many of them show place, time or possession:

He stood *on* the stage [place].

She arrived *before* the debate [time].

He preferred the sound *of* the flute [possession].

Note that some words that are used as prepositions here can fill other roles – *before*, for example:

She arrived before [preposition] the debate.

She arrived before [conjunction] the debate began.

We have been here before [adverb].

I'd prefer to see you after lunch but before [noun] will do.

Prepositions can consist of more than one word, but some composite prepositions are unnecessarily verbose:

I sat *in front of* the fire.

I moved back *because of* the heat.

*but* I walked over *with* [rather than *together with*] my friend.

*and* They are uncertain *of* [rather than *with regard to*] your intentions.

The position of prepositions in a sentence has been the subject of much dispute among grammarians, some of whom have claimed that a preposition should never end a sentence. The rigid application of this 'rule' has often resulted in unnatural or stilted constructions, inspiring the comment attributed to Winston Churchill: 'This is the sort of English up with which I will not put'. English usage has in fact always permitted the preposition to fall where it sounds most natural, and that position is often at the end of a sentence; in some sentences, like the middle one of the next three, there is no alternative position for it:

Where have the children come *from*?

Peace is worth striving *for*.

That is the shop she works *in*.

Nevertheless there are occasions on which it is appropriate to turn a sentence round. If the situation demands formal speech or writing, choose:

He is the person *to* whom we owe our lives.

*rather than*

He is the person we owe our lives *to*.

Take care not to repeat a preposition already included: *the studio in which the band recorded their music in*. Delete the first *in* if writing informally, the second if writing formally.

It is also important to include necessary prepositions:

Is she opposed *to* or in favour *of* the purchase?

*not* Is she opposed or in favour of the purchase?

Note that when a pronoun such as *I*, *he*, *she*, *we*, *they* or *who* follows a preposition, the pronoun must be in the objective case: *me*, *him*, *her*, *us*, *them* or *whom*. There is generally little trouble over this requirement when only one pronoun follows: *for me*; *with her*; *through us*. But mistakes are common when more than one word is governed by the preposition, or the sentence is complex:

This is between *you* and *me* [not *I*].

She sold a puppy to *him* [not *he*] and his brother.

He is a librarian *whom* [not *who*] researchers have come to rely on.

The last example is less likely to cause problems if expressed more formally, with *on* preceding *whom* instead of coming at the end of the sentence.

There is a special rule for *whoever* and *whomever*, which can simultaneously follow a preposition and introduce a clause. You can only put the objective form, *whomever*, after the preposition when the objective case is required in the following clause too:

Pin the ribbon on *whomever* they choose.

In the last sentence *whomever* (the objective form) follows the preposition *on* and is also the object of the verb *choose*. But note the following:

Pin the ribbon on *whoever* wins.

In this sentence *whoever* (the subjective form) follows the preposition *on* but is the *subject* of the verb *wins*.

Many people who are otherwise well versed in the English language are insecure about the most idiomatic preposition to use with a particular word. Here is an assortment of combinations, some of which are notoriously tricky:

| | |
|---|---|
| agonise *over* a decision | bend *under* a weight |
| live *in* Australia | bend *with* the wind |
| live *at* Coober Pedy | compare lawn *to* a billiard table |
| calculated *by* the hour | compare Townsville *with* Cairns |
| liable *for* tax | enthuse *over* an idea |
| liable *to* migraine | demur *at* [not *about*] a suggestion |
| a report *on* [not *about*] pollution | the spokeswoman *on* [not *about*] health |
| oblivious *of* [not *to*] criticism | place the pie *in* [not *into*] the oven |
| ignorant *of* [not *about*] the rules | throw the bag *into* [not *in*] the bin. |

See also **case (grammar)**; **pronouns**.

**prerequisite** See **perquisite/prerequisite/requisite**.

**prerogative** Spell this word correctly and you will pronounce it correctly (not 'perogative'). It means a right or privilege.

**prescribe/proscribe** These two verbs are almost opposite in meaning. To *prescribe* is to recommend, order or dictate. To *proscribe* is to recommend against, denounce or prohibit:

The doctor prescribed daily walks but proscribed violent exercise.

The related nouns are *prescription* and *proscription* respectively.

**prescribed payments system** Frequently abbreviated to *PPS*, this system is a form of withholding tax designed to prevent tax evasion. People who employ contractors such as cleaners and gardeners are required to deduct, and forward to the Australian Tax Office, a percentage of payments made to the workers. Industries such as building, with its high percentage of contract labour, are particular targets of PPS provisions.

**presently** Many people in Australia have begun, in recent years, to adopt the US usage *presently* (rather than *at present*) when they mean now. They would once have used *presently* only to mean in a short while. The traditional usage is recommended:

My cousins will arrive presently.

*but not*

My cousins are presently at Alice Springs.

See also **current/currently**.

**press/pressure/pressurise** Do not forget that you can often use *press* rather than *pressure* when you mean put pressure on:

We will press [*or* pressure] Felicity to join us tomorrow.

Restrict *pressurise* to its literal meaning, to maintain or increase the pressure of air, liquids and so on:

We know that the air in the cabin has been pressurised.

**prestigious** Because it has been applied so frequently to people and things lacking inherent *prestige* (that is, influence or distinction), *prestigious* has lost much of its power and value. Real-estate agents and recruitment firms are the worst offenders. Today's *prestigious property development* is often tomorrow's jerrybuilt eyesore; a *prestigious position* in a *prestigious company* is often just a job in a debt-burdened conglomerate heading for receivership. Choose instead one of the numerous synonyms, such as *influential*, *important* or *outstanding*.

**Preston, Tas. and Vic.** Compare with *Prestons*, NSW.

**presume** See **assume/presume**.

**presumptive/presumptuous** The adjective *presumptive* primarily means probable, or presumed to be true:

His written confession was presumptive evidence of his guilt.

An *heir presumptive* is one whose right to succession or inheritance can be superseded by the birth of an heir with a stronger claim.

*Presumptuous*, the more common word, means unduly forward or arrogant:

It is presumptuous of this newcomer to expect to become a director so soon.

*Presumptuous* is frequently misspelt and mispronounced. Watch the spelling, and pronounce it 'pre-**zump**-tewus'.

See also **heir**.

**pretence/pretension/pretentious** The noun *pretence* means pretending or affectation; the first sense can bring it close to *pretension*, and the second to *pretentious*:

Nick really believed he was an astronaut: it was no pretence.

Gordon's remarks on finance are pure pretence; he knows nothing about it.

The noun *pretension* means laying claim, with or without justification; it is often used – with a similar meaning – in the plural:

The advertising agency's pretensions to excellence were justified by the success of its campaign.

*Pretension* is not necessarily derogatory but its adjective *pretentious* is always critical in tone, implying an affectation of dignity or importance:

The agency is pretentious about its record, but it has had some deplorable failures in recent years.

See also **portentous/pretentious**.

**preternatural/supernatural** Both words broadly mean above or beyond nature but *preternatural*, the less common of the two, is often legitimately used as a synonym for *abnormal*:

Rajiv had a preternatural awareness of other people's feelings.

*Supernatural* is more appropriately used where it stands in contrast to notions of the material or temporal:

Carrie regarded her cloudless birthday as a sign of supernatural intervention, but her mother called it luck.

**prevaricate/procrastinate** To *prevaricate* is to behave or speak evasively:

Sheila hid the letters and prevaricated over their whereabouts.

To *procrastinate* means to delay:

Angus procrastinated for so long that his contract was cancelled.

**prevent** Be careful when using the verb *to prevent*. Follow it with *from* or an *-ing* word:

Let's prevent them from leaving.

*or* Let's prevent their escaping.

See also **-ing words**.

**preventative/preventive** Either spelling is acceptable but *preventive* is preferred: *preventive medicine*.

**previously** See **hitherto/previously**.

**prewar/postwar** A hyphen is not necessary in either of these adjectives. *Prewar* means before a war: *prewar affluence*. *Postwar* means after a war: *postwar reconstruction*. Neither can act as an adverb:

Life was very different before the war [*not* prewar].

Always indicate to which war you are referring if there is any doubt about it.

See also **World War I; World War II**.

**prey** See **pray/prey**.

**price** See **cost/price**.

**Prichard, Katharine Susannah** Note the spelling of the name of this famous Australian author.

**prima facie/prima-facie** The Latin phrase *prima facie* means on first appearances or at first sight. With the addition of a hyphen, it is used in law to describe evidence that is strong enough at face value to establish a fact without further proof, though additional evidence may undermine it:

The prima-facie evidence of the defendant's neighbour brought about an acquittal in the first week of the trial.

The term is best avoided in general contexts, where suitable substitutes include *at first sight*, *at first glance* and *on the face of it*.

**primarily** Put the stress on the first syllable.

**principal/principle** *Principal* can be an adjective or a noun. As an adjective it means chief or most important:

Good value is our principal aim, but good service is important too.

The noun *principal* may mean the leading or highest-ranking person; another meaning is a capital sum of money, as distinct from profit or interest:

The college principal was chosen by the teaching staff.

The principal in this account had small amounts of interest added to it.

A *principle* is a rule of conduct or a fundamental truth. The word is always a noun:

He is a man of high principles but he fails to meet his own standards.
Equality is an essential principle of democracy.

**printer** A *printer* is a person who runs a printing business. In the context of computers a *printer* is also a device that prints output from a computer onto paper. There are various types of printers, the main ones being laser printers (non-impact printers) and dot-matrix printers (impact printers).

Laser printers can output in traditional black or other single colours in a limited range, and can also produce full-colour pages using a four-colour film cartridge. Bond paper is needed for single-colour output, and thermal or specially coated paper for full colour. Laser printers output to A4 or A3 size paper, and their resolution ranges from 300 dots per inch (dpi) to 1000 dpi.

Dot-matrix printers produce output of lower quality than can be provided by laser printers. They are either 'sheet fed' (using individual A4 bond pages) or they operate on 'continuous feed', using paper with sprocket holes along both sides to feed it through a series of bars to the printer roller.

Print quality is not the only thing to consider when buying a printer. Print speed (for both text and graphics), paper-size and paper-tray capacity, the suitability for use with popular software and font packages and so on are also important.

See also **dots per inch**; **image setter**; **input/output (computer)**.

**printer font/screen font** *Printer fonts* used in computers are required for printing out *screen fonts*, which are the typefaces you see on a computer screen.

See also **downloadable font**; **font**; **resident font**; **type**.

**printout** See **input/output (computer)**.

**print run** The number of copies of a publication to be printed at the one time is called its *print run* (or *run* for short).

**prioritise** Try to avoid this new verb.

**prior to** This is a cumbersome way of saying *before*, which is to be preferred in all but the most formal of contexts:

Guests are invited to view the exhibition prior to dining with the gallery director.
We had a few drinks before [*not* prior to] going to the theatre.

**prise/prize** *Prise* is the preferred spelling for the verb meaning to force open. The variant spelling *prize* is acceptable; the US English *pry* is not. *Prize* is the spelling of the verb meaning to treasure; the adjective meaning valued; and the noun meaning a reward, or something secured or valued.

**pristine** Though it once only meant pertaining to the original state, this adjective has taken on the meaning unsullied, new or clean – a logical development:

Su-Li kept her books in a pristine condition, hoping to sell them later.
We picked daisies of pristine whiteness.

**privilege** Note the spelling.
See also **contempt**.

**prix fixe** See **à la carte/prix fixe/table d'hôte**.

**prize** See **prise/prize**.

**pro** This word may be used as a preposition to mean much the same as the Latin *pro*, in favour of: *She is pro the idea*. In the phrase *pros and cons* it is a plural noun meaning the arguments (or people) in favour of something, while the *cons* – abbreviated from the Latin *contra*, against – are the arguments (or people) opposed to something: *Tell us the pros and cons of the situation*. *Pro* is also a colloquial abbreviation, which needs to be used carefully because it may be complimentary: *a real pro [professional] of a chef*; or it may be derogatory: *a pro [prostitute] working in Kings Cross*.

**pro-** The prefix *pro-* is attached to other words to supply the meaning in favour of: *pro-decentralisation*; *pro-Tory*. See also its opposite *anti-* in the entry **ante-/anti-**.

**pro-am** This adjective is used to describe sports involving both professionals and amateurs.

**probability** Except when emphasis is essential, avoid the phrase *in all probability*. Prefer *probably*.

**probe** Do not overlook synonyms for the verb, such as *search*, *investigate*, *examine* and *explore*.

**problematic** In normal use *problematic* (or *problematical*) means having the nature or appearance of a problem; or it may mean questionable. Using *questionable* when that is your drift will ensure that you are understood.

**proboscis** Note the spelling of this noun, which is applied to an elephant's trunk, the snout of some smaller animals, and the tubelike feeding organ of some insects. It is used in jocular slang to mean the human nose. The pronunciations most often heard are 'pro-**boss**-kis' and 'pro-**boss**-is'.

**proceed** See **precede/proceed**.

**process colours** The *process colours* are cyan (blue), magenta (red) and yellow, used together with black in four-colour printing.

**procrastinate** See **prevaricate/procrastinate**.

**prodigal** The adjective *prodigal* means recklessly extravagant – hence the *prodigal son* who, in the New Testament parable, wasted his inheritance. The expression *prodigal of* means lavish with: *prodigal of his favours*. Because the *prodigal son* stayed away for years, the noun *prodigal*, which means spendthrift, is sometimes used to describe a person who has returned home after a long time:

> The prodigal is back after ten years on the London stage.

Since this usage is not supported by many authorities, it is best restricted to informal contexts.

**profession/professional** The term *profession* was once restricted to a pursuit requiring academic qualifications, such as engineering, law or medicine. A *professional*, as opposed to an *amateur*, was one who earned a living (not merely dabbled) in the fine arts, performing arts, literature or sport. Today the trend is to call any trade a profession and to label anyone in a paid occupation as professional: *a plumber by profession*; *a professional gardener*. Many people who do not necessarily favour social distinctions object to the blurring of this linguistic distinction.

**professor** Note the spelling. The abbreviation *Prof.*, used with a professor's name, is strictly informal, like the designation – facetious or friendly – *the prof.*

See also **ranks, titles, honours and awards**.

**proffer** Note the spelling, and that of *proffered* and *proffering*. The verb *to proffer* is just a longer and slightly old-fashioned way of writing *offer*.

**pro forma** This Latin phrase means according to the form or pattern, and it is generally used to describe something done in accordance with established procedure. Note that the phrase does not mean 'for form's sake', as some people seem to think:

> The visas were checked and passports stamped pro forma.

As an adjective (*pro-forma licences*) it has a hyphen.

**prognosis** See **diagnosis/prognosis**.

**program/programme** Either spelling is acceptable, but *program* is now preferred by many people. Some dictionaries confine the use of *program* to computer contexts, although *program* was the spelling in British English up to the beginning of the nineteenth century, when the French *programme* was introduced. Note that the *m* is always doubled for other forms of the word such as *programmed*, *programming* and *programmer*. The use of *program* as a verb is relatively new and stems largely from computer jargon. It appears frequently in the context of planning and scheduling, and is generally acceptable:

The course is programmed to fit in with field trips.

**program (computer)** A *program* is a sequence of instructions written in a programming language, to be carried out by a computer in order to perform particular tasks or to solve a particular problem.

**prolific** This adjective means abundantly productive or fruitful – not merely abundant – and should be applied to someone or something that produces, not what is produced:

He was a prolific director who made at least one film a year.

*not* His prolific films have had only minority appeal.

**prolix** Either speech or writing may be described – unflatteringly – as *prolix*, which means excessively lengthy and wordy.

**prompt** This is the term for a message or symbol on a computer screen indicating that some action by the user is needed before the next stage can proceed.

**prone/prostrate/supine** In reference to the position of a body, *prone* and *prostrate* mean lying face-downward (or simply lying flat), but *supine* means lying face-upward. (Be careful not to confuse the spelling of *prostrate* with that of the male *prostate* gland.)

See also **apt/liable/prone/likely**.

**pronouns** A *pronoun* is the part of speech that can take the place of a noun. In the following example the pronoun *they* avoids repetition by replacing the noun *actors*:

The actors will enter separately, then *they* will move off together.

Nouns that are replaced often do not appear at all, however:

*He* and *I* catch the same train.

The following are the main kinds of pronoun:

- personal

  I, me, you, he, him, she, her, it, one (sometimes classed as an indefinite pronoun), we, us, they, them

- reflexive

  myself, yourself, himself, herself, itself, oneself, ourselves, yourselves, themselves

- possessive

  mine, yours, his, hers, its, ours, theirs

  and the closely related possessive adjectives

  my, your, his, her, its, one's, our, their

- demonstrative
  this, that, these, those
- relative, including
  who, whom, whose, which, that, whoever
- interrogative, including
  who? whom? which? what?
- indefinite, including
  anyone, someone, no one, each, such, everybody
- reciprocal
  each other, one another

Pronouns can cause various problems, and the following are some guidelines and explanations.

- The form of the pronoun varies. If it occurs before the verb in its clause, or if that verb is *to be*, the pronoun is subjective; otherwise it is objective.

  *I* [subjective] hit the ball.  The ball hit *me* [objective].

  *He* [subjective] is the leader.  The leader is *he* [subjective] who has most talent.

  The matter is discussed in the entries **subject/object** and **case (grammar)**. But see also **I/me** for informal usage, and **who/whom** for some particular traps. Note that pronouns following prepositions must (with the exception of *whoever*, in circumstances described in the entry **prepositions**) be in the objective case.

  with *her*  under *whom*  towards *us*  among *them*
- The personal pronoun, not the reflexive pronoun, is the correct one in examples such as the following (see also **self**):

  They will only find *me* [not *myself*] at home.
- Before words ending in *ing*, the choice of *me* or *my* depends on whether the *-ing* word is a present participle or a gerund (verbal noun):

  Mother photographed *me* carrying [present participle] cases.

  *but* Mother appreciates *my* coming [gerund] home.

  This is further illustrated in the entry **-ing forms.**
- The absence of a sex-inclusive third-person singular pronoun in English – that is, one that can apply equally to both sexes – causes difficulties for those who try to avoid discriminatory language:

  If Ben or Julia wants to come, he or she must pay now.

  The *he or she* is awkward, but its replacement by *they* – an increasingly common ploy – is grammatically unacceptable in formal contexts. Rewording is often the only way out:

  Ben or Julia must pay now if either wants to come.

  Indefinite pronouns can be troublesome in the same way when they refer to a person whose sex is unknown; they are best avoided:

  You can invite your best friend to the party.

  *rather than*

  Anyone is allowed to invite his [*or* his or her, *or* their] best friend to the party.

Several aspects of the sex-inclusive problem are dealt with in entries such as

**anybody/anyone**; **discriminatory language**; **each**; **each other/one another**; **every/everybody/everyone**; **he/she**; and **their/them/they**.

- Pronouns linked with collective nouns such as *group*, *committee* and *staff* may be singular or plural depending on the context. This is discussed under **collective nouns**.
- Be careful to avoid ambiguity when a pronoun refers to a preceding noun:

Pack the plums, without squashing *them*, into the jars.

*not* Pack the plums into the jars without squashing *them*.

See also **anybody/anyone**; **case (grammar)**; **collective nouns**; **discriminatory language**; **each**; **each other/one another**; **every/everybody/everyone**; **gender**; **he/she**; **I/me**; **-ing forms**; **myself**; **nouns**; **oneself**; **possessives**; **prepositions**; **self**; **their/them/they**; **who/whom**.

**pronunciation** Spell this word correctly and you will pronounce it correctly (not 'pronounciation').

See also **Australian English**; **stress**.

**proofs** In the context of publishing, the term *proofs* applies to the first copies of typeset material; corrected versions of those proofs; and the dyelines (sometimes called *ozalids*) supplied by printers for the final checking of imposition. Proofs are also provided for approval before the printing of jackets, covers and coloured illustrations.

Text proofs always require careful checking, whether the copy was typeset from manuscript or keyed into a word processor and then transferred by disk or modem into a typesetter's computer.

First proofs were traditionally supplied by the typesetter in the form of galleys, their length matching that of the tray of hot-metal type from which they were pulled (now they may be of any length). After correction, these *galley proofs* were and still often are turned into *page proofs* by the typesetter or designer, and then returned to the publisher (or other client) for a second checking. Today, particularly in desktop publishing, proofs are more often supplied in paged form at the initial stage.

Several sets of first proofs are required. Typesetters usually have proofs checked by their own proofreader, who works at high speed and therefore cannot be expected to find every error. A set of proofs goes to the author, who more than anyone else needs to be reminded that proofs do not constitute a new draft of the manuscript. Typesetting errors must be corrected, and minor amendments may be made, but major rewriting at this stage is very expensive and can rarely be justified. Authors are not obliged to learn the standard proofreading marks – corrections and requests may be simply written on the proofs.

The designer of the publication must check that the type specifications have been followed in every detail: correct typeface, size and leading, line length and so on. The general appearance of the text also needs the designer's approval at this point.

A set of proofs is usually read by the editor of the publication, or it may be handed over to a specialist proofreader. Checking the accuracy of the typesetting is the primary function of proofreaders; however, since the galley proofs stage is the latest at which corrections can be made at reasonable cost, other problems need to be pointed out before it is too late.

It is normally the editor's role to decide which corrections are appropriate and to prepare the master set of proofs for correction by the typesetter. For costing purposes, typesetter's errors should be marked in one colour (usually red) and publisher's emendations in another (usually blue); a key explaining the meaning of each colour is essential. Ink, ballpoint or felt-tip pen may be used. The standard proofreading marks, explained in the entry **marks in proof correction**, are required for the master set.

Proofreading may involve one person or two. If you are proofreading alone, with your eyes constantly moving from manuscript to proofs, it is necessary to devise some way of keeping your place in both so that no line is overlooked. Most people find it necessary to have a piece of card or a ruler to move down as each line of the proofs is checked. When two people share the job, one follows the proofs while the other reads the manuscript aloud, pointing out matters such as punctuation, capital letters and design instructions.

Proofs need to be checked for the following:

- the sequence of galleys or pages
- departures from the manuscript
- errors in spelling and grammar that were overlooked in the manuscript
- gross inconsistencies or contradictions (inconsistencies in spelling, capitalisation or hyphenation may be checked against the editor's style sheet if it is available)
- the sequence and position of any artwork, tables, footnotes or captions
- correct setting in headings and display type, where errors are easily overlooked
- appropriate word breaks
- visual problems with the setting, such as uneven word spacing or letter spacing; excessively short lines in unjustified setting; rivers of white space running through the text; a dash at the beginning of a line (to be avoided if possible); runs of dashes, hyphens or the same word (three or more) occurring at the beginning or end of a line; orphans or widows

Each proof should be initialled as it is checked.

Unpaged galley proofs are given back to the typesetter for correcting, and are then rechecked. Turning galleys into pages may be done by the typesetter, instructed by the designer. But if the publication includes elements such as illustrations that require one aesthetic decision after another, paging is a job that only the designer can do.

Any corrections to page proofs must if possible be confined to the page on which they occur. This is of course more difficult when the first proofs are already paged. Carrying text over to the next page is expensive, and exceedingly troublesome to the indexer if an index is being prepared from the page proofs.

The printer's dyeline proofs (ozalids), which usually look like blueprints (and are therefore colloquially known as 'blues'), need checking for the sequence of pages; the completeness and correct positioning of the text and all its elements; and freedom from dirty marks. A final perusal of the preliminary pages is advisable. Printers can usually allow only about twenty-four hours for the scrutiny of dyelines, and delays at this stage can ruin a production schedule.

Useful reference books for proofreaders include the AGPS *Style Manual for Authors, Editors and Printers*; *The Australian Writers' and Editors' Guide* (Oxford); *The Penguin Macquarie Dictionary of People & Places* (Penguin); *Collins Gem Dictionary of Spelling & Word Division*; and, of course, a good general dictionary. One or more typeface books of the kind produced by commercial typesetters would also be helpful.

See also **author's corrections**; **copy editing**; **Cromalin proofs**; **dyelines**; **imposition**; **justified type/unjustified type**; **kerning**; **marking up**; **marks in proof correction**; **orphans and widows**; **page numbering**; **publications, parts of**; **type**; **word division**.

**proofs, marks for correcting** See **marks in proof correction**.

**propaganda** Note the spelling of this noun, which does not occur in the plural. Its principal meaning is information (often misleading or false) systematically disseminated, usually in order to damage an enemy or promote a cause.

**propellant/propellent/propeller** A *propellant* is a propelling agent such as gunpowder or compressed gas; *propellent*, an adjective, means able to push forward:

Despite their excellent propellent qualities, CFCs fell out of favour as propellants.

*Propeller* is the accepted spelling in Australian English for the device with radiating blades; or a person or thing that propels.

**proper nouns** The names of individual people or specific peoples, places and things are all *proper nouns*. They are distinguished from *common nouns* by having an initial capital letter, as in the following:

- people, real or fictitious

  Daisy Bates 'Weary' Dunlop Blinky Bill Mowgli
- nationalities, races, inhabitants of towns, religions

  Hungarian Caucasian Parisian Hinduism
- places and public buildings

  Antarctica Tasman Sea Pitt Street the Mint

- things such as organisations, trade names, historical or cultural landmarks, months, and days of the week

    the United Nations  Vegemite  the Eureka Stockade

    the Renaissance  November  Tuesday

When a proper noun becomes plural, the rule is simple: add *s* to all words except those that end in *s*, *ss*, *sh*, *ch*, *x* or *z*, which require an *es* ending:

    the Smiths  the Robinsons  the Clearys  the Davieses

    the Basses  the Bushes  the Lynches  the Foxes  the Lutzes

The apostrophe has no part in forming the plural, although many examples of its incorrect use may be seen: *the Smith's*; *the Jones'*. If possession has to be shown, however, an apostrophe follows the plural form of the name: *the Smiths' caravan*; *the Joneses' geese*. Note also *the two Germanys* not *the two Germanies*.

See also **apostrophe**; **capitalisation**; **nouns**; **nouns, plurals of**; **possessives.**

**prophecy/prophesy** *Prophecy*, pronounced '**proff**a-see', is the noun: *She seemed to have a gift of prophecy. Prophesy*, pronounced '**proff**a-sie', is the verb: *He prophesied better times.*

**proportion** A *proportion* is a ratio, or the relationship between two or more things in some respect:

    The hotel tower was tall in proportion to nearby buildings.

*Proportion* should not be used in place of words like *some*, *many* or *most*, but it is legitimate to refer to *a small proportion* or *a fairly large proportion*:

    Some [*not* A proportion] of the audience left at the interval.

*or* A small proportion of the audience left at the interval.

**proportional spacing** This typesetting term refers to the horizontal relationship between the individual characters of a typeface. For example, the letter *w* is wider than the letter *o*, *m* wider than *i*. In proportionally spaced type narrower letters and other characters are given less horizontal space, resulting in a tighter and more visually pleasing line of type. In typesetting and desktop-publishing programs, including word-processing packages, most fonts are proportionally spaced. Some typewriters and old word-processing packages do not have proportional spacing and their characters all occupy the same horizontal distance.

See also **type**.

**pro rata** This Latin phrase means proportionate (adjective) or proportionally (adverb). It is written as two words without a hyphen: *pro rata salary rises for juniors and seniors.*

**pros and cons** See **pro**.

**proscribe** See **prescribe/proscribe**.

**prosecute** See **persecute/prosecute**.

**prospective** See **perspective/prospective**.

**prostate gland** Not 'prostrate'.

**prostrate** See **prone/prostrate/supine**.

**protagonist** A *protagonist* is the leading character in a play, novel, or episode in history; or the leader in a movement or cause:

This novelist preferred to depict her protagonist as an anti-hero.

The word is frequently used incorrectly. It does not mean a supporter; its prefix is derived from the Greek *protos*, meaning first (as in *prototype*), not *pro-*, meaning in favour of (as in *pro-Australian*). *Protagonist* is not the opposite of *antagonist*.

Curtis is a proponent [*not* protagonist] of trade protection.

Do not use *protagonist* in the plural, as there can only be one in any story or episode; and do not qualify it with *main*, *chief*, or *leading*, as the word already contains these meanings.

**protégé** This French word is usually not italicised but it retains its accents. It means someone who is protected or under patronage, and may refer to a male or female even though this is the masculine form in French.

**pro tem** This phrase means for the time being (Latin: *pro tempore*):

The draft report is the best we can do pro tem.

It is written as two words without a hyphen, and is not italicised. Prefer the English equivalent.

**protest** Write and say *protest against the decision*, not *protest the decision* (US usage).

**protrude** See **intrude/obtrude/protrude**.

**proved/proven** Either *proved* or *proven* (a rather more formal word) may be used as the past participle of the verb *to prove*:

Hassam has proved [*or* proven] his quality as a painter.

*Proven* is the usual form of the adjective:

Ascorbic acid is a proven remedy for scurvy.

**provided/providing** *Provided* or *providing*, often followed by *that*, may be used to introduce a stipulation; it puts more emphasis on the conditional element than *if* does. *Provided* is preferred by some authorities to *providing*, but either is acceptable:

He will inherit everything provided [*or* providing] that he marries Clara.

Use *if*, not *provided*, where no stipulation is involved:

We'd have visited you if [*not* provided] we'd known you were at home.

Use *provided* when the phrase *on the proviso that* could reasonably be substituted for it:

I will give you the money provided [on the proviso that] you sign the contract.

In the following examples *provided* and *providing* are strictly speaking *dangling participles*, but they have become accepted idioms:

Provided we have enough food, you can stay the weekend.

Providing you come too, I'll attend the conference.

**proviso** The plural of this noun meaning condition is *provisos*.

**PS** postscript (Latin: *postscriptum*); Public Service.

**PSA** Prices Surveillance Authority.

**p's and q's** Note the position of the apostrophes in this odd expression. The phrase means behaviour or manners in *minding your p's and q's*.

**PSB** Public Service Board.

**psychology/psychiatry** Note the spelling of these two words.

**PT** physical training.

**PTA** parent–teacher association.

**Pte** private (soldier).

**PTO** please turn over.

**Pty** Proprietary (company).

**publications, parts of** There are three main parts to a publication such as a book: the *preliminary pages* or *front matter*, the *text* and the *endmatter* (sometimes called *back matter*). Works of fiction do not normally include endmatter. While non-fiction publications may be as simply structured as a novel, they sometimes have many pages preceding and following the actual text. The sequence suggested here is the traditional one but it is not inviolable; moreover additional components may sometimes need to be included.

***Preliminary pages or front matter*** These pages (colloquially known as the 'prelims') are usually given lower-case roman folios (that is, page numbers),

although arabic folios are acceptable. The folios actually appear, however, only on the preliminary pages that come after the contents list and contain text.
*Half-title page* This right-hand page serves to protect the title page. It usually displays only the title (excluding any subtitle) of the book, but in paperback editions may also have a biographical note on the author or editor.
*Reverse of the half-title page* This is a left-hand page, which is usually blank but may be used for an illustration or a list of previous publications by the author.
*Title page* The title of the work (including the subtitle if there is one), the name of the author or editor, and the name of the publisher appear on this right-hand page.
*Imprint page* On the reverse of the title page is the left-hand page that contains the publisher's name and address or addresses; details of editions and reprints; the copyright notice; the ISBN number; the CIP (cataloguing-in-publication) data, if included; design and editorial credits; the names of the typesetter and printer; and, occasionally, typographical information.

The details of editions and reprints were traditionally printed in full, a practice that enabled both publisher and reader to interpret them. Today, however, many publishers have adopted the US system of presetting a row of numerals (usually 1 to 10, often in reverse order), the relevant one of which is obliterated on the printing film at each reprint. Although this saves the setting of a line of type for each printing, it does not tell either publisher or reader the year in which the reprint occurred. Some variations on this method are more informative.

See the entries **CIP**, **copyright** and **ISBN** for information about these items on the imprint page. The CIP data (an aid to librarians) is supplied, on request, by the National Library of Australia.
*Foreword* If a foreword is desirable, its best position is the right-hand page following the imprint page. It is an introduction written by someone other than the author, sometimes a considered appraisal of the book by an authority, sometimes simply a piece of hyperbole commissioned from a well-known name.
*List of contents* This occupies the right-hand page following the imprint page if there is no foreword, and the subsequent right-hand page if there is a foreword. For readers it is usually the most important part of the preliminary pages. The contents list covers all parts of the book, giving the page number for the beginning of each component. It is particularly important for the contents list to be informative if the work does not have an index. Many works of fiction no longer include a contents list, but it is indispensable in non-fiction.
*Other lists* Various non-fiction publications require the detailing of components such as illustrations, tables and maps; the listing of consultants or contributors; and keys to conventions or abbreviations used in the text. These should begin on the left-hand page following the contents list. If the explanation of conventions or abbreviations can be made in or just after the preface, either of those positions may be preferable.

*Preface* The preface may begin on a left-hand or right-hand page and is written by the author. It explains the purpose of the book and provides any information that might be valuable to a reader – for instance, an interpretation of specialist terms. Acknowledgement of any help received in the production is often included in the preface, which should be revised for each new edition.
*Acknowledgements* If these are too extensive to be included in the preface, a separate section, under its own heading, may follow the preface (not necessarily on a new page).
*Introduction* Some publications require an introduction, in which the author sets down more detailed or more specific information than is normally put in a preface. It should follow the preface, beginning on the next right-hand page. A substantial introduction may become part of the text – even its first chapter.
***Text*** This should always start on a right-hand page and be numbered with arabic folios (numbers). Any half-title page introducing main divisions such as sections or parts should start on a right-hand page and have a blank reverse (folios do not appear on either). Chapters usually start on a left-hand or right-hand page in accordance with the way the text falls.
***Endmatter*** Most non-fiction works have at least an index following the text, and some have substantial endmatter.
*Appendix* Many reference books need one or more appendixes, which are sections that supplement the text in a substantial way. Unless short, each appendix should start on a new page, the first being preferably a right-hand page.
*Glossary* A glossary (beginning on a left-hand or right-hand page) is an explanatory listing of technical or unusual words and phrases used in the text.
*Endnotes* Explanatory notes and references to sources are sometimes grouped at the back of a publication. They may begin on a left-hand or right-hand page.
*Bibliography* A bibliography is normally a list of works consulted or referred to by the author, but in some publications it is solely a guide for readers, often designated *Further reading*. It may start on a left-hand or right-hand page.
*Index* The index preferably begins on a right-hand page. It may be a single listing of words arranged alphabetically, or a number of listings for specific purposes.

See also **acknowledgements**; **bibliographies**; **CIP**; **copy editing**; **copyright**; **foreword/preface**; **indexing**; **introduction**; **ISBN**; **notes**; **page numbering**; **references**; **reports and submissions**.

**public holidays, Australian** The following are the national holidays observed in all States and territories (except where indicated), together with the dates on which they occur:

| | |
|---|---|
| New Year's Day | 1 January |
| Australia Day | 26 January |
| Anzac Day | 25 April |
| Queen's Birthday (except WA) | 2nd Monday in June |
| Christmas Day | 25 December |

| | |
|---|---|
| Boxing Day (except SA) | 26 December |
| Good Friday and Easter Monday | Vary from year to year* |
| Easter Tuesday (some States) | Follows Easter Monday |

*The date of Easter depends on that of Easter Sunday, which must be the first Sunday after the full moon that occurs on or after 21 March.

There are also numerous holidays (including Labour Day, Canberra Day, Victoria's Melbourne Cup day) observed in different States and territories. Consult a local diary for the dates. In general, if a holiday falls on a weekend it is taken on the day or days following the weekend.

**publicly** Not 'publickly' or 'publically'.

**puerile** See **juvenile/puerile**.

**pumpkin** When you spell and pronounce this word, remember the second *p*.

**pun** A *pun* is a kind of word play in which related words are juxtaposed with unrelated meanings, and letters or syllables are often transposed. All puns require shared knowledge: *A cannonball took off his legs, so he laid down his arms* needs little explanation, but *Horrid Manly Jepkins* means nothing if you have never heard of Gerard Manley Hopkins.

**punctuation** *Punctuation* is the use of major dividing marks, such as full stops and question marks, to group words into sentences, with less weighty marks such as commas and semicolons subdividing the sentences. The purpose of punctuation is to make coherent a flow of words that cannot be immediately and clearly understood without it.

Although there are a number of important rules for punctuation, set out in the entries on the major punctuation marks, personal writing styles allow some flexibility. Moreover a trend has been evident in the twentieth century towards sparser punctuation, allied with shorter sentences, than was fashionable earlier. Some people have used this evidence of flexibility to disregard the rules altogether, so that their prose has become impenetrable. Effective punctuation is therefore an essential part of good writing, not an optional addition to it.

A useful rule of thumb is to punctuate as lightly as possible without holding up or misleading the reader. Consider the following examples, in which the main punctuation marks other than full stops, question marks, exclamation marks and ellipses are illustrated. In each case the mark is essential, and the best one for its context:

- the comma

While he was cooking, the baby started crying.

*not* While he was cooking the baby started crying.

- the semicolon

Let me hold the baby; you need to stir the sauce.

*not* Let me hold the baby, you need to stir the sauce.

- the colon

  It was a splendid meal: deep-fried zucchini flowers, duck with mangoes, then pear soufflé.

- brackets

  She sat down (on the best chair as usual) and lectured us on unselfishness.

- dashes

  He agreed – how could he do otherwise? – to set us a good example.

See also **brackets**; **colon**; **comma**; **dashes, types of**; **dashes, use of**; **ellipsis**; **exclamation mark**; **full stop**; **question mark**; **semicolon**; **sentence**.

**purchaser** Note the *-er* (not '-or').

**purport** This verb is used to mean claim, especially when there is a gap between the claim and the reality. Although its *-ing* form is legitimate (*a book purporting to be comprehensive*), it cannot be used in the passive voice:

The book purports to cover every aspect of embroidery.

*not* The book is purported to cover every aspect of embroidery.

**purposefully/purposely** Prefer *purposefully* when you mean resolutely or with determination:

She purposefully sought out the judges and challenged them when they failed to choose a winner.

Prefer *purposely* when the meaning is intentionally or for an express purpose:

The judges purposely kept all the entrants in suspense.

**put/putt** *Put* the shot but *putt* the golf ball (the first rhymes with *foot*, the second with *but*).

**put an end to** *Stop* is usually better.

**putrefy** Note the *-efy* in this verb, which means to rot or cause rotting. The noun is *putrefaction*.

**PVA** polyvinyl acetate.

**PVC** polyvinyl chloride.

**pygmy** See **pigmy/pygmy**.

**pyjamas** Note the spelling; *pajamas* is the US version of the word.

# Qq

**Qantas** This acronym stands for the original name of the Australian international airline, which was *Queensland and Northern Territory Aerial Services*.

**QC** This abbreviation for the legal distinction *Queen's Counsel* (when the monarch is a woman) has the plural form *QCs*; *Queen's Counsel* has no plural form: *four QCs*; *four Queen's Counsel*.

See also **KC**; **ranks, titles, honours and awards**.

**QED** This abbreviation stands for *quod erat demonstrandum*, Latin for *which was to be shown or proved*. It is rarely seen today.

**Qld** Queensland.

**quadriplegic** See **paraplegic/quadriplegic**.

**quad sheet** See **paper sizes and weights**.

**quality** The adjective *quality* is now somewhat overused, especially in advertising and commerce, as a synonym for *good* or *excellent*: *quality service*; *a quality product*. Note the spelling of *qualitative*, which means relating to quality and is frequently mispronounced and misspelt 'qualitive'.

**quandary** Do not spell this noun 'quandry'. A *quandary* is a state of uncertainty or a dilemma, not just a problem:

> The farmers are in a quandary – should they sow the oats now or wait for rain?

**quango** Note the spelling (preferred to *qango*). This is an acronym for **qua**si-autonomous **n**on-**g**overnmental **o**rganisation – originally **qua**si **n**on-**g**overnmental **o**rganisation. Of British origin, the term was first used to describe advisory bodies that drew some or all of their funding, and much of their direction, from government. In Australia the term is sometimes broadened to include statutory authorities such as power utilities.

**quantify** This verb means to measure or express the quantity of something. It may be used figuratively but should not refer to countable items, which denote number, not quantity. A simpler word is often more appropriate.

We must quantify the opposition to this proposal.
*but* We must count [*not* quantify] the objections to this proposal.

**quantum leap** In physics a *quantum leap* is a sudden transition, and the phrase has leapt into the English language. Often those who use it mean a huge change or jump (in, for instance, prices, policy or fortune) rather than an abrupt one. The expression may thus be inaccurate as well as increasingly overworked.

**quarrel/quarrelled/quarrelling** Note the single *l* in the first and the *-ll-* in the others.

**quarto** The plural is *quartos*. *Quarto* is the page size that results when a broadsheet is folded to make four leaves.

See also **paper sizes and weights**.

**quasi-** The Latin word *quasi* means as if, and it is combined (almost always using a hyphen) with other words in English to mean resembling or seeming: *quasi-official*; *quasi-independent*. It is pronounced '**kway**-zie' or '**kwar**-zee'.

**quay** See **key/quay**.

**query** Because the noun or verb *query* implies doubt or uncertainty, the word *question* or *ask* is often more appropriate:

The telephone account was so high that we queried it.
*but* My question about the exchange rate [*rather than* query] is important.
*and* 'Do you come here often?' he asked [*not* queried].

**question** The correct phrase is *the question whether*, not *the question of whether*.

See also **beg the question**; **leading question**; **question mark**; **rhetorical question**.

**question mark** This punctuation mark (?) is used at the end of a direct question, whether or not it is in the interrogative form:

Are you coming? You are coming?

A question mark does not, however, follow a reported or indirect question:

I asked whether you were coming.

In an unspoken question in the present tense, the preferred position of the question mark is at the end of the sentence:

How is she, I wonder?

*not* How is she? I wonder.

No question mark is used if the thought is in the past tense:

How was she, I wondered.

Question marks can, however, occur in the middle of sentences in certain circumstances, such as the following:

The weather will be cold (isn't it always?) for our beach holiday.

The question mark would remain if dashes replaced the brackets in that example. Note also:

Do you have everything you need: bathers? suncream? a hat and a towel?

A question mark usually follows a short request: *Would you come this way?*. But a full stop is preferable at the end of a longer request that resembles an instruction:

Would you please acknowledge this letter as soon as possible.

A question mark placed after a piece of information expresses doubt about its validity: *the poet John Donne* (*1572?–1631*).

**questionnaire** Note the *-nn-*. Pronounce the word 'kwes-ch'n-**air**' rather than 'kes-ch'n-**air**'.

**queue/queued/queuing** Note the spelling.

**quick** The comparative and superlative forms of the adjective *quick* are *quicker* and *quickest*: *the quicker of the two ways home*; *the quickest way home*. The adverb *quickly* requires the comparative and superlative *more quickly* and *most quickly*:

You will get home more quickly by cycling than by walking.

You will get home most quickly by taking the car.

The common use of *quick*, *quicker* and *quickest* as adverbs (*You will get home quickest by walking*) is not recommended even as a colloquialism. *Fast*, *faster* and *fastest*, on the other hand, always have the same form for adjective and adverb.

**quieten** Do not use the equivalent US verb *quiet* in sentences such as the following:

The speaker attempted to quieten [*not* quiet] the crowd.

**quisling** *Quisling* is an eponym derived from the name of Vidkun Quisling (1887–1945), the pro-Nazi leader of Norway during World War II. The word quickly came to mean a traitor, or a collaborator with an enemy. It is written with a lower-case initial letter.

**quit/quitted** Use *quit* for the past tense of the verb *to quit* when it is metaphorical:

We quit while the going was good.

Prefer *quitted* when there is a literal meaning:

We quitted the shopping centre before it became too busy.

**quite** The adverb *quite* may mean absolutely or fairly, and there is a considerable difference. Intonation usually indicates the sense in conversation, but in writing you will have to make sure that the context conveys your meaning if there is any chance of ambiguity:

We sat on the floor because it was quite clean.

Does this mean absolutely or fairly?

The phrase *quite a* is correctly used instead of *a quite* before adjectives to mean rather: *quite a large car*; *quite a popular resort*. However, if there is no adjective, restrict the expression to informal contexts: *quite a character*.

**quitted** See **quit/quitted**.

**quiz** Plural *quizzes*.

**quondam** Choose an English word such as *former* instead of the Latin word *quondam* wherever possible. It might, however, supply a desirable touch of irreverence in some contexts:

My former [*not* quondam] business partner has died.

*but* Our quondam host has moved on to another party.

**quorum** The plural is *quorums*, never 'quora'. A *quorum* is the number of members required at a meeting for business to be conducted legally.

**quotation/quote** As a noun *quotation* (and *quotation mark*) is preferable to *quote*:

I intend to read a quotation [*not* quote] from Oodgeroo Noonuccal.

Put quotation marks [*not* quotes] around that phrase.

*Quote* is the verb:

You could quote Marshall or Morrison on life in the bush.

*Quote* and *unquote* are used in reported speech to indicate the beginning and end of a quotation:

The mining engineer said, quote, I will resign if I am proved wrong, unquote.

See also **quotation marks/inverted commas**; **quotations**.

**quotation marks/inverted commas** Single *quotation marks* ('  ') are used in many Australian books today and recommended here. Some book publishers, and many publishers of newspapers and magazines, prefer double quotation marks, however. Quotation marks are otherwise known as *inverted commas*. The first of a pair of quotation marks, called a turned comma, is an upside-down version of the apostrophe that is the second of the pair. Double quotation marks are used for material quoted within single quotation marks; a quotation within the inner quotation reverts to single marks, and so on. The sequence is reversed if house style requires double quotation marks for normal use.

Quotation marks are used primarily to indicate:

- direct speech

  'Please come with me', she said.

- the quoting of spoken or written words belonging to people other than the author

  The number of marchers was 'outrageously exaggerated', according to a bystander.

  '"Outrageously exaggerated", did you say?' asked the journalist.

  As John Douglas Pringle wrote, 'Categories are the curse of the art critic'.

Some of the rules for the positioning of punctuation in relation to quotation marks vary according to the authority consulted, but most agree on the following.

- Quoted words and short phrases (like 'outrageously exaggerated', above) are simply enclosed in quotation marks.
- Sentences that consist entirely of quoted material are treated similarly (and so is quoted material in parentheses):

  'Categories are the curse of the art critic.'

  The bystander's remark ('outrageously exaggerated') was reported in the newspaper.

- Punctuation – *other than the final full stop* – belonging to a quotation goes inside the quotation marks:

  'Will you come?' she asked.

  'Please don't go!' I begged.

  'By the way,' he said, 'we are right out of salt'.

  But note that in the next example the comma is placed after the quotation mark following *will* because it belongs to the sentence as a whole, not to the quotation:

  'They will', we declared, 'need some salt'.

- Quoted material that is only part of a sentence may be preceded by a comma or a colon, depending on matters such as the degree of formality and the bulk of the quoted material; or it may not need any preceding punctuation at all:

  She said, 'Please come with me'.

  Pringle wrote: 'Categories are the curse of the art critic. Very few artists feel that they belong to a group or to a school; they are individual by definition'.

  She went on murmuring 'Please'.

There are conflicting views on the placing of the *full stop* at the end of quotations that conclude a sentence, but the rule recommended is used in the examples above: *the final full stop is put after the closing quotation mark rather than before it* (only the one full stop is needed). It is worth noting, however, that in the publishing of fiction there is a strong tradition, widely maintained today, for all the punctuation to be placed inside quotation marks that are used to convey conversation between characters:

> 'Please come with me,' she said.
>
> 'Please,' she said, 'come with me.'
>
> She went on murmuring 'Please.'

The following is another area in which the procedure recommended is not universally accepted. When a sentence that is a question ends with a quotation that is also a question, the only question mark required is the one within the quotation; the same applies to exclamations:

> Do you want her to ask bluntly, 'What's for lunch?'
>
> Don't you dare say 'What rubbish!'

Treat quotations ending in ellipsis in the same way:

> His voice faltered: 'I don't think . . .'

But when two different punctuation marks fall side by side, both need to be printed:

> Would you have expected her to say 'What rubbish!'?
>
> Don't you dare ask 'What's for lunch?'!
>
> His voice faltered: 'May I ask . . .?'.

Where procedures are optional, the important thing is to follow the chosen one carefully and consistently.

Do not put quotation marks around quotations that are:

- indirect

  He said that the story could not be true.

  *but* He said, 'The story cannot be true'.
- introduced by another device, such as italicised names, to indicate direct speech

  *Grattan:* Can you tell us the likely date of the election?

  *PM:* Not yet.

When a quotation is longer than about thirty words (or likely to run to more than two printed lines), it is usually typeset as a block without quotation marks but in a smaller size than the rest of the text. A block quotation of this kind may be indented a couple of ems from the left-hand margin, or set at the same measure as the text with extra space above and below the passage. The first line of the quotation is not usually given the normal paragraph indent even when it begins a paragraph. The text following the quotation is usually set full out.

When poetry is quoted in a text it looks better in a central position than indented from the left-hand margin as if it were a block quotation.

A lengthy piece of direct speech is set the same size and measure as the text, with an opening quotation mark at the beginning of each paragraph but a closing one only at the end of the concluding paragraph. Long extracts from, for instance, Acts or regulations, may also be treated in this way.

Quotation marks, rather than italics, are used for the titles of short poems, songs, short stories, essays, lectures, chapters, articles in magazines and newspapers, and programs on radio and television. They are used in addition to italics in cases where it is necessary to indicate that the word or words would normally be printed in italics – for instance, the name of a ship in a book title:

*'Falie': Portrait of a Coastal Trader*

Quotation marks are also placed around words or expressions when you wish to establish that the words are not of your choosing; are being used in a special way; or are colloquialisms of a particularly extreme or unusual kind. Letters to be emphasised are sometimes put inside quotation marks too. Italic type is often an alternative to quotation marks in such cases.

The bus driver addressed my uncle as 'old son'.

It is a common error to say 'infer' when you mean 'imply'.

He's a complete 'computer-head'.

Smyth pointed out the 'y' in his name.

Quotation marks are often used just once to introduce a special name ('Bullocky Jim'; 'The Laurels'); subsequent mentions do not require them.

See also **ellipsis**; **quotations**; **titles of publications, and literary, artistic and musical works**.

**quotations** Quotations from other works can illuminate or enhance a writer's prose; in academic publications they frequently play an essential role in supporting and illustrating arguments. But quotations are often unnecessary, distracting, inaccurate or pretentious. Fowler in *Modern English Usage* cites the main pitfalls of using quotations as 'manglings' (misquotations), 'quotation sandwiches' (text interspersed with fragmentary quotations) and 'foreign oil and English water' (a disconcerting blend of English and foreign-language quotations).

All these traps can be avoided, however. Scrupulous care in copying will eliminate misquotations and, if there is already an error in the material, the insertion of *sic* (Latin for so or thus) in square brackets will point it out (see the entry ***sic***).

Quotations scattered throughout a passage are very distracting, and concise and careful paraphrasing (putting the content of a quotation into your own words) can reduce the problem; you must nevertheless remember to indicate the source of the ideas used in this way. Very short quotations are best paraphrased unless they are particularly striking or important, and very long ones may be reduced by ellipsis – three dots substituting for the least important words. There is no need to insert ellipsis at the beginning or end of a short quotation:

The report revealed that '52 per cent of residents participated regularly' in kerbside recycling.

Longer quotations do not require ellipsis at either end unless an incomplete sentence is in danger of being misunderstood, or it seems important to show that the quotation breaks off in mid-sentence. Ellipsis in quotations, like the quotations themselves, should be used judiciously.

Even when the publication is intended for a well-educated readership, quotations from languages other than English should be kept to a minimum.

If you wish to quote passages from other people's writings, do it accurately, effectively and appropriately.

See also **ellipsis**; **misquotations**; **quotation/quote**; **quotation marks/inverted commas**; ***sic***.

**quote** See **quotation/quote**.

**q.v.** Used mainly for cross-referencing in encyclopaedias and in dictionaries of various kinds, *q.v.* is the abbreviation of a Latin phrase meaning which see. It is not usually italicised.

# Rr

**R** king *and* queen (Latin: *rex* and *regina* respectively; see also **ranks, titles, honours and awards**); repeat (TV classification); restricted exhibition – 18 years and over (film classification).

**RA** Royal Academy (London); Royal Academician.

**RAAF** Royal Australian Air Force.

**RAASA** Royal Automobile Association of South Australia.

**RAC** Royal Automobile Club (UK).

**RACA** Royal Automobile Club of Australia.

**RACGP** Royal Australian College of General Practitioners.

**racism/racialism/racist/racialist** Prefer the term *racism* (rather than *racialism*) for views or behaviour that is prejudiced against members of another race; and *racist* (rather than *racialist*) for the person guilty of racism.

See also **discriminatory language**.

**rack/wrack** As a noun and verb *rack* has many meanings, including wreck or destruction: *rack and ruin*. *Wrack* is an alternative spelling for *rack* in that expression, but note the spelling in *racked with pain* and *rack one's brains*. *Wrack* is also a particular kind of seaweed, or any seaweed that has been washed ashore.

**racket/racquet** Either spelling may be used for a tennis or squash bat, but only *racket* for an illegal scheme or a loud noise.

**RACP** Royal Australasian College of Physicians.

**RACQ** Royal Automobile Club of Queensland.

**racquet** See **racket/racquet**.

**RACS** Royal Australasian College of Surgeons.

**RACT** Royal Automobile Club of Tasmania.

**RACV** Royal Automobile Club of Victoria.

**RACWA** Royal Automobile Club of Western Australia.

**RADA** Royal Academy of Dramatic Art (London).

**radar** radio detection and ranging.

**radius** Plural *radii* or *radiuses*.

**RADM** Rear Admiral.

**RAF** Royal Air Force (Britain).

**ragged type** See **justified type/unjustified type**.

**raise/rise/raze** The verbs *raise* and *rise* can both mean to move to a higher position. *Raise* takes an object: *I raise myself from my bed*; its past tense and past participle are *raised*. *Rise* takes no object: *I rise from my bed*; it is an irregular verb with the past tense *rose* and past participle *risen*. As nouns, both *raise* and *rise* can mean an increase in pay.

The verb *raze* means to erase, or demolish completely:

> The houses were razed to make way for a new road.

Note that the expression *raze to the ground*, although well established, is a tautology.

**raised capital** See **capital letters, decorative initial**.

**raison d'etre** The French phrase *raison d'être* means the reason or justification for existence; it is not just a synonym for *reason*:

> His raison d'etre was a passionate search for truth.

Anglicised, it is generally written without an accent and need not be set in italics; pronounce it 'ray-zon **det**tra'.

**RAM** See **random-access memory**.

**Ramadan** Note the spelling of this name for the Muslim month of fasting.

**ramification** This noun, most commonly seen in the plural, strictly means the arrangement of branches, and even used figuratively should not move too far from that image. Do not use it, therefore, when you simply mean consequences.

> The ramifications of the pay rise for the cleaners were that every employee in the network demanded an increase.

**RAN** Royal Australian Navy.

**R & B** rhythm and blues.

**R and D** research and development; also *R & D*.

**random-access memory** The *random-access memory* (*RAM*) of a computer is an internal memory area used to store programs and data while the computer is in use. Random-access memory is so called because it can, on average, access data from one point as quickly as from any other. Most RAM is termed volatile, which means that it holds data only until the computer is turned off. It is therefore important to *save* such data if it will be needed again. A computer's RAM is measured in kilobytes or megabytes, and its size is an important indicator of the computer's capacity.

See also **memory**; **read-only memory**; **save**.

**R and R** rest and recreation; also *R & R*.

**ranks, titles, honours and awards** For a country with a strong tradition of egalitarianism Australia has a surprising wealth of official titles and honorifics signifying rank and status. The standard references to consult for a complete assessment of this bewildering subject are the latest editions of *Debrett's Handbook of Australia* and Sir Asher Joel's *Australian Protocol and Procedures*.

***Modes of address*** Titles of rank and status – *Professor*, *Sir*, *Dame* – should precede a person's name but follow honorific terms of address: *His Excellency*; *the Honourable*; *His Grace*. Vice-regal, armed services and clerical titles are usually given precedence over others:

> His Excellency Professor Roland Thomas
> Major-General the Honourable Sir John Carlton
> The Reverend Dr Bernice Williams

Note that *the Reverend* may be abbreviated to *the Rev.* or *the Revd* (less common), but the definite article *the* must be included. When addressing or referring to a person holding the title *Sir* or *Dame*, it is correct to use the given name before the surname:

Dame Mabel Northcote Sir Joseph Paddington

When shortened, these become:

Dame Mabel [*not* Dame Northcote] Sir Joseph [*not* Sir Paddington]

The wife of a knight may use the honorary title *Lady*, but not with her given name:

Sir Joseph and Lady Paddington Lady Paddington and her friends

To make a distinction between two Lady Paddingtons, it is permissible to say:

Sarah, Lady Paddington *or* Lady (Joseph) Paddington

To use the title *Lady Sarah Paddington* would imply that the woman in question was the daughter of a duke, marquess or earl, or that she had been the wife of a knight but was now divorced from him. Note, however, that the wife of a baron who has no title in her own right is referred to as *the Lady*, not just *Lady*: *the Lady Clegwidden*. This is an acceptable abbreviation of her formal title, *the Right Honourable the Lady Clegwidden*.

Members of the Privy Council, peers of the realm (dukes, marquesses, earls, viscounts and barons), and the lord mayors of Adelaide, Brisbane, Hobart, Melbourne, Perth and Sydney (while in office) are entitled to be called *the Right Honourable*.

In Australia *the Honourable* (abbreviated *the Hon.*) is the customary honorific for Executive Councillors; the President of the Senate; the Speaker of the House of Representatives; Ministers of State Governments; State Executive Councillors; Presidents and Members of the Legislative Councils; the Speakers of the Legislative Assemblies; members of the Commonwealth Judiciary; Chief Justices and Puisne Judges of State Supreme Courts; and the President and judges of the New South Wales Court of Appeal.

Members of the Federal Executive Council and Executive Councillors of Victoria and Tasmania automatically keep the title *the Honourable* on retiring. Certain other MPs and members of the judiciary may appeal to the Crown to retain the title after retirement.

The following are the recommended modes of address for correspondence and conversation with selected dignitaries. For reasons of simplicity only one form of title has been provided for certain positions, even though they are open to either women or men. Readers can easily replace the chosen form with the appropriate title for a member of the opposite sex where necessary.

It is important to remember that the basic forms of address – *Mr*, *Mrs*, *Miss*, *Ms* – are used only if the person has no higher title. When Miss Brown receives a doctorate of any kind she is addressed as Dr Brown; on her appointment to an academic chair she becomes Professor Brown. A wide range of titles is possible for the Chancellor of a university, for instance: for a man they include *Professor*, *Mr* and *Judge*; for a woman, *Mrs*, *Lady* and *Dame*.

The entries are arranged in alphabetical order, not by category.

| *Person being addressed* | *Envelope, and superscription in letter* | *Salutation in letter* |
|---|---|---|
| ALDERMAN | Alderman Clare Brown (or Alderman James Porter) | Dear Alderman *or* Dear Alderman Brown (or Dear Alderman Porter) |
| In conversation: Alderman *or* Madam Alderman (or Mr Alderman) | | |
| AMBASSADOR | His Excellency Mr James Porter, Ambassador of Australia to Pacifica | Your Excellency *or less formally* My dear Ambassador |
| In conversation: Your Excellency (or, in the ambassador's country of origin, Mr Porter) | | |
| ARCHBISHOP, ANGLICAN | The Most Reverend the Archbishop of Smithsvale | Dear Archbishop *or* Your Grace |
| In conversation: Your Grace *or* Archbishop | | |
| ARCHBISHOP, CATHOLIC | His Grace the Most Reverend James D. Porter, Archbishop of Smithsvale | Your Grace *or* Dear Archbishop |
| In conversation: Your Grace *or* Archbishop | | |
| ARCHBISHOP, GREEK ORTHODOX | The Most Reverend Archbishop Spiros Georgiou | Your Eminence Archbishop Georgiou *or less formally* Dear Archbishop Georgiou |
| In conversation: Your Eminence, Your Grace *or* Archbishop | | |
| ARCHBISHOP, RUSSIAN ORTHODOX | The Most Reverend Archbishop Vassili Karipov | Your Eminence *or less formally* Dear Archbishop Vassili |
| In conversation: Your Eminence *or* Archbishop Vassili | | |
| ARCHDEACON | The Venerable the Archdeacon of Smithsvale *or* The Venerable James D. Porter, Archdeacon of Smithsvale | Dear Archdeacon |
| In conversation: Archdeacon | | |
| BARON | The Right Hon. the Lord Porter of Smithsvale *or* The Lord Porter | The Lord Porter *or* Dear Lord Porter |
| In conversation: My Lord *or* Lord Porter | | |

| *Person being addressed* | *Envelope, and superscription in letter* | *Salutation in letter* |
|---|---|---|
| BARONESS (in her own right) | The Right Hon. the Baroness Brown *or* The Baroness Brown *or* The Right Hon. the Lady Brown | Madam |
| In conversation: Baroness Brown *or* Lady Brown | | |
| BARONESS (wife of Baron) | The Right Hon. the Lady Porter *or* The Lady Porter | Madam |
| In conversation: Madam *or* Lady Porter | | |
| BARONET | Sir James Porter, Bt (the abbreviation Bart is used sometimes) | Sir *or* Dear Sir James |
| In conversation: Sir James | | |
| BARONET'S WIFE | If the daughter of a commoner, Lady Porter; of a viscount or baron, The Hon. Lady Porter; of a duke, a marquess or an earl, Lady Clare Porter | Madam *or* Dear Lady Porter |
| In conversation: Madam *or* Lady Porter | | |
| BISHOP, ANGLICAN DIOCESAN | The Right Reverend James Porter, the Bishop of Smithsvale *or* The Right Reverend the Lord Bishop of Smithsvale | Dear Bishop |
| In conversation: Bishop (preferred) *or* My Lord Bishop | | |
| BISHOP, CATHOLIC | His Lordship, the Most Reverend James D. Porter, Bishop of ........................... | My Lord *or* Dear Bishop Porter |
| In conversation: My Lord *or* Bishop | | |

| *Person being addressed* | *Envelope, and superscription in letter* | *Salutation in letter* |
|---|---|---|
| BISHOP, GREEK ORTHODOX | The Right Reverend Bishop Spiros Georgiou | Your Grace *or less formally* Dear Bishop Georgiou |
| In conversation: Your Grace *or* Bishop | | |
| BISHOP, RUSSIAN ORTHODOX | The Right Reverend Bishop Vassili Karipov | Your Grace *or* Bishop Vassili |
| In conversation: Your Grace *or* Bishop Vassili | | |
| BROTHER | Brother James Porter | Dear Brother James |
| In conversation: Brother *or* Brother James | | |
| CANON | The Reverend Canon James Porter | Dear Canon *or* Dear Canon Porter |
| In conversation: Canon *or* Canon Porter | | |
| CARDINAL | His Eminence, Cardinal James Porter, Archbishop of Smithsvale | Your Eminence *or* Dear Cardinal Porter |
| In conversation: Your Eminence *or* Eminence | | |
| CHAIRMAN, LOCAL GOVERNMENT | The Chairman of the Smithsvale Council (note that the form *chairperson* is often used for either male or female) | Mr (or Madam) Chairman *or less formally* Dear Mr (or Madam) Chairman |
| In conversation: Chairman *or* Mr Chairman (or Madam Chairman) | | |
| CHANCELLOR OF A UNIVERSITY | The Chancellor of the University of Smithsvale (or of Smithsvale University) | Dear Chancellor *or less formally* Dear Professor (or appropriate title) Porter |
| In conversation: Chancellor *or* Mr Chancellor | | |
| CHARGE D'AFFAIRES | Mr James Porter, Chargé d'Affaires, Embassy (or Legation) of Australia in Pacifica | Sir *or less formally* Dear Mr Porter |
| In conversation: Mr Porter | | |

| *Person being addressed* | *Envelope, and superscription in letter* | *Salutation in letter* |
|---|---|---|
| CHIEF JUDGE, DISTRICT COURT NSW | His Honour Judge James Porter | Dear Chief Judge *or less formally* My dear Chief Judge |
| In conversation: Chief Judge | | |
| CHIEF JUDGE, FAMILY COURT OF AUSTRALIA | The Hon. Justice Porter | Dear Chief Judge *or less formally* My dear Chief Judge |
| In conversation: Chief Judge | | |
| CHIEF JUDGE, FEDERAL COURT OF AUSTRALIA | The Justice Brown | Dear Chief Judge *or less formally* My dear Chief Judge |
| In conversation: Chief Judge | | |
| CHIEF JUDGE, SUPREME COURT OF THE ACT | The Hon. Mr Justice Porter | Dear Chief Judge *or less formally* My dear Chief Judge |
| In conversation: Chief Judge | | |
| CHIEF JUSTICE, HIGH COURT | The Hon. Justice Brown | Dear Chief Justice *or less formally* My dear Chief Justice |
| In conversation: Chief Justice | | |
| CHIEF JUSTICE, SUPREME COURT OF SA | The Hon. Justice Clare Brown | Dear Chief Justice *or less formally* My dear Chief Justice |
| In conversation: Chief Justice | | |
| CHIEF JUSTICE, SUPREME COURT, STATE COURTS OTHER THAN SA | The Hon. Mr Justice Porter | Dear Chief Justice *or less formally* My dear Chief Justice |
| In conversation: Chief Justice | | |
| CHIEF MINISTER, LEGISLATIVE ASSEMBLY OF ACT | Ms Clare Brown, MLA, Chief Minister ACT Legislative Assembly | Dear Chief Minister *or less formally* My dear Chief Minister |
| In conversation: Chief Minister | | |
| CHIEF MINISTER, LEGISLATIVE ASSEMBLY OF NT | The Hon. Clare Brown, MLA, Chief Minister NT Legislative Assembly | Dear Chief Minister *or less formally* My dear Chief Minister |
| In conversation: Chief Minister | | |

| *Person being addressed* | *Envelope, and superscription in letter* | *Salutation in letter* |
|---|---|---|
| CONSUL-GENERAL | Mr James Porter, Consul-General of Australia to Pacifica | Sir *or less formally* My dear Consul-General |

In conversation: Consul-General *or* Mr Consul-General

| | | |
|---|---|---|
| COUNCILLOR | Councillor Clare Brown (or Councillor James Porter) | Councillor *or* Dear Councillor *or* Dear Councillor Brown (or Dear Councillor Porter) |

In conversation: Councillor *or* Madam Councillor (or Mr Councillor)

| | | |
|---|---|---|
| COUNTESS | The Right Hon. the Countess of Smithsvale *or* The Countess of Smithsvale | Madam *or less formally* Dear Lady Smithsvale |

In conversation: Madam *or* Lady Smithsvale

CURATE See PRIEST (or CURATE or DEACON), ANGLICAN

| | | |
|---|---|---|
| DAME OF AN ORDER OF CHIVALRY | Dame Clare Brown (add initials GCB, GCMG, GCVO, GBE, DCB, DCMG, DCVO or DBE as the case may be) | Madam *or* Dear Dame Clare Brown *or* Dear Dame Clare |

In conversation: Dame Clare

DEACON See PRIEST (or CURATE or DEACON), ANGLICAN

| | | |
|---|---|---|
| DEAN | The Very Reverend the Dean of Smithsvale | Dear Dean Porter *or* Dear Mr Dean |

In conversation: Sir *or* Mr Dean

| | | |
|---|---|---|
| DEAN OF A UNIVERSITY | Professor Clare Brown, Dean of Music, University of Smithsvale (or of Smithsvale University) | Dear Dean |

In conversation: Dean

| *Person being addressed* | *Envelope, and superscription in letter* | *Salutation in letter* |
|---|---|---|
| DUCHESS | Her Grace the Duchess of Smithsvale *or* The Duchess of Smithsvale | Madam *or* Dear Duchess of Smithsvale *or* Dear Duchess |
| In conversation: Your Grace | | |
| DUKE | His Grace the Duke of Smithsvale *or* The Duke of Smithsvale | My Lord Duke *or* Dear Duke of Smithsvale *or* Dear Duke |
| In conversation: Your Grace | | |
| EARL | The Right Hon. the Earl of Smithsvale | My Lord |
| In conversation: My Lord | | |
| EARL'S WIFE | The Right Hon. the Countess of Smithsvale *or* The Countess of Smithsvale | Madam *or* Dear Lady Smithsvale |
| In conversation: Madam *or* Lady Smithsvale | | |
| GOVERNOR | His Excellency Sir (or Mr) James Porter | Your Excellency *or less formally* My dear Governor |
| In conversation: Your Excellency | | |
| GOVERNOR'S WIFE | Lady (or Mrs) Porter | Dear Lady (or Mrs) Porter |
| In conversation: Lady (or Mrs) Porter | | |
| GOVERNOR-GENERAL | His Excellency Sir (or Mr) James Porter | Your Excellency *or less formally* My dear Governor-General |
| In conversation: Your Excellency | | |
| GOVERNOR-GENERAL'S WIFE | Her Excellency Lady (or Mrs) Porter | Your Excellency *or less formally* Lady (or Mrs) Porter |
| In conversation: Your Excellency *or less formally, after introduction,* Lady (or Mrs) Porter | | |

| *Person being addressed* | *Envelope, and superscription in letter* | *Salutation in letter* |
|---|---|---|
| HIGH COMMISSIONER | Her Excellency<br>Ms Clare Brown,<br>High Commissioner for Australia to Pacifica | Your Excellency<br>*or less formally*<br>My dear High Commissioner |
| In conversation: Your Excellency | | |
| THE HONOURABLE | The Hon. James Porter (or The Hon. Clare Brown) | Dear Sir (or Madam)<br>*or less formally*<br>Dear Mr Porter (or Ms Brown, or title chosen by her) |
| In conversation: Sir (or Madam) *or less formally* Mr Porter (or Ms Brown, or title chosen by her) | | |
| JUDGE, DISTRICT or COUNTY COURTS | His Honour Judge Porter | Dear Judge Porter |
| In conversation: Judge | | |
| JUDGE, FAMILY COURT OF AUSTRALIA | The Hon. Justice Brown | Dear Judge<br>*or less formally*<br>My dear Judge |
| In conversation: Judge | | |
| JUDGE, FEDERAL COURT OF AUSTRALIA | The Hon. Justice Porter | Dear Judge<br>*or less formally*<br>My dear Judge |
| In conversation: Judge | | |
| JUDGE, SUPREME COURT OF THE ACT | The Hon. Mr Justice Porter | Dear Judge<br>*or less formally*<br>My dear Judge |
| In conversation: Judge | | |
| JUSTICE, HIGH COURT | The Hon. Justice Brown | Dear Judge<br>*or less formally*<br>My dear Judge |
| In conversation: Judge | | |
| JUSTICE, SUPREME COURT OF SA | The Hon. Justice Brown | Dear Justice Brown |
| In conversation: Judge | | |

| *Person being addressed* | *Envelope, and superscription in letter* | *Salutation in letter* |
|---|---|---|
| JUSTICE, SUPREME COURT, STATE COURTS OTHER THAN SA<br>In conversation: Judge | The Hon. Mr Justice Porter | Dear Justice Porter |
| KNIGHT BACHELOR<br>In conversation: Sir James | Sir James Porter | Sir<br>*or* Dear Sir James |
| KNIGHT OF AN ORDER OF CHIVALRY<br>In conversation: Sir James | Sir James Porter (add the recognised letters of the Order, such as GCB or KCB) | Sir<br>*or* Dear Sir James |
| KNIGHT'S WIFE See BARONET'S WIFE | | |
| LORD MAYOR (Brisbane, Hobart, Sydney)<br>In conversation: Lord Mayor | The Right Hon. the Lord Mayor of ........................, Alderman Clare Brown | My Lord Mayor<br>*or less formally*<br>Dear Lord Mayor |
| LORD MAYOR (Melbourne)<br>In conversation: Lord Mayor | The Right Hon. the Lord Mayor of Melbourne, Councillor James Porter | My Lord Mayor<br>*or less formally*<br>Dear Lord Mayor |
| LORD MAYOR (Adelaide and Perth)<br>In conversation: Lord Mayor | The Right Hon. the Lord Mayor of ........................, Ms (or title chosen by her) Clare Brown | My Lord Mayor<br>*or less formally*<br>Dear Lord Mayor |
| LORD MAYOR (Darwin)<br>In conversation: Lord Mayor | The Right Worshipful the Lord Mayor of Darwin, Mr Porter | My Lord Mayor<br>*or less formally*<br>Dear Lord Mayor |

| *Person being addressed* | *Envelope, and superscription in letter* | *Salutation in letter* |
|---|---|---|
| LORD MAYOR'S WIFE (or person undertaking duties of Lady Mayoress, for example Lord Mayor's daughter) | The Lady Mayoress of Smithsvale, Mrs (or title chosen by her) Clare Porter | My Lady Mayoress<br>*or less formally*<br>Dear Lady Mayoress |
| MAYOR Note that when a woman is elected Mayor she is never addressed as Mayoress | His Worship the Mayor of Smithsvale, Councillor (or Alderman) Porter (but Geelong uses the title The Right Worshipful the Mayor of Geelong, Alderman Porter) | Mr Mayor<br>*or less formally*<br>Dear Mayor |
| In conversation: Mr Mayor *or* Mayor | | |
| MAYOR'S WIFE | The Mayoress of Smithsvale, Mrs (or title chosen by her) Clare Porter | Madam Mayoress<br>*or less formally*<br>Dear Mayoress |
| In conversation: Madam Mayoress | | |
| MEMBER, HOUSE OF REPRESENTATIVES | Mr James Porter, MP (or if a member of the Privy Council, The Right Hon.; if a former Minister, The Hon.) | Dear Sir<br>*or less formally*<br>Dear Mr Porter |
| In conversation: Mr Porter | | |
| MEMBER, LEGISLATIVE ASSEMBLY or HOUSE OF ASSEMBLY | Mr James Porter, MP (or MLA or MHA as appropriate) | Dear Sir<br>*or less formally*<br>Dear Mr Porter |
| In conversation: Mr Porter | | |
| MEMBER, LEGISLATIVE COUNCIL | The Hon. Clare Brown, MLC | Dear Madam<br>*or less formally*<br>Dear Ms (or title chosen by her) Brown |
| In conversation: Ms Brown (or title chosen by her) | | |
| MINISTER, HOUSE OF REPRESENTATIVES | The [Right] Hon. James Porter, MP, Minister for ........................ | Dear Minister<br>*or less formally*<br>Dear Mr Porter |
| In conversation: Mr Minister *or* Minister | | |

| *Person being addressed* | *Envelope, and superscription in letter* | *Salutation in letter* |
|---|---|---|
| MINISTER, SENATE | Senator the [Right] Hon. Clare Brown, Minister for ........................ | Dear Minister *or less formally* Dear Senator |
| In conversation: Minister | | |
| MINISTER, STATE PARLIAMENT | The Hon. James Porter, MP (or MLA, MHA or MLC as appropriate), Minister for ........................ | Dear Minister *or* Dear Mr |
| In conversation: Mr Minister *or* Minister | | |
| MINISTER, UNITING CHURCH | The Reverend James Porter | Dear Sir *or less formally* Dear Mr Porter |
| In conversation: Mr Porter | | |
| MONSIGNOR | The Reverend Monsignor James Porter (add initials PP if also a parish priest) | Dear Monsignor Porter |
| In conversation: Monsignor | | |
| NUN | Sister Clare Brown | Dear Sister Clare |
| In conversation: Sister *or* Sister Clare | | |
| POLICE COMMISSIONER | Commissioner of Police for ........................ | Dear Commissioner *or* Dear Commissioner Porter |
| In conversation: Commissioner *or* Mr Porter | | |
| PREMIER | The Hon. James Porter, MP (or in SA alternatively MHA), Premier of .................... | Dear Premier *or less formally* My dear Premier |
| In conversation: Mr Premier *or* Premier | | |
| PRESIDENT-GENERAL, BAPTIST CHURCH | The Reverend James Porter (or, if a layman, Mr James Porter) | Dear Sir *or less formally* Dear Mr Porter |
| In conversation: Mr President-General *or less formally* Mr Porter | | |

| *Person being addressed* | *Envelope, and superscription in letter* | *Salutation in letter* |
|---|---|---|
| PRESIDENT, LEGISLATIVE COUNCIL | The Hon. James Porter, MLC, President of the Legislative Council | Dear Mr President *or less formally* My dear President |
| In conversation: Mr President | | |
| PRESIDENT OF THE ASSEMBLY, UNITING CHURCH | The Reverend James Porter | Dear Mr President *or less formally* Dear Mr Porter |
| In conversation: Mr President *or less formally* Mr Porter | | |
| PRESIDENT, SENATE | Senator the Hon. James Porter, President of the Senate | Dear Mr President *or less formally* My dear President |
| In conversation: Mr President | | |
| PRIEST, CATHOLIC | The Reverend Father Porter (add initials PP if a parish priest) | Dear Father Porter |
| In conversation: Father | | |
| PRIEST (or CURATE or DEACON), ANGLICAN | The Reverend James D. Porter *or sometimes* The Reverend Father James D. Porter | Dear Mr Porter *or sometimes* Dear Reverend Father *or less formally* Dear Father Porter |
| In conversation: Mr Porter | | |
| PRIEST, GREEK ORTHODOX | The Reverend Father Georgiou | Dear Father Georgiou |
| In conversation: Father | | |
| PRIEST, RUSSIAN ORTHODOX | The Reverend Father Vassili Karipov | Dear Father Vassili |
| In conversation: Father Vassili | | |
| PRIMATE OF AUSTRALIA | | |
| *If an Archbishop* | The Most Reverend the Archbishop of ..............., Primate of Australia | Dear Archbishop *or* Your Grace |
| In conversation: Your Grace *or* Archbishop | | |
| *If a Bishop* | The Right Reverend the Bishop of .................., Primate of Australia | Dear Bishop |
| In conversation: Bishop *or* My Lord Bishop | | |

| *Person being addressed* | *Envelope, and superscription in letter* | *Salutation in letter* |
|---|---|---|
| PRIME MINISTER | The [Right] Hon. James Porter, MP, Prime Minister | Dear Prime Minister *or less formally* My dear Prime Minister |
| In conversation: Prime Minister *or* Mr Prime Minister | | |
| PRIVY COUNSELLOR | The Right Hon. James Porter (if also a peer, the name is followed by the initials PC after all other orders and decorations) | According to the rank of the individual |
| In conversation: according to the rank of the individual | | |
| PROFESSOR AT A UNIVERSITY | Professor Clare Brown, University of Smithsvale (or of Smithsvale University) | Dear Madam *or less formally* Dear Professor Brown |
| In conversation: Professor *or* Professor Brown | | |
| QUEEN | The Queen's Most Excellent Majesty *or* Her Majesty The Queen (for formal and state documents; all other correspondence is addressed to The Private Secretary to Her Majesty The Queen) | Madam *or* May it please Your Majesty *A letter should conclude:* I have the honour to remain, Madam, Your Majesty's most humble and obedient servant |
| In conversation: Your Majesty *and subsequently* Ma'am | | |
| QUEEN'S COUNSEL | Mr James Porter, QC | Dear Sir *or* Dear Mr Porter |
| In conversation: Mr Porter | | |
| RABBI | Rabbi Abrahams | Dear Sir *or less formally* Dear Rabbi Abrahams |
| In conversation: Rabbi Abrahams *or less formally* Rabbi | | |
| SALVATION ARMY COMMISSIONER | Commissioner Porter | Dear Commissioner Porter |
| In conversation: Commissioner *or* Commissioner Porter | | |

| *Person being addressed* | *Envelope, and superscription in letter* | *Salutation in letter* |
|---|---|---|
| SENATOR | Senator (or Senator the [Right] Hon.) Clare Brown | Dear Madam *or less formally* Dear Senator |
| In conversation: Senator | | |
| SHIRE PRESIDENT | The Shire President, Councillor Clare Brown | Dear Madam President |
| In conversation: Madam President | | |
| SPEAKER, HOUSE OF REPRESENTATIVES | The Honourable James Porter, MP, Speaker of the House of Representatives | Dear Mr Speaker *or less formally* My dear Speaker |
| In conversation: Mr Speaker | | |
| VICE-CHANCELLOR OF A UNIVERSITY | The Vice-Chancellor of the University of Smithsvale (or of Smithsvale University) | Dear Vice-Chancellor *or less formally* Dear Professor (or appropriate title) Porter |
| In conversation: Vice-Chancellor | | |
| VISCOUNT | The Right Hon. the Viscount Porter *or* The Viscount Porter | My Lord *or* Dear Lord Porter |
| In conversation: My Lord *or* Lord Porter | | |
| VISCOUNTESS | The Right Hon. the Viscountess Porter *or* The Viscountess Porter | My Lady *or* Dear Lady Porter |
| In conversation: My Lady | | |

***Honours and awards*** Honours, awards, degrees and so on are usually indicated by their initial letters, placed after a person's surname. The correct sequence for post-nominal initials is:

orders
decorations
medals (war medals in campaign sequence)
civil distinctions
university degrees and diplomas (in the order conferred)
membership of associations and societies
membership of parliament

Since 1975 Australia has had its own honours system, the Order of Australia, which has largely replaced the imperial honours system. Below is a list of the main Australian and British honours and awards (and their abbreviations where applicable) in order of precedence. Note that the honours Knight of the Order of Australia (AK) and Dame of the Order of Australia (AD) were abolished in 1986.

The honours and awards that come under the Australian Order of Precedence are italicised.

| | |
|---|---|
| *VC* | *Victoria Cross* |
| GC | George Cross |
| *CV* | *Cross of Valour* |
| *KG* or *LG* | *Knight* or *Lady of the Garter* |
| *KT* or *LT* | *Knight* or *Lady of the Thistle* |
| GCB | Knight *or* Dame Grand Cross of the Order of the Bath |
| *OM* | *Order of Merit* |
| *AK* or *AD* | *Knight* or *Dame of the Order of Australia* |
| GCMG | Knight *or* Dame Grand Cross of the Order of St Michael and St George |
| *GCVO* | *Knight* or *Dame Grand Cross of the Royal Victorian Order* |
| GBE | Knight *or* Dame Grand Cross of the Order of the British Empire |
| *AC* | *Companion of the Order of Australia* |
| CH | Companion of Honour |
| KCB *or* DCB | Knight *or* Dame Commander of the Order of the Bath |
| KCMG *or* DCMG | Knight *or* Dame Commander of the Order of St Michael and St George |
| *KCVO* or *DCVO* | *Knight* or *Dame Commander of the Royal Victorian Order* |
| KBE *or* DBE | Knight *or* Dame Commander of the Order of the British Empire |
| Knight Bachelor | |
| *AO* | *Officer of the Order of Australia* |
| CB | Companion of the Order of the Bath |
| CMG | Companion of the Order of St Michael and St George |
| *CVO* | *Commander of the Royal Victorian Order* |
| CBE | Commander of the Order of the British Empire |
| *SG* | *Star of Gallantry* |
| *SC* | *Star of Courage* |
| DSO | Companion of the Distinguished Service Order |
| *DSC* | *Distinguished Service Cross* |
| *AM* | *Member of the Order of Australia* |
| *LVO* | *Lieutenant of the Royal Victorian Order* |
| OBE | Officer of the Order of the British Empire |
| ISO | Companion of the Imperial Service Order |
| *MVO* | *Member of the Royal Victorian Order* |
| MBE | Member of the Order of the British Empire |

| | |
|---|---|
| *CSC* | *Conspicuous Service Cross* |
| *NSC* | *Nursing Service Cross* |
| RRC | Royal Red Cross (1st Class) |
| DSC | Distinguished Service Cross |
| MC | Military Cross |
| DFC | Distinguished Flying Cross |
| AFC | Air Force Cross |
| ARRC | Royal Red Cross (2nd Class) |
| *MG* | *Medal for Gallantry* |
| *BM* | *Bravery Medal* |
| *DSM* | *Distinguished Service Medal* |
| *PSM* | *Public Service Medal* |
| *APM* | *Australian Police Medal* |
| *AFSM* | *Australian Fire Service Medal* |
| *OAM* | *Medal of the Order of Australia* |
| *Order of St John* | |
| DCM | Distinguished Conduct Medal |
| CGM | Conspicuous Gallantry Medal |
| GM | George Medal |
| *CSM* | *Conspicuous Service Medal* |
| *Antarctic Medal* | |
| QPM | Queen's Police Medal for Gallantry |
| QFSM | Queen's Fire Service Medal for Gallantry |
| DSM | Distinguished Service Medal |
| MM | Military Medal |
| DFM | Distinguished Flying Medal |
| AFM | Air Force Medal |
| QGM | Queen's Gallantry Medal |
| *RVM* | *Royal Victorian Medal* |
| BEM | British Empire Medal |
| QPM | Queen's Police Medal for Distinguished Service |
| QFSM | Queen's Fire Service Medal for Distinguished Service |

*Commendation for Gallantry*
*Commendation for Brave Conduct*
Queen's Commendation for Brave Conduct
*Commendation for Distinguished Service*
*War Medals/Australian Active Service Medal (in order of date of qualifying service)*
*Australian Service Medal*
*Police Overseas Service Medal*
Polar Medal
Imperial Service Medal
*Coronation and Jubilee Medals (in order of date of receipt)*

*Defence Force Service Medal*
*RFD* *Reserve Force Decoration*
*Reserve Force Medal*
*National Medal*
*Champion Shots Medal*
*Long Service Medals*
Independence and Anniversary Medals (in order of date of receipt)
*Foreign Awards (in order of date of authorisation of their acceptance and wearing)*

See also **degrees and diplomas; Doctor, the title; KC; MHA; MHR; MLA; MLC; MP; Ms; professor; QC; reverend/the Reverend/reverent.**

**RAOU** Royal Australasian Ornithologists Union.

**rapacious/voracious** *Rapacious* means greedy for money or possessions, and liable to seize them:

A bank that was open-handed in the boom became rapacious in the recession.

*Voracious* means hungry for food or (figuratively) cultural nourishment:

Clarissa is a voracious reader and theatregoer.

**rapt/wrapped** Both *rapt* and *wrapped* (more colloquially) can now mean engrossed, enraptured or full of enthusiasm. The association between *rapt* and *enraptured*, and *wrapped* and *enveloped*, seems to have helped two similar-sounding words to converge.

The audience paid rapt attention to a performance of *The Display*.

Tracy saw Julian Lennon and was wrapped [*or* rapt].

Note that *wrapt* is an obsolete form of *wrapped*.

**rarefy/rarefied/rarefying** Note the spelling.

**rarely** Avoid the phrase *rarely ever*.

**rather** It is correct to use *rather* with either *would* or *had* to express preference, although *would* is much more common than *had*:

He would [*or* had] rather play than study.

Note that both *a rather good meal* and *rather a good meal* are correct. Be careful how you handle the construction *rather than*; do not duplicate the comparison:

We wanted to visit Broome rather than Darwin.

*but* We were more eager to visit Broome than [*not* rather than] Darwin.

**ravage/ravish** The verb *ravage* means to devastate or cause havoc in:

The bushfire ravaged the pine plantation near the town.

*Ravish* is a peculiar word, having two meanings that stand in stark contrast. One is to enchant or enrapture:

We were ravished by the beauty of the east coast.

The other is to carry off (a female) by force or to rape (her).

**raze** See **raise/rise/raze**.

**RBL** reasonable benefit limit (superannuation).

**RC** Roman Catholic.

**RDO** rostered day off.

**re** The preposition *concerning* is often replaced by the Latin word *re*, which means with regard to, but this should be restricted to legal writing and headings in business correspondence. *Re* may be set in italic or roman type, and is pronounced 'ree'.

**re-** This prefix means again. It is generally linked to its root word without a hyphen except when followed by *e*: *readmit*, *redefine*, *re-elect*, *re-employ*. Sometimes a hyphen is essential for distinguishing between two otherwise identical-looking words – for example, *recount* (to narrate) and *re-count* (to count again). In speech the distinction is usually easy to make because emphasis can be placed on particular syllables. When *redress* means to make amends, for example, only the second syllable is stressed, but when it means to dress again, *re-* is pronounced to rhyme with *tree* and both syllables are stressed.

Be careful not to repeat the *again* idea when using a *re-* word:

Practice matches can now revert [*not* revert back] to their fortnightly pattern.

The goalkeeper was recalled to the position of captain [*not* again].

**reaction** Some authorities are of the view that *reaction* should be used to describe an immediate or spontaneous response rather than a considered one:

The horse's reaction to the kangaroo was to bolt.

*but* Analyse the costs and give me your response [*rather than* reaction] next week.

However, the second usage is now so common that it should probably be regarded as a mere peccadillo.

**readable** See **illegible/unreadable**.

**reader** In the world of publishing there are three distinct kinds of reader. The one the publisher woos is the indispensable reader of publications, preferably also a buyer. The reader who examines and reports on manuscripts submitted to publishers may be an outside expert or an editor, but the role of this kind of reader is to help the publisher to decide whether or not to accept the work. The third kind of reader, more often called a *proofreader*, is the person who checks typesetters' proofs for the publisher. Some editors fill all three roles.

**read-only memory** A computer's *read-only memory* (*ROM*) is an internal memory area where programs that control the computer's functioning, such as the start-up routines, are stored. The ROM of a computer is installed in memory chips by the manufacturer and cannot be altered by the user. Switching off the power to the computer does not affect the ROM.

See also **memory; random-access memory**.

**real/realistic/really** This trio of words is much abused in modern usage; all three are overworked, and in many instances they are superfluous. All can be deleted from the following examples without loss of meaning: *a real problem*; *a realistic likeness*; *a really good attempt*. When an intensifier is needed, try to find more specific or less hackneyed words, for example *a serious problem*; *a dramatic likeness*; *a particularly good attempt*. The expression *Get real!* is a relatively new piece of slang.

**reason** Although frequently heard, the phrase *the reason is because* is tautological:

The reason I am leaving is that I am tired.

*not* The reason I am leaving is because I am tired.

Most authorities consider *the reason why* idiomatic and acceptable, although *why* (or *reason*) can often be omitted:

That was the reason [*or* That was why] I left the meeting.

Avoid this common but particularly clumsy misconstruction:

The reason why I am leaving is because I am tired.

The simplest substitute leaves out *reason* altogether:

I am leaving because I am tired.

See also **because**.

**rebut** See **deny/refute/rebut**.

**receipt** Note the *-ei-* and *-pt*.

**receivership** See **bankruptcy/factoring/liquidation/receivership**.

**reciprocal** See **common/mutual/reciprocal**.

**recompense** Note the *-se*.

**recount/re-count** The verb *recount* means to relate or narrate; *re-count* (with a hyphen) means to count again.

See also **re-**.

**recoup/recover/recuperate** These three verbs can have the same meaning, but they are not all used in exactly the same way. *Recoup* may mean to recover in the context of financial loss:

The gambler barely managed to recoup [*or* recover] his stake.

It may also mean to recompense:

The company will recoup you for the loss of your time.

*Recover* and *recuperate* can be used synonymously in the context of health as well as finance; they are both followed by *from* in the next construction:

She was recovering [*or* recuperating] from an operation.

The broker recuperated [*or* recovered] from his losses on the stock exchange.

See also **recover/re-cover**.

**recourse/resort/resource** These three nouns (the middle one can also be used as a verb) all broadly refer to something called on for help. They are rarely interchangeable, however.

Arthur could not buy the book but had recourse to the school library.

*Resort* implies more extreme need than the other words:

The book was not there, and the university library was his last resort.

Arthur resorted to the university library when he could not find the book elsewhere.

*Resource* and its plural, *resources*, can sometimes be interchanged, and both have more general application than the other two:

The library provides a rich resource [*or* provides rich resources] for researchers.

**recover/re-cover** *Recover* means to regain something lost or taken away; *re-cover* (with a hyphen) means to provide with a new cover.

See also **re-**; **recoup/recover/recuperate**.

**recreation/re-creation** *Recreation* means a relaxing activity or a pleasurable pastime; *re-creation* (with a hyphen) is reconstruction, or the creation of something again.

See also **re-**.

**recto** See **page numbering**.

**recuperate** See **recoup/recover/recuperate**.

**recur/recurrence** Note the spellings; 'reoccur' and 'reoccurrence' are common errors.

**Redcliffe, Qld and WA** Compare with *Red Cliffs*, Vic.

**Red Hill, ACT, Qld, Vic., WA** Compare with *Redhill*, SA; *Red Hills*, Tas.

**Reds** This term is now an out-of-date Cold War synonym for *communists*, and should not be used except in, for instance, a quotation.

**redundant** This adjective means superfluous; avoid using it where *irrelevant*, *unnecessary* or *unimportant* would be more appropriate:

> His report on whale sightings was redundant because we already had the information.
>
> His report on whale sightings was irrelevant [*not* redundant] because funding for the campaign had been cancelled.

**reference** There are several rather verbose phrases that include this word, but most have simple substitutes. Instead of *in reference to* and *with reference to*, consider using *on*, *about*, *respecting* or *regarding*; and rather than *have reference to*, try *mean* or *are about*.

See also **references**.

**reference marks** Footnotes providing supplementary information in a publication may be keyed to the text by the following *reference marks*, in standard sequence:

| | |
|---|---|
| asterisk | * |
| dagger | † |
| double dagger | ‡ |
| section mark | § |
| parallel rules | ‖ |
| paragraph symbol | ¶ |

If there are more than six footnotes the symbols may be doubled (** and so on) but superior figures ([1] and so on) are preferred, as they usually are for notes whose main function is to supply references to the author's sources rather than to convey additional information. Reference marks are placed after the text to be referenced, preferably at the end of a sentence and after the final punctuation mark. These characters are usually available in desktop-publishing programs.

See also **asterisk**; **inferior characters/superior characters**; **notes**; **references**.

**references** References to an author's sources in a non-fiction work may be sparse enough to be incorporated informally:

> Trevor Nottle has some useful appendixes in *The Cottage Garden Revived*, published by Kangaroo Press in 1984.

Where a substantial number of precise references are necessary, the *note system of referencing* is recommended for general use and for scholarly works in the humanities. The *Harvard system of referencing* (otherwise referred to as the *author–date system*) is favoured for other publications, particularly scientific and technical ones.

See the entry **notes** for the separate role of footnotes under either of these systems.

***The note system*** The main advantage of this mode of referencing is that it allows text to flow with virtually no interruption. To keep costs down, the references – keyed to the text with small numbers (superior figures) – are now usually printed at the end of articles, chapters and books rather than at the foot of the relevant page.

The conventions for the system are detailed in the third edition of the AGPS *Style Manual*, but an outline follows.

You should place the superior figures ([1] and so on) at the end of the sentence (or paragraph) referred to where possible. The format for citing the first reference to a work is very similar to the traditional format for items in a bibliography, as set out under the entry **bibliographies** in this book. There are four differences: the superior figure keying the note to the text precedes the item; the name of the author is in its natural sequence (*not* with surname first); commas rather than full stops divide up the note; and page details are included where required. Here is an example of text followed by the references relating to it:

> There are many opportunities for senior citizens to acquire income-producing skills.[1] Such skills, often learnt in difficult times,[2] can be picked up from one's parents and subsequently revived.[3] They have been known to give life an entirely new meaning.[4]

The actual references would read thus:

> [1]P. I. Croxford, *Woodworking for Retirees*, Prack Press, Sydney, 1992, pp. 164–95.
>
> [2]*Argus* (Melbourne), 1931.
>
> [3]Brian Tilly, Reminiscences of Adelaide in the 1950s, taped in Sydney 12–15 January 1990, transcript in writer's possession, pp. 7–10.
>
> [4]Sol Tennant, 'Living Alone', *Oldies Journal*, vol. 3, no. 2, 1989, pp. 41–5.

Second references to the same sources can be much abbreviated:

> [5]Croxford, p. 169.
>
> [6]*Argus*, 1931.
>
> [7]Tilly, pp. 15–20.
>
> [8]Tennant, p. 44.

Subsequent references are set out similarly, unless there are consecutive references to the same source – in which case there are two options:

> [9]Tennant, p. 42.

*or* [9]ibid., p. 42.

The use of other Latin abbreviations such as op. cit. and loc. cit. is now largely outmoded.

***The Harvard (author–date) system*** The *Harvard system* is more disruptive to a narrative than the *note system*, but it does away with the tedious checking of superior figures for sequence and completeness. The textual references supply minimal detail; however, though its format is slightly different, the alphabetically arranged *list of references* contains information similar to that in the note system references. Here is a brief summary of procedure.

The references are placed within parentheses at the end of sentences (or paragraphs) where possible. Here is the passage quoted above, with references given the Harvard system treatment:

> There are many opportunities for senior citizens to acquire income-producing skills (Croxford 1992). Such skills, often learnt in difficult times (*Argus* 1931), can be picked up from one's parents and subsequently revived (Tilly 1990). They have been known to give life an entirely new meaning (Tennant 1989).

The alphabetical *list of references* would read as follows:

> *Argus* (Melbourne) 1931.
>
> Croxford, P. I. 1992, *Woodworking for Retirees*, Prack Press, Sydney, pp. 164–95.
>
> Tennant, Sol 1989, 'Living Alone', *Oldies Journal*, vol. 3, no. 2, pp. 41–5.
>
> Tilly, Brian 1990, Reminiscences of Adelaide in the 1950s, taped in Sydney 12–15 January, transcript in writer's possession, pp. 7–10.

Additional reading recommended may be set out separately in a bibliography. Note, however, that under the Harvard system a bibliography has exactly the same format as the list of references, whereas the format for bibliography and references differs in several respects under the note system.

See also **bibliographic style; bibliographies; et al.; ibid.; loc. cit.; notes; op. cit.; reference marks; titles of publications, and literary, artistic and musical works.**

**referendum** The accepted plural is *referendums*.

**reform/re-form** The verb *reform* means to bring reform or to amend, but *re-form* (with a hyphen) means to form again.

See also **re-**.

**refute** See **deny/refute/rebut**.

**regard** Several idiomatic phrases include the word *regard*, and they all need to be checked, in context, for possible verbosity. *In regard to* can often be replaced by *about*; *with regard to* by *concerning*; and *as regards* by *regarding*.

In constructions such as the following, where the verb *regard* means to consider, it must be followed by *as*:

> She regards him as her son.

*not* She regards him her son.

Do not follow *as* with a participle or an infinitive, however: *She regards him as being her son*; *She regards him to be her son.*

See also **consider**.

**regardless** See **irregardless/regardless**.

**Regency Park, SA** Compare with *Regents Park*, NSW.

**register marks** In the preparation of artwork for a publication, *register marks* – very short printed lines at right angles to each other – act as a guide for alignment at the printing stage.

**regretfully/regrettably** *Regretfully* means with regret, sadly:

He remembered his rash words regretfully.

*Regrettably* (note the *-tt-*) means unfortunately:

Regrettably he could not cancel the effect of his rash words.

**regularly** Pronounce the four syllables clearly ('reg-yoo-lar-lee', not 'reg-yoo-lee').

**regular type** See **type**.

**rein/reign** A *rein* is a restraint: *a horse's rein*; *a rein on the imagination*. Note the spelling of the idiomatic *free rein*. A *reign* is the period of a sovereign's rule, or of a dominating power or influence: *Queen Juliana's reign*; *the reign of protectionism*.

**reiterate** This verb means to say or do again, or repeatedly. Note that *reiterate again* is a tautology.

**relation/relationship/relative** When *relation* and *relationship* mean link, prefer *relation* for abstract connections: *the relation between instinct and imagination*. Use *relationship* for human connections, including those of kin: *the father–son relationship*; *a lasting relationship between colleagues*. The plural *relations* is preferable when you mean dealings: *good employer–employee relations*. Use either *relation* or *relative* to refer to people connected by blood, marriage or adoption: *relations [*or *relatives] staying over Easter*.

**relatively** See **comparatively/relatively**.

**relay/re-lay** The verb *relay* means to transmit; *re-lay* (with a hyphen) means to put down again. Note that the past tense and past participle of *relay* are spelt *relayed*, whereas those of *re-lay* are spelt *re-laid*.

See also **lay/laying/lie/lying**; **re-**.

**relevant** See **germane/material/relevant**.

**relocate** Public servants and business people persistently overwork this verb: *The office will relocate to Brisbane next month*. Prefer *move* or *shift*.

**REM** rapid eye-movement.

**remain** Avoid the tautological phrases *continue to remain* and *still remain.*

**remediable/remedial** *Remediable* means capable of being put right; its opposite, *irremediable*, is probably used more frequently in spite of being harder to spell: *remediable erosion problems*; *irremediable cracking*.

*Remedial* means providing a remedy: *remedial education*.

**remembrance** Not 'rememberance'.

**reminiscent** Note the *-sc-*.

**renaissance/renascence** A *renaissance* is a rebirth or revival; *renascence* is a less common form of the word. When used in reference to the revival of classical learning and art in Europe, beginning in the fourteenth century, *renaissance* is often spelt with an initial capital. Pronounce it 're-**nay**-sonce'.

**rendezvous** This is both the singular and plural form. Derived from the French phrase *rendez-vous* (present yourself) the word means a meeting. It is often used as a verb but some forms of it (*rendezvousing*, for example) are clumsy. Pronounce it 'ronday-**voo**'.

**renege** This awkward-looking verb means to fail to carry out (a promise or agreement), and is followed by *on* when a preposition is required:

> Our council agreed to subsidise a new road then reneged on the deal.

Pronounce the word 're-**neg**' or 're-**nig**'.

**rental** Prefer *rent*.

**repair** See **fix/repair**; **repairable/reparable**.

**repairable/reparable** Both these adjectives broadly mean capable of being repaired, but only *repairable* is used of material objects:

> The broken television set was repairable.

*Reparable* is used with abstract nouns, and implies remedy rather than repair:

> The damage to her pride was reparable, but the friendship was doomed.

Note that the opposite of *repairable* is *unrepairable*; of *reparable*, *irreparable*. Stress the second syllable in *repairable*, the first in *reparable*.

See also **fix/repair**.

**repeat** Avoid the tautological phrase *repeat again*.

**repel/repulse/repellent/repulsive** The verbs *repel* and *repulse* can both mean to drive back:

> We asked the toughest-looking guest to repel [*or* repulse] gate-crashers.

While the adjectives *repellent* and *repulsive* can both mean distasteful or repugnant, *repulsive* is the stronger of the two:

I find the dentist's chair repellent, but my dentist's haughty manner is positively repulsive.

As an adjective *repellent* can also mean repelling: *water-repellent cloth*. The noun *repellent* means an article or substance that repels: *mosquito repellent*.

**repercussion** This is an excessively weighty noun to use if *result*, *effect* or *consequence* would be adequate:

A result [*not* repercussion] of the strike was a shortage of milk.

Save *repercussion* (often in the plural) to describe the after-effects of important or serious incidents:

The Chernobyl nuclear accident had lasting repercussions.

**repetitious/repetitive** While both these adjectives broadly mean repeated, *repetitious* always suggests undue and tedious repetition: *a boringly repetitious speech*. *Repetitive* does not usually have negative implications: *repetitive hand movements*.

**replace/substitute** *Replace* means to take the place of; note the idiomatic use of prepositions:

I will replace the old video *with* a new one.

Pam was replaced *by* Lara *as* receptionist [use *by* when verb passive].

*or* Lara replaced Pam *as* receptionist.

*Substitute* means to put in the place of, and is always followed by *for*:

I will substitute the new video *for* the old one.

**replete** This adjective means abundantly supplied or full (particularly of food): *replete after Christmas dinner*. Avoid using it when you simply mean provided or fitted with, unless irony is intended:

The bathroom was fitted [*not* replete] with gold taps and gilt mirrors.

**report** Refer to a report *on*, not *into*.

**reports and submissions** These two kinds of document may be differentiated by their respective purposes. A *report* is usually requested by an individual or organisation wanting answers, information and recommendations. A *submission* is made up of a collection of arguments put forward to support or object to certain actions, and is designed to persuade or convince.

Accuracy, relevance and clarity are the essential elements of good reports and submissions. Both are often the product of a long process of investigation, analysis and sorting of information. The sifting out of non-essential material is one of the keys to the readability of a document, and only a small proportion of the data gathered may remain in it.

Two things will help to keep a writer on track when drafting a document: constant checking of the material against the subject to ensure that it is appropriate; and constant awareness of its audience. Reading the text out loud is a good test of both relevance and clarity.

Language and structure are of prime importance. Straightforward language, expressing clearly what the writer wants to say, is the most effective. Unless a report is intended only for specialists all technical terms should be explained, preferably within the body of the text (or, if necessary, in footnotes or a glossary). Information needs to be presented in a logical sequence so that the reader is led easily from one point to the next. For example, in a document dealing with housing problems you could organise information chronologically (1890s to the present), by area (inner, middle and outer suburbs) or by type (private and public).

The way a document of this kind is arranged depends on the topic and intended readership. However, most reports and submissions include the following parts.

Title page (bearing the title, author's name, place and date of publication)
Terms of reference (if applicable)
Acknowledgements (where necessary)
List of contents (which should be fairly detailed if there is no index)
Summary (if the text is complex and long)
Introduction (which explains what the report or submission is about)
Text (divided into sections or chapters)
Conclusions or recommendations (or both)
Appendixes (containing details that would not be appropriate in the text)
Glossary (if necessary)
Bibliography or list of references
Index (if the document is long)

See also **circumlocution**; **commercialese**; **copy editing**; **officialese**; **publications, parts of**.

**represent/re-present** *Represent* may mean to stand for or act in place of, exemplify or portray:

My sister will represent me at the shareholders' meeting.
My mother represents all that is gracious.

When *represent* means portray, *is* may be the better word:

This story is [*not* represents] the truth.

*Re-present* (with a hyphen) means to present again.

See also **re-**.

**reprint** See **edition/impression/reprint**.

**repulse/repulsive** See **repel/repulse/repellent/repulsive**.

**reputable** Put the stress on the first syllable.

**requisite** See **perquisite/prerequisite/requisite**.

**research** For both noun and verb, put the stress on the second syllable.

**reservoir** Pronounce this word 'rezza-**vwar**' rather than 'rezza-**vor**'.

**reside** Use *live*.

**resident font** A *resident font* is a typeface that is supplied with and resident in your computer system. The fonts most commonly included for desktop publishing are Times, Helvetica, Palatino, Avant Garde and Zapf Dingbats. The corresponding printer fonts are also necessary and are often supplied.

See also **downloadable font**; **font**; **printer font/screen font**.

**resolution** See **dots per inch**; **pixel**.

**resort/re-sort** The verb *resort* means to have recourse to: *resort to legal action*. *Re-sort* (with a hyphen) means to sort again.

See also **re-**; **recourse/resort/resource**.

**resource** See **recourse/resort/resource**.

**respective/respectively** These words are used to clarify the relationship between two or more things referred to:

> The children placed their respective gifts on the table.

Here *respective* indicates that each child brought a separate gift, rather than that the children as a body brought gifts.

> The Art and Music departments are situated in A and B blocks respectively.

Here *respectively* removes the possibility that the departments share A and B blocks. Do not use these words unnecessarily, however:

> The children climbed onto their horses [*not* respective horses].

The children are unlikely to climb onto more than one horse at a time, or to do it collectively.

> She travelled to Singapore, Hong Kong and Tokyo [*not* respectively].

As only one traveller is mentioned, there is no confusion to avoid.

Certain officials may need to be reminded that *respectively* and *respectfully* are far from synonymous:

> Patrons are respectfully [*not* respectively] requested to leave quietly.

**respite** As this noun means temporary relief, do not double up by using the term *temporary respite*. The second syllable rhymes with *bit* (the *i* is barely sounded) or *bite*.

**restaurateur** Someone who runs a *restaurant* is a *restaurateur*, not a 'restauranteur', although the latter is such a common error that its existence is noted in some dictionaries.

**restive/restless** Both these adjectives can mean agitated, fidgety, unable to keep still. Prefer *restive* if there is some indication that the agitation is a reaction against restraint.

The tethered horse was restive.
Inge had a restless night because of the humidity.

**restrictive clause** See **clause**.

**restrictive phrase** See **phrase**.

**résumé** Note that this French word meaning brief description or summary is not italicised, but retains its accents in English to distinguish it from the verb *to resume*.

See also **c.v.**

**resuscitate** Note the *-sc-*.

**retro-** No hyphen is used to link this prefix, meaning backwards, with root words. Compounds include *retrograde* (going backwards); *retrospective* (directed to the past); and *retroverted* (tilted backwards).

**return** Avoid the tautological phrases *return back* and *return again*.

**return key** The *return key* on a computer (or typewriter) keyboard is used to take the operator from the end of one line to the beginning of the next. It is also often used to confirm computer commands.

**Reuters** The British news agency is called *Reuters Ltd*, but note the following forms: *AAP-Reuter*; *a Reuter correspondent*; *a Reuter report*.

**Revelation, Book of** The shortened title is *Revelation*, not the common but incorrect 'Revelations'.

**revenge** See **avenge/revenge/vengeance**.

**reverend/the Reverend/reverent** *Reverend* means worthy of or entitled to reverence: *the reverend gentleman*. With an initial capital, and preceded by *the*, this is the general title for a minister of religion or priest. *The Reverend* is often abbreviated to *the Rev.* or *the Revd* (which is less common). It should always be used with a secondary title, given name or at least one initial: *the*

*Reverend Father Doyle*; *the Reverend Dr Jones*; *the Reverend Peter Morgan*; *the Reverend P. Morgan*. It is incorrect to address a clergyman simply as *Reverend* or *Reverend Morgan*, whatever the circumstances. Informally, the appropriate style for the priest is *Father Doyle*; for the others, *Dr Jones* and *Mr Morgan*. The same rules apply when the clergy are women; the informal style will depend on the preference of the woman, which might be *Dr*, *Mrs*, *Miss* or *Ms Wilson*. Note that *the Reverend* precedes any other title.

*Reverent* means feeling or characterised by reverence, and is used to describe deep respect or piety:

The pilgrims knelt before the relics in a reverent hush.

See also **ranks, titles, honours and awards**.

**reversal/reversion** A *reversal* is the act of reversing something – that is, turning it about:

The inflationary budget meant a reversal for the country's economy.

The related verb is *to reverse*.

A *reversion* is the act of going back – to former practices, conditions and so on:

Despite promises, his present actions indicate a reversion to past habits.

*Reversion* also has specialised meanings in biology, law and insurance. The relevant verb is *to revert*.

Remember not to combine any of these words with *back* as they already contain this sense.

**reverse** See **converse/inverse/obverse/reverse; reversal/reversion**.

**reverse type** See **desktop publishing; type**.

**reversion/revert** See **reversal/reversion**.

**review/revue** A *review* is any examination of something, in the form of, for instance, a report or critique; or a periodical containing articles on current affairs, books and so on. Note that you undertake a review *of* not *into* a matter. A *revue* is a theatrical entertainment consisting usually of songs and satirical sketches.

**revolting** This word can mean in revolt or disgusting. Be sure that the context makes your meaning clear. *Revolting* peasants are not necessarily disgusting.

**revue** See **review/revue**.

**-re word endings** See **US spelling**.

**rf** radio frequency; also *r.f.*

**RFDS** Royal Flying Doctor Service.

**rhetorical question** A *rhetorical question* is one that does not require an answer. Its purpose is not to ask for information, but rather to make a point more effectively than a statement would. Consider the dramatic flourish of this question:

> Which of you would not do the same?

And compare it with the dullness of a mere statement:

> You would do the same.

A rhetorical question assumes that there is only one answer, an answer that is implicit in the question. Lawyers and politicians use the device freely:

> Was there ever such a clear-cut case of fraud?
>
> Has this country ever been governed so badly?

The implied answer in both cases is *Of course not*.

See also **beg the question**; **leading question**.

**rheumatism** Note the *rheu-*.

**Rh factor** rhesus (or Rhesus) factor.

**rhinoceros** *Rhinoceros* is the singular and a collective term: *one rhinoceros*; *a large herd of rhinoceros*.

**RHSA** Royal Humane Society of Australia.

**rhyme/rhythm** Note the *rhy-* in both words.

**Richter scale** The *Richter scale* (devised by Charles Richter) measures the total energy or magnitude of seismic disturbances such as earthquakes. The scale is logarithmic, with an earthquake differing by one unit on the Richter scale for every factor of ten in magnitude.

**ricochet/ricocheted/ricocheting** Note the spelling. *Ricochet* means to rebound, and it is normally applied only to projectiles such as bullets. The *chet* in all forms is pronounced 'shay'.

**riesling** Note the *-ie-* in the name of this wine, which is sometimes given an initial capital. Common pronunciations are '**rees**-ling' and '**reez**-ling'.

**right/rightly** The meanings of *right*, when it is used as an adverb, include correctly (*Have I guessed right?*); straight (*Drive right through*); immediately (*Come right away*); fittingly (*It serves you right*); completely (*to drop right off*);

and very (in certain titles): *the Right Reverend*. *Rightly*, which can only be an adverb, has a narrower range of related meanings: correctly, properly, and in accordance with a code of behaviour.

> I rightly guessed that Ee-Ling would not stay long.
> They were rightly concerned by the change in the weather.
> She rightly obtained a permit before entering the conservation zone.

Note that *right* tends to follow verbs, while *rightly* generally precedes them.

See also **right?**.

**right?** The irritating conversation filler *right?* should be avoided by any speaker wishing to retain a listener's interest:

> 'You see what I did, right? I told him his ideas were wrong, right?, and that the plan wouldn't work, right?, unless you were involved as well . . . right?'

The listener is sometimes expected to murmur a confirming *right*. To answer *wrong* would be bad form, but might help to break the speaker of a bad habit.

See also **right/rightly**.

**rightly** See **right/rightly**.

**rigor/rigour** Either spelling is acceptable for the noun meaning hardship, severity or strictness, although *rigour* is preferred. The adjective, however, is always spelt *rigorous*.

In the Latin phrase *rigor mortis* (which means the stiffening of a body after death) the spelling *rigour* is not an option.

**RIP** This abbreviation of the Latin phrase *requiescat [*or *-ant] in pace* means may he or she (or they) rest in peace. It often appears in death notices and on headstones, especially those belonging to members of the Catholic Church.

**rip-off/scam** *Rip-off* is a lively colloquialism meaning a swindle. It is popularly applied to overpriced goods and services that cheat the consumer. A *scam* is a racket or swindle in which people are tricked out of their money. The noun *rip-off* should always be hyphenated; the verb should not.

**rise** See **arise/rise**; **raise/rise/raze**.

**rival/rivalled/rivalling** Note the single *l* in the first and the *-ll-* in the other two.

**the Riverina** *The Riverina* is an extremely fertile and agriculturally productive area between the Murray and Lachlan rivers in southern New South Wales. It extends west from a line drawn to connect Condobolin, Junee, Wagga Wagga and Albury, and includes the Murrumbidgee Irrigation Area.

**rivet/riveted/riveting** Note the single *t* in all forms, including the related noun *riveter*.

**RLSSA** Royal Life Saving Society of Australia.

**RMC** Royal Military College (Duntroon, ACT).

**RMIT** Royal Melbourne Institute of Technology.

**RNA** ribonucleic acid.

**rob** See **burgle/rob/steal**.

**Rocklea, Qld** Compare with *Rockley*, NSW.

**rococo** Note that the *c* is single in both places. Ornamentation that is unattractively florid is sometimes described as *rococo*, but the term derives from an eighteenth-century vogue, originating in France, for elaborate though graceful design in art and architecture.

**rollover** The word *rollover*, used generally, refers to the renewal of a loan or the continuation of a deposit at the maturity date, usually requiring a revision of interest rates. The term is now frequently applied to the investment of a superannuation payout with a government-approved institution, thereby deferring payment of the tax on the lump sum. It has come to be used as a verb, noun or adjective.

**Rolls-Royce** Note the hyphen.

**ROM** See **read-only memory**.

**Roman Catholic** See **Catholic/catholic**.

**roman numerals** *Arabic numerals* (1, 2, 3 and so on) predominate in the English-speaking world, but *roman numerals* are still used for purposes such as the numbering of the preliminary pages in a book, and of appendixes, volumes, and acts and scenes in plays. They appear on old-style clock and watch faces, and in the names of monarchs, popes and certain events: *Elizabeth II*; *Pius XI*; *World War II*. They are written as upper-case or lower-case letters, depending on their purpose. The following are the most frequently used of the letters that make up roman numerals.

| *Upper case* | *Lower case* | *Arabic equivalent* |
|---|---|---|
| I | i | 1 |
| V | v | 5 |

| *Upper case* | *Lower case* | *Arabic equivalent* |
|---|---|---|
| X | x | 10 |
| L | l | 50 |
| C | c | 100 |
| D | d | 500 |
| M | m | 1000 |

These letters may be combined in various ways. Apply the following principles to build up more complex numbers.

- Add identical numerals (up to three of them) and place them side by side:
  I + I = II = 2 *or* i + i = ii = 2
  X + X + X = XXX = 30 *or* x + x + x = xxx = 30
- Add a smaller numeral to a larger numeral, and put the smaller one second:
  V + I = VI = 6 *or* v + i = vi = 6
  C + III = CIII = 103 *or* c + iii = ciii = 103
- Subtract a smaller numeral from a larger numeral, but put the smaller one first:
  X – I = IX = 9 *or* x – i = ix = 9
  D – C = CD = 400 *or* d – c = cd = 400

Follow this procedure for combinations such as IV (4), IX (9), XIV (14), XIX (19), XXIV (24), XXIX (29), XLIX (49) and XCIX (99). A large number such as 574 is formed in the following way:

500 + 50 + 24 = 574
D + L + XX + IV = DLXXIV = 574

The date 1993 becomes MCMXCIII:

1000 + 900 + 90 + 3 = 1993
M + CM + XC + III = MCMXCIII = 1993

Expressing dates in roman numerals is not recommended, however. Leave that to the film producers who are under the delusion that a date expressed as MCMLXXXVII adds more class to their product than a simple 1987. Runs of roman numerals are not abbreviated in the way that arabic numerals are: *XXI–XXV* (*21–5*), not *XXI–V*. Note too that *-th* never follows: *Edward VII*, not *Edward VIIth*.

Take care not to use the arabic figure 1 instead of the letter I when the roman numeral one is required: *Elizabeth II*, not *Elizabeth 11*.

See also **numbers in figures or words**; **page numbering**.

**roman type** See **type**.

**roof** Plural *roofs* (not 'rooves').

**rough** A *rough* is a preliminary depiction of a design or illustration, intended to convey a general idea of the final work.

See also **layout**.

**round** See **around/round**.

**rouse** See **arouse/rouse**.

**rout/route** The noun *rout* means a comprehensive defeat involving disorderly flight:

Only a few wounded men found their way back to camp after the rout.

The related verb means to drive (out): *rout out the rats*. *Rout* (in the following senses more commonly spelt *root*) can also mean to rummage: *rout around in the shed for paint*; or to dig (out): *buried bones for the dog to rout out*.

The noun *route* means a way or road planned or taken:

The inland route is faster than the coastal route.

The verb means to send by or establish such a road. Because the past tense of both verbs is *routed*, ensure that the context makes your meaning clear. *Rout* is pronounced like *out*; *route* is pronounced like *root*.

**ROW** This is the abbreviation for right of way (plural *rights of way*), the name given to a path or road legally traversed by the public; the form *RoW* is sometimes seen.

**royal commission** A *royal commission* is held *on* a matter, not *into* it.

**royalties** See **contracts**.

**RP** Received Pronunciation.

See also **Australian English**; **British English**.

**RRP** recommended retail price; also *rrp*.

**RSI** This is an abbreviation of *repetition* (or *repetitive*) *strain injury*, which is caused by performing the same or similar movements frequently over a period of time and results in inflammation of the tendon sheath or tendon of a muscle. Two types of RSI are *tenosynovitis*, which is inflammation of the tendon sheath (especially of the wrist); and the so-called *carpal tunnel syndrome*, which results from excessive or prolonged inflammation of the wrist tendons causing pressure on the nerves running through the wrist tunnel.

**RSL** Returned & Services League (before September 1990, Returned Services League).

**RSM** regimental sergeant-major.

**RSPCA** Royal Society for the Prevention of Cruelty to Animals.

**RSVP** This abbreviation of the French words *répondez s'il vous plaît* means please reply.

**rugby** Two different codes of football go by this name in Australia. *Rugby Union* is abbreviated as *Rugby*; *Rugby League* is abbreviated as *League*.

**rules** In typography a horizontal or vertical line used to separate columns or lines of text, or to create boxes, is called a *rule*. The thinnest is called a hairline rule. Rule measurements are specified in points, and half-point and one-point rules are commonly used in books. In desktop publishing all page-makeup programs and most word-processing programs have a rule facility.

See also **underlines/underscores**.

**running heads/running feet** *Running heads* (or *running headlines*) are often printed at the top of the pages in a non-fiction publication to provide location guidance for the reader. Pages such as blanks, the imprint and title pages, and those that open a chapter are not given running heads. Normally the book's title appears at the top of the left-hand page (or verso) and the chapter heading on the right-hand page (or recto). If the text is divided into several parts, the title for each may go on the left-hand pages and the chapter heading on the right. But if chapters have a number of distinct sections, it may be more helpful to put the chapter headings on the left and the section headings on the right.

Running heads are usually ranged right or left, depending on whether they lie on right-hand or left-hand pages, and are often aligned with the page number. If heads are typeset the same size as the text, they should be in a different face or style; it is also desirable to avoid using exactly the same size and style as text headings. If the line of copy is too long it may be abbreviated.

*Running feet* (or *running footlines*) have the same function but appear at the bottom of pages; they occur less often in books than in magazines, where they identify the title and often the date of publication.

**run-up** This compound, used to mean a time preceding a significant event, has won qualified acceptance in formal contexts: *the run-up to the election*; *the Christmas run-up*.

**rural/rustic** Both adjectives mean pertaining to the countryside (a *rural scene* is often *rustic*), but they are not always interchangeable. *Rustic* often has an additional sense – quaint, unsophisticated or crude.

**RV** Revised Version (of the Bible).

# Ss

**S** supertext subtitles for the deaf (TV classification).

**SA** South Africa; South Australia.

**sac/sack** A *sac* is a bag-like structure, usually containing fluid, in an animal or plant; for other kinds of bags, use *sack*. As a verb, *sack* means to pillage or loot: *The victors sacked the city*. Informally it means to dismiss: *He was sacked from his part-time job*.

**saccharin/saccharine** The preferred spelling of the sugar substitute is *saccharin*, although either is acceptable. The adjective meaning sweet or sugary is spelt *saccharine*.

**sack** See **sac/sack**.

**sacrilege/sacrilegious** *Sacrilege* involves the violation of something regarded as holy. Both the noun and its adjective, *sacrilegious*, are frequently misspelt, probably because of an incorrect association with the word *religious*.

**s.a.e.** stamped addressed envelope.

**salary/wage** Both words refer to fixed payments made to employees: professional or non-manual workers usually receive a fortnightly or monthly *salary*; other workers receive a weekly or daily *wage*.

**SALT** This is an acronym for *Strategic Arms Limitation Talks*. To refer to *SALT talks* is, of course, tautological.

**salubrious/salutary** Although both these adjectives mean beneficial (especially to health), each has a specific application. Use *salubrious* to describe a healthy climate or environment:

We enjoyed the salubrious air of Kosciusko in summertime.

Use *salutary* literally or figuratively:

Bev thought that the sea water had a salutary effect on her rheumatism.

Shopping while on holiday gave him a salutary lesson in the cost of food.

**SAM** surface-to-air missile.

**same** As an adjective, *same* is best followed by *as* before a clause:

Please give us the same caravan as we occupied last year.

It is acceptable, however, to replace *as* with *that* or to omit the conjunction altogether.

*Same* used as a pronoun is an out-of-date piece of commercialese: *Please forward same by return post*. Put *it* or *them* instead.

**sanatorium** A *sanatorium* is a health resort, an institution for convalescence; the plural is *sanatoriums* or, more rarely, *sanatoria*. But note the spelling chosen by the *Sanitarium Health Food Company*.

**sanction** The word comes from the Latin *sancire*, to decree, which explains why in English *sanction* has such apparently contradictory meanings as permission and penalty. To sanction something is to decree that it is permitted, authorised, even encouraged. To sanction against something is to decree that it is not permitted – as happens when the United Nations imposes trade sanctions on a country that is flouting international law.

**Sanderson, NT** Compare with *Sanderston*, SA.

**sank/sunk** The recommended past tense of the verb *to sink* is *sank*, although *sunk* is acceptable:

The ship sank [*or* sunk] in the typhoon.

*Sunk* is the normal past participle; *sunken* is the preferred form of the participle for use as an adjective, especially preceding a noun:

The ship has sunk; it hit a sunken reef.

**sans** The French word *sans* means without. Its currency in English is mainly jocular:

After the stormy crossing most passengers arrived sans breakfast.

**sanserif type** See **type**.

**sarsaparilla** The name of the plant, the soft drink made from it, and Patrick White's fictional township is often misspelt. Note the second *a*.

**satellite** Note the spelling.

**satire** *Satire* is the use of words to denounce by means of ridicule or exaggeration. Vehicles for satire include books, cartoons, plays and revues, and their targets range from people and their failings to institutions and their follies. Do not confuse *satire* with the *satyr* of mythology (pronounced 'sayt'r').

**save** Every computer program has a *save* function for transferring data into the memory, on a hard or floppy disk. It is one of the most crucial functions, together with backing up. To save material – text, graphics, charts – means to store it on disk. Saving should be done frequently, in fact several times per hour, because work unsaved can be lost if the computer crashes or a power failure occurs. Note that saving is not the same as *backing up*, which is a matter of duplicating stored data.

See also **backup**; **crashed/gone down**; **data retrieval**.

**sb** solid brick (house); also *SB*.

**SBLT/Sub. Lt** Sub-Lieutenant.

See also **lieutenant**.

**SBS** Special Broadcasting Service.

**scam** See **rip-off/scam**.

**scanner** A *scanner* is a device used to convert text or graphics to digital format suitable for storage on a disk. Text for scanning may be typed, word processed or handwritten; graphics may include photographs, pictures, maps and diagrams. The higher the quality of the text or image to be scanned, the better the result.

Optical character recognition software is required to scan text, and different software is needed for scanning graphic or photographic images.

See also **optical character recognition**.

**scarcely** See **double negative**; **hardly**.

**scarify** This word has nothing to do with the verb *to scare*. It means to make scratches or incisions in a surface and, by extension, to lacerate with criticism:

> The tough-coated seeds were scarified to aid sprouting.
>
> In his report the Royal Commissioner scarified politicians and was critical of the bureaucracy.

Pronounce the *a* as in *cat*, or make it rhyme with the *ai* in *fair*.

**scenario** Many people prefer this word to be confined to the context of theatre or cinema, where it refers to the outline of a plot. The wider meaning – imagined course of action or series of events – is acceptable, but the word should not be overworked as a synonym for just any *plan*, *action* or *situation*.

**sceptic** See **cynic/sceptic**.

**SCG** Sydney Cricket Ground.

**schedule** Prefer the traditional Australian pronunciation '**shed**-yool' to the US-derived '**sked**-yool'.

**schism** This noun means a serious splitting of a group into opposing parties or a complete breakaway, not a minor division or disagreement. It may be pronounced '**sizm**' or '**skizm**' but not 'shizm'.

**schizophrenic** Note the spelling. *Schizophrenic* means suffering from *schizophrenia*, a psychiatric disorder. It should not be used simply to mean *contradictory*, *capricious*, *unreliable* or *confused*.

**scissors** *Scissors* is a plural noun, taking a plural verb:

Are the scissors in the drawer?

*A pair of scissors* is the closest you can get to the singular.

**SCM** Student Christian Movement.

**Scotch/Scots/Scottish** *Scotch* as adjective and noun is disliked by many of the people of Scotland, who prefer *Scottish* (*the Scottish people*; *Scottish music*) and *Scot* (*a Scot*; *all the Scots*). The terms *Scotsman* and *Scotswoman* are acceptable, and so is *the Scottish* (as a collective noun). *Scots* is also used as an adjective where tradition or law dictates: *Scots Guards*; *Scots law*; *a Scots pint*. However, *Scotch* is generally used to describe the whisky, broth, mists, tweed and terrier. As a derogatory colloquialism *Scotch* (or *Scottish*) also means stingy.

**Scott Creek, SA** Compare with *Scotts Creek*, Vic.

**Scottish** See **Scotch/Scots/Scottish**.

**screen** In the context of printing a *screen* is a photographic device by means of which even-toned images can be given a dot pattern that allows them to be printed.

**screen font** See **printer font/screen font**.

**screen saver** In computer terminology a *screen saver* is a moving graphic image that comes onto the screen at a set time (specified by the operator) after the mouse or keyboard was last used. The purpose of a screen saver is to prevent phosphor burn-in, which may result if a screen is left on for long periods of time with no change in the image (the burn-in appears as a ghost of that image on the screen).

**scrolling** In computer terminology *scrolling* is the moving of text on a screen so that parts of a document not visible can be brought into view.

**scrutiny** As a *scrutiny* is a searching or minute examination, common expressions such as *detailed scrutiny* and *close scrutiny* are tautologies.

**scull/skull** *Scull* for the oar and boat; *skull* for the bony framework of the head.

**SDA** Seventh-Day Adventist.

**SDI** Strategic Defense Initiative (the US nuclear defence project commonly called *Star Wars*).

**Seaford, SA and Vic.** Compare with *Seaforth*, NSW and Qld.

**seasonable/seasonal** *Seasonable* means appropriate to or in keeping with the seasons and, by extension, timely:

> Frost in low-lying areas was seasonable in winter.
> Because of our broker's seasonable advice we sold our shares before the crash.

*Seasonal* means depending on a particular season of the year:

> Fruit-picking is a seasonal occupation: apricots in summer, pears in autumn.

**seasons** Give a lower-case initial to *summer*, *autumn*, *winter* and *spring*, unless they are personified, as sometimes happens in poetry.
See also **midday**.

**SEATO** This is an acronym for *South-East Asia Treaty Organization* (dissolved 1977); also *Seato*.

**secateurs** The name of the small pruning implement is pronounced '**sekka**-t'z' or 'sekka-**terz**'.

**second/secondly** See **first/firstly**.

**Second World** See **Third World/First World/Second World**.

**Second World War** See **World War II**.

**seeing that** *Seeing that* is an acceptable substitute, in informal contexts, for conjunctions such as *because* or *since*:

Seeing that tomorrow is Saturday, we can sleep in.

*That* should not be replaced by *as*, *as how* or *as to how* in this construction, but in very informal contexts it may be omitted provided that there is no ambiguity.

**seize** Note the *-ei-*.

**self** This word may be used as a noun in expressions such as *not her usual self*. But allowing it to act as a pronoun in the following kind of phrase is not recommended: *ballet tickets for self and friend*.

The suffix *-self* (and its plural, *-selves*) produces reflexive pronouns: *He injured himself*. Reflexive pronouns are often used for emphasis (*She herself is responsible*), but this should not be overdone. The personal pronoun should be used in the following constructions:

He and his brother [*not* Himself and his brother] will be there.

Joan and I [*not* myself] will do the flower arrangements.

Note that when *self-* is a prefix it always has a hyphen: *self-reliant*, *self-appointed*, *self-congratulatory*. Avoid using *self-* compounds that are tautological: *self-confessed*, *self-conceit*.

See also **myself**; **oneself**; **pronouns**.

**self-starter** A *self-starter* is best kept for engines. Many people dislike the use of this compound word to describe a person who has initiative or who can work effectively without encouragement. It is, of course, an advertising cliché: *Self-starter required for responsible position*. *Self-starters* are usually good at *kick-starting*. They are also often *high-flyers* in the *fast lane* who are *head-hunted*. The majority of such bizarre terms from the jargon of recruitment advertising would be best placed permanently *on the back-burner*.

**semicolon** The *semicolon* (;) is the punctuation mark whose weight falls between that of the decisive *full stop* and the weaker *comma*. Although one of the most useful punctuation marks, the semicolon is today one of the least popular, partly because the more readily understood *dash* has increasingly replaced it. If overused, as it sometimes was in nineteenth-century writing, the semicolon tends to have a clogging effect on prose. It is best used sparingly, but can be very effective in the following situations:

- to separate main clauses (clauses that can stand alone and make sense) that are closely related in content or theme; a semicolon is used here in preference to a joining word like *as* or *for* – a full stop would make too strong a break

  She caught me by the sleeve; she had something else to tell me.

- to separate contrasting clauses

  He was a huge, muscular fellow; yet he was a coward.

- before certain connecting words and phrases (except when they are parenthetical) that traditionally demand a semicolon rather than a comma – for instance *however*, *moreover*, *therefore*, *thus*, *nevertheless*, *what's more* and *in the circumstances*

  Guests are free to depart; however, we advise against it.

  This room is reserved for members; moreover they may smoke here.

- to eliminate confusion in a complex sentence where there are already many commas

  Those of us who were eager to see the sights, even those of us who had travelled all night, set out on arrival in search of adventure; but others, less keen, sought the comforts of the hotel.

- to separate complex items in a list, particularly when they are already broken up by commas

  He spent the money wildly: ribbon for his daughter's hair, though it was now cut very short; lengths of flowered silk, though the colours were vulgar; lace, cottons, and 12 metres of bias binding.

  Fuel, and spare oil, for the car; sandwiches and fruit, for lunch; games for the children – all needed her immediate attention.

See also **clause; colon; comma; dashes, use of; full stop.**

**Semite/Semitic** A *Semite* is someone who speaks a *Semitic* language, as do both Arabs and Jews, although the terms *anti-Semite* and *anti-Semitic* have come specifically to mean anti-Jewish.

**sensibility/sensitivity** These nouns are broadly synonymous. Both describe a capacity for sensation or feeling, but they are not interchangeable in the following examples. *Sensibility* is most often used in the plural, and it generally suggests refined or artistic feeling. *Sensitivity*, on the other hand, is more broadly applied and can attract criticism if regarded as over-sensitivity.

The graffiti in the train offended my aunt's sensibilities.

The delicacy of the watercolours showed a high level of sensibility.

Kevin's sensitivity on the subject of vivisection made us wary of mentioning it.

**sensual/sensuous** Often used interchangeably, these adjectives have differences of meaning that are worth preserving. Although both refer to the senses, *sensual* applies to physical arousal or gratification, particularly sexual. *Sensuous* applies to all the senses, but has traditionally been used in reference to aesthetic rather than physical arousal. Note that *sensual* often has sleazy overtones that are not conveyed by *sensuous*:

The movements of the scantily clad belly-dancer were sensual.

The rich scent and velvety texture of gardenias are sensuous.

The respective nouns are *sensuality* and *sensuousness*.

**sentence** A *sentence* is a group of words that makes complete sense. It can be:

- a statement

    The night is dark.

- a command

    Turn on the light.

- a question

    Can you see me?

A sentence begins with a capital letter and ends with a full stop, a question mark, an exclamation mark or ellipsis. The traditional rule that a sentence must contain a subject and a verb continues to apply generally to formal writing, though the subject or verb may be 'understood' when words are omitted through ellipsis:

[You] Turn on the light. [I'll do it] With pleasure!

In fiction the verbless sentence is a legitimate device for approximating the informality of speech, representing a thought process, or for dramatic effect:

Listening. Listening. He counted the steps. Coming . . . nearer.

Use this kind of style sparingly, however: too much of it can irritate the reader.

Advertising copy makes flagrant misuse of verbless sentences or sentence fragments punctuated as complete sentences: *China holds much fascination. Especially for tourists*. This sort of headline prose should be avoided in formal contexts.

A common error is the so-called *run-on sentence*: *We have a problem with pollution, it is also a global problem.* The comma makes too weak a link between the two clauses in this example, and they must either be joined by a conjunction or semicolon, or clearly separated by a full stop:

We have a problem with pollution, but it is also a global problem.

*or* We have a problem with pollution; it is also a global problem.

*or* We have a problem with pollution. It is also a global problem.

See also **clause**; **colon**; **comma**; **full stop**; **phrase**; **semicolon**.

**separate** Not 'seperate'.

**septic** See **cynic/sceptic**.

**serendipity** This word means the gift for discovering pleasant things by accident: the accidental aspect should not be overlooked.

**serge/surge** *Serge* is a twilled fabric. A *surge* is a strong, wave-like forward or upward movement.

**serial** See **cereal/serial**.

**serial numbers** The *serial numbers* given to computer hardware and software should be recorded by the owner. You may need to quote the serial number of software to the supplier when upgrading it, and will have to key it in when installing either new or upgraded software. A copy of the numbers should also be lodged with your insurance company.

**series** The noun may be either singular or plural:

This television series is good.

These television series are good.

**serif type** See **type**.

**serve/service** Perhaps because it sounds slightly less servile, the verb *service* is often used today instead of *serve*. The traditional and more appropriate word should be retained, however:

The local council is here to serve [*not* service] the municipality.

If you mean maintain and repair, *service* is the right word; you may also *service* a debt and your stallion may *service* (or serve) a mare.

**sewage/sewerage** *Sewage* is the waste matter; *sewerage* is the system of pipes and fittings that gets rid of it.

**sexism** See **discriminatory language**.

**SF** science fiction; single-fronted (house; see also **sf**).

**sf** This is the abbreviation (also *SF*) for *single-fronted*, a real-estate term meaning that a house (especially a Victorian or Edwardian terrace house) is only one room wide (usually with a passage down one side).

**SGC** superannuation guarantee charge.

**SGT/Sgt** Sergeant.

**shall/will** Many people are unaware of or ignore the traditional distinction between *shall* and *will*, using whichever comes into their heads first when writing, and abbreviating them (*I'll*, *you'll* and so on) when speaking. There are subtle differences between the two words in certain contexts, but the following fairly straightforward rules are worth noting.

- To express the future without emphasis, use *shall* for the first person (*I* or *we*):

  I shall leave tomorrow.

  Use *will* for the second person (*you*) and third person (*he*, *she*, *it* or *they*):

  You and he will leave tomorrow.
- To express determination or a promise, use *will* for the first person:

  I will go if it kills me. We will be there, you can be sure.

To indicate determination, a promise, a command or the granting of permission, use *shall* for the second and third person:

You shall go tomorrow whether you like it or not!

They shall go tomorrow since they have worked so hard today.

See also **should/would**.

**shammy** See **chamois/chammy/shammy**.

**she/her** The correct pronoun to use before and after various verbs is explained in the entry **case (grammar)**.

See also **he/she**.

**sheaf** Plural *sheaves*.

**shear/sheer** The verb *shear* means to remove (hair, wool and so on) with instruments such as scissors or shears, or to deprive (of). Its past tense is *sheared* or *shore*:

We sheared [*or* shore] the sheep last week.

Its past participle is normally *shorn*, but for something forcibly taken away, ripped or broken off, use the form *sheared*:

The government was shorn of its tax-raising powers.

The ship's rudder was sheared off in the collision.

The adjective *sheer* means transparent and light (of fabrics: *sheer silk*); steep (*a sheer drop*); or absolute (*a sheer waste of time*). As a verb it means to deviate or swerve:

The ship sheered away from the dock at the last moment.

**sheik/sheikh** Either spelling is acceptable. Pronounce the word 'sheek' or 'shake'.

**Shelley, Vic. and WA** Compare with *Shelly Beach*, NSW, Qld and Tas.

**shibboleth** *Shibboleth* means a special word or phrase that marks off the members of a particular group.

As Scott became upwardly mobile, he used 'lunch' as a shibboleth: anyone calling the midday meal 'dinner' was dropped.

Strictly speaking the word should not be applied to a group's habits or beliefs, as it commonly is today (*a shibboleth of that faction*).

*Shibboleth* was drawn into the English language from an Old Testament story about the role played by this Hebrew word as an identifier. Those who could pronounce it correctly were sorted out from those who could not; the latter were killed.

**shined** See **shone/shined**.

**ship** See **boat/ship**.

**shone/shined** *Shone* is the past tense and past participle of the verb *to shine*, except when it means polished:

> Olivier's name shone like a beacon among actors.
> The children have shined their shoes.

**shorn** See **shear/sheer**.

**short-sighted** See **long-sighted/short-sighted**.

**should/would** *Should* and *would* once followed the same pattern as *shall* and *will*, with *should* for the first person (*I* or *we*) and *would* for the second person (*you*) and third person (*he*, *she*, *it* or *they*). In the case of *should* and *would* the distinction seems to have been largely lost, however, and *would* tends to be used in either case:

> I would [*or* should] like to come.
> She would like to come.

There is another use for the word *should* – to mean ought to. In this sense it cannot be replaced by *would*:

> I should [ought to] leave now, but the visitors should [ought to] be fed first.

When *would* means used to, *should* is not an alternative:

> When I was a child, I would [used to] hide under the house and my mother would [used to] coax me out.

The same contraction serves for both *should* and *would*: *I'd*, *we'd*, *you'd*, *they'd* and so on. Note that the contractions *should've* and *would've* stand for *should have* and *would have*, not 'should of' and 'would of'.

See also **have/had**; **of**; **ought**; **shall/will**.

**showthrough** In the context of printing *showthrough* is the degree to which print on one side of a page is visible from the other side; the word is also applied to the visible print itself:

> We asked about the showthrough of the proposed paper.
> We saw the showthrough on a sample page and rejected the paper.

**shrank/shrunk/shrunken** *Shrank* is the past tense of the verb *to shrink*:

> They shrank from revealing his hiding place.

*Shrunk* is the past participle:

> The hot water has shrunk the blanket.

*Shrunken* is the adjective: *shrunken gums*.

**SI** International System of Units (French: *Système International d'Unités*).
See also **metric system**; **weights and measures**.

**sibling** Your *sibling* may be either your sister or your brother. The word frequently appears as an adjective in the phrase *sibling rivalry*.

***sic*** The Latin word *sic*, meaning so or thus, is placed within square brackets after an oddity or error in quoted material to indicate that the original has been transcribed accurately. It is always italicised. This is a concise and handy device, but it should be used selectively. It is often more sensible to avoid erroneous words and phrases by paraphrasing or ellipsis than to highlight them with *sic*:

> Grey wrote that victory was 'inevitable but evasive'.

*rather than*

> Grey wrote that 'victry [*sic*] was inevitable but evasive'.

See also **quotations**.

**SIDS** sudden infant-death syndrome.
See also **syndrome**.

**siege** Note the *-ie-*.

**signature mark** A *signature mark* is printed at the beginning of each section of a book to indicate sequence at the binding stage. Signature marks are sometimes numbers or letters, sometimes printed bars.

**silicon/silicone** In the age of the computer the distinction between these words is worth noting. *Silicon* is a non-metallic element (found in sand), from which a *silicon chip* is made. *Silicone* is a compound of silicon and other substances used in, for example, some oils, greases, resins and synthetic rubber. Pronounce *silicon* '**sill**a-c'n' and *silicone* 'silla-**cone**'.

**silvan/sylvan** Either spelling is acceptable but *sylvan* is recommended. This adjective means of, or pertaining to, trees and forests.

**simile** A *simile* is a figure of speech in which the meaning of a word is enhanced by its comparison with something else. *As* or *like* is used in forming the comparison. A *metaphor*, by contrast, does not include either of these link words – its imagery is less direct, implying rather than comparing. Our language is filled with idioms that are similes: *as black as coal*; *as dull as ditchwater*; *flat out like a lizard drinking*. Striking similes are created by comparing unlike things:

> 'Like a small gray coffee pot sits the squirrel' (Humbert Wolfe)
>
> 'Seventy summers are hived in him like old honey' (Judith Wright)

See also **analogy/analogous**; **idiom**; **metaphor**.

**simplistic** This word is not a synonym for *simple*. *Simplistic* means over-simplified, and its use implies criticism:

Franca's plan is neat and simple.

Pietro's plan is so simplistic as to be ineffectual.

**simply** See **even**.

**since** See **ago/since**; **as/since/because/for**.

**sine qua non** This Latin phrase literally means *without which not* – that is, something essential, or an indispensable condition:

It was a sine qua non of our agreement that the firm paid all expenses.

Do not use the phrase where it will not be understood.

**singular or plural** In the English language the rule of *number agreement* means that a verb must agree with its subject. A singular subject takes a singular verb:

This tree grows quickly.

A plural subject, or more than one subject, takes a plural verb:

These trees grow quickly.

This eucalypt and this wattle grow quickly.

Note that words like *this*, *that*, *these* and *those* must also agree with the number of the noun they accompany: *this tree* but *these trees*; *this sort* but *these sorts*.

Common difficulties arising from the rule of number agreement are dealt with in the following ways.

- When the subject is separated from the verb by a noun of different number, the verb must not be misdirected towards the closer noun:

  The end [subject] of all our problems was [*not* were] in sight.

- When you have to choose between *there is* and *there are* in a sentence the number of the verb is decided by what follows:

  There is a hot wind blowing.

  There are cooling breezes near the sea.

- When nouns joined by *and* represent separate units, the verb is plural, even when one of the nouns is only implied:

  The horse and its rider were injured.

  The hot [tap] and cold tap are clearly distinguished from each other.

  But note that when *or* joins singular units the verb is singular:

  The hot tap or the cold tap is [*not* are] faulty.

- When nouns joined by *and* together represent a single entity, the verb is singular:

  My friend and comforter [one and the same person] has returned.

  Rum and Coke [the one drink] is his favourite.

- When *and* introduces something in parenthesis – that is, a section between commas, dashes or brackets that could be deleted from the sentence without loss of sense – the verb agrees with the principal subject:

  My barrister – and possibly her associates – is [*not* are] attending.

  Words or phrases introduced by *as well as*, *plus*, *along with*, *together with*, *in addition to* and so on are also treated as parenthetical – whether or not they are marked off by commas:

  My barrister, as well as her associates, is attending.

  My brother as well as my son is attending.
- Linked units introduced by *each* or *every* require a singular verb:

  Each dog and cat in the pound has [*not* have] been inoculated.
- The phrase *a number of*, meaning several, is followed by a plural verb:

  A number of ducks have landed on the dam.

  *The number of* means the total, and is followed by a singular verb:

  The number of ducks on the dam is twenty or so.
- Measurements of time, length, weight and so on, when regarded as a single entity, require a singular verb:

  Thirty kilometres [a single distance] was as far as he could run that day.
- Some nouns ending in *-ics*, such as *politics*, *statistics* and *acoustics*, are singular when referring to an activity or field of study:

  Politics is his main interest.

  Statistics is a subject requiring mathematical skills.

  Acoustics is an important study for those who plan large buildings.

  But they become plural when used in ways such as the following:

  Your politics are unacceptable.

  His statistics are verifiable.

  The acoustics of the hall were detrimental to the performance.
- The title of a book, film and so on is always treated as a single entity:

  *Milo and Otis* is popular with children.

  *The Birds*, directed by Alfred Hitchcock, was an ornithologist's nightmare.

See also **and**; **brackets**; **collective nouns**; **commas**; **dashes, use of**; **discriminatory language**; **each**; **each other/one another**; **either**; **every/everybody/everyone**; **kind of/type of/sort of**; **neither**; **none**; **nouns, plurals of**; **one**; **or**; **there are/there is/ there's**.

**Sinhalese** See **Sri Lanka/Sinhalese**.

**siphon/syphon** Either spelling is acceptable for the name of the instrument that draws off water (or the action involved).

**site** See **cite/site**.

**situation** This noun means location, condition, or a combination of circumstances:

> The situation of the gym is to be changed from basement to ground floor.
> The bushfire situation is serious.

*Situation* is often superfluous in stock phrases such as *crisis situation*; *work situation*; and *home situation*. This usage seems to have been first popularised during the Vietnam War, when Pentagonese was heard nightly on television:

> The Marines have a battle situation on their hands at Hue.

The cliché *ongoing situation* should be avoided, even as a joke.

**sizable/sizeable** Either spelling, with or without the *-e* of *size*, is acceptable for this word.

**SJ** Society of Jesus (Jesuits).

**skein** Note the *-ei-*.

**ski/skied/skiing** Note also the spelling of *skis* and *skier*.

**skulduggery** This is the recommended spelling (rather than *skullduggery*).

**skull** See **scull/skull**.

**slander** See **defamation**.

**slang** The most informal, and often the most vigorous, form of a language is its *slang*. Colourful and ever-changing, it is the terminology of the street, the factory, the pub, the sports field, the home – in fact, of any place where people get together. Slang ranges from the simply descriptive or amusing to the grossly obscene. It may break with tradition or challenge authority, or it may simply be a matter of playful or exuberant expression. It exploits every linguistic device, including metaphor (*bomb* = car); rhyme (watching out for *Noahs* = *Noah's arks* = sharks); onomatopoeia (*splat*, *whiz*); word modification (*bewdy*); word abbreviation (*max* = maximum); word opposition (*classy* = vulgar); and the adoption of foreign words (*pronto*, *macho*).

It is usually easy to distinguish between formal language, colloquial expressions and slang. *He is inebriated* is formal. *He's had a drop too much* is colloquial – that is, relatively informal. *He's pissed as a newt* is slang. Many slang words and phrases eventually become part of standard English: *joke* and *mob*, for instance, were once considered low speech. Others disappear for a time, only to be revived years later. Australian slang terms such as *ratbag*, *galah* and *nervous Nelly* are hardy perennials. Most slang has a short life, however, quickly becoming outdated or boring through overuse. Writers who wish their work to stay fresh should therefore remember that yesterday's slang served up today can be comical at best, incomprehensible at worst.

See also **argot/dialect/jargon/lingua franca**; **Australian English**; **British English**; **colloquialisms**; **idiom**; **neologisms/nonce words**; **US English**.

**slash** See **solidus.**

**sleight/slight** *Sleight* is a noun meaning skill or dexterity; it is rarely used other than in the expression *sleight of hand*. Do not confuse its spelling with that of the noun *slight*, meaning indifference, contempt or a snub:

> Thomas saw his aunt but ignored her – a slight she never forgave.

Both words rhyme with *kite*.

**slow** The adjective *slow* is correctly used as an adverb in certain idiomatic constructions: *a go-slow campaign*; *a slow-moving river of lava*. Otherwise use *slowly*:

> You are reading too slowly [*not* slow] to finish that book tonight.

Colloquialisms in which the strictly incorrect *slow* or *slower* replaces the correct *slowly* or *more slowly* arc common but by no means universally accepted: *Drive slower!*.

**small capitals** See **capital letters, small.**

**smelled/smelt** Either word may be used as the past tense and past participle of the verb *to smell*.

***SMH*** *Sydney Morning Herald.*

**Smithton, Tas.** Compare with *Smithtown*, NSW.

**so** The use of the conjunction *so* to introduce a result is very common but not universally approved of in formal prose: *They left supplies, so [as a result] we didn't starve*. In a formal context prefer *and so* or *therefore* (without the comma).

To express purpose use *so that* rather than *so*, thus avoiding ambiguity:

> They left supplies [why?] so that we wouldn't starve.

An alternative in a slightly different construction is *so as* followed by an infinitive:

> They left supplies so as to prevent us starving.

*So as* can often be omitted in examples such as the last because the infinitive supplies the idea of purpose adequately. Note that the common construction *so as we wouldn't starve* is wrong.

Watch out for ambiguity when you use *so* as an adverb:

> The noodles were laced with chillies and so hot.

Does *so* mean *therefore* or *extremely*?

**so and so's** Note the position of the apostrophe, which is regarded as essential in this expression.

**so-called** In formal contexts the compound adjective *so-called* should be used only when someone or something has no right to a name:

The so-called architect Smith was really only a builder.

This is correct usage if Smith had no architectural qualifications. It is incorrect if Smith was actually an architect whose designs merely seemed unprofessional.

**sociable/social** Although both adjectives refer to relationships and have the general meaning companionable or friendly, *social* alone has the sense pertaining to society or to 'smart' society: *social security*; *social ambitions*. *Sociable* and *social* may be used with the same noun, but they have distinct meanings:

We had a sociable [*or* social] night down at the club.

Here *sociable* means convivial while *social* simply suggests some form of organised gathering.

***SOED*** *Shorter Oxford English Dictionary*.

**soft hyphen** See **hard hyphen/soft hyphen**.

**soft page break** See **hard page break/soft page break**.

**soft return** See **hard return/soft return**.

**software** See **hardware/software**.

**software copyright** *Software copyright* operates along similar lines to book copyright; the author of the software usually owns the copyright. It is illegal to copy any software you have purchased other than for backing up, and software companies do random checking for illegal software duplication.

See also **copy protection**; **copyright**; **pirating**.

***soi-disant*** This French expression (usually italicised) means self-styled: *a soi-disant author*. Note that it is not a synonym for *so-called*. Use it only where it will be understood. Pronounce it 'swa-**dee**zon'.

**solecism** The origin of *solecism* is a Greek word meaning incorrectness of speech. In a linguistic context a *solecism* is a blunder in speech or writing – gross mispronunciation in the case of speech or a violation of grammar or idiom in either: *She and I was alone*; *We jumped off of the diving-board*. In a social context *solecism* means a breach of good manners or etiquette. Pronounce the word '**soll**a-sizm'.

**solidus** There are various names for this diagonal, forward-slanting stroke (/), for instance *diagonal*, *oblique* and *slash*. One of its purposes is to separate alternatives: *male/female*; *night/day*. It is also used for fractions (¾); percentages expressed by the symbol %; to form standard abbreviations (a/c, c/-); to replace *per* in measurements (80 km/h); and to indicate the end of a line in verse when a poem is run on: 'After the whey-faced anonymity/Of river-gums and scribbly-gums and bush,/After the rubbing and the hit of brush,/You come to the South Country/'(Kenneth Slessor). Today we prefer dashes, full stops and apostrophes to the solidus in the following:

Sydney–Hobart [*not* Sydney/Hobart] yacht race
the fiscal year 1991–92 [*not* 1991/92]
13.10.91 [*not* 13/10/91]
£20 7s 6d [*not* £20/7/6]
P'nesia [*not* P/nesia]

Do not confuse the solidus with the back-slanting diagonal stroke (\) found on many computer keyboards, which has a specific software-control use only.

See also **and/or**.

**soliloquy** See **monologue/soliloquy**.

**soluble/solvable** *Soluble* means both able to be dissolved and able to be solved. *Solvable* has only the second meaning. Thus powder may be *soluble* but not *solvable*, whereas a problem may be *soluble* or *solvable*.

**somebody/someone** *Somebody* and *someone* are interchangeable, followed by a singular verb, and written as one word:

Somebody [*or* someone] is going to head office later today.

When these singular indefinite pronouns are followed by personal pronouns the latter should be singular too, but the sex of the *somebody* or *someone* is not always known. Informally it has become acceptable to use a plural: *If someone needs a drink we can offer them beer.* But the correct (if more cumbersome) *him or her* is preferred in formal contexts.

See also **anybody/anyone**; **discriminatory language**; **every/everybody/everyone**; **gender**; **he/she**; **pronouns**; **their/them/they**.

**somersault** Note the spelling.

**soprano** Plural *sopranos*.

**sort of** See **kind of/sort of/type of**.

**sorts** See **pi font**.

**SOS** morse code distress call (plural *SOSs*).

See also **May Day/mayday**.

**source** This is a noun; many authorities do not yet accept it as a verb.

**South/south** See **compass points**.

**South-East Asia** Note the hyphen, and the initial capitals for each part of this compound name. *South-East Asia* is said to include Brunei, Burma, Cambodia, Indonesia, Laos, Malaysia, the Philippines, Thailand and Vietnam.

See also **Far East/Middle East/Near East**.

**sowed/sown** The past tense of *sow* is *sowed*. The past participle can be either *sown* or *sowed*:

> I sowed the back paddock after rain.
> They have sown [*or* sowed] the wheat since the rains.

**SP** starting price (bookmaking).

**spate** A *spate* is a flood – of water or anything else that can come in a deluge:

> The river in spate was an awesome sight.
> A spate of inquiries jammed our switchboard.

**SPC** South Pacific Commission.

**SPCK** Society for Promoting Christian Knowledge.

**-speak** George Orwell coined the word *newspeak* to describe the official language of the nightmare society of his 1949 novel *Nineteen Eighty Four*. Since then the suffix *-speak* has been tacked onto numerous words to describe varieties of jargon or typical speech: *doublespeak*, *computerspeak*, *Haigspeak*, *Hawkespeak*. The novelty of the idea has worn off, but the device is so useful that it is unlikely to go away.

**speciality/specialty** These two words are often used interchangeably, but *speciality* is recommended for the noun:

> The chef's speciality is local fish, poached in white wine.

*Specialty* is the preferred form when the word is used adjectivally:

> The arcade is full of specialty shops.

**specially** See **especially/specially**.

**specialty** See **speciality/specialty**.

**species** The biological classification is spelt *species* in both the singular (abbreviated sp.) and plural (abbreviated spp.). The less common word *specie* means coined money.

**specious** Note the spelling. This adjective means misleadingly attractive, or untrue but appearing to be true. It is pronounced '**spee**-shus'.

**spectre** Note the spelling; the word means ghost, or something else that is terrifying or to be dreaded.

**spectrum** The plural of this term for the colours of a rainbow is *spectra*, but *spectrums* is sometimes seen. There are other technical uses for the word, and it is somewhat overworked figuratively as a synonym for *range*, *extent* or *scope*:

Our field officer reported a brilliant spectrum after the showers.

*but* The accounts covered the complete range [*rather than* spectrum] of our purchases.

**sped/speeded** Either *sped* or *speeded* may be used as the past tense and past participle of the verb *to speed*.

**spelled/spelt** Either *spelled* or *spelt* is acceptable as the past tense and past participle of the verb *to spell*, when it means to identify the components of a word, but *spelt* is recommended:

They spelt Katharine's name wrongly.

Only *spelled* is used when the word means to give a rest to:

We have spelled our showjumper for a year.

**spelling** Australian spelling is generally based on that of British English, though US spelling has had some influence on both. Whatever the predominant tradition, the spelling of words in the English language is notoriously difficult. Attempts to regularise and simplify spelling have all failed, and it is unlikely that the language will be changed suddenly or radically in any way.

Though there are certain rules, there are many exceptions. Because of this, and because English spelling is not phonetic, words usually have to be learnt individually. In the end, the most useful aid is a good dictionary. This book contains entries for a large number of words that are often misspelt or have optional forms; more general entries cover word endings such as *-or/-our* and *-ise/-ize*.

See also **-able/-ible word endings**; **Australian English**; **British English**; **US English**; **US spelling**; and individual entries.

**spelt** See **spelled/spelt**.

**spilled/spilt** Either *spilled* or *spilt* may be used as the past tense and past participle of the verb *to spill*, but *spilt* is recommended.

**spirituous/spiritual** Note the *-uous* in *spirituous*. The word refers to alcohol; do not confuse it with *spiritual*, which refers to the supernatural.

**split infinitive** An *infinitive* is the basic form of a verb, usually preceded by *to*: *to walk*; *to fly*; *to grow*. When an infinitive is broken by an adverb or phrase immediately following the *to*, it is said to be *split*: *to slowly walk* instead of *to walk slowly*.

Most authorities agree that the *split infinitive* should be avoided in formal writing wherever possible – particularly when the insertion involves more than one word – but for stylistic rather than grammatical reasons. They also maintain, however, that a split infinitive is sometimes necessary in order to avoid ambiguity or a strained, unnatural sentence.

The simple expedient of avoiding a split infinitive by placing the adverb at the end of a sentence seems to be overlooked by many writers:

> The driver began to study the map carefully.

*rather than*

> The driver began to carefully study the map.

Occasionally it is advisable to rephrase a sentence rather than resort to a split infinitive:

> The council decided that it would at least maintain the present system.

*rather than*

> The council decided to at least maintain the present system.

In the first example *would maintain* is a compound verb. It can be split without objection because it is normal for adverbs to be inserted between the parts of compound verbs that are not infinitives.

Some split infinitives are colloquial in origin, especially those broken by *really*: *to really try hard*. In formal contexts it is better to avoid even these if it can be done gracefully:

> I intend to try really hard.

*rather than*

> I intend to really try hard.

See also **adverbs**; **infinitive**; **verbs**.

**spoilage/spoliation** These two words are not synonymous. *Spoilage* means spoiling (usually of foodstuffs), while *spoliation* means plunder:

> Lack of refrigeration meant the spoilage of all fresh food.
>
> The spoliation of the ship by pirates ended the hopes of the refugees.

Note the spelling of *spoliation* (not 'spoiliation').

**spoiled/spoilt** Either word may be used as the past tense and past participle of the verb *to spoil*, but *spoilt* is preferred. *Spoilt* is the usual adjectival form: *a spoilt brat*; *spoilt milk*.

**spokesperson** If the sex of the person referred to is known, the term *spokesman* or *spokeswoman* is recommended. *Spokesperson* is now widely used as the sex-inclusive term, but *advocate* or *representative* may be preferred.

See also **chair**; **discriminatory language**; **-person**.

**spoliation** See **spoilage/spoliation**.

**spooler** A *spooler* is a computer facility that allows the user to continue working on a document while another document is being processed in the background.

See also **buffer**.

**spoonerism** This is a kind of oral dyslexia, in which the initial letters, syllables or sounds of words are accidentally transposed: *under the affluence of incahol*. *Spoonerisms* derive their name from that of the Rev. W. A. Spooner (1844–1930), who claimed not to be an ornithologist but was certainly a word-botcher.

See also **malapropism**.

**spoonful/spoonfuls** Note the single *l* in both, and the form of the plural (not 'spoonsful' or 'spoons full').

See also **compound nouns, plurals of; -ful**.

**spouse** A *spouse* is one of the partners in a marriage. The word has some jocular currency but is normally reserved for use in forms, applications and so on. If the sex of the person referred to is known, prefer *husband* or *wife*.

**spread** See **layout**.

**spreadsheet** A *spreadsheet* is a program used for accounting and scheduling purposes in general computing and desktop publishing. The screen or page in a spreadsheet is divided into columns to make boxes called cells. When the value in one cell is changed, all other values that are affected by the change are automatically recalculated.

**spring** The past tense of this verb is *sprang*; *sprung* is the past participle.

**spun** *Spun* is the past tense and past participle of the verb *to spin*. *Span* is an archaic form no longer recommended.

**SQNLDR/Sqn Ldr** Squadron Leader.

**squalor** Note the *-or*.

**SRC** Students' Representative Council.

**Sri Lanka/Sinhalese** *Sri Lanka* is the present name of the former British colony of Ceylon, an island situated at the foot of the Indian subcontinent. *Sinhalese* (not 'Singhalese') is the language of the people of the same name, who form the majority of the country's population.

**SRN** State Registered Nurse.

**SS** Nazi elite corps (German: *Schutzstaffel*); steamship.

**SSGT/S. Sgt** Staff Sergeant; also *S/Sgt.*

**St** saint; street.

**St George, Qld** Compare with *St Georges*, SA; *St Georges Basin*, NSW.

**staffer** US companies often have *staffers*. Australian companies have *employees* or *staff members*.

**stalactite/stalagmite** *Stalactites* hang from the roofs of caves; *stalagmites* rise from their floor. Some people remind themselves of the relative positions of the two by linking the *c* of the *stalactites* with that of *ceiling* and the *g* of the *stalagmites* with that of *ground*.

**stanch** See **staunch**.

**stanchion** An upright bar or post is a *stanchion*, not a 'staunchion'.

**stand-alone computer** A *stand-alone computer* is not connected to a network.

**stank/stunk** Either *stank* or *stunk* may be used as the past tense of the verb *to stink*; *stunk* is the past participle:

> The farmyard stank [*or* stunk] of pigs.
> These pipes have stunk for so long that they must be flushed clean.

**state** When *state* means nation or government it is normally given a lowercase initial: *member states of the European Community*; *affairs of state*; *state schools, not private ones*. To avoid confusion or ambiguity, an initial capital is recommended when the word refers to an independent region within a country: *the State of Queensland*; *New York State*; *a conference involving all States*.

**state-of-the-art** This compound adjective is synonymous with *up-to-date*, *modern* or *technically advanced*, and these terms should sometimes replace it to give it a rest.

**stationary/stationery** *Stationary* means not moving: *a stationary train*. *Stationery* means writing materials (pens, paper, envelopes and so on).

**status quo** Since *status quo* (Latin for *the state in which*) means the existing situation, it is tautological to refer to *the present status quo* or *a status quo situation*.

**staunch** The alternative spelling *stanch* for both the verb (meaning to stop the flow) and the adjective (meaning steadfast) is now unusual. You can *staunch* either a flow of blood or the bleeding wound itself.

**STD** sexually transmitted disease; subscriber trunk dialling.

**steal** See **burgle/rob/steal**.

**Stewart, Vic.** Compare with *Stuart*, Qld.

**stg** sterling (currency).

**stiletto** Plural *stilettos*.

**still** It is tautological to combine *still* with words like *remain*, *persist* and *continue*.

**stimulant/stimulus** A *stimulant* is any drug, drink or food that stimulates activity. A *stimulus* can be anything – but generally something abstract – that sparks action or exertion.

> The runner was disqualified for having taken a stimulant before the race.
> Fear was his stimulus for leaping the fence ahead of the bull.

The plural of *stimulus* is *stimuli* (or, more rarely, *stimuluses*).

**storey/story** A *storey* is a level in a building; the plural is *storeys*. A *story* is a tale; the plural is *stories*.

See also **floor/storey**.

**straightjacket/straitjacket** Either spelling is acceptable for the name of the confining jacket, but *straitjacket* is preferred.

**straitlaced** Note the spelling of this adjective, which means prudish.

**stratagem/strategy** A *stratagem* is a plan or trick. It can be part of a *strategy*, which is an overall plan of campaign; both words were originally military but are now also used generally.

**strategic** This adjective, which means important to a plan, is often superfluous, and in fact has become rather a joke word. A *strategic redeployment* is Pentagonese for a military defeat; the terms *strategic restructuring* and *strategic* *re-evaluation* are euphemisms often used in business to describe the shuffling of assets by bankrupt companies in order to confuse shareholders, bankers and receivers.

**strategy** See **stratagem/strategy**.

**stratum** A *stratum* is a layer (plural *strata* or, more rarely, *stratums*). In non-scientific contexts *strata*, like *data*, is often used as a singular noun, though this practice is not recommended because *stratum* (unlike *datum*) is well known as the singular noun.

**stress** When a word has more than one syllable, it is not always easy to decide which syllable to stress. Is it '**ro**-mance' or 'ro-**mance**', for example? (The answer is *either*.) In English the patterns of stress are so irregular that any guidelines are as likely to confuse as to help.

However, one aspect of stress consistent enough to warrant mention concerns the many words that, although spelt the same, are pronounced differently according to whether they are nouns or verbs. Here is the general rule.

- Stress the first syllable for the noun: **re**ject
- Stress the second syllable for the verb: re**ject**

The following are among those treated similarly:

| | | | | |
|---|---|---|---|---|
| combat | convert | ferment | pervert | rebound |
| conduct | convict | import | present | refuse |
| conflict | discharge | increase | progress | suspect |
| contest | exploit | insult | protest | survey |
| contract | extract | object | rebel | transfer |

There are plenty of exceptions, however, including *cluster*, *result* and *venture*, which have the same stress whether noun or verb.

Stress variation sometimes also distinguishes verbs from adjectives, as in *alternate*: '**orl**ta-nate' (verb) and 'orl-**tern**it' (adjective); and nouns from adjectives, as in *invalid*: '**in**va-lid' (noun) and 'in-**va**llid' (adjective).

For help with pronunciation or stress, consult a good dictionary or one of the numerous pronunciation guides on the market. *The Macquarie Dictionary* uses phonetic alphabet symbols to provide comprehensive pronunciation guidance, based on usage in the Australian community, for every headword. The simple non-phonetic pronunciation system used in the *Heinemann Australian Dictionary* is recommended for those who find phonetics difficult.

See also **Australian English**; **re-**.

**strip-in** In the context of typesetting a *strip-in* is a line of corrected type stuck over an incorrect line on finished art. A large strip-in is called a *patch*. So that the strip-in can be finely adjusted, hot wax instead of glue is used as an adhesive. Strip-ins should be avoided as much as possible because they are easily dislodged. In desktop publishing it is quicker and safer to reprint a whole page containing a correction than to use a strip-in.

**structure** Remember alternatives for this verb such as *organise*, *set up*, *prepare* and *construct*.

**Strzelecki** Note the spelling of the surname of the explorer and places called after him.

**stunk** See **stank/stunk**.

**stupefy** Note the *-efy* (not 'stupify').

**stupor** Note the *-or*.

**style sheet** See **copy editing**.

**subconscious/unconscious** As nouns and adjectives, both words are terms used in psychology and also generally. *Subconscious* refers to the part of the mind that is not fully conscious (*sub* meaning under) though it may influence behaviour: *repressed desires of the subconscious*. The psychological concept of the *unconscious* relates to the 'forgotten' memories that cannot be recalled by the conscious self but still determine behaviour. In everyday usage, *subconscious* means not fully aware (*subconscious fear*) and unconscious means insensible (*an unconscious patient*) or intellectually or emotionally unaware (*unconscious of the danger*).

Avoid using *unconsciously* as a synonym for *unintentionally* in this kind of expression:

> His humour was unintentionally [*not* unconsciously] cruel.

**subject/object** The *subject* of a verb is the noun or noun-substitute that 'directs' the action of the verb; the *object*, on the other hand, is the noun or noun-substitute that 'receives' the action:

> The carrier [noun subject] delivered the parcels [noun object].
> He [pronoun subject] delivered them [pronoun object] early.

A noun or noun-substitute attached to a preposition is also called the *object*: *from the treetops*; *into the mist*; *against us*. The last example demonstrates the change of form that some pronouns (but not nouns) undergo when they are objects rather than subjects: *us* is the object form (in the *objective case*), while *we* is the subject form (in the *subjective case*). More detail on this matter is provided in the entry **case (grammar)**.

See also **active voice/passive voice**.

**subjective** See **objective/subjective**.

**subjective and objective case** See **case (grammar)**; **subject/object**.

**sub judice** This Latin phrase (meaning under a judge) is a piece of legalese. A matter that is *sub judice* is before the courts and therefore cannot be discussed elsewhere until it is settled.

Pronounce the second word '**joo**-da-see'.

**subjunctive mood** A verb in the *subjunctive mood* expresses the possible, conditional or desirable: the hypothetical as opposed to the factual (called the *indicative mood*). When you say *If I were you I'd wear a dark suit* you are using the subjunctive form *were* instead of the indicative form *was*. The verb *to be* is conspicuous among examples of the subjunctive mood because it changes all its present-tense forms (*am*, *is* and *are*) to *be*, and the past form *was* to *were*. Other verbs undergo only one change of form: the third-person singular of the present tense loses its *s* – for example, he, she or it *pays* becomes *pay* (as illustrated below).

The more natural-sounding of expressions in the subjunctive mood – such as the *If I were* of the first example – cause little trouble and are as common in speech as in print. But note the following, in which the subjunctive form is the correct one for expressing a possibility; in spoken English the incorrect version is appropriately informal and widely accepted:

> Wanda proposes that her employer pay [*not* pays] compensation.

An attractive alternative to the subjunctive in such constructions is the use of *should*:

> Wanda proposes that her employer should pay compensation.

*If* often introduces clauses having a conditional sense that requires the subjunctive form of a verb:

> If Ky were [*not* was] a little older he could come to work with me.

*As if* is followed by the subjunctive when the clause has a hypothetical air:

> The apprentice talked as if he were [*not* was] the master electrician.

In 'wish' constructions such as the following you should always use the subjunctive when writing; the indicative is more natural in speech:

> She wished that she were [*not* was] home in bed.

The subjunctive mood occurs in some very common expressions, whether or not we recognise it there. The following all have some sense of desire:

> Lest we forget   Be that as it may.   God bless you.

The first is really a contraction of the words *So that we may not forget*, the last *May God bless you*.

See also **as if/as though**; **if it was/if it were**; **mood**.

**Sub. Lt** See **SBLT/Sub. Lt**.

**submissions** See **reports and submissions**.

**subpoena** A *subpoena* is a writ summonsing a witness 'under penalty'; as a verb it means to summons as a witness (note the spelling of the forms *subpoenaed* and *subpoenaing*). The word is pronounced 's'**pee**na'.

See also **summoned/summonsed.**

**subscribe** See **ascribe/subscribe.**

**subscripts** See **inferior characters/superior characters.**

**subsequent** See **consequent/consequential/subsequent**.

**substitute** See **replace/substitute**.

**subsume** This verb means to place in a larger group or category:

> The proposal to widen the corner was subsumed under the road reconstruction scheme.

Do not use *subsume* as a synonym for *include* or *contain*:

> The road reconstruction scheme included [*not* subsumed] some widening of corners and improving of drains.

**successive** See **consecutive/successive.**

**succinct** Note the spelling of this adjective, which means concise. It is pronounced 'suk-**sinkt**'.

**such/such as/like** *Such* may be used in the following example, but *that* or *this* often sounds more natural:

> That is the story of my life.

*rather than*

> Such is the story of my life.

When *such* introduces an example it must be followed by *as*, not *that* or *who*:

> Arrange for such refreshments as [*not* that] will be needed for the guests.
>
> Invite such people as [*not* who] will enjoy good music.

If ambiguity is possible, or the context is formal, introduce examples with *such as* rather than *like*:

> She sold novels such as *The Twyborn Affair*.

*not* She sold novels like *The Twyborn Affair*.

Using *like* could mean that she sold novels similar to but not including *The Twyborn Affair*. In the same kind of construction *like* is preferably confined to informal use:

> They wear colours like orange and red.

As is explained in the entry **phrase**, phrases that are said to be 'defining' must not be marked off from the rest of the sentence by a pair of commas. Because the meaning of *such as* suggests that it always defines something, it may appear without commas in *any* simple sentence:

> Novels such as *The Twyborn Affair* may sell as fast as science fiction.

Bulkier sentences may require the pair of commas in order to be easily read, and the *such as* phrase becomes parenthetical without losing its sense of defining something:

> Topical Australian novels, such as Patrick White's *The Twyborn Affair*, may sell as fast as science fiction.

*Such as* may be regarded as a preposition (taking the objective case) or a conjunction (taking the subjective case) in the following kind of example:

> There are many out-of-work bricklayers such as him.

*or* There are many out-of-work bricklayers such as he [is].

Note that *such as* is incorrect in the following example:

> Where the snowfields are famous, as [*not* such as] in New Zealand, many tourists arrive in winter.

It is correct but misplaced here:

> Fruit is canned at Shepparton, such as pears and apricots.

The phrase *such as pears and apricots* should follow the word *Fruit*.

See also **case (grammar)**; **like**; **phrase**; **pronouns**.

**suddenness** Note the *-nn-*.

**suffixes** See **prefixes and suffixes**.

**suit/suite** The meanings of the noun *suit* include an item of clothing, one of the sets in playing-cards (clubs, for example), a petition, a lawsuit, and the courting of a woman. A *suite* may be a group of followers, a series (including a series of rooms), a set of furniture or a type of musical work. Pronounce *suit* to rhyme with *boot* and *suite* to rhyme with *beet*.

**Summer Hill, NSW** Compare with *Summerhill*, Tas.

**summoned/summonsed** A person is called to come or *summoned* except after receiving a *summons* to appear in court, when *summonsed* is the correct verb.

See also **subpoena**.

**sunk** See **sank/sunk**.

**Sunraysia** The *Sunraysia* is a district centred on Mildura in north-western Victoria; it is the home of Australia's dried-fruit industry.

**Sunshine Coast** The *Sunshine Coast* is the popular name for a resort 100–150 kilometres north of Brisbane and extending from Caloundra to Noosa Heads. Its main urban centre is Nambour.

See also **Gold Coast**.

**super-** The prefix *super-* means above or beyond, as in *superstructure* and *supernatural* (no hyphens). It has been cemented to many words and product names to give them a lift: *superstar*, *super-store*, *super-train* (sometimes in such words hyphens are used).

**supercilious/superficial** *Supercilious* means haughtily disdainful or contemptuous:

> His manner was supercilious but he felt inferior.

*Superficial* means of or pertaining to the surface or – in reference to people – shallow:

> She had no close friends because she was capable only of superficial relationships.

**superior characters** See **inferior characters/superior characters**.

**superlative** See **comparative and superlative**.

**supernatural** See **preternatural/supernatural**.

**superscripts** See **inferior characters/superior characters**.

**supersede** *Supersede* – meaning to supplant – must be one of the most frequently misspelt words in the English language. The last syllable is *-sede*, not '-cede'.

**supervisor** Note the *-or*.

**supine** See **prone/prostrate/supine**.

**supplement** See **complement/compliment/supplement**.

**suppose/supposing** Either *suppose* or *supposing* can introduce a question or statement:

> Suppose [*or* Supposing] we run out of beer?
> Suppose [*or* Supposing] they can't finish the job, we'll have to do it ourselves.

**surge** See **serge/surge**.

**Surrey Hills, Vic.** Compare with *Surry Hills*, NSW.

**susceptible** Note the *-sc-* and *-ible*.

**sustainable development** Development that meets the needs of the population in one generation without compromising the ability of future generations to meet their own needs is called *sustainable development*. The term *ecologically sustainable development* is often used to emphasise the crucial role of the natural environment in the fostering of sustainable development.

**Sutherland, NSW** Compare with *Sutherlands*, SA; *Sutherlands Creek*, Vic.

**swam/swum** *Swam* is the past tense of the verb *to swim*; *swum* is the past participle:

We swam in the river all day.

The children have swum in this river before.

In Australian English the past participle *swum* is often used instead of *swam* for the past tense, but this is incorrect.

**swap** *Swap* is the correct spelling of the word meaning to exchange or barter; *swop* is common but not recommended.

**SWAPO** South-West Africa People's Organization.

**swat/swot** Both words are colloquial, and both may be verbs or nouns. To *swat* means to inflict a sharp blow: *swat a fly*; *to swot* means to study hard: *swot for my exams*. A *swat* is a blow, and *swot* is a term often used half scornfully and half enviously of someone who is studying hard.

**swelled/swollen** *Swelled* is the past tense of the verb *to swell*:

My sprained ankle swelled.

When *swelled* simply means increased, it is also the correct form of the past participle:

Three busloads of tourists have swelled the attendance.

*Swollen* is the past participle in cases of injury or excess:

His face has been swollen by the blow.

The creeks were soon swollen by the melting snow.

*Swollen* is also the usual form of the adjective (*a swollen ankle*), but *swelled* is often used instead of *swollen* in the phrase *a swollen head*.

**swot** See **swat/swot**.

**swum** See **swam/swum**.

**syllabus** Plural *syllabuses* or, more rarely, *syllabi*.

**sylvan** See **silvan/sylvan**.

**symmetry** Note the *-mm-* and *-etry*. The word means balance in form or arrangement.

**sympathy** See **empathy/sympathy**.

**syndrome** This medical term describes the pattern formed by a group of symptoms in a disease or disorder: *Down syndrome*; *manic-depressive syndrome*. Used generally, it refers to any combination of characteristics or symptoms: *the Lolita syndrome*; *the spoilt-child syndrome*. As the word has become something of a cliché, try not to overuse it.

**synergy** This is the joint action of two or more substances such as drugs, each of which increases the effect of the other. It is also known as *synergism*. The word has been adopted by business commentators and has been overused as a substitute for *cooperation* or *collaboration*. It is pronounced '**sinn**a-jee'.

**synonymous** Note the spelling. In the context of grammar this adjective means having the same meaning.

**synonyms** See **antonyms and synonyms**.

**synopsis** The plural of this noun meaning summary is *synopses*. Writers asked to provide a synopsis for their publisher should ascertain the size and scale required. A couple of paragraphs outlining the plot, in the case of fiction, or describing the content, in the case of non-fiction, might be sufficient.

**syntax** This grammatical term refers to the arrangement of words in sentences. If your *syntax* is faulty your meaning is likely to be unclear.

**synthesis** See **analysis/synthesis**.

**syphon** See **siphon/syphon**.

# Tt

**T-** Use an initial capital and a hyphen in words such as *T-shirt*, *T-bone*, *T-junction* and *T-square*.

**TAB** Totalizator Agency Board.

**Tabilk/Tahbilk** Note the spelling variation: *Tabilk* is the Victorian locality in which the winery *Chateau Tahbilk* is found.

**tableau** The plural of this French noun meaning scene is *tableaux* or *tableaus*.

**table d'hôte** See **à la carte/prix fixe/table d'hôte**.

**TAFE** Technical and Further Education.

**Tallwood, NSW** Compare with *Talwood*, Qld.

**Tarana, NSW** Compare with *Taranna*, Tas.

**target** The noun target is a synonym for *goal*, *aim* or *objective*, and the verb is all too popular in commercial English:

> Consultants were hired to target the company's market.

Note the single *t* in the forms *targeted* and *targeting*.

**Tarong, Qld** Compare with *Taronga*, Tas.; *Taronga Park*, NSW.

**Tas.** Tasmania.
See also **Van Diemen's Land**.

**Tattersall's** The name of this lottery has an apostrophe, but its abbreviation *Tatts* does not. Note also *Tattslotto.*

**taught/taut** *Taught* is the past tense and past participle of the verb *to teach. Taut* means tightly drawn (that is, not slack): *a taut bowstring*; *the play's taut plot.*

**tautology/pleonasm** *Tautology* is a redundancy of words. More specifically, it is the needless repetition of an idea, often within the same phrase. Many tautological phrases are so much part of everyday speech that they are used unthinkingly by most people:

| | | | |
|---|---|---|---|
| join together | cooperate together | true facts | descend down |
| in actual fact | continue on | divide up | a fast sprint |
| final outcome | revert back | repeat again | a new innovation |
| follow after | temporary respite | unite together | noxious poisons |
| climb up | two twins | return again | a brief moment |
| a free gift | a paid professional | sufficient enough | a feline cat |

Tautologies often arise because of a faulty understanding of the meaning of words, as in the following examples:

The council outlined a new, all-embracing, *comprehensive* [which means all-embracing] plan.

They all agreed *unanimously* [which means totally in agreement] with the plan.

We live in close *proximity* [which means closeness] to the school.

*Pleonasm* is a much less common term denoting redundancy, or an unnecessary repetition, of words. Some authorities consider *pleonasm* synonymous with *tautology*; others state that it more correctly describes simple verbosity – the use of more words than are necessary to express the intended meaning.

See also **truism**.

**taxi/taxied/taxiing** Note the spelling (the plural of the noun is *taxis*).

**TB** tuberculosis.

**TEAS** Tertiary Education Assistance Scheme.

**tea-tree** This spelling is preferred to *ti-tree* because of the use Captain Cook and others made of the leaves as a tea-substitute. Both *Leptospermum* and *Melaleuca* species were used for this purpose, but *tea-tree* is now applied to the first more generally than to the second. Though the spelling *ti-tree* is not recommended, it has had some currency in Australia since at least the 1870s.

**Teatree, Tas.** Compare with *Tea Tree Gully*, SA ; *Ti Tree*, NT.

**technical/technological** The adjective *technical* often describes the practical skills and terms of reference involved in art, craft or science: *technical training*; *technical books*. It has a second meaning – according to the strict interpretation of rules: *a technical knock-out*; *a technical assault*. The noun is *technicality*. *Technological* means relating to the practical application of science and engineering to industry: *a technological breakthrough*; *technological wizardry*. The noun is *technology*.

**teetotal** Note the spelling (not 'tea-'). Someone who is *teetotal* abstains from drinking alcohol and is called a *teetotaller*. Of US colloquial origin, the words are formed by the duplication of the initial letter of *total* for the sake of emphasis.

**Telecom** Australian Telecommunications Commission.

**telephone numbers** When writing telephone numbers, use the spacing indicated; ask typesetters for a *thin space*:

1 1234
11 1234
111 1234
(03) 111 1234
1800 111 123

The area code – but not the toll-free code 1800 – should be placed within brackets.

International codes and telephone numbers should be typeset on letterheads as follows:

+612 111 1234

The + sign indicates the position of the international access code for the country from which a call is made. For example, a person phoning Sydney from the US would first dial the US international access code 011, then 61 (the country code for Australia) and 2 (the code for Sydney), followed by the local number (111 1234). To ring overseas countries from Australia you begin with the Australian international access code 0011, then dial the relevant country code, area code and telephone number.

**temerity/timidity** Although not strictly opposites, these two words have contrasting implications. *Temerity* means rashness or audacity:

> Sister Branson had the temerity to park her car in the senior surgeon's space.

*Timidity* means shyness or fearfulness:

> His timidity made him easy prey for practical jokers.

**temperature** See **Celsius/centigrade/Fahrenheit**.

**template** In desktop publishing a template is the grid (or layout pattern) for a specific job. If you use a particular template regularly, it can be stored on your hard drive or on a floppy disk ready for use as required. High-end page-makeup programs allow the operator to incorporate in the template design specifications such as text area (line length and number of lines per page), left and right margins, gutter width, the font and size of text and headings, the leading, indents, rules, crop marks and so on. The method for setting up a template varies from program to program.

See also **crop marks**; **desktop publishing**; **layout**.

**tend** Say *tend* the bar, not *tend to* the bar; but you must *attend to* the customers.

**tenosynovitis** See **RSI**.

**tenses** The *tense* of a verb tells us *when* an action takes place. Tense is indicated by the form of the verb or the addition of auxiliary (helping) verbs. The basic tense formations are as follows:

- the *present simple*, which indicates *now*

  I *work* in the city.

  but note that a permanent fact may be expressed in the present tense, even though the narrative is in the past

  The women *learnt* [past] that the plan *works* [present] well.
- the *present continuous*, which indicates *now but continuing for a while*

  I *am working* long hours at the moment.
- the *past simple*, which indicates *a time in the past*

  I *worked* in the city a long time ago.
- the *past continuous*, which indicates *a time in the past that continued for a while*

  I *was working* when you phoned.
- the *present perfect* (and its continuous form), which connects *past time with the present*

  I *have worked* [or *have been working*] here for years.
- the *past perfect* (and its continuous form), which indicates *a time before a time in the past*

  I *had worked* [or *had been working*] here before the war.
- the *future* (and its continuous form), which indicates *a time in the future*

  I *shall work* [or *shall be working*] here from tomorrow.

  but note that *future* tense may be indicated by the *present* form in some circumstances:

  I *am working* at Tweed Heads next week.

In telling a story, be consistent in the tense you use – for instance, do not jump from past tense to present tense without good reason.

See also **verbs**.

**terminal** A computer *terminal* consists of a keyboard and a screen; the actual computer to which they are linked may be some distance away.

**terminus** The plural is *termini* or *terminuses*. Note that we usually have a tram or bus *terminus* but an air *terminal*.

**textual/textural** *Textual* means of or pertaining to a text: *textual amendments*. *Textural* means relating to texture: *the textural coarseness of hemp*.

**than** *Than* may be a conjunction, introducing a clause:

They asked more questions than we did.

Or it may be a preposition, preceding a noun or pronoun:

We would rather have Hank in the team than you.

Or its function may be disguised because a verb has been left unstated:

They asked more questions than us [than we did].

In formal prose the correct pronoun in this last case is *we*, not *us*, whether or not the verb is expressed. But for conversational and informal purposes it is acceptable to use the more natural-sounding *us* (or *me*, *him*, *her* and so on rather than *I*, *he*, *she* and so on). But watch out for ambiguities:

You pay her better than me.

Does this mean that you pay her better than you pay me, or that you pay her better than I do? Introducing the relevant verb will dispel any doubts.

Note that the combination *than what* is always wrong:

The manager has a bigger car than I have.

*not* The manager has a bigger car than what I have.

For other constructions in which *than* is the wrong word see **different**, **hardly**, **prefer** and **rather**. In the following example *as* is the correct word:

These mountains are three times as rich in minerals as [*not* than] those.

**thankfully** The adverb *thankfully* means in a thankful way:

The underpaid porter accepted the tip thankfully.

Some people also use it colloquially to mean *it is a matter for relief that*:

Thankfully my daughter passed her exams.

Ambiguity is possible here: was she simply thankful that she passed her exams, or was it a great relief to everyone that she did? Avoidance of this usage is recommended.

See also **hopefully**.

**thank you** Write *thank you* as two words, except when you are treating it as an adjective or noun: *a thankyou note*; *saying our thankyous*.

**that** *That* may sometimes be understood, rather than expressed, in a sentence:

I'm sure [that] you're right.

The kitten [that] I bought is thriving

These are informal, unambiguous examples in which *that* might sound rather stilted. In general, however, the conjunction or relative pronoun *that* is indispensable. Even in spoken English its omission can cause confusion, and formal verbs such as *ensure*, *announce* and *request* demand it:

The government will ensure *that* hospital funding continues.

They announced *that* the guest comedian was sick.

We requested *that* our tickets be refunded.

In the absence of *that*, ambiguity may put readers on the wrong track at least temporarily: *He felt her face, throat, arms and legs suited her for the leading role.* Or the meaning intended may be permanently elusive: *Reagan said for several years the United States was too soft on Russia.* Did he make the remark a number of times over a period of several years, or did the lenient attitude persist for several years? Similarly: *She said on leaving we must shut the door.* Did she tell us that we must shut the door when we left, or was her remark made as she was departing?

Be careful not to duplicate *that* in a complex sentence: *Amanda has found that, when you learn one foreign language, that others become easier.*

Avoid using *that* as an adverb in formal speech and writing:

It's not so cold.

*or* It's not as cold as that.

*not* It's not that cold.

See also **and which**; **clause**; **that/which**; **who/that**.

**that/which** Choosing *that* or *which* depends on whether it introduces a defining (restrictive) or non-defining (non-restrictive) clause. This question is discussed in the entry **clause**. The choice of the construction *and that* or *and which* is discussed under **and which**. The use of *that* for people is explained under **who/that**.

See also **comma**; **phrase**; **that**; **which**.

**the** The little word *the* is grammatically known as the definite article. Like the indefinite article *a* or *an*, it accompanies many nouns: *the bushranger*; *the Snowy*; *the generosity*; *the florist*. In the first of the following examples, however, the idiom *man and boy* does not require *the* before either noun; in the second, *the* is an option before *spring*:

The florist, man and boy, loved flowers.

He was happiest in [the] spring.

But *the* should always be included in this rather different construction:

The local florist, Otto Schultz, enjoyed his work.

*not* Local florist Otto Schultz enjoyed his work.

*The* is often attached to only one noun even though it applies to more than one: *the daffodils and hyacinths*. The addition of an adjective may bring with it the chance of ambiguity: *the golden daffodils and hyacinths*. Since golden hyacinths exist but are uncommon, it is best to insert *the* before *hyacinths* if you really mean hyacinths in general.

The pronunciation of *the* was a simple matter before broadcasters discovered that the most common word in the language could be used to give their utterances a more imposing sound: *Thee prime minister has announced that thee deficit has been reversed.* Ignore the broadcasters. Before initial consonants, as in *prime* and *deficit*, pronounce *the* with the weak sound of the second syllable of *mother*. It is only before initial vowels, as in *eggs* and *apples*, that it is correct to pronounce *the* as 'thee'.

See also **a/an**; **titles of publications, and literary, artistic and musical works**.

**their/them/they** The grammatically incorrect practice of using *their*, *them* and *they* with singular subjects like *anyone*, *everyone*, *nobody* and *person* is widespread today as people attempt to avoid using the sex-specific *he* or *she*:

Ask everyone if they have seen the dog.

Nobody carried water with them on the hike.

Each person has a right to their own opinion.

While such usage has gained a qualified acceptance, it should be avoided in formal writing. For suggestions of ways around this problem see **he/she**.

See also **anybody/anyone**; **each**; **every/everybody/everyone**; **discriminatory language**; **gender**; **-ing forms**; **pronouns**; **they're/ there/ their**.

**them/their** See **-ing forms**; **their/them/they**; **they're/there/their**.

**thence** *Thence* is a somewhat outdated adverb meaning from that place; the *from* is not repeated:

We rowed as far as the bay and thence [*not* from thence] sailed north.

*Thence* may also be used to mean therefore, but few people would opt for it nowadays:

The phone was dead and we concluded thence that the cable had been cut.

Note that *thenceforth* and *thenceforward* mean from that time onwards:

Thenceforth [*or* thenceforward] they were never to meet without embarrassment.

See also **hence**; **whence**.

**there** See **there are/there is/there's**; **they're/there/their**.

**there-** Many compound words beginning with *there* are considered archaic today, and they smack of legalese or officialese when used – for example *thereat*, *thereby*, *therefor*, *therein*, *thereof*, *thereon*, *thereto*, *theretofore* and *therewith*. Exceptions are *thereabouts*, *thereafter* and *therefore*, which are all in common and idiomatic use. Note the slight difference in spelling between *therefor* (meaning for that) and *therefore* (meaning thus).

**there are/there is/there's** Breaking the following rule is pardonable in conversation but not in written English. You should use *there are* when what follows is plural (note that two or more singular items add up to a plural):

> There are [*not* there's] three points to consider.
>
> There are [*not* there is] a vase, two mirrors and a painting in the room.

*There is* or *there's* is correct only when what follows is in the singular or may be regarded as a single unit:

> There is an unusual moth near the light.
>
> There is 3 tonnes of sand in the yard.

See also **singular or plural**.

**The Rock, NSW** (2655) Compare with *The Rocks*, NSW (2000).

**thesaurus** The name *thesaurus* comes from a Greek word meaning treasure or treasury. As a book, a thesaurus is a treasury of language. Unlike an ordinary dictionary, it does not give the precise meaning of words, but lists words that are similar in meaning (synonyms) and their opposites (antonyms). A good thesaurus will go beyond merely providing synonyms and antonyms; it will also give a wide variety of phrases that have similar or contrasting connotations. Thus a thesaurus is a useful tool for a writer wanting the most apt word or phrase for expressing an idea or feeling. A thesaurus is usually arranged alphabetically, although the famous one published by Peter Roget in 1852 sorted expressions into groups of related meanings. Extensive alphabetical indexing in later editions made Roget's classic work easier to use. Today a high-end word-processing program will usually have an integrated thesaurus linked to a dictionary.

See also **antonyms and synonyms**; **dictionary**.

**thesis** Plural *theses* (pronounced '**thee**-seez').

**they/them** The correct pronoun to use before and after various verbs is explained in the entry **case (grammar)**.

See also **their/them/they**; **they're/there/their**.

**they're/there/their** Although these words are often used incorrectly, it is generally through carelessness rather than ignorance. This is particularly so in the case of the contraction *they're* (short for *they are*), which is regularly written as *there* (an adverb) or, occasionally, as *their* (a possessive adjective). Compare the three in the following correct sentence:

> *There* are some who, though *their* mistakes are numerous, will tell you that *they're* never wrong.

Note also the possessive *theirs* (not 'their's').

See also **-ing forms**; **their/them/they**; **there are/there is/there's**.

**thin space** See **word spacing**.

**third/thirdly** See **first/firstly**.

**Third World/First World/Second World** The term *Third World* is sometimes applied to underdeveloped countries – that is, those with insignificant manufacturing sectors, low literacy rates and a low per capita income. Into this category would come parts of Latin America, Africa, Asia and the Middle East. Although there is some debate over definitions for the *First World* and *Second World*, the First is generally regarded as including most of Europe, North America, Japan, Australia and New Zealand. The Second is considered to comprise the developed countries of what used to be the communist bloc.

**though** See **although/though**.

**three Rs** Note the capital *R* and no apostrophe.

**threshold** Although this word is pronounced 'thresh-hold', note that there is only one *h* joining the syllables.

**thus** Do not use the peculiar US variant *thusly*.
See also **nevertheless/nonetheless**; ***sic***.

**tiling** Most printers used in desktop publishing are based on the size of an A4 page. If you want to produce pages that are larger than A4, for example A3 or tabloid, you will need to print out the larger-sized page in A4-size pieces and *tile* them – that is, manually paste the pieces together to make a whole page.

**till/until** Both words mean up to the time *of* (preposition) or up to the time *that* (conjunction). In formal writing *until* is perhaps the more common word, particularly at the beginning of a sentence. *Till*, being thought less formal, is possibly the more frequent in speech. Note that *till* is a word in its own right; it is not a mere contraction of *until*, which has no contracted form: the often seen *'till* and *'til*, and the advertiser's *til*, are all incorrect.

Since *up* is part of the sense of *till* and *until*, it is undesirable to duplicate it in the phrases *up till* and *up until*. Similarly, *until such time as* is an unnecessarily wordy extension of *till* or *until*.

**time** This word is often superfluous: say *in three days* rather than *in three days' time*, for example.
See also **time of day**; **time zones**.

**time of day** There are two ways of expressing the hours and minutes of a day. The *12-hour system* is one: *7.15 a.m.*, *3.30 p.m.*; and the *24-hour system* is the other: *0715*, *1530*.

*The 12-hour system* The 12-hour system is generally favoured for narrative text. Complete hours, half-hours and quarter-hours are usually written in full:

Sophie caught the bus at a quarter past ten.

The meeting was at half past eleven.

Approximate times should always be expressed in words rather than figures:

We left at about seven [*not* 7] o'clock.

Note that *o'clock* (of the clock) is used only after complete hours: *nine o'clock*, not *a quarter past nine o'clock*; and preferably not with figures: *four o'clock*, not *4 o'clock*. More precise times must be expressed in figures:

Sven always arrives home at 6.35 p.m.

Inclusion of the full stops and a space after the figures is recommended for the abbreviations *a.m.* (Latin: *ante meridiem* – before noon) and *p.m.* (Latin: *post meridiem* – after noon): *7.23 a.m.*; *9.34 p.m.* The abbreviations may, however, be written without full points and set solid with their related figures (*7.23am*; *9.34pm*) if there are many of them and space is at a premium. It is not necessary to use two noughts to indicate full hours: *7 p.m.*, not *7.00 p.m.*

Strictly speaking *12 p.m.* is *noon* and *12 a.m. is midnight*, but it is more helpful to write *12 noon* or *12 midday* (or preferably just *noon* or *midday*) and *12 midnight* (or just *midnight*). On the other hand it is unnecessary to add *in the morning* to *3 a.m.* or *afternoon* to *5.10 p.m. tomorrow*.

The US constructions *a quarter of ten* for *a quarter to ten*, and *a quarter after nine* for *a quarter past nine* are not acceptable in Australian usage.

*The 24-hour system* Because of its precision the 24-hour system – which had military origins – is becoming more popular. It is the time system for the telecommunications and airline industries, and involves numbering the hours from 1 to 23 using four digits (the first pair refers to hours, the second pair to minutes). A day starts at midnight, which is 0000 hours, and ends at one minute to midnight, 2359 hours. No punctuation or spacing is used between the digits:

0315 (3.15 a.m.)  1305 (1.05 p.m.)  2250 (10.50 p.m.)

The numbers from 1300 hours are quickly converted to the 12-hour system by deducting 1200 from the number: 1300 hours would be 1 p.m.

Because the 24-hour system is precise and universally understood, there is a case for suggesting its adoption in business communications generally, and particularly those involving non-English-speaking people. The vague *You'll get the fax at nine* would become the precise *You'll get the fax at 0900* (pronounced 'oh-nine hundred').

See also **a.m./p.m.**; **daylight saving**; **GMT**; **numbers in figures or words**; **time zones**.

**time zones** Australia has three standard time zones: *Eastern Standard Time* (*EST*), which is ten hours ahead of Greenwich Mean Time (GMT) and covers Queensland, most of New South Wales, the Australian Capital Territory, Victoria and Tasmania; *Central Standard Time* (*CST*), which is nine and a half hours ahead of GMT and covers South Australia, the Northern Territory and the far west of New South Wales; and *Western Standard Time* (*WST*), which is eight hours ahead of GMT and covers Western Australia.

See also **daylight saving**; **GMT**; **time of day**.

**timidity** See **temerity/timidity**.

**tirade** See **harangue/tirade**.

**titillate/titivate** Although *titillate* literally means to tickle, it is now most often used figuratively to mean stimulate or excite in a pleasant way:

> The idea of leading a secret life titillated her fancy.

Because *titillate* these days tends to have sexual overtones, it is sometimes confused with *titivate*, which means to adorn or make smart:

> Our cousins have gone to titivate before the visitors arrive.

The variant spellings *tittivate* and *tidivate* are not recommended.

**titles of publications, and literary, artistic and musical works**
When the titles of newspapers, magazines and journals occur in text they should be set in italic type (underlining indicates italics in handwritten or typed copy):

> *Canberra Times*   *Elle*   *Landscape Australia*

Note that roman type is used for a possessive or plural *s* following italicised titles:

> the *West Australian*'s editorial   several *Tribune*s

When such a title includes the definite article (*the*), the word is usually given a lower-case initial and set in roman type – the *Daily Telegraph* – though exceptions have traditionally been made for *The Times* and *The Economist*. The house style of newspapers, magazines and journals may, of course, differ in some ways from what is recommended here for the broader publishing scene. However, it is generally agreed that the definite article should be omitted altogether when its inclusion would be awkward:

> She had been a journalist for the *Age*.
> *but* She had been an *Age* journalist.
> He worked as a photographer for *The Times*.
> *but* He was a *Times* photographer.
> We had the *Advertiser* delivered every morning.
> *but* We read our *Advertiser* over breakfast wherever possible.

The titles of books, plays, long poems, films, operas, musicals, paintings, sculptures and other art works are also set in italic type:

> *The Vivisector*   *Emerald City*   *The Divine Comedy*
> *Strictly Ballroom*   *La Traviata*   *Cats*
> Leonardo's *La Gioconda*   Michelangelo's *David*

Single quotation marks are used for the titles of short stories, essays, articles, lectures, chapters (quoted in references), short poems, songs, and television and radio programs:

Lawson's short story 'The Union Buries Its Dead'
Walter Murdoch's essay 'On Sitting Still'
Auberon Waugh's *Spectator* article 'The laziest people on earth'
the Dyason Memorial Lecture 'China's Policy and Outlook'
chapter 2, 'Single storeys'
Wordsworth's 'The Solitary Reaper'
'Waltzing Matilda'
the TV soap opera 'Neighbours'
the radio program 'Green and Practical'

The titles of unpublished material, including diaries, theses and transcripts, are neither italicised nor enclosed within quotation marks:

The thesis was entitled Community Relations in Small Towns.

The names of musical works such as concertos and symphonies are usually set in roman type without inverted commas. The descriptive titles of such works, however, are set in italic type:

Beethoven's Piano Concerto No. 3 in C minor
*but* Beethoven's Symphony No. 6 in F major – the *Pastoral*
*and* Vivaldi's *The Four Seasons*

The names of books such as the Bible and the Koran are treated similarly.

The first word in all these titles is always given an initial capital, but there are two common systems for dealing with the other words in a title.

***Dominant words only*** This is the traditional style for books, and the recommended style for all the kinds of title dealt with here except the names of articles and chapters. Under this system you capitalise the dominant words in the title: nouns, pronouns, adjectives, adverbs, interjections, most verbs, long prepositions, and conjunctions other than *and*, *but* and *or*. The remainder begin with a lower-case letter:

- the definite article – *the*
- the indefinite article – *a*, *an*
- the *to* of an infinitive
- the verb *to be* in all its forms – including *am*, *are*, *is*, *was* and *will be*
- short prepositions – including *for*, *with*, *in* and *of* (but not long ones like *towards* and *underneath*)
- coordinating conjunctions – *and*, *but* and *or* (but not subordinating conjunctions like *when* and *if*)

The following book titles are capitalised under the 'dominant words' system:

*How to Adopt a Child*
*Sleep is for the Rich*
*Marching Towards the Future*
*Cruden's Complete Concordance to the Old and New Testaments*
*Call Me When the Cross Turns Over*

When a title consists of three words or fewer it is usual to give each an initial capital regardless of the normal rules:

*We Were There*
*Women In Jeopardy*

***Essential words only*** This is an optional treatment (favoured by libraries, for example) for book titles, and the recommended style for the names of articles and chapters. Under this system, only proper names are capitalised after the first word:

*How to adopt a child*
*Sleep is for the rich*
*Cruden's complete concordance to the Old and New Testaments*
*We were there*
an article in the *Scots Magazine* called 'The beautiful menace'
a chapter entitled 'People dreaming dreams'

A common device in some newspapers and magazines today is to set all titles in bold roman type, in order to make them stand out from the body of text. This can be effective provided there are not many of them one after the other.

See also **capitalisation**; **italics, use of**; **quotation marks/inverted commas**.

**ti-tree** See **tea-tree**.

**TKO** technical knock-out (boxing).

**TLC** tender loving care; Trades and Labour Council.

***TLS*** *Times Literary Supplement*.

**TNT** TNT Limited (formerly Thomas Nationwide Transport Limited); trinitrotoluene (explosive).

**to/too/two** The preposition *to* is frequently confused with the adverb *too*, and some people even confuse it with the number *two*. They are used as follows:

We went to the concert and Elise did too.
The two houses were too dilapidated to restore.

**together** *Together* is often added unnecessarily to words such as *assemble*, *combine*, *join*, *gather*, *link* and *cooperate* – all of which contain this meaning already.

**together with** See **singular or plural**.

**toggle** In computer terminology a *toggle* is a key or combination of keys that turns a command (such as a command for bold type) on as well as off.

**toilet** See **lavatory/toilet**.

**toing and froing** Note the absence of hyphens in this expression.

**tomato** Plural *tomatoes*.

**ton/tonne/tun** An *imperial* (or *long*) *ton* is equal to 2240 pounds or about 1016 kilograms. A *US* (or *short*) *ton* is equal to 2000 pounds or about 907 kilograms. A *metric tonne* is equal to 1000 kilograms or about 2204 pounds. To differentiate between the imperial or the US *ton* and the metric *tonne*, the latter is often pronounced to rhyme with *on*. But many people prefer to retain the traditional pronunciation (rhyming with *fun*), and to precede the words *ton* and *tonne* with *imperial*, *US* or *metric* as appropriate.

A *tun* is a large cask that holds 210 imperial gallons or about 955 litres.

See also **weights and measures**.

**tonsillitis** Note the *-ll-*.

**too** See **to/too/two**.

**the Top End** This is the colloquial name (sometimes given lower-case initials) for the northern part of the Northern Territory – hence a *top-ender* (sometimes given an initial capital), someone who lives there.

**tornado** Plural *tornadoes* or *tornados*.

**torpedo** Plural *torpedoes*.

**torso** Plural *torsos*.

**tortuous/torturous** The primary meaning of the adjective *tortuous* is winding or twisting:

> They followed a tortuous track over the mountain.

Figuratively it means not straightforward – that is, devious:

> Duncan's account of his movements was too tortuous to be credible.

*Torturous* means involving torture and is generally used to describe something very painful:

> The survivors of the shipwreck had experienced torturous thirst.

**total/totally** Take care when using the adjective *total* and the adverb *totally*. Although people sometimes feel they need them for emphasis, the words are usually redundant, as in the phrases *total devastation*, *total absence*, *totally empty*, *totally bankrupt* and *totally unnecessary*.

**to the tune of** Avoid this cliché.

**toward/towards** Either form is acceptable for this preposition, but *towards* is recommended.

**TPC** Trade Practices Commission.

**TPI** totally and permanently incapacitated (used for former defence force personnel who qualify for a *TPI pension*).

**trackball** A *trackball* is a device available for use on computers for moving the cursor around the screen. Some operators prefer it to a *mouse* because it is usually located on the keyboard and does not use desk space.

See also **cursor**; **mouse**.

**tracking** In typesetting or desktop publishing, *tracking* (also known as *letter spacing*) refers to the general tightening or loosening of the spaces between characters – often for aesthetic reasons. It is usually global (that is, occurs throughout the setting), though it can be used on individual lines to help shape a paragraph. Tracking does not change the appearance of the actual letters. Compare it with *kerning*, which refers to the adjustment of spacing between pairs or groups of letters to achieve evenness of appearance (as is illustrated in the entry **kerning**), and with the *condensing* and *expanding* of type (as illustrated in **type**).

| | |
|---|---|
| *Tracking –12* | **The magpies were carolling in Gosford.** |
| *Tracking normal* | **The magpies were carolling in Gosford.** |
| *Tracking +6* | **The magpies were carolling in Gosford.** |
| *Tracking +12* | **The magpies were carolling in Gosford.** |

**track record** Numerous sporting terms adopted into common usage have rapidly become clichés through overuse, and *track record* is one of them. *A good track record in sales* is simply and more accurately *a good sales record*. A few others to be wary of are *level playing field*, *lineball decision* and *a new ballgame*.

See also **level playing field**.

**trade names/trademarks** See **business names/trade names/trademarks**.

**trade unions** The preferred plural is *trade unions* rather than *trades unions* or *trades union*.

See also **compound nouns, plurals of**.

**traffic/trafficked/trafficking** Note the *-c* in the first and the *-ck-* in the other two.

**trait** A *trait* is a distinguishing feature or quality: *an unexpected trait of personality*. The traditional pronunciation 'tray' is preferred to 'trayt'.

**tranquil** Note the *-ll-* in *tranquillity*, *tranquilly*, *tranquillise* and *tranquilliser*.

**transfer/transferred/transferring** Note the single *r* in the first and the *-rr-* in the other two. In law, one who makes a transfer (for instance, of property) is a *transferor*; the normal spelling is *transferer*.

**transient/transitory** Both these adjectives mean temporary, passing after a short time. They are often interchangeable, but *transient* is a better choice when there is an uncomplicated sense of something passing quickly: *transient visitors*; *a transient thought*. *Transitory* is preferred when a sense of regret over the impermanence is to be conveyed: *the transitory nature of childhood innocence*.

**translucent/transparent** Substances that allow light to penetrate them may be *translucent* (as frosted glass is) or *transparent* (as clear glass is). *Transparent* is also used figuratively to mean open, candid or obvious:

> Stefan's transparent honesty was well known.
>
> The promoter's recital was transparent nonsense.

**transpire** Many authorities object to the use of the verb *transpire* to mean happen or take place, but it was first recorded in this sense very early in the nineteenth century and has surely established itself by now:

> I wonder what transpired at the meeting in June.

The basic meaning is to become known:

> It transpired that she had not attended the May or June meeting.

In physiological contexts *transpire* means to give off waste matter (through the pores of the skin, for example), but it should not be used as a synonym for *perspire*.

**transverse/traverse** The adjective *transverse* means lying crosswise, and usually at right angles to something: *transverse roof joists*. Although *traverse* may be an adjective synonymous with *transverse*, its most common use is as a rather formal verb meaning to pass across or over:

> The explorers traversed the desert without difficulty.

**trauma/traumatic** The noun *trauma* and its adjective *traumatic* correctly apply to any serious injury or to shock that has long-term repercussions:

> The specialist warned the fast bowler that further trauma to his spine would end his career.
>
> Many residents of Darwin found the wartime bombing a traumatic experience.

Neither should be used merely as a buzz word to describe everyday upsets or unpleasantness, but they are acceptable in conversational hyperbole:

Christmas shopping is a traumatic experience.

The plural of *trauma* is *traumas* or, in medical contexts, *traumata*. Pronounce the *au* with an 'or' sound.

**travel/travelled/travelling** Note the single *l* in the first and the *-ll-* in the next two.

**travel disk/security disk** A *travel disk* or *security disk* is a replica of the 3½ inch or 5¼ inch disk that comes with a new computer. These disks are made from either firm plastic or heavy cardboard and it is recommended that you insert them into the floppy disk drives to protect the driver heads when moving machines from one place to another. If you are buying a computer secondhand, try to obtain the travel disks from the original owner, though a floppy disk – new or used – can be substituted. Some newer disk drives will automatically secure the driver heads without the need for travel disks.

**traverse** See **transverse/traverse**.

**treble/triple** These words both have special meanings as musical terms but are close to interchangeable when used to mean threefold. Prefer *treble* when you mean three times the size, and *triple* when referring to something in three parts:

This year's profit is treble that of last year.

Clare's horse took the first obstacles easily but refused the triple jump.

Both words function as nouns and verbs as well as adjectives.

**trek/trekked/trekking** Note the single *k* in the first and the *-kk-* in the other two (not '-ck-').

**tremor** Note the *-or*.

**tri** The prefix *tri-* indicates the number three: *tripod*, *triangle*. Avoid its use in measurements of time such as *tri-monthly*, as the reader may not be sure whether you mean three times a month or every three months.

See also **bi-**.

**trial** The new verb *to trial* (*Let's trial this product in the shops*) probably arrived in Australia via Madison Avenue. Do not forget the older verbs *test* or *try*.

**triple** See **treble/triple**.

**triumphal/triumphant** The adjective *triumphal* describes something marking a victory or triumph: *a triumphal arch*; *a triumphal fanfare*. *Triumphant* means victorious or successful; it is by far the more frequently used of the two words:

The medal-winning gymnast returned triumphant from the Olympic Games.

**trivia** *Trivia* means trifles and should take a plural verb. It is, however, used with a singular verb so frequently that the grammatically correct plural verb has come to sound unidiomatic. To avoid this problem it is often better to replace *trivia* with *trivialities* or *trivial matters*.

**trompe l'oeil** Note the spelling of this French phrase, which literally means 'trick the eye' and is used of paintings and decorations that have an illusionary effect. It does not need to be italicised. Pronounce the phrase 'tromp **ler**ya', with the 'a' virtually swallowed.

**troop/troupe** A *troop* is a military unit, or any group of people or animals. *Troupe* is the spelling if you mean a company of actors or other performers. A *trooper* is a mounted police officer or cavalry soldier (or the horse of either). A *trouper* is a performer, but the term *old trouper* can be extended to any person who shows great devotion or loyalty.

**true facts** Avoid this tautology.

**truism** A *truism* is not simply something that is true. In its strictest sense a truism is a type of redundancy: it repeats what is already implied, yet purports to give additional information. Consider the following truism:

He is an idle person who does not work.

Since *idle* implies that he does not work, the statement is the equivalent of saying *He is a person who does not work who does not work*. In its wider sense a truism is a self-evident truth: *We need food if we are to eat*. Do not use the word *truism* when you merely mean *fact*:

It is a fact [*not* truism] that the divorce rate is climbing.

See also **tautology/pleonasm**.

**try to** A common error, to be avoided in all contexts, is to follow the verb *try* with *and* instead of the *to* of an infinitive:

You must try to help her. *not* You must try and help her.

Try to see it my way. *not* Try and see it my way.

**TSS** toxic shock syndrome.

**TT** teetotal (see also **teetotal**); tuberculin tested.

**Tuggeranong, ACT** Compare with *Tuggerawong*, NSW.

**tumor/tumour** Either spelling is acceptable but *tumour* is recommended.

**tun** See **ton/tonne/tun**.

**tunnel/tunnelled/tunnelling** Note the single *l* in the first and the *-ll-* in the other two.

**turbid/turgid** *Turbid* means unclear, muddy or disturbed: *a turbid pool*; *turbid thoughts*. *Turgid* means swollen or distended: *turgid cells*. It is often used in reference to pompous or bombastic speech or writing: *turgid prose*.

**two** See **to/too/two**.

**2IC** second in command.

**2LT** 2nd Lieutenant.
See also **lieutenant**.

**-t word endings** See **-ed/-t word endings**.

**TWU** Transport Workers' Union.

**type** The terms used to describe the two broad families of modern typefaces are *serif* and *sanserif*. A *serif typeface* is one that has short strokes crossing the ends of the stems, arms and tails of characters.

The typeface used in this book, Times, is a serif face.

Typefaces without serifs are called *sanserif*. The *sanserif face* was popularised by the Bauhaus movement, which in the interests of functionalism sought a simple, uncluttered letter form. Very few sanserif faces are suitable for text work as they are difficult to read in long stretches. They are best reserved for headings, subheadings and captions. Being exceptionally clear, they are ideal for signposts.

The typeface used in this line is Helvetica, a sanserif face.

*Type nomenclature* The most important characteristic of a typeface is the *x-height*, which is the height of the lower-case x measured from baseline to meanline. For example, of the letters *h*, *i*, *j*, *k*, *l* and *m*, only *m* represents the *x-height* of the typeface. The x-height of the others is the part of each that equates with the height of the *m*. A typeface with a tall x-height will appear larger than a face of the same point size with a smaller x-height. Because of this, the x-height is often a more realistic measurement of a typeface than the point size. The following examples are set in the same point size, but Cheltenham has a greater x-height than Bembo.

This line is set in Cheltenham book.

This line is set in Bembo.

*Ascenders* are the parts of lower-case letters that rise above the x-height: letters with ascenders are *b*, *d*, *f*, *h*, *k* and *l*. *Descenders* are the parts of characters that descend below the baseline: letters with descenders are *g*, *j*, *p*, *q* and *y*. It is important that sufficient leading be allowed between lines for ascenders and descenders not to touch. The *cap height* is simply the height of a capital letter of the chosen font measured baseline to cap line. In computer setting the cap height acts as a standard of measurement between different typefaces. The most accurate comparisons are obtained by using a capital E of a font.

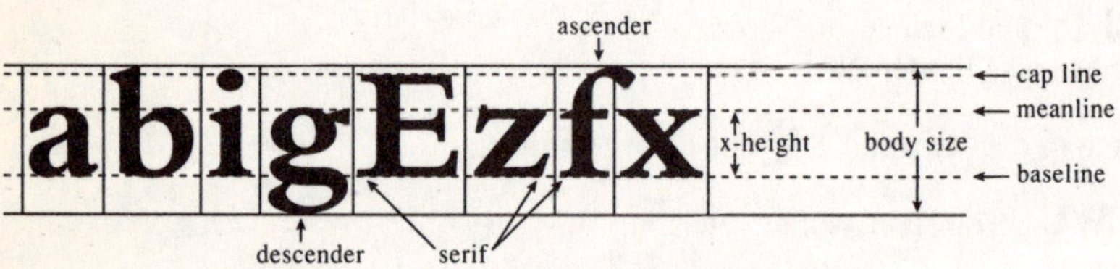


***The parts of a serif type***

***Basic type*** *Roman type* is the term for any upright type (as opposed to an italic type). It originally described the serif faces developed by the Romans.

This line is set in roman type.

*Italic type* (sometimes called *cursive* or *oblique* type), was developed in the sixteenth century from handwriting.

*This line is set in italic type.*

Italic type has special uses described in the entry **italics, use of**. It should not be chosen for long runs of text. Nearly all typefaces have italic fonts, although italic is better suited to serif than sanserif faces. Most italic type is slanted 12° from the vertical.

*Condensed type* is available in most fonts. Because more characters are fitted into the measure, condensed type is narrower than uncondensed type. Condensed typefaces should be used sparingly, in headings or display work, for example, or where space considerations demand them. Condensed fonts that have all the controlled stroke weights of the fonts used by traditional typesetters are sold by desktop-publishing and software suppliers.

This type is condensed.
This type is not condensed.

Note that the condensed and uncondensed versions are the same size although they look different. The same applies to the expanded and unexpanded type in the following examples.

*Expanded* (or *extended*) *type* is available in most fonts. Expanded typefaces should normally be used only for headings, and then sparingly, as they are less legible than normal type. Expanded fonts that have all the controlled stroke weights of traditional fonts are also available for desktop publishing.

This type is expanded.
This type is not expanded.

***Type weights*** *Light type* is the finest type in most fonts.

This line is set in light type.

*Book type* (sometimes called *regular* or *normal* type) is the standard against which other weights in a font family are measured. It is the type that is generally used for text.

This line is set in book type.

*Medium type* is an intermediate weight, usually between book and bold. In some faces it replaces *demi-bold*; in others, both medium and demi-bold are found, with medium the lighter of the two.

This line is set in medium type.

*Bold type* is found in every typeface, and nearly all typefaces have a range of these heavyweight fonts. For emphasis in text, demi-bold is often preferable to bold. Bold is most effective when used sparingly.

**This line is set in bold type.**
**This line is set in demi-bold type.**

***Display and special type*** For display and other special purposes (required in advertising matter, for example) there is a range of faces available to both traditional typesetters and desktop-publishing operators. They include brush script, copperplate, novelty type and outline type.

**Videos at sale price!**

*Reverse type* – type that is white against a dark background – is used for special effects but may be difficult to read, particularly when it is small.

This line is set in reverse type.

See also **capital letters, decorative initial; capital letters, setting of; capital letters, small; desktop publishing; font; kerning; leading; marking up; points; proportional spacing; tracking; typesetting**.

**type of** See **kind of/sort of/type of**.

**typesetting** The modern graphics-based typesetting machine, be it a mainframe or personal computer, allows an enormous variety of ways of setting type. Graphics-based word-processing and desktop-publishing programs have turned many labour-intensive and difficult tasks into automatic processes. It is now easy to swirl type around a graphic image or set it in a circle but, on the whole, all forms of trick typesetting are best left in the hands of an experienced typographer.

See entries throughout that relate to typesetting.

**type size** See **points; type**.

**typo** This is an abbreviation for *typographical error*. A *typo* is sometimes called a *lit*, short for *literal*.

# Uu

**u.c.** upper-case (that is, capital) type: S, T, in contrast to s, t (lower case). See also **capital letters, setting of; type**.

**UCC** Universal Copyright Convention (first adopted in 1952).

**UCLA** University of California at Los Angeles.

**UFO** unidentified flying object.

**uhf** ultra-high frequency (electromagnetic waves, as in radio and TV); also *UHF*, *u.h.f.*

**UHT** ultra heat tested (long-life milk).

**UK** United Kingdom.
See also **Britain/Great Britain/United Kingdom/British Isles**.

**ultimate** The adjective and noun *ultimate* has been distinctly overworked as a colloquial synonym for *best*, *most advanced* or *trendiest*: *the ultimate vintage wine of the 1960s*; *the ultimate in central heating*. A more specific word is usually available.

**ultimatum** An *ultimatum* is a last-ditch proposal, the turning down of which carries some threat of serious consequences. Prefer the plural form *ultimatums* to the uncommon alternative *ultimata*.

**Ultima, Vic.** Compare with *Ultimo*, NSW.

**ultraviolet** This is one word, but *infra-red* is hyphenated.

**Uluru** The Aboriginal name superseding *Ayers Rock* (note that there is no apostrophe in *Ayers*).

**UN/UNO** These are both abbreviations of *United Nations Organization*; the shorter form *UN* is preferred.

**un-** See **non-**.

**unanimous** This adjective means completely in agreement; it is not a synonym for *enthusiastic* or *wholehearted*:

> There was a unanimous decision to paint the bowling-club fence.

*but not*

> The paint-shop owner gave the club's decision his unanimous support.

Note that a motion is only carried *unanimously* if everyone votes in favour of it (otherwise it is carried by a majority).

**unaware/unawares** Both the adjective *unaware* and the adverb *unawares* convey a lack of awareness, but ignorance makes a person *unaware* while there is an element of surprise conveyed by the word *unawares*:

> He was unaware that the storm had passed.
> They were a socially unaware group.
> The train strike caught the travellers unawares.

**uncharted** *Uncharted* territory, not 'unchartered'.

**unconscious** See **subconscious/unconscious**.

**under** See **below/beneath/under/underneath**.

**under-** The prefix *under-* has three meanings: below or underneath, as in *underground*, *underpinning*; lower in dignity or rank, as in *undergraduate*, *undersecretary*; and to a lesser degree, as in *underdone*, *underfed*. The prefix and the root usually form one word, but there are exceptions such as *under-age* and *under-utilise*, where a hyphen is required to avoid misleading or ugly letter combinations.

**underhand/underhanded** These adjectives are interchangeable in most contexts when the meaning dishonourably secretive, or underarm (as in bowling), is intended:

> Advertising Philip's job while he was working interstate was an underhand [*or* underhanded] action.
> Gail threw the ball underhand [*or* underhanded].

*Underhanded*, but not *underhand*, can also mean short of hands (that is, staff):

> The factory is usually underhanded on Mondays.

In this sense *understaffed* is more commonly used, however.

**underlay/underlie** The verb *underlay* means to give support or protection to something from below:

The builder will underlay the concrete with plastic.

*Underlie* literally means to lie under:

Various rock strata underlie the shale.

Figuratively it means to exist beneath the surface of something:

What motives underlie his present actions?

Note the correct verb parts:

| | | |
|---|---|---|
| underlay (present) | underlaid (past) | underlaid (past participle) |
| underlie (present) | underlay (past) | underlain (past participle) |

The present participle of *underlie – underlying* – is often used adjectivally before a noun: *underlying tensions*. The same does not apply to *underlay*: *underlaying* can be part of the verb (*He is underlaying the carpet*) but cannot be an adjective.

See also **lay/laying/lie/lying**.

**underlines/underscores** These are interchangeable typesetting terms for lines printed beneath type. Underlining is available in all word-processing and page-makeup programs.

If you want to use underlining as a design feature in a heading it may be better to use the rule tool. Italic or bold type is preferable to underlining when emphasis is needed in text.

**underneath** See **below/beneath/under/underneath**.

**unders** This printing term means the number of copies of a publication by which a customer's order has fallen short.

**underscores** See **underlines/underscores**.

**under the circumstances** See **circumstances**.

**undertones** See **overtones/undertones**.

**under way** This expression, which means in progress, should not be run together to make one word:

Construction of the new bridge is under way [*not* underway].

Note that *way* is not spelt 'weigh'.

**undiscriminating** See **indiscriminate/undiscriminating**.

**undo command** The *undo command* is the saviour of many desktop and word-processing operators. If you accidentally delete anything from your document, you can immediately select the *undo* function and the deleted material will be returned to the screen, provided you have not made any additional keystrokes.

**undoubtedly** See **doubtless/undoubtedly/indubitably**.

**uneconomic/uneconomical** See **economic/economical**.

**unequivocal** This adjective means clear, plain or unambiguous:

When he was asked to help his answer was an unequivocal *no*.

The adverb is *unequivocally*. Note that there are no such words as 'unequivocable' and 'unequivocably'. Similarly, the antonym of *unequivocal*, *equivocal* (not 'equivocable'), has the adverbial form *equivocally* (not 'equivocably').

**UNESCO** United Nations Educational, Scientific and Cultural Organization.

**unexceptionable/unexceptional** See **exceptionable/exceptional**.

**UNICEF** United Nations International Children's Emergency Fund.

**uninterested** See **disinterested/uninterested**.

**uninterruptible power supply** In computer terminology an *uninterruptible power supply* is an electrical device attached to the same power point as a computer. It prevents work being lost if there is a power failure or surge, at which point it takes over and provides a continuous, even supply.

**Union Jack** The national flag of the United Kingdom is made up of the crosses of St George, St Andrew and St Patrick (symbolising England, Scotland and Ireland). Its present form dates from the Act of Union of 1 January 1801, a fact that has sometimes escaped the notice of Hollywood film producers.

**unique** Something that is *unique* is one of its kind and has no like or equal. Therefore a thing cannot be *very*, *rather*, *more* or *less unique*, although it can be *nearly* or *almost unique*.

**United Kingdom** See **Britain/Great Britain/United Kingdom/British Isles**.

**United States** See **America/United States/Latin America**.

**unjustified type** See **justified type/unjustified type**.

**unknown** Think before you use the word *unknown*. When referring to a person, in particular, you probably mean *little-known*. The *hitherto unknown politician Jim Brown who was brought into Cabinet today* must have been known by someone, even if it was only his mother.

**unlike** See **like**.

**unmistakable/unmistakeable** Either spelling, with or without the *-e* of *mistake*, is acceptable.

**unparalleled** See **parallel**.

**unpractical** See **practicable/practical**.

**unprecedented** Something that is *unprecedented* has never happened before; the word is not merely a synonym for *unusual*, *different*, *rare*, *novel* or *remarkable*. While it is true that the use of atomic weapons in World War II was *unprecedented*, it is a misuse of the word to say that the human misery suffered in that war was *unprecedented* when all the wars of history have brought misery to many people.

**unreadable** See **illegible/unreadable**.

**unrepairable** See **repairable/reparable**.

**unsatisfied** See **dissatisfied/unsatisfied**.

**until** See **till/until**.

**untrammelled** Note the spelling.

**unveil** Public figures like to *unveil* new policies or schemes; they could simply *reveal* or *announce* them.
See also **vale/veil**.

**unwanted/unwonted** *Unwanted* means not wanted. *Unwonted*, now old-fashioned if not archaic, means unusual, not customary:

> Beth's advice is unwanted since it is so unreliable.
> Glen's incivility was unwonted given his earlier friendliness.

Pronounce the *-want-* of *unwanted* 'wont'; the *-wont-* of *unwonted* is, however, pronounced 'wohnt'.

**unwieldy** Note the *-ie-*.

**unwonted** See **unwanted/unwonted**.

**up** Take care when using *up* in conjunction with verbs. It may be an inseparable part of the verb, or a reasonable substitute for *all*, but it is often superfluous:

> Please clean up the mess.
> I have used up my monthly allocation.
> I'll phone [*not* phone up] after lunch.
> He has tightened [*not* tightened up] the screws.

**up-** Although disliked by many people, the numerous compounds beginning with *up-*, such as *upcoming*, *update*, *upfront* and *upgrade*, are acceptable in commercial English. However, such telegraphese has gained only qualified acceptance in formal contexts.

**upcoming** See **forthcoming**.

**UPI** United Press International.

**upon** See **on/upon**.

**upside** See **downside**.

**upward/upwards** The adjective is *upward*: *an upward glance*. Either form is acceptable for the adverb, but *upwards* is recommended: *moving upwards*. *Upwards of* is a rather awkward way of saying *more than*: *upwards of 30 tonnes*.

**urban/urbane** *Urban* is the opposite of rural and means pertaining to, or occurring in, a city: *urban dwellers*; *urban planning*. *Urbane* means smoothly polite, suave or sophisticated: *the urbane Noël Coward*.

**URTI** upper respiratory tract infection.

**us** See **we/us**.

**us/our** See **-ing forms**.

**US/USA** United States of America.
See also **America/United States/Latin America**.

**usable/useable** Either spelling, with or without the *-e* of *use*, is acceptable.

**usage/use** Prefer *use* for all senses of the word except when referring to treatment, custom or rules: *harsh usage*; *historical usage*; *English usage*.

**useable** See **usable/useable**.

**used to** When *used to* refers to happenings in thc past, its negative and interrogative (question) forms can cause problems. The recommended negative forms are as follows:

They used not to compete.
*or* They never used to compete
*not* They didn't use [*or* used] to compete.
*or* They usen't to compete.

The recommended interrogative forms are as follows:

Used they to compete? Used they not to compete?

*or* They used to compete, didn't they? They used not to compete, did they?

It will often be more idiomatic to avoid *used to* altogether:

Did they ever compete? Didn't they ever compete?

Since the formal rules for negative and interrogative require rather stiff constructions, people understandably disregard them when conversing.

**US English** *US English* is now a highly conspicuous form of the language: more people speak and write it than any other variety, although British English is still spread more widely throughout the world.

Because of the commercial dominance of the United States since the 1950s particularly in communications, entertainment, and defence and computer technology, US English has infiltrated not only other varieties of English, but different languages too. Computer technology alone has given rise to hundreds of foreign adaptations such as *les applications batch* (French), *der Highbyte* (German) and *debuggare* (*to debug* in Italian).

Just as the United States grew out of a rebellion, so did its language. A refractory child of British English, it sprang from the enthusiasm for all things distinctively American that followed the War of Independence. In 1828 Noah Webster (1758–1843) published his *American Dictionary of the English Language* after decades of work. In it he incorporated what we now call American spellings: *color*, *fiber*, *wagon*, *defense*; he also introduced new rules for pronunciation, giving due emphasis to each syllable so that the British word 'secr't'ry' became 'sec-re-tary'. Like Samuel Johnson's dictionary in England, Webster's was a linguistic landmark. Paradoxically it preserved in US English much that had disappeared from British English. The spellings *color* and *colour*, and *center* and *centre*, for instance, coexisted in Shakespeare's day; *cute*, *mad* (angry), *mugging* and *moonshine* (whisky) were all old British terms.

While written US English has much in common with British and Australian English, and speakers are mutually intelligible, there are numerous differences in vocabulary, pronunciation and, to some extent, grammar. Differences between US vocabulary and that of British and Australian English range from slight variations, as in *crawfish*, *dollhouse* and *math*, to separate words, such as *elevator* (lift), *druggist* (chemist), *realtor* (estate agent) and *sidewalk* (footpath). The greatest confusion occurs when the same words have different meanings in different parts of the world, as in *vest*, which is a *waistcoat* in US English and, traditionally, a *singlet* in British and Australian English.

American slang has quickly found its way into other languages through popular music, films and television, and Australians have picked up many such colloquialisms, absorbing some and adapting or rejecting others.

American pronunciation differs in varying degrees from the range of British and Australian versions, the main difference being in the vowel sounds. Although US English has nothing like the number of dialectal variations that occur in the

English of the British Isles, there are marked differences between, for example, Northern and Southern regional dialects, and less conspicuous differences within regions. Probably the best-known accents are those of New England; the Southern drawl with its stretched vowels; the nasal twang of the Midwest; and the Brooklynese of New York City made famous by Damon Runyan.

See also **Australian English**; **British English**; **US spelling**.

**user-friendly** Anyone who has ever read a computer software manual will be aware that while the manufacturer may have produced software that is kind to users, the manual itself may be *user-hostile*. The overworked term *user-friendly* is now applied to virtually anything that is easy to use or understand, from bottle-openers to atlases. Advertisers have also plundered the expression to woo the public with descriptions such as *environmentally friendly* and *customer-friendly*.

**user groups** *User groups* are non-profit associations of people using a particular computer platform or piece of software. Members meet regularly to increase their knowledge of their computer and its software. The groups are usually independent of the manufacturers, dealers and distributors, though representatives of computer companies may sometimes be guest speakers. Information on user groups can generally be found in trade magazines or obtained from a major computer dealer or your personal network.

**US spelling** The following are the main areas of difference between US and British (and therefore Australian) spelling.

***Words ending in -or/-our*** US spelling favours *-or* in most cases: *armor*, *behavior*, *color*, *flavor*, *neighbor*, *vigor*. Exceptions include *glamour* and *saviour*, which sometimes retain the *u*.

***Words ending in -er/-re*** US spelling favours *-er* in most cases: *theater*, *specter*, *goiter*, *miter*, *somber*, *fiber*. Exceptions include *acre*, *lucre*, *macabre*, *massacre* and *ogre*.

***Words ending in -ise/-ize and -yse/-yze*** US spelling favours the *-ize* form in words such as *civilize* and *organize*, and *-yze* in words such as *analyze* and *paralyze*. Exceptions to the *-ize* form include *advertise*, *advise*, *exercise*, *supervise* and *televise*. (In Australian English we may put *civilise* or *civilize*, *organise* or *organize*; but we must use the *-yse* spelling in *analyse* and *paralyse*.)

***The digraphs ae and oe*** In most cases US spelling uses the simple *e* rather than *ae* or *oe* in words such as *anemia*, *encyclopedia*, *esophagus*, *archeology* and *medieval*; but it retains the digraph in *aerobics*, *amoeba* and *oedipal*.

***Words ending in -l or -ll*** In US spelling the *-l* is usually not doubled for compounds of two-syllable or longer words: *dueling*, *labeled*, *marvelous*, *quarreled*, *traveled*. Note, however, the US English forms *install/installment*; *enthrall/enthralling*; *fulfill/fulfilling/fulfillment*; and *enroll/enrollment*.

***Words ending in -ce/-se*** In US English some British English words ending in *-ce* are spelt with an *-se*: *defense*, *offense*, *pretense*. The noun *licence* becomes *license* as a verb in British English, but the Americans use *s* for both noun and verb. On the other hand, they use the spelling *practice* for both noun and verb while we distinguish between them by spelling the noun *practice* and the verb *practise*.

***Words ending in -able*** While British spelling allows options in this matter, US spelling consistently drops the *-e* of the root word in *likable*, *livable*, *sizable*, *movable* and *unshakable*, for example.

Other US spellings occasionally seen in Australia include *aluminum* (aluminium); *analog* (analogue); *ax* (axe); *check* (cheque); *curb* (kerb); *epilog* (epilogue); *kidnaped* (kidnapped); *mold* (mould); *mustache* (moustache); *pajamas* (pyjamas); *pedagog* (pedagogue); *skeptic* (sceptic); *sulfur* (sulphur); and *tire* (tyre). All these spellings are non-standard in Australian English.

See also **US English**.

**USSR** Union of Soviet Socialist Republics (dissolved 1991–92).

See also **CIS**.

**UT** This is the abbreviation for *Universal Time*, which is another name for Greenwich Mean Time (GMT). Before 1925 GMT was reckoned as beginning at noon; since then it has been reckoned from midnight. To avoid confusion, the term *Universal Time* was adopted for the second system in 1928.

See also **GMT**.

**utilise/utilisation** These heavyweight words are rarely necessary. If you need to emphasise an opportunist element, *make use of* is less pompous than *utilise*:

> We made use of [*rather than* utilised] the leftover ham in sandwiches.

Generally, however, *use* will do for both noun and verb.

**utility** A *utility* is a comparatively simple program that enhances or assists the operation of your computer. For example, any virus-detector program is a utility that tells you if there is a virus on your hard or floppy disks.

**uv** ultraviolet.

See also **ultraviolet**.

# Vv

**V** five (roman numeral).
See also **roman numerals**.

**v.** verse; versus (also vs.; both abbreviations are sometimes italicised).

***v.*** This abbreviation means refer to (Latin: *vide*).

**vacation** Although the word is used in reference to breaks in the legal or academic year, Australians generally still take *holidays* rather than *vacations*.

**VADM** Vice Admiral.

**vain/vane/vein** *Vain* can mean futile, without real value; applied to people it means conceited:

The irrigation scheme was a vain attempt to farm desert land.
He was so vain he couldn't walk past a window without glancing at it.

A *vane* is a blade-like device moved by wind or water: a *weather vane*; *a broken vane in the propeller*. A *vein* is a vessel that carries blood; a body of ore; or the striations in materials such as wood and marble. Figuratively it can mean streak (*a vein of ruthlessness in her character*); or manner (*a speech in lighthearted vein*).

**vale/veil** A *vale* is a valley. A *veil* is a transparent or semi-transparent covering for the head; figuratively, it is something that covers, screens or conceals: *a veil of silence*.

See also **unveil**.

**value added** This term means the difference between the cost of the raw materials from which a product is made and its final value.

**Van Diemen's Land** Note the spelling of the name of Tasmania before November 1855 (not 'Dieman's').

**vane** See **vain/vane/vein**.

**vapor/vapour** Although either spelling is acceptable, *vapour* is recommended; but note *vaporise* and *vaporous*.

**vapourware** *Vapourware* is computer software that has been promoted by the manufacturer but is not yet available to the purchasing public for some reason (usually because it is full of bugs).
See also **bug**.

**variegated** Note the *-ieg-*.

**various** Since *various* means a number of different kinds of, it is tautological to combine *various* and *different* in phrases such as *various different bargains*.

**VAT** value added tax.

**VC** vice-chancellor, Victoria Cross (see also **ranks, titles, honours and awards**); Vietcong (or Viet Cong).

**VCR** video cassette recorder

**VD** venereal disease.

**VDC** Volunteer Defence Corps.

**VDT** visual display terminal.

**VDU** visual display unit.
See also **monitor**.

**V-E Day** This is the day commemorating the World War II Allied Victory in Europe (8 May 1945).

**vegan/vegetarian** A *vegan* is a person who eats no animal products at all; a *vegetarian* eats no meat but may eat fish, and animal products such as eggs, milk and cheese. *Vegan* is only a noun, but *vegetarian* can be used adjectivally too.

**veil** See **vale/veil**.

**vein** See **vain/vane/vein.**

**venal/venial** The Latin word *venalis*, from which *venal* is derived, literally means for sale, but this adjective is now applied only to people or systems that are 'bought' in the sense of being corrupt:

Even the mayor's best friends abandoned him when his dealings were found to be venal.

*Venial* means excusable:

Her offence was considered venial in one so young and the case was dismissed.

**vengeance** See **avenge/revenge/vengeance.**

**veranda/verandah** Either spelling, with or without the *-h*, is acceptable.

**verbal/oral** See **aural/oral; oral/verbal.**

**verbal nouns** See **gerunds; -ing forms; participles; verbs.**

**verbs** A verb is the part of speech that denotes action or a state:

She *is* the woman who *lives* next-door.

No true sentence is complete without a verb.

The most important grammatical point about verbs is that they change their forms. A major reason for change is *agreement*, which means that a verb agrees with its subject in person and in number:

I [*or* you, we *or* they] *live* here.
He [*or* she *or* it] *lives* here.
The Browns *live* here.

A second reason for change is *tense*, which tells us when an action takes place. The main tenses are as follows:

| | |
|---|---|
| present | I live, I do live, I am living |
| past | I lived, I did live, I was living |
| future | I shall live, I shall be living |
| present perfect | I have lived, I have been living |
| past perfect | I had lived, I had been living |
| future perfect | I shall have lived, I shall have been living |

The *-ing* version of each tense is called the continuous form.

Most verbs are described as *regular*, their forms following the same pattern as that of the regular verb *to live*: *I live*; *I lived*; *I have lived. Irregula*r verbs (of which there are hundreds) are unpredictable because the past tenses stray from the standard pattern. Three of the most common are the verbs *to be*, *to do* and *to eat*:

| | | |
|---|---|---|
| I am | I was | I have been |
| I do | I did | I have done |
| I eat | I ate | I have eaten |

The following are some of the terms used of verbs and their functions.

- An *infinitive* is the basic form of a verb; it is usually introduced by *to*, though this may be hidden:

  We hope *to live* here now. We can [are able *to*] *live* here now.

- A verb has a *present participle* and a *past participle*, both of which can act as nouns or adjectives when they are not forming part of certain tenses.

| ***Participle*** | ***Noun*** | ***Adjective*** |
|---|---|---|
| He *is pampering* her. | *Pampering* is unwise | He has *pampering* ways. |
| He *has pampered* her. | The *pampered* are ungrateful. | She is a *pampered* girl. |

- *Phrasal* verbs are verbs combined with other parts of speech; many phrasal verbs are somewhat informal:

  He *fell over*. What will they *come up with*?

- *Auxiliary* (or 'helping') verbs include *be*, *do*, *must*, *have*, *can* and *could, will* and *would*, *may* and *might*; a verb formed with an auxiliary is often called a *compound* verb:

  I *must invite* the whole family. You *have visited* us before.

  She *would like* this house. They *may stay* to dinner.

- A *transitive* verb has a direct object:

  The rules *restrict* residents.

- An *intransitive* verb does not have a direct object:

  The rules *exist* for the benefit of residents.

- The *voice* of a transitive verb such as *restrict* may be *active* or *passive*, but that of an intransitive verb such as *exist* can only be *active*. Thus you can say:

  The residents *are restricted* by the rules.

*but not*

  The benefit of residents *is existed* by the rules.

- Some verbs are transitive in one construction and intransitive in another:

  She *lives* a full life [transitive]. He *lives* through his son [intransitive].

- The *mood* of a verb reveals attitudes. The *indicative mood* states facts or asks questions:

  We are singing. Are you singing?

  The *subjunctive mood* expresses the possible, conditional or desirable:

  I only ask that you sing. We hoped that you might sing.

  The *imperative mood* indicates commands:

  Sing! Don't wait for the others.

Many verbs have the same form as related nouns: *a holiday* or *to holiday*; *bends in the river* or *the river bends here*. Other verbs are constantly being created by *back formation*, which means adapting or shortening nouns and using them to express action, as the noun *oration* has been abbreviated in the verb *to orate*. The phenomenon of changing nouns, and adjectives too, into verbs has long been a part of the flexible nature of the English language; if a new verb filled a need, it was accepted by the majority of users in time. Consider the expressions *bridge the gap*, *feather your nest* and *bridle your temper*. Newer verbs include *to moisturise*, *to immunise* and *to fax*. Today the practice is rapidly increasing –

far too rapidly for some, who object to neologisms such as *to trial*, *to prioritise*, *to interface* and *to action*. Careful users of English will try to distinguish between the new verbs that are worth having and those that should be discouraged.

See also **active voice/passive voice**; **back formation**; **infinitive**; **-ing forms**; **participles**; **subjunctive mood**; **tenses**.

**vermilion** Note the single *l* in the name of this strident red colour.

**vermin** This noun is both singular and plural. One mouse is *vermin*, and so are twenty rats.

**verso** See **page numbering**.

**very** Do not use *very* unless it adds something. Often a strong adjective is more effective when used alone: to describe pain as *excruciating*, for example, is more telling than to say that it is *very excruciating*. Nor should *very* be overworked in intensifying weak or commonplace words; it is better to search for a more vivid adjective than to be content with *very good*, *very bad* or *very nice*, for instance.

**veto** A *veto* is a prohibition, or the power to enforce a prohibition; the plural is *vetoes*.

**vhf** very high frequency (electromagnetic waves, as in radio and TV); also *VHF*, *v.h.f.*

**via** This Latin word literally means by the path, and is used in English to mean by way of; it is not italicised:

> We flew to Los Angeles via Fiji and Hawaii.

It is also a neat way of saying by means of:

> I'll send the information via my fax machine.

Pronounce it '**vie**-a'.

**viable** There was a time when this adjective only meant capable of independent existence or of survival: *a viable foetus*; *viable plant stock*. The word is now somewhat overused as a synonym for others such as *feasible*, *effective*, *workable*, *practicable*, *usable*, *profitable*, *promising*. One of these words may often be more appropriate:

> Is the project workable [*rather than* viable]?
>
> The company's new plans seem promising [*rather than* viable].

**Vic.** Victoria.

**vice/vice-** In Australian and British English the word *vice* in all its meanings, and the prefix *vice-*, are spelt with a *c* (*vise* is the US spelling for the double-jawed clamp).

**vice versa** This Latin phrase means in reverse order; it is not italicised:

Will I telephone you or vice versa?

Pronounce it 'vice **ver**-sa' or '**vie**-sa **ver**-sa'.

**vie/vied/vying** Note the spelling.

**vigor/vigour** Either of these spellings is acceptable, but *vigour* is recommended. Note *vigorous* and *vigorously*, however.

**vilify** Note the single *l* in this verb meaning to blacken the name of (someone).

**VIP** very important person.

**virtuoso** A *virtuoso* (plural *virtuosos* or *virtuosi*) is someone who displays a high level of skill or knowledge; the word is particularly applied to outstanding musical performers and (as an adjective) to performances.

**virus** In computer terminology a *virus* is a program that interferes with the regular functioning of a computer. The presence of a virus may not be readily apparent to the user, although symptoms such as the slowing of responses to commands or unexpectedly altered screen displays often indicate that something is wrong. Facetious or irrelevant messages appearing on the screen are merely annoying, but a virus may be more serious and involve the deletion of data or programs from the computer's memory. Virus detection programs now available can be installed in such a way that they automatically check any disk inserted into a floppy drive.

See also **bug**.

**vis-à-vis** This phrase means face to face in French and in English too, but it is also used to mean concerning:

They could not understand the government's philosophy vis-à-vis immigration.

The grave accent is often dropped in English, and there is no need to print the phrase in italics. Pronounce it 'veez-ar-**vee**'.

**visible** *Visible* means capable of being seen: *visible results*. Used, like *high-profile*, to mean conspicuous, the word has become a cliché in its application to public figures: *a visible prime minister*; *a highly visible role*.

**visit** Unlike the Americans, Australians do not add *with*:

I will visit you soon.

*not* I will visit with you soon.

**visual** See **layout**.

**visual display unit** See **monitor**.

**viz.** This odd little abbreviation (from the Latin word for clearly or namely, *videlicet*) introduces an explanatory phrase. Note the comma before but not after it:

> The children could hardly wait for the most important event of the evening, viz. the pizza delivery.

Many people prefer *namely*.

**V-J Day** This is the day commemorating the World War II Allied Victory over Japan (15 August 1945; in the US, 2 September 1945).

**vogue words** See **buzz words**.

**voice** To *voice* means to express: *She voiced her criticism*. Note that the expressing may be vocal or written.

**voice (grammar)** See **active voice/passive voice**.

**volcano** The plural is *volcanoes* or *volcanos*. Note the spelling of *vulcanology*, the study of volcanoes, and *vulcanologist*, an authority on them.

**voluntarily** Put the stress on the first syllable (*vol-*), not on the *-tar-*.

**voracious** See **rapacious/voracious**.

**vortex** A *vortex* (plural *vortexes* or *vortices*) is a powerful whirling mass such as a whirlpool or, figuratively, a situation or event into which anybody or anything nearby is inescapably drawn.

**vowel/consonant** *Vowels* and *consonants* refer to speech sounds and the letters that represent them. A *vowel* is a voiced sound shaped in the mouth as the outgoing air passes unrestricted by the lips, tongue or teeth. The basic vowel sounds are represented in the alphabet by the letters *a*, *e*, *i*, *o*, *u* (and sometimes *y*, as in *happy*). In English all these letters represent more than one sound, which makes English spelling difficult and inconsistent. There are, for example, three different sounds represented by the letter *a* in the sentence *Sam came last*. Conversely the following words contain the same sound, but it is represented by different letters: *fought*, *caught*, *sort*, *lawn*.

Because the vowel sounds are much more numerous than the five basic letters would suggest, dictionaries use well-known words to indicate pronunciation. Thus *a* may be as in *lad*, *lard*, *late* or the first (abbreviated) *a* in *again*.

A *consonant* is a sound made when the outgoing air is wholly or partly blocked by the lips, tongue or teeth. All the letters of the alphabet that are not vowels are consonants.

See also **consonants, doubling of**.

**VSOP** very special old pale (brandy).

**vulgarisms/four-letter words** Vulgarisms can be defined as words that have generally been avoided, except privately, in polite society. A list of such words would cover many innocuous colloquialisms, but would certainly include the four-letter words *arse*, *piss*, *shit*, *turd*, *fart*, *fuck* and *cunt*. These words were, to varying degrees, regarded as coarse in the Middle Ages and they became increasingly unacceptable. The most offensive seems to have been *cunt*. Eric Partridge says in *A Dictionary of Slang and Unconventional English* that since about 1700 'it has, except in the reprinting of old classics, been held to be obscene, i.e. a legal offence, to print it in full'. Even the 1811 *Dictionary of the Vulgar Tongue* entered the word as *c**t*. The first general dictionary to include it is believed to have been *The Penguin English Dictionary* in 1965.

It goes without saying that vulgarisms of every kind have always been much more freely used in spoken English than in print.

Times and attitudes change, and today nearly all the four-letter words have a reduced capacity to shock and may regularly be seen in many newspapers and magazines. The exceptions are *fuck*, which is still printed as *f*— in some publications, especially newspapers, and *cunt*, which remains a banned word in mainstream publications but turns up occasionally in the fringe press. Following the unsuccessful prosecution for obscenity of D. H. Lawrence's *Lady Chatterley's Lover* in England in 1960, all four-letter words have been used freely in fiction.

In general many people regard such words as completely acceptable in fiction today, and in non-fiction when used in quotations from direct speech or if the context calls for them. They should not be used gratuitously, however, and they remain unacceptable in headlines or titles.

See also **obscenity**; **slang**.

**vulnerable** Remember the first *l* when you spell and pronounce this word and its opposite, *invulnerable*: not 'vunerable' or 'invunerable'.

**v.v.** vice versa.

See also **vice versa**.

# Ww

**WA** Western Australia.
See also **Western Australia**.

**WAAAF** Women's Auxiliary Australian Air Force.

**WACA** This is an acronym for *Western Australian Cricket Association*. Its ground in Perth is known as *the WACA* (pronounced 'wacka').

**wage** See **salary/wage**.

**wagon** This (rather than *waggon*) is the preferred spelling in Australian English.

**wait** See **await/wait**.

**waive/wave** To *waive* means to relinquish, forgo or dismiss:

> Brian waived his right to appeal against the appointment of his rival.

The correct word in the following example is, however, *waved*, in spite of the sense of something being dismissed:

> Magda's protests were waved aside as being trivial.

**wake/waken** See **awake/awaken/wake/waken**.

**Wakeley, NSW** Compare with *Wakerley*, Qld.

**want** The meanings of the verb *to want* include to desire, to lack or to need, and it is impossible to guess which is intended in the following sentence:

> He wants a good dressing-gown.

To make your meaning clear you will have to change the word: try *would like to have* if you mean the first, *lacks* if that is what you mean, and *needs* or *requires* if you mean the third.

It is only in colloquial contexts that you may use *want* to mean should or ought (to):

You want to fill up with petrol on the way home.

*but* Applicants should [*or* ought to] ask for the correct form.

**-ward/-wards** The suffix *-ward* is used for adjectives: *forward planning*; *a backward glance*. There is much more variation when it comes to adverbs: *skipping forwards* but *We carried forward the total to the next column*. Such words need to be checked individually.

**WASP** White Anglo-Saxon Protestant.

**wastage/waste** These two nouns are not synonymous. *Wastage* means loss by decay, wear, leakage, evaporation and so on:

The hot weather caused food wastage at the market.

*Natural wastage* means reduction in employee numbers through means other than retrenchment.

*Waste* (also an adjective or verb) has a range of meanings relating to literal or figurative rubbish, ruin, squandering, or careless use:

Retyping that letter was a waste of time.

There is usually an element of human culpability connected with *waste* (but rarely with *wastage*).

**wave** See **waive/wave**.

**-ways/-wise** Both these suffixes form adverbs of direction or manner, and they are sometimes interchangeable: *lengthways/lengthwise*; *crossways/crosswise*; *endways/endwise*. The suffix *-wise* is the more versatile of the two, forming words such as *clockwise*, *likewise* and *otherwise*. Occasionally *-wise* is used in its literal sense in a compound: *streetwise*. The practice of attaching *-wise* to every conceivable noun when you mean *with reference to* is widely criticised. In formal contexts avoid the temptations of *travelwise*, *foodwise*, *clotheswise*, *moneywise* and so on.

**wb** weatherboard (house); also *WB*.

**WC** water closet.

**W/Cdr** *or* **WGCDR** Wing Commander.

**WCTU** Woman's Christian Temperance Union (not 'Women's').

**we/us** Choosing the correct pronoun before and after various verbs is explained in the entry **case (grammar)**.

**WEA** Workers' Educational Association.

**weather conditions** The phrase is a tautology as various atmospheric *conditions* contribute to the *weather*.

**weaved/wove/woven** The verb *to weave* has two distinct meanings and a different past tense and past participle for each. When cloth, baskets or stories are referred to, use *wove* for the past tense and *woven* as the past participle:

She wove the cloth at the loom.

Grimm's fairy tales were woven with great skill.

When *weave* means to take a devious course or to move from side to side, use *weaved* for both the past tense and past participle:

He weaved his way through the dancing couples.

**weights and measures** The abbreviations used in the following conversion table are internationally recognised symbols. They do not take a full point, nor do they become plural when used with numbers higher than one: *4 kg* not *4 kgs*. In metric measurements involving numbers lower than one, place a nought before the decimal point: *0.75* not *.75*. Abbreviated weights and measures should be separated from related numbers by a thin space: *10 ha*; *60 km*; *5243 t*. But note *31°C*; *90°F*; an angle of *45°*; a height of *5′6″* (no space between parts of the measures).

Further information is provided in individual entries for some weights and measures, and in the entries **imperial system**; **metric system**; **numbers in figures or words** and **SI**.

## Metric Conversion Table

| *Quantity* | *Metric unit* | *Imperial unit* | *Metric to imperial units* | *Imperial to metric units* |
|---|---|---|---|---|
| LENGTH | millimetre (mm) *or* centimetre (cm) | inch (in) | 1 cm = 0.394 in | 1 in = 25.4 mm |
| | centimetre (cm) *or* metre (m) | foot (ft) | 1 m = 3.28 ft | 1 ft = 30.5 cm |
| | metre (m) | yard (yd) | 1 m = 1.09 yd | 1 yd = 0.914 m |
| | metre (m) | rod | 1 m = 0.2 rod | 1 rod = 5.03 m |
| | metre (m) *or* kilometre (km) | furlong (fur) | 1 km = 4.97 fur | 1 fur = 201 m |
| | kilometre (km) | mile | 1 km = 0.621 mile | 1 mile = 1.61 km |

## Metric Conversion Table

| *Quantity* | *Metric unit* | *Imperial unit* | *Metric to imperial units* | *Imperial to metric units* |
|---|---|---|---|---|
| MASS | gram (g) | ounce (oz) | 1 g = 0.0353 oz | 1 oz = 28.3 g |
| | gram (g) *or* kilogram (kg) | pound (lb) | 1 kg = 2.20 lb | 1 lb = 454 g |
| | kilogram (kg) | stone | 1 kg = 0.16 stone | 1 stone = 6.35 kg |
| | tonne (t) | ton | 1 t = 0.984 ton | 1 ton = 1.02 t |
| AREA | square centimetre ($cm^2$) | square inch ($in^2$) | 1 $cm^2$ = 0.155 $in^2$ | 1 $in^2$ = 6.45 $cm^2$ |
| | square centimetre ($cm^2$) *or* square metre ($m^2$) | square foot ($ft^2$) | 1 $m^2$ = 10.8 $ft^2$ | 1 $ft^2$ = 929 $cm^2$ |
| | square metre ($m^2$) | square yard ($yd^2$) | 1 $m^2$ = 1.20 $yd^2$ | 1 $yd^2$ = 0.836 $m^2$ |
| | square metre ($m^2$) | perch (p) | 1 $m^2$ = 0.04 p | 1 p = 25.3 m |
| | hectare (ha) | rood | 1 ha = 9.9 rood | 1 rood = 0.101 ha |
| | hectare (ha) | acre (ac) | 1 ha = 2.47 ac | 1 ac = 0.405 ha |
| | square kilometre ($km^2$) | square mile (sq. mile) | 1 $km^2$ = 0.386 sq. mile | 1 sq. mile = 2.59 $km^2$ |
| VOLUME | cubic centimetre ($cm^3$) | cubic inch ($in^3$) | 1 $cm^3$ = 0.0610 $in^3$ | 1 $in^3$ = 16.4 $cm^3$ |
| | cubic decimetre ($dm^3$) *or* cubic metre ($m^3$) | cubic foot ($ft^3$) | 1$m^3$ = 35.3 $ft^3$ | 1 $ft^3$ = 28.3 $dm^3$ |
| | cubic metre ($m^3$) | cubic yard ($yd^3$) | 1 $m^3$ = 1.31 $yd^3$ | 1 $yd^3$ = 0.765 $m^3$ |
| | cubic metre ($m^3$) | bushel (bus) | 1 $m^3$ = 27.5 bus | 1 bus = 0.0364 $m^3$ |
| VOLUME (fluids) | millilitre (mL) | fluid ounce (fl oz) | 1 mL = 0.0352 fl oz | 1 fl oz = 28.4 mL |
| | mililitre (mL) *or* litre (L) | pint (pt) | 1 L = 1.76 pt | 1 pt = 568 mL |
| | litre (L) *or* cubic metre ($m^3$) | gallon (gal) | 1 $m^3$ = 220 gal | 1 gal = 4.55 L |
| FORCE | newton (N) | pound-force (lbf) | 1 N = 0.225 lbf | 1 lbf = 4.45 N |

## Metric Conversion Table

| *Quantity* | *Metric unit* | *Imperial unit* | *Metric to imperial units* | *Imperial to metric units* |
|---|---|---|---|---|
| PRESSURE | kilopascal (kPa) | pound per square inch (psi) | 1 kPa = 0.145 psi | 1 psi = 6.89 kPa |
| (meteorology) | millibar (mb) | inch of mercury (inHg) | 1 mb = 0.0295 inHg | 1 inHg = 33.9 mb |
| ANGULAR VELOCITY | radian per second (rad/s) | revolution per minute (r/min, rpm) | 1 rad/s = 9.55 r/min | 1 r/min = 0.105 rad/s |
| VELOCITY | kilometre per hour (km/h) | mile per hour (mph) | 1 km/h = 0.621 mph | 1 mph = 1.61 km/h |
| TEMPERATURE | Celsius temp (°C) | Fahrenheit temp (°F) | $°F = (\frac{9}{5} \times °C) + 32$ | $°C = \frac{5}{9} \times (°F - 32)$ |
| ENERGY | kilojoule (kJ) | British thermal unit (Btu) | 1 kJ = 0.948 Btu | 1 Btu = 1.06 kJ |
| | megajoule (MJ) | therm | 1 MJ = $9.48 \times 10^{-3}$ therm | 1 therm = 106 MJ |
| | kilowatt hour (kWh) | | 1 MJ = 0.28 kWh | 1 kWh = 3.60 MJ |
| POWER | kilowatt (kW) | horsepower (hp) | 1 kW = 1.34 hp | 1 hp = 0.746 kW |
| FREQUENCY | hertz (Hz) | cycle per second (c/s) | 1 Hz = c/s | c/s = 1 Hz |

Adapted from 'Metric conversion table', *The Macquarie Dictionary*, 2nd edn, The Macquarie Library, Sydney, 1991, p. 2045.

**weird** Note the *-ei-*.

**WEL** Women's Electoral Lobby.

**well-** When *well-* is part of a compound adjective preceding a noun, the comparative and superlative forms are expressed as *better-* and *best-* (not 'more well-' and 'most well-'):

| | | |
|---|---|---|
| a well-known cafe | a better-known cafe | the best-known cafe |
| a well-built shed | a better-built shed | the best-built shed |

Note that when such compounds follow the noun they refer to, the hyphen is omitted:

> This cafe is well known.
> That cafe is better known.
> Mario's cafe seems to be the best known.

**Wendoree Park, NSW** Compare with *Wendouree*, Vic.

**West/west** See **compass points**.

**Western Australia** The people of *Western Australia* are *Western Australians* or *West Australians*. The terms *Westralia* and *Westralian* are decidedly unofficial. Perth's long-established newspaper is the *West Australian*.

**Westlake, Qld** Compare with *West Lakes*, SA.

**wet/whet** The verb *to wet* means to dampen or saturate with liquid (both the past tense and the past participle may be either *wet* or *wetted*):

> She wet [*or* wetted] the tissue with a solvent.
> We have wet [*or* wetted] the soil well.

*Whet* means to sharpen or make keen:

> Whet the knife on that whetstone.
> Have an hors d'oeuvre to whet your appetite.

**WGCDR** See **W/Cdr *or* WGCDR**.

**wharf** The plural is *wharves* or *wharfs*. A waterside worker is colloquially a *wharfie* (rather than *wharfy*).

**what** The relative pronoun *what* can stand for one thing or more than one, and the verb following it must agree. When *what* means the thing that, it takes a singular verb:

> What he lacks is courage.

When *what* means the things that, we use a plural verb:

> What she needed most were blankets.

Sometimes, however, it is impossible to judge whether the reference is to one thing or more than one. In doubtful cases the singular should be used:

She told us what was needed.

See also **what/which**.

**what/which** In a question, use *what* if the inquiry is general because it implies open choice:

What will suit us best? What book do you want?

Use *which* if the inquiry is more specific, because it implies alternatives:

Which will suit us best? Which book do you want?

See also **clause**; **what**; **which**.

**what ever/whatever** See **how ever/however**.

**when** Do not use *when* to introduce a definition; there is usually an alternative construction.

*Put* In hydroponics, plants are grown in a medium such as gravel rather than soil.

*not* Hydroponics is when plants are grown in a medium such as gravel rather than soil.

**whence** *Whence* (an old-fashioned word) means from where or from which place. Since from is part of the meaning of *whence*, it should not be repeated:

I shall inquire whence [*not* from whence] he came.

See also **hence**; **thence**.

**when ever/whenever** See **how ever/however**.

**whereabouts** *Whereabouts* is always one word, and as a noun it can take a singular or plural verb:

His whereabouts is [*or* are] unknown to his family.

**where ever/wherever** See **how ever/however**.

**whet** See **wet/whet**.

**whether or not** The phrase *or not* is often necessary after *whether* because it suggests an alternative. If there is little sense of an alternative, *or not* can be omitted:

Voula asked her visitor whether or not she liked sugar in her tea.

*but* Chloe's mother asked her whether she would like a cool drink.

See also **if**.

**which** *Which* can introduce an explanatory clause relating not only to a preceding noun or phrase but to a whole clause:

It was a very heavy rain, which filled the reservoirs.

*or* Rain caused the reservoirs to fill, which ended water restrictions.

*but not (because ambiguous)*

The reservoirs were filled by the rain, which ended water restrictions.

Choosing between *which* and *that* is discussed in the entry **clause**.

See also **and which**; **what/which**; **who/that**.

**which ever/whichever** These words follow the pattern of *how ever* and *however*, *what ever* and *whatever*, and so on, but the single-word form is far more common than the two-word form.

See also **how ever/however**.

**while/whilst** Either spelling is acceptable for this conjunction, but *while* is recommended because *whilst* sounds rather old-fashioned. *While* can mean during the time that, or although. Occasionally the dual meanings give rise to ambiguity: *While we ate our lunch we were not hungry*. Write instead:

During the time that we were eating our lunch we were not hungry.

*or* Although we were not hungry we ate our lunch.

**whiskey/whisky** The *whiskey* that is produced in the US and Ireland is spelt with an *-ey* and its plural form is *whiskeys*. All other *whisky* has the plural form *whiskies*.

**WHO** World Health Organization.

**who/that** The relative pronoun *who* primarily refers to human beings, while *that* can refer to people or things (*which* refers only to things):

The children who [*or* that] arrived early saw a platypus.

Some authorities condone the use of *who* for animals: *This is a stray dog, who keeps me company*; and for a body of people: *We formed a subcommittee, who meet on Fridays*. Others prefer to regard both animals and groups as things, replacing *who* in these examples with *which*.

Although *who* and *that* can both refer to people, *who* comes more naturally in most cases. *That* is often preferable after words that you might think of as people-substitutes – *someone*, *anyone*, *everyone* and so on: *everyone that came*. Use *that* also where people and things are linked: *the luggage and passengers that were left behind*.

See also **clause**; **that/which**; **who/whom**; **whose/who's**.

**who/whom** *Who* is the subjective form, acting as the subject of a verb; *whom* is the objective form, acting as the object of a verb:

Who [subject] will mow the lawns?

Whom [object] did they pay for the job?

It is widely accepted that in conversation the strictly ungrammatical *who* sounds more natural than *whom* in sentences such as the last:

Who did they pay for the job?

In the following kind of sentence *whom* may often be omitted:

Joe is the man [whom] the council pays to mow the lawns.

Prepositions should be followed by *whom*, not *who*:

To whom should Joe report?

In conversation, however, *who* sounds more natural than *whom* (and the preposition moves to the end of the sentence):

Who did Joe report to?

In their anxiety to give *whom* its due, some people make the error of attaching it to the wrong verb. In the following example *who* is the subject of *mows*, not the object of *think*:

Joe is the man who we think mows the lawns most carefully.

*not* Joe is the man whom we think mows the lawns most carefully.

Mentally inserting brackets around *we think* in such a sentence should steer you towards the right word (sometimes, as here, *who* may be omitted altogether).

On the other hand, *whom* is correct when an infinitive (*to be* in the following example) takes the place of the second verb (*mows*):

Joe is the man whom we believe to be the council's choice.

In this construction, too, *whom* may be omitted.

See also **and which**; **case (grammar)**; **clause**; **who/that**.

**who ever/whoever/whomever** See **how ever/however**; **prepositions**; **who/whom**.

**wholly** Note the *wh-* and the *-ll-*.

**whom** See **who/whom**.

**whose/who's** *Whose* is the possessive form of *who*:

Whose books are those on the bench?

*Who's* is the contracted form of *who is* or *who has*:

Who's coming to the shops with us?

Who's taken my lunch?

Note that *whose* can apply to things as well as to people – it is far less clumsy to say *the shop whose pies are famous* than *the shop of which the pies are famous*.

See also **and which**; **who/that**.

**why** See **reason**.

**-wide** *Worldwide*, *nationwide* and *statewide* should be written as one word. Compounds such as *Australia-wide* and *Tasmania-wide* are hyphenated.

**widow** The expression *the widow of the late Jeff Jones* is tautological. Instead, say *the widow of Jeff Jones* or *the wife of the late Jeff Jones*.

See also **orphans and widows**.

**wield** Note the *-ie-*.

**wilful/wilfulness** Note the *ful* in these two words, but the *full* in *wilfully*.

**will** See **shall/will**.

**Williamstown, Vic** Compare with *Williamtown*, NSW.

**WIMP** A computer acronym for *window*, *icon*, *mouse*, *pointer*.

**window** In computer terminology a *window* is an area on a screen in which particular tasks are delineated. Windowing enables the user to display several files at once, and this means that various parts of a word-processing document can be viewed and worked on together, or word processing may be carried out in one window while a spreadsheet program, for example, is ready for use in another. Data can also be moved from one window to another: a table from a spreadsheet, for example, may be quickly and easily inserted into a word-processing document.

See also **file**.

**-wise** See **-ways/-wise**.

**with** When a singular subject is linked to something else by the preposition *with*, the verb is singular:

> The bride with her two bridesmaids has [*not* have] just arrived at the church.

Using the conjunction *and* instead of the preposition *with* would change the verb from *has* to *have*.

See also **along with/together with**; **singular or plural**; **with/by/of**.

**with/by/of** The journalistic device that places a phrase at the head of a sentence to attract attention often falls foul of the preposition *with*, using it when *by* or *of* is required:

> By [*not* With] the present government, a fleet of cars is regarded as unnecessary expenditure.
>
> Of [*not* With] Brahms, as of [*not* with] Mahler, he proved to be one of the foremost exponents.

Ending rather than beginning these sentences with the phrases would, of course, make them more elegant as well as less accident-prone.

See also **of**; **with**.

**withhold** Note the *-hh-*.

**WMC** Western Mining Corporation Holdings Limited.

**WO1** Warrant Officer Class 1.

**WO2** Warrant Officer Class 2.

**WOFF/W. Off.** Warrant Officer.

**woman** In general references *woman* is more acceptable than *lady* or *female* for describing an adult female human:

Do you know the woman who lives in the corner house?

*Lady* is used to describe a person of notably good manners or breeding, and when speaking about a woman in her presence:

My grandmother always behaved like a lady.

Please show this lady to the table.

*Female* is used in describing animals and the sexual organs of plants:

We took three rabbits – a male and two females.

The female part of the flower is out of sight.

It is also a convenient term for female humans of mixed age – that is, when some in a group are too young to be called *women* (or too old to be called *girls*):

There were three females (aged five, twelve and forty-one) in the lifeboat.

The whole subject of terminology for the female sex is under discussion today. The best course may be to use *woman*, *lady*, *female* and *girl* in contexts where the opposite-sex equivalents *man*, *gentleman*, *male* and *boy* would be appropriate.

See also **discriminatory language**; **female/feminine/feminist**; **gender**; **madam/madame**; **male/masculine**; **man/mankind**; **Ms.**

**wondrous** This slightly archaic adjective (note the spelling – not 'wonderous') means wonderful or marvellous.

**Woodberry, NSW** Compare with *Woodbury*, Tas.

**Woodford, NSW, Qld and Vic.** Compare with *Woodforde*, SA.

**woodfree papers** See **paper sizes and weights.**

**wool/woolly/woollen** Note the *-ll-* in the compounds of the word *wool.*

**Woolloomooloo** Note the tricky spelling of the name of this Sydney locality.

**word count** See **character count/word count**.

**word division** In justified text a word often has to be broken at the end of a line and hyphenated in order that the spacing between words should remain reasonably comparable line by line. Even when text is unjustified, hyphenation is sometimes necessary if excessively short lines are to be avoided. When the appearance of typeset text is unacceptable, rewording is sometimes necessary; a word division rule may occasionally have to be broken if there is no other solution to a problem.

One of the fundamentals of sensible word division is that, where possible, words should be broken according to pronunciation so that the reader is led naturally from the part of a word at the end of a line to the tail of the word on the line below. For example, the word *problem* should be broken *prob/lem*, while *program* should be broken *pro/gram*. The following are the main rules for word division.

- Divide a compound between its parts:
  house/keeper   soft/hearted   truck/load
- Divide after a prefix of two or more letters:
  ex/periment   hyper/active   sub/limate   con/struct
- Divide before a suffix of two or more letters:
  add/ed   content/ment   mani/fold   adapt/ing
- Divide after a double consonant that belongs to the root word:
  miss/ing   sell/ing   express/ion
- When a word doubles the final consonant to change form, divide between the consonants:
  submit/ting   permit/ted   occur/ring
- Divide syllables according to sound so that the reader can easily recognise the word:
  frac/tion *not* fract/ion
  miti/gate *not* mitig/ate
  pli/able *not* plia/ble
  gor/geous *not* gorg/eous
- Do not break words of one syllable.
- Do not retain fewer than three letters at the end or beginning of a line unless they constitute a prefix or suffix.
- Do not break a person's given name or surname (and try to avoid breaking between initials and a surname).
- Do not break a word that is already hyphenated.
- Letters that represent the one sound must never be divided:
  pneu/matic *not* pne/umatic
  beau/tiful *not* bea/utiful
  crea/ture *not* cre/ature
- Take care not to create misleading part-words on either side of the break:
  bum/per   bear/ded   pee/ress   the/rapist

Do not divide numbers, or separate abbreviations and symbols from the numbers with which they are combined:

008 810 211   69 km   52%

Divide dates as follows: *30 April / 1973* not *30 / April 1973*. But do not split dates expressed in figures: *30.4.73*.

While most high-end word-processing and desktop-publishing programs have the capacity to hyphenate automatically, care should be taken when using this facility as many of the word divisions differ from those favoured in Australia. Manual word division will often be necessary. The *Collins Gem Dictionary of Spelling & Word Division* and *The Oxford Spelling Dictionary* are invaluable aids for this purpose.

See also **hard hyphen/soft hyphen; hyphenation; hyphenation dictionary; justified type/unjustified type**.

**word spacing** For maximum legibility in typeset material, the *word spacing* of each line should be consistent and even. While this is always attainable in unjustified setting, it is rarely so in justified setting, even when all the available end-of-line word breaks are used.

As a general rule, the optimum word space in text-size faces (9 point to 11 point) is no more than 25 per cent of the type size, which may be seen as approximately the width of a lower-case i of the chosen font. In the case of 10 point type this would mean 2.5 point word spacing. The optimum space between words is, in fact, surprisingly small and it is a common fault to exaggerate it. Too much word space makes the copy difficult to read and can create distracting rivers of white space that run vertically through the text, as the following illustrates.

> As a general rule, the optimum word space in text-size faces (9 point to 11 point) is no more than 25 per cent of the type size, which may be seen as approximately the width of a lower-case i of the chosen font. In the case of 10 point type this would mean 2.5 point word spacing. The optimum space between words is, in fact, surprisingly small and it is a common fault to exaggerate it. Too much word space makes the copy difficult to read and can create distracting rivers of white space that run vertically through the text, as this example illustrates.

The correct spacing is also important after punctuation marks, apostrophes and quotation marks, and space will often have to be subtracted to obtain a visually even effect. Word-processor operators who use two spaces after the full stop at the end of a sentence should not do so if their work is to be converted to type.

In larger point sizes, particularly in headline and display type, some manual juggling of word space is often required to get the desired effect.

The term *thin space* or *hair space* is sometimes used when a fine space is needed – for example between a letter and a full stop (or a reference mark such as a superior dagger).

Page-makeup and word-processing programs allow the operator to control the amount of word spacing used in a document.

See also **justified type/unjustified type; kerning; points; tracking; type.**

**working title** In the context of publishing a *working title* is a conveniently short name given to a book during the production process: *Nineteenth-century Porcelain and Its Manufacture*, for example, might have the working title *Porcelain.*

**World War I** The 1914–18 war was once widely known as the *Great War*, but it is now most often referred to as *World War I* or the *First World War.* Prefer *World War I*, and use a roman I for the number.

See also **prewar/postwar**.

**World War II** The war of 1939–45 may be called *World War II* (with a roman II) or the *Second World War*, but *World War II* is recommended.

See also **prewar/postwar**.

**worm's-eye view** See **bird's-eye view**.

**worth/worth while/worthwhile** It is permissible to use *worth*, but not *worth while* or *worthwhile*, before an *-ing* word:

> The photography exhibition is worth visiting.

You cannot describe something as simply being *worth*, but you can say that it is *worth 30 cents*, or *worth much more*.

Either *worth while* or *worthwhile* can stand alone, however, after a verb:

> All those discussions proved worth while [*or* worthwhile] in the end.

*Worthwhile* (but not *worth while*) can go before a noun: *worthwhile discussions*.

**would** See **should/would**.

**wove/woven** See **weaved/wove/woven**.

**w.p.b.** waste-paper basket.

**wpm** words per minute.

**WRAAC** Women's Royal Australian Army Corps.

**WRAAF** Women's Royal Australian Air Force.

**wrack** See **rack/wrack**.

**WRANS** Women's Royal Australian Naval Service.

**wrapped** See **rapt/wrapped**.

**write protection** In computer terminology this is a form of temporary data protection in which the information on a disk can be read but not altered. Boxes of 5¼ inch disks include stickers that are folded over a notch near the top right-hand corner to prevent any further material being written to the disk (coloured adhesive dots, obtainable from stationers, are good substitutes). There is a small plastic slider on the back of the 3½ inch disk that, when pushed into place, locks the disk to prevent further writing.

When the write-protect gap is blocked by a sticker or slider, the disk drive is physically prevented from operating because the sensor fails to receive the light that it recognises as permission to write to a disk.

Files and folders can also be write-protected, or locked, to prevent work in them from being written over, altered or accidentally destroyed.

**WST** Western Standard Time.
See also **time zones**.

**WWF** Waterside Workers' Federation

**WYSIWYG** These initials (forming an acronym pronounced 'whizzy-wig') stand for *what you see is what you get*, which refers to the capacity of computer screens to show how text or graphics will appear on the printout.

# Xx

**X** ten (roman numeral; see also **roman numerals**); non-violent explicitly sexual material (film classification in ACT, NT).

**x-height** See **type**.

**Xmas** There is nothing inherently unchristian or insulting about this abbreviation for *Christmas*, although some advertisers and newspapers avoid it for fear of giving offence. The Greek letter *X* (or *chi*) introduces the Greek word for Christ (*Christos*), and should therefore be regarded as an acceptable substitute for it. Pronounce *Xmas* in the same way as *Christmas*, however.

**X-ray** The word always has a hyphen, and *X-ray* is preferred to *x-ray*.

# Yy

**yet** One way of indicating contrast is to use the word *yet*:

She says she likes flowers yet she grows none.

*Although* has the same effect:

Although she says she likes flowers she grows none.

The combination of *although* and *yet* would duplicate the sense of contrast unnecessarily: *Although she says she likes flowers, yet she grows none*. For the same reason the combination *but yet* should be avoided: *The heat was unbearable but yet we had to walk the dog*.

Another meaning of *yet* is so far, and it may be followed by the present or perfect tense but not the simple past tense:

Are you tired yet? *not* Were you tired yet?
Have you slept yet? *not* Did you sleep yet?

**YHA** Youth Hostels Association.

**Yiddish** See **Hebrew/Yiddish**.

**yield** Note the *-ie-*.

**YMCA** Young Men's Christian Association.

**yoghurt/yogurt** Either spelling is acceptable, but *yoghurt* is recommended. The word is pronounced with either a short or long *o*.

**yoke/yolk** The noun *yoke* has a number of related meanings – from the device for joining a pair of animals such as horses or oxen working in tandem to the kind of yoke people may be subjected to (*the yoke of a dictator*). A *yolk* is the central part of an egg, the yellow as distinct from the white in a hen's egg.

**Yolngu** See **Aborigine/Aboriginal**.

**Yom Kippur** The Jewish Day of Atonement (note the spelling).

**Yorke Peninsula, SA** Compare with *Cape York Peninsula*, Qld.

**Yorketown, SA** Compare with *York Town*, Tas.

**you** *You* is more natural than *one* in most references to people in general:

> You [*not* One] must do what is necessary to achieve your [*not* one's] goal.

Whichever is used, it is important to be consistent:

> When you are enjoying an evening you don't notice the time.

*not* When one is enjoying an evening you don't notice the time.

See also **one**.

**you/your** See **-ing forms**; **you**; **your/you're/yours**.

**Young, NSW** Compare with *Youngs*, WA.

**your/you're/yours** The first two are sometimes confused. *Your* is the possessive adjective relating to *you*:

> Do you have your books with you?

*You're* is the contraction of *you are*:

> I believe you're coming to the party.

There is no apostrophe in the possessive pronoun *yours*:

> These socks are yours.

**you've** Because the contraction of *you have* is often (wrongly) pronounced 'yorv', it is sometimes misspelt 'your've'.

**yuppie** *Yuppie* (or *yuppy*) is a near-acronym for *young urban professional*. A variation on this rather tired colloquialism is *yumpie* (or *yumpy*) for *young upwardly mobile professional*. Childless couples of the same ilk are sometimes referred to as *dinkies* (*double income, no kids*).

**YWCA** Young Women's Christian Association.

# Zz

**z** Pronounce this letter 'zed' (not 'zee' as the Americans do).

**zenith** See **nadir/zenith**.

**zero** The plural is *zeros* or *zeroes*.
See also **naught/nought**.

**zoologist/zoology** Pronounce the *zool-* in two parts: 'zoe-ol' (not 'zoo-ol').

**ZPG** zero population growth.

**zucchini** The plural is *zucchini* or *zucchinis*; this vegetable is sometimes known as a *courgette*.